TALES OF
THE OLD WORLD

IT IS A dark age of war and bloodshed. Monsters roam the land unchecked, daemons whisper promises into the hearts of men and evil forces plot the overthrow of the Old World. In the Empire, the greatest realm of men, the Emperor Karl Franz musters his armies. Together with the dwarfs of the Worlds Edge Mountains and the high elves from the island of Ulthuan, they stand united against the common foe: the Chaos hordes from the north, the greenskin tribes of the mountains and the restless dead. Rumours persist of ratmen living in the sewers, bandits gathering in the wilds and other foul creatures that shun the light of day. Only courage will out and from the fires of war, great heroes rise. For in these dark times heroes are needed more than ever.

By popular demand we've collected some of the best fantasy short stories ever written for the Black Library into one mighty tome and added some brand-new stories!

More Warhammer omnibuses from the Black Library

GOTREK & FELIX: THE FIRST OMNIBUS
by William King

(Contains the novels
Trollslayer, Skavenslayer and *Daemonslayer*)

GOTREK & FELIX: THE SECOND OMNIBUS
by William King

(Contains the novels
Dragonslayer, Beastslayer and *Vampireslayer*)

GENEVIEVE
by Jack Yeovil

(Contains the novels
Drachenfels, Genevieve Undead, Beasts in Velvet and *Silver Nails*)

THE AMBASSADOR CHRONICLES
by Graham McNeill

(Contains the novels
The Ambassador and *Ursun's Teeth*)

THE KONRAD SAGA
by David Ferring

(Contains the novels
Konrad, Shadowbreed and *Warblade*)

A WARHAMMER ANTHOLOGY

TALES
OF THE
OLD WORLD

Edited by
Marc Gascoigne
& Christian Dunn

A Black Library Publication

The majority of these stories appeared in the following anthologies: *Realm of Chaos* (© 2000, Games Workshop Ltd) and *Lords of Valour* (© 2001, Games Workshop Ltd).

Shyi–Zar first appeared in the *Chaos Rising* booklet (© 2004, Games Workshop Ltd). *Freedom's Home or Glory's Grave, Haute Cuisine, Dead Man's Hand, The Man who Stabbed Luther van Groot, Rat Trap, Rotten Fruit,* and *Ill Met in Mordheim* have not before appeared in print.

This omnibus edition published in Great Britain in 2007 by
BL Publishing,
Games Workshop Ltd.,
Willow Road, Nottingham,
NG7 2WS, UK.

10 9 8 7 6 5 4 3 2 1

Cover illustration by David Gallagher.
Map by Nuala Kinrade.

ISBN 13: 978 1 84416 452 3
ISBN 10: 1 84416 452 7

Distributed in the US by Simon & Schuster
1230 Avenue of the Americas, New York, NY 10020, US.

See the Black Library on the Internet at
www.blacklibrary.com

Find out more about Games Workshop
and the world of Warhammer at
www.games-workshop.com

THIS IS A DARK age, a bloody age, an age of daemons and of sorcery. It is an age of battle and death, and of the world's ending. Amidst all of the fire, flame and fury it is a time, too, of mighty heroes, of bold deeds and great courage.

AT THE HEART of the Old World sprawls the Empire, the largest and most powerful of the human realms. Known for its engineers, sorcerers, traders and soldiers, it is a land of great mountains, mighty rivers, dark forests and vast cities. And from his throne in Altdorf reigns the Emperor Karl Franz, sacred descendant of the founder of these lands, Sigmar, and wielder of his magical warhammer.

BUT THESE ARE far from civilised times. Across the length and breadth of the Old World, from the knightly palaces of Bretonnia to ice-bound Kislev in the far north, come rumblings of war. In the towering World's Edge Mountains, the orc tribes are gathering for another assault. Bandits and renegades harry the wild southern lands of the Border Princes. There are rumours of rat-things, the skaven, emerging from the sewers and swamps across the land. And from the northern wildernesses there is the ever-present threat of Chaos, of daemons and beastmen corrupted by the foul powers of the Dark Gods. As the time of battle draws ever near, the Empire needs heroes like never before.

North of Here Lie The
Dreaded Chaos Wastes.

f Claus

Grengrad.

Here Be Trolls...

Praag.

middle mountains.

Kislev

Kislev.

denheim.

Wolfenburg.

Talabheim

Altdorf.

The Empire

Karak Kad

Nuln.

The
Moot.

Sylvania.
Dracken
-hof.

Zhufbar.

Averheim.

Black
Water.

Karak
Norn.

Black fire Pass.

CONTENTS

Editor's Introduction
Christian Dunn

So I've just finished going over the running order for this anthology (or should that be über-anthology?) and there's so much I want to say.

Should I tell you about the time that I was literally an hour away from the submissions deadline for issue 22 of *Inferno!* and still a story down when the mail arrived containing CL Werner's synopsis for 'A Choice of Hatreds'? It blew us all away and was commissioned on the spot (thanks Clint!).

Or should I tell you about how Robert Earl's 'Rattenkrieg' was originally rejected by an over-zealous assistant editor only to be rescued when another staff member read the synopsis and realised how great the twist is (it's on page 429 but at least do me the decency of finishing this introduction before you rush off and read it)?

I could tell you how happy I am that most of the stories that were commissioned to keep 'on the shelf' for *Inferno!* (see, I learned my lesson from issue 22) have now finally been committed to print in this volume.

I could also tell you that because I didn't get to write a farewell editorial for *Inferno!*, I'm ecstatic to finally have the chance to thank Marco and all of the authors and artists for making it such a success for so many years.

Would it be worth mentioning how, like a gym teacher whose protégé goes on to win the FIFA golden boot or Heismann Trophy, how proud I am that many of these authors have gone on to become top-selling novelists for the Black Library and other publishers and imprints?

Maybe I could tell you that although I miss *Inferno!* like a faithful family pet or a kidney, it's great to see the tradition of uncovering new talent being continued through the Black Library short story competitions.

I could even tell you that these thirty-six stories represent the finest writing from almost a decade of Warhammer short fiction and will take you on a journey from the heartland of the Empire to the madness-inducing landscape of the Chaos Wastes.

Or maybe I should just step away from the keyboard and just let you read the stories?

I hope you enjoy them as much as I do.

TALES OF
HONOUR & HEROISM

FREEDOM'S HOME OR GLORY'S GRAVE

Graham McNeill

SHADOWS LEAPT LIKE dancers around the tall garrets of the crumbling towers and Leofric Carrard was starting to think that it had been a bad idea to agree to Lord d'Epee's request to venture into the abandoned depths of his castle.

The blade of Leofric's sword shone with a milky glow in the moonlight, its edge like a razor despite him never having taken a whetstone to it. The Blade of Midnight was elven and Leofric hoped that whatever enchantments had been woven in its forging would be proof against the monster they were hunting, a creature of the netherworld, neither alive nor dead.

The ruined inner walls of the gatehouse reared above Leofric, the ramparts empty and dusty, and the merlons broken and saw-toothed. The gateway before him sagged on rusted iron hinges, the timbers splintered and yawning like an open mouth. Beyond the gateway, he could see one of the inner keeps, its solid immensity a brooding black shape against the sky.

'Do you see anything, Havelock?' he called to his squire.

'No, sir,' whispered the squire, his voice sounding scared, and Leofric hoped that this venture would not see Havelock meet as grisly a fate as his previous squire, Baudel. Leofric still saw the bloody image of Baudel in his nightmares, his belly ripped open by the forest creatures of Athel Loren.

15

'Very well,' he said, keeping his voice even. 'Let's keep on.'

Leofric advanced cautiously through the gateway, keeping his head moving from left to right in search of anything out of place. It saddened and angered Leofric to see such a fine castle left to such neglect. In its day, this would have been an almost impregnable fastness, but its glory days had long since passed and its current lord, the lunatic Lord d'Epee was in no fit state to restore it. Where would the local peasants find shelter in times of war? Every lord and noble of Bretonnia had a sacred duty to preserve the natural order of things in his lands, and that could not happen were he to allow the peasants of his lands to be butchered by orcs or beastmen because they had nowhere to run to.

True, Aquitaine was a largely peaceful dukedom – aside from the fractious populace – but that was no excuse for a noble lord to let his castle fall into disrepair. When Leofric had commanded a castle of his own, back in Quenelles, he had spent a goodly sum from his coffers to ensure the castle remained defensible at all times.

But there was more than simple neglect at the heart of Castle d'Epee's abandonment. The lord and his family dwelled in the outermost gatehouse, fearful of the darkness and the creatures of evil that had taken the inner reaches of their ancestral home, and unwilling to risk their own lives to recover the treasures and heirlooms that lay there.

One such heirloom was the object of Leofric and Havelock's quest, a stuffed stag's head said to be hung within the great hall of the third keep. Privately, Leofric thought it a frivolous use of his knightly skills to retrieve such a folly, but the twitching Lord d'Epee had offered Leofric and Havelock shelter on their journey in search of the Grail and his code of honour bound him to accede to his host's request for aid.

Beyond the gate, Leofric found himself in a cobbled courtyard with ruined outbuildings leaning against the walls, their roofs collapsed and open to the sky. Rotted straw was strewn across the cobbles and the derelict keep loomed like an enormous black cliff before him. Moonlight pooled in the courtyard and glittered from the silver of his plate armour, but the keep remained resolutely dark and threatening, its casement windows invisible against its darkness and its crumbling towers like spikes of black rock.

Havelock moved to stand beside him; the man's presence reassuring even though his skill with the bow he carried would be negligible in the darkness. His rough peasant clothes were dull and blended with the gloom so that only the light reflecting from his eyes stood out.

'I don't like this place,' said Havelock. 'I can see why they abandoned it.'

'It's a grim place, right enough,' agreed Leofric. 'Someone should come here in force and reclaim it. It's not right that a castle this strong should be left like this.'

Havelock nodded and started to reply, but Leofric raised his hand to silence him as he caught sight of something moving at the base of the keep, a darting shadow that had nothing to do with those cast by the moon and drifting clouds above.

Leofric pointed to where he had seen the movement and set off towards the shadow, hoping to discover some way of entering the keep or a foe he could defeat.

He drew closer to the keep and with every step he took, it seemed to him that he could smell the aroma of roasting meat and hear the sounds of revelry. He turned to Havelock and saw that his squire's senses were similarly intrigued.

'Sounds like a feast,' whispered Havelock.

Leofric nodded and returned his attention to the keep as he saw a soft light emanating from beneath a door of thick wood and banded black iron. He heard a woman's laughter and felt an ache of loss as it summoned unbidden memories of his lost wife, Helene. He reached to his gorget, beneath which he wore the blue, silken scarf she had given him on the tilting fields outside Couronne after he had unhorsed Duke Chilfroy of Artois.

He could not feel the soft material through the metal of his gauntlets, but just knowing it was there was enough to warn him of the falsehood of the woman's laughter. Even as they drew near, a warm and friendly glow built from the windows of the keep, spilling like warm honey into the courtyard. The sound of voices grew louder, laughter and ribald jokes echoing from the walls around them. Though he knew it was but an illusion, his heart ached to go to these revellers and join their carousing, to throw off the shackles of discipline enforced upon him by his quest for the Grail.

Havelock took a step towards the keep, the bowstring going slack as he lowered the weapon. 'My lord... should we ask the people within whether they've seen the stag's head? Maybe we can stop for a while, rest and get some food?'

Leofric shook his head and reached out to pull Havelock back. He felt resistance and pulled harder, stopping the squire in his tracks. The man twisted in his grip, sudden hostility flashing in his eyes.

'Let me go!' hissed Havelock. 'I want some food and wine!'

Leofric's palm snapped out and cracked against Havelock's jaw. The squire staggered and Leofric said, 'Use your head, man. There *is* no food or wine, it is all an illusion to ensnare us.'

Havelock spat blood and shook his head in contrition as he saw that Leofric spoke the truth. He pulled his bowstring taut once more. 'Sorry, my lord.'

'Remember,' said Leofric. 'Lord d'Epee said the creature would attempt to make us lower our guard by promising us a warm welcome and attempting to confuse our senses with friendly images. We must not let that happen.'

'No, my lord,' said Havelock.

Satisfied his squire understood the threat before them, Leofric once again advanced on the door. Light streamed from the windows and at the threshold, but it was a dead light now, bereft of warmth or sustenance. He could feel it calling to him, bidding him enter with promises of comfort and an easement of burdens, but knowing it for the lie it was, the illusory light had no power over him.

He reached out to grip the black ring that opened the door, and was not surprised when it turned easily beneath his hand. Cold, glittering light enveloped him as the door swung open with a grinding squeal of rusted hinges and he felt its attraction grow in power as he saw what lay within the keep.

Where he had expected emptiness and desolation, instead there was life and people. The great hall stretched out before him, its tables groaning with wild meats and fruit of all descriptions. Earthenware jugs overflowed with wine and a colourful jester capered madly in the centre of the chamber, juggling squawking chickens. Children played 'smell the gauntlet', a game banned in Bretonnia after it had incited a peasant revolt, and a laughing nobleman clapped enthusiastically to a badly played lute. Above the nobleman, Leofric saw a stuffed stag's head, its antlers drooping and sad, and shook his head at the idea of risking his and Havelock's life for such a tawdry prize.

Leofric took a step inside, wary at the sight of so many apparitions and forced himself to remember that they were not real. Lord d'Epee had only mentioned one creature, calling it a Dereliche, a spectral horror that sucked the very life from a person with its deathly touch. He had said nothing about a host of creatures...

The revellers appeared to ignore him, but having attended the court of the king and been on the receiving end of courtly snobbery, Leofric recognised their studied disinterest as false. Whoever or whatever these ghostly people were, they *knew* he was there.

'Lord d'Epee didn't say nothing about a party,' whispered Havelock.

'No,' said Leofric grimly, 'he didn't.'

Each of the revellers glimmered with a sheen of silken frost and Leofric approached the nearest, a man dressed in the garb of a minor noble, his clothes bright and well cut, though of a fashion even Leofric knew had passed out of favour many hundreds of years ago.

Leofric slowly extended his sword arm towards the apparition, the blade white in the reflected light of the hall. The tip of the sword passed into the outline of the man, and it had penetrated barely a fingerbreadth when the man hissed and leapt away, the guise of humanity falling from his features in a heartbeat.

Instantly, the gaudy banquet vanished and Leofric was plunged into utter darkness. A low moaning soughed on the cold, dry air and he felt the hairs on the back of his neck rise at the sound. He heard Havelock cry out in fear and spun around, trying to pinpoint the sound of the moaning voice.

'Havelock!' commanded Leofric. 'Where are you?'

'Right here, my lord!' shouted Havelock, though Leofric could see nothing in the blackness.

'Find a wall and get to the door, I don't want to hit you by mistake!'

'Yes, my lord,' replied Havelock.

Leofric blinked and rubbed a hand across his eyes as he attempted to penetrate the gloom. He turned quickly on the spot, keeping his sword extended before him until his eyes could adjust. He heard a hissing behind him and spun to face it, but another sound came to him from behind and he realised he was surrounded by a host of creatures that were as insubstantial as mist.

He cried out as something cold brushed against the skin of his back, flinching in sudden pain and surprise. His flesh burned as though with frostbite, but he could tell his armour was still whole. Whatever powers these creatures possessed was such that his armour was useless and he cursed d'Epee for sending them on this fool's errand. He remembered the same deathly chill touch when shadow creatures of the dark fay had attacked him when he had journeyed to the lair of the dragon, Beithir-Seun. Cu-Sith had saved him then, but the Wardancer was long dead and Leofric was on his own now.

Another cold touch stole into his flesh from the side, but he was ready this time and swept his sword down and the white blade cut through something wispy and soft like wadded cheesecloth. A sparkle of light fell to the stone floor like a rain of diamond dust and Leofric heard a shriek torn from what sounded like a dozen throats simultaneously.

'So you can be hurt?' taunted Leofric as he heard a chorus of hisses drawing nearer.

'Yes, we can,' said a sibilant voice that came from many places, 'but your flesh is ours, your spirit is ours...'

He could see the faint outlines of perhaps a dozen figures drifting towards him, their outlines blurred and indistinct, but that was enough. Ever since his time in Athel Loren, his sight had been keener and he had been sensitive to the proximity of magic in the air. He narrowed his eyes, letting his awareness of the approaching creatures steal over him like a warm blanket.

'Come on… ' he whispered as he saw they all moved in perfect concert, as though they were but fragments of a whole… as though orchestrated by a single will.

He could see that the apparitions were unaware that he could see them in the darkness and continued turning blindly to maintain the deception.

You're not the only ones who have the power of illusion, he thought.

When the nearest creature was an arm's length from him, Leofric lunged, spearing it with the point of his sword. The multitude cried out in pain as it vanished in a puff of light, but by then Leofric was amongst them, his sword slashing left and right and destroying each creature it cut into. Shrieks and wails of pain filled the hall and Leofric saw the apparitions whip through the air like smoke in a storm.

'Now, Havelock!' shouted Leofric.

Once again the rusted hinges squealed as Havelock threw open the door to the banqueting hall and bright moonlight streamed inside. Further illuminated by the light of the night sky, the apparition was bathed in white; its spectral outline limned in glittering light as its ghostly avatars returned to it and became part of the whole once more.

So this was a Dereliche, thought Leofric. Its features were twisted in hatred as its form grew in power, though Leofric knew he must have hurt it with those he had destroyed.

With a shriek of rage, the Dereliche hurled itself forward, its arms extended and ending in ghostly talons that reached for his heart. Its speed was astonishing, but Leofric had been expecting its attack and twisted out of its reach and swung his sword for its head.

His blade cut into the monster and he felt its rage as the Blade of Midnight burned its ethereal body with its keen edge. The Dereliche spun behind him and its claws raked deep into his side as it passed and Leofric cried out in pain as he felt his strength flow from his body and into his foe.

'Your strength fills me, knight!' laughed the Dereliche. 'I will feast well on you.'

Manic laughter followed him as Leofric spun to face his foe once more, launching a deadly riposte to its body. The sword sailed past the creature and it darted in again with a predatory hiss of hunger.

The Blade of Midnight snapped up and Leofric shouted, 'Lady guide my arm!' as he leapt towards the Dereliche and felt the blade pierce its unnatural flesh.

It shrieked in agony as the magical blade of the elves dealt it a dreadful wound, the powerful enchantments breaking its hold on the mortal realm. Even as it wailed and spat in its dissolution, Leofric spun his sword until it was held, point down, before him. He dropped to one knee and whispered his thanks to the Lady of the Lake.

'She will not save you!' hissed the Dereliche. 'You are already marked for death, Leofric Carrard.'

Leofric's eyes snapped open and he saw the fading form of the Dereliche as it sank slowly to the stone floor of the chamber, its form wavering and fading with each passing second.

'How do you know my name?' demanded Leofric.

The Dereliche gave a gurgling chuckle and said, 'The Red Duke will rise again in Châlons and his blade will drink deeply of your blood. The realm of the dead already knows your name.'

Leofric rose to his feet and advanced on the creature, but before he could demand further explanation, its form faded completely until only a dimming shower of sparkling light remained.

With the Dereliche's destruction, the last vestiges of the hall's illusion fell away and Leofric saw it for the faded, forgotten place it truly was. Neglect and despair hung over everything and the wan moonlight only served to highlight the melancholic air of decay.

He looked up and saw that the stag's head was still there, looking even more pathetic than it had before, its fur fallen out in clumps and one antler broken. Havelock moved to stand beside him and followed his gaze.

'Looks like he's seen better days, my lord.'

'Haven't we all?' said Leofric, sheathing his sword and turning from the stag, his thoughts dark and filled with foreboding.

A LIGHT RAIN fell and Leofric shivered beneath his armour as he rode along the muddy, rutted road north-east from Castle d'Epee towards the squat brutal mountains of the Massif Orcal. He rode a magnificent elven steed, its flanks as white as virgin snow on a mountain top and a mane like fiery copper. Aeneor had consented to be his steed after a great battle in the heart of Athel Loren when his original rider had been killed and Leofric had ridden him into battle to defend the elves of Coeth-Mara.

Bretonnian steeds were widely regarded as the finest mounts of the Old World, but even the mightiest horse in the king's stables would be humbled by Aeneor's beauty and power.

Havelock rode behind him on a considerably less imposing beast, grumbling and miserable as the rain soaked through his oiled leather cape.

Castle d'Epee was many miles behind them and Leofric was glad to see the back of it. Upon presenting the mouldering stag's head to Lord d'Epee, the man had hurled it to the floor and screamed at the pair of them that they had brought him the wrong one.

Manners forbade Leofric from responding, but even had the vow he had sworn upon embarking on his quest for the Grail not forbidden him to rest more than a single night in any one place, he would not have remained for fear of his temper causing an unforgivable breach of etiquette.

He and Havelock had ridden from the castle as soon as the sun rose over the World's Edge Mountains, a distant smudge of dark rock on the eastern horizon. Castle d'Epee was now several days behind them, and they had made good time until the rains from the coast had closed in, turning Bretonnian roads to thick, cloying mud. The grim weather suited Leofric's mood perfectly and he had brooded long over the last words the Dereliche had said to him.

Normally he would give no credence to the utterances of a creature of evil, but it had known his name and spoken of the Red Duke, and such things were not to be taken lightly.

As they had made camp on their first night away from Castle d'Epee, Havelock had started a fire and begun polishing Leofric's armour. Leofric himself had found a nearby spring and offered prayers of thanks to the Lady for protecting them from the foul Dereliche.

The sky above was dark by the time Havelock had prepared a thin stew for him and as he sat on his riding blanket, Havelock said, 'This Red Duke, who's he then? Someone you crossed before?'

Leofric shook his head, blowing to cool the hot stew. 'No, Havelock, he's not. He's something far worse. I'm surprised you haven't heard of him. He was quite the terror of Aquitaine in his day.'

'Maybe he was, but I'm from Gisoreux and we got enough troubles enough of our own to bother with them quarrelsome types from Aquitaine.'

'And you've never heard the Lay of the Red Duke?' asked Leofric.

Havelock shook his head. 'Can't says I have, my lord. Me and mine, well, we worked the land, didn't we? All we had was a red horse and a black pig. Didn't have no time for fancy stories like that.'

Leofric hadn't known exactly what the reference to coloured farm animals meant, but assumed it was some Gisoren expression for poverty. Havelock was of peasant stock and Leofric had to remind himself that his squire was unlikely to have been exposed to any culture or heard any courtly tales.

'So who was he then, my lord?' asked Havelock.

'The Red Duke was a monster,' began Leofric, wishing he remembered more of the flowery passages of the Lay, 'one of the blood drinkers. A vampire knight. No one really remembers where he came from, but he terrorised this land over a thousand years ago, murdering hundreds of innocents and slaying any who dared to stand against him, then raising them up to join his army of the dead.'

'Sounds like a right bad sort,' said Havelock, making the sign of the horns to ward off any evil spirits that might be attracted by such tales of dark creatures of the night.

'He was,' agreed Leofric. 'His blood drenched debaucheries are said to have shamed the Dark Gods themselves.'

'So what became of him?'

'Like all creatures of evil, he was eventually defeated,' said Leofric. 'The noble knights of the day fought the great battle of Ceren Field and the king himself skewered the fiend on the end of his lance.'

'So he's dead and gone then?' asked Havelock, scooping up the last of his stew with his fingers and wiping his mouth with his sleeve.

'So they say,' said Leofric, grimacing at Havelock's lack of manners. Uncouth and peasant born he most certainly was, but he was a fine squire and was the only other human that Aeneor allowed near him. 'It's said that he rose again nearly five hundred years later, but he was defeated once again, though the Duke of Aquitaine was killed in the battle on the edge of the Forest of Châlons. Accounts of the battle differ, but some say that the Red Duke's spirit escaped the battle and fled into the depths of the forest, where it remains to this day.'

'And that ghost thing you killed says he's going to rise again? That don't sound good.'

'No, it does not, and as a knight sworn to the quest it is my duty to see if there is any truth to what it said. And if evil is rising there, I must defeat it.'

FINE WORDS, REMEMBERED Leofric as a droplet of rain fell into his eye and roused him from the memory of his recounting of the Red Duke's infamy. The Forest of Châlons was still some days distant and there were more uncomfortable days ahead. Leofric had no clear idea of where to seek the Red Duke, but the Barrows of Cuileux lay crumbling and forgotten in the south-western skirts of the mountain forests, and such a place was as good as any to seek the undead.

A low mist hugged the ground as the rain eased off and Leofric caught a scent of woodsmoke carried on the evening's breeze. The landscape around him was undulating, but mostly flat and devoid of landmarks to help him find his bearings.

'Havelock?' said Leofric, turning in the saddle. 'Do you know where we are? What villages are around here?'

His squire stood high in the saddle, cupping his hand over his eyes as he surveyed the bleak landscape around him.

'I'm not rightly sure, my lord,' apologised Havelock. 'I don't know this part of the country, but I think this road, more or less, follows the border between Aquitaine and Quenelles.'

Leofric felt homesick as he looked eastwards towards the realm of his birth, the lands that had once been his, and the heartbreaking memory of his family.

'So that means there's maybe a few villages a few miles north of here, round the edges of the Forest of Châlons. Maybe even...' said Havelock, his voice trailing off.

Leofric heard the faint longing in Havelock's voice and said, 'Maybe even what?'

'Nothing, my lord,' said his squire, staring at the mud.

'Don't lie to me, Havelock,' warned Leofric.

'It's nothing, my lord, just something the servants at Castle d'Epee were talking about.'

'And what might that be?' demanded Leofric, tiring of Havelock's reticence. 'Out with it, man!'

'A village they talked about,' said Havelock. 'A place they called Derrevin Libre.'

The name rang a bell for Leofric, but he couldn't place it until he remembered the long, rambling discourses of Lord d'Epee. The man had mentioned something about the place, but his ravings had been too nonsensical to take much of it in. Clearly the servants had been talking about it too, and probably with more sense.

'Well, what did they say about it?'

Havelock was clearly uncomfortable talking about what he'd heard and Leofric supposed some peasant code of honour kept his tongue in check.

He wheeled Aeneor to face his squire and said, 'Tell me.'

THEY MADE CAMP for the evening and after finishing a meal of black bread and cheese, Havelock told him what he'd heard in the sculleries of Castle d'Epee. Derrevin Libre, it turned out, was indeed a village on the southern edge of the Forest of Châlons, but it was a most remarkable village. Some six months ago, Havelock said, the peasants there had risen up in revolt and overthrown their rightful lord and master before killing him. Once over his initial hesitation, his squire had relished the chance to tell the tale of the peasant revolt, embellishing his tale with lurid details of how truly repellent the local lord had been, even going so far as to link the man with the dark gods of the north.

Leofric sighed as Havelock continued with yet more details of the lord's vileness in an attempt to justify the overthrow of the natural order of things.

'So why didn't the local lords just ride in and crush the rebellion?' interrupted Leofric. 'Why aren't those peasants strung up by their necks from the top of the Lace Tower?'

'They would have been, you see,' said Havelock, wagging his finger at Leofric, before a stern glance warned him not to continue doing so. 'Aye, they would have been, except that the local lords was in the middle of not one, not two, but three different feuds! You know how these Aquitaine folks are, they don't have to fight for their land so they fight each other.'

That at least was true, reflected Leofric. The nobles of Aquitaine were ever in the grip of some internal feud or war and no sooner would one die down than a new one would flare up.

'So the peasants were just left to rule the village themselves?' said Leofric, horrified at the idea of such a thing. Were word of this to travel beyond the borders of Aquitaine, who knew what might happen if peasants were allowed to get the idea that their noble masters could be overthrown at will...

'More or less,' agreed Havelock. 'Though Lord d'Epee's scullion told me that they'd managed to attract the attention of a few bands of Herrimaults to help them fight to keep their freedom.'

'Herrimaults?' snapped Leofric, spitting into the fire. 'I might have known. Criminals and revolutionaries, the lot of them.'

'But sir,' said Havelock. 'They's good men, the Herrimaults. They only rob from them's as can afford the loss and give what they take to feed the poor. They's good men.'

Leofric could see the admiration in Havelock's eyes, and shook his head.

'No, Havelock, they are nothing more than bandits who no doubt perpetuate the stories of their code of honour and reputation as underdog heroes to gullible people like you in order to secure their help in keeping them beyond the reach of the law. Honestly, Havelock, if a dwarf asked you to invest in the Loren Logging Company you'd say yes.'

The smile fell from Havelock's face at Leofric's dressing down, but Leofric could still see the spark of defiance there, fuelled by the romantic notion of peasants casting off their noble masters, and knew he had to crush it.

'Very well, Havelock,' said Leofric. 'I have no issue with people wishing a better life for themselves, but there is a natural order to things that cannot be upset or the land will descend into anarchy. If every peasant wanted to rule his village who would till the fields, gather the crops or rear the animals? Nobles rule and peasants work the land, *that's* the proper order of things.'

'But, that's not–'

Leofric held up his hand to stifle Havelock's protests and said, 'Let me tell you of the last time a peasant tried to rise above his station. He was a young man of Gisoreux, and though you say you never had time for fancy stories, I think you'll know it.'

'You're talking about Huebald, my lord?' said Havelock.

'I am indeed. Yes, he was a brave and handsome young man who saved the Duke of Gisoreux's bride from the terrible beasts of the forest, but the thanks of the fair Lady Ariadne should have been enough for him. Instead he used his friendship with the lady to have her go begging to her husband to dub him a knight of the realm. A peasant becoming a knight, I mean whoever heard of such a thing?'

'I don't think that's quite what happened,' said Havelock, clearly hesitant about contradicting a questing knight.

'Of course it is,' said Leofric, 'This Huebald, despite the armour, weapons and squire he was gifted with by the duke, was still a peasant at heart and his true nature was what was to undo him when he sought to move in higher circles. With the noble knights of Gisoreux, he rode into battle against a horde of beasts and was slain as he fled the field of battle.'

'My lord, with respect, I do know this story, and if I might be so bold as to say so, I think you might have heard a different version from mine.'

'Oh?' said Leofric. 'And what happens in your version?'

'The way I heard it,' said Havelock, 'was that Huebald was shot in the back by his squire as he charged the monsters.'

'Shot by his squire?' exclaimed Leofric. 'Why in the world would a squire shoot his knight?'

'Rumour has it the nobles paid him to do it,' shrugged Havelock. 'Gave him a gold coin, more wealth than anyone like him would see in five lifetimes, to do it. The nobles didn't want some uppity peasant thinking he could be as good as them and they put him back down in the mud with the rest of us.'

'I had not heard that version of the story,' said Leofric.

'Well you wouldn't have, would you, my lord,' said Havelock, absently stirring the embers of the fire. 'You nobles hear your version 'cause it puts us peasants in our place, and we hear our version and it gives us something to hope for. Something better than grubbing in the mud and shit, which is what we normally do.'

'So which version do you think is true?' asked Leofric.

Havelock shrugged, 'Honestly? I don't know, probably somewhere in the middle, but that doesn't matter, does it? All that matters is we each have our own version that keeps us happy I suppose.'

Leofric said nothing, staring at Havelock with a little more respect than he had done before. When Havelock had come to him and begged to be his squire, Leofric had initially refused, for a questing knight traditionally travelled alone, but something in Havelock's demeanour had changed his mind. Perhaps it was his newly acquired sense for things yet to pass that had made him change his mind, a disquieting gift, he presumed, of his time spent beneath the boughs of Athel Loren. Whatever the reason, he had allowed Havelock to accompany him and, thus far, had no cause to regret the decision.

'Maybe you're right, Havelock,' said Leofric. 'I suppose each strata of society perceives past events through its own filters and hears what it wants or needs to.'

His squire looked blankly at him and Leofric cursed for expressing himself in ways beyond the ken of a peasant. He smiled and said, 'I'm agreeing with you.'

Havelock smiled back and said. 'Oh. Good.'

'Don't get used to it,' said Leofric and stretched, looking up into the darkness of the night sky. The Forest of Châlons was still some days off and as he watched a shooting star streak across the heavens, he wondered whether it was a good omen or not.

THE FOREST OF Châlons stretched out before Leofric in a wide swathe of emerald green that lay in the shadow of the rearing crags of the Massif Orcal. The outer trees were stripped of their leaves on their lower reaches by a technique Havelock informed him was known as pollarding, and the dawn light didn't make the forest look any more appealing than it had when they had arrived last night.

Dawn was only an hour old and there was no point in wasting the light, so Leofric pressed his heels to Aeneor's flanks. He disdained the use of spurs, for to use such things on an animal as wondrous as an elven steed would be grossly insulting to it.

'Come on,' said Leofric as Havelock's horse displayed more reluctance to approach the forest before them. 'We have to make as much progress before night falls.'

'I know, my lord, but there's not a man alive who wouldn't be a bit wary of entering a place like this. We're heading towards barrows, ain't we? A man oughtn't to mess with the resting places of the dead.'

'That might be difficult if we're to hunt down a vampire knight, Havelock,' said Leofric, though he understood his squire's reticence The forests of Bretonnia were notorious havens for orcs, brigands and the mutated beasts of Chaos, their dark depths unknown by men for hundreds of years. Many a brave, if foolhardy, duke had attempted to clear out the deep forests of his lands only to fail miserably and lose many of his knights in the process. The depths of the forests were the domains of evil and none dared walk beneath their tangled branches or follow their forgotten pathways without good reason.

Leofric was no stranger to mysterious forests, having spent a span of time with the Asrai of Athel Loren, but even he had to admit that the darkness within the Forest of Châlons was unnerving, as though the forest itself looked back at him with hungry eyes.

He shook off the sensation and guided Aeneor between the tall, thin trees on the outer edges of the forest. The undergrowth was thin and wiry, the forest floor hard packed and well trodden, as though many people had come this way recently, and Leofric fancied he could see hoof prints in the soil.

They rode for several hours before stopping for some food and water, though Leofric had quite lost track of time in the gloomy half-light of the forest. Havelock walked the horses before feeding them grain that had cost Leofric more than most peasants would see in a month.

'I don't like this place,' said Havelock, as he always did. 'Feels like someone's watching me all the time.'

Leofric looked up from the blue scarf wrapped around the hilt of his sword and cast his eyes around the clearing they had stopped in. The trees in this part of the forest were larger than those at the fringes, older and gnarled with age. They grew thicker here too, blocking the light and wreathing the forest in a perpetual twilight that blurred the passage of time and hung a pall of wretchedness upon the soul.

But Havelock was right. As much as Leofric tried to dismiss his concerns as that of a superstitious peasant, he knew enough to know that in places like this, someone – or some*thing* – might very well be watching them. Since they had left the sunlight behind them at the edge of the forest, his warrior's instinct had been screaming at him that they were not alone in this dark place.

'I don't like it much, either, Havelock,' agreed Leofric, 'but for some reason, creatures of evil never make their lairs in beautiful groves or in the middle of golden corn fields. It's always a haunted forest or deserted castle atop a forbidding crag of black rock.'

Havelock laughed, 'Yes, not very original are they?'

'No, but there's a certain evil tradition to uphold I suppose,' said Leofric, rising from the log he sat upon to climb onto the back of his horse once more.

The barrows were at least another day's ride away and Leofric had no wish to stay within the forest any longer than was absolutely necessary.

FOR THE REST of the day and much of the next, Leofric and Havelock rode deeper into the Forest of Châlons, their passage growing slower with each mile as though the trees themselves sought to impede their progress. The sensation of being watched remained with them the whole way and Havelock's nervousness was not helped when they came upon the first of the barrows.

The burial mound had long since been ransacked, its stone door lying splintered and mossy beside its overgrown entrance. Mouldering bones lay scattered around, not even the animals of the forest wishing to gnaw on the dead of this place. A broken sword blade of corroded bronze lay wedged in the dark earth and Leofric guessed that this tomb had been open to the elements for hundreds of years.

They passed on, lest some wild beast had made its lair within the barrow, but the forlorn sight of the plundered barrow depressed Leofric. What hope was there for an honourable warrior if his grave was certain to be robbed by greedy delvers? A warrior should be allowed his rest when he finally made the journey through Morr's gates, not disturbed by thieves seeking gold or treasures of ancient magic.

He and Havelock said little as they passed onwards, seeing more and more of the gloomy barrows the further they travelled. Bleached bones, grinning skulls and rusted weaponry littered the forest floor and though they heard the sounds of animals and beasts through the trees, they saw nothing of the forest's fauna.

As dusk approached on the second day of their travels, Leofric felt a subtle shift in the forest around them, as though the very air and landscape had suddenly become less hostile to their presence. He could see patches of purpling sky above him and the scent of honeysuckle came to him, where before he had smelled only death and desolation.

He raised his hand to halt their progress as he saw a gleam of low sunlight catching on something ahead. From here he could not yet see what had reflected the light, but its pale gleam was like a beacon through the darkness of the tree canopy.

'There's something ahead,' said Leofric, his hand sliding towards the hilt of his sword.

Havelock did not reply, his mood too gloomy after the monotonous ride through the forest, though he raised his head to look. As he caught sight of the reflected light, Leofric saw his spirits rise, as though the sight of something bright was enough to rouse him from the melancholy the darkness of the forest had laid upon him.

'What do you think it is?' he asked.

'I don't know,' replied Leofric. 'This deep in the forest, it could be anything.'

He eased Aeneor forward, the undergrowth and trees growing thinner and more scattered the closer they came. Yet more bones and ancient shards of rusted armour lay strewn around, too many to simply be the result of despicable grave robbers, though Leofric saw that these were no ordinary bones or weapons.

'Was there a battle fought here?' asked Havelock.

Leofric had been wondering the same thing, though if there had been a battle, it had not been fought by men, for the fleshless cadavers and the accoutrements of war that lay here were those of elves and orcs. Graceful, leaf-shaped swords and snapped bowstaves lay strewn all about, and long kite-shields were splintered by monstrously toothed cleavers that would take two strong men to lift.

Narrow elven skulls of porcelain white mingled with thickly ridged and fanged skulls of orcs and it was clear that no quarter had been asked or given in whatever battle had been fought here.

And this was no ordinary battlefield either, saw Leofric as they emerged into a wide, overgrown space of undulating barrows and ruined structures. The remains of a tall tower stood upon a rugged spur of silver rock, its once noble battlements cast down and forgotten. Fashioned from a stone of pale blue, it was clear that no human hand had been part of its construction, for its curves and smooth facing was beyond the skill of even the most gifted stonemasons.

'It's beautiful...' breathed Havelock, his gaze sweeping around the cluster of overgrown buildings.

'These are elven,' said Leofric, riding into the centre of what must once have been an outpost of the Asrai in the Forest of Châlons, forgotten and abandoned hundreds of years ago or more. Weeds and grass grew up through the remains of stone roads and each of the fine buildings that once gathered around the foot of the tower had been smashed and burned in the fighting. The setting sun threw a golden light over the scene and Leofric thought it almost unbearably sad to see such beauty destroyed.

'Do you think your Red Duke is here?' asked Havelock nervously and Leofric shook himself from his contemplation of the ruined elven outpost.

'Perhaps,' he said. 'We should explore this place and see what we can find.'

'Yes, my lord,' said Havelock, looking into the dusky sky, 'but shouldn't we do that with the sun at our backs? Don't seem like sense to go delving into a place like this in darkness.'

Leofric nodded, wheeling his horse to face his squire. 'Yes, you're right. We'll make camp a few miles distant and return at first light.'

He saw the relief on his squire's face and chuckled, 'I may be a knight sworn to destroy evil wherever I find it, Havelock, but I'm not going to go charging off into a ruined tower as night falls looking for the undead. I learned my lessons as a Knight Errant.'

The smile fell from his face as he heard a dry crack, like that of a snapping branch. His sword flashed into his hand and Leofric was amazed to see a cold fire slithering along the length of the blade. The liquid flames gave off no heat, and Leofric could feel the powerful magic surging within the enchanted blade.

'What's happening?' cried Havelock, as Leofric heard more dusty cracks and the scrape of metal on metal. He spun his mount to identify the source of the noises, seeing that the sun was now almost vanished beneath the western treetops.

Before Leofric could answer, the source of the noises was revealed as a host of shambling warriors emerged from the collapsed and greenery-draped buildings. Their skeletal forms marched with a horrid animation, for each of the warriors was a dead thing, a revenant clad in the armour of forgotten times and bearing a rusted sword or spear. They rose from the undergrowth with the powdery crack of bone and their empty eye sockets were pools of darkness that burned with ancient malice.

'The living dead!' shouted Leofric, his revulsion and fury at these abominations rising in his gorge like a sickness. Havelock's mount reared in terror, its ears pressed flat against its skull. His squire had drawn his bow and, without a firm grip on the reins, he tumbled from the saddle as the horse bolted from the clearing. Leofric cursed and angled Aeneor towards the fallen Havelock as more of the skeletal warriors picked themselves up from the ground or emerged from the ruined structures.

He held out his hand and Havelock took hold of his forearm, swinging up onto Aeneor's back as Leofric caught sight of two figures emerge from the tower that stood above them. The first was a warrior in gold and silver armour, and where there was a mindless malevolence to the warriors that rose around them, Leofric saw a black will and dark purpose at the heart of this creature. Though the flesh had long since rotted from its bones, it was clear that it had once been a mighty warrior, its thin skull and gleaming hauberk marking it out as one of the Asrai. The creature bore two ancient longswords and a high helm of tarnished silver reflected the last dying rays of the sun.

The second was a hunched man robed in black who bore a long, skull-topped staff and whose face was gaunt to the point of emaciation. Leofric saw the skeins of powerful magic playing over his pallid flesh.

'Let's go, my lord!' begged Havelock, his primal terror of the undead making his voice shrill as the skeletal warriors closed the noose of bone around them.

Leofric dug his heels into Aeneor's flanks, knowing that speed was more important than manners now. The horse leapt forwards, smashing the nearest of the dead warriors to the ground. Leofric's white blade clove the skull of another and he cut left and right as the armoured skeletons pressed in around them.

The fire of his blade surged with every blow and Leofric felt the hatred of the weapon as a potent force that guided his arm and struck the head from his every opponent with a deadly grace. Clawed hands tore at Aeneor and the horse lashed out with his back legs, its hoofs caving in brittle ribcages and shattering rusted shields.

Havelock loosed arrows from the back of the horse, though most of his shots flew wide of the mark. Leofric chopped with brutal efficiency at the grimly silent horde of undead, battling to get enough space to fight with all the skill he possessed.

But the long dead warriors were too numerous and even Aeneor's strength was insufficient to forge them a path.

'Lady protect us!' shouted Leofric, smashing his sword through a skeleton warrior's chest and dropping it to the ground as another slashed a spear across Aeneor's chest. The steed screamed foully, rearing up and almost toppling them from its back. The spear was knocked from the dead warrior's grip and Aeneor's hooves crushed his attacker as they came back down to earth.

Leofric cried out as he saw the blood spray from the wound and kicked the skull from another warrior's shoulders as he saw that they were pulling back, forming an unbreakable ring of blades and bone around them. He heard Aeneor's breath heave and saw blood-flecked foam gather at the corner of his mouth.

'What are they doing?' asked Havelock, his survival instincts overcoming his fear for the moment.

'They are waiting for that,' said Leofric as he saw the armoured warrior that had emerged from the ruined tower striding towards him with grim purpose and murderous intent.

Clearly this was one of the champions of the undead, an ancient warrior bound to the mortal plane by evil magic. It would not attack mindlessly, but with malice and all the skill it had possessed in life. Closer, Leofric could see the skill wrought in every link of its armour and the fine workmanship of its weapons. An obsidian charm hung around the champion's neck, gleaming and polished to a mirror finish.

Leofric risked a glance towards the tower, seeing the robed figure extend his hand towards the silent horde, now understanding that he was surely a practitioner of the dark arts of necromancy. The will of this necromancer was what held the dead warriors at bay while his champion took the glory of the kill. Did such a creature even understand the concept of glory or honour?

The armoured champion stopped and spun his swords in an elaborate pattern of swirling blades that Leofric recognised as elven. He had seen the Hound of Winter perform similarly intricate blade weaving and fervently hoped that this warrior was not as skilled as the venerable champion of Lord Aldaeld had been.

'You will fight me,' said the creature, its voice dusty and lifeless. 'And you will die.'

Leofric did not deign to reply, he had no wish to trade words with this creature of darkness. A dark pall of fear sought to envelop him at the unnatural horror of this dead warrior, but he fought against it, raising his sword as a talisman against such weakness.

The undead champion raised its swords and dropped into a fighting crouch. 'You *will* fight me. The Red Duke will have need of warriors like you and I when he rises.'

'The Red Duke…' said Leofric, suddenly understanding. 'He has not risen.'

'No,' agreed the champion, 'he bides his time, but you have been brought here to die like many before you to swell the ranks of his army for when that day comes.'

Leofric cursed his impetuous decision to ride towards Châlons from Castle d'Epee in such haste. How many other knights had fallen into this trap and been slain only to rise again as one of the living dead? For all his smug words to Havelock earlier, he knew that he was not as far from his days as a Knight Errant as he had thought.

Further words were useless and he gave a cry of rage as he charged towards the undead champion. His sword speared towards its chest, but a black-bladed sword intercepted the blow and the champion slashed high towards Leofric's neck. The edge clanged on the metal gorget of Leofric's armour, but with the force of the blow he almost fell. He swayed in the saddle as Aeneor turned nimbly on the spot as the champion came at them again.

With Havelock behind him, Leofric was nowhere near as mobile as he would normally be, but he could not simply push him from the horse. Twin longswords stabbed for him, but the Blade of Midnight moved like a snake, blocking each blow and sending blistering ripostes towards the champion's head.

The dark warrior circled Leofric and he thought he could sense its dark amusement at their plight. He felt his anger rise and quashed it savagely, knowing that such anger would lead him to make a fatal error. He felt Aeneor's chest heave with exertion and hoped his faithful mount could bear them away from this evil place.

Once again, he charged towards the warrior, using the mass of his steed to drive his sword home. The Blade of Midnight smashed aside the first of the warrior's longswords and plunged towards his chest. Leofric yelled in triumph, then cried out in pain as a shock of

numbing cold flared up his sword arm and his sword slid clear
without having caused any harm to the undead warrior.

He circled around, gritting his teeth against the pain and stared,
uncomprehending, at his foe. His strike had been a good one, he was
certain of it. The monster should even now be cloven in twain upon
the ground, yet it stood unharmed before him, the amulet on its chest
burning with afterimages of dark fire.

The sun had now dropped behind the horizon and Leofric felt a
cold weight settle in his belly as he realised that this warrior was protected from harm by powerful dark magic.

'My lord,' begged Havelock from behind him. 'We must flee. Please,
I don't want to die here.'

'No, I will not run from this evil. I will defeat it,' said Leofric with a
confidence he did not feel. Before the pall of fear that still sought to
crush his courage could take hold, he attacked once more, a cry for
aid from the Lady of the Lake bursting from his lips. Once again,
Leofric's white blade and the warrior's black swords traded blows. The
champion's skill was great, but so too was Leofric's and he bore the
enchanted blade of the Hound of Winter.

They fought within the circle of the undead warriors, Leofric finding his attacks thwarted time and time again by the skill of his foe and
the unnatural magic that protected it.

When the end came it was sudden, Leofric raising his sword to
block a lightning riposte a fraction of a second too late. The black
blade glittered with evil runes and Leofric cried out in agony as it
smashed through the waist lames of his breastplate. Numbing cold
and pain spread from the wound, the hurt increased tenfold by the
spiteful runes inscribed onto the champion's blade. Leofric swayed in
the saddle as his vision greyed and only Havelock's grip and Aeneor's
sure footing kept him from falling.

Aching cold spread from where the champion's blow had landed,
blood streaming down the buckled strips of laminated plate that had
protected his midriff.

'You have great skill for a mortal,' hissed the undead warrior. 'You
will make a fine addition to the Red Duke's army.'

'No...' whispered Leofric, attempting to lift his sword, but his arm
was leaden and useless.

'Yes,' promised the champion, its grinning skull face alight with
triumph as it drew back its arm to deliver the deathblow. Leofric
felt the fear that had threatened to seize him earlier rise in a suffocating wave at the thought of rising to become one of the living
dead.

But before the undead warrior could strike Havelock cried, 'Aeneor!
Ride! Carry us away!'

The elven steed reared once more, his lashing hooves forcing the champion back, before turning and galloping towards the ring of skeletal warriors who stood sentinel around the duel. Havelock held Leofric tightly as the steed thundered onwards and closed his eyes as he felt the horse surge into the air.

Aeneor smashed through the ranks of the dead with the clang of metal and the snap of bone as he crushed those he landed upon and scattered the others with the power of his charge. Swords and spears stabbed, but none could touch the fast moving steed as it battered its way clear of its rider's enemies.

Then they were clear and Leofric felt a measure of his senses returning as they rode clear of the dark fear that filled the air around the undead.

He raised his head and said, 'We have to go back and fight!'

'With all due respect,' wheezed Havelock, 'don't be a fool! Don't listen to him, Aeneor, keep going!'

Leofric wanted to protest, but his strength was gone. He gripped his sword hilt tightly and looked down at his wound, where blood pumped weakly down his leg. He had suffered worse in his time as a knight, but the real damage had been done – and was *still* being done – by the evil magic worked into the champion's blade.

He heard the mournful howl of wolves echoing from the furthest reaches of the forest and knew that the minions of the Red Duke were not about to let him escape that easily.

'Havelock...' gasped Leofric.

'My lord?' said his squire.

'Get me clear of this place...'

'That's what I'm doing, my lord,' confirmed Havelock as the elven steed thundered through the forest and away from the domain of the undead. 'Though I think Aeneor's doing a better job of it than I am.'

Leofric nodded weakly as the cold spread to his chest and he felt the pain deep in his heart. 'We have to warn the lord of Aquitaine...'

Aeneor galloped onwards.

How long they had ridden for, Leofric could not say; his only memories blurred and pain-filled. Deathly cold filled his limbs and his every movement felt like it would be his last. He was dimly aware of the forest flashing past him and the howling of wolves in the night. The passage of time became meaningless to him as the pain of his wound threatened to overwhelm him.

Waking dreams plagued him in which he saw Helene once more, alive and wrapped in her favourite red dress as she danced for him and held his son, Beren, out before her. He wept to see such visions and though they showed him wondrous memories, he cast them from his thoughts as he knew they were the vanguard of the journey to Morr's embrace.

In moments of lucidity, he tried to converse with Havelock and ask of the health of Aeneor, but each time he tried to speak, he found his words slurred and unintelligible.

An eternity or a heartbeat passed in silent, cold agony and it was with a start Leofric opened his eyes to see that they were no longer beneath the oppressive branches of the forest. Golden fields of corn stretched away for miles in all directions and warm sunlight streamed from the sky.

He smiled as he wondered if this was what it was like to die. He had heard that Morr's realm was cold, but he felt the warmth of the sun on his skin as a sweet nepenthe.

Thin columns of smoke rose from a pleasant looking walled hamlet in the distance and he wondered what fine fellows dwelled within. He realised that he was still riding a horse, feeling the grip of another holding him upright and with that realisation came the pain again.

He groaned, remembering the battle in the forest and the dire warning they had to bring to the knights of Aquitaine.

'Havelock…' he gasped, seeing a handful of hooded peasants walking towards them from the direction of the hamlet.

'I see them,' said Havelock.

Leofric squinted through the bright sunshine and his heart sank as he saw that the men were all carrying longbows fashioned from yew.

And as his consciousness finally slipped away, he saw that every arrowhead was aimed unerringly towards him.

WHEN NEXT LEOFRIC opened his eyes, he saw woven straw bound by twine above him and the animal stench of livestock was thick in his nostrils. He blinked, his eyes gummed by sleep and his mouth felt unbearably dry. His head rested on a pillow of wadded hessian and he saw that a thin blanket covered his body.

He lay still for several moments, piecing together the events of the last few… days?

How long had he lain here?

And where *was* here?

Leofric rolled his head to the side, seeing that he lay in a small room with a floor of hard-packed earth and walls formed from wattle and daub. His armour lay neatly stacked in the corner of the room and the Blade of Midnight stood propped against one wall.

He tried to rise, but a wave of nausea rose and threatened to make him vomit, so he lay back down and marshalled his strength as memories began to return to him. He remembered the fight against the undead warrior and reached below the blanket to where he recalled the monster's diabolical sword had cut him.

He could feel the wound was stitched, and that it was no more than a couple of days old. Of the flight from the undead, he remembered almost nothing, save a frantic ride through the dark groves of the forest towards what he supposed was safety.

'So where in the name of the Lady am I?' he whispered.

From the look of the room, he surmised he was in a peasant village somewhere near the edge of the Forest of Châlons, but which one he had no idea. Perhaps Havelock would know...

Havelock!

What had become of his squire? Leofric was overcome by a sudden horror that Havelock had met the same fate as Baudel, and vowed that never again would he ride into danger with a squire.

Even as the thought formed, a shadow moved at the entrance to the room and the blanket that covered the door and afforded him a little privacy moved aside and Havelock entered, carrying a steaming bowl that smelled delicious.

'Havelock!' cried Leofric. 'You're alive!'

'Well, begging your pardon, my lord, of course I am,' replied Havelock. 'It's you that almost didn't make it out of the forest in one piece.'

Leofric smiled to see his squire alive and well, pushing himself slowly upright. He winced at the numb stiffness in his side, but could already feel that it was a fading hurt. Havelock sat at the end of the cot bed and handed him the bowl, together with a hunk of hard bread. He saw the bowl was filled with a thin soup and dipped the bread in to moisten it before chewing it slowly.

He said nothing for a while, content just to wolf down the soup and bread, feeling stronger already as it reached his stomach. At last he put aside the bowl and said, 'How long have I lain here?'

'Two days,' replied Havelock. 'You were unconscious before I brought you in.'

'I was badly hurt,' said Leofric, again touching the stitches in his side.

'Aye, my lord,' nodded Havelock. 'That you were. I stitched the wound easy enough, but there was something about that wound that I couldn't fix.'

'The undead warrior,' said Leofric. 'He carried a blade of dark magic. I should be dead. Why am I not dead?'

'Always looking for the cloud around every silver lining, eh?' smiled Havelock. 'There's a woman here, knows her herbs and a thing or two about the human body. More than a thing or two in her younger years, if you take my meaning.'

'What?' said Leofric, utterly nonplussed.

Havelock sighed. 'Sometimes I swear trying to get the nobles to understand something simple's like duelling an avalanche.'

'What are you talking about, Havelock?'

'I'm saying that there's a grandmother here with more than a touch of the fay about her,' whispered Havelock conspiratorially. 'Her eyes are different colours and she's as quick on her feet as a Bordeleaux tavern wench.'

'What about her?' asked Leofric. 'What did she do?'

'Well I don't know,' shrugged Havelock. 'You don't go asking about those with the fay upon them, you just accept it and hope they don't turn you into a frog. She dug up some herbs from the edge of the forest and made you some kind of poultice. Rubbed it on your wound and mumbled some mumbo-jumbo I never ever heard before. Fair put the wind up me.'

'Put the wind up you?'

'Aye, my lord,' nodded Havelock, appearing more reluctant to continue. 'Once she'd finished, you was raving for the whole night, shouting about Morr's gate and... well.... how you had to get back to Athel Loren to save her... '

Leofric lay back down on the bed, well able to imagine how his ravings must have appeared to one who knew that his wife was dead.

'But anyway,' continued Havelock. 'Whatever it was she did seems to have worked, eh?'

'So it would appear,' agreed Leofric, sitting upright again as another thought occurred to him. 'Two days? The undead? Is there any sign of them?'

'No,' said Havelock. 'We got away from them. I think Aeneor would have outrun Glorfinial himself.'

'Aeneor!' cried Leofric.

Havelock held up a hand and said, 'He's fine. I took care of him myself. He's a tough old beast that one, the hard muscles of his chest kept the spear from going too deep. He'll have a nasty scar to show off, but he'll live.'

Relieved beyond words, Leofric swung his legs from the bed and said, 'My thanks, Havelock, you have done me proud. I'll not forget this. Nor the kindness of the peasants of... actually, where are we?'

'Ah...' said Havelock. 'Funny you should ask that.'

'Funny?' said Leofric. 'Funny how?'

Havelock was spared from answering by the arrival of another man at the door, his build powerful and his bearing martial. Dressed in the rough clothing of a huntsman, he carried a quiver of arrows over his shoulder and had a long bladed sword partially concealed beneath his hooded cloak. Beneath his peaked and feathered hunter's cap, his face was rakishly handsome and Leofric saw a glint of mischief there that he instantly disliked.

'Who are you?' asked Leofric. 'And where am I?'

The man smiled. 'My name is Carlomax and you are in the Free Peasant Republic of Derrevin Libre.'

LEOFRIC SAT ON the wall on the edge of the village, his breath coming in shallow gasps as he walked the circumference of the village to regain his strength. He wore his armour, for a knight of Bretonnia had to be able to fight in his armour as though it weighed nothing at all, though he felt very far from such fitness.

The blade of the undead champion had wounded him grievously, and despite the healing power of this village's fay woman, it was going to take time for his strength to fully return. He set off again, feeling stronger with each step and casting an eye around the village of Derrevin Libre.

Two score buildings of a reddish orange wattle and daub comprised the village, though at its centre stood a largely dismantled stone building that must once have belonged to the noble lord of this village. Only the nobles of Bretonnia were permitted to use stone in their dwellings, but such laws obviously held no sway in this place as Leofric watched gangs of peasants chipping away the mortar and ferrying the stone to the ground via a complicated series of block and tackle.

A tall palisade wall of logs with sharpened tops formed a defensive wall around the village and Leofric knew that this was higher and stronger than most villages could hope for. Having climbed to the top of the wall earlier, he had seen a bare swathe of the forest where the logs had come from and knew that the revolting peasants had put their brief time of freedom to good use in preparing for the inevitable counterattack. Hooded Herrimaults with longbows patrolled the walls and land beyond the village, alert and ready for the attack from the local lords that must surely come soon.

The village was thronged with laughing peasants and Leofric found the effect quite unsettling. Men and women worked in the fields beyond the walls and children played in the earthen streets, chasing hoops of cane or teasing the local dogs. The villages Leofric remembered from Quenelles were a far cry from Derrevin Libre, their peasants surly and hunched with their faces to the soil.

The sun was hot and he could feel his skin reddening, though he had refused Havelock's offer of a hooded Herrimault cloak, seeing it as an acceptance of what had happened here. The few people he encountered in his slow circuit of the village were amiable, if wary of him, as they had good right to be. For Leofric represented exactly what they had rebelled against six months ago.

Leofric still found it hard to believe that a peasant revolt had managed to survive this long, but if there was anywhere it could do so, it

was the fractious dukedom of Aquitaine. He did not know the names
of the local lords, but knew it was only a matter of time until they
came with fire and sword and put an end to this futile dream of freedom. Strangely, the thought of the status quo being restored here did
not give him as much comfort as he expected it would. People would
die and the ringleader of this revolution would be hanged.

Speaking of the ringleaders, he saw Carlomax, the charismatic Herrimault who appeared to be the self-appointed leader of this revolt
walking towards him, a longbow clutched in one hand, while his
other hand gripped the hilt of his sword.

'Mind if I walk with you?' asked Carlomax.

'Do I have a choice?' asked Leofric.

'This is Derrevin Libre,' smiled Carlomax. 'Everyone has a choice.'

'Did the local lord have a choice before your little revolution killed
him?'

Carlomax's lips pursed and Leofric saw him bite back a retort
before his easy composure reasserted itself. 'You are angry with me,
yet I have done nothing to you, sir knight.'

'You are a revolutionary, that is enough to make me angry.'

'A revolutionary?' said Carlomax. 'Yes, I suppose I am. But if I am,
then I fight for honour and justice, that is the true revolution here.'

'Honour and justice now includes murder does it?' spat Leofric.

Again Carlomax struggled to stay calm, and said, 'If you'll allow me
to show you something, I think you might change your mind.'

'Show me what?'

'Come,' said Carlomax, indicating that Leofric should follow him.
'It's easier if you see it first.'

THE ICE ROOM of the former lord of Derrevin Libre was dug deep
into the earth, far below ground level, and as Leofric descended
the stairs he relished the drop in temperature after the heat of the
day. A compact room of rough-hewn stone blocks, there was, of
course, no ice left, but it was still nevertheless pleasantly cool
though the shelves were empty of meat and vegetables as he might
have expected.

In fact the room was empty save for the bloated shape of the corpse
concealed beneath a large blanket. Despite the cool air, the stench
was appalling and Leofric was forced to cover his nose and mouth to
keep it at bay.

'You kept the body?' said Leofric, aghast. 'Why?'

'You'll see,' promised Carlomax. 'Take a look.'

Against his better judgement Leofric approached the covered body,
keeping one hand pressed over his mouth as Carlomax took hold of
the blanket and pulled it back to reveal the dead body beneath.

Leofric dropped to his knees at the horror that was revealed, his stomach turning in loops as he fought to prevent himself from vomiting. The body was that of a man, but a man so bloated and repellent that Leofric could barely believe such a thing was human. Sagging folds of flab hung slackly from the man's frame, his skin discoloured and ruptured in numerous places, each long gash encrusted with filth and dried pustules. The man had clearly been diseased and he backed away lest some contagion remained in the rotted flesh.

'You need to burn this,' said Leofric. 'It has become rank with corruption.'

'No,' said Carlomax. 'The body has not changed since we killed him.'

Leofric looked back at the repulsive corpse and said, 'Impossible. The body has rotted from within.'

'I swear to you, Leofric, that this is exactly how this... thing was put here. Look at his arms, he was a worshipper of the Dark Gods.'

Leofric was loath to look again at the horrendous sight, but bent once again to the body. His eyes roamed the purulent, flabby arms, at last seeing what Carlomax was referring to. All along the length of the man's arms were a regular series of blisters, each formed in a triangular pattern of three adjoining circles. Each cluster was arranged in the same pattern.

'I have seen this before,' said Leofric.

'You have? Where?'

'I fought alongside the king at the great battle against the northern tribes at the foot of the Ulricsberg. I saw this symbol painted on the banners and carved into the flesh of the warriors who worshipped the Dark God of pestilence and decay.'

Carlomax made the sign the protective horns as Leofric saw that many of the open wounds on the man's body had more than a hint of mouth to them, some even having twisted vestigial teeth and gums protruding from the grey meat of the body.

'The man was an altered,' said Carlomax. 'He deserved to die.'

Leofric nodded. The mutating power of Chaos had warped the dead man's flesh into this morbidly repulsive form for some unguessable purpose and the horror of it sickened him.

The power of Chaos was a foulness that infected the minds of the weak with promises of easy power and immortality, but it inevitably led to corruption and death, though such a fate never seemed to deter others from believing they could master it.

'I've seen enough,' he said, turning and marching up the stairs. He needed to be out of that foetid darkness and away from the disgusting vision of the mutated corpse. He emerged into the sunlight, taking a deep breath of fresh air and feeling his head clear almost instantly as he moved away from the building.

'You see now why this happened?' asked Carlomax, following Leofric back into the daylight above.

Leofric nodded, but said, 'It won't make any difference though.'

Carlomax shook his head. 'It has to. When people see what happened here and why, justice will prevail.'

'Justice?'

'Yes, justice,' snapped Carlomax. 'That is the code of the Herrimaults, to uphold justice where the law has failed and to reject the dark gods and to fight against them at all times.'

'The Herrimaults truly have a code of honour?'

'We do,' said Carlomax defiantly.

'Tell me of it,' said Leofric.

As the last rays of sunlight faded from the sky, Leofric sat on the edge of the palisade wall looking out over the surrounding lands, his thoughts confused and uncertain. When he had first heard of Derrevin Libre, he had been horrified at the upsetting of the natural order of things and branded the Herrimaults as little better than brigands, but the day spent with Carlomax had disabused him of that notion.

The man's brother had been hung for smiling at a noble's daughter and his mother crippled by a beating for weeping at the execution. Small wonder he had turned to the life of an outlaw.

Carlomax had told him how he had later abducted the noble's daughter, intending to rape and torture her, but had found that he had not the stomach for such vileness, and had released her unharmed.

How much of that story was true, he didn't know for sure, but Carlomax had an integrity to him that Leofric had quickly recognised and despite his initial misgivings, he found he believed the man. The code of the Herrimaults had impressed him, its tenets not unfamiliar to a knight such as he; to protect the innocent, to uphold justice, to be true to your fellows and to fight the powers of Chaos wherever they are found.

Following such a code, Carlomax might himself have been a knight were it not for his low birth. And from what Leofric had seen around Derrevin Libre, he couldn't argue that Carlomax had created a functioning society for its people that was superior to the lot of the majority of Bretonnian peasants.

The night's darkness was absolute and Leofric knew that come the morning he and Havelock would ride to the city of Aquitaine itself to warn the duke of the threat gathering in the north of his lands.

Filled with such gloomy thoughts, Leofric did not hear Havelock approach, his squire appearing absurdly cheerful, though he was not surprised. To another peasant, Derrevin Libre must seem like paradise and Leofric found that he could not find it in himself to disagree.

'You should get some sleep, it's going to be a long day tomorrow and you still haven't got your strength back yet… my lord,' said Havelock and Leofric couldn't help but notice the tiniest hesitation before he had added 'my lord'.

'I know,' said Leofric.

Havelock nodded, suddenly awkward and Leofric said, 'Do you want to stay here, Havelock? In the village, I mean?'

His squire frowned and shook his head. 'No, my lord. Why would I want to do such a thing?'

Leofric was surprised and said, 'I thought you admired the Herrimaults?'

'I do, my lord,' agreed Havelock. 'But I swore an oath to you and I plan on honouring that. It's nice here, don't get me wrong, but…'

'But what?'

'But it won't last,' whispered Havelock sadly. 'You know it and I know it. When the local lords finally get over whatever feuds are keeping them busy, they'll come in force and burn this place to the ground. Can't have the peasants believing that there might be other ways of life than the one they're born to, eh? Tell me I'm wrong.'

Leofric shook his head. 'No, you're not wrong. I just wish the notions that underpin the knightly code and the Herrimaults' code could be put into practice beyond the conduct of a single knight or outlaw.'

'Well, it's a noble dream, my lord, but we live in the real world, don't we?'

Leofric said, 'That we do, Havelock, that we do. Here, help me up.'

Havelock pulled Leofric to his feet, the pair of them freezing as a chorus of wolf howls echoed through the darkness.

Leofric's gaze was drawn to the edge of the forest as he heard new sounds beyond that of the howling wolves, the tramp of feet and the crack of snapping branches as armed warriors marched through the trees.

'Oh no… ' whispered Leofric as he saw scores of armoured skeletons emerge from the treeline, packs of snapping wolves at their heels.

Standing in the centre of the battle line, dimly illuminated by the flickering glow of the torches set on the palisade walls of Derrevin Libre, was the gold and silver armoured champion of the dead and the hooded necromancer. The champion rode the monstrous carcass of the blackest horse, its eyes afire with the flames of the damned.

'Run, Havelock!' shouted Leofric. 'Get Carlomax! Tell him to get every man who can hold a sword to the walls. We're under attack!'

WITHIN MOMENTS, A hundred men were at the wall, some armed with longbows, but most with peasant weapons: axes, spears and scythes.

The army of undead had not moved since Leofric's warning, their utter stillness draining the courage of the men at the walls with every passing second.

'Where have they come from?' asked Carlomax, standing beside Leofric with his bow at the ready and a quiver full of arrows.

'From deep in the forest,' said Leofric. 'They are the heralds of the Red Duke.'

'The Red Duke!' hissed Carlomax, his handsome features twisted in the fear that such a name carried for the people of Aquitaine. 'He rises again?'

Leofric nodded. 'I believe he will soon. Havelock and I were riding for the duke's lands bearing warning when we came upon your village.'

'Can we hold them?' asked Carlomax. 'There are quite a lot of them...'

'We'll hold them,' promised Leofric, casting his gaze along the length of the palisade wall. 'By my honour, we will hold them.'

Like a wind driven before a storm, the fear of these dreadful creatures reached outwards, and Leofric could see that each man's heart was icy with the chill of the grave at the very unnaturalness of the risen dead.

Though the men on the walls were clearly brave, Leofric knew that their courage balanced on a knife-edge and that they needed some fire in their bellies if they weren't to flee in terror from the first charge.

Leofric marched along the length of the wall facing the undead, lifting his white bladed sword high so that every man could see its purity in the face of such evil.

'Men of Bretonnia!' he shouted. 'You will hold these walls!'

'Why should we listen to you?' cried a voice in the darkness.

'If you want to live, you will listen to him!' returned Carlomax.

Leofric nodded his thanks and continued. He had thought to appeal to their duty to the king, but had thought the better of it when he saw the number of Herrimault cloaks among the villagers. As much as he had considered them little more than bandits before today, he was savvy enough to know that their skill with a bow would be useful in the coming fight.

'You are right to question me, but I say this not as an order, but as a statement of fact. You *have* to hold these walls, for if you do not, your families will die and your homes will become your graves. At least until fell sorcery brings your spirit back to your dead flesh and you are denied eternal rest.'

He could see the horror of such a thought writ large on every face, knowing that the fear of such a fate would rouse each man to great deeds.

'Your courage and strength will decide if you live or die tonight, so if you fight not for the king or your lord, fight for that. No grand gestures or lordly ambitions will be satisfied by this battle, only survival. I have fought things like this before and I tell you now they *can* be defeated. Cut them down as you would an orc or beast, but be wary of them rising again. Destroy the head if you can or smash the ribcage. Though these things have no hearts that beat as ours do, a mortal blow will still destroy them. Fight hard and may the Lady guide your arms!'

'Derrevin!' shouted Carlomax, seeing that Leofric had finished.

'Libre!' cheered the men of the village in response.

'Nice speech, my lord,' said Havelock, nocking an arrow to his bow, 'but I think his was punchier.'

'Evidently,' agreed Leofric as the chant of 'Libre! Libre! Libre!' echoed through the darkness.

Leofric gripped his sword a little tighter as he saw that the time for speeches and waiting was over as the army of undead began its advance on the village. Marching in ordered squares a general of the Empire would have been proud of, the dead warriors tramped in silence towards the walls, the only sound the clink and scrape of rusted chainmail on bone.

'Steady!' shouted Carlomax, nocking an arrow and pulling his bowstring tight. For a moment Leofric wished he had a bow, but then shook his head at such foolishness... a knight with a bow! He chuckled at the idea and knew he had spent too much time in Derrevin Libre if its revolutionary ideals were starting to put such thoughts in his head.

'Loose!' shouted Carlomax and a flurry of arrows slashed towards the marching warriors.

As Leofric had said, the undead could indeed be brought down, and a dozen skeletons collapsed into jumbled piles of bone as the magic binding their form together was undone. The remainder paid these losses no heed and came on, uncaring of the volleys of shafts that punched through skulls or severed spines.

Though dozens fell with each volley, there were hundreds more and Leofric knew that within moments the enemy would be at the walls. Dark fear spread like a bow wave before the undead and Leofric could see many shafts loosed in haste from shaking hands thud harmlessly into the ground.

'Bretonnia!' he shouted. 'The spirit of Gilles le Breton is in each of you! Do not give in to the fear! Remember that your loved ones depend on your courage!'

Further words were wasted as the undead warriors slammed into the wall and Leofric felt the logs sway as the implacable will of the Necromancer gave the undead strength. Ancient sword blades hacked into the timbers and skeletal hands dug into the gnarled bark as dead warriors hauled themselves towards the parapet.

A leering skull encased in a fluted helmet of bronze appeared before Leofric and he swept his sword through the neck, sending the body tumbling to the earth. No sooner had it vanished than yet more appeared. The Blade of Midnight smote them down, but armoured skeletons clambered over the sharpened logs all along the length of the wall.

The villagers of Derrevin Libre hacked at them with axes and stabbed them from the walls with their spears, but for some the horror of the living dead was too much and they broke and ran from the battle. Havelock sent shaft after shaft into the horde at the bottom of the wall as they chopped at the logs or slithered over the bones of the fallen.

Screams of fear and pain filled the air as ancient blades and clawed hands tore at warm flesh and Leofric hacked his way through the dead to where the fighting was thickest, bellowing cries to the Lady and the King as he smashed the undead from the walls.

Carlomax held a section of wall above the gate, his sword battering skeletons from the walls with every stroke. Leofric could see that the man was reasonably skilled with a sword, and what he lacked in elegance, he made up for in ferocity.

The night rang to the clash of iron on bronze, the battle fought in the flickering glow of torches set on the wall. Leofric heard wailing screams and turned to see the men on the wall to his right shrieking like banshees and clawing at their flesh in agony. Age-withered flesh slid from their muscles and wasted organs blistered as they ruptured and turned to dust.

'No!' shouted Leofric, tasting the rank odour of dark magic on the air. He risked a glance to the hillside where the undead champion and the necromancer watched the battle below. Leaping scads of power swirled around the dread sorcerer.

Even as he returned his gaze to the battle, he saw it was hopeless. Skeletal warriors had footholds along the wall and the men of Derrevin Libre who had fallen were even now climbing to their feet to hurl themselves at their former comrades with monstrous hunger.

'Carlomax! Havelock!' shouted Leofric. 'The sorcerer!'

He had no way of knowing whether or not his words had been heard as he fought his way along the wall, hacking a path through the living dead. He saw Havelock pinned against the inner face of the wall by a skeleton attempting to throttle the life from him, while Carlomax battled a trio of armoured skeletons. Leofric killed the first and kicked the second over the wall as Carlomax despatched the last.

He hacked his sword through the spine of the skeleton attacking Havelock and, together with Carlomax, the three of them formed a fighting wedge above the gate.

'My thanks,' breathed Carlomax. 'I don't think I could have taken them all.'

Leofric nodded and said, 'We can't hold them like this.'

'No,' agreed Carlomax. 'What do you suggest?'

'Something more direct,' said Leofric, pointing to the two dark figures that observed the battle from their vantage point at the treeline. 'I need to get them down here!'

'What?' said Carlomax. 'Are you mad?'

A thunderous crash and crack of shorn timbers sounded from below and Havelock shouted, 'The gate!' as a white blur galloped through the village towards the wall.

'Be ready for my shout!' yelled Leofric as he dropped from the parapet and onto the back of Aeneor. Leofric yelled an oath to the Lady, and rode into the gateway, where a dozen skeletons pushed through with spears lowered. He smashed their blades aside and bludgeoned them to splinters with the weight of his charge and the brutality of his sword blows.

Aeneor reared in the gateway before the advancing horde of the dead, Leofric's Blade of Midnight throwing off loops of white fire that reflected from the insides of the skulls of the warriors before him.

'Come on then, you dead bastards!' he shouted. 'I'll kill you for good this time!'

A shadow loomed beyond the gateway and he urged Aeneor onwards, leaping the splintered ruin of the gate and scattering the skeletal warriors before him. His sword cut skulls from necks and arms from shoulders as he cut a deadly swathe through the enemy, but beyond the press of bone and bronze at the gateway, he saw what he had been hoping for.

Mounted on his dark steed, the undead champion awaited him, the necromancer hunched in his shadow and dark coils of magic leaping from his wizened fingers.

'Carlomax! Havelock!' called Leofric. 'Now! Shoot!'

A pair of arrows leapt from the walls and hammered into the champion's breastplate, but the dead warrior appeared not to notice them.

'Not him!' shouted Leofric, but further words were impossible as the champion charged towards him, the eyes of his terrifying black steed burning with dreadful malice. Leofric knew his strength was not the equal of this warrior, but he was no man's inferior on horseback. He had toppled Chilfroy of Artois and would be damned if this creature of darkness was going to be the death of him.

The distance between the two warriors closed rapidly and Leofric swayed aside at the last possible second as the champion's sword struck to deal him a mortal blow. The Blade of Midnight turned aside the blow and Leofric lunged, the tip of the blade spearing the heart of the champion's obsidian amulet and splitting it apart with a hideous crack of thunder.

The champion gave a cry of fury as Aeneor turned on the spot and Leofric swept his sword out in a wide arc as a pair of arrows slashed through the air above him.

Even amid the clamour of battle and the screams of the dying, Leofric heard the thud of arrows striking flesh and the hollow clang as his sword smashed the undead champion's helmet and skull to shards.

The dark steed rode on for a moment before its substance began to unravel and it finally collapsed into a clattering pile of dead flesh and bones. The fallen champion was pitched from the saddle, his own form coming apart as the will that held him to the mortal world fled his ruined shell.

Leofric lifted his sword in victory as he saw the necromancer struggle to pull Carlomax and Havelock's arrows from his chest, but it was a futile gesture and Leofric watched as dissolution rendered his flesh down to naught but dust.

The sounds of battle began to fade and Leofric saw the undead horde begin to collapse before the walls of Derrevin Libre as the dark magic that empowered them faded from their long-dead bones.

He sighed in relief and felt his spirits rise as he realised that the night's horror was over.

The Battle for Derrevin Libre had been won.

'SO WHAT WILL you tell the duke of us, Leofric?' asked Carlomax as Leofric and Havelock prepared to ride from the village the following morning. Havelock's horse had been lost in the depths of the forest, but he had been furnished with one of the previous master of the village's prize steeds.

With the defeat of the undead, Leofric felt that the sky was clearer and he could smell the scent of wild flowers carried on the back of a delightfully crisp breeze.

Leofric considered the question for a moment before answering. 'I will tell him the truth.'

'And what is that?'

'That Derrevin Libre has no lord,' said Leofric. 'And that it might be better were it to be allowed to go on without one for a while.'

Carlomax nodded. 'Thank you, that is more than I would have asked for.'

'It won't change anything though,' warned Leofric. 'They *will* come with bared swords.'

'I know,' agreed Carlomax. 'But now we have a few battles under our belts and even if they do kill us all, what we achieved here will be spoken of for years. Even the mightiest forest fire begins with but a single spark...'

Leofric shook his head. 'Then Derrevin Libre will be freedom's home or glory's grave.'

He turned Aeneor for the southern horizon and said, 'And I do not know which one I fear the most.'

ANCESTRAL HONOUR
Gav Thorpe

THICK, BLUE-GREY pipe smoke drifted lazily around the low rafters of the tavern, stirred into swirls and eddies by the dwarfs sat at the long benches in the main room. Grimli, known as the Blacktooth to many, hauled another keg of Bugman's Firestarter onto the bar with grunt. It wasn't even noon and already the tavern's patrons had guzzled their way through four barrels of ale. The thirsty dwarf miners were now banging their tankards in unison as one of their number tried to recite as many different names of beer as he could remember. The record, Grimli knew, was held by Oransson Brakkur and stood at three hundred and seventy-eight all told. The tavern owner, Skorri Weritaz, had a standing wager that if someone named more beers than Oransson they would get a free tankard of each that they named. The miner was already beginning to falter at a hundred and sixty-three, and even Grimli could think of twenty others he had not mentioned yet.

'Stop daydreaming, lad, and serve,' Skorri muttered as he walked past carrying a platter of steaming roast meat almost as large as himself. He saw Dangar, one of the mine overseers, at the far end of the bar gazing around with an empty tankard hanging limply in his hand. Wiping his hands on his apron, Grimli hurried over.

'Mug of Old Reliable's, Dangar?' Grimli offered, plucking the tankard from the other dwarf's grasp.

'I'll wait for Skorri to serve me, if'n you don't mind,' grunted Dangar, snatching back his drinking mug with a fierce scowl. 'Oathbreakers spoil the head.'

Skorri appeared at that moment and shooed Grimli away with a waved rag, turning to Dangar and taking the proffered tankard. Grimli wandered back to the Firestarter keg and picked the tapping hammer from his pocket. Placing a tap three fingers' breadth above the lower hoop, he delivered a swift crack with the hammer and the tap drove neatly into the small barrel. Positioning the slops bucket under the keg, he poured off the first half-pint, to make sure there were no splinters and that the beer had started to settle.

As he wandered around the benches, picking up empty plates, discarded bones and wiping the tables with his cloth, Grimli sighed. Not a single dwarf met his eye, and many openly turned their back on him as he approached. Sighing again, he returned to the bar. A shrill steam whistle blew signalling a change of shift, and as the incumbent miners filed out, a new crowd entered, shouting for ale and food.

And so the afternoon passed, the miners openly shunning Grimli, Skorri bad tempered and Grimli miserable. Just as the last ten years had been. Nothing had changed in all that time. No matter how diligently he worked, how polite and respectful he was, Grimli had been born a Skrundigor, and the stigma of the clan stayed with him. Here, in Karaz-a-Karak, home of the High King himself, Grimli was lucky he was even allowed to stay. He could have been cast out, doomed to wander in foreign lands until he died.

Well, Grimli thought to himself, as he washed the dishes in the kitchen at the back of the tavern, perhaps that would be better than the half-life he was leading now. Even Skorri, who was half mad, from when a cave-in dropped a tunnel roof on his head, could barely say three words to him, and Grimli considered him the closest thing he had to a friend. In truth, Skorri put up with having the Blacktooth in his bar because no other dwarf would lower themselves to work for the mad old bartender. No one else would listen to his constant muttering day after day, week after week, year after year. No one except Grimli, who had no other choice. He wasn't allowed in the mines because it would bring bad luck, he'd never been taken as an apprentice and so knew nothing of smithying, stonemasonry or carpentry. And as for anything to do with the treasuries and armouries, well no one would let an oathbreaker by birth within three tunnels of those areas. And so, bottle washer and tankard cleaner he was, and bottle washer and tankard cleaner he would stay for the rest of his life, perhaps only two hundred years more if he was lucky.

That thought started a chain of others in Grimli's mind. Dishonoured and desperate for release, from this living prison of disdain and hatred, the dwarf's thoughts turned to the Slayer shrine just two levels above his head. He was neither an experienced nor naturally talented fighter. Perhaps if he joined the Slayers, if he swore to seek out an honourable death against the toughest foe he could find, then he would find peace. If not, then his less than ample skills at battle would see him dead within the year, he was sure of it. Grimli had seen a few Slayers; some of them came to Karaz-a-Karak on their journeys and drank in Skorri's tavern. He liked them because they would talk to him, as they knew nothing about his family's past. They would never talk about their own dishonour, of course, and Grimli didn't want to hear it; he was still a dwarf after all and such things were for oneself not open conversation even with friends and family. But they had talked about the places outside of Karaz-a-Karak, of deadly battles, strange beasts and mighty foes. As a life, it would be better than picking up scraps for a few meagre copper coins.

He was decided. When his shift finished that evening, he would go up to the shrine of Grimnir and swear the Slayer oath.

As HE STEPPED through the large stone archway into the shrine, Grimli steeled himself. For the rest of the day he had questioned his decision, looking at it from every possible angle, seeing if there was some other solution than this desperate measure. But no other answer had come to him, and here he was, reciting the words of the Slayer oath in his mind. He took a deep breath and stared steadily at the massive gold-embossed face of Grimnir, the Ancestor God of Battle. In the stylised form of the shrine's decoration, his beard was long and full, his eyes steely and menacing, his demeanour proud and stern.

I am a dwarf, Grimli recited to himself in his head, *my honour is my life and without it, I am nothing*. He took another deep breath. *I shall become a Slayer, I shall seek redemption in the eyes of my ancestors*. The lines came clearly to Grimli's keen mind.

'I shall become as death to my enemies until I face he that takes my life and my shame,' a gravely voice continued next to him. Turning with a start, Grimli was face-to-face with a Slayer. He had heard no one enter, but perhaps he had been so intent on the oath he had not noticed. He was sure that no one else had been here when he came in.

'How do you know what I'm doing?' asked Grimli suspiciously. 'I might have come here for other reasons.'

'You are Grimli Blacktooth Skrundigor,' the Slayer boomed in his harsh voice. 'You and all your family have been accused of cowardice and cursed by the High King for seventeen generations. You are a serving lad in a tavern. Why else would you come to Grimnir's shrine other than to forsake your previous life and become as I?'

'How do you know so much about me, Slayer?' Grimli eyed the stranger with caution. He looked vaguely familiar, but even if Grimli had once known him, his transformation into a Slayer made him unrecognisable now. The Slayer was just a little taller than he was; though he seemed much more for his hair was spiked with orange-dyed lime and stood another foot higher than Grimli. His beard was long and lustrous, similarly dyed and woven with bronze and gold beads and bands, which sparkled in the lantern light of the shrine. Upon his face were numerous swirling tattoos – runes and patterns of Grugni and Valaya, to ward away evil. In his hand, the Slayer carried a great axe, fully as tall as the Slayer himself. Its head gleamed with a bluish light and even Grimli could recognise rune work when he saw it. The double-headed blade was etched with signs of cutting and cleaving, and Grimli had no doubt that many a troll, orc or skaven had felt its indelicate bite.

'Call me Dammaz,' the Slayer told Grimli, extending a hand in friendship with a grin. Grimli noticed with a quiver of fear that the Slayer's teeth were filed to points, and somewhat reddened. He shuddered when he realised they were bloodstained.

Dammaz, he thought. One of the oldest dwarf words, it meant 'grudge' or 'grievance'. Not such a strange name for a Slayer.

He took the offered hand gingerly and felt his fingers in a fierce grip which almost crushed his hand. Dammaz's forearms and biceps bulged with corded muscles and veins as they shook hands, and it was then Grimli noticed just how broad the other dwarf was. His shoulders were like piles of boulders, honed with many long years of swinging that massive axe. His chest was similarly bulged; the harsh white of many scars cut across the deep tan of the Slayer's bare flesh.

'Do you want me to accompany you after I've sworn the oath?' guessed Grimli, wondering why this mighty warrior was taking such an interest in him.

'No, lad,' Dammaz replied, releasing his bone-splintering grip. 'I want you to come with me to Karak Azgal, and see what I have to show you. If, after that, you want to return here and be a Slayer, then you can do so.'

'Why Karak Azgal?' Grimli's suspicions were still roused.

'You of anyone should know that,' Dammaz told him sternly.

'Because that is… was where…' Grimli started, but he found he couldn't say the words. He couldn't talk about it, not here, not with this dwarf who he had just met. He could barely let the words enter his own head let alone speak them. It was too much to ask, and part of the reason he wanted to become a Slayer.

'Yes, that is why,' nodded Dammaz with a sad smile. 'Easy, lad, you don't have to tell me anything. Just answer yes or no. Will you come with me to Karak Azgal and see what I have to show you?'

Grimli looked into the hard eyes of the Slayer and saw nothing there but tiny reflections of himself.

'I will come,' he said, and for some reason his spirits lifted.

It wasn't exactly a fond farewell when Grimli told Skorri that he was leaving. The old dwarf looked him up and down and then took his arm and led him into the small room next to the kitchen which served as the tavern owner's bed chamber, store room and office. He pulled a battered chest from under the bed and opened the lid on creaking hinges. Delving inside, he pulled out a hammer which he laid reverentially on the bed, followed by a glistening coat of chain-mail. He then unhooked the shield that hung above the fireplace and added it to the pile.

'Take 'em,' he said gruffly, pointing to the armour and hammer. 'Did me good, killed plenty grobi and such with them, I did. Figure you need 'em more 'n me now, and you do the right thing now. It's good. Maybe you come back, maybe you don't, but you won't come back the same, I reckon.'

Grimli opened his mouth to thank Skorri, but the old dwarf had turned and stomped from the room, muttering to himself again. Grimli stood there for a moment, staring absently out of the door at Skorri's receding back, before turning to the bed. He took off his apron and hung it neatly over the chair by the fire. Lifting the mail coat, he slipped it over his head and shoulders where it settled neatly. It was lighter than he had imagined, and fitted him almost perfectly. The shield had a long strap and he hooked it over one shoulder, settling it across his back.

Finally, he took up the hammer. The haft was bound in worn leather, moulded over the years into a grip that his short fingers could hold comfortably. The weight was good, the balance slightly towards the head but not ungainly. Hefting it in his hand a couple of times, Grimli smiled to himself. Putting the hammer through his belt, he strode out into the busy tavern room. The conversation died immediately and a still calm settled. Everyone was looking at him.

'Goin' somewhere, are ye?' asked a miner from over by the bar. 'Off to fight, perhaps?'

'Perhaps,' agreed Grimli. 'I'm going to Karak Azgal, to find my honour.'

With that he walked slowly, confidently across the room. A few of the dwarfs actually met his gaze, a couple nodded in understanding. As he was about to cross the threshold he heard Dangar call out from behind him.

'When you find it lad, I'll be the first to buy you a drink.'

With a lightness in his step he had never felt before, Grimli walked out of the tavern.

FOR MANY WEEKS the pair travelled south, using the long underway beneath the World's Edge Mountains when possible, climbing to the surface where collapses and disrepair made the underground highway impassable. For the most part they journeyed in silence; Grimli used to keeping his own company, the Slayer unwilling or unable to take part in idle conversation. The night before they were due to enter Karak Azgal they sat camped in the ruins of an old wayhouse just off the main underway. By the firelight, the stone reliefs that adorned the walls and ceiling of the low, wide room flickered in ruddy shadow. Scenes from the great dwarf history surrounded Grimli, and he felt reassured by the weight of the ancient stones around him. He felt a little trepidation about the coming day, for Karak Azgal was one of the fallen Holds, now a nest of goblins, trolls, skaven and many other foul creatures. During the nights they had shared in each other's company, Dammaz had taught him a little of fighting. Grimli was not so much afraid for his own life, he was surprised and gladdened to realise, but that he would fail Dammaz. He had little doubt that the hardened Slayer would not need his help, but he fancied that the old dwarf might do something reckless if he needed protecting and Grimli did not want that on his conscience.

'Worried, lad?' asked Dammaz, appearing out of the gloom. He had disappeared frequently in the last week, returning sometimes with a blood-slicked axe. Grimli knew better than to ask.

'A little,' Grimli admitted with a shrug.

'Take heart then,' Dammaz told him, squatting down on the opposite side of the fire, the flames dancing in bright reflections off his burnished jewellery. 'For fear makes us strong. Use it, lad, and it won't use you. You'll be fine. Remember, strike with confidence and you'll strike with strength. Aim low and keep your head high.'

They sat for a while longer in quiet contemplation. Clearing his throat, Grimli broke the silence.

'We are about to enter Karak Azgal, and I'd like to know something,' Grimli spoke. 'If you don't want to answer, I'll understand but it'll set my mind at rest.'

'Ask away, lad. I can only say no,' Dammaz reassured him.

'What's your interest in me, what do you know about the Skrundigor curse?' Grimli asked before he changed his mind.

Dammaz stayed silent for a long while and Grimli thought he wasn't going to get an answer. The old dwarf eventually looked him in the eye and Grimli meant his gaze.

'Your distant forefather Okrinok Skrundigor failed in his duty many centuries ago, for which the High King cursed him and all his line,'

Dammaz told him. 'The name of Skrundigor is inscribed into the Dammaz Kron. Until such time as the honour of the clan is restored, the curse will bring great pain, ill fortune and the scorn of others onto Okrinok's entire heritage. This I know. But, do you know why the High King cursed you so?'

'I do,' Grimli replied solemnly. Like Dammaz, he did not speak straight away, but considered his reply before answering. 'Okrinok was a coward. He fled from a fight. He broke his oaths to protect the High King's daughter from harm, and for that he can never be forgiven. His selfishness and betrayal has brought misery to seventeen generations of my clan and I am last of his line. Accidents and mishaps have killed all my kin at early ages. Many left in self-exile, others became Slayers before me.'

'That is right,' agreed Dammaz. 'But do you know exactly what happened, Grimli?'

'For my shame, I do,' Grimli replied. 'Okrinok was sworn to protect Frammi Sunlocks, the High King's daughter, when she travelled to Karak Azgal to meet her betrothed, Prince Gorgnir. She wished to see something of her new home, and Prince Gorgnir, accompanied by Okrinok and the royal bodyguard, took her to the treasuries, the forges, the armouries and the many other great wonders of Karak Azgal. Being of good dwarf blood, she was interested in the mines. One day they travelled to the depths of the hold so that she could see the miners labouring. It was an ill-chosen day, for that very day vile goblins broke through into the mines. They had been tunnelling for Grugni knows how long, and of all the days that their sprawling den had to meet the wide-hewn corridors of Karak Azgal it was that one which fate decreed.'

Grimli stopped and shook his head with disbelief. A day earlier or a day later, and the entire history of the Skrundigors may have been completely different; a glorious heritage of battles won and loyal service to the High King. But it had not been so.

'The grobi set upon the royal household,' continued Grimli. 'Hard fought was the battle, and bodyguard and miners clashed with a countless horde of greenskins. But there were too many of them, and their wicked knives caught Frammi and Gorgnir and slew them. One of the bodyguards, left for dead by the grobi, survived to recount the tale to the High King and much was the woe of all the dwarf realm. Yet greater still was the hardship for as the survivor told the High King with his dying breath, Okrinok Skrundigor, upon seeing the princess and prince-to-be slain, had fled the fight and his body was never found. Righteous and furious was the High King's anger and we have been cursed since.'

'Told as it has been to each generation of Skrundigor since that day,' Dammaz nodded thoughtfully. 'And was the High King just in his anger?'

'I have thought of it quite a lot, and I reckon he was,' admitted Grimli, poking at the fire as it began to die down. 'Many a king would have had us cast out or even slain for such oathbreaking and so I think he was merciful.'

'We will speak of this again soon,' Dammaz said as he stood up. 'I go to Kargun Skalfson now, to seek permission to enter Karak Azgal come tomorrow.'

With that the Slayer was gone into the gloom once more, leaving Grimli to his dour thoughts.

THE STENCH OF the troll sickened Grimli's stomach as it lurched through the doorway towards him. It gave a guttural bellow as it broke into a loping run. Grimli was rooted to the spot. In his mind's eye he could see himself casually stepping to one side, blocking its claw with his shield as Dammaz had taught him; in reality his muscles were bunched and tense and his arm shook. Then the Slayer was there, between him and the approaching monster. In the darkness, Grimli could clearly see the blazing axe head as it swung towards the troll, cleaving through its midriff, spraying foul blood across the flagged floor as the blade continued on its course and shattered its backbone before swinging clear. Grimli stood in dumbfounded amazement. One blow had sheared the troll cleanly in two. Dammaz stood over the rank corpse and beheaded it with another strike before spitting on the body.

'Can never be too sure with trolls. Always cut the head off, lad,' Dammaz told him matter-of-factly as he strolled back to stand in front of Grimli.

'I'm sorry,' Grimli lowered his head in shame. 'I wanted to fight it, but I couldn't.'

'Calm yourself, lad,' Dammaz laid a comforting hand on his shoulder. 'Next time you'll try harder, won't you?'

'Yes, I will,' Grimli replied, meeting the Slayer's gaze.

FOR TWO DAYS and two nights they had been in Karak Azgal. The night before, Grimli had slain his first troll, crushing its head with his hammer after breaking one of its legs. He had already lost count of the number of goblins whose last vision had been his hammer swinging towards them. Over twenty at least, possibly nearer thirty, he realised. Of course, Dammaz had slain twice, even thrice that number, but Grimli felt comfortable that he was holding his own.

Dammaz had been right, it did get easier. Trolls still scared Grimli, but he had worked out how to turn that fear into anger, imbuing his limbs with extra strength and honing his reflexes. And most of all, it had taught Grimli that it felt good to kill grobi. It was in his blood, by race and by clan, and he now relished each fight, every battle a chance to exact a small measure of revenge on the foul creatures whose kind had ruined his clan so many centuries before.

They were just breaking camp in what used to be the forges, so Dammaz informed him. Everything had been stripped bare by the evacuating dwarfs and centuries of bestial looters and other treasure hunters. But the firepits could still clearly be seen, twenty of them in all, spread evenly across the large hall. Grugni, God of Smithing, was represented by a great anvil carved into the floor, his stern but kindly face embossed at its centre. Dammaz told him that the lines of the anvil used to run with molten metal so that its light illuminated the whole chamber with fiery beauty.

Grimli would have liked to have seen that, like so many other things from the days when the dwarf realms stretched unbroken from one end of the World's Edge Mountains to the other. Such a great past, so many treasures and wonders, now all lost, perhaps never to be regained and certainly never to be surpassed. Centuries of treachery, volcanoes, earthquakes and the attacks of grobi and skaven had almost brought the dwarfs to their knees. They had survived though; the dwarfs were at their fiercest when hardest pressed. The southern holds may have fallen, but the northern holds still stood strong. In his heart, Grimli knew that the day would come when once more the mountains would resound along their length to the clatter of dwarf boots marching to war and the pound of hammers on dwarfish anvils. Already Karak Eight Peaks was being reclaimed, and others would follow.

'Dreaming of the golden age, lad?' Dammaz asked, and Grimli realised he had been stood staring at the carving of Grugni for several minutes.

'And the glory days to come,' replied Grimli which brought forth a rare smile from the Slayer.

'Aye, that's the spirit, Grimli, that's the spirit,' Dammaz agreed. 'When we're done here, you'll be a new dwarf, I reckon.'

'I'm already...' started Grimli but Dammaz silenced him with a finger raised to his lips. The Slayer tapped his nose and Grimli sniffed deeply. At first he could smell nothing, but as he concentrated, his nostrils detected a whiff of something unclean, something rotten and oily.

'That's the stink of skaven,' whispered Dammaz, his eyes peering into the darkness. Grimli closed his eyes and focused his thoughts on his senses of smell and hearing. There was breeze coming from behind him, where the odour of rats was strongest, and he thought he could hear the odd scratch, as of clawed feet on bare stone, to his right. Opening his eyes he looked in that direction, noting that

Dammaz was looking the same way. The Slayer glanced at him and gave a single nod of agreement, and Grimli stepped up beside him, slipping his hammer from his belt and unslinging his shield from his back.

Without warning, the skaven attacked. Humanoid rats, no taller than Grimli, scuttled and ran out of the gloom, their red eyes intent on the two dwarfs. Dammaz did not wait a moment longer, launching himself at the ratmen with a wordless bellow. The first went down with its head lopped from its shoulders; the second was carved from groin to chest by the return blow. One of the skaven managed to dodge aside from Dammaz's attack and ran hissing at Grimli. He felt no fear now; had he not slain a troll single-handedly? He suddenly realised the peril of overconfidence as the skaven lashed out with a crudely sharpened blade, the speed of the attack taking him by surprise so that he had to step back to block the blow with his shield. The skaven were not as strong as trolls, but they were a lot faster.

Grimli batted away the second attack, his shield ringing dully with the clang of metal on metal, and swung his hammer upwards to connect with the skaven's head, but the creature jumped back before the blow landed. Its breath was foetid and its matted fur was balding around open sores in places. Grimli knew that if he was cut, the infection that surrounded the pestilential scavengers might kill him even if the wound did not. He desperately parried another blow, realising that other skaven were circling quickly behind him. He took another step back and then launched himself forward as his foe advanced after him, smashing the ratman to the ground with his shield. He stomped on its chest with his heavy boot, pinning it to the ground as he brought his hammer smashing into its face. Glancing over his shoulder, he saw Dammaz was still fighting, as he'd expected, a growing pile of furry bodies at his feet.

Two skaven then attacked Grimli at once, one thrusting at him with a poorly constructed spear, the other slashing with a wide-bladed knife. He let his shield drop slightly and the skaven with the spear lunged at the opportunity. Prepared for the attack, Grimli deflected the spearhead to his right, stepped forward and smashed his hammer into the skaven's chest, audibly splintering ribs and crushing its internal organs. He spun on the other skaven but not fast enough, its knife thankfully scraping without harm along the links of his chainmail. He slammed the edge of the shield up into the skaven's long jaw, dazing it, and then smashed its legs from underneath it with a wide swing of his hammer. The creature gave a keening, agonised cry as it lay there on the ground and he stoved its head in with a casual backswing.

The air was filled with a musky scent, which stuck in Grimli's nostrils, distracting him, and it was a moment before he realised that the rest of the skaven had fled. Joining Dammaz he counted thirteen skaven corpses on the ground around the Slayer, many of them dismembered or beheaded.

'Skaven are all cowards,' Dammaz told him. He pointed at a darker-furred corpse, both its legs missing. 'Once I killed their leader they had no stomach for the fight.'

'Kill the leader, I'll remember that,' Grimli said as he swung his shield back over his shoulder.

FOR THE REST of the day Grimli felt the presence of the skaven shadowing him and the Slayer, but no further attack came. They passed out of the forges and strong rooms down into the mines. The wondrously carved hallways and corridors led them into lower and more basically hewn tunnels, the ceiling supported now by pit props and not pillars engraved with ancient runes. The stench of skaven became stronger for a while, their spoor was littered across the floor or of the mineshafts, but after another hour's travel it faded quickly.

'This is grobi territory, lad. The skaven don't come down these ways,' Dammaz informed Grimli when he commented on this phenomenon.

As they continued their journey Grimli noticed even rougher, smaller tunnels branching off the workings of the dwarfs, and guessed them to be goblin tunnels, dug out after the hold fell. There was a shoddiness about the chips and cuts of the goblin holes that set them apart from the unadorned but neatly hewn walls of dwarf workmanship, even to Grimli's untrained eye. As he absorbed this knowledge, Dammaz led him down a side-tunnel into what was obviously once a chamber of some kind. It was wide, though not high, and seemed similar to the dorm-chambers of Karaz-a-Karak.

'This is where it happened,' Grimli said. It was a statement, not a question. He realised this was where Dammaz had been leading him.

'Aye, that it is, lad,' the Slayer confirmed with a nod that shook his bright crest from side to side. 'This is where Okrinok Skrundigor was ambushed. Here it was that Frammi and Gorgnir were slain by the grobi. How did you know?'

'I'm not sure as I know,' Grimli replied with a frown. 'I can feel what happened here, in my blood, I reckon. It's like it's written in the stone somehow.'

'Aye, the mountain remembers, you can be sure of that,' Dammaz agreed solemnly. 'You can rest here tonight. Tomorrow will be a hard day.'

'What happens tomorrow?' asked Grimli, unburdening himself of his shield and pack.

'Nothing comes to those who hurry, lad, you should know that,' Dammaz warned him with a stern but almost fatherly wag of his finger.

THAT NIGHT, GRIMLI's dreams were troubled, and he tossed and turned beneath his blanket. In his mind he was there, at the betrayal so many centuries before. He could see Frammi and Gorgnir clearly, inspecting the bunks of the wide dormitory, protected by ten bodyguards. Gorgnir was wide of girth, even for a dwarf, and his beard was as black as coal and shone with a deep lustre. His dark eyes were intelligent and keen, but he was quick to laugh at some jest made by Frammi. The princess, to Grimli's sleeping eye at least, was beautiful; her blonde hair tied up in two tresses that flowed down her back to her knees. Her pallor was ruddy and healthy, her hips wide. Clad in a russet gown, a small circlet of gold holding her hair back, she was unmistakably the daughter of a High King.

In his dream-state, Grimli sighed. The lineage of those two would have been fine and strong, he thought glumly, had they but been given the chance to wed. At the thought, the deadly attack happened.

It seemed as if the goblins sprang from nowhere, rushing through the door with wicked cackles and grinning, yellowed teeth. Their pale green skin was tinged yellow in the lamplight, their robes and hoods crudely woven from dark material that seemed to absorb the light. The bodyguards reacted instantly, drawing their hammers and shields, forming a circle around the royal couple. The goblins crashed against the shieldwall like a wave against a cliff, and momentarily they were smashed back by the swings of the bodyguard's hammers, like the tide receding. But the press of goblins was too much and those at the front were forced forward into the determined dwarfs, crushed and battered mercilessly as they fought to get at the prince and princess. Soon they were climbing over their own dead, howling with glee as one then another and another of the bodyguard fell beneath the endless onslaught. The shield wall broke for a moment, but that was all that was needed. The goblins rushed the gap, pushing the breach wider with their weight of numbers.

This was it, the dark moment of the Skrundigor clan. It was Gorgnir who fell first, bellowing a curse on the grobi even as his axe lodged in one of their skulls and he was swarmed over by the small greenskins. Frammi wrenched the axe free and gutted three of the goblins before she too was overwhelmed; one of her tresses flew through the air as a sword blade slashed across her neck.

Almost as one the three remaining bodyguards howled with grief and rage, hurling themselves at the goblins with renewed ferocity. One in particular, a massive ruby inset into his hammer's head, smashed a bloody path into the grobi, every blow sweeping one of the tunnel-dwellers off its scampering feet. His helm was chased with swirling designs in bronze and gold and he had the faceplate drawn down, showing a fierce snarling visage of Grimnir in battle. The knives and short swords of the goblins rang harmlessly off his mail and plate armour with a relentless dull chiming, but they could not stop him and he burst clear through the door.

The other two bodyguards fell swiftly, and the goblins descended upon the dead like a pack of wild dogs, stripping them of every item of armour, weapon, jewellery and clothing. They bickered and fought with one another over the spoils, but soon the pillaging was complete and the goblins deserted the room in search of fresh prey. For what seemed an eternity, the looted bodies lay where they had been left, but eventually a low groan resounded across the room and one of the bodies sat up, blood streaming from a dozen wounds across his body. Groggily he stood up, leaning on one of the bunks, and shook his head, causing fresh blood to ooze from a gash across his forehead. He staggered for a moment and then seemed to steady.

'Skrundigorrrr!' his voice reverberated from the walls and floor in a low growl.

THE DREAM WAS still vivid when Grimli was woken by a chill draught, and he saw that the fire was all but dead embers. He added more sticks from the bundle strapped to his travelling pack and stoked the ashes until the fire caught once again. As it grew it size, its light fell upon the face of Dammaz who was sitting against the far wall, wide awake, his eyes staring intently at Grimli.

'Did you see it, lad?' he asked softly, his low whisper barely carrying across the room.

'I did,' Grimli replied, his voice as muted, his heart in his throat from what he had witnessed.

'So, lad, speak your mind, you look troubled,' Dammaz insisted.

'I saw them slain, and I saw Okrinok fight his way free instead of defending their bodies,' Grimli told the Slayer, turning his gaze from Dammaz to the heart of the fire. The deep red reminded Grimli of the ruby set upon Okrinok's hammer.

'Aye, that was a terrible mistake, you can be sure of that,' Dammaz grimaced as he spoke. The two fell into a sullen silence.

'There is no honour to be found here,' Grimli declared suddenly. 'The curse cannot be lifted from these enduring stones, not while mighty Karaz-a-Karak endures. I shall return there, swear the Slayer oath and come back to Karak Azgal to meet my death fighting in the caverns that witnessed my ancestor's treachery.'

'Is that so?' Dammaz asked quietly, his expression a mixture of surprise and admiration.

'It is so,' Grimli assured the Slayer.

'I told you not to be hasty, beardling,' scowled Dammaz. 'Stay with me one more day before you leave this place. You promised you would come with me, and I haven't shown you everything you need to see yet.'

'One more day then, as I promised,' Grimli agreed, picking up his pack.

THEY ENTERED THE goblin tunnels not far from the chamber where Grimli had slept, following the sloping corridor deeper and deeper beneath the World's Edge Mountains. They had perhaps travelled for half a day when they ran into their first goblins. There were no more than a handful, and the fight was bloody and quick, two of the grobi falling to Grimli's hammer, the other three carved apart by the baleful blade of Dammaz's axe.

'The goblins don't live down here much. They prefer to live in the better-crafted halls of Karak Azgal itself,' Dammaz told Grimli when he mentioned the lack of greenskins. 'But there are still plenty enough to kill,' the Slayer added with a fierce grin.

True enough, they had not travelled more than another half mile before they ran into a small crowd of greenskins moving up the tunnel in the opposite direction. The goblins shrieked their shrill war cries and charged, only to be met head-on by the vengeful dwarfs. In the confines of the goblin-mined cavern, the grobi's weight of numbers counted for little, and one-on-one they were no match for even Grimli. As he smashed apart the skull of the tenth goblin, the others turned and ran, disappearing into the darkness with the patter of bare feet. Grimli was all for going after them, but Dammaz laid a hand on his shoulder.

'Our way lies down a different path, but there will be more to fight soon enough,' he told Grimli. 'They will head up into Karak Azgal and fetch more of their kind, and perhaps lie in wait for us somewhere in one of the wider spaces where they can overwhelm us.'

'That's why we should catch them and stop them,' declared Grimli hotly.

'Even if we could run as fast as they, which we can't, lad, the grobi will lead us a merry chase up and down. They know these tunnels by every inch, and you do not,' Dammaz countered with a longing look in the direction the goblins had fled. 'Besides, if we go chasing willy-nilly after every grobi we meet, you'll never get to see what I have to show you.'

With that the Slayer turned away and continued down the passage. After a moment, Grimli followed behind, his shield and hammer ready.

* * *

GRIMLI WAS SURPRISED a little when the winding path Dammaz followed led them into a great cavern.

'I did not think the grobi could dig anything like this,' he said, perplexed.

'Grobi didn't dig this, you numbskull,' laughed Dammaz, pointing at the ceiling. Grimli followed the gesture and saw that long stalactites hung down from the cave's roof. The cavern had been formed naturally millennia ago when the Ancestor Gods had fashioned the mountains. Something caught the young dwarf's eye, and he looked futher into the hall-like cave. A massive mound, perhaps a great stalagmite as old as the world itself, rose from the centre of the cavern.

Grimli walked closer to the heap, and as he approached his eyes made out the shape of a small arm stuck out. And there was a tiny leg, just below it. Hurrying closer still, he suddenly stopped in his tracks. The mound was not rock at all, but built from the bodies of dozens, even scores of goblins, heaped upon one another a good ten yards above his head. Walking forward again, amazed at the sight, Grimli saw that each goblin bore at least one wound, crushed and mangled by what was obviously a heavy hammer blow. He looked over his shoulder at Dammaz, who was walking towards Grimli, axe carried easily in one hand.

'You recognise the handiwork, lad?' Dammaz asked as he drew level with Grimli and looked up at the monumental pile of greenskin corpses.

'Okrinok did this?' Grimli gaped at the Slayer, wondering that he could be even more astounded than he was before.

'Climb with me,' Dammaz commanded him, stepping up onto the battered skull of a goblin.

Grimli reached for a handhold and as his fingers closed around the shattered arm of a goblin, it felt as hard as rock beneath his touch. There was no give in the dead flesh at all and his skin prickled at the thought of the magic that obviously was the cause. Pulling himself up the macabre monument, Grimli could almost believe it had been fashioned from the stone, so unyielding were the bodies beneath his hands and feet. It was a laborious process, hauling himself up inch by inch, yard by yard for several minutes, following the glow of Dammaz's axe above him. Panting and sweating, he pulled himself to the top and stood there for a moment catching his breath.

As he recovered from his exertions, Grimli saw what was located at the very height of the mound. There stood Okrinok. He was unmistakable; his ruby-encrusted hammer was still in his grasp, lodged into the head of a goblin that was thrusting a spear through the dwarf's chest. The two had killed each other, and now stood together in death's embrace. Grimli approached the ancient dwarf slowly, almost reverentially. When he was stood an arm's length away, he reached out and laid a trembling hand upon his ancestor's shoulder. It was then that Grimli looked at Okrinok's face.

His helmet had been knocked off in the fight, and his long, shaggy hair hung free. His mouth was contorted into a bellow, his scowl more ferocious than any Grimli had seen before. Even in death Okrinok looked awesome. His beard was fully down to his knees, bound by many bronze and gold bands and beads, intricately braided in places. Turning his attention back to his ancestor's face, he noted the familiar ancestral features, some of which he had himself. But there was something else, something more than a vague recognition. Okrinok reminded him of someone in particular. For a moment Grimli thought it must be his own father, but with a shiver along his spine he realised it was someone a lot closer. Turning slowly, he looked at Dammaz, who was stood just to his right, leaning forward with his arms crossed atop his axe haft.

'O-Okrinok?' stuttered Grimli, letting his hammer drop from limp fingers as shock ran through him. He staggered for a moment before falling backwards, sitting down on the goblin mound with a thump.

'Aye, lad, it is,' Dammaz smiled warmly.

'B-but, how?' was all Grimli could ask. Pushing himself to his feet, he tottered over to stand in front of Okrinok. The Slayer proffered a gnarled hand, the short fingers splayed. Grimli hesitated for a moment, but Okrinok nodded reassuringly and he grasped the hand, wrist-to-wrist in warriors' greeting. At the touch of the Slayer, Grimli felt a surge of power flood through him, suffusing him from his toes to the tips of his hair.

GRIMLI FELT LIKE he had just woken up, and his senses were befuddled. As they cleared he realised he was once again in the mine chamber, witnessing the fight with the goblins. But this time it was different – he was somehow *inside* the fight, the goblins were attacking *him*! Panic fluttered in his heart for a moment before he realised that this was just a dream or vision too. He was seeing the battle through Okrinok's eyes. He saw Frammi and Gorgnir once more fall to the blades of the goblins and felt the surge of unparalleled shame and rage explode within his ancestor. He felt the burning strength of hatred fuelling every blow as Okrinok hurled himself at the goblins. There were no thoughts of safety, no desire to escape. All Grimli could feel was an incandescent need to crush the grobi, to slaughter each and every one of them for what they had done that day.

Okrinok bellowed with rage as he swung his hammer, no hint of fatigue in his powerful arms. One goblin was smashed clear from his feet and slammed against the wall. The backswing bludgeoned the head of a second; the third blow snapped the neck of yet another. And so Okrinok's advance continued, his hammer cutting a swathe of pulped and bloodied destruction through the goblins. It was with a shock that Okrinok realised he had no more foes to fight, and looking about him he found himself in an unfamiliar tunnel, scraped from the rock by goblin hands. He had a choice; he could return up the tunnel to Karak Azgal and face the shame of having failed in his sacred duty. Or he could keep going down, into the lair of the goblins, to slay those who had done this to him. His anger and loathing surged again as he remembered the knives plunging into Gorgnir and he set off down the tunnel, heading deeper into the mountain.

Several times he ran into parties of goblins, and every time he threw himself at them with righteous fury, exacting vengeance with every blow of his hammer. Soon his wanderings took him into a gigantic cavern, the same one where he now stood again. Ahead of him the darkness was filled with glittering red eyes, the goblins mustered in their hundreds. He stood alone, his hammer in his hands, waiting for them. The goblins were bold at first, rushing him with spears and short swords, but when ten of their number lay dead at Okrinok's feet within the space of a dozen heartbeats, they became more cautious. But Okrinok was too clever to allow that and sprang at the grobi, plunging into the thick of his foes, his hammer rising and falling with near perfect strokes, every attack crushing the life from a murderous greenskin.

To Okrinok the battle seemed to rage for an eternity, until it seemed he'd done nothing but slaughter goblins since the day was born. The dead were beyond counting, and he stood upon a mound of his foes, caked head-to-foot in their blood. His helmet had been knocked loose by an arrow, and several others now pierced his stomach and back, but still he fought on. Then, from out of the bodies behind him rose a goblin. He heard a scrape of metal and turned, but too slowly, the goblin's spearshaft punching into him. With blood bubbling into his breath, Okrinok spat his final words of defiance and brought his hammer down onto his killer's head.

'I am a dwarf! My honour is my life! Without it I am nothing!' bellowed Okrinok, before death took him.

TEARS STREAMED DOWN Grimli's face as he looked at Okrinok, his expression grim.

'And so I swore in death, and in death I have fulfilled that oath,' Okrinok told Grimli. 'Many centuries have the Skrundigor been blamed for my act, and I have allowed it to happen. The shame for the deaths of Gorgnir and Frammi was real, and the High King was owed his curse. But no longer shall we be remembered as cowards and oathbreakers. The goblin king was so impressed that he ordered his shamans to draw great magic and create this monument to my last battle. But in trapping my flesh they freed my soul. For many years my spirit wandered these tunnels and halls and brought death to any grobi I met, but I am weary and wish to die finally. Thus, I sought you out, last of the Skrundigor, who must be father to our new line, in honour and in life.'

'But how do I get the High King to lift the curse, to strike our name from the Dammaz Kron?' asked Grimli.

'If you can't bring the king under the mountain, lad, bring the mountain over the king, as we used to say,' Okrinok told him. He pointed to his preserved body. 'Take my hammer, take it to the High King and tell him what you have seen here. He will know, lad, for that hammer is famed and shall become more so when my tale is told.'

'I will do as you say,' swore Grimli solemnly. Turning, he took the haft of the weapon in both hands and pulled. Grimli's tired muscles protested but after heaving with all his strength, the dwarf managed to pull the hammer clear.

He turned to thank Okrinok, but the ghost was gone. Clambering awkwardly down the mound of bodies, Grimli's thoughts were clear. He would return to Karaz-a-Karak and present the hammer and his service to the current High King, to serve him as Okrinok once did. It was then up to the High King whether honour was restored or not. As he planted his feet onto the rock floor once more, with no small amount of relief, Grimli felt a change in the air. Turning, he saw the mound was being enveloped by a shimmering green glow. Before his eyes, the mound began to shudder, and saw flesh stripping from bones and the bones crumble to dust as the centuries finally did their work. Soon there was nothing left except a greenish-tinged haze.

Hefting Okrinok's hammer, Grimli turned to leave. Out in the darkness dozens of red eyes regarded him balefully. Grimli grinned viciously to himself. He strode towards the waiting goblins, his heart hammering in his chest, his advance quickening until he was running at full charge.

'For Frammi and Gorgnir!' he bellowed.

A GENTLEMAN'S WAR
Neil Rutledge

THE SUN BEAT down relentlessly. Otto von Eisenkopf felt the back of his neck burning. He dare not shift the position in which he had secreted himself though, he thought, as his neck burnt even hotter – this time with shame as he remembered the ants' nest. His first action with this confounded crew and he had to try and conceal himself on an ants' nest! That huge fellow – Lutyens, or whatever his name was – he hadn't laughed, he hadn't made a single sound, in fact, adhering to thrice-cursed Captain Molders's silence order! The man may not have laughed aloud, but Otto had seen the mirth in his eyes all right. Bah! A pox on all of them!

By Sigmar, what was he doing lying here like a bandit, the rocks digging through his padded brigandine as the distant hoofbeats came closer? A mere brigandine! Where was his own armour? And his scalp itched enough to drive him insane. Only the gods knew what manner of lice were in the lining of the battered arming cap he'd been given. A steel arming cap! So much for the fine armet which his squire, Henryk, had polished until it shone. So much for the wonderful plumes, all the way from Araby, which his sister had carefully dyed in the family colours. How proud of them he had been, even wearing them in his hat as he travelled up to join his father. Where was the glorious war he was promised?

Despite the faint sounds of the approaching enemy, Otto risked a slight movement, in quest of comfort alone of course, but a dislodged pebble clicked against another. He sensed the hidden eyes of Lutyens boring into him. By the Hammer, this wasn't what he had prepared for!

His mind drifted back to that journey of just two days ago. How different his mood had been then! He remembered the final stretch especially. They had travelled up and across open moor country, so very different from the fields and forests of his home. It had been like chancing upon a new land, bathed in sunshine, ringing with unfamiliar, haunting bird calls and the continual chatter of water over countless rocky stream beds. Water, to his mind, far sweeter and cooler than anything he had ever drunk at home. His heart had been as high and as bubbling as the larks that rose to sing as their horses had passed. He remembered that he had sung too, the old war ballads of the Empire. They had made Otto swell with pride, as he had thought he would soon be joining those illustrious ranks of legend. He had imagined himself charging head-to-head with the knightly orders.

So much for that! Here he was, baking on hot stones like a flat cake. Lurking, lurking with a tattered handful of mercenary pistoliers, fully half of them from outside the Empire. Even that fellow, Molders, the captain, had an accent which sounded more than half Bretonnian. How could his father trust such men? Trust them to reliably scout out which route the invading Bretonnian scoundrels would take?

Otto reflected that the Graf must be under terrible stress. His father had been made ill, perhaps, by the strain of having to defend their glorious homeland with only men such as these. Not a single knight! By Sigmar, what an insult! He resolved to himself to strive all the harder to not let his father down, to at least be a reliable pair of eyes and ears on this confounded mission. He was certainly confident he was more trustworthy than that scurvy Captain Molders. What manner of upstart was he to consider ambushing a Bretonnian noble like this? Lurking to trap a man whose code of honour would not permit him to flee even if outnumbered and who, if bested in fair combat, would certainly graciously submit to honourable capture and ransom.

Otto's anger began to rise. No, by Sigmar the Blessed, he would not permit this! It was his first combat and he was not going to enter it like a bandit. He would behave honourably, even if these low sellswords would not. He could hear the hoof beats of the approaching Bretonnian party coming nearer. Abruptly he rose to his feet and crashed through the shrubs to stand on the path.

He stood straight and proud, sweeping the path with his eyes. The Bretonnian knight was just down the track, the scarlet of his horse's caparison dazzling in the sunlight. Riding beside him on a shaggy pony was a rough, leather-clad man with an eye patch, clutching a light crossbow, undoubtedly a local enlisted as a guide.

Otto raised his hand. 'Ho, sir knight,' he began. The Bretonnian reined in, his hatchet face looking startled. But it was the blur of movement to one side which caught Otto's eye. Just in time he ducked, and a crossbow bolt hissed past him. The guide, still holding the bow, had now swept out his sword with his free hand and was charging him. Otto struggled to draw his own blade. The knight was shouting something. Otto cursed and stepped smartly to one side, only narrowly avoiding the guide's murderous sword swipe. His own sword now in his hand, the young nobleman whirled to face the horseman who, rearing his mount, had turned with incredible speed to attack him again. His gaze locked by his enemy's one blazing eye, Otto desperately prepared to dodge again but suddenly the guide fell as Lutyens burst from the scrub and discharged a pistol into the side of his head.

Otto's mind reeled. The huge, rather slow pistolier had transformed into a raging colossus of action. He didn't seem to pause, even as he coolly dropped the knight's war-horse with his other pistol. Blonde hair streaming from under his burgonet, he charged to where the squires were riding up to protect their fallen master. He glanced back at Otto and shouted, 'Get at them, fool!'

Otto hesitated. He was staring aghast at his borrowed brigandine, splattered with blood from the slain guide. He looked up as a squire charged him. Gasping aloud, Otto just managed to roll behind the dead guide's horse. He barely parried a spear thrust from the Bretonnian and luckily managed to seize the weapon with his free hand. He stared up at the face of the squire: a grizzled, scarred man who hissed with exertion as he tried to wrest the weapon from the young noble's hand.

Otto stepped forward, trying to jab his sword at the Bretonnian's arm but he stumbled over the body of the dead guide, which was hanging, one foot trapped in the stirrups. Frantically, Otto tried to pull himself upright using his enemy's spear but he fell, twisting, amongst the horses' hooves. Through the stamping legs and dust, he stared into the scarred face as the squire grinned and stabbed down with his spear. Otto writhed but once more a pistol discharged close by and the Bretonnian, grin still fixed in place, toppled from his horse. His killer, a wiry pistolier in a dented helmet, paused just long enough to seize the horse's bridle and pull the beast away from the young noble, before running towards the main body of the Bretonnians. Otto, panting aloud, struggled to his feet and stumbled after him.

The knight, protected by a close knot of squires, was on his feet and ordering his men to the attack. Standing screened by his warriors, with one hand the Bretonnian attempted to beat the dust from his crimson surcoat, while with the other he held his sword aloft. 'They are only brigand dogs!' he yelled. 'Kill them!'

Charging forward, Otto almost screeched as he shouted with indignation, 'I am no brigand, but Otto von Eisenkopf of Barhaus! Defend yourself, insolent knight.'

Dimly, Otto was aware that there seemed to be very few pistoliers on the road or moving through the shrubs and boulders, but now his attention was fixed on the tight group of men immediately facing him. The squires hesitated, looking to their master for guidance. Slowly the knight gestured them aside and stepped forward. 'Very well,' the Bretonnian hissed, 'whatever honour you have, von Eisenkopf, prepare to test its mettle.'

The knight stood before him, looking almost warily at his young opponent. He held his sword – a fine, jewel-hilted affair – loosely by his side while his free hand toyed with a corner of his silk jupon. Otto sized his opponent up. The man was older and taller, very tall in fact, but sparsely built, with a thin face and hawk nose.

His reach would be long, Otto thought, but he himself had inherited his father's bull-like physique and he reckoned that, young though he was, he himself was perhaps the stronger. They were both shieldless but the Bretonnian was well armoured while Otto had only his brigandine. Otto smoothly raised his sword and took up his stance. He felt calmer now, on familiar ground. Just like the fencing hall, he thought to himself.

'A swordsman, eh?' Was there surprise in the thin features of the Bretonnian's face, or even hesitancy? Then the knight seemed to compose himself and took up his own stance and immediately attacked. It was not the speed of the thrust that caught Otto off guard, but its clumsiness. He parried, almost, and, had he not been so startled, could have finished the fight there and then. The knight lunged again and this time Otto was ready. Smoothly parrying and riposting, driving the knight back so quickly that he tripped, falling backwards with a grunt.

'Rise, sir,' Otto said, stepping back graciously and preparing for another bout. The knight rose slowly, but when he bent to retrieve his sword he lifted it by the blade, not the hilt.

'I yield, von Eisenkopf. You have bested me.' The knight's words were drowned out in a sudden crashing of pistol and arquebus fire. Otto looked up. Molders must have sent men from further down the track up and over the outcrop to the north of the path. Now the pistoliers were firing down on the squires who were attacking their few, hard-pressed comrades around the track. Otto could hear the captain's voice booming, even through the gunfire. 'The horses, shoot the horses! Don't let them away, lads.'

The knight looked around too. 'Yield, my brave men!' he ordered. 'We are undone. Yield.'

The squires began dropping their weapons and, although somewhere further along the track there was still some shouting, the skirmish was over. Otto could see Molders standing on a boulder yelling, 'Round them up, you sluggards! Get moving!' He was shaking a wheel lock in the air in his strange staccato manner, the brandishes seeming to underline his words.

The Bretonnian knight turned back to Otto and bowed, 'Sir Guillame de Montvert. I am honoured to make your acquaintance.'

Otto smiled, somewhat surprised by the ease of his victory, 'And I yours, Sir Guillame.' Here at last was proper courtesy. Even in defeat, even as his men were being rounded up by the ragged pistoliers, this man could observe the proper formalities. The young nobleman continued, 'I should be delighted if you could dine with me tonight.'

The Bretonnian grinned. 'I seem to find myself with time to spare,' he shrugged modestly. 'I fear you find me inconvenienced, though. I regret my wardrobe is limited.'

'Fear not! Some arrangements will be made. Besides, my table is at present quite simple enough.'

At that moment Molders strode up. He moved with the typical briskness which had begun to irritate Otto so much. Molders was not a tall man and he seemed to Otto to compensate for his short stature with an exaggerated cockiness of movement, the jut of his chest only exceeded by the jaunt of his chin and bristling beard.

'You are our prisoner,' he addressed the knight sharply. Then turning to one of his men, 'Take him and tie him like the rest.'

'Indeed not!' Otto protested, 'This man is my prisoner and a knight of honour. He is to dine with me this evening.'

The captain gasped and stared. His pale blue eyes seemed to protrude from his face in an effort to out-reach the grizzled spade of a beard now thrust accusingly at Otto. The pistolier behind him snorted as he attempted to suppress a laugh. Molders, used only to being obeyed without question, stood silent, glaring in astonishment at the young man before him.

Otto dared continue, 'Furthermore, I have found your conduct this day most reprehensible. We have brought dishonour on the good name of the Emperor and the reputation of his troops.' He looked at the trooper standing behind Molders. 'You, man! Fetch my mount and obtain a horse for Sir Guillame, and be quick about it!'

The trooper, the wiry man who had saved Otto earlier in the skirmish, had been grinning in buck-toothed amusement but now his expression changed to one of discomfiture. He had lost his helm; now he pulled his somewhat greasy curls in perplexity as he glanced at Molders. The captain shrugged in rare indecision as Otto once more turned to him. 'We will ride ahead, captain. See to the rest of the prisoners and follow as fast as you can.'

The confused pistolier had returned with Otto's horse and another. 'Sir Guillame? Please?' Otto gestured to the second horse, smoothly vaulted into his own saddle and, with an imperious gesture, hurled the battered arming cap off his head and into the scrub. He turned to address Molders once more. The captain's face was the colour of pickled red cabbage. He was silently gesturing for Lutyens to mount and accompany Otto. Otto was about to protest but the captain looked up and his glare was so fierce that the young man held his tongue.

'Lutyens will see to your needs… young sir.' Molders's voice was clipped even more than usual and barely audible. Without a further word he turned his back and began issuing orders to his men.

'Well, Sir Guillame, shall we ride?' Otto said brightly, amused by what he took as Molders's pique at being reprimanded. 'We must ride hard if we are to be back at the forward camp by dusk.' The Bretonnian nodded and they set off briskly, Lutyens following behind.

At first they conversed lightly, exchanging details of their family, discussing the moor country and its prospects for falconry. Otto felt wholly at ease with the older Bretonnian but, his heart high once more, he was aware of his duties. Behind the bright chat, his mind was working furiously. Otto was far too good mannered to question the knight regarding military matters, but as the conversation went on, his prisoner, seemingly disarmed by his own good cheer, let slip a few clues. These clues pointed to what Otto already suspected; that Sir Guillame and his squires were scouting the route for the main Bretonnian attack. It was the obvious route, really! The one Otto would have taken, were he in their opponent the Duke de Boncenne's place. A far better route than the narrow, difficult southern pass or the long swing, deeper into the Empire to the north. A bold, direct approach across the moors and a sharp, honourable conflict to decide the issue.

'You are preoccupied, young sir.' Sir Guillame's voice broke into Otto's thoughts.

'Yes, yes, I am sorry. Please excuse my ill manners. It is no way to treat an honoured guest.'

'Perhaps you are missing a lady?' the Bretonnian asked smiling.

Otto blushed, 'I have been training hard, Sir Guillame, and hope for a commission in the Reiksguard.'

The Bretonnian laughed. 'Ah, you Imperials,' he chided mockingly, 'You are much too serious. A man must strive for honour, yes, but he can love too! What is life without a little romance?' Sir Guillame went on, expanding the other aspects of what he regarded as the highlights of a knightly life.

Otto nodded and occasionally added a polite word but his mind was elsewhere once more. The mention of the Reiksguard had reminded him of the opportunities which lay before him. His father would be well pleased. He had tempered the baseless actions of the pistoliers with honour, captured an important prisoner with due decorum and was now gaining valuable information. He could see the conflict unfolding. The Bretonnians would advance and be brought to battle on the moors. Otto himself would fight bravely and the whole affair would end in a most satisfactory manner. He was still vaguely worried about how reliable the pistoliers really were, but he was confident that his father would act quickly on his suspicions. Yes, all would be well. For the time being he set his concerns aside and determined to enjoy the ride, the scenery and the Bretonnian's company.

THEY ARRIVED BACK at the forward camp just as the dusk was deepening into night. Otto swelled with pride as they passed the pickets and he was able to declare himself and report he was returning with an honoured prisoner, Sir Guillame de Montvert. They made their way through the camp, Otto riding with head held high. He felt almost proprietorial as he looked around, eyes scanning the activity that was revealed only in fire-lit, flickering patches. Men huddled in their tent groups, cooking, polishing weapons, binding arrow fletchings. Troops engaged in the myriad small tasks necessary when preparing for battle. Otto's spirits soared with the thrill of it all. How he had waited for this, to serve with honour his Emperor, land and family! His ears heard the camp sounds almost as music. The subdued voices with the occasional laugh or burst of song, the clink of a ladle against a cooking pot, the heavier ringing from a distant field forge, the noises from the tethered horses. Aye, horses. Horses, not knights' chargers!

Otto's good spirits promptly vanished and he was suddenly glad that they had arrived at sundown, so Sir Guillame could not see the rag-tag composition of his father's advanced force. He winced as he thought of it and remembered his own shock at his first sight of the troops: scruffy woodsmen from Stirland, ruffianly-looking local light horse and a large contingent of mercenary hackbut men and pistoliers. He had protested to his father that their forces were inadequate. The memory of his father's response still made the blood flush hot under his skin. His father, nobleman of the Empire and respected general, had actually stated that pistoliers were cheaper to field than knights and were a good deal more useful. Otto's very ears burned as he remembered his father's curt words, 'This isn't a crusade against Araby, Otto! It's a border squabble, provoked by the greed of that adventurer, de Boncenne. He's using the usual territory problems as an excuse to get his hands on the coal mines by Grunwasser. You don't call out the Reiksguard to deal with bandits!'

Otto's worries for his father returned in a rush. How could he think such of a duke, a pillar of Bretonnian chivalry? He was obviously ill, worn out by the stress of attempting to defend this difficult border with such paltry forces and, perhaps, was subtly misled by these unreliable mercenaries in which he seemed to place such faith. Again, Otto resolved not to let his father down. He, at least, was dependable and he had the information that was so badly needed. But first he had his chivalrous duties to attend to.

He guided Sir Guillame to his own tent where he found his youthful squire busy polishing the buckles of his charger's harness. They shone in the firelight but the sight, far from pleasing Otto, only reminded him of how distasteful he found it to ride the rough-looking, if hardy, mount he had been given to accompany the pistoliers. Young Henryk rose immediately. Even in camp, his dapper form was immaculate in the red and white Eisenkopf colours. His face seemed to shine pristine in the firelight. 'Welcome home, sir! I see you have a guest.'

Otto's irritation showed in the brusqueness with which he ordered the squire to see to his distinguished prisoner. He ordered that the Bretonnian should have the use of his own tent, while his personal effects were to be transferred to the tent of his servant. He repented almost at once when he saw how courteous the good-natured Henryk was in addressing and attending to the Bretonnian and, to try and save the servant extra labour, looked for Lutyens to order him to see to the horses, but the mercenary was nowhere to be seen.

'Typical,' Otto muttered to himself. 'Uncouth, uncultured and unreliable!' He gave further instructions to Henryk, excused himself to Sir Guillame and went to wash and change, before presenting himself to his father.

Inside the cramped tent of his servant, Otto cleaned and arranged himself as best he could in the flickering lamp light. It was somewhat awkward but he was smiling to himself as he stepped outside to gain the headroom necessary to attach his plumes to his hat. He imagined receiving his father's congratulations on the capture of Sir Guillame. He pictured the Graf's serious face, as his beloved son explained the ill-dealings of the pistoliers and his suspicions of them. He saw in his mind's eye his father's pride and relief that he had such a son to count on. Still smiling, he checked briefly that his prisoner was comfortable, then made his way to his father's quarters.

The Graf's tent was in the very centre of the camp. It was large but made of plain leather, as tough and unpretentious as the man within.

Otto straightened himself as he saw his father's standard hanging above the door, bloodied by the light of the great braziers in front of the tent, and his heart filled with pride as the two halberdiers on guard smartly saluted him and stepped aside to let him pass.

Immediately within was a large chamber, well lit with lanterns and furnished with a variety of folding wooden stools and tables. Otto smiled as Gunther, his father's veteran aide-de-camp, greeted him. It was hard to tell the scars from the lines of age on the old man's face but he still had a sprightly step as he moved to salute Otto.

'Greetings, sir,' the old soldier said warmly. 'You have captured an honourable prisoner, I believe.'

Otto found it hard not to grin like a schoolboy. 'I have won some very little honour,' he replied. 'I must report to my father.'

'The general is in conference,' Gunther told him. 'With Herr Lutyens, one of your comrades in the affray.'

'Comrade?' Otto clicked his tongue, his good humour dispelled. What was that oaf doing plaguing his father? Concocting some tale to cover the mercenaries' reprehensible behaviour, no doubt.

'Some warm wine, sir?' The aide was offering him a somewhat battered but gleaming pewter goblet, a gently steaming flask in his other hand.

'What?' Otto asked, preoccupied with what the dubious Lutyens might be telling his father. 'Ach, yes, why not?' he said grimly. Lutyens could have his crow but Otto would see his father got the true story! He settled himself irritably on a stool by the tapestries that curtained off his father's inner chamber and sipped at his wine. Gunther, ever the tactful servant, busied himself quietly at the far side of the chamber.

Otto could distinguish two voices on the far side of the tapestry – the deep drone of Lutyens and his father's terse speech. Habitually polite, the young noble was about to move to another stool out of earshot, when he again wondered what tale Lutyens might be spinning. He had best listen, he thought to himself. His father was obviously worn down by his onerous duties as warden and was already placing too much reliance on these brigands. He had better learn as much as he could if he was to help his father. Still sipping his wine, he surreptitiously leant a little closer to the tapestry.

'So they put up little fight?' the Graf was asking.

'Little enough, sir. They seemed of scant quality.'

Otto nearly choked on his wine. Scant quality! Who was this rustic to judge a knight of Bretonnia?

'And where is Captain Molders?'

'He is following with the main body, sir.'

'I expected a prompt report from him, Lutyens. Not advanced warning from you.'

'Young Master Eisenkopf was in haste to bring back the Bretonnian knight, sir.'

Otto coloured as he heard his father snort, 'Not that much haste, it seems! He hasn't reported yet! Your opinion, Lutyens: what of this Bretonnian party?'

'I'm not sure, sir, but they didn't seem up to much to me and Captain Molders reckoned they were odd too, sir. I believe he thought them some kind of ruse.'

Otto stood up rapidly. His father was listening to nonsense, or worse, treachery. Without waiting further, he brushed aside the hanging and strode into his father's quarters. Lutyens sat nearer, his huge bulk balanced precariously on a camp stool. Facing him across a folding table sat Otto's father, the Graf von Eisenkopf. The Graf was a powerful man but even he looked small compared to Lutyens. Perhaps it was this that seemed, to Otto's eyes, to lend him a shrunken air. To his anxious son, the Graf's broad, open face looked pale even in the warm lamp light. And was there more grey in that close cropped hair and beard?

'Father,' Otto began breathlessly, 'I have additional information regarding the Bretonnians' plans.'

Lutyens swung his ice-blue eyes towards him and his father looked up coolly, fixing Otto with the same stern gaze that had met his childhood misdemeanours.

'It must be important information, indeed, for you to have forgotten your normal courtesy,' the Graf observed, calmly.

Otto coloured but began again. 'This man...' He was about to berate the pistolier as a completely untrustworthy source of information but something in the gaze of his father made him change his mind. 'This man may not have all the facts. He has not spoken with our noble prisoner, Sir Guillame de Montvert.'

'I do not doubt it,' the Graf agreed. 'But he has made his report promptly, as a dutiful trooper should and I myself had hoped to speak with de Montvert, at least before too long.' His voice was soft but the rebuke was not lost on Otto. The young man knew better than to try to make excuses to his father, but inside he felt a burning sense of injustice. The general was still speaking, now to Lutyens. 'Thank you, trooper, for your report. You are dismissed for the present.'

The big pistolier rose and bowed somewhat awkwardly. 'Yes, sir.' He was usually slow of movement but Otto thought he detected reluctance in his measured step as he departed.

On pretence of straightening the curtain, Otto checked that Lutyens had indeed left. He turned and the Graf gestured to him. 'Sit down, my son. Congratulations on the capture of the prisoner. But I am surprised you have not brought him to me.'

'I... I thought it good manners to allow a man of his rank to prepare himself properly before presenting himself.'

'You are thoughtful but we are not at court, my son. We are defending our land. It is more important for me to get information quickly.'

'Sorry, father.'

'No matter. Make your report.'

Much of the fire and anger had been chastened out of Otto. He related his views to his father a great deal more quietly than he had imagined when riding back. He described the ambush, mentioning his distaste for such skulking tactics and telling how he had sprung forth and challenged the Bretonnian knight. He considered voicing his suspicions about the loyalty of Captain Molders, but the grim set of his father's jaw made him change his mind. He would keep his fears to himself for the present, and wait and see what actions were to be taken.

'So you sprung the ambush too soon.' His father's voice was steely.

'I acted as a gentleman, father.'

'I placed you under the orders of Captain Molders and expected you to obey him.'

Otto's resentment boiled over: 'Father! The man is a mercenary! He knows nothing of honour. Listen to his accent, he sounds more like a Bretonnian! You know the trouble these locals cause you. Brigands, as much a thorn for us as for their enemies. How can he be trusted?'

His father banged his fist on the table, silencing him. He was about to speak and then passed his hand wearily across his brow. Otto regarded him warily. He did look tired. These past months since he had been appointed warden must have been hard. Battling orcs or defending against beastmen in the east was arduous but at least you knew where you stood with an orc. Here the damned locals on both sides of the border were always feuding, raiding and seemingly caring little for Emperor or King.

'Father, I am here to serve you loyally.'

The Graf returned his earnest gaze. 'I know, Otto, but war isn't like the ballads or the parade ground. Molders is no knight but he is a veteran of this border squabbling and I'll stake my sword he is not false. I'm far from sure about just how chivalrous this opportunist the Duke de Boncenne is. What I am sure of is that the Emperor runs the South March on a tight purse and I have precious few forces to impede Boncenne. If he pushes up to the Grunwasser, he'll lodge himself like a halfling in a bakery and be twice as difficult to shift.'

Listening, Otto was a tumult of emotions: shame yet resentment at this chastisement, worry for his father and a tingling sense of excitement at being involved in such tense matters.

'I must have more information,' his father was continuing. 'Molders will report as soon as he arrives. Meanwhile bring me the knight and I will question him.'

'Yes, father. Will he be dining with us?'

'No he will not!'

Otto winced. 'I will fetch him at once.'

As Otto left, Molders was just coming into the tent. The pistolier captain pulled his shoulders back even further than normal and gave a strangled snort as he passed. The young noble glared at him before stiffly walking to his tent.

When he arrived, the Bretonnian was sitting by the fire, wrapped in Otto's second cloak and thanking Henryk who had just topped up his goblet. The knight looked up, 'Ah, greetings, Otto. I compliment you on your hospitality.' He gestured with his goblet.

'I fear I must interrupt your rest, Sir Guillame. My father...' Otto hesitated slightly, 'My father desires to speak to you. I am sure he will not detain you long. I will wait until you return and we can dine together. I shall escort you to the Graf at once.'

Otto's plans to dine were to be frustrated, however, and scarce three hours later he was in the saddle again.

OTTO PRIDED HIMSELF on his horsemanship and was indeed reckoned a natural in the saddle, but he had never encountered riding like this before. Throughout the scant hours of darkness that were left they pressed on like men possessed. There was no moon and Otto wondered how his horse could see to pick his way over the rough hillsides, never mind how Molders was guiding the troops. Dawn brought easier going as they reached the moorland plateau which marked the no-man's land on the south march between Bretonnia and the Empire, but there was no change in pace. The pistoliers dispersed themselves more widely but they did not even stop for breakfast, the men sipping from their flasks and eating on the move instead.

Otto was very weary but inside he was a conflicting mass of emotion. Pride that his father had seen fit to dispatch them to check his own theory and scout for a Bretonnian force coming over the moor. But there was anger at Molders's barely concealed contempt for what he saw as a wasted errand. The captain firmly believed that the main Bretonnian attack was coming by the southern route. The man was mad, or worse, an enemy agent. How could he doubt the honour of knights such as Sir Guillame? No! They would locate the Bretonnian force, his father would marshal his troops and battle would be joined on the moor.

It would be Otto's first battle. Not a large one admittedly, in fact more of a border skirmish over a couple of valleys and those wretched coal mines, but what mattered the size of the conflict when true honour was at stake? He had heard the pistoliers talk of the Duke of Boncenne as an upstart, keen to get his hands on the profits of those mines. How could they think so of a duke? They were the mercenaries! More likely the duke viewed the whole venture as a test of honour, an adventure to prove himself in his new post of march warden and quite right too! Any noble of courage and mettle would do similarly.

The day wore on. They had halted briefly but Molders was relentless, and by late afternoon they had picked up the cart road which ran from Dreiburg across the border. The pistoliers followed the road but were still well spread out in a long skirmish line. Otto looked to his right where Lutyens was riding, blonde hair streaming out behind him in the stiff breeze, his huge form dwarfing his small mount. It was worrying how the giant had always been somewhere near. Had Molders posted the big man to keep a special watch over him? Was the pistolier captain aware of Otto's suspicions? Anxiety twisted in his stomach. If the pistoliers proved to be traitors it would be very easy for them to kill him. He would stand no chance against so many. A cloud passed over the sun and the wild, open landscape of the moors seemed suddenly bleak. The craggy rock outcrops took on the guise of sinister watching heads, roughly haired with heather, peering at Otto. The incessant chatter of the chill streams, a babble which had once echoed Otto's bubbling spirits now seemed to mock him as they approached the rise to the scarp edge where the moor descended in a rocky jumble to the Bretonnian plains. Here Molders halted his men, and, leaving most with the horses, led a few forward on foot to look out over the land ahead.

The captain signalled that Otto should come too, and again the young man was irked to find himself chaperoned by the hulking Lutyens. Using the rough, boulder-strewn slope as an excuse, Otto tried to pick a route that led him away from his unwelcome shadow but wherever he moved Lutyens's slow footfall followed. Otto's heart beat faster, faster than the climb should have occasioned, as he wondered what lay at the scarp edge. Would this be the scene of his death at the hands of traitors? A supposed accident on the cliff edge? Apprehensively his hand rested on his sword hilt but he felt powerless. He hung back when, approaching the skyline, the pistoliers dropped and crawled towards the edge. Lutyens stopped beside him. Ahead, Molders was cautiously peering through the gap between two rocks. He reached down to a pouch at his belt and pulled out a small brass tube. A spyglass, an item of expense and rarity, looted doubtless! The captain scrutinised the land ahead.

There seemed to be a ripple of expectation amongst the pistoliers. Several glanced back. Their faces showed interest, expectation. Were they Molders's most trusted henchmen, here to witness Otto's murder? The captain turned impatiently and even behind that spade of a beard, Otto could clearly detect a wolfish grin. He gestured imperiously for Otto to come forward. The young noble moved forward, tensed for action. There was a touch on his shoulder and he whirled, sword half-drawn before his arms were caught in Lutyens's iron grip.

'Get down, by Sigmar! You will reveal us!' the giant hissed.

Shaking, bewildered, Otto crawled to where Molders beckoned with his spyglass. There was a glint in the captain's eye as he gestured to Otto to look ahead. Heart pounding and trying to watch the pistolier out of the corner of his eye, Otto glanced around the boulder in front of him.

He gasped at what he saw and his fears vanished in a rush of vindicated pride. Some distance from the bottom of the slope a long line of horsemen was trotting towards them, the sun glinting off their helmets and spear points. Squires screened the advance of the main force which was arranged along the road behind. He had been right! He glanced over to where Molders was lying but the captain did not look round. Molders was scrutinising the slowly advancing Bretonnians. Otto looked at them too. The main force was quite a distance away and some dust was rising but Otto could see a collection of bright banners floating above the head of the procession and beneath them a splash of colour he took to be the caparisons of the knights' chargers. Behind marched a column of infantry, a mixture of archers and men-at-arms most probably.

Molders just kept staring through the spyglass and the outriders were nearly at the bottom of the slope before he made any move, silently gesturing to Meyer, his lieutenant, to take the glass. Otto smiled to himself. Most probably the captain was sour at being proved wrong. Meyer looked for some minutes before lowering the instrument, his thin lips pursed and dark brow creased with concern. He passed the glass to Lutyens with a soft oath, 'By Sigmar! A ruse.'

Molders grinned harshly at Otto before wriggling backwards with Meyer, gesturing to Lutyens to pass the glass to Otto. The young noble paused to admire the instrument. It was crafted exquisitely; dwarf-made, Otto thought. Lutyens was impatiently signing to him to hurry so he lifted it to his eye. It took him a second to focus it and when he did he let out an involuntary whistle, immediately cut short by a vicious jab from Lutyens. The image was miraculous, far superior to that given by his father's own prized telescope, one of the best the craftsmen of the Empire could produce. He could see every detail of the faces of the horsemen, now beginning to pick their way up the long slope, and he was surprised at what an unkempt crew they appeared. This was nothing to the shock he got when he trained the glass on the knights leading the column further back along the road. He picked out the Duke by his banner and horse trappings but through the Dwarfish instrument he could see that the figure on the charger was not the darkly handsome, moustached warrior he'd heard of. Indeed it was only a young stripling of a youth, gawky and pale. The rest of the procession was equally startling. There was the occasional warlike veteran but most seemed youths or old men and many of the spearmen seemed armed with farm implements, not weapons of war. Lutyens was tugging at his boot. His mind in turmoil, Otto squirmed back and then ran over to where Molders was issuing a furious stream of orders.

The captain was addressing Meyer. 'Make sure they see you. Act just as if you had contacted their real force. Don't get too close, so that they stay confident we haven't spotted their ruse. You'll not have trouble with their skirmishers if you keep back, they're only there to try to make sure we don't get close enough to spot their damned deception. The rest of us must get back to the main camp at once. Sigmar knows, this will be too close!'

THE RIDE OUT had set a hard pace; the ride back was punishing. They slowed to a walk only where the going was so rough as to demand it, otherwise it was a constant gallop. Otto, who had been disdainful of the pistoliers' wiry mounts, was forced to concede that even if the small horses looked rough, their endurance was exceptional. His mind was filled with the face of the youth that had been masquerading as the Duke – and under the Duke's own banner! What perfidy! He felt almost physically sick when he thought of the base nature of the trick. Even now the Bretonnian force must be advancing unhindered, probably by the southern route, as Molders had predicted, damn him! Otto shivered when he thought of the implications for the honour of the Empire and for his father. How wrong he had been! He looked ahead, to where Molders was riding, resolute but seemingly unperturbed. A blush of shame coloured the young noble's face as he remembered his judgement of the pistolier captain. By the Hammer, what were they to do?

The long summer dusk was just deepening into night proper when Molders barked a curt command and most of the pistoliers wheeled off towards the south. There were only six of them now, still pressing on towards his father. Some of Otto's old anxieties resurfaced. Where were the others going? Was he now riding with traitors who would turn on him to ensure the news of the Bretonnians' vile trick never reached his father? Once more his hand toyed with his sword hilt and he began to try and scrutinise his companions as best he could in the closeness of the night. Each seemed entirely oblivious of him, silent automatons ploughing through the gathering darkness. He was exhausted and his mind was whirling. Would they be in time? Again he felt nauseous. How could a man fight with honour in times like these? The jolting as the horse pushed steadily over the rough ground seemed to shake him to the bone. Each shock from the saddle emphasised the jarring of his thoughts: perfidy, treachery, failure, dishonour! By Sigmar, they had to be on time! Instinctively he tried to spur his mount faster but the horse tossed its head and whinnied in protest.

'Patience!' came Lutyens's slow voice out of the darkness from Otto's left. 'The horse won't rush the broken ground in the dark.'

'Sigmar!' Otto hissed bitterly, 'What kind of world is this, where even a horse can act more aptly than I can?'

The nightmare hours dragged on, the ground studded with rocks, the miles with self-recriminations and doubt as Otto desperately tried to picture where the Bretonnians might have reached and their possible plans. If they successfully pushed through the southern passes onto the flat lands along the Grunwasser all would be lost! The Graf's ill-assorted force of light troops, even stiffened by his own household halberdiers, couldn't face Bretonnian chivalry on the plains. Chivalry! The word had bitter ring to it now. Would they be in time? Otto's thoughts whirled on. The pistoliers were supposed to be able to doze in the saddle. He couldn't have slept now for worry even if he could keep his seat. Where was the camp? How much further?

The challenge from their own picket lines came suddenly and Otto almost cried aloud with relief. They hastened to report to his father. 'Fresh horses and prepare yourselves to be away again at once,' Molders ordered before he dismounted and strode into the Graf's headquarters. Confused by a sense of mingled anxiety and shame, Otto thought of returning to his own tent, but instead he trotted after Molders.

The captain was sitting on a stool in the foyer talking hurriedly with Otto's father. The Graf paced in front of him while old Gunther served the pistolier a hasty meal of bread and cheese. Otto studied his father nervously. His shoulders were still squared and he stood straight but his face was drawn and his fists were clenched. Once Otto would have bristled with indignation that a mere mercenary captain should sit while his father stood, but now the young man just waited awkwardly, the sick feeling in his stomach stronger than ever.

His father heard him enter and turned. 'Sit, Otto,' he gestured to a stool by Molders, 'and eat quickly. Gunther, send word to Otto's manservant to prepare for his master to depart again quickly.' He resumed talking to Molders. 'So, an elaborate ruse! You were right to suspect them. We may just be able to stop them if we despatch a fast force at once. I have the troops ready. It all hinges on how far the Bretonnians have proceeded on the southern route.'

'If they have taken that route,' Molders said through a mouthful of bread, crumbs falling from his beard. A twinge of Otto's old resentment returned. Such familiarity from a mere captain! The Graf showed no resentment, however, and spoke, even respectfully, to the pistolier.

'No, they will have. You are right about that too, I am sure. Besides, the Magister of Dreiburg is well placed to intervene in the unlikely event they have swung north.' The Graf clenched his fists. 'It is a matter of timing. I'll send ahead yourself and your men, two hundred of the Stirlander archers, all of the hackbut men who have mounts, von Grunwald with his light guns and fifty local horse. The Stirlanders will have to manage on foot or double up on horses; they've done it before. You will attempt an ambush in the foothills. I have alerted Dreiburg and I will follow you with the remaining hackbut men and the halberdiers. We will take up a defensive position at Ravensridge, should you need to fall back. If you are caught on the plain, it could go very ill for you!'

'We must hope against that, my lord, but by my reckoning we have a good chance of getting there.' Molders looked at Otto sarcastically. 'The lads set a good pace when their lives and booty depend on it.' The captain took a swig of ale and, standing up, abrupt as ever, continued, 'Right, swilling ale doesn't prime pistols. We'll be off.' He stared pointedly at Otto again. 'Besides I can't afford to fail you, I haven't had my full pay yet!' He gave a strangled noise that might have been a laugh and went out.

'Sigmar go with you!' the Graf called after the pistolier. Otto felt himself flush at the memory of his mistakes as his father turned to him. There were traces of worry around the Graf's eyes but there was no reproach in his face as he said, 'You had best hurry and join them, my son. You will acquit yourself well, I am sure. My thoughts go with you.'

Otto stammered, 'I am… sorry, father.'

'Sorry?'

'Sorry for my misjudgement.'

'We all misjudge things, lad. You are here to learn. Now go.'

'Thank you.' Otto turned.

'Otto, one other thing. Sir Guillame has disappeared, and so has your best palfrey. I fear the two disappearances may be connected. Don't blame Henryk. It is I who should have ensured a stricter guard.'

This news stung Otto more than anything he had yet heard. 'But… but he was a knight, a man of honour!'

His father shrugged. 'You can't keep ward over the honour of others. Just keep your own intact, son – and your hide! Now go and serve your Emperor and your father.'

'Yes, sir.'

But Otto was perplexed as he left the tent. The man whom he had trusted, looked to as an example of chivalry, had coldly manipulated him. Duped him! As he made his way to join the pistoliers, he felt sick in his heart.

IT WAS ANOTHER tough ride and, in truth, Otto was weary to his very core as they trotted through the darkness. This time they had a road to follow, albeit a rough one, and Molders was driving his men hard. Otto rode at the front of the column in the same group as the captain. To his discomfiture, even through his tiredness, he noticed Lutyens was still his shadow. Now, though, the discomfort wasn't fear of treachery but bitterness that he could have been so wrong. Lutyens was his chaperone – not to cloak some dark plot, but instead to look after him, and he had needed him! The memory of Lutyens saving him in that first action returned with the sharpness of a spear thrust and he squirmed in his saddle. The whirling succession of tortured thoughts returned again: perfidy, treachery, failure, dishonour! Above all was the incessant question: *would they be in time?*

His head slumped to his chest, Otto ground his teeth and left control to his mount; the hill pony he thought, with another wave of bitterness, that could act more appropriately than he, Otto von Eisenkopf, noble of the Empire!

The night wore on, measured out by the drumming of hooves, and the pounding thoughts: perfidy, treachery, failure, dishonour! Would they be in time? Otto looked to his side and there, sure enough, was Lutyens. The giant's head lolled. By Sigmar! He was asleep in the saddle! Otto had an urge to hurl his dagger at him. How could he sleep? Otto's fingers clenched the reins until they hurt. Couldn't they make better speed? The old notion of a traitorous Molders deliberately delaying progress came back into his head. Angrily Otto forced it aside, knowing it to be wrong, but a shred of the notion persisted. The young noble cursed himself. By the Hammer, was he himself so shallow? Was he so base as to hope for the imagined treachery to be true just so as to have the gratification of salving his own pride? His world seemed to have crumbled; was he now crumbling too? The hooves, and his thoughts, drummed on.

By dawn they were climbing into the foothills but the light brought no relief to Otto. The sunrise hurt his tired eyes and as he looked back over his shoulder he took little comfort in what he saw. The dust-shrouded column wound after them, now slowed by the narrowed and steep road. The slower pace was bad enough but Otto wondered, with a twinge of what felt disturbingly like fear, what was going to happen when they did contact the Bretonnians? How could this rag-tag force defeat battle-hardened knights? Boncenne may have behaved like some base, fairground mountebank but he was an experienced general who had stood in the lists against the most martial of Bretonnian nobility.

Who could they set against this formidable warrior? Molders, compensating for his short stature with an aggressive swagger and that ridiculous beard? Von Grunwald, head of an ancient noble family but a crank obsessed with the pack horse-toted light guns he had designed? Himself, a young fool who had once hoped for a commission in the Reiksguard and was now riding only with mercenary pistoliers?

Daylight or not, the hooves, and the thoughts, drummed on: perfidy, treachery, failure, dishonour!

Suddenly there was a stir. One of the advance scouts came cantering back towards them. Otto tensed wondering if they had contacted the Bretonnians. Was all lost, their opponents already descending into the plains? The man rode up to Molders. He was breathless, his jerkin plastered with dust that had also stiffened his sweat-soaked hair into absurd tufts. Otto edged his mount closer to Molders to hear the scout's report. The man was gathering breath. Was his gap-toothed mouth a grimace of worry or a triumphant grin?

'Report man, for Sigmar's sake,' Otto muttered under his breath.

'The valley is clear, captain,' the man grinned. 'It's the perfect spot for an ambush. The track is quite broad, steep slope one side, more gentle hills the other, but it's only an illusion of openness. The river is swift and deep, a formidable barrier to fleeing troops. Armoured men would never get across it'

'Very good, trooper,' Molders replied. He turned and began quickly issuing orders, marshalling his troops.

The road became steeper, winding up the rocky, wooded hillside. The sun was shining strongly and the woods rang with birdsong but there was a tension in the air and Otto noted nervous movements all around him as even the seasoned pistoliers checked and rechecked their wargear.

At the top of the hill Molders gave more orders. 'Von Grunwald, his guns and the archers will block off here where the path climbs steeply to the hilltop. The hackbut men will hold the steepest craggy slopes, yonder in the valley centre. The pistoliers and the light horse will close off the rear and block the Bretonnians' retreat. They must keep especially well up slope bar some few, well hidden, to signal when the last of the enemy pass. It is our best plan; we must hope they don't scout properly in their haste.'

Von Grunwald and his guns began deploying to cover the road up out of the valley. Watching the old man working with his men unloading the guns Otto's anxieties returned. 'This is an Empire noble?' he mused, bewildered, as he stared at the short, wiry old man

wearing only tattered hose, his face grimy and his head crowned with
an amazing shock of white hair.

BEWILDERED HE MIGHT have been but Otto was still impressed by the
speed with which the troops deployed, and at such quiet determination and discipline. Even if they were rough and ready, unpolished
and mercenary by calling, they certainly seemed apt to their work.
Indeed it seemed to him that he was the one out of place as he
handed his mount to one of the local horsemen assigned to keep
their horses safely out of sight down slope, away from the line of Bretonnian advance. All of his training had been to fight from the saddle
and in the open and here he was facing his second action, once more
on foot, and once more in hiding. Woodenly, Otto followed the other
pistoliers down from the boulder-strewn crest.

They descended into the woods that overlooked the valley but stayed
well up the slope, picking their way with some difficulty through the tangle. At one point Otto looked down through a narrow break in the trees;
even with his inexperienced eye, he could see what a splendid site for an
ambush it was. Lutyens, scrambling alongside him, was grinning from
ear to ear and Otto was amazed to hear the normally taciturn pistolier
whisper to him, 'They are finished! This will be butchery.'

'We can hold back armoured knights?' Otto panted.

'Here,' the giant replied, 'here we won't hold them, we'll destroy
them!' He gave Otto a pat on the back which almost knocked him
down the slope.

'But if they scout ahead?' Otto feared that the worry he felt might
sound in his voice but Lutyens just grinned more broadly.

'When have Bretonnians ever scouted properly? They ride into battle as brazen as Marienburg harlots. Besides, they will feel they have
no reason to. They think they have duped us. It takes more than some
gilded duke to fool old Molders though!'

Otto was amazed at the affection in the big man's voice as he spoke
of his captain. But he had little time for reflection as he scrambled up
the steep slope, his hose tearing on the brambles, branches scoring
his face. He was almost trembling with exhaustion before, quite some
distance higher, they came on Molders directing his forces down the
steep, wooded slope to their final hiding place. The captain was
jammed, seemingly at ease, in against a tree trunk, beard thrust out,
his arms a jerky windmill of action as he signed his men into position. Where did these men get their endurance?

'Get comfortable,' Lutyens advised him as they reached their allotted position. 'And watch out for the ants!' The memory conjured up
by the jibe stung even more than the ants had. Otto found a likely
spot, settled down and began the wait.

Hours dragged past. As Otto brushed a fly away from his face yet again, he was glad he had taken Lutyens's advice and found a comfortable spot. Nestled behind the roots of a fallen tree, he was well hidden and could shift his position easily and without danger but it was still sweltering and it seemed as if he had been stuck here for days, not just hours.

The waiting cast a gloom over him. The nausea he had felt back at his father's tent was back. He lay listless, staring up at the shifting patterns of sunlight streaming down through at the waving screen of leaves. It bewildered him and made the sick feeling worse. The whole world bewildered him now. He was dog-tired but as he carefully rolled over, turning his eyes from the light, he knew he couldn't sleep. What if this was a mistake too? Had the Bretonnians really taken this route? He thought of their trickery and it depressed him. He thought of Sir Guillame stealing his best horse and fleeing like a common soldier, and his gloom was mixed with shame and anger.

More hours seemed to pass. He stared at a beetle crawling along a tree root. It was all right for the beetle, it just crawled around and did, well, whatever beetles did. It could live its life as it ought. But what about him? How should he live his life? What had happened to the rules and codes he had learned and loved? How could he live with honour? Eventually, as the time crawled past, these feelings turned into self-pity, as Otto remembered his joyful anticipation of battle as he rode up to join his father. Five days ago, or five years? A vast gulf at any rate. Where were the fine plumed armet and shining plate he had imagined? No lance by his hand either, but a clumsy wheel lock pistol. Sigmar save him! It had come to this, lurking again. His second ambush! Two actions, both sprung from skulking. He almost let out a bitter laugh but choked it back just in time.

Otto saw Lutyens's head turn. The blonde giant was wedged in what seemed like a tortuous position, yet he hadn't moved once. Otto expected a reproachful glare over his choked laugh but Lutyens didn't even look at him. He was concentrating on something else. Otto listened, straining to hear above the noise of the river, and eventually caught, faint but unmistakable, the sound of horses' hooves and the jingle of harness. His tiredness vanished instantly; he started to peer around the roots of the tree but Lutyens shook his head. The young noble felt the tension in the pit of his stomach. His pulse raced. They waited.

Were the Bretonnians just an advance guard? Had they sent squires to scout the steep slope? The faint noises continued. The minutes passed. They waited.

Lutyens looked as if he was dozing, confound the man! The noise of the hoof beats got louder. Was this the main party? Still no noise of alarm. They waited.

Otto's hand strayed to his pistol and closed on the grip. The sound of the unseen Bretonnians' progress continued. Still they waited.

Suddenly it came: the notes of a Stirland hunting horn drowned almost immediately by crashing blasts. Von Grunwald's falconets, Otto assumed. Lutyens was on his feet and skidding down the slope. Otto rose but almost tripped over his own stiff legs. Cursing, he plunged after the pistolier. The gorge now echoed with shouting men and neighing horses. On the right there was a continuous cracking as the hackbut men rained fire down on the unfortunate Bretonnians.

Otto was dimly conscious of other men charging downhill but through the tangle of trees and boulders he could see little. He tripped again, rolled and scrambled up. The noise all seemed to be ahead of him now. He skidded on towards the shouting and clash of fighting but was brought up on the edge of a crag far too high to jump. Down through the greenery he could catch glimpses of combat. Cursing again, he tried to make his way around the top of the crag.

There was a great crashing sound and a blood-stained figure appeared, struggling up through the trees. Otto stared into the wide eyes of a young Bretonnian squire. The squire fumbled with his bow. Otto raised his wheel lock and pulled the trigger. Nothing! Blast it! He hadn't cocked the weapon. The squire had an arrow nocked as Otto, yelling with frustration, hurled the pistol at him. The heavy weapon hit the youth full in the face and with a cry he staggered back. Otto, sword drawn now, lunged after him but the squire had tripped on a rock. The man clutched vainly at the branches, and screaming, fell over the crag. Otto bent to retrieve his pistol. His hands shook slightly as he wound back the lock.

Sigmar! What kind of war was this?

WHEN OTTO FINALLY burst out of the thick undergrowth at the edge of the road he could scarcely believe his eyes. A heaving mass of mounted men had been hemmed in against the river by the Empire forces. Molders's men were scrambling over a mounting wall of dead horses and men to get at the Bretonnians, who seemed scarcely to be putting up a fight at all. Some of the pistoliers were lifting spears from their dead enemies, that they might better goad the seething whirl of panic-stricken men and horses towards the torrent gushing behind them. Otto, horror struck, just stood and stared, his head ringing with the shrieks of the dying men and horses, the reports of pistols and the strident cries of the pistoliers and their local allies. This butchery could not be battle! How could a man of honour fight like this?

Further up the path, the situation was different. The hackbut men were well protected by the crags that lined the road at that point and could fire down on their opponents almost with impunity. This very protection, however, meant that they could not press the Bretonnians so closely, and amongst the milling crowd a more purposeful wedge of cavalry was being formed. A leader of authority was gathering his most experienced knights and rallying them to attempt a break out back along the road. In the confined space and press of men there was scant room to use their lances, never mind charge, but with determination born of hardened experience and desperation they fought their way along the road. Otto could see the line of Empire troops buckle. Shaken into action, he rushed to aid them.

'Sigmar and the Empire!' he yelled, entering the fray.

Almost at once he was in trouble. Knocked backwards by a blow from a lance shaft swung like a club, he narrowly escaped the flailing hooves of a knight's horse. The pistolier next to him was not so lucky and a hoof glanced off his burgonet bringing him to his knees. Seemingly frozen, Otto realised the felled pistolier was Captain Molders. With what seemed like unearthly slowness, Otto watched the knight raise the brass-bound lance haft. He recognised the arms on the surcoat as those of the Duke of Boncenne, himself. A wheel lock flashed; with amazement, Otto realised that it was he himself who had fired. The shot missed the Duke but felled his mount. The world sped up once more as Otto, consumed with rage, charged his foe.

The Duke's horsemanship was superb and he was out of his stirrups and saddle and leaping to his feet even before his dead mount had crashed to earth. He flung the broken lance at the still reeling Molders, knocking him flat. Then he swept out his sword and leapt at Otto.

'Base cur!' the young Empire noble cried as he aimed a vicious thrust at the man's head. 'Are you warrior or charlatan to resort to such trickery?'

The Duke was a skilled and powerful warrior, and he blocked Otto's thrust with ease, riposted and knocked the young noble back. Otto just kept his footing and the Duke, following up his own thrust, slipped in turn. He regained his balance but had to step back and for a moment the two opponents stared at one another. The Duke's face was as blank as the plates of his armour, his hard, dark features hardened yet further by the steel frame of his helm. The thin moustache and thinner lips seemed graven on his visage and, along with the stiff guard the Bretonnian had adopted, gave Otto the momentary but disconcerting impression that he was facing some form of animated, metallic statue.

'Base cur!' Otto repeated. The Duke made no reply but suddenly lunged forward in a lightning attack. Otto did well to turn or dodge the flurry of blows but was unable under this relentless storm to press his own attack. The young noble burnt with righteous indignation but, even through his fury, he realised the danger of this awesome warrior and the need for calm and concentration. The noise and confusion of the rest of the battle had faded, leaving Otto facing his enemy in a private minia-ture world as wide only as the stretch of their blades. Otto regained his rhythm but against the power and longer reach of the taller Bretonnian was able only to keep up a stout defence.

As he parried blow after blow, the young noble, lighter armoured though he was, began to be conscious of his waning strength as the strain of the past days caught up with him. The Duke seemed to sense it, too, and pressed his attack even more relentlessly. Thrust followed thrust and Otto was driven back, away from the main action. Using every shred of his skill, Otto turned the attacks and desperately strove to find an opening for his own blade. He was breathing heavily and realised he could not long maintain his defence. Pushed back, step by step, he strove to maintain his concentration on the Bretonnian's lightning blade. Focused on his opponent he failed to see the dip behind him and suddenly pitched backwards, landing winded, his sword clattering away across the pebbles. He stared helplessly up as the Duke, face still impassive, stepped over him, changing his grip in readiness to drive his blade down.

There was a gasp of pain but it was the Duke who cried out as a giant, gauntleted fist smashed into the side of his head from behind. The Bretonnian crashed over and frantically scrabbled for his sword as he stared up at Lutyens, who had pulled a wheel lock from his sash and levelled it at the knight. The shot cracked but flew wide as Otto struggled up and knocked the pistolier's arm aside.

'No, Lutyens, I will finish this… to my code,' the young man panted. Pointing to the fallen Bretonnian with his recovered blade, he put what strength he had into his voice and commanded, 'Rise and defend yourself, de Boncenne!'

The Duke lifted his own sword and rose. He face was still blank but, as he resumed his attack, his thrusts seemed to have lost some of their power. Whether it was due to Lutyens's blow or shock from his young opponent's actions, he was definitely less resolute in his offence.

Otto, despite panting with near exhaustion, realised he had a chance. Desperately he gathered his strength and smashed a thrust aside far harder than he had done before. Feinting quickly, he stepped back a pace and, wielding his sword in two hands, swung it around in a great circle, and hewed the head from his enemy with one blow. His face splashed with hot blood, he barely registered his victory. He recovered his swing and raised his sword for another blow, before swaying and collapsing, saved only from toppling over the lifeless body of his enemy by the strong arms of Lutyens.

The huge pistolier dragged Otto to the shelter of some large boul-ders and prepared to defend him. With the death of the Duke, however, what little fight there had been in the Bretonnians was gone. Some few of the determined knot of men which the Duke had rallied had broken through and spurred back down the road. Some others, lightly equipped squires, had somehow swam across the river and were fleeing away over the hill to the other side, but very few. It had been, as Lutyens had predicted, butchery.

Otto gradually came to his senses. He was propped against a boulder and looking out on a river where a raft of drowned men and horses had jammed against jutting rocks. Struggling to recall what had happened he turned to the bank and saw hackbut men laughing, already stripping the dead.

He looked himself up and down. He was drenched with blood and wondered vaguely if was it his own. He felt a sudden rush of weakness and leant back against the warm stone, staring down at his bloodied sword.

Gradually, Otto remembered his struggle with the Duke and looked to where the crumpled body of his foe lay. So this was victory. So much for honour!

Dazed, he struggled to stand up, leaning heavily on his sword. He remembered Molders and Lutyens and wondered what had happened to them.

He found them sitting by the river, Lutyens bathing his captain's badly bruised head with his soaking neckerchief. Molders looked pale and rather dazed but otherwise fine; at any rate, his chin was still thrust firmly forward. Lutyens looked up, grinning again; action obviously improved his spirits. Addressing Otto, the big pistolier said, 'You look more stunned than the captain and your head is intact!'

Otto slumped onto a rock, shrugged and gestured weakly around him with his sword. 'I didn't expect this,' he mumbled.

Molders met his eyes and suddenly, in spite of his pop-eyes and spade beard, he seemed less ridiculous to Otto. The captain said softly, 'My first battle wasn't what I expected either.'

'I have been so wrong,' the young noble went on. 'So many mistakes!' He sat down facing Molders. 'You have done the Empire a great service, Captain Molders. And you, Lutyens, you've now saved my life twice and I have never even thanked you. How dishonourable!'

'Dishonourable?' Molders asked. 'There is more honour in a man admitting his errors and facing them, than in his battling a hundred foes. I owe you my life and the Graf will be proud of you. No, sir; your honour is intact.'

'Yes,' agreed Lutyens, stepping over and thumping Otto on the back, making him wince. 'You fought by your code, remember?'

The blond giant paused and looked Otto in the eyes. 'I think you will always fight by your code,' he stated seriously.

Then stepping back, he added with a guffaw, 'But in spite of that, we'll make a soldier of you yet!'

THE DOORWAY BETWEEN
Rjurik Davidson

'I WANT THEM dead and my property returned to me.' Baron von Kleist leaned forward as he spoke, the light throwing shadows across his thin face. He was a tall, gaunt man fast approaching middle age, clean shaven, his black hair slicked back like a raven's wing. And although he wore a simple cloak, secured over his shoulder with a plain clasp, he had the air of nobility about him. Perhaps this was due to the very simplicity of his attire, for true nobles have no need to dress flamboyantly, to show off with frills and lace. Only the new nobility needed to prove their credentials with gaudiness and show.

Or at least, that's what Frantz Heidel thought as he sized up the man opposite him. The witch hunter leaned back against his chair and glanced around the inn. Logs crackled in an open fireplace, yellow flames lazily throwing out heat. A few old-timers leaned up against the bar, heads drooping forwards as if they were gaining weight by the minute. In the opposite corner, a group of young men sat and laughed, their faces ruddy from cheap wine. The innkeeper's daughter served them, making her way from behind the bar, through a wave of suggestive comments, to the young men's table. Bechafen, Heidel thought to himself, could be any town in the Empire.

Heidel dressed plainly himself, his clothes a series of simply-cut browns and greens, perfect for the wilderness. His face mirrored his attire, brown straggling hair falling around his ears, lines etched into

93

his skin, thin lips. The only remarkable feature were his eyes, deep and dark. It was as if behind them whole vistas of passion and zealotry were concealed. Only the pupils allowed a glimpse, as if through a keyhole into a blazing room. He turned back to regard the nobleman.

'The destruction of evil, that is the task I've set myself. It is my vow to seek out this cancer that grows daily in the world. And when I find it...' Heidel let his voice trail off.

'A noble cause, undoubtedly.' The baron smiled slightly. 'I understand you burned a man just three days ago. Tell me, have you ever destroyed an innocent by mistake?'

'Never.'

'And how can you be sure?' The baron's eyes were alive with the challenge.

'Witchcraft, sorcery and other forms of corruption are revealed by the stench that wafts before them. Evil betrays itself at every turn. Those who are sensitive feel its presence – I know I am in darkness when I cannot see,' Heidel said rather distractedly. He leaned forward, his voice gaining conviction. 'The innocent have nothing to fear, for they walk in the light. But the guilty will reveal themselves, and they should tremble because only the gods and light and truth can cleanse the world of the foul existence of corruption.'

The baron seemed satisfied with Heidel's reply and leaned back, sipping his dark red wine. A moment later he placed the glass back onto the table. 'So this job is suited to you? You can track down this evil band and – how do you put it? – cleanse them. The Dark Warrior has the heirloom, no doubt. When you have cleansed this foul brood and retrieved it, you will return it to me. Seven hundred crowns for its safe return. You can find me here when you return.'

'Tell me, baron, when this band attacked your wagon, how did they know to take the heirloom?' Heidel poured himself another small measure of wine from the ceramic carafe.

'I brought all my valuables with me when I chose to settle here, in Bechafen. They took us by surprise on the road and my men fled, the cowardly fools, leaving the follower of Darkness and his band to take what they wanted. Naturally I am somewhat embarrassed, so I trust that your task will be kept private.' The baron covered one thin hand with the other, as if to show what he meant.

'And what does this heirloom look like?'

'It is a pendant, silver, set with a blue gem. It is beautiful like a clear sky above the ice-stilled Reik in winter. When caught in the light it throws a thousand tiny sparks of silver into the air, and the blue becomes as deep and rich as the oncoming night.'

'A beautiful object.' Heidel smiled, picturing the gem in his head with its changing blues and its flashing silver reflections.

'My most precious,' the baron said earnestly.

'You must be quite concerned.'

'I am sick with worry that I might never see this precious thing again.' Then the baron shook his head from side to side, as if in disbelief that the pendant could ever have been stolen.

'Well fear not, your lordship. I shall return your heirloom to you, and in doing so, give these foul obscenities their just desserts: an eternal sleep in a long, cold grave.' Heidel's voice was firm, solid, emphatic. 'I will need to find a guide of course, someone who knows the land–'

'Ah, I have already thought of that,' the baron interrupted with a wave of his hand. 'I know just the man. He's a tracker, familiar with these parts. Karl Sassen. I shall send him word to meet you here at the inn.'

'Well, if this Sassen is able to do the job, then we should be able to leave tomorrow.' The witch hunter raised his glass high. 'To success in our mission,' he said.

'To success,' von Kleist echoed, smiling broadly.

THE TRACKER, SASSEN, arrived mid-morning. Heidel was reading *The Confessions of Andreus Sinder*, a book full of the most personal and incisive perceptions into the nature of evil and darkness when there was a sharp rat-tat-tat on the door. He placed the heavy volume aside almost reluctantly and admitted him.

Sassen was a little man, sprightly like a small animal. His body seemed perpetually tense, as if he might need to spring from danger at any moment. Heidel couldn't help but think he looked like a weasel, a view accentuated by his long nose and soft, thin, facial hair.

'Come in,' Heidel invited and Sassen followed him into the room. Heidel sat down but he was disconcerted when the tracker, instead of doing likewise, began to walk around, stopping only to inspect Heidel's possessions.

'A nice long-coat,' Sassen said in a soft high voice, more gentle and articulate than one would expect from a tracker. He rubbed the fur of the lapel between thumb and forefinger.

Heidel agreed uncertainly, unsure of what to make of the little man.

Sassen touched the hilt of the dagger on the small table by the side of the bed, but Heidel, getting increasingly annoyed, noticed that the tracker had cocked his head and that his eyes were on *The Confessions of Andreus Sinder*.

'When do we start?' The tracker turned and, for the first time since entering the room, looked Heidel straight in the eye.

Heidel, by this time, was struggling to contain his anger. The tracker had no manners. How dare he wander into Heidel's room and begin to peruse at his leisure! Heidel bit his tongue and struggled for a moment before responding. 'You realise the danger of the task?'

The little man scrunched his face up. 'I'm not a warrior.'

'It is our joint task to recover the baron's heirloom, so together we must do whatever is necessary. If that means you fight, then so be it. I will not complain about having to help with the tracking.'

Sassen looked confused for a moment, as if there was something faulty in Heidel's logic, then nodded in agreement. 'Very well,' he said before sitting down on the bed and picking up the heavy tome which lay there. 'This book,' the tracker said. 'I have heard of Andreus Sinder.'

'You are an educated man?' Heidel was both impressed and curious.

'Oh, not really,' Sassen said with a self-deprecating smile. 'I've learned to read a little: just a word here and there.'

For the first time Heidel warmed to the man with the rodent's face. Humbleness had always been a virtue to Heidel.

Sassen continued: 'I heard that Sinder was something of a sinner in his youth. Corrupted, they say, before he understood the true nature of evil.'

'But he renounced the darkness,' Heidel countered instantly, 'and believed that his knowledge could be used the better to combat it.'

Sassen smiled momentarily, revealing sharp white teeth. 'Could that be true? That a man could turn his back on darkness, when once he revelled in it?'

'It appears to be the case,' Heidel admitted.

'Then you have entertained the thought, Herr Heidel, that you might benefit from delving into forbidden acts and unhealthy practices?' Sassen smiled and his leathery face was cunning and mischievous.

Heidel's eyes flashed dangerously. 'There are some,' he noted, 'who say that they would never consider such a possibility. They argue that one can never be sure of one's resilience, that only the strongest can return to the light after tasting such sweet and poisoned fruit.'

Sassen stood and began to pace, intensely interested in the discussion. 'And you agree with this position?'

'No,' Heidel stated resolutely.

'There is surely no alternative.' The tracker seemed pleased. Evidently he believed he had cornered Heidel. 'Only such a position can be held if you wish to avoid experimenting with the Darkness yourself, and yet see some value in the *Confessions*. Otherwise what would your approach to Sinder be?'

'I would have killed him.' Heidel's voice was steady, adamant.

'Even–'

Heidel finished Sassen's question: 'Even after he had confessed the error of his ways.'

Sassen stared fixedly, as if in disbelief, his small mouth open, revealing the small, sharp teeth. Heidel himself sat quite still, feeling almost guilty to have crushed what little intellectual argument the tracker had mustered – but knowing without question that he would have done just what he had declared.

Later, after the pair had worked out a basic plan for the task ahead, Sassen left to organise the supplies: saddle-bags, his sword, blankets, food, and so on. Heidel, too, readied himself. He put on his old brown leather coat, hiding the chainmail he had donned for the battle that was surely to come. On his head he placed a black, broad-brimmed hat, weather-beaten and stained with sweat. He attached his sword to his waist and checked the long bow and quiver that he would carry on the saddle of his grey mare.

Was it true, Heidel wondered, that he would have killed Andreus Sinder, the author of one of the most erudite tracts on the nature of evil, a text filled with piecing insights into the darkness in all its manifestations? Almost without realising it, he picked up the *Confessions* from where it lay on the table. He turned the cover over in his hands, feeling its weight. He rubbed his fingers across its cover. The leather was soft and supple. Instinctively he opened to the first page where the manuscript began. He read the first lines:

Only by my participation in these unnatural events did I understand the true gravity of these horrors. Only then did I know the need to burn twisted evil with the bright flame of the sword.

Heidel placed the book down, lost in thought.

HEIDEL MET SASSEN by the gates of Bechafen in the early afternoon as the sun was just beginning to break through the lumbering clouds overhead.

From Bechafen they rode out on the road that ultimately led to Talabec, passing through a series of small hamlets surrounded by green rolling fields. Their path ran south, though later it would turn gradually west. Cattle and sheep stood lazily about, munching on the grass and occasionally turning their soft dull eyes towards the two men and their horses as they rode by. Beyond the cows stood fields of wheat and barley, turning gold in the late summer. A farmer steering a cart carrying grain passed in the opposite direction; when he saw Heidel he bowed his head and would not look at him. Then a merchant train carrying barrels and furs clanked by, its heavily armed outriders giving them hard, silent stares.

Finally a couple of young nobles on dashing black horses galloped across the fields and crossed the road in front of them without greeting, disappearing into the distance in pursuit of some unseen prey. After that they were alone on the worn path which meandered through the tree-dotted scrubland. Slowly, inexorably, the road turned westwards.

As they rode Heidel felt distinctly happy. At last, he told himself, on the trail of evil again.

'Lord Sigmar,' he prayed under his breath, 'protect me on this journey. Let me return safely, the scalps of my enemies in my hand.' He never knew if the gods heard his prayers, but praying always seemed a wise idea. For if they did hear, perhaps they would deign to look over him.

As if trying to fill the silence, Sassen began to tell Heidel about his life, though the witch hunter would have been quite happy not to hear it. The little man had lived in the country hereabouts for many years and had spent time hunting and clearing the land. Once, though, he had sailed the seas with a group of Norsemen, raiding unprotected towns, pillaging fat merchant ships. But since then, he assured Heidel, he had decided to work permanently around Bechafen. Heidel was not sure whether to believe the tracker. Sailing with Norsemen? Sigmar keep him, he thought; let the little man have his fantasies.

'The baron told me that the attack on his goods occurred some ten miles from Bechafen,' Sassen continued. 'He says the band of brigands headed east into the forest, towards the mountains.'

'How did he discover that?'

'After the attack he and his men returned to the carts, only to find them plundered. A fresh trail led off into the woods.'

Heidel nodded silently and disappeared back into his own thoughts as they rode on.

The scattered vegetation around the road slowly transformed into forest: first a copse of trees here; then a slightly larger copse there, then they came quicker and faster until there was only a wall of thick greenery. Heidel was most comfortable in the wilderness. There was something about its simplicity. Danger was swift and direct: wild beasts searching for food; the descent of the winter snows; the surge of the stormy sea. Heidel's worries were equally simple: finding a camp-site out of the weather; keeping warm and dry; saving enough provisions for the journey. Evil was stark, clear, easy to locate; creatures of darkness wandering the woods, raiding small villages, or hiding in the mountains. Heidel's task was simple: to find them, and to eliminate them.

Cities were another story. Affluence made Heidel uneasy. The machinations and intrigues of the courts, great glittering balls with ladies hiding their pockmarks under white paint and rouge, lords and princes wallowing in a sordid world of whores and white powders. Nothing was simple, everything was veiled and obscured. People spoke and acted according to complex codes and signs that had to be interpreted. A friendly greeting could conceal a serious insult. Your best friend could be your worst enemy. Simplicity and directness were seen as colloquial and quaint. Danger came in all sorts of guises, all manner of forms. He could never move in that society. They brought malevolence upon themselves. He could not, he would not, protect them. Better to leave that to witch hunters like Immanuel Mendelsohn.

Heidel leaned over and spat on the ground at the thought of the man.

Mendelsohn, a self-proclaimed witch hunter, was a nobleman by birth. He had grown up amongst the lords and the ladies – and the whores. He could move with ease in high society: with his frilled silk shirts, his brown curly locks, his floppy hats and pointed leather boots. And, for all this, Mendelsohn was not above suspicion. After all, it is a short step from silk shirts to other pleasures of the flesh. First came the finery, then the women and the illicit substances. Then came corruption, sure as night followed day. No, Heidel did not like him or his kind. Heidel did not like the aristocrat's search for fame, his love of publicity, his attempt to turn everything into a drama. Mendelsohn gave witch hunters a bad name and it would not surprise Heidel if one day he would have to go after the noble himself. That stray thought brought an ironic smile to his lips.

Heidel shook his head and banished Mendelsohn from his thoughts. He recognised that such thoughts had a habit of turning him distinctly surly. He looked around at the forest. The trees seemed to be getting thicker, more twisted, the underbrush more prickly and uninviting. Sassen rode beside him in silence, tracker's eyes now intent on finding the trail of the quarry.

Maybe four hours after they left Bechafen, Sassen suddenly called a halt. He reined in his horse and leaped down to the road. He crept, head down along the edge of the forest. It appeared to Heidel as if the little man was actually sniffing for the trail. Then the tracker looked up suddenly and stated: 'Here it is.'

Heidel dismounted too and walked over to him. On the ground were a series of scuffled tracks leading into the forest. Without Sassen he would have ridden straight past it.

The way into the forest was marked by several broken branches and the tracks, still distinct after two days without rain, leading into the darkness. Once into the trees it would be hard going. Branches hung low like outstretched arms barring the way; roots twisted like tentacles from the ground, threatening to trip them.

'Do you know this area well?' Heidel asked the tracker.

'Fairly well. It's all pretty much like this, I'm afraid. But that means it will hamper the band as much as us. We'll have to walk, anyway.'

Sassen wrinkled his eyes, an annoying habit that Heidel had noticed; the little man always squinted when he spoke.

'It doesn't look like we'll be able to travel at night,' Heidel said. He looked to the sky, as if night was about to fall then and there. But it was still deep and blue with clumpy white clouds rolling slowly overhead.

'Unlikely,' Sassen agreed. 'We'll just have to make the best of the day.'

'Fine. Then we had better begin.'

FOR FOUR DAYS they pushed through the forest, the gnarled branches of the trees blocking them and their horses, thorns and bushes scratching against their legs, drawing blood wherever the skin was exposed. In no time Heidel's hands were covered in a delicate latticework of dried blood. The days were dark as the sun was shut out by the canopy overhead. But if the days were dark, the nights were blacker still. Even the shadowy forms of the trees disappeared into the night.

Every day passed the same. They awoke at first light and departed as quickly as possible. During the day they pushed on as hard as they could for, according to the baron, the bandits would have two days' start on them. If Heidel and Sassen pressed on with this pace they could catch them within a week at most, less if the band had made more permanent camp somewhere. When they caught them, surprise would be the key. Heidel would stand no chance against a united group; he would have to pick them off one by one.

On the morning of the fourth day since entering the forest, Sassen stopped and inspected the tracks, an action that had become increasingly regular. 'They are less than a day away from us.' He peered up at Heidel and squinted.

Ahead of them they could see twenty feet at the most. At any moment they might stumble upon the prey. That could mean death or worse. In these close confines, the hunters would become the hunted, and the black warrior's horde would surely crush them. Often Heidel heard rustling close to them in the forest or fluttering amongst the branches above, but whatever it was remained unsighted. He assumed they were just the movements of birds and animals, but they made him jittery anyway.

Perhaps to ease his tension Sassen kept trying to strike up a conversation, trying to get Heidel to tell of his exploits as a witch hunter.

'How many have you put to death?' he asked one time.

Heidel glared at him.

'You are grim, Herr Heidel.'

'Better to say nothing at all, than to say nothing using many words.' The witch hunter spoke plainly.

Undeterred, Sassen continued: 'I hear you burnt a man only last month. What for?'

'He was in league with corruption.' Heidel practically spat the sentence out, the words so filled with revulsion and disdain.

'What did he do?' Sassen inquired timidly.

'When I arrived in this particular village many were falling ill. It was like a plague.' Heidel's voice rose in intensity as he spoke, passion beginning to creep into his account. 'At first I could not discern the cause of this illness. I studied the victims and found that they had great red swellings beneath the skin. Under the armpits, on the neck, between the legs. As a test I punctured one of the victim's swellings, and from the wound squirmed a writhing mass of worm-like creatures, all purple and yellow and bulbous. Alas, the victim died. Later I tried to cleanse a victim by applying fire to his swellings. But the strain was too much on his body.'

Heidel glanced at Sassen, who looked on with a mix of disgust and excitement.

'Continue, continue,' the tracker said, pulling his thin beard with his fingers and licking his lips.

'I realised that the only victims were men, and so turned to the origins of the illness: if I could determine the cause then perhaps I could save these poor people. It took me but a day to find the truth. I interviewed the men and found that those who fell ill first had something in common. All were suitors of a woman, a particular woman. Searching her house I found nothing. But I was undeterred. I pressed the woman for the names of all who courted her. Under duress she produced a list, and all on that list were ill… all save one, the keeper of the inn. I found in that man's cellar a cauldron full of writhing, squirming larvae. These he would feed to the men when they were drunk, placing them in their ale. Somehow they would eat their way through the flesh and the insides. And so he was burnt at the stake that very night.'

'But why, why did he do it?'

'He called it an act of love. He loved her, but she did not return his feelings. As a result he hated her other lovers and decided to kill them. But as he acted out his drama he lost his mind. His hatred for these particular men turned into a hatred of all men. Soon it would have become a hatred of all the world and everything within it. That way is the path to darkness.'

After he finished there was silence for a moment, and then Sassen burst into a high fit of uncontrollable laughter.

'You think it funny?' Heidel's eyes flashed and his hand moved unconsciously to his sword.

'No, no, of course not.' Sassen suddenly looked worried and did not ask any more questions of Heidel.

* * *

AROUND NOON ON the fourth day, the trail they had been following suddenly met a path, wide enough for two carts, leading away to left and right. Once it must have been well used, but now was overgrown, with the trees threatening to close in once more. Sassen handed his horse's reins to Heidel and bent down to examine the tracks.

'They passed to the left,' he said, 'but there are other tracks here, that come from the right. Someone on a horse. It looks like he dismounted, for there are new footprints. Here, see?' Sassen pointed to the new tracks. 'Perhaps he met the group here and has joined them.'

Heidel peered down. There was a small group of hoof-prints, one over the other, as if the horse was made to wait for some time. Next to them were the fresh prints of a boot.

'They are soft-soled,' Sassen noted. 'See how faint the tracks are.'

'Well, with only one horse they can't have gone far. If we mount here we may catch them today. How old are these tracks?' Heidel peered down at the tracks himself.

'Perhaps half a day.' Sassen squinted in the direction that the tracks led, as if he might yet see the band travelling away from them.

'Then we shall ride slowly – and tonight we shall come upon them in a hail of fire and light.' Heidel's eyes flashed at Sassen. The tracker smiled grimly and looked away.

They rode throughout the rest of that day and, as it became dark, Heidel turned to Sassen: 'You must set up camp here. We do not know how far away the band is, but we must take no chances. I shall walk ahead and begin the work, using my bow. I'll be back before morning. Do not light a fire, for I want you here when I return. Otherwise...' Heidel had nothing more to say, so he nodded, dismounted, took his bow and quiver, and began the walk.

Sassen left the path behind him for a clearing, the two horses in tow. 'Good luck,' he called out to the witch hunter, who did not acknowledge him.

THE NEW PATH was wide and above him he could see the stars. It was a relief to feel the open air again and to feel the fresh wind. 'Sigmar,' he prayed under his breath, may the forest be kind to me tonight. 'And Ulric, god of battle, to you I pray also: together may we come down upon these abominations and cleanse them with blood and steel.'

And his heart began to sing, as it always did before he went into battle. For something stirred in him before he killed. It was as if his soul was suddenly in harmony with the world, as if there was some secret melody, some logic, which things and events travelled along. Truth, that was what it was. When a foe squirmed upon his sword – that was truth. When the light in a mutant's eyes dimmed slowly, and then faded to black.

The road opened out into a large clearing. He found them there, camping around a small fire. Already they were drunk or intoxicated, and he smiled silently. Baron von Kleist had been right: these were evil things that needed cleansing. Darkness undermines itself, he thought.

There were seven of them. Six things: neither men nor beasts but something in between, twisted and vile. And the warrior, dull in his black and heavy armour, his face hidden by a great helmet. Some nameless black meat was charring on a spit above the fire. Bottles of liquid lay strewn amongst the creatures, who rolled around on the ground amongst the dirt and their own filth. Only the warrior sat calmly on an overturned log, contemplative and evil.

When three of the corrupted men-things began to make their way from the clearing down a slope away to the right of him, Heidel seized his chance and followed them. He crept as quietly as possible, a shadow in the darkness, yet cursing under his breath as he heard the twigs breaking beneath his feet. But the creatures didn't hear him, for they were crashing down the slope carelessly. After a minute they came to a small stream flowing gently, the sound of water over rocks floating through the air. All three dipped waterskins into the water, splashing their filth into the clear stream, and turned to carry them up the hill.

It was then that Heidel struck. His first arrow hit the leading beast-man in the neck, piercing its soft fur and sending blood gushing through its bear-mouth.

Pandemonium broke loose. In a whirr of motion a second arrow whisked through the air, another close behind. Two hits and a thing with tentacles fell groaning. A last beastman hissed like a gigantic snake; something heavy crashed into it from behind, screaming and lashing out. Then Heidel retreated back into the darkness. An excellent initial foray; three creatures dead.

Praise be to Sigmar. Blessings upon the name of Ulric.

WHEN HE ARRIVED back at the clearing where he had left the tracker, he found Sassen sitting silently between the horses. It was still dark and the chill bit at his face. Sassen was shivering despite being wrapped in a blanket.

'A fine night, Sassen. In the darkness I struck against malevolence, and Sigmar was on our side.' Heidel spoke fast, breathlessly recounting the night's events. 'We must ride before dawn. The sun will soon rise and we must catch them again before they have a chance to move or find us unawares. The darkness will give us cover.'

The crisp air was motionless as they rode. Before long the eastern sky began to lighten. Finally, as they came close to the quarry's camp, the sky had turned gold and red and pink, but the sun was still hiding behind the tree-line.

Heidel glanced at Sassen and wondered if the tracker would be of any use in the fight. The little man had a short sword at his side, but until now it had only been used to hack at bushes and branches. It had not yet tasted blood, unless the stories of sailing with Norsemen were true. Perhaps this would be the morning of its baptism.

When Heidel judged that they were close to the camp, he hissed for them to halt, and they tied their horses to a tree.

'Let's hope that they have not heard us,' he whispered to Sassen. 'Are you ready for this?'

The tracker looked at the ground, then to the sky, and finally nodded briefly, pursing his lips. The fear emanated from him like a scent.

Heidel's mood had changed since his joyous return from his initial foray. Perhaps he could feel Sassen's fear, and somehow he had taken it as his own: an uncomfortable, dissolute, emotion. He felt a terrible sense of foreboding. And though he prayed to Sigmar and Ulric once more, his heart refused to lighten. Instead it was weighed down, leaden. For a moment Heidel felt the inevitability of defeat. How could he face that dark warrior, that faceless, soulless thing – all darkness and metal, terrible and sublime? The warrior had seemed just another man in the night. But as the sky became light, its image in his head to grow in stature; it was as if the very light was eaten by evil, which turned the warrior into something else entirely. Now he was ten feet tall, his armour hardened, impenetrable.

Heidel shook himself. 'Fool,' he muttered under his breath. But despite his reassurances he still felt the sands of uncertainty shift beneath his feet.

They crept along the side of the track and before long came to the camp. Heidel was almost surprised that the creatures were still there. Three corrupted mutants sat in a circle facing outwards, in their hands jagged and vicious blades. There was a chicken-man. Behind him crouched something with what Heidel first took to be a shield on his back, before he realised that it was a shell that has grown from the man's flesh. And finally there was another, a truly foul, corrupt thing which made Heidel rage with fury and sick with revulsion when he a saw it. Where its head should have been there was merely a gaping mouth dripping ooze and slime, pink and putrescent.

The warrior was nowhere to be seen.

'Sassen,' he said, 'the time has come to mete out justice.'

They began.

HOW BEAUTIFUL, HEIDEL thought, as his arrows arched their way across the clearing in the still, crisp dawn air: rising ever so slightly in their flight, and then dropping subtlety, before plunging into flesh and blood. For a moment he forgot the combat, and was content simply to watch the arrows sail, their beauty as they fulfilled their purpose, to fly and to strike.

Then the serenity of the arrows was broken and everything became violence and death. The chicken-man suddenly began hopping uncontrollably, thrusting himself into the air, surprisingly high. The manic leaping was disturbing to watch, the body pulling tight, thrusting repeatedly against the ground. The corrupt body, thrusting and twisting, twisting and thrusting, blood spraying under incredible pressure; the last actions of a doomed creature in agony. So much blood.

Heidel's next arrow struck the second monstrosity, piercing its shell, forcing it to thrash and grasp aimlessly at the shaft protruding from its back.

The witch hunter charged, his sword in hand, Sassen scurrying alongside him, howling at the top of his voice. Heidel quickly lost sight of the tracker as the third creature came at him. He realised with disgust that its body was covered with gaping, slavering, teeth-filled orifices. Its arms were tough and wiry, and the witch hunter knew that if it clutched him those mouths would suck his life. There would be no escape from its clutches.

'You are doomed, spawn!' he cried as he thrust his sword forward, driving it into the creature's belly. It slid along his blade, up to the hilt, yet there was life in it still. It grasped at him, and held him in its wiry arms, pulling him closer, ever closer still. The strength of its arms was immense, and he felt the mouths as they bit into his flesh.

'Sigmar!' he screamed, and tried to push himself away. But it held him fast.

Desperately he twisted his sword and dragged it upwards, and he felt warm blood and entrails on his hands. There was a terrible bird-screech wail. The fiend's grasp weakened. It slid to the ground.

Heidel staggered back, sword hanging loosely in his hand, sweat and blood dripping over his eyes. He was vaguely aware of Sassen fighting something on the other side of the clearing. Weakly he spun around – and something huge and black loomed before him.

The warrior was seven feet tall, a great battle-axe in its mailed fist. Heidel felt dwarfed by it, as if he stood before something from another age, something eternal. For a moment he was motionless, paralysed by awe. He realised that this would be the moment of his death. From behind his opponent the sun had risen all red and gold. Its rays gleamed off the black armour and blinded him. The only thing he could see was the silver pendant, set with a brilliant blue gem, hanging tantalisingly around the warrior's neck.

Then a mailed fist struck him in the face, throwing him backwards. Heidel scrambled desperately to the side as the great battle-axe plunged into the earth. He felt the rush of air as it flew past him. Heidel swung his sword sideways and felt it clatter off armour. A deep laughter followed, a laughter so unnatural and mocking that it filled Heidel with rage. The rage became strength and he leaped to his feet and jumped backwards. The axe whirled close to his belly, threatening to gut him.

'Laugh now! But you will die screaming!' Heidel screamed.

But only laughter was returned.

Side-stepping to the right, Heidel lashed out, aiming at the elbow where only the black plates separated revealing only chainmail. He connected, and felt the sword bite, before stumbling sideways and backwards away from the lethal axe whirling towards him. As he stumbled his foot clipped something – a stone, a root – and his balance shifted, his leg remained stationary, yet his body lurched forward. Desperately he tried to pull his foot forward. Finally he succeeded, in time for his knee to brace his fall.

The warrior was now behind him, unsighted. The terribly notion seized him that something huge and sharp would plunge into his back or cleave his skull. He threw himself to the side and heard a great roar, felt the rush of air on his cheek as if it was a spring breeze.

With great effort he leaped back onto his feet, twisted his body, arcing his sword in one great circular motion. There was a clang as the blow struck his opponent's chest, denting his breastplate and forcing the monstrosity back a step. Glancing around, Heidel noticed the slim figure of Sassen duelling lithely with a beastman, sword flashing time and time again.

Heidel raised his hand to wipe the sweat from his forehead eyes. Soon it would blind him. He lashed out at the colossus as it advanced once more, and again found himself dodging the deadly axe. The witch hunter struck and struck again, and each time the same pattern repeated itself. He thrusting and slashing, his sword glancing off the black armour. The warrior heaving his great axe and plunging it into the thin air: air in which only an instant before Heidel had stood.

Heidel had struck well, denting the armour, drawing blood from between the plates where only chainmail protected the fiend. Yet he knew he stood no chance. One blow from the axe would fell him. Then it would be over. His blows were too small, too weak. Perhaps they drew some strength from the warrior, but Heidel was tiring faster.

Then the inevitable happened: Heidel fell backwards over a corpse. Sweat dripped down into his eyes so everything became a blur. Above him the huge black-armoured warrior stood. Behind the monster, the sun shone with a surreal beauty and the immense, ancient axe glinted cruelly. Heidel knew he was dead. There would be no escape.

A sudden explosion, and it was like time slowed to a crawl. A massive dent appearing in the side of the warrior's helmet. Another explosion: the dent pushed further in, and a thousand tiny holes appeared, as if someone had thrust needles repeatedly through the metal. The warrior backed away, suddenly staggering, blood and streams of yellow filth dribbling from beneath the vast helmet. The huge body fell like the edge of a cliff into the sea; foul steam and dust was thrown into the air with a gigantic crash. The dust seemed to hover in the air for a second and then was whisked away from the enormous body by a sudden gust of wind.

Heidel sat and stared, his ears ringing, sweat dribbling into his eyes. Through the ringing came a startling voice.

'Just in time, hey? You know, Heidel, old man, you really should pick better odds.'

Heidel turned his head. There stood a fop: dressed in a frilled silk shirt, a floppy soft hat on top of hair curled into ringlets, a tiny perfectly trimmed moustache, and wearing soft, pointed leather boots. The man held two smoking pistols in his hands.

'Mendelsohn,' Heidel said flatly.

SASSEN HAD TAKEN care of the shell-creature and was now busy piling the bodies together. Heidel was relieved that the tracker had not been killed in the fight. He had lost track of the little man for most of it, but apparently Sassen could handle his sword after all, and though a trickle of drying blood ran down his left arm, he was not badly injured.

'Only a scratch,' the little man had said quietly when Heidel asked about it. The tracker seemed distracted, as if something was on his mind. Heidel assumed it was the result of the combat. He had seen many men shaken after a battle; some were so distraught they were speechless, wept like children, or moaned worse than the wounded.

They were determined to burn the foul bodies. Mendelsohn and Heidel began collecting wood and building the fire up into a pyre.

'You must have passed me in the night,' Mendelsohn grinned. 'I must say, I'm a bit upset that you only left the warrior for me.'

'Have no fear, Mendelsohn. The Empire is crawling with corruption. You should know that, from the circles you move in,' Heidel snapped.

Mendelsohn smiled for a reply and picked up a fallen log, swathed with damp and rotting bark. 'Damn this, it'll ruin my shirt.' He held the log away from his body but bits still fell onto the silk cuffs.

'I'll go and fetch the horses,' Sassen called out from the clearing. He had finished piling the bodies together as best he could and seemed anxious to be away from this place of death and corruption. Heidel nodded in agreement and the tracker disappeared off down the path.

When they had built the fire high enough, Heidel began to throw on the corpses, cringing as he touched their diseased bodies. He was in turmoil. Mendelsohn, the aristocratic dandy, had saved his life. Had the flamboyant fop not arrived, he would now most certainly be dead. But Heidel felt humiliated, bested, and could not bring himself to show gratitude. He had known Mendelsohn some years, long enough to realise that the paths they walked were different ones. He did not entirely approve of that which the noble had taken. Begrudgingly he turned to the other man.

'You arrived at an important time. Thank you, Mendelsohn.'

Mendelsohn raised his head and gave him a brilliant, handsome smile. 'You make it sound like we had a merchant's meeting. "You arrived at an important time…" – otherwise I would never have sold the silver spoons!' A moment passed. 'Oh, call me Immanuel; "Mendelsohn" sounds so formal.'

Heidel struggled for a moment with his manners, then said: 'And you, you can call me Frantz… I suppose.' A moment later, 'So the baron, he hired you too?'

'The baron?'

'Baron von Kleist? He set me upon this task.'

'I know of no Baron von Kleist.'

Heidel stopped for a moment, thinking. 'The baron hired me to recover an heirloom, a most precious thing, that these foul beasts stole. They attacked the caravan which he was taking to Bechafen.'

Mendelsohn looked concerned for a moment and pulled on his small moustache with his fingers. 'This band attacked no caravan. I followed them from Bechafen myself, all the way. Never let them stray far from my sight the whole journey. Where is this von Kleist from?'

'From Altdorf or somesuch. He was moving here to escape the pressures of the capital.'

Mendelsohn pulled harder on his moustache. 'I know most of the nobles in Altdorf, but I have never heard of a Baron von Kleist. What was this heirloom of which he spoke?'

Heidel walked to the massive armoured corpse of the dark warrior. The thick metal plates which covered the body were impressive. Great strength would be needed to carry such weight. Even now the enormity of the body and the armour were frightening, as if the Warrior might suddenly leap once more into life.

Heidel was also struck by the stench that emanated from the corpse, flies buzzed and disappeared into the cracks between the plates. He shuddered, imagining what was beneath the armour. The flies preferred what was hidden beneath the plates to the bloody mass that had been the warrior's head.

'A pendant, spectacular. It was around the neck of this–' Heidel began, then stopped. There was nothing: the pendant was not there. He looked up at the noble.

'Gone?' Mendelsohn raised his eyebrows inquiringly.

Heidel nodded and turned slowly.

'Sassen.'

IT TOOK THEM half a day to find trace of Sassen's flight. They rode two in line, Heidel sat behind Mendelsohn, clinging as lightly to the man's back as he could. At twilight they came across Sassen's roan, dead by the side of the path.

'He took my grey mare,' Heidel said impassively.

'Aye, and this poor beast looks a little grey itself.' Mendelsohn smiled brilliantly.

Heidel could not understand this incessant cheerfulness. 'Immanuel, how in this world of darkness, do you remain so–'

'Happy?'

'Yes.'

'It's not happiness, it's...' One of his slender hands described a little circle as he thought of the right word. 'It's a sense of humour.'

Heidel thought about that for a moment.

'A sense of humour is one of the ways to fight the darkness, Frantz. If the world is a duality, caught between light and dark, day and night, good and evil, then we understand humour as the opposite of... Damn, I can't think what it's an opposite of right now but...' Mendelsohn threw his arms in the air. 'It's a good opposite anyway.' He laughed to himself.

'Immanuel?' Heidel said seriously.

'Yes.'

'You're a very strange man.'

They rested for a while as the sun went down, ate some dried fruit, salted pork and bread, and let the horse graze. They had reached the point at which Heidel and Sassen had broken through the forest and reached the wider path. To the north lay the thin track along which they had followed the evil band. To the east the wider path continued, the way Mendelsohn had ridden. Both led to the Talabec-Bechafen road.

'Did you follow me all the way?' Mendelsohn asked.

'No, we cut through the forest from the north. It looks like Sassen is returning that way. Perhaps he thinks it will be quicker.'

'Well, if we follow the wretch directly he will stay much the same distance ahead of us. If we return to Bechafen on the trail that I took, we will cover more distance but will be able to ride. It's a risk, but it means we have a chance of cutting him off. If however, he reaches Bechafen before us, I fear we will have lost him.'

For three days they rode and it was like a nightmare broken only when they stopped to eat or sleep at night. But sleep was hard to find. To his great irritation, Heidel would doze off only momentarily before being jolted awake. As he lay half-asleep he felt the constant motion of the horse beneath him, as if he was still riding. At other times he felt the roots and rocks digging into his back, every knot and twist. So he spent most of his time in a strange twilight world of insufferable insomnia.

When sleep finally took him, he dreamed strange dreams: of riding the same horse as a cloaked figure. He was too afraid to talk to the man, for he knew that something was not quite right. Once, in the dream, he touched the figure on the shoulder, and the man turned. The face was for a moment caught in the shadows. But as the wan moonlight touched the face Heidel screamed: for it was a corpse, cadaverous and rotten, and curling down from its shrivelled scalp was a cascade of perfect brown ringlets. It had touched its cheeks with rouge, in a gesture monstrous and sickening, and on its face was a grin of yellow, decaying teeth.

'Humour,' it said to him, 'humour is the opposite of...' And those words echoed in frightful ways. But no matter how he tried, Heidel could not get off the horse.

ON THE FOURTH day they reached the road, and there they bought fresh horses from a passing merchant for a thousand crowns. More, thought Heidel, than he had been offered for this task. They enquired and found that a small, weaselly man, riding a grey mare, had passed within the hour.

They caught their first distant glimpse of Sassen as he entered Bechafen – the tracker riding slowly towards the town's great wooden gates.

'My poor mare,' Heidel muttered, noticing the beast's head drooping with fatigue.

The sun was going down behind them, the chill in the air starting to bite. They followed Sassen's route through the gates, past the two guardsmen who looked indifferently on all those who entered the town. They trailed Sassen as inconspicuously as they could, trying to keep groups of people between them. They were fortunate that there were many on the streets: labourers heading for their favourite tavern, street vendors packing up their goods for the day, farmers driving their carts towards the gates and the hamlets surrounding Bechafen. In any case, Sassen did not check behind him; he did not seem mindful of pursuit, as far as they could tell.

As the two witch hunters made their way through the busy streets, they kept as far behind as they could, and at times feared that they had lost the tracker. But just as they were losing heart, peering desperately into the distance, one of them would notice Sassen heading away down a side street, or just turning a corner in the distance. On and on he went, leading them across the centre of the town, and finally they entered the wealthier quarters, trotting past great rows of town houses, hidden from the road by high walls.

Sassen entered the grounds of a decrepit and decaying building, its eaves cracked and splintered, tiles missing from its roof, a garden overgrown with weeds and grasses. The tracker tied the exhausted horse to a dying tree and disappeared around the side of the house.

'Do we enter now, or rest and return later, refreshed?' Mendelsohn asked.

Heidel noticed that Mendelsohn's handsome face was weary and lined; his eyelids looked leaden, weighed down.

'We could rest now and return later,' Heidel replied. 'If we do we will be able to deal more easily with whatever evil we find. However I fear to tarry, for evil left alone can prosper and grow.' He paused wearily and squinted. 'I say we enter now, and administer the cure for whatever corruption we may find.'

Mendelsohn nodded his head emphatically. 'Let us finish this business. Later we may rest.'

They tied their horses to the front gate and walked into the front garden of the house. Mendelsohn loaded his pistols while Heidel looked around, sword drawn.

'There must be a back way in,' Heidel whispered.

They crept around the building, daring a peek through the side windows. The place seemed empty; no furniture cluttered the rooms, no fire warmed the air.

The back door, peeling paint clinging to its wooden panes, swung loosely on its hinges. Beyond they could see an empty corridor leading into a shadowy room. As they entered, it occurred to Heidel that the place seemed even more decaying from the inside. The floors were covered with grime and dust, and thick, matted cobwebs hung low from the ceiling. For a moment he felt that he had entered something dead, as if he stood in the dry entrails of something that had once moved and lived. Colour had once adorned these walls; people had once laughed in these rooms and hallways.

They searched the ground floor, and found nothing. Upwards they ventured, but all the rooms were empty.

'It seems we must enter the cellar,' Mendelsohn ventured. 'Though the prospect displeases me.'

The stairs led down into the deepest darkness. Into the very bowels of this dead creature, thought Heidel. He pushed the idea from his mind, for it unnerved him. He was not usually quite so morbid.

Eventually they reached the floor of a dry and empty room. A burning torch hung on the wall facing them, holding back the darkness. Heidel strode across and took it. To his left a narrow tunnel, chiselled through the rock, descended into yet deeper darkness.

'I do not like this, Immanuel,' Heidel whispered.

'Me neither. Yet I fear the solution to which we seek lies deeper down this tunnel. We are left with but one option. Light the way for me.' Mendelsohn walked through the tunnel opening.

Heidel followed, holding torch in one hand, blade in the other. To himself he began to pray: 'Ulric, watch over me. Sigmar, guide me.'

The tunnel descended slowly for a hundred paces or so, then levelled out. The floors were smooth as if worn by years of use, but the narrow walls and the roof overhead were craggy. Many times Heidel or Mendelsohn clipped outcrops of rock with their shoulders, arms or knees. The air down here was fetid and foul. Moisture, cold and clammy, clung to the walls and dripped down from the roof, while small puddles splashed underfoot. The two witch hunters could not see very far ahead of or behind them, and the unseen weight of the earth overhead enclosed them. Heidel was in gloomy spirits and Mendelsohn said nothing. Though remaining level, the tunnel wound now left, now right, and before long Heidel had lost all sense of the direction in which they moved. With every step the sense of utter foreboding grew in him.

The stale odour of the still air seemed to increase with each step. With nowhere to go, no fresh air cleansing the tunnel, the smell accumulated into a gagging, noxious, stench that began to sicken Heidel. It brought to mind worms wriggling in dead meat – warming slowly in the sun. Nausea washed over the witch hunter in waves until finally he could bear it no longer and exploded into a fit of coughing.

The noise echoed weirdly down the tunnel. Mendelsohn jumped at the sudden break in the silence and turned. For a confused moment, Heidel's fears leapt from his unconscious: as Mendelsohn had turned, he had imagined his face to be emaciated and cadaverous, a rotting skull, just like the face in his dreams. He gasped and his heart leapt in his chest. But as soon as he had started, he realised that it was no so. Mendelsohn was just himself.

'What will the ladies of the court think of me now?' Mendelsohn smiled his handsome smile, trying to brush the smell from him with fluttering shakes of his hands. 'I shall have to buy myself some expensive Bretonnian perfume to rid myself of this foetid odour.'

Heidel could not help himself and broke into a shy smile. He did not mention his nightmarish vision, however, and Mendelsohn's words did little to allay Heidel's fears. The pair began walking again and after twenty paces or so the dread had returned. All was the same as before: the stench, the darkness, the water, the loss of a sense of direction. Then just when Heidel felt like suggesting they turn back, a dim light beckoned before them.

HEIDEL AND MENDELSOHN crept forwards until they could peak into the chamber beyond. It was a cavern, smooth walled and dry, perhaps two hundred feet long and just as wide. The towering roof disappeared into the darkness above. It must have been a mausoleum of some sort, or perhaps a part of the Bechafen catacombs. Desiccated corpses lay on great stone slabs; bones littered the floor, jutting up at odd angles, in a veritable sea of human remains. Hundreds of narrow holes were cut into the walls, from which more bones protruded. From everything rose the stench of death and decay.

In the middle of the room stood a stone contraption, somewhat like an arch, maybe ten feet high, beneath which stood Sassen. The little man looked up towards the top of the archway, stepped back, turned on his heels and walked out of Heidel's sight. To the witch hunter, the tracker had never seemed so like a weasel, with his pointy, pinched little face, his furry little beard, his beady eyes squinting.

From somewhere out of sight, a familiar voice rose to break the deathly stillness, and echoed down the tunnel. 'Come in, Heidel, I've been expecting you. And bring your friend.' It finished with a burst of uncontrollable laughter.

All hope of surprise was gone, if they ever had it, and Heidel felt bitter defeat. Wearily he and Mendelsohn stumbled through into the shadowy mausoleum, arms limply hanging by their sides.

'You've come to witness my triumph, of course. Welcome, Herr Heidel, to the Bechafen catacombs.' Baron von Kleist stepped into the flickering torchlight towards the arch. A few paces behind him, Sassen loitered more shyly. Swathed in a black robe, the baron appeared tall and thin to Heidel, much like a cadaver himself. The torches that lit the mausoleum threw great shadows over his body. His skin seemed to be pulled too tightly over his head, and his eyes and mouth seemed to disappear into gaping blackness. His face seemed transformed into a skull. The baron laughed again.

'Witness my work: from here Bechafen shall fall! Here I shall open the doorway between life and death. I will conquer death, vanquish nature, and these pitiful bones will rise once more!' The baron turned slowly around in a circle and raised his arms up in triumph. He was looking at all the bones and corpses as if they were all the riches of the world; as if, instead of lifeless, rotting bodies, they were gems inlaid with silver and gold.

Heidel's face twisted in fury. 'This is blasphemy, infernal sorcerer! And for that you will pay! Sigmar damn you!'

'Why such harsh words, witch hunter? In condemning me you are only damning yourself. It was you, after all, who was responsible for the return of the key to that doorway between.' The baron dangled the pendant before him, taunting the witch hunter. 'My so-called "guards" ran away with it. So I turned to an employee of an entirely different kind. I thank you for its safe return.'

Von Kleist gave a mocking half-bow. Behind the baron, Sassen gave a strange little high pitched laugh. Heidel gripped the hilt of his sword in anger. He yearned to swoop upon the little man and repay him for his betrayal. Heidel could feel Mendelsohn tense and tremble in fury beside him.

'You have been corrupted, necromancer, and for that you will be sent screaming to the abyss,' Mendelsohn stated simply, as if he was passing sentence. For a moment the baron was taken aback by the confidence in the witch hunter's voice.

But then von Kleist smiled. 'And what of this?' he asked as he reached up and implanted the brilliant blue gem of the pendant into the top of the stone archway. A harsh light arced from the gem, sulphur-bright, searing away the shadows of the cavern. A rank smell, as if of burning metal, filled the stale air. Slowly the entire floor seemed to move; the sea of bones swelled into waves. A jaundiced murmuring rose discordantly on the air – and the bones began to move!

Heidel felt unhinged, delirious at the sight, as ages-dead bones ordered themselves: as thighs re-attached themselves to hips, as jaws began chatter, as mottled arms and withered skulls rejoined their bodies. The cavern echoed with the hideous scraping of bones as they slid, as if sentient, in search of the right joint, the correct aperture, with which to connect. The horrendous reek of death choked the air as the entire collection of corpses and body parts shifted and roiled around each other. To Heidel it seemed a hallucination, yet he knew its awful reality. This was no time for dreaming; they must act, or they would die here.

The witch hunters moved with lightning speed. They leaped high and scrambled over moving skeletons, slashing out with their rapiers at claws which tried to grasp them. Heidel kicked at cadaverous hands, pushed himself further forward using skulls as hand-holds, ribs as footholds. He struggled to balance himself on the shifting sea of bones beneath his feet, which seemed to lurch ten feet one way, then ten feet another. He felt nails begin scratch at him, jaws bite. More than once he felt sharp pain and his blood flow.

Heidel heard two explosions in swift succession, and watched Sassen fall howling, his face ghastly white, two holes blasted in his chest. He glanced around wildly, but could not see Mendelsohn. The witch hunter had only moments before he would be drowned in a sea of gnashing corpses. Desperately he tried to reach the baron, slashing frantically as he tried to carve a path through the shifting bones.

Baron von Kleist was prepared. Beneath his breath he muttered something arcane and guttural. From his suddenly outstretched hand a ball of livid red flame shot towards Heidel, who ducked uselessly as searing fire wrapped itself around his body. Someone screamed agonisingly, a wail which rose and rose until Heidel wished that whoever it was would stop. Then, as it finally died out, the witch hunter realised that he, Heidel, had been the one screaming. He raised his head to see another fireball speeding from the baron's hand. The fire embraced him again; his agonised wail broke unbidden from him once more. As the pain died he saw, from the corner of his eye, Mendelsohn, who had scrambled rapidly over the rising bones and reached the arch. The other witch hunter stood behind the baron, arm raised with a stone in hand.

No, Heidel screamed inside, mouth barely able to form the words. Mendelsohn! You're facing the wrong way...

Mendelsohn faced not towards the baron, but towards the arch. The stone came down, with all the force that Mendelsohn could muster in his body – directly onto the blue gem of the pendant set into the arch. A third vast fireball exploded around the hellish cavern, but this time the fire did not touch Heidel. This fire was white and searing, and it flowed from the gem in the archway like a river of flame. Flame that engulfed Mendelsohn and tossed the baron aside with its force.

Around Heidel the bones shuddered, as if in memory of agonising pain. Then they collapsed like puppets with their strings severed.

With renewed vigour, Heidel leaped forward and landed before the baron, who was struggling onto his hands and knees amidst the scorched cadavers. Heidel kicked out and von Kleist was flung backwards. The baron scrabbled, belly exposed, hands desperately searching for purchase on the carpet of bones. The witch hunter thrust downwards, feeling the sword pierce vital organs, slip between bones.

A look of shock crossed the baron's face. 'No!' he howled. 'This cannot be!'

'Know this, necromancer!' Heidel cried. 'I am a witch hunter. I will seek out evil wherever it raises its misshapen head, and I will wipe its pestilence from this world. You are leprous and corrupt. Return to the abyss from whence you came.'

When his words finished, the baron was dead.

Heidel rushed over to Mendelsohn's side, but was too late. In destroying the pendant, the flamboyant witch hunter had destroyed himself.

HEIDEL DID NOT stay long. He muttered a few words under his breath, a prayer of sorts:

'What is it to be a witch hunter?
To toil endlessly against the dark.
What then will be our reward?
We ask for none and none is received.
When can ever we stop?
When the cold grave eternal calls us to rest.'

Heidel stood and turned to leave. But he stopped himself, bent down and picked up a metal object from the floor. It was an ornately carved pistol, the silver a little blackened with soot. He turned it over in his hand. It was heavy, yet fit well in his palm.

Well weighted, he said to himself. I think I will learn to use this, he said. Yes, I think I will. Then he placed it beneath his belt.

I might not buy a silk shirt though.

In his head he heard Mendelsohn's voice. *Humour is one of the ways to fight the darkness*, it said.

Heidel smiled briefly and began the long walk back to the surface of the town.

BIRTH OF A LEGEND
Gav Thorpe

'GRUNGNI'S BEARD, I wish they'd quieten down! I've got one hell of a hangover!' King Kurgan spat derisively at the burly greenskin watching over them.

The four dwarfs were tied to stakes, their hands and ankles bound with crude rope. A huge bonfire raged not far off and the orcs were celebrating their victory. The air was filled with the sound of beating drums and the woods reverberated with the constant pounding. As the night passed, they broke open huge barrels of their foul intoxicating brew to wash down the hunks of charred dwarf flesh they had eaten earlier. The flames of the fire leapt higher and higher and the orcs shouted louder and louder.

Kurgan's blood boiled. He strained at his bonds with all his strength. It was to no avail; the knots remained as tight as ever. He was condemned to look on despondently while the foul creatures made a banquet of his household. Over to his left, Snorri slumped semi-conscious against his pole. The others, Borris and Thurgan, seemed similarly dazed. The king's gruff voice cut across the laughter and shouts of the orcs.

'Snorri! Hey, Snorri! A curse upon us for being captured rather than killed, wouldn't you say?'

The venerable advisor groaned and looked up at his king, one eye screwed shut with pain, the lids stuck together with congealed blood from a cut on his brow.

'Aye, a pox on the green devils for not ending it honourably, sire. I'll see them all rotting in hell 'fore I'm for the pot! Mark my words!'

Despite their predicament, Kurgan was heartened by Snorri's defiant words and he grinned to himself. Out beyond the fire he could see the orcs smashing open the barrel of ale he had been taking with him to his cousin in the Grey Mountains. A tear glistened in Kurgan's eye as he thought of that fine brew, made over five hundred years ago and matured in oak casks stored in Karak Eight Peaks, wasted in stunted orc throats. What he had paid for that small keg could have trained and equipped an army for a month. The potent ale had seemed like a good investment at the time, but when the orcs had poured from their hiding places yelling their shrieking war cries, he had realised that perhaps the money should have been spent on an army after all.

Kurgan pushed aside thoughts of ale and studied the orc camp, trying to figure out a plan of escape. Most of the orcs – he wasn't sure how many there were – sat in small groups, dicing, squabbling or just sprawling, bloated. The smaller goblins scurried to and fro, fetching and carrying for their bigger cousins, who would occasionally kick or punch one of them for raucous entertainment. A particularly inventive black orc used his spear to elicit a yelping noise which the orcs found amusing.

Kurgan could see that most of the dwarfs' stolen weapons, armour and treasure was piled all over the camp, with no plan or order. In one part of the clearing, Kurgan's mighty field tent had been crudely erected for the orc leader, although the sides of the massive marquee had not been unfurled. Inside, gold and gems were piled high, but Kurgan was looking for the magical weapons and armour that had been stripped from him and his Longbeard retainers. Across the darkness Kurgan could make out the massive warlord, sitting on a fur-backed throne at one end of the tent while his drinking cronies squatted around him. A mass of glittering treasure was spilled around them. They laughed heartily at some brutal jest. Perhaps the warlord felt Kurgan's gaze lingering on him, for the orc slowly turned his heavy head to fix the dwarf king with evil red eyes. That malevolent glance fastened Kurgan to the wooden stake as surely as the ropes which bound him. For a short moment he stopped struggling.

Kurgan regained his composure, scowling at the dark savage with what he hoped was his most frightening glare. The warlord backhanded one of his subordinates for some misdemeanour, sending the orc sprawling in a spray of teeth. The huge brute stood up abruptly, shouting something to his subordinates, his bosses. He grabbed a passing goblin and tossed the unfortunate creature into the blazing campfire. As the warlord's comrades laughed at this jest, the huge orc began stomping towards Kurgan. His glowing eyes never left the dwarf for a moment. The milling throng of orcs and goblins parted effortlessly before the stride of the mighty warlord, closing in behind their leader as he marched towards his most prized captives.

The orc warlord was dressed in heavy black mail and studded plates, and even Kurgan found himself thinking that he presented a fearsome sight. At his belt hung a string of grisly trophies: severed heads, hands, feet and ears dangled from a chain looped around a thick leather strap. The warlord's skin was dark green in colour, almost black, and slab-like muscles rippled beneath the surface. The orc's bucket-jawed head thrust forward from between two chain-bedecked shoulder pads, his red eyes burning with fierce power. They were pinpoints of pure hatred, smouldering with a barely-repressed violence that made Kurgan tremble with fearful anticipation. Switching his gaze before he betrayed any weakness to the advancing orc, he looked at the huge column of smoke pouring into the sky, lifting burning fragments of his comrades' clothes into the chill night air.

ACROSS THE WOODS, other eyes had seen the smoke. Now they moved silently through the forest towards its source.

Ansgar turned to the youth leading the hunting party and asked the question which had been nagging him.

'Are you sure this is a good idea? We've got no clue as to what's out there!'

The burly young man simply turned to him and winked, before pressing forward along the rough track. Ansgar sighed and beckoned the rest of the party to follow, swapping worried glances with a couple of the older members, veterans of no few battles. Eginolf passed by and Ansgar fell into step with his twin brother.

'I don't like this at all, Eginolf. He's a fine lad, but he's not ready for something like this. Headstrong, if you ask me.'

'I didn't,' came the grunted reply.

Ansgar shrugged and padded along the game trail in silence, his hand holding his sword to his thigh to stop it making any noise. The hunting party included warriors of all ages, from veterans in their thirties like Eginolf and himself, to seasoned warriors in their early twenties and untried boys who had seen only a dozen summers.

Their leader, perhaps surprisingly, fell nearer that end of the scale. The youth was a fine-looking young man. Only fifteen, he was already over six feet tall and his well-muscled body put any man to shame. It wasn't only his physical prowess that impressed Ansgar, though. The hunt lord was clever and canny, with an experience of hunting and battle that belied his age. The lad had a toughness inside too, a resolute stubbornness to overcome any problem.

Ansgar fondly recalled a time, maybe five years ago, when a party had gone to the river to catch fish. The group had been confronted by a massive bear, there for the same purpose. Everybody else had frozen, but the young lord had strode forward, hands on hips, until he was a few paces from the huge beast. 'These are our waters, fish somewhere else!' he stated in a level voice. Ansgar had expected the bear to swipe the boy's head off, but instead it had looked at the youngster's unwavering stare and had turned and lumbered into the woods without a growl.

From that day, the young lord had become known as Steel-eye, and his reputation had done nothing but grow. He was a good leader, generous to those who served him well, swift to act against the enemies of the tribe. He was very much like his father and when that great man was eventually ushered into the halls of the dead, his successor would bring a time of equal prosperity. But that was for the future. All that mattered now was finding out who was trespassing on their lands.

The warriors of the hunting band were dressed for the cold night, their brightly patterned woollen breeches and fur-lined leather jerkins protecting them from the biting north wind. Most of the men wore their hair in one or two long braids down their back, woven with bright ribbons and beads to match their chequered leggings.

As the lord's hunting party, they were equipped with the finest weapons forged from sturdy metal mined in the south-eastern foothills. Each of the men also had a short hunting bow, carved from the horns of mountain cattle. The warriors of the tribe were taught how to use the bows from the time they were able to lift one, and even in the darkest night they rarely missed their mark. Ansgar was proud to carry the champion's bow, edged with gold and silver thread, which he had won four times in the last six years. Whatever his words of caution, Ansgar was as eager for a fight as any of them, looking forward to the promise of more glory in battle. If there was some fighting to be done this night, he would be ready for it.

The party moved on in silence, the forest around them in almost total darkness as the cloudy sky obscured the twin moons. Now that they had dropped into the dale the distant flicker of fire could no longer be seen, but the scouts had taken their bearings well and they were headed almost straight to the north to investigate the intrusion. Soon they would find out just who it was who thought they could camp within their borders.

BY THE TIME the warlord was stood in front of his dwarf captives, most of his warriors were behind him. His head cocked to one side with concentration, the large orc looked at each of them in turn, assessing their remaining strength. Noticing Snorri's injury, the massive black orc's mouth twisted in a cruel smile and he stepped forward for a closer look.

It was just the opportunity Snorri had been waiting for. Lashing forward with his head, the old dwarf delivered a smashing butt to the bridge of the orc's nose, sending a spatter of green blood spilling through the night air. The mumbling throng behind him fell silent except for a few gurgling gasps of horror and the clatter of the odd weapon or cup dropped in stunned disbelief. As the chieftain shook his head to clear the dizziness, one of his lieutenants stepped forward, a bared scimitar lifted above his head. His intent was clear. Angrily, the chieftain pushed the orc back into the mob and grinned evilly at Snorri. Wiping away the mixture of blood and mucus dripping down his long top lip with the back of his gnarled, scarred hand, the battle-hardened orc chuckled. 'I likes dis wun – 'e's gorra lorra spirit, hur hur!'

When the stunned silence continued, the warlord slowly turned on his heel to glare at his warriors. Under his hostile gaze, the mob broke into howls of sycophantic laughter. Satisfied with this display, their leader turned back to the dwarfs, his attention now firmly fixed on Kurgan.

'Wotcha, stunties! Are we cumfurtabble? Do yooze knows what I'm gonna do wiv yooze lot? Dere's lots of fings we can do togevver, and it'll be a lorra fun. We 'ad a lorra fun wiv yer mates!'

To illustrate his point, the warlord let rip with an enormous belch, spattering Kurgan with spittle. The stench of charred dwarf flesh and fungus beer was nauseating and the dwarf king felt his stomach lurch uncontrollably. With some effort, Kurgan quelled the bile rising in his throat and grimaced at the warlord.

'Course, we woz 'ungry den, so we 'ad to be pretty quick wiv da butcherin'. Yooze fellas, we's gonna take our time over, ain't we lads?'

The warlord turned to his ragtag army, his cavernous mouth yawning open to display an impressive set of yellowing, cracked fangs in what Kurgan assumed was the orc equivalent of a grin. This time the mob cheered on cue, laughing heartily. Kurgan tried once more to loosen his bonds, without success.

'Da furst fing we's gonna do is put yer feet inna fire. Dat'll warm yer up fer sure. Den we can stick fings in yer eyes, so's you don't see no more. Den we's gonna chop off yer fingas and toes and ears and noses and hack off yer luvverly beards. I fink yer king's beard will go well wiv me uvver mates.'

The orc stretched and grabbed a handful of Kurgan's hair, dragging his head forward until it was level with the vile decaying decorations on the orc's belt. The stench of rotting blood and filth emanating from the warlord's unwashed fur leggings made Kurgan want to retch, and he had to muster every ounce of self-control not to heave up his breakfast. The warlord released his grip and continued.

'Den I fink we'll start boilin' bits of yer inna pot, and we'll feed 'em to yer so's yer don't go 'ungry. Yooze stunties are tough 'uns, no mistake, and I reckon dere'll still be plenty of life left in yer after dat. So den we start peelin' yer skin off an' feedin' it to da boarz. Da last fing we's gonna do is cut out yer tongues, cos by dat time yer'll be screamin' really loud and musical, beggin' us ta stop 'avin so much fun.'

Kurgan spat again, and raised his head to stare straight at the old orc. Clearing his throat of smoke and ash, the dwarf king's voice rang clearly out over the camp.

'You have plagued us for many years, Vagraz Head-Stomper, and we have never been afraid of you. You don't frighten us now! You will never get me to beg anything from you, you worthless dung-head! I'd bite off my tongue before I would give you that pleasure. You can torture us, but you'll never break our spirits.'

The warlord frowned at the interruption. With a non-committal grunt, the orc delivered a short punch to Kurgan's jaw, smashing his head back against the post and splitting his lip.

'You mite not fink I'm very smart, but I knows a few fings about yooze stunties. F'rinstance, I knows dat da worst fing for you is gonna be to watch yer mates gettin' it furst.' Gazing at the roaring fire and then back to the dwarfs, Vagraz gave an evil chuckle. 'Enough words. Let's get started!'

With that he spun and delivered a mighty kick to Snorri's midriff. The ancient counsellor fell to his knees, doubled up with pain. Another kick from the iron-capped boots knocked Snorri sideways, spiralling down the pole until he was left choking in the mud. Eager to regain his lost standing, the burly orc with the scimitar pushed forwards again, two swift hacks severing through the ropes binding Snorri. As a goblin darted forward to wind more cord around the dwarf's wrists, the orc subordinate leant down and snarled into Snorri's ear.

'Lucky you, da boss wants yer furst!'

THE MOONS BROKE from the cloud and the party halted briefly by a swift-running brook. The men sat down in the undergrowth along the bank, splashing the cold water onto their faces, swallowing a few gulps of the cool, refreshing liquid and chewing on the odd meat twist or fruit they had brought along. Soon they were moving again. Slipping silently into the darkness, disturbing the bushes and branches less than the touch of a breeze, the scouts ran off ahead.

Soon the first of them returned, melting back from the shadowy darkness. They gathered around the hunt lord to report. The oldest of them, Lando, spoke first.

'It's an orc camp, lord. It's difficult to say how many, they keep moving around, but by my reckoning it's odds of at least four to one in their favour. They've got a few guards, but they're all drunk. We could slit their throats without any problems. From the trails they seem to be heading westward, from the mountains.'

Frodewin carved a picture of the scene in the dirt. 'The most sheltered approach is from the west. We can circle round the Korburg and move up Aelfric's Vale to attack. The moons are almost set; soon it'll be completely dark. With that massive fire they've got burning, their night vision is going to be worthless. We should be able to pick off half of them before they realise there's anything amiss.'

The blond curly hair of Ringolf bobbed up and down with excitement as the young lad pushed his way to the front to add his news.

'They've captured somebody, but I couldn't get close enough to find out who.' The young man gulped a breath. 'There's a whole horde of them. Maybe we should wait for the others to arrive.'

Steel-eye sighed and looked at each of his men. Without a word, he turned and started off towards the orc camp at a run. The others exchanged confused glances and then followed without protest. The going was easy, following a deer track to the west through the ferns that studded the base of the mound known as Korburg. The scouts slipped ahead once more, spreading out to silence the slumbering sentries they had located. The main party continued around the tor, breaking to the north when it reached a small stream which splashed down the steep slope from a high spring.

Quickly and carefully, the hunters passed through the woods without a sound. The twin moons dipped out of sight and the forest was plunged into blackness. Steel-eye signalled a stop and then moved forward, tapping Ansgar and Eginolf to indicate they should accompany him. They half crouched, half ran towards the clearing. Ansgar could hear the drums and the chants of the orcs quite clearly now – and smell the stench of burning flesh on the breeze. The old huntsman uttered a whispered curse and Eginolf placed a warning finger to his lips. He pointed towards a small thicket where a dozing orc leant against a tree, its crude club lying next to it.

Without a sound, Eginolf drew his long hunting knife and slipped into the trees. A moment later he was rising out of the bushes behind the orc. His hand clamped around its long jaw and the knife flashed down in one swift stroke. Eginolf laid his prey down carefully before rejoining his fellow huntsmen who lay in a clump of ferns at the edge of the clearing. From here they could clearly see four dwarf prisoners tied to stakes, two of them pretty badly wounded. As they watched, an immense black orc walked over to the dwarfs, followed by almost the entirety of his warband. There was a brief exchange, during which the chieftain was knocked sprawling by a head butt from one of the captives. All three of the humans grinned in appreciation of this act of defiance, and both Eginolf and Ansgar nodded when their lord started to string his bow and gestured for them to fetch the other warriors. Before long, the whole war party was hiding along the western face of the clearing. In the centre of their line, Ansgar and Eginolf flanked the hunt lord. One of the dwarfs was being dragged from his post and they watched as he started to fight with his captors before being savagely beaten into acquiescence.

Ansgar spat and whispered another curse, before shooting an inquiring look at his master.

'As much as it riles me to see such creatures on our lands,' he whispered urgently, 'why should we risk ourselves for the stunted beardlings? They've never offered a hand to us.'

Steel-eye spoke for the first time that evening. His voice was strong but quiet. It had an authoritative ring to it which forestalled any quarrel.

'I don't like orcs. Any being, man or dwarf, who can still put up a fight when bound certainly earns my respect.'

He pulled an arrow from his quiver and rose to one knee.

SNORRI WAS HAULED roughly to his feet. As the orcs jostled him towards their leader, the venerable dwarf lashed out with his foot, smashing the knee of one of his guards. As the other orcs grabbed him, Snorri stamped on the fallen orc's neck, producing an audible crack. He was bundled to the ground, the orcs kicking him and jabbing him with the butts of their spears. Throughout the cruel, mocking laughter of the warlord cackled out over the roar of the fire. Bloodied, smeared with mud and half-fainting from pain, Snorri was dragged across the camp towards the fire. The orc mob gathered around, whooping and cheering, eager for blood.

The air was suddenly thick with black-feathered arrows, each picking out a separate target with lethal accuracy. The orcs had no time to scream before they were dead. Even as the others in the camp looked around with dumbfounded disbelief, a second hail of shafts picked off another swathe of greenskins. The air was filled with startled, raucous cries. The drunken orcs fumbled to get their weapons ready, stumbling over their dead companions and tripping over the stashes of loot that littered the clearing. Another deadly volley poured from the dark trees, followed by a series of whooping cries as a band of humans broke from their cover, dropping their bows and drawing long knives and swords from their belts.

Kurgan strained again at his bonds, then looked up at Thorin's yell.

'This is our chance, uncle! Let's try to get out of here while the greenskins are diverted by these primitives.'

A glance to his right confirmed to Kurgan that Borris was still unconscious, hanging from the ropes like a tattered rag doll. The massive bruise on Borris's head was as dark as coal and dried blood stained the whole side of his face. Escape didn't look very likely, but Kurgan was not one to look a gift pony in the mouth. He clenched his teeth and wrenched at the ropes once again.

The orcs had now recovered from their initial surprise and had started to organise themselves. Compared to the mass of greenskins, Kurgan thought the humans looked pitifully few. Gnashing his teeth in frustration, he strained at his bonds until his arms went numb, but there was no give in the ropes. Despite their lack of numbers, the humans were taking a heavy toll of the stunned, drunken orcs. One young man in particular was cutting a bloody path through the horde, slaying another orc with every swing of his sword. The greenskins were beginning to surround their attackers though, and Kurgan feared the reprieve from the orcs' bloody attentions would be short-lived.

ANSGAR WAS GRINNING with the rush of battle, even as he parried another serrated orc sword. Lunging forward with his left hand he buried his hunting knife in the savage's midriff. As the orc dropped gurgling to the floor another stepped forward, only to be felled by a blow from Eginolf, who fought to his brother's right. The twins looked around for more foes. Their hunt lord was surrounded by a throng of greenskins, but even if they'd been sober the orcs would have been poor match for the mighty human lord. Although covered in a dozen light scratches and bruises, he paid no heed to his wounds and fought with the ferocity of a bear. Roaring the tribe's battle cry, he plunged his sword through the neck of a goblin and, with a backhand blow of his knife, disembowelled another.

Most of the goblins were dead or fleeing into the welcoming darkness of the forest, and no few orcs too. Nevertheless, Ansgar could see that the surprise attack would peter out unless they could break the main orc horde. Suddenly his attention was drawn to Steel-eye. Screaming in anger, the youth leapt over the heads of his attackers to come crashing down in the middle of their impromptu shield-wall. Ansgar lost sight of him behind a wall of green bodies and flailing swords.

Concerned for his lord, Ansgar shouted for his trusted veterans to follow him. He set off through the throng, hacking his way towards the youth. Ansgar's worry was short-lived. The muscled young man

burst into view, rearing up from a tangle of corpses to hack at the
exposed backs of his would-be attackers. Breaking in panic, the orcs
tried to run, only to be cut down as Ansgar and Eginolf led their seasoned fighters to support their leader. There was an open route to the
captives now, and Ansgar directed some of the men to act as a rear-
guard while the rest followed Steel-eye as he hurried towards the
dwarf prisoners.

KURGAN COULDN'T HELP but be awed by the fighting prowess of the
young human, obviously their leader from the way the savages clustered around him. Even as the dwarf king watched, the youngster
effortlessly dodged a clumsy spear thrust, before stunning his attacker
with the pommel of his sword. Ducking beneath a wild axe swing to
slash the hamstrings of another greenskin, the youth stabbed
upwards with his knife, showering himself in a fountain of orc blood.
Kurgan almost felt like a spectator at some macabre dance, watching
carefully choreographed moves executed with grim precision. The
young man was constantly moving, weaving between the blows of his
adversaries while his own weapons bit deep with every strike. A powerful kick to the spine sent a black orc crumpling to the ground, while
the lad headbutted another adversary, snapping the orc's spiked helmet back with a jarring crack.

Kurgan noted that the other humans weren't faring badly either. A
few had fallen, but nowhere near as many as the orcs. The lithe huntsmen darted through the throng in pairs and trios, singling out a foe
to gang up on. After dispatching one individual they would find
another, and so on, moving through the orc camp with ruthless efficiency. For all their primal savagery, the humans were brave fighters.

Kurgan heard Thorin spit a curse and he turned to see his nephew
glaring angrily at the approaching humans.

'What's wrong, lad?'

'Those damned pinkskin humans. They're fighting over us with the
orcs. I don't know which of them is worse. With orcs you know
they're a bunch of cut-throat scum, but these humans are all false-
hoods and backstabbing. They've probably come to cart us off to
whatever foul pit they call a home. And they'll take the treasure too,
I'll warrant.'

'Mayhap, lad. Whatever their reasons, as long as they're killing
greenskins I've no quarrel with them. I'll give them their dues, they
know how to swing a sword when the going gets tough. Quit belly-
aching and try to get free!'

Kurgan turned his attention back to the battle. Some of the humans
had broken through the orc line and their leader now led a small
group of their oldest warriors towards the dwarf king. Seeing their

painted faces, foam-flecked lips and wild, bloodthirsty eyes, Kurgan was unsure he wanted to be the object of their attentions. Still, these stupid humans might unwittingly provide him and the others with some chance of getting away. Without a word, one of the youngest warriors ran behind the posts and Kurgan winced as he anticipated a dagger thrust to his kidneys.

It never came. Instead, Kurgan felt the rasping of a knife against his ropes. They were wound loosely around the pole itself, looped many times over and the lad was having difficulty cutting through them as they slipped and slithered up and down the rain-slicked pole. Kurgan exerted all his strength in one last mighty effort. With a snap the ropes parted and he pitched forward into the mud. In another few moments his legs were free and he looked up to see how the battle was progressing.

A quick glance showed Kurgan all he needed to know. Despite the casualties inflicted on the orcs, things still looked grim. Skill and speed was one thing, but in this battle raw muscles and numbers counted for more and the pressure was beginning to tell on the men. Almost half the humans had fallen; now only the toughest and most skilful fighters remained. Hoarse war-cries were drowned out by the clash of metal on metal and the screams of the wounded and dying. Foot by foot, the humans were being pushed back.

Thorin was free now, but the humans were having trouble cutting loose the bonds on the unconscious Borris. With a snarl, their blood-drenched leader sheathed his sword and grabbed the stake itself. He heaved upwards, muscles bulging under the pressure. His legs were slowly straightening, even while his booted feet sank into the mud. Kurgan looked on in astonishment as the top of the pole begin to rock from side to side, first only a few inches, and then a foot, and then it was swaying wildly. With a grunt and a twist, the stake came free and toppled to the ground. A tall human with plaited hair and a drooping moustache stepped forward, slipped off the ropes holding Borris to the stake and draped the inert dwarf over one shoulder.

The young human leader was about to start back towards the fight, but Kurgan grabbed his cloak. He formed the unfamiliar words of the human language with difficulty, speaking in a thick accent.

'You not hold them off by your own. Thorin and I can help. Ancient dwarf weapons here, lots of runes. Magic. Understand me?'

The young man stepped back in astonishment, then grinned widely. Kurgan was surprised by the calm strength in his voice, even though his chest was rising and falling rapidly from his recent exertions.

'You've got magic weapons here? Why are we standing talking? Let's go get them!'

They set off at a run towards the warlord's ramshackle tent, even as
the human line began to falter under the constant onslaught of the
orcs. A few of the greenskins broke through and raced across the
muddy clearing, eager to intercept the freed prisoners. Kurgan and
Thorin both looked around for something to fight with, stopping to
grab a couple of axes and shields from the piles of loot left over from
the orcs' ambush.

By now the main fight was raging around the part of the camp given
over to the warlord, and the humans were being pressed back to
within an arm's reach of the tent. Vagraz wasn't about to give up the
treasure and prisoners he had already fought for once that day. The
humans around Kurgan shouted their battle-cry once more and
charged into the fray. The human leader was leaping amongst the
orcs, sweat gleaming off his rippling muscles in the flickering firelight.
He moved with a grace rarely found in one of his size, darting
through the crowd and hacking down a mountain of foes.

Now Vagraz himself led the greenskins, a mob of black orcs
around him. They were fearsome foes and the heavily armoured
orcs smashed into the humans with terrible ferocity. The warlord
cleaved through a handful of humans with a single blow from his
massive axe. Vagraz's backswing beheaded another unfortunate
before the orc strode forward to deal more death. The humans fell
back before him.

Having gained the warlord's tent, Kurgan and Thorin rummaged
through the treasures stolen by the orcs, searching frantically for their
ancient weapons and armour. Nothing else would hold back the tide
of greenskins now. Beside them lay the still form of Borris, whose
deathly pallor did little to cheer Kurgan. Looking up briefly, he saw
the orc warlord crush the face of a hunter with a mighty punch,
before swinging his axe round in a deadly arc that left three more
fighters dismembered. Cursing his befuddled head and aching limbs,
the dwarf king redoubled his search.

BEFORE THE TENT, Ansgar and Eginolf fought back to back, surrounded
by a crowd of orcs whose blows rose and fell with relentless ferocity.
Each of them was marked by a dozen light cuts, but the pile of bodies around them testified that each drop of blood had been drawn at
a heavy price.

As Ansgar gutted one orc and stepped back to avoid the swipe of a
sword, he felt Eginolf stumble behind him. Hacking wildly at his foes
to push them back momentarily, Ansgar glanced over his shoulder.
Eginolf, his twin brother, was on his knees. A spear had punched
through his stomach; its barbed point now jutted from his back. Eginolf still swung his sword and screamed at the orcs.

'It'll take more than a green scum twig like this to end me. I'm going to bathe in your blood, you cowardly wretches!'

Time slowed for Ansgar as he saw a black orc push forward from the throng, a mighty cleaver in each hand. Even as Eginolf weakly fended off one blow, the other arm swept down with unstoppable force. Helpless to intervene, Ansgar watched with horror as the head of his twin tumbled to the ground.

Something inside Ansgar snapped. Yelling incoherently with pure rage, he threw himself at the orcs with renewed vigour. He was berserk, giving no thought for his own life, as he hacked and slashed, stabbed and jabbed with his sword. Startled by this unexpected fury, the orcs fell back.

Ignorant of everything except his raging hatred of his brother's murderers, Ansgar pressed on wildly, each step taking him further from the sanctuary of his comrades. As he shouldered one foe aside, Ansgar's blade was knocked from his grasp and was lost beneath the orcs' stamping feet. Ansgar tossed his knife from his left to his right hand and ducked his head down. In the press, the orcs' heavy weapons were useless. Ansgar's hunting knife was far more deadly; opening arteries, severing windpipes, ripping tendons and puncturing vital organs.

DESPITE THE VETERAN'S frenzied counter-attack, Kurgan thought the humans looked close to fleeing. The dwarf king was hastily hauling on his rune-encrusted armour, feeling its ancient plates fold over him like an old lover's embrace. Thorin was busy strapping on his studded gauntlets when he gave a cry of dismay. Turning, Kurgan watched in horror as Vagraz burst through the ranks of humans. The orc's massive axe glittered with dark magic, black flames playing along its edges. A few foolhardy men tried to interpose themselves between the awesome killing machine and the dwarfs, but in a few swift heartbeats they were dead, their blood seeping into the forest floor to mix with the gore of a hundred other warriors, orc and human.

Then the humans' youthful leader was there, leaping over the axes and swords of the orcs to attack their warlord. The young warrior stood with his legs slightly apart, ready to face the oncoming butcher. Still staring at the approaching orc, the human shouted to Kurgan.

'Where's your magic, beardling? I think now would be a good time to see it!'

Bellowing his wrath, Vagraz charged. Rolling beneath a wild swing of the warlord's baleful axe, the human youth dived to one side, then swung his long sword down at the orc's neck with his whole weight. The blade shattered on the enchanted armour of the warlord, who turned slowly and grinned at his would-be killer. Without hesitation the hunt lord flung the shattered stump of his sword into the orcs' face and leapt, his feet thudding into the warlord's jaw with a sickening crunch. The orc was knocked sprawling by the unexpected blow.

Allowing the hulking brute no time to recover, young Steel-eye moved behind Vagraz and started raining punches into the back of his thick neck. Roaring in anger, the orc spun around, smashing a plate-sized fist into the lord's chin, hurling him to the ground. Shaking his head to clear it, Vagraz lifted an immense booted foot to stamp on the young warrior, but he was too slow and the hunter rolled to his feet with fluid grace. The young man delivered a sweeping kick that made the warlord buckle at the knees.

Kurgan was cursing constantly now, throwing heaps of gold and gems aside in his frantic quest for his ancient weapon.

'Where the hell are you?' he spat, but even as he spoke his hand fell upon sturdy stitching wound around cold steel. With a yelp, he pulled the rune-forged warhammer from the concealing pile of glittering treasure. Kurgan fervently prayed he wasn't too late.

He span around to see the beleaguered human leader slip on the slick of mud and blood that covered the ground. As the orc chieftain lifted his massive axe above his head, its blade shining with unearthly energies, Kurgan flung his hammer to the young man. It arced across the campsite, spinning slowly, its head flashing in the glow of the bonfire. The youth's long arm snapped up to grab it, his fingers closing round the hilt. As Vagraz's dark axe swept down, the barbarian leader brought up the rune hammer to meet it. The weapons clashed with a shower of black and blue sparks and the two fighters were locked together.

The orc had the advantage and pressed down with all his weight, bringing the sorcerous axe blade ever closer to the young man's throat. The youth's arms trembled with the strain, sweat poured across his body and his face was purple with effort. His huge muscles twitched and veins stood out like cords across his neck and shoulders. With a scream Steel-eye thrust the orc back with all his remaining strength, swinging the hammer to one side to knock the warlord off balance. Howling, the hunter leapt to his feet and the two adversaries stood facing each other again. The human was grinning wolfishly, his eyes ablaze. The orc's hand constantly clenched and unclenched on the haft of his massive axe in agitated anticipation. Gauging each other carefully, the two leaders circled slowly.

'Your axe is very pretty, scum, but this hammer will be your doom. Even unarmed I was besting you and now I have this, you have only a heartbeat left to live! Enjoy your last moments, greenskin offal!'

'Keep talkin', pretty boy! Froat Biter hasn't finished wiv yer yet. Perhaps yer voice won't be so dainty once I've cut yer froat from ear ta ear!'

'I'll bathe in your blood and count the heads of your friends before that clumsy lump of pig iron touches my skin!'

'Let's see if yer muscles are as big as yer mouf!'

As one, both combatants swung. Their mighty weapons rang against each other with an explosion of magical energy. Steel-eye ducked Vagraz's swing and brought the warhammer around in a mighty blow that smashed off one of the warlord's shoulder pads. Amazed that his magical armour had been penetrated, the warlord was thrown off-guard. Vagraz barely had time to throw a hasty parry as the warhammer swung upwards again, knocking the orc backwards. Without pause, the young human leapt forward to sustain his attack, raining blow after blow against the orc.

Vagraz was not going to fall easily. A wild swing opened up a gaping cut in the hunter's side, but left the orc leader's defences open. With a defiant yell, the young man ignored his injury and swung again, the head of the hammer sweeping Vagraz off his feet with an audible cracking of bones. A second blow snapped the orc's head backwards and sent his axe tumbling from his grasp. Somehow the orc still clung to life. With a grunt it raised itself to its shattered knees and held up a hand. Confused and suspecting treachery, the hunt lord checked his next blow, staring distrustfully down at the broken creature on the ground before him.

To Steel-eye's surprise, the warlord started laughing, a dull chuckling that rose to a guttural thunder. Vagraz snorted contemptuously, spitting several teeth into the mud, and he raised a hand to form one final, vulgar gesture.

His patience gone, the hunt lord stepped forward. 'Was that really the best you could do?' Steel-eye taunted, stepping on the orc's other hand with a crunching of bones, as it stretched towards the fallen axe. Steel-eye steadied himself and swung one final blow. As the body slumped to the ground, the hunter stepped absent-mindedly to one side to avoid a rivulet of green, viscous fluid that drained towards the trees. He was staring intently at the body, as if suspecting it still presented some danger.

After a moment's pause, Steel-eye turned to look around him. Kurgan strode up, laughing heartily. The dwarf king tugged hard on the hunter's ragged, bloodstained cloak, stopping him as he took a stride towards the fight. The lad turned quickly to glare at the dwarf, his wide, battle-crazed eyes full of questions, the hammer in his hand half-raised to attack.

'Woah there, it's only me! You're a fine fighter, lad, and no mistake. Perhaps you pinkskins aren't so bad as we thought.'

Steel-eye looked down at the dwarf and held out the hammer, haft first. When he spoke, his words came in panting gasps, his breath carving misty shadows in the cold air.

'Thank you for… your weapon… Talk later… orcs to kill… Take it back… I'm sure I can find… something else.'

The dwarf king shook his noble head. Stroking the tangles out of his long beard, he looked up at the human with a wry smile on his face and a mischievous glint in his eye. Kurgan took the proffered warhammer and patted its rune-encrusted head. With a short chuckle, he handed it back to the surprised youth.

'I think he likes you better than me. Keep him. His name is Ghal Maraz, or Skull Splitter. You've done us a great service today. A small gift hardly compares to the life of a dwarf king, now does it?'

The youngster nodded his thanks and turned to rejoin the fight. The remaining orcs were falling back into the woods, all thoughts of battle gone now their warlord was dead. Kurgan laid a hand on the hunt lord's arm and halted him again.

'This day will be recorded in our annals with joy. What's your name lad, that we might honour you?'

Steel-eye hefted the hammer in his hand, his eyes straying towards the fleeing orcs. He looked at the dwarf king again, his eyes smouldering with energy. The rest of his face was in darkness and as the flames flickered in those intense grey eyes, they took on an eerie light. Even the baleful gaze of the orc warlord hadn't exuded the raw power of the youth's stare. His reply was short and simple.

'Sigmar.'

TALES OF ADVENTURE & MYSTERY

HAUTE CUISINE

Robert Earl

DURING THE SUMMER when the ship *Destrier* limped back into Bordeleaux, the heat was everywhere and always. In the daytime it throbbed down from the blinding sun, grilling the skin of those forced to toil beneath it. At night it lay heavy in the air, radiating from bricks and cobbles so that the city felt like a giant kiln.

Even in the docks, where Manann's breath blew chill from the ocean beyond, the heat greased the air. The open sewers that fed into the harbour oozed beneath it, and the waste that finally dripped into the thick waters was as warm as blood. Methane fires occasionally flared above the stew of filth and brine, although they did nothing to dispel the stink.

But to Florin d'Artaud the foetid air of the harbour was sweeter than any rose. After all, it was the smell of home, and after thousands of miles of ocean and jungle and danger and pain, what could smell sweeter?

He lent over the railings of the *Destrier* and gazed longingly at the sweltering city that rose up around them. Lorenzo, who stood behind him, was not to be distracted by such sentiments. The older man stared at the deck instead, his eyes glittering in the oil lamps that had been set around the gunwales of their ship.

The treasure glittered, too. It had been spread out on the battered timber of the deck, and now, as the survivors of the expedition watched like hawks, it was being divided.

'Gold,' said the captain, weighing a misshapen yellow statue that looked a little like a frog. 'Sixteen pounds and nine ounces.'

The assembled men, gaunt and ragged and fabulously wealthy, nodded approvingly. They watched the quarter master scratch the weight into the lump of metal, then turned back as the captain lifted the next piece. It was a medallion as big as a breastplate, the perfect oval spoiled only by a bullet hole right in the centre.

'Gold,' the captain said. 'Twelve pounds and six ounces.'

The men shifted appreciatively. Only Florin looked impatient. He paced around behind them, gazing hungrily at his city. Even at this late hour it would be teeming with life, he knew. There would be fresh women and fresh food, tailors and bathhouses and wine merchants.

Behind him the captain paused over the next part of the inventory. A murmur of disquiet passed through the men as they watched him turn the bauble this way and that. Then he shrugged and put the thing into the scales.

'Egg,' the captain said as he weighed it. 'Twenty-four pounds.'

Florin's brow creased and he turned around.

'What did he just say?' he asked Lorenzo, who was frowning. It made him look even more like a monkey.

'Egg,' he said, and there was no mistaking the disgust in his voice. 'More gold than we could carry, and what does some idiot decide to save?'

There was a murmur of angry agreement, and the captain held the egg up. It took two hands to lift it, and although it was obviously worthless it was pretty. Intricate shapes patterned the glazed surface, and he could see why, in all the panic, somebody might have snatched the bauble up.

The men, however, seemed less understanding.

'Well, whoever brought this should take it as their share,' the captain announced. 'Who was it?'

The men fell silent. The Bretonnians glared suspiciously at the Kislevites, and the Kislevites sneered at the Tileans. The captain, realising that the fuse of racial tension had been relit, decided to douse it.

'Nobody? Right then, as nobody wants it we'll throw it away.'

Before anybody could reply he lifted the egg high over his head and hurled it over the side of the ship. It plopped into the sewage-choked water, bobbed once, then disappeared from view.

'Gold,' the captain said, moving hurriedly on to the next piece. 'Nine pounds and four ounces.'

It was almost dawn by the time the spoils had been divided, and as the shipful of rich vagabonds hove into Bordeleaux, not a single one of them gave another thought to the egg that had been added to the rich stew of the city's harbour.

* * *

One Year Later

THE MEN WHO worked in these depths toiled as hard as any miners. They strained and swore and struggled, their brows oiled with sweat as they practised their craft beneath the hiss of brass lanterns.

The patissier, his skin grey after a lifetime spent in clouds of flour, battered his pastry with a blacksmith's strength. The saucier wielded a long-handled tasting spoon amongst his apprentices, driving them on like so many galley slaves. Meanwhile the rotissier, his arms scarred by fire and boiling grease, sliced apart a roast piglet with a swordsman's skill.

And through this inferno, his face red and his eyes savage, strode the chef. In one hand he held the rolling pin that served as his marshal's baton. The other was empty, although it flexed nervously. After all, although every dinner party involved the sort of perfect timing that would make a juggler dizzy, tonight was even worse. Tonight his master, Monsieur Lafayette, was entertaining his arch rival, Monsieur Griston.

Which was to say that perfection was no longer enough.

The chef idly whacked his rolling pin down on a porter who had been foolish enough to cross his path. The impact of wood onto flesh soothed him. So did the thought that tonight he would indeed give his master more than perfection.

'How's the porc au miele provençal?' he asked the rotissier. The man, who was using two knives simultaneously, answered without looking up.

'Needs to rest for twenty minutes,' he said.

The chef looked at his timepiece, a burnished brass lump that was as big as his palm.

'Twenty minutes,' he repeated. 'Good. saucier?'

The saucier swivelled at the sound of his master's voice. 'Chef?'

'Twenty minutes for the sauce florette de porc.'

'But it's ready in five.'

'Twenty minutes!' the chef screamed, and all around him quailed.

'Twenty minutes it is,' the saucier said, already shoving his apprentice out of the way to take personal charge of that particular cauldron.

The chef forgot him as he hurried towards his own bench. It was a marble slab, as big as a coffin, and a porter stood beside it in constant attendance. With a feeling of pride the chef put his rolling pin to one side and opened the box of eggs that waited for him on the slab. He hoisted one out, turning it to admire it in the lamplight.

He still wasn't sure what the thing was. The size put him in mind of the giant chickens that were said to live in the Southlands. On the other hand, the colours that striped it were like nothing he'd seen on any mere bird's egg before. They looked almost ceramic.

It didn't really matter. All that mattered was what lay inside the strange shell. The one that he had sampled before purchasing the box had been as smooth as the richest mousse. And the taste… For the first time in his life, the chef believed that he had found something that couldn't be improved upon by any artifice of his.

He smiled happily, secure in the knowledge that he would get the credit anyway. And all he had to do was to poach the eggs, slice them, and then cover them with clear sauce translucid for appearance's sake.

'Garçon,' he bellowed, despite the fact that the porter was standing right behind him.

'Yes, chef?'

'Bring me the poaching kettle and the entrée silverware.'

The porter didn't reply. Instead, he choked.

'The entrée silverware?' he finally managed to repeat.

The chef turned to glare at him, fury in his eyes.

'It's just that we don't have it. Entréeier Reinald has already sent the entrées up.'

The chef's look became murderous.

'He gave them oysters in sauce escargot,' the porter stuttered, and started to edge away.

For a moment it seemed that he might have to run, but the chef's fury found its lightning rod in the person of the entréeier himself. He had just returned from supervising the waiters' handling of his creations, and had the relieved look of a man who had done a difficult job well.

The expression vanished beneath the chef's animal howl of outrage. Assuming that his master had been driven to madness by the pressures of his office, Reinald attempted to defend himself from the assault.

Unfortunately, such defiance did little to improve his superior's mood. As the two men fought their way through the shadows, fists blurring and teeth flashing, the rest of the kitchen worked on. Most remained oblivious to the violence going on around them as, sweating and swearing and struggling, they created perfection.

But on that night, as their chef had known all along, perfection wasn't enough.

'THESE OYSTERS ARE very good, Lafayette,' Count Griston nodded across the dining table towards his host. 'And the sauce is just right. It just goes to show that you can prepare quite a decent dish without worrying about any creativity whatsoever.'

Baron Lafayette smiled grimly at the insult. The worse thing about it was that it was true. The oysters escargot were faultless, but apart from that they were the same as oysters escargot anywhere.

'I'm glad you are enjoying them,' he told Griston. 'I knew that you would. Many people say that the true gastronomer is a man of simple tastes.'

'I quite agree,' Griston's wife said. 'When we last ate at the castle we had oysters for an entrée there, too.'

'Oh, how is the duke?' Lafayette's wife enquired sweetly. 'Have you seen him recently?'

'Two years ago, wasn't it Griston?' her husband added.

'Yes,' Griston admitted. 'I really should take more time for these social engagements. But you know how it is when things are going so well, eh Lafayette?'

Lafayette, who had lost an entire cargo of dates just the month before, nodded. To change the subject he turned to the fifth man at the table. The Harbour Master was working his way through his plate of oysters with the same silent diligence which had taken him to his present rank.

He was hardly the most sparkling of guests, Lafayette thought. But then, he didn't have to be. Only a merchant who was a fool would risk offending the Harbour Master with a missed invitation, and whatever else they were, the merchants of Bordeleaux were no fools.

'How are you finding the oysters, Harbour Master?' he asked.

The man grunted, and nodded. Then he swallowed.

'Passable,' he allowed. 'Very passable indeed.'

Griston tried not to grin too widely.

'A toast,' he called, raising his glass. 'To our host, and his passable food.'

'Very passable,' the Harbour Master corrected, but it was too late. Lafayette downed his wine in a single gulp, and scowled as he waited for the waiter to refill his glass.

'What's for the meat course, my dear?' his wife asked, hoping to lighten his mood.

'Oh. I think that it's porc au miele provençal.'

'Lovely,' Griston said. 'Meat and potatoes. Haven't had that since I was an esquire.'

'Really? Then I can see that you're well dressed for it.'

Griston flushed. 'What do you mean by that?' he asked.

'What do you think I mean?'

'Gentlemen,' the Harbour Master sighed. 'I wonder if we might talk about something else instead of fashion? I am a simple man, and it makes my head spin.'

'Yes, of course,' Lafayette said. There was a moment of thoughtful silence, which Griston's wife broke.

'Has anybody seen the latest play about Florin d'Artaud?'

'Oh yes,' Lafayette's wife replied. 'Wasn't it good? Somebody said that he even went to the opening night. My friend Myrtle actually saw him. She said that he was wearing those new skin-tight Tilean hose.'

The two women sighed in unison. Their husbands frowned.

'D'Artaud.' Lafayette waved his fish knife dismissively. 'The man's a complete fraud.'

'Damn right,' Griston said. 'I knew his father once. A decent enough fellow for a commoner. Hard working. Always paid the agreed price. Manann alone knows what he'd think of his son's gallivanting.'

'Gallivanting indeed,' Griston's wife scolded him. 'You're just jealous. Monsieur d'Artaud is the hero of Lustria. Everybody knows that.'

'Sounds more like a pirate than a hero to me,' Griston said, and Lafayette nodded his agreement.

'Got it in one, Griston,' he said. 'Turns up in a ship full of Tileans and gold and tells everybody some story about cities in the jungle. Man's a rogue, simple as that.'

'I heard that he challenged somebody to a duel for insulting him last week,' Lafayette's wife said.

As Lafayette coughed on a slip of oyster, Griston came to his aid.

'What we mean, mademoiselle, is that nobody can be sure of the exact provenance of d'Artaud's wealth.'

Lafayette looked at him gratefully.

The Harbour Master relaxed. Now that he had navigated the conversation back to safer waters he could turn his attention back to the food. And just in time, too. As the merchants argued with their wives about Florin d'Artaud, the smell of honeyed pork filled the dining chamber. This perfume was closely followed by a huge silver platter of the fragrant meat itself.

These dinners were hard work, the Harbour Master thought as he tucked in, but well worth it.

LATER THAT NIGHT, Lafayette's chef sat alone in his kitchen. Although the stoves had burned low the furnace heat of these depths remained constant, the masonry ever warm with the memory of fire. The chef remained oblivious to the temperature as he poked about in the embers of the roasting pit. He had spent his whole life in such infernos, and anyway he had other things on his mind.

Although he had left the entréeier battered and bruised, it had been no victory. Not really. Tonight he had had the chance to prove his superiority over every other chef in Bordeleaux. Yet all it had taken had been the stupidity of one man and the chance to present the perfect entrée had been lost. Despite his promise to bring another batch the strigany who had sold them to him had disappeared. As far as the chef knew that meant that the eggs were unique, irreplaceable. Now he would have to pickle them. What a waste.

A fat tear rolled down the chef's florid face and he poured himself another goblet of wine. For a while he toyed with the idea of having the entréeier murdered, but eventually he decided against the plan. He was too depressed.

He sighed miserably, drained his cup, and staggered off to the wine cellar to fetch another bottle. When he returned he opened it, enjoying the greasy squeak of the reluctant cork, and was about to pour himself another goblet when a sudden, sharp report echoed around the deserted kitchen.

He stood still for a moment, his eyes glittering in the darkness as he listened. He was rewarded with more noise, a series of sudden cracks that sounded like breaking twigs.

The chef put down the bottle and picked up his rolling pin. This wouldn't be the first time that urchins or thieves had slipped in to steal a meal from this dark labyrinth.

The chef squared his jaw as another volley of impacts rang out, and he realised that they were actually coming from his own workbench. This time they sounded more like breaking porcelain, and he was seized with a horrible suspicion.

It was the eggs. Somebody was breaking those cursed eggs. And who could be responsible for such vandalism but the entréeier, bent on revenge?

Pale with outrage the chef put down his rolling pin and picked up a cleaver instead. The razored rectangle of steel had been sharpened that very evening and shone with a murderous intent. He examined the edge approvingly then moved stealthily forward towards his workbench.

In the gloom he couldn't see the perpetrator, but he could already see the crime. The wooden crate that the eggs had been in had been smashed open and fragments of precious cargo lay all about, lustrous with colour even in the gloom.

The chef hissed, eyes flitting around as he stepped forward. He peered into the remains of the box and saw that every single egg had been broken. Every single one.

His self-control snapped.

'Entréeier!' he roared, waving the cleaver in challenge. 'Where are you, you scoundrel? Where are you?'

But there was no reply. The chef, his breath ragged with the passion of his wine-fuelled rage, peered into the darkness. For a moment he was afraid that the entréeier had escaped, somehow slipping past him in the darkness. Then he saw a flicker of movement in the cold store that lay ahead, and a predatory grin split his face.

'Come here, Jacques,' he said, trying to keep the hatred out of his voice. 'Let's have some wine and talk about this.'

There was a rustle of further movement, and the shatter of a pot knocked off a shelf.

'Come out into the light,' the chef said. 'I know that you're in there. Let's be mature about this.'

He edged further forward, cleaver raised. There was a moment of silence, and then the patter of approaching footsteps, rapidly approaching footsteps.

'Got you, you... oh.'

The chef's mouth fell open in a perfect circle of surprise at the things which had emerged from amongst the butter vats and cured hams.

For a split second he took them for cats. They were about the right size, and they moved with the same sinuous grace. But even through the fog of wine and rage, the chef could see that there was nothing feline about these things. They were more like the house lizards that hunted through the kitchen in the summer. Or maybe, he thought vaguely, the swamp frogs that graced so many of his dishes.

At the thought of such delicacies he hefted the cleaver. It was a mistake. Moving with a blur of speed the strange intruders flitted about him, leaping onto shelves or scuttling under tables to encircle his lumbering form.

'Get out of my kitchen!' the chef shouted at them, and waved his cleaver menacingly. The creatures watched the makeshift weapon, heads cocked and eyes aglitter. Gradually, with the slow assurance of a crossbowman winching back his string, the crests on their heads rose and their tails twitched excitedly.

But it wasn't until the chef tried to strike one of them that they attacked.

Although they were still sticky with the yolk of their birth, the creatures moved with an instinctive viciousness. The chef screamed as he felt his tendons torn out from the back of his legs, and even as he collapsed needle teeth were ripping open the arteries in his arms. Blood spurted as he dropped his weapon, and he raised his hands to defend himself.

It was already too late. The things were already sinking their teeth into his throat, puncturing through the flab to bite into the arteries beneath. Blood sprayed as the dying man thrashed around, too shocked to realise that he had become offal in his own kitchen.

With his throat torn open it didn't take the chef long to die. Seconds, perhaps. But his assailants lacked even that amount of patience, and even as the chef's heart pattered its last they were feasting upon his still living flesh, relishing the taste of their very first meal.

It was to be the first of many that night.

* * *

Three Months Later

'By MANAAN'S CODPIECE, I'm bored.'

Florin d'Artaud, hero of Lustria and proprietor of the Lizard's Head, gazed miserably around his domain. It was mid afternoon and the tavern was almost deserted. There were a handful of drovers nursing their beers, a group of hooded men talking intensely but softly in a corner, and a pair of silently drinking longshoremen.

There were also two serving girls who were passing the time by braiding each other's hair. Florin watched them for a while. Then he sighed.

Lorenzo, who was busily gutting mackerel into a wooden bucket, looked up at him.

'If you're bored, then you can give me a hand.'

Florin glanced over to see his friend slice open a fish's belly and hook the innards out with a practiced thumb.

'Why don't you let the girls do that?' he asked.

Lorenzo shrugged.

'I like to keep in practice. Anyway, it's quite relaxing.'

Florin frowned and looked back towards the barmaids. Now they had changed places, and the brunette had started working on the blonde's hair. It looked as smooth as mead in the dusty light of the tavern, and as he watched the locks being teased out she looked up and caught his eye. He smiled at her and she flushed and looked away.

Florin's smile grew wider.

'Think I'll just go and see how the staff are getting on,' he told Lorenzo as he got to his feet.

But before Lorenzo could reply, the doors of the tavern banged open and a squad of men marched into the room. Their boot steps echoed off the wooden walls with a flawless rhythm, and their steel harnesses gleamed with the polish of professional soldiers. Florin looked from the blank slates of their faces to the weapons that were scabbarded at their belts, then looked back to their faces.

Whatever these men wanted, he decided, it wasn't wine.

The room fell silent as the rest of the clientele came to the same conclusion. Several of the customers were already scurrying out of the back entrance. The squad of mercenaries watched them go and turned their attention to Florin.

'Good afternoon, gentlemen,' Florin said, nodding to them. They said nothing. Instead they fanned out to form a crescent around him.

Florin balanced on the balls of his feet, let his hand brush against the hilt of his dagger and glanced back towards Lorenzo. The older man had already risen to his feet, his fish-slimed gutting knife now held underhanded.

'I said,' Florin said, his fingers itching to draw his weapon. 'Good afternoon.'

This time there was a reply. It came from behind the broad shoulders of the mercenaries, and the man stepped forward as he spoke.

'Good afternoon, Monsieur d'Artaud,' the figure said. To the uninitiated he would have appeared to be no more than a prosperous craftsman. A minor merchant, at most. There was no adornment on his simple leather tunic, or on the canvas clothes he wore beneath it. He wore a cutlass on one side of his belt, wooden handled like most others, and his head was shaved, as was the fashion in the messier professions.

Inconspicuous as he was, Florin recognised him immediately.

'Harbour Master,' he said, trying not to sound too surprised. It wasn't every day that the Harbour Master visited a tavern such as the Lizard's Head. In fact, it wasn't ever. 'How can we be of service?'

'I'm not sure yet,' the Harbour Master replied. He took a seat and pulled it up to the table. 'That's what I'm here to talk to you about. You don't mind clearing your establishment for a few moments do you? Just while we talk?'

Florin looked at Lorenzo, who waved a hand towards the room. Somehow, beneath the shadow of the Harbour Master's enforcers, it had already cleared itself. Even the serving girls were gone.

'I'll lock the door,' Lorenzo said. The Harbour Master waited until Lorenzo had bolted both front and back doors. Then, with a curt call, he ordered one of his men forward. The man carried a stained hessian sack over one shoulder, and Florin wondered what was in it.

He didn't have to wonder long. At another command from his master the man hoisted the sack off his shoulder and upended it over the table. There was a soggy thump as a severed head fell out and bounced on the woodwork.

'So tell me, monsieurs,' the Harbour Master asked, watching their expressions with a hungry intensity. 'What do you make of that?'

The two men leant forward to examine the grisly trophy. When Florin realised what it was a jolt of adrenaline shot through him. The last time he had seen one of these cursed things it had almost been the death of him. Of all of them.

Feeling the Harbour Master's eyes on him he bit down on his excitement and arranged his features into a careful nonchalance. Then he made a show of examining the head.

Although it was almost the same size as a human's, there could be no doubt that it was from a much more exotic victim. Even in the dim light of the tavern the scales that covered it gleamed, and the flat iron shape of the skull beneath suggested something serpentine or aquatic.

'I never thought I'd see one of these bastards again,' Lorenzo swore suddenly.

Florin nudged him, but it was too late. The Harbour Master was looking at them with the expression of a weasel who has found a pair of snared rabbits.

He licked his lips. 'So you *do* know what this thing is.'

It was more statement than question, and Florin had no choice but to nod.

'Yes,' he said and, ignoring the queasiness in his stomach, he peeled one of the scaly eyelids open. The orb within stared back at him. The deep yellow of the alien eye was already starting to cloud, which was some relief. Florin squared his jaw and prised open the thing's mouth. Its needle teeth were just as sharp as he remembered.

'Well?' demanded the Harbour Master, who was not used to being kept waiting. 'What is it?'

Florin dragged the back of his hand across his brow and shrugged.

'I don't know if they have a name. But we did come across something like them in Lustria. Vicious things they were. Vicious and damned near invisible.'

'So the stories about you are true,' the Harbour Master said.

'Not all of them,' Florin and Lorenzo said in perfect, paranoid harmony.

The Harbour Master smiled.

'Oh, don't worry,' he said with a conspiratorial wink. 'I'm not an outraged father. I'm here purely in my official capacity. The thing is, these things have infested the area around the warehouses by the main harbour. We first started noticing them a couple of months ago, and since then they've been nothing but trouble. They've been destroying stock, ruining thatch, killing porters. I lost two myself, which wouldn't be so bad if the rest hadn't used it as an excuse to demand more wages.'

The Harbour Master frowned at the injustice of it all, then continued.

'And then yesterday, things got even worse. The things have actually dared to kill one of the merchants. You know the candle importer, old "Nine Bellies" Flangei? He was taken whilst he was inspecting his stock. Now all of his fellows are complaining. I hear some of them are even thinking about withholding their anchorage contributions. It would never happen, of course, but all the same they need reassurance. And as you can guess, Monsieur d'Artaud there aren't many people who can reassure men who've seen what these things can do.'

Florin nodded with false sympathy.

'I don't see how they could have reached Bretonnia from Lustria, though.' He frowned. 'I mean, I can assure you that we didn't bring any back. Did we, Lorenzo?'

'Course not,' Lorenzo replied. 'They're bad enough a thousand leagues distant let alone on our own doorstep.'

'Yes, I know none were on your ship's manifest.' The Harbour Master waved a soothing hand. 'I've already checked. But however these things got here, get here they did. So now we need somebody qualified to hunt them down and eradicate them. My men are excellent soldiers, but they lack expertise.'

'You want us to do it?' Florin cast a doubtful eye towards the monster's severed head. It glared up at him, a challenge still gleaming in its dead eye.

'That's right,' the Harbour Master said. 'Who better to reassure the merchants and deal with these vermin than the man who knows them best, Captain Florin d'Artaud, hero of Lustria?'

He beamed with the happy enthusiasm of a man who has found the perfect solution.

Florin fidgeted, torn between pride and sincerity. For once, sincerity won out. 'I'm sorry to disappoint you, but I really don't know anything about these creatures. In fact, the man who killed this one probably knows more than me.'

'Not any more. He's dead. But anyway, you're too modest, Monsieur d'Artaud. Your tavern is called the Lizard's Head.'

'Yes, but…'

'And you admit to knowing what these things are?'

'I wouldn't say admit…'

'And to knowing their provenance.'

'What does provenance…?'

'Good. So all you have to do is to decide how best the worried merchants of Bordeleaux should view your relationship with these vermin. As the man who will earn a fine bounty for their extermination. Or as the man who has some other connection with them.'

The three men sat in contemplative silence. The Harbour Master didn't bother to enunciate the threat any further. He didn't need to.

'Well, it would be quite an interesting hunt,' Florin suggested, a smile starting to play across his face.

'Interesting.' Lorenzo's voice was full of disgust. 'Lethal more like.'

'That's all settled, then,' the Harbour Master said, getting to his feet. 'We can stop wondering about how these things followed you back from Lustria, and start paying you a crown a head. Now, if you will excuse me, I have other business to be about. If you would like to go to the customs house at dawn, I'll get my clerk to show you what happened to poor old Nine Bellies.'

'You mean that you aren't going to give me your men?' Florin asked, casting an eye over the polished warriors of the Harbour Master's entourage. They stood as still as stone, each man a part of a perfect formation.

'Gods no,' the Harbour Master chuckled. 'These are the finest warriors in Bordeleaux. Apart from our knightly masters, of course.' He paused to glance over his shoulder before continuing. 'In any case, they have other fish to fry. Well, good day to you.'

A moment later Florin and Lorenzo were alone in their tavern. They glared at the lizardine head with the concentration of fortunetellers forced to share a single crystal ball.

'At least we won't be bored,' said Florin.

Lorenzo just spat.

THE NEXT MORNING was grey and damp. Sunrise had been lost beneath a warm fog that was as wet as rain, and beneath his mail Lorenzo's tunic was soon as damp as his spirits. He grumbled and cursed as he trudged along behind Florin, his head bowed and his shoulders up around his ears.

Florin, on the other hand, looked like a man on his way to a day at the races. Despite the sodden humidity of the streets the last hours had seen his spirits rising like mercury in a broken thermometer.

It was the promise of action that did it. That and the possibility of bloodshed. It was always the way, he thought. Life was never better than when lived in the glorious terror of mortal risk, never sweeter than when Morr himself followed in your shadow.

Florin grinned and looked back towards Lorenzo. 'Lizards, hey? Should be just like the good old days.'

Lorenzo shot him a sour look. 'Not unless you want to starve yourself and then shove some leeches down your breeches.'

Florin laughed uproariously and slapped Lorenzo on the back.

'I hate it when you're in a good mood,' the older man grumbled.

'Why?'

'Because somebody always ends up getting hurt.'

'Well then.' The humour bled from Florin's face to leave a wolf's grin of anticipation. 'Let's make sure it isn't us. You remember what those things did in Lustria. Imagine if they start taking over the city. Our city.'

'I'm sure your civic conscience does you credit,' Lorenzo snorted. 'But why couldn't we have bought a window for a chapel instead? Or had a sewer dug? Or made a donation to the priestesses of Shallya? Or...'

'Look, there's the customs house,' Florin interrupted.

Lorenzo looked up to see the great granite blockhouse looming out of the mist ahead. Officially, being no more than a commoner's building, it wasn't a fortress. It had no battlements, no drawbridge, no turrets or murder holes or crenellations.

What it did have were massively thick walls and a battery of cannons on the reinforced roof.

'Ever seen the gunners practise a volley from there?' Florin asked. Lorenzo shook his head.

'No. Can't see the Harbour Master wasting any black powder either. Anyway, I don't think that the cannons are supposed to exist. Our noble masters might not like it.'

Florin grunted with shared contempt, and looked around. The streets were becoming busier the closer to the docks they came, although nobody seemed to be paying them much attention.

'I hear that in l'Anguille some of the merchants are talking about changing all that. You know that in Marienburg they're ruled by the most able men in the city, not by aristocrats? Well, in l'Anguille... never mind.' He broke off as a man hailed them through the crowd that had gathered around the customs house.

'Monsieur d'Artaud?'

'And who might be asking?'

'I'm Couraine,' the man said as he hurried forward. 'Apprentice to the undersecretary of the Harbour Master's office.'

'You're a clerk?'

'Yes,' Couraine said as he gawped at Florin. 'At least, almost. I still haven't finished my apprenticeship.'

Florin could well believe it. Couraine was barely old enough to grow a beard, and he was as pale and skinny as a shaved rat. He had the face of one too, pinched and bucktoothed. But what really made him stand out amongst the leather-skinned bruisers who crowded around the customs house was that he was unarmed. Whereas other men bristled with cutlasses and boathooks and daggers, the only thing the apprentice carried was a massive leather-bound ledger.

'So,' Florin said, slapping him on a bony shoulder. 'You're to be our guide.'

Couraine swallowed nervously.

'Oh no,' he stuttered. 'I'm just going to show you where the attacks have taken place.'

Florin looked at Lorenzo, who rolled his eyes.

'Oh, and the body of Monsieur Flangei. My master said you might want to take a look. Do you?'

'Yes. Where is it?'

'If you'd just follow me, monsieur,' Couraine said, and scuttled back towards the customs house. Florin and Lorenzo followed him through the waiting merchants and captains, past the guards at the entrance, and into the echoing hall beyond. Even now, in the height of summer, it was cool inside the granite-built fortress.

'Down here,' Couraine called back over his shoulder, and disappeared down a flight of stairs. They followed him past the last slitted window and into the darkness of the cellars. Couraine paused to take an oil lamp from a cubby hole. He lit it, and looked back at his two charges, the three men's faces now bathed in a warm, butter yellow glow.

'We're only allowed to use one lamp per party,' Couraine apologised in the gloom. 'My master says that it is all we need. Also,' he took a deep breath, and narrowed his eyes in concentration 'any extra expenditure can only lead to an increase in harbour duties, which would damage the great trading tradition of our city.'

Lorenzo snorted, and Couraine looked at him nervously.

'You said that very well, Monsieur Couraine,' Florin soothed him. 'Now, let's take a look at this body, shall we?'

'Yes. Yes, of course.' The apprentice looked at him gratefully, and led the way into the darkness. 'We've kept it in this room here.'

As soon as Couraine opened the door the smell hit them. Even to men used to living amongst the constant stink of Bordeleaux the odour of the rotting corpse was eye-watering. The horrible sweetness of it clung to the back of their palates and turned their stomachs.

'We brought him in here two days ago,' Couraine explained, his features wrinkling with disgust. Reluctantly he led the way through a long, empty room towards the covered remains. The flies that buzzed above the blanket looked horribly plump.

They were half way down the room when the clerk staggered to a halt. He swallowed twice, pressed one hand to his stomach, and wretched. Florin looked at him. Even in the yellow lamplight he looked as white as wax.

'Let me take the lamp,' he said, taking it from the cold sweat of Couraine's trembling fingers. 'And perhaps you could do me a favour and wait outside the door? Make sure we aren't disturbed.'

'Yes. Yes, of course, monsieur,' Couraine said gratefully, and fled back out of the room.

Florin took the lamp from him and marched forward to the stinking bundle. The flame flickered into new colours beneath the corpse gas. Without giving himself time to think, Florin knelt down beside the body and pulled the blanket off it.

'Oh, sweet Manann,' Lorenzo whispered, his eyes as wide as copper coins in the lamplight.

Florin said nothing. He just gagged as he stumbled back from the thing. When he was back on his feet he pulled the hem of his tunic up over his mouth and exchanged a horrified glance with Lorenzo.

Then he swallowed, fixed his features into a look of bravado, and forced himself to kneel down again to examine the corpse.

'I see why Couraine was so jumpy,' he said, drawing a dagger from his boot and prodding the putrefying mass before him. Maggots writhed enthusiastically around the point of the blade, and Florin's stomach rolled.

'Do you think that happened after he was dead?' Lorenzo asked, peering over Florin's shoulder.

'What?' Florin asked, his voice a squeak.

'The way that the body… the way he was flayed.'

'Before and after,' Florin decided. 'Look at the way some of the teeth marks jump. Looks like he was moving while they were tearing slivers off.'

Lorenzo looked and wished he hadn't. Beneath the melting flesh there were flashes of bone, the cuts on it still fresh and yellow.

'Look at the way they stripped him of his fat,' Florin said, using his dagger to brush a cluster of squirming maggots from the corpse. 'See the way they've eaten between his sinews? And look, they've eaten his lights but left his heart intact.'

He prodded the horribly swollen organ that remained within the pink bars of the ribcage. It was as grey and bloated as some poisonous fungus, and the surface glistened with slime. Florin's brow furrowed as he examined it. It burst suddenly, and Florin and Lorenzo jumped back from the spray of black liquid.

'I think we've seen enough,' Florin said, his voice level. Lorenzo was already half way to the door, so Florin picked up the lantern and followed him. Something popped as he did so, and there was a squelch as the rotting remains settled further.

Couraine was waiting for them in the corridor outside. He was holding his ledger in front of him, twisting at the corners nervously.

'The summer's no time to be killed. It's only been two days and your friend in there looks like spare ribs in jelly.' Florin winked.

'Oh, he wasn't my friend.' Couraine shook his head. 'I didn't know him at all, in fact.'

'I know. I was just… never mind. Just tell me, do you know why was he called Nine Bellies?'

Couraine's mouth fell open.

'I didn't know. He was fat, but I didn't think that he really had nine bellies.' The clerk lowered his voice and looked suspiciously around 'Does that make him a mutant?'

'No,' Lorenzo cut in. 'It makes you an idiot.'

'Don't worry about him,' Florin said, clapping Couraine's bony shoulder. 'He's just being friendly. Now, where exactly was it that Monsieur Flangei was slaughtered?'

The clerk opened his book and, with a nervous look at Lorenzo, he started shuffling through the pages.

'Here it is,' he muttered, and began to read: 'Monsieur Flangei, a commoner of some substance, was devoured by diverse monstrosities on the day of the seventh quarter moon. The place of his misfortune was the pier which extends from his warehouse, commonly called the Dragon Wharf. Several commoners witnessed his misfortune, none of whom are worthy of note. Reward posted – none as yet.'

Florin frowned.

'I know where the Dragon Wharf is. But what about the people who saw the attack. Who were they?'

'Peasants,' Couraine said. 'Not worthy of note.'

Lorenzo opened his mouth to say something, but Florin gestured him to silence. 'Why were they unworthy of note?'

Couraine shrugged helplessly.

'It is the way the page has to be filled in. Only knights are worthy of note.'

'But Flangei wasn't a knight, and you have his name down there.' Florin pointed to the spidery scrawl of the unfortunate merchant's epitaph.

'Yes, but that's different. We have to know who his family are.'

'So they can give him a burial,' Florin nodded.

'So they can pay for expenses incurred. In fact, his wife is due to collect him later. Somebody said she was quite upset. She saw the whole thing, apparently.'

Lorenzo opened his mouth to say something else, Florin nudged him into silence.

'And where does the poor woman live?' Florin asked.

'Oh no.' Couraine's narrow features twisted into a look of fresh anxiety. 'She's not too poor, is she? Only if she can't pay, she can't have the body, and when that happens my master always makes me deal with them. It's terrible. People don't seem to understand that good accountancy practices are vital to the lifeblood of the city's trade. In fact, the last widow even tried to hit me when I was trying to explain that to her.'

This time Lorenzo didn't say anything. Instead he just rolled his eyes. Florin tried not to smile.

'I'm sure she'll be fine. In fact, if you remind me where Madame Flangei lives, I'll explain it to her for you.'

Couraine's face lit up.

'I think she lives over her husband's warehouse. Although I suppose it's her warehouse now. You will explain to her, won't you? I mean, it's the same for everybody.'

'Relax,' Florin told him with an easy grin. 'We'll do just that.'

And with a bow that was barely sarcastic, he left Couraine to his relief, and led off into the thickening crowds.

By the time Florin and Lorenzo had reached the district which ended at the Dragon Wharf the morning mist was long gone. It had been burned away by the blinding sun, and already Bordeleaux was roasting.

In the alleyways that the two lizard hunters pushed through the air was thick with the perfume of stale sweat and raw sewage. Fortunately the merchants and tradesmen that lined every street in this quarter seemed immune to the heat-greased stench. They shouted and cajoled and lied as eagerly as ever, seemingly oblivious to the sweat which dripped from them.

Even the courtesans who idled on the balconies above were sodden with perspiration. Runnels of sweat cut through their powder and paint, leaving them as striped as barracuda as they eyed the throng below.

Hardly any surprise then, Florin thought as he elbowed his way past a cluster of longshoremen, that tempers were already starting to fray. Screams and curses floated through the usual hubbub, and he'd stepped over two bleeding bodies in as many minutes.

Another fight was just breaking out ahead. Resisting the urge to watch he skirted the knot of spectators and emerged onto the Dragon Wharf. The wet slap of sea air was like a cool hand on a fevered brow, and even the smell of stagnant brine was a relief after the vaporous interior of the city. Florin wiped his brow with relief and marched forward.

'Which one is Flangei's warehouse?' Lorenzo asked as the two men walked along the wharf. Cobbles and earth had given way to the wooden platform of its construction, and their boot heels joined in with a hundred others to beat a constant tattoo on the stained timber. To one side the waters of Bordeleaux's harbour oozed, the turgid waters forested by the masts of countless ships. On the other side the warehouses squatted. Their brick walls were blind of any windows and their wide doors were guarded by listless groups of watchmen.

'I can't remember which one was his,' Florin answered, his eyes sliding over the shingles that hung outside most of the warehouses, 'but I'm sure these gentlemen can help us. Good morning, monsieurs.'

The two men he had addressed were dressed in the same sea boots and tabards as most of the men here. Cudgels hung at their belts, and they were leaning on the iron-banded door of their master's warehouse.

'Monsieurs, is it?' one of them asked with a sneer.

'Yes,' Florin replied. 'It is.'

He stepped closer to the guard and smiled with the warm good humour of a lion who has cornered a wolf. For a moment the guard held his gaze. Then he looked away and shuffled his feet. Florin, telling himself that he wasn't disappointed by the lack of challenge, produced a coin.

'We're looking for the warehouse of Nine Bellies Flangei,' he said, turning his smile onto the second guard. 'Do you know where it is?'

'Just down there,' the man said cautiously, and pointed down the wharf. 'It's got a shingle with some candles on it.'

'Thank you,' Florin said and handed him the coin. 'Monsieurs.'

The guards nodded and watched as Florin and Lorenzo prowled down the wharf. When they were out of earshot the first guard regained his voice.

'He's lucky,' he told his mate, gesturing towards the lizard hunters. 'If it wasn't so damned hot I'd have given him a bloody nose. Cheeky sod.'

The other man grunted noncommittally and pocketed the coin. It was, after all, too hot to argue.

THEY FOUND THE widow Flangei busy with a delivery. A barque had tied up outside her late husband's warehouse, and a stream of porters were carrying barrels from the vessel's hold to the store. Despite the sweat that plastered their rags to their gaunt frames the men moved with the eagerness of worker ants, their bony bodies bent double beneath their loads.

Lorenzo didn't blame them. Under the stern gaze of their mistress, he would have worked with the same diligence.

Madame Flangei stood on a handcart, watching her little empire with sharp blue eyes. The fact that her face looked like a well-used hatchet did nothing to compliment her figure. She was a robust woman, and whatever charms she might have had were concealed beneath a functional canvas shift. The cleaver that she wore on her belt didn't add much to her feminine appeal either. The weapon was, after all, hardly the latest in Bordeleauxan fashion.

Only her hair showed any trace of vanity. It was as red as copper, and she had bound it into a coiffure that looked tight enough to serve as a helmet.

In fact, Lorenzo decided, she looked so formidable that the quartet of guards who stood behind her seemed almost superfluous. Their hands rested easily on their cudgels, but their eyes were everywhere. They had noticed Florin and Lorenzo as soon as the pair had paused to watch their mistress's goods being unloaded, and now one of them pointed the two men out to her.

'Something you boys want?' Madame Flangei asked with a voice like a bullwhip. She stared down at them with eyes that Lorenzo thought must be the coldest things in a thousand miles.

But If Florin shared his friend's uncharitable opinion he gave no sign of it. Instead he swept off his hat and bowed.

'Yes, thank you, Mademoiselle. We're looking for the widow Flangei.' He held his pose as he spoke, although the dark brown intensity of his eyes never left the blue ice of hers.

And even as she answered Lorenzo was amazed to see that that ice had already started to melt.

'Why are you looking for her?' the widow asked. Her voice remained a blunt instrument, but now the fist which had been resting on one hip fluttered up towards her tightly bound hair to pat at an imaginary stray lock.

'We are looking for Madame Flangei to discuss a matter relating to her late husband's death,' Florin told her, his own voice as smooth as honey.

The widow frowned, and her jaw jutted out like the ram of a galley.

'I'll collect that old fool's bones tomorrow. As you can see, I'm busy at the moment.'

Florin shook his head and smiled ruefully. 'Please, mademoiselle. On another day I would happily spend all afternoon being mocked by you. It would be a small price to pay for your presence. But today our business is too important. And unfortunately it revolves around the widow of an aged merchant, not a lady as young as yourself. Would that it did!'

Lorenzo watched in amazement as the widow's mouth fell open, then shut with a snap. At the same time, a red flush crept up from beneath her collar and she scowled furiously.

Lorenzo could never understand why Florin had this effect on women. It couldn't be what he said, the older man decided, because what he said was usually complete nonsense. So if it was nothing he said, it must just be the way he said it.

'Well, *I* am the Widow Flangei.' The widow finally recovered her voice. By now the blush had reached her hairline, and without any warning her scowl suddenly collapsed into a delighted smile.

Florin feigned embarrassment.

'Madame Flangei, I am so sorry. I hope you didn't take any offence. I certainly meant no disrespect. Can you forgive me?'

The widow silenced his apologies with a giggle that had her men looking at her in frank astonishment. She remained oblivious to them, though. She was too busy wishing that she'd worn something a little more flattering than her canvas shift. She fidgeted with her belt so that it tightened around her waist, but then Florin approached and she forgot all about even that.

'You are most gracious,' he purred, 'although now that I have acted like a perfect fool, I am almost too embarrassed to introduce myself.

I am Florin d'Artaud, Hero of Lus… I mean, agent of the Harbour Master. This is my comrade, Lorenzo.'

So saying he took her hand, which was as calloused as a sailor's, and caressed it as he pressed it politely to his lips. He gazed up at her as he did so, and she sighed.

'Is there somewhere a little more private we can go?' he asked, forgetting to release her hand. Madame Flangei, forgetting to take her hand back, licked her lips and nodded.

'Henri,' she said, turning to her nearest henchman. 'See that all hundred and twelve barrels are weighed and tested. All of them, understand? Then you can send the skipper up for payment. Me and Monsieur d'Artaud are going up to the backroom to discuss business.'

The henchman, trying not to look too amazed at this transformation of his mistress, snapped a salute as the widow, leading Florin by the hand, retreated to the cooler confines of her inherited building.

Lorenzo watched them go, exchanged a bemused look with the guard, then found a patch of shade and tried to make himself comfortable. He knew Florin well enough to know that he would be gone for a fair while.

It was afternoon by the time Florin emerged from the warehouse. He nodded happily to the guards who waited at the gates, then strolled over to Lorenzo with a friendly smile. But Lorenzo, who had spent the afternoon watching the heat haze flicker over the rotting stew of the harbour, was in no mood to smile back.

'What took you so long?' he snapped as Florin gave him a hand up from where he had been squatting against a wall.

'What?' Florin asked, the smile never leaving his face as he gazed across the harbour to the sea gates.

'I said, what took you so long?' Lorenzo repeated, and violently dusted himself down.

'Oh that,' said Florin, and made some vague gesture. 'Well, you know how it is. And the widow Flangei is certainly an incredible woman.'

Lorenzo looked at him sourly. 'Incredible is one word for it. She looked like she'd eat a man alive.'

Florin turned to look at the older man, a strange expression on his face. Then, for no reason at all, he burst into a fit of wild laughter.

'I don't see what's so funny,' Lorenzo muttered. 'I've been out here baking in the midday heat while you've been in there faffing around for hours on end. I mean, I suppose at some point you did ask her about what happened to old Nine Bellies.'

'Yes, of course,' Florin said, wiping his eyes. 'Of course I did. He was eaten by the lizards alright. They took him right off the wharf. Just by where you're standing now.'

Lorenzo turned to look suspiciously at the water that slopped against the scaffolding that supported the wharf.

'She said they climbed up from below here and started eating him while he was still struggling. She and the guards went to save him, but it was too late. They stripped him to the bone in seconds. Nine bellies and all.'

Lorenzo spat into the harbour. 'She didn't seem overly concerned by her loss.'

'Let's just say that Monsieur Flangei didn't have enough of an appetite for his good lady wife.'

'He didn't have the appetite? But I thought the man ate like a pig. Oh. I see what you mean.'

Florin winked at Lorenzo, who shook his head.

'I'll never understand women,' he said.

Florin clapped him on one bony shoulder. 'Don't worry,' he said. 'As long as you understand boats.'

Lorenzo's look of confusion gave way to one of suspicion. 'You're not thinking of paddling about beneath the wharf, are you?'

'It's the only way,' Florin said. 'Remember how it was in the jungle? Those things love water. It's nice and shady for them down there, too. No wonder they do all their hunting around the docks. Bet you anything you like we find them down there.'

'More likely they'll find us. And I do remember exactly what it was like in the jungle. We might as well swim out to the manacles to hunt sharks. Look, I've been thinking. Tilea is supposed to be nice, and if we didn't mind taking a low price for the tavern we could...'

'No.' Florin shook his head. 'It wouldn't be right. After all, I am Florin d'Artaud, Hero of Lustria. I can't turn and run when these things are threatening my own city.'

Lorenzo looked at him, appalled. 'Please tell me you aren't serious,' he said.

Florin just shrugged.

'Of course I'm serious. What Bordeleauxan man would leave the fair damsels of this great city to the mercy of monsters?'

'Manann's scrotum!' Lorenzo swore. 'You've finally cracked up. Was it the heat?'

'Something like that.' Florin, refusing to take offence, just grinned. 'Anyway, we'll get hold of a boat from Couraine tomorrow morning. Now we should eat. I've got an ogre of an appetite, and I think I saw a fish stew shop just back there.'

'The condemned men ate a hearty meal,' Lorenzo muttered, but Florin was already heading hungrily back into the swarming alleyways that led off from the wharf.

* * *

THE GUARDS STUDIED the vessel that had emerged from the steaming morning mist. It had seen better days. Even in the grey light they could see that the hull was a mildewed patchwork of ancient planking and new timber.

The mast had been lost, too, so the boat wallowed inelegantly forward under the power of the oarsman. He was grunting with exertion and the smell of his sweat was fresh amongst the miasma of rot that hung about the wharf.

The second occupant of the boat was more relaxed. He was not rowing. Instead he was watching. He leant forward over his crossbow, eagerly peering through the mist towards the pilings that supported the Dragon Wharf.

The guards watched him watch. Their heads floated amongst a confusion of bobbing detritus, and their eyes remained as still and unblinking as pebbles. They examined the boat as it splashed ever nearer with a cold-blooded patience, moving only to keep their bodies steady in the lazy current.

When the intruders had almost reached the dark waters beneath the wharf, their boat stopped. The two men barked at each other for a while, then set about lighting a pair of lanterns. Only then did the oarsman continue, slowly edging the boat between the forest of slimed timber that supported the wharf above.

The lamplight was sharp in the guards' eyes, although they ignored the temptation to blink. With an instinctive wisdom they realised that even that tiny movement might be too much. Instead they suffered, and watched the strange patterns that the reflected lamplight sent dancing around the roof of this drowned underworld.

The boat splashed and echoed its way between the pillars, the oarsman cursing as he rowed. His companion remained silent, his senses as taut as the arms of his crossbow. Occasionally he would hold one of the lanterns up to study the mildewed underside of the wharf above. Mostly he just squinted into the surrounding darkness.

Silently, and with barely a ripple, the guards followed in the intruders' wake.

Hunters and hunted progressed, and the waters grew more treacherous. Beneath the carpentry of the wharf, the city had spilled into the sea. Collapsed masonry and islands of refuse formed reefs in the stagnant water between the pilings. Strange fungi glistened in the lamplight, and every dip of the oar brought a fresh waft of rotting brine.

It wasn't until the intruders had reached the crumbling foundations of the warehouses that they stopped. The rotting masonry seemed to send them into some confusion, and they started barking at each other again.

The guards' eyes glistened in the lamplight as they drifted to a halt around the vessel. Two of them, moving with the silent grace of poured treacle, slipped from the water and slithered into the timber-work above the boat. Those that remained submerged themselves so that only their eyes remained above water. It had been a day since they'd eaten, and that had only been a skinny dockhand. Now their tails twitched with excitement at the thought of the feast to come.

Their prey continued to bark meaninglessly as the guards closed in on them from all sides. Within seconds they were in position as, completely oblivious to their peril, the humans continued to bicker.

'Now THAT WE'VE come to the end of this lunacy', Lorenzo said, gesturing towards the solid masonry before them, 'can we go and start putting our affairs in order? Belmeier is coming to value the tavern at noon, and I want to make sure we have everything done by high tide tonight. If we don't find a ship leaving for Tilea we could end up anywhere.'

Florin didn't bother to reply. Instead he carried on squinting through the lamp-lit darkness, fidgeting with his crossbow all the while.

'They're definitely down here', he said, and bit the inside of his lip. 'I can almost smell them. They'll love all this. The heat. The dankness. Just like the jungle.'

Lorenzo looked at his partner. In the reflected lamplight his expression could have almost been joyful.

'Whether they love it or not', Lorenzo said, 'we have to go. Today. We don't have any more time. If we don't sell up and go now, we might not have another chance. Are you listening to me?'

'Yes, of course', Florin lied, and turned to where he thought he had heard a splash.

'If we don't go, the Harbour Master will use us as a scapegoat to fob off the merchants. He told us as much himself.'

'No point in that.' Florin's ears twitched at the sound of something slithering through the darkness. 'Hanging us won't solve anything.'

'Of course there's a point. It will provide the merchants with a… Oh, by Ranald's dice bag, I'm sick of this', Lorenzo yelled, his patience snapping and his anger sudden and ferocious. 'Why do you always have to be such a damned fool? It was bad enough with the cards. Then the madness with those mercenaries, and that stinking jungle. Now this. Why is it that every day with you is like with Morrslieb rising?'

Florin looked at his companion. For the first time he could see the genuine anger in the older man's battered features. The anger and the fear.

'Lorenzo,' Florin said, his features icy with a terrible patience. 'I am not a fool.'

And with that he lifted his crossbow, pointed the steel barbed bolt towards Lorenzo, and pulled the trigger.

There was a hum and a blur, and Lorenzo's mouth fell open as he felt the flash of the bolt whisper past his cheek. But he didn't have time to be surprised. Before he could even gasp the bolt had bit home with a dull thud and the water behind him erupted into a desperate thrashing.

'Told you they were here!' Florin exulted, his voice echoing around the drowned depths. He swapped one crossbow for another and looked around for a fresh target.

'Look up,' Lorenzo yelled, seizing the boat hook that lay between his feet. Florin threw back his head in time to see a confusion of scales and talons shining in the lamplight. He aimed and fired the crossbow in a single sweep, and the bolt pinned the lizard to the woodwork beyond it as neatly as a butterfly on a pin.

Before he had time to admire his handiwork another scaled body was falling from above. This time it was Lorenzo who took it. Thrusting up with the boat hook he pierced its stomach then flipped it into the turgid water beyond, a manoeuvre which tipped the boat terrifyingly close to capsizing.

Even as they tried to balance their weight in the yawing vessel, the two men realised that the water around them was alive. As soon as the sharp tang of fresh blood had seasoned the water, the lizards had thrown off all caution. They were hungry, and driven on by their appetites they arrowed towards the boat, the water churning up behind them.

'Damn,' said Lorenzo as he tried to count them. Florin just grinned, a lethal crescent in the darkness. The twin cutlasses he unsheathed shone their own eager welcome as the first scaly body vaulted over the oarlocks, teeth bared.

Florin bellowed as he scissored the heavy blades towards the creature. Steel met scale a whisper before fangs met skin, and the serpentine head went flying back into the water.

'Be careful not to capsize us,' Lorenzo cried, and grabbed a hold of the oars to steady the rocking vessel. He kicked the decapitated body back over the side, and ducked as an arc of bloodied steel flickered overhead. By now the swarm was upon them, and Florin was fighting with an abandon that had the boat rolling like a barrel. Lorenzo could only dodge the blades and pray as, throwing his weight this way and that, he tried to keep them from capsizing.

'There's loads of them,' Florin cried as, with a pirouette worthy of an acrobat, he twisted to simultaneously lop the arm off one opponent and the head from another. 'Try to see where the heads are going.'

He turned and stabbed at something behind Lorenzo's bowed back. The boat reared alarmingly, then splashed back down. A spray of cold brine dashed across the back of Lorenzo's neck, followed by a spray of hot blood. He tried to ignore both as the boat bucked beneath him.

'We'll need the heads,' Florin grunted as he punched the steel guard of one cutlass into a serpentine snout and hacked down on another. 'To collect the full bounty.'

Lorenzo cursed this fresh insanity, and tried not to think about what would happen if the boat was flipped and the lanterns extinguished.

But already the ambushers seemed to be retreating. Florin prised his cutlass from the skull of his last victim and looked around him, confusion furrowing his blood-spattered brow.

'They're going,' he decided as Lorenzo kicked another body into the water.

'Yes. Let's join them.'

'Good idea. We'll have to be quick though. Come on, start rowing. That one's wounded, so we should be able to follow it.'

Florin dropped a cutlass into the bloodied bilge that slopped around his boots, leant over the prow, and lifted a lantern overhead.

'Come on, they're getting away,' he complained.

Lorenzo didn't have the energy to argue. Instead he threw his meagre weight behind the oars and, praying that Manann would continue to offer his traditional protection to lunatics, he rowed.

HAD THE SURVIVOR not been so badly wounded, Florin and Lorenzo would never have kept up with it. Every part of the creature, from the smoothly scaled arrow of its head to the powerful rudder of its tail, was built for speed in the water.

What hampered it were its injuries, and they were horrific. A cutlass stroke had sliced open its back, so that as it moved the severed muscles slipped and tore over the chipped ribcage beneath. Its left arm was also gone, lopped off at the shoulder by a butcher's blow that had been aimed at its head.

A warm-blooded creature would surely have succumbed to the shock and pain of these twin mutilations, but not this one. As its pursuers closed in it struggled on, ignoring the agony that sang through its nerves as easily as it ignored the pieces of flotsam that churned beneath its remaining limbs.

'Slow down a bit,' Florin hissed, waving his hand at Lorenzo.

'Slow down?' the older man repeated, surprised.

'We're getting too close,' Florin whispered, as if afraid that their quarry could understand. If it did it gave no sign. The serpentine shape of its bleeding body writhed through the black water ahead, its head tilted to one side as it crawled lopsidedly through the rotting brine. As Florin watched a flash of reflected lamp light glittered in one of its eyes. It reminded him of the gold at the bottom of a prospector's pan.

'It's turning right,' Florin hissed as the thing rolled to one side and made its way through a row of pilings. Lorenzo heaved on the oars and followed it. Florin helped him, pushing the boat away from one of the timber columns before looking back to the rippled water of their quarry's track.

For one heart-stopping moment he thought that he'd lost it. Then he saw that the only thing he'd lost was the churn of water. The lizard itself had crawled out onto a tumble of silt-choked debris. The spit of rubble sloped gradually up from the water and at the top of it, fanged with broken masonry, the mouth of a tunnel yawned hungrily open.

Florin grinned as he watched the wounded lizard crawl into the entrance. He was still grinning as he turned back to Lorenzo, who was concentrating on shepherding the boat between a fallen piling and a floating island of refuse.

'What did I tell you?' Florin exulted. 'We've got them. See over there!' He lifted the lantern up so that the flickering yellow light leapt after the retreating lizard. 'See all those claw marks on the silt outside the hole? This is where they live, alright. Here, pass me the boathook and row us up to it. I'll find a place to land.'

Lorenzo muttered as he pulled on the oars, and the battered boat nosed its way to the mess that served the lizards as a pier. Florin squinted at the spill of detritus. He tried a couple of places before finally chopping the boathook down into a fallen pile and fastening the boat to it.

'Right then,' he said, turning to Lorenzo and lifting a lantern to light his face. 'Let's reload the crossbows, get in there.'

'Alright.' Lorenzo shrugged, and warily eyed the dark maw of the tunnel as he winched back one of the crossbows. 'Alright, let's finish them. We don't have time to sell the tavern now anyway.'

Florin nodded distractedly. He had already armed his bow, checked his cutlasses were loose in their sheaths, and turned up the wick on his lantern. He waited for Lorenzo to do the same then bounded out of the boat and scrabbled up the crumbling slope towards the cave.

He paused at the edge of it, lantern held in one hand and crossbow in the other. When he heard Lorenzo at his back he passed the bow back and drew his cutlass instead. Lorenzo reluctantly extinguished his own lantern and, as the darkness drew tighter about them, he slung one crossbow over his shoulder and held the other at the ready.

Thus armed the two men stepped into the tunnel.

After the stink of the rotting world beneath the wharf, the still air within these burrowed walls was almost refreshing. So was the silence. There was no drip of water or scrape of driftwood or rumble of wagons passing overhead. Apart from the smear of blood along the floor it might have been as empty as a tomb.

They had gone perhaps thirty paces when Lorenzo started to wonder why the tunnel was so big. The lizards themselves had been no bigger than a man, and from what he had seen of them he guessed that they walked on all fours, or perhaps stooped over in orcish fashion.

So why, he wondered, was the ceiling so high? It was maybe ten feet in all, and the light of the lantern barely touched it. All that Lorenzo could see was that it was covered with the regular claw marks of its excavation.

Suddenly Lorenzo was seized with a terrible suspicion. He swallowed nervously, tapped Florin on the shoulder and leant forward to whisper into his ear.

'Why is this place so big?' he asked, eyes rolling up towards the ceiling.

Florin shrugged. 'Who knows? Maybe they like the ventilation.'

'I thought you said they liked humidity.'

'Maybe they like both.'

'How,' Lorenzo said, forgetting to whisper, 'can they like both?'

'Look,' said Florin, 'what's that up ahead?'

He lifted his lantern and, with his cutlass held as still as a viper about to strike, he edged forward. Lorenzo was about to continue the discussion when he realised that there was something up ahead after all. It sparkled on the floor of the tunnel, flecks of lantern light catching metallic edges.

'Treasure,' the two men told each other in perfect harmony. Then they were hurrying forward, the oddities of lizardine architecture forgotten in the face of the creatures' fabled wealth.

But when they reached the treasure it was not the sort they had hoped for. Florin knelt down to examine their find.

'Eggs.' He spat the word and rolled one of the things out of the muddy hollow that served as its nest. It was heavy, although not heavy enough to be gold, and the pattern that sparkled so seductively was no more precious than a dragonfly's scales.

'Are you sure they aren't something else?' Lorenzo asked with an air of unaccustomed optimism.

'I'm sure. Remember that idiot who brought an egg back on the *Destrier*? That was the same as these.'

Lorenzo looked down at the nest, disappointment creasing the satchel of his face.

'I remember. I remember the captain throwing it overboard too. But I don't remember there being more than one.'

Florin sighed, his hopes of riches dashed. 'Maybe the first one hatched and laid the rest. Look at the size of them. Bet it made their eyes water, hey?'

Lorenzo just shook his head.

'At least we should get a bounty for them,' Florin consoled him. 'Let's finish off the escapee first, though. I wouldn't mind keeping his head as a trophy.'

He got back to his feet, lifted the lantern, and continued along the bloody trail of his quarry. Lorenzo followed him, pausing only to stamp down on one of the eggs.

The crunch was surprisingly loud in the confined space.

But what was even louder was the answering howl of agony that reverberated out of the darkness ahead.

'Damn,' said Florin, and for once Lorenzo was in total agreement. The roar that even now echoed around them bore little relation to the wounded thing they had chased into this pit. It didn't sound hurt so much as enraged. It also sounded big.

'Let's go back,' said Lorenzo, edging nervously back between the eggs. This time he was careful not to stand on any of them.

'Listen,' Florin said. 'Footsteps.'

Lorenzo listened. He felt rather than heard the beat of footsteps that were drumming through the hard-packed earth. As they drew nearer he licked his lips and tried to swallow.

'Here it comes,' Florin said. He put his lantern down and reached for the bow Lorenzo passed him. The two men aimed at the unknown, the hairs on the back of their necks rising as another roar split the air and the thing emerged from the darkness.

At first it was no more than a darker patch in the darkness beyond. Then it was a field of glittering stars as lamplight caught the edges of its scales. And then it was upon them.

Neither man had seen its like before. Even in their memories the saurian warriors of Lustria had never grown so big. The thing that thundered towards them was actually stooped beneath the high ceiling, the boulder-sized muscles of its forearms rippling as it reached out towards them. But if the talons were terrifying, the crocodilian slab of its head was worse. It leered down at them, a serpentine mask of glistening fangs and murderous rage.

For a split second the two men stared at the horror, mesmerised by the ferocity of its charge. Then, a second before the daggers of its talons reached them, they fired.

The bowstrings hummed as the two bolts blurred towards their target. The first struck the scales that rippled down its belly and bounced off as harmlessly as hail. But the second, which both men later swore they had fired, found a softer target in the vicious slit of the monster's eye.

It screamed as it lunged to one side, and both men smelt the rotten meat stink of its breath. Florin snatched up the lantern as they leapt away from the thrashing claws and scurried back up the tunnel.

'Reload,' he told Lorenzo as a fist the size of a small pig closed around the arrow that was imbedded in the lizard's eye. It plucked it out with a horrible pop that was lost beneath a fresh scream of agony. Then it turned its remaining eye on the two intruders.

'Duck,' Lorenzo said and, as the beast lowered its head for a fresh charge, he fired again.

He almost hit his target. Almost. But this time the beast whipped its head aside at the last moment, and the steel-tipped bolt bounced harmlessly off the top of its head.

Lorenzo tried to reload, but Florin knew it was too late. As his comrade fumbled with the bow the beast vaulted over the nest of eggs and hurled itself towards them.

Florin stopped thinking. Instead he let instincts take over. Even as the great lizard fell upon him he dropped his cutlass, slipped a thin stiletto from his boot, and leapt forward to meet it.

He ignored the pain of the talons that cut through his flesh to slide across the ribs beneath. He ignored the hot stink of its breath as its jaws snapped shut an inch beside his head. He even ignored the terror of its bulk, and the roll of the impossibly strong muscles beneath the impossibly thick hide.

He ignored everything apart from the slit of the beast's remaining eye.

As the lizard wrapped its forearms around him for a final embrace, Florin used its knee as a toe-hold and sprang upwards, twisting his body as taut as a bow before its release. There was only one chance, he knew. Only one roll of the dice.

But as soon as he struck, he knew that it would be enough.

The stiletto hit the serpentine eye dead centre, severing the black pupil and punching through the jelly beneath. A cutlass blow would have ended there, bouncing off the skull. But the stiletto was thin enough to follow the optical nerve through the tunnel of bone and into the brain.

The lizard didn't even have time to scream as the splinter of steel ended its life. It just swayed for a last, dying heartbeat, then collapsed forward as dead as a falling tree.

There was a boom as the massive carcass hit the tunnel floor, and a sprinkle of falling earth from the ceiling above.

Lorenzo, who couldn't quite believe he was still alive, rushed forward to wrestle Florin's body out from beneath the carcass.

'Are you alright?' he asked, dragging him clear.

Florin coughed and spat out a mouthful of blood. 'Apart from all the broken bones, you mean?'

'Don't worry about them,' Lorenzo reassured him. 'They're a small price to pay for getting the job done. See, I told you it was a good idea to track them down here.'

Florin opened his mouth to argue. But before he could, the pain, the blood loss, and the knowledge that he was safe conspired to send him into grateful oblivion.

'WELL I'LL SAY this for young d'Artaud,' said Baron Lafayette as he examined the colour of his claret. 'He's certainly resourceful.'

Count Griston, who sat across the dining table from his host, shrugged his half-hearted agreement. It was another one of their dinner parties, and he was wondering if Lafayette would be able to top the vin et bile d'aigle and os de poisson gellés he had served last month.

'Ah yes, d'Artaud. I forgot about him. Didn't he help you out with some business in the docks, Harbour Master?'

The Harbour Master, who had been enjoying the way that the claret complemented the mixed gastropods of the entrée, nodded.

'Yes, there was something he helped me with. We had some problems with a particularly vicious gang on the Dragon Wharf. D'Artaud did a bit of scouting and discovered their lair.'

Lafayette's mouth dropped in surprise, and he exchanged a glance with his wife. But before he could say anything she kicked him neatly on the shin.

'Yes, crime around the docks is expensive.' Griston seized upon the subject with a real enthusiasm. 'In fact, Harbour Master, only last week I lost a substantial amount of stock. Very substantial. Perhaps when you come to calculating next month's docking fees…'

'Please, count.' The Harbour Master held up his hands. 'Let us not ruin this fine meal with talk of business. And anyway, docking fees aren't related to any lapses in warehouse security.'

'As you say,' Griston nodded. 'Now is not the place to talk about how lapses in warehouse security weren't to blame for my loss.'

Lafayette saw the Harbour Master's displeasure, and on another occasion he would have happily left Griston to make it worse. Tonight, though, he didn't have the patience.

'Well, if we have all finished,' he said, looking around the table and then snapping his fingers for the servants. They cleared the table with a quiet efficiency that wouldn't have shamed a gun crew, then scurried away to fetch the main course.

Griston, his wrangle with the Harbour Master temporarily forgotten, watched them go.

'What is the main course this evening, Lafayette?' he asked. 'Pork again?'

Lafayette smiled at the insult, rocked back on his chair, and cracked his knuckles.

'To be honest, Griston,' he lied, 'I can't remember. I left it to chef to decide on the menu. But look, here it comes now.'

The aroma that preceded the silver platter was mouth watering. It was spicy enough to conjure up thoughts of Araby, although not too spicy to mask the scent of roast meat and a hint of something citric.

The servants set the platter down on the table, so that the assembled diners could see their anticipation reflected back from the silver dome of the lid. The butler placed a silk-gloved hand on the handle on top of it, and looked at his master.

Lafayette waited, drawing out the moment for another delicious second, then gave the nod.

With a practiced flourish the flunky lifted the silver dome off the platter beneath, then stepped back so that the diners could savour the sight of the dish. When the sweet-smelling steam had cleared the guests did just that, staring at the creation before them with three identical expressions of shock.

Lafayette and his wife exchanged a glance of absolute triumph.

'Ah,' said Lafayette with a carefully affected nonchalance. 'One of chef's foreign dishes.'

Griston looked at his host then back to the platter before him. The carved meat oozed succulence, and it was so white as to be almost translucent. But it was the appearance of the dish that really drew the eye.

'That head,' he couldn't help asking. 'Is it real?'

'Yes, of course,' said Lafayette as the servants began to serve his guests. 'I always insist on having the head sent up with the meat. You can always tell the freshness of the animal by the gold of its eyeballs. See how they shine even after having been roasted?'

'Yes,' said Griston miserably. He tasted a forkful of the meat, and his misery deepened. It was superb. Unique.

But the Harbour Master had other concerns.

'Where did you get that thing?' he asked, staring at the scaled head with something approaching panic.

Lafayette shifted uncomfortably until his wife saved him.

'I couldn't possibly reveal my sources,' she said, smiling sweetly. 'I'm just glad that Monsieur d'Artaud got rid of all those thieves at the dock, aren't you? They might have stolen it from our importer.'

The Harbour Master met her gaze, understanding. Then he shrugged, and tasted a sliver of the white flesh. It melted on his tongue.

'I propose a toast,' he said. 'To our host, Count Lafayette, and to the excellence of his table. This delicacy is certainly a rare treat. Shallya willing.'

The diners clinked their glasses, and returned to the succulence of Lafayette's triumph.

PARADISE LOST

Andy Jones

'WELL, JOHAN, Y'SEE, it's like this…' The gruff dwarf voice hung for long moments in the hot tropical air. 'Sometimes yer has to take the big chance…' The voice trailed off. 'Ain't half hot, though.'

'Snowkapt Mountinz, I see Snowkapt Mountinz.' Indecipherable babble escaped from Keanu the Reaver like steam from a leaky kettle. 'Ja, und schtreams, und kold, kold fountinz…' Even the barbarian's delirium was thickly accented.

Johan Anstein, ex-Imperial envoy, groaned inwardly and manoeuvred a fragment of sailcloth to shade himself from the merciless ravages of the sun. The young, would-be warrior peered with squinting eyes at the dwarf sitting stoically at the rowlocks.

'But Grimcrag, what are we going to do?' Anstein's voice was little more than a croak, his tongue thick and furred in his mouth. He could feel the sun hammering down on his head, even through the thick tarpaulin he had draped across his blistered shoulders.

The young man pointed what was (to his mind at least) quickly becoming a skeletally thin arm at the recumbent elf lying in the bilges. Jiriki rolled softly with the swell of the sea. 'He hasn't moved all day, and Keanu thinks he's back home in Norsca.'

Johan studied the barbarian lolling in the steersman's seat. Wearing nothing but a loin cloth and horned helmet, the Reaver glistened menacingly.

'Take mich Home, Momma!' the barbarian gargled, his teeth chattering uncontrollably.

'Don't you be worryin' about yon elf, lad,' Grimcrag interjected. 'He's always doin' that suspendered animalation trick of his when things get tricky.' The dwarf deftly prodded the comatose Jiriki with a boat hook. 'See, nothing!'

Grimcrag scratched at his beard and spat overboard. 'It's old musclehead I'm worried about. I don't think he can take many more days without anything to drink. He's getting beerhydrated, and it'll be the end of him, mark my words.'

'No sign of land?' Johan asked hopelessly.

The dwarf performed what under normal circumstances would have been an almost comical double take. 'Oh yes, didn't I mention it? We're about thirty yards away from a lovely landing berth. I can see the tavern from here... OF COURSE THERE'S NO BLOODY LAND!' Grimcrag snorted in derision, and continued scratching despondently at his beard.

Johan slumped back under the tarpaulin. 'That's it then, we're done for.'

Minutes later, he had drifted off into a restless, sun-driven daydream.

'GOLD, LAD, GOLD! More than you can imagine!' The dwarf voice resonated with barely controlled excitement.

'Yes, but it's not Lustrian, or from the Lost Kingdoms at all: it's in a storm-wrecked Bretonnian galleon.'

'Never mind that, it's ours for keeps now.'

'It's sinking fast!'

'We've got time, lad, and this boat can hold plenty.'

'Wouldn't we be better scavenging water and food?'

'VOT? S'YOU MAD?'

A madly canted deck, so far down in the water that it was not much of a climb at all even in their weakened state. Crazy angles, creaking hawsers, the desolate flapping of ripped and tattered sailcloth. Not so different from their own recent fate.

Keanu barging the others aside impatiently, muscles straining as he pulled at the iron ring on the deck hatch. Nothing... then the screech of swollen wood on rusted metal.

A black square leading down into nothingness. The stench of stagnant death and decay. The slap of lazy waters in the dark bilges below.

Heat-bloated bodies gently bumping against him in the darkness. Foetid water climbing quickly over their waists. Fish swimming blindly about their legs. The discomforting feel of being ghoulish carrion, unwelcome visitors intruding upon the rest of the dead. Heavy crates. A race against time and the horror of joining the bodies in the hold for ever.

A portion saved. Exhaustion. The sad sight of a once-noble vessel slipping ignominiously below the waves, leaving at its last nothing more than bubbling froth and a few shards of timber.

The endless sun by day and the chill blackness of night. Day after day after day in a boat piled high with nothing but gold. Death's shadow never seemed far away. Who would succumb first?

'Sail ahoy!'

Hope!

'You sure, elfy?'

'Yes, it's some kind of corsair.'

'Wave everything! We're saved!'

'Hide the gold, lad!'

'Where, for heaven's sake?'

'Halloo! Halloo!'

A brine- and barnacle-encrusted tramp. A patchwork of old repairs over older repairs. A grimy grey sail. Tar and smoke-blackened timbers. A ruined figurehead jutting like a broken tooth. The most beautiful ship Johan had ever seen.

A grizzled, suspicious face. A toothless grin, a hooked hand. A swarthy bunch of no-hopers. Angels in disguise, no doubt.

'Well 'pon my soul, if it ain't the great mister lardy-dardy I-wouldn't-hire-your-ship-if-I-was-in-the-middle-of-the-Great-Ocean-on-a-tea-chest Grunsonn himself...'

'Vot?'

'Grimcrag, you didn't?'

'Not exactly, lad... I think he missed out the bit about the tea chest leaking...'

A diplomatic elvish voice: 'Look here, Black Hook Pugh Beard or whatever your name is, are you going to help us or not?'

'Depends, eh, lads? Shall we help the hoity-toities?'

A chorus of despicable cheers and catcalls.

'Dependink on vot, 'zactly?'

'Got'ny gold in those boxes?'

'Ja!'

'No!'

'For heaven's sake, Grimcrag. Yes, yes, yes, just get us off this blasted boat!'

'You'll be wantin' water then?'

'Ja.'

'Yes.'

'Mmph!'

'Definitely.'

Ropes and grapples snaking down. Chests brim full of Bretonnian gold hauled up on board. A fishermen's net lowered. Salvation in sight. Four sun-bleached souls about to end their week-long torment. Heaven is nigh.

JOHAN STIRRED IN his heat-drenched half-sleep. He already knew the ending of this particular dream. He'd seen it for real, and dreamed it a hundred times a day since. His eyes opened a crack, as he wondered yet again if maybe, somehow, this was all a dream, a very bad one. Perhaps he was really lying on silk sheets at home in Castle Baltenkopf? Pitiful hope seized his heart.

But no, here was the boat, and there sat the disconsolate form of the renowned Grimcrag Grunsonn, unceremoniously stripped down to filthy grey vest and long johns. The lugubrious dwarf still wore his iron-shod boots and his helmet, but his armour and precious axe were tucked under his bench for safe-keeping. Johan blearily noticed that today the dwarf had rolled his sleeves up. Perhaps the sun was finally getting to even him.

Johan turned over and quickly drifted off into fitful sleep again, the endless monotony of the slap-slapping of the sea against the boat's flimsy side a familiar lullaby. After a few hours of blissful oblivion, the dream came on again.

THEY ARE SCRAMBLING up the net, grinning madly to one another. Even Grimcrag has forgotten the thought of his gold in the joy of rescue. Fresh water? A bath? Food? What it is to have friends!

Halfway up and disaster strikes – the net falls away, plunging them down into the sea. Uproarious laughter from above

When they surface, the ship is already drifting away. Their small, sorry boat is dragged alongside by the current for a moment, as if forlornly hoping for a tow.

The corsairs laugh cruelly, jeering at the Marauders from the safety of the gunwale.

'Come back!' Johan gurgles.

'MY GOLD!' shrieks Grimcrag.

Jiriki and Keanu swim with strong, accomplished strokes towards the boat.

The pirates throw down some water skins and a few barrels of salted fish.

The Marauders clamber, exhausted, into their floating prison cell once more. Ironically enough, there is more room without all the gold. At least Johan can stretch his long legs.

Grimcrag is inconsolable, shouting curses southwards long after the pirates' sail has dipped below the distant horizon. The sharks circle. In the boat they all know they are doomed.

* * *

JOHAN WOKE WITH a start, a sharp stabbing pain in his heart warning him that finally his time was nigh. He had hoped that he would not be the last to die. He didn't think he could stand that. At least they hadn't eaten each other. They still had their honour.

It was so hot he could barely breathe. Eyes closed, he groaned softly. What a way to go. The stabbing pain intensified, followed by a repetitive dull thumping ache in his head. After a moment, Anstein opened his eyes.

Grimcrag stood over him, staring open-mouthed at the horizon. Waking up to the view of a dwarf's badly-sewn long johns crotch revealed secrets to the young adventurer that lesser men had died for merely talking about in casual conversation. The dwarf was absent-mindedly stabbing him in the chest with a marlin spike, whilst simultaneously stomping nervously up and down on the ex-envoy's head with a heavily booted foot.

'Pack it in, Grimcrag,' Johan croaked through sun-dried lips. 'Just lie down and die quietly like the rest of us.'

The dwarf mumbled something through his salt-encrusted beard.

Johan thought he had misheard. He painfully raised his head, and pawed feebly at the dwarf's long johns. His breath came in rasping sobs. 'What did you say?' He was surprised to see that the dwarf was weeping. Must be a delayed reaction to the loss of so much gold.

Salty tears ran down the grizzled dwarf's cheeks, mingling with that already tangling his beard. Johan strained to hear his cracked whisper. 'Land, lad. Marvellous, green, grassy, diggable bloody LAND!'

KEANU WAS MOSTLY awake and rowing hard by the time they approached the beach, rounding the rugged headland into the sheltered cove beyond. So far, the island had seemed an impenetrable fortress, with cliffs on every side, but the sight of this sheltered cove took Johan's breath away. A strip of white, white sand stretched for perhaps a quarter of a mile, with projecting horns of rock sheltering the cove from the open ocean. Coral reefs made bizarre living citadels in the clear water, and also created a natural barrier against any heavier swells.

Negotiating towards a gap in the reef, Keanu muttered something about catching a chill, and Johan could see whisps of steam escaping from beneath the barbarian's helm. Clearly the man needed rest soon.

'See all that green, lad?' Grimcrag shouted, pulling on an oar. 'That shows there must be water on the island somewhere.' The dwarf was wearing a relieved grin along with his boots and underclothes, and had obviously heroically put the matter of his gold to the back of his mind for a while.

Despite Johan's best efforts, and the crazed shouting and whooping of them all, they had failed to rouse Jiriki from his deep slumber. Grimcrag had explained that it sometimes happened like that – and the Reaver had grunted something about 'Vontink a lie in, praps' – but Johan could see that the dwarf was concerned.

Johan trailed a finger in the clear waters, watching the myriad schools of fish flash in the sunlight beneath him. He had taken an hour at the oars, rowing around what looked to be a huge lump of jungle-covered rock, and now he was taking a well earned rest. So many fish.

Then Grimcrag shouted for him to grab a boat hook and be ready to fend off. 'We're going through the gap in the reef, lad, and we don't want to hole her.'

As they navigated safely through, the elf slept on, snoring softly, his feet at the tiller and his head just behind Grimcrag's seat.

A few moments later and they were into the lagoon, five hundred feet or so from the white sands of the beach. Johan had once read a book from Araby about exotic fruits. Surely what he was seeing now were indeed the fabled, erm, barnarnowls or something; the exact name eluded him.

'Looks like we're in for a sojourn in paradise, eh, Grimcrag?' he shouted excitedly, pointing shorewards. 'See, corker nuts.'

The dwarf grinned deliriously, 'Yes, and jimjam trees too!'

Johan sighed contentedly, sat back at the tiller and peered at the fish again.

A moment later, Anstein, Grimcrag and Keanu made simultaneous exclamations.

'Grimcrag, there's no fish at all in the lagoon! Why d'you think that might be?'

'Hell, lad, what's that coming from the jungle?'

'Achtung! Valkink Lizarts!'

Johan's question was forgotten as all eyes swung forwards. All, that is, except for Jiriki, who was facing the wrong way and asleep anyway. A strange procession was making its way through the jungle and onto the beach. What indeed looked to be four- to five-foot tall, walking lizards were emerging in small groups, carrying bows, blow pipes and crude swords. Others were throwing quantities of fruit and flowers into the lagoon, while slightly larger lizards began blowing on trumpets fashioned from polished shells.

In all, Johan soon estimated there to be upwards of a hundred lizard men on the beach. So engrossed were the reptilians, that they didn't seem to have noticed the intruding boat. In fact, and Johan thought this most peculiar, they seemed to be studiously avoiding looking up or out to sea at all, as if terrified of what they might see.

'They won't be expecting us, make no mistake,' giggled Johan, his fish spotting momentarily forgotten.

'Vot is dey?' Keanu asked. 'Never seeink Nothink like dat before.'

'Dunno, Keanu, but best be on the safe side,' Grimcrag growled, reaching instinctively for Old Slaughterer, his trusty axe. Only once the mighty blade was wedged firmly between his stumpy legs did he recommence rowing. 'Johan, you're an envoy, this should be right up your street,' the dwarf grunted over his shoulder. 'Do something useful for a change.'

'Ja, Usevul.'

Johan looked at the throng of lizard men they were fast approaching, and racked his brain for the appropriate phrase or saying. Visiting ambassadors he was fine with, or representatives of the merchants' guild, but a hundred apparently semi-civilised lizards throwing fruit into a lagoon on a desert island was something different altogether.

'Well?'

'Ja, say Somzink.'

Feeling that his talents were obviously being called into question, Johan stood up and made his way to the front of the boat with what he hoped was an air of quiet confidence. From the way Grimcrag beamed toothily and nudged the steaming barbarian, he had succeeded so far.

Standing at the very prow, Johan cupped his hands to his mouth.

'HALLOO! HALLOO! DON'T KILL US – WE, ER, COME IN PEACE!'

Judging by the collective intake of breath from behind him, his speech had a dramatic effect on Grimcrag and Keanu. The lizards on the beach were immediately thrown into a state of high panic. Some buried their heads in the sand, others ran off into the jungle. Others feverishly threw more and more fruit into the lagoon. Johan saw one of them biting large chunks out his trumpet. A few braver souls, who unfortunately all seemed to carry bows, stood uncertainly on the shoreline, arrows knocked and ready.

'Now you've gorn and done it, lad,' Grimcrag muttered. 'At least try and smile, nice, like.'

Johan fixed his best diplomatic grin as Keanu and Grimcrag continued to row.

A moment later, something triggered the lizards into even more frenzied behaviour. Within a few seconds all save a dozen or so lonely warriors had vanished into the jungle. The creatures raised their bows uncertainly. Johan could see that they were still trying to avoid looking directly out to sea, which couldn't do much for their chances of hitting anything.

'Bound to be poison-tipped. I heard once that...' Grimcrag was rudely interrupted by an unmistakable elven shriek from the rear of the boat.

'AAAAAARGH! What in Tiranoc and the sunken realms is that!!!??'

'Oh good, Jiriki, you've woke–' began Johan as he turned, but the words died on his lips.

Perhaps fifty feet behind the boat, approaching them in a huge welter of spume and spray, was the biggest, most fearsome looking beast he had ever seen.

CONSCIOUSNESS SLOWLY SEEPED back into Johan Anstein's wiry frame, like reluctant treacle leaching through the stygian depths of an old gravel bed. Something was tickling his face.

'Two sugars in mine, Grimcrag,' Johan groaned, keeping his eyes screwed firmly shut as he clutched his head to stop it falling off. Johan's skull felt as if the dwarf was enthusiastically excavating for gold somewhere behind his frontal lobe. 'Must have been some party,' he thought, groggy from what could only have been last night's excesses of ale. Cosy in his blanket, Johan desperately tried to let sleep reclaim him.

Something slimy and cold began wriggling up into Johan's nose. It was only then it occurred to a sluggish Anstein that he hadn't been to a party for weeks, not since three days before they set sail on that accursed boat. 'Boat...'

Johan frowned inadvertently in his slumber, as dislocated thoughts fell like dominoes through his drowsy brain: 'Boat... shipwreck... pirates... island... lizards... MONSTER!!!'

A swift moment later, Johan was very much awake and cautiously opening an eye, whilst keeping the other screwed firmly shut, just in case. He sneezed to clear his nose of what could only be an inquisitive worm, and blinked his one open eye. Total darkness. Either he was blind, or somewhere black and smelling of sandy earth. Somewhere black, sandy and with worms. Johan briefly wondered if maybe it was better to imagine he was blind.

Cautiously he edged onto his back, immediately encountering another problem. He seemed to be roughly wrapped in some sort of coarse material. It enveloped him in a manner most unlike a blanket. The word 'shroud' drifted through the backwaters of Anstein's stunned mind, on an unavoidable collision course with his conscious thoughts. Struggling free of his 'blanket', Johan gingerly reached upwards with his right hand. Almost immediately his nails scraped rough wooden planks in the dark. Panic struck as quickly as the Dwarf Mineworker's Guild when the pit-head bar ran out of Bugman's.

'Buried alive!' Johan gasped, thrashing out wildly about him in the inky blackness. In every direction he hit wood almost immediately. 'Oh No Oh No Oh No!' he shrieked, before lying very still, like a desperate and cornered beast. 'Think, Anstein, think!' he muttered, teeth chattering uncontrollably. A terrible fear gnawed at his innards, threatening to return the blind panic which had all but overwhelmed him a moment ago.

Johan recapped the situation aloud, in a vain attempt to calm his pounding heart. 'The monster – that's why there were no fish in the lagoon. That's what the strange lizardy men were making offerings to.' Johan stopped for a moment as a violent trembling fit seized his frame. It passed.

'We almost reached the beach, then it was upon us,' Johan whispered slowly to himself, as the recollection of the dread fanged monstrosity which had assaulted their tiny boat flooded back into his memory.

He remembered it roaring in insensate fury. He remembered its tiny, bestial eyes, staring fixedly at him from a cart-sized head atop a mast-high neck. He remembered the water streaming in frothy torrents from its crustacean-encrusted back. Johan remembered Jiriki loosing arrow after arrow at the beast. He smiled as he remembered Grimcrag's axe, a whistling arc of gold and red in the bright sunlight. He remembered the barbarian's war cry as the Reaver struck again and again with his wicked longsword. He remembered the moment when the beast began to know fear. He even recalled his own blade – a cold sliver of silver pricking at the gargantuan monster's side.

Johan gulped in the darkness of his tomb as he recalled what must have been seen as the moment of his own death. Tears welled in his eyes, tears of sadness and frustration. At least he would be remembered as a hero, killed fighting a great beast. And they had slain it, of that he had no doubt at all.

Even buried alive, on a far distant isle, for that he surely was, Johan allowed himself a grim smile as he remembered the sea monster's death throes. Bleeding from a hundred or more wounds, it had threshed the water to a pinky red froth. Its cries had echoed around the cove over which it must have been undisputed lord for many years.

And Johan remembered its massive tail swinging round as if time had slowed, clearing the water like a fifty-foot yard arm. The others had instinctively ducked just in time, but Johan could clearly see in his mind's eye that he, alone, had not. He could remember a flash of pain and a great many stars, then nothing more, but now he nursed the bump on his head and silently wept salty tears of pain, fear and frustration. Buried alive! Johan desperately hoped he had been given a good send off at least...

Mad, blind panic swept over Johan again, carrying him like a broken twig before a mountain river in flood. He screamed, he yelled, he cried insanities at the darkness as he hammered and clawed weakly at his coffin lid for what seemed like hours.

Eventually he was exhausted, and lay panting in the darkness. It was no good. He was surely doomed to die, probably of asphyxiation when the air in the foetid hole ran out.

Johan slumped, beaten and dispirited in the cool blackness. He was ready, at last, to die. As one of Grunsonn's Marauders.

ON THE BEACH, the Marauders sat around a small fire and devoured chunks of half-cooked sea monster with gusto, as the eventful day drew to a close. On the distant horizon, the sun sank beneath the waves, its angry red orb extinguished for another day.

'Marooned in the middle of nowhere!' Jiriki muttered, picking delicately at a tender morsel.

Grimcrag stared wistfully out to sea, hot fat running down his bearded chin. 'Reckon that was as good a fight as any I've had for a while – thought it had us fer a moment or two.'

'Nah!' spat the barbarian through stringy haunch, black eyes gleaming in the firelight. ''Ve voss just Veak, dat's all, uddervise ve're killink it pretty damm Qvick, ja?!'

'S'pose so,' Grimcrag answered after a moment's chewing, before shaking his shaggy head as if to clear cobwebs away. 'Eeh, though, we're gettin' all maudlin and no mistake, aren't we?' The dwarf's eyebrows furrowed and he gestured with stubby fingers at the feast which lay before them. 'Look at this lot, 'nough to keep us going for weeks.' He turned to the others and smiled his broken-toothed, bearded grin. 'S'not all that bad, is it lads? Old Grimcrag saw you right in the end.'

Jiriki threw back his head and laughed sarcastically. The silvery note rang clear across the cove. He wagged a slender finger reproachfully. 'Oh yes, Grimcrag, everything's just fine!' The elf looked around them pointedly. 'Here we are, stuck in the middle of nowhere, with no boat, no hope of rescue, not even a map!' It wasn't often that the elf betrayed much emotion at all.

At this sudden outburst Keanu and Grimcrag sat open-mouthed, fat and saliva dribbling from their chins in equal measure. Jiriki sighed and kicked languidly at the sand before looking up and smiling sadly. 'Oh what's the use, we're stuck here!' Looking stern, the elf continued in an admonishing tone. 'Bear in mind though, Grimcrag, it's no use trying that "I'm your caring father" routine with us any more, you sneaky old miscreant, we've known you far too long for any of that nonsense to work – we're not young Anstein, you know.'

At the mention of Johan, the conversation ground to a halt. Keanu reached a ham-sized fist into the fire and lugged out a huge, crisped slab of meat, sizzling hot and dripping fatty juices onto the sand.

'Johan would like that bit, I'll wager,' Grimcrag grunted, nodding at the hunk of flesh. 'He always did like a nice bit of crackling.'

They paused in unison, the unspoken bond of untold shared adventures and brushes with death uniting the Marauders' thoughts.

A dull thumping and muffled shrieking intruded upon their reverie, and Keanu stood up, rack of monster in hand. He padded lithely across the beach to the spot where their battered rowing boat lay over-turned on the sand. The thudding and shouting quite clearly came from beneath the upturned hull. Keanu reached down and carefully lifted up one side of the boat, peering underneath through the small firelit crack. A pair of wild and staring eyes greeted him, accompanied by animalistic growls and mewlings.

JOHAN'S PANIC WAS rudely interrupted by one edge of his coffin being lifted away. Ruddy light seeped through the crack. A hulking shape awaited, accompanied by the unmistakable smell of charred and burning flesh.

'This is it then, Hell it is for me,' Johan burbled, terrified and mis-erable. At least he wouldn't be stuck in the dark for ever, which perhaps was some small consolation.

'Avake, jung 'un?' The unmistakable voice ripped through Johan's mind, and reality rapidly readjusted itself in his brain.

'Gghhh?' the ex-envoy burbled, wondering how Keanu came to be down in Hell too. Perhaps he had a visitor's day-pass.

'Head betta? Hungry?' Keanu's voice cajoled, but Anstein knew that devils and daemons could be very convincing if they wanted. He backed off to the far side of his coffin, trying to remember suitable holy signs or gestures. Something outside sighed patiently.

'Kom on out, you're Schleepink too long, ja? Nitemares also, by da look of it. All tangled unda da tarpaulin you are.'

The delicious tang of roasting meat reached Johan's nostrils and his grumbling stomach decided the matter in lieu of his concussed mind.

'Keanu?' he whimpered hopefully, 'Is it really you?'

Whatever stood beyond the coffin seemed to pause and ponder the question.

'Ja, 'f Korse, schtupid!' With one mighty heave, the barbarian lifted the boat away from Johan, who lay revealed, blinking in the firelight.

Johan shivered uncontrollably, wrapped in his tarpaulin-shroud, dazed and confused. An all-important question rose to the fore of his battered mind, back as he was, from the dead. Before he could stop them, his cracked and swollen lips had formed the fateful words.

'Can I smell... crackling?'

* * *

THE PATHWAY FROM the beach into the jungle was obviously well trodden, but the Marauders trod it with exceptional care. As they wound onwards through leafy glades, one moment they were drenched in tropical sunlight, the next they were plunged into the greeny darkness of the humid forest canopy.

Jiriki took the lead, gliding with silky footfall along the jungle track. The elf sniffed the air, listening intently at every turn. It was a source of some contention between Keanu the hulking barbarian and Jiriki the elf as to which had the most highly attuned senses. No one would argue that in the natural state, an elf's senses were keener than those of man or dwarf, but the Reaver had long proven himself to be something of an exception. His ability to pinpoint danger was second to none (except maybe Jiriki on a very good day), and he too moved catlike in the jungle, but staying perhaps ten feet from the path itself.

Grimcrag was still rumbling about 'All that sixth senses nonsense!' and snorting derisively to himself. He made no attempt at quietness, clattering along in his trusty armour, the clanks and bangings interspersed with frequent hearty belches. This disregard of any possible danger, to Johan's way of thinking, made something of a nonsense of the others' theatrical movements.

'Let me tell you, young Anstein,' bellowed the dwarf, receiving a recriminating stare from Jiriki and a muffled 'Qviet!' from a nearby bush. 'There's some senses what is 'stremely useful, and others,' the dwarf pointed at Jiriki's frozen form, 'what isn't.' Johan noticed that for all his brevity, the second part of Grimcrag's utterance was little more than a whisper. The dwarf belched, shrugging apologetically. 'Pardon me, lad, sea monster. Always repeats something awful, in my 'sperience.' The dwarf pushed his warhelm back and scratched vigorously at his grizzled scalp. 'Hot, innit?'

Johan nodded, peering cautiously into the gloomy canopy on either side. Everywhere, things were moving; unseen things that flapped, or scrabbled, or crawled, or just made atonal cooing noises in the distance. Sword drawn, the envoy felt decidedly uncomfortable as they made their way down the beaten track. He didn't want to go first, as that way lay almost certain first contact with them, and he didn't want to go last, as that way he was almost certain to be picked off without anyone else noticing. In actual fact, he didn't much like the idea of being on the track at all, as it was such an obvious place to set a trap (even the words trap and track were strangely similar), and the very thought of plunging off into the forest, as Keanu had, filled the young man with queasy unease.

'Anyhow,' Grimcrag carried on, waving his axe vaguely at the vegetation, 'what's the use of being able to creep about in the jungle?' Johan was about to enter a plea on behalf of forest lore, tracking, hunting and so on, but Grimcrag was in full flow. 'No, heightened and truly useful senses relate to real things, things you can touch...' The dwarf's voice tailed off, and Johan had a pretty good idea what he was contemplating, and it wasn't dusky maidens from Araby.

'Such as... gold?' He ventured, prodding Grimcrag from his reverie.

'Well, I s'pose that's as good an example as any,' Grimcrag whispered hoarsely. 'My senses can detect gold – and beer too, for that matter – from a distance of...' The dwarf stopped in his tracks and frowned.

Johan looked puzzled. Surely Grimcrag was not about to be overcome by a fit of honesty regarding his claims? Looking over his shoulder at the dwarf, Johan almost bumped into Jiriki. The elf had stopped dead still, managing to meld almost invisibly into the background. Only his bright red jerkin gave him away, and the best the elf could manage under the circumstances was to vanish to the extent that it looked as though someone had left their shirt out to dry on the bole of a tree. Of Keanu there was no sign.

Over his shoulder, Johan could see Grimcrag standing still as stone, eyes closed, nostrils dilated as he sniffed the leaden air. Sending darting glances all around in search of trouble, all Johan saw was further evidence of paradise. Yellow-white shards of sunlight flashed through the greenery, catching the heavy moisture in the laden air like glittering gemstones. Nearby, unseen, a stream trickled and gurgled seductively. A multi-coloured bird with huge wings sang sweetly as it glided between treetops far overhead. Water trickled off the mound of stark white skulls sitting by the bend in the pathway.

'Skulls?'

'A village!'

'Qviet, dammit!'

'BEER!'

THE SETTLEMENT APPEARED deserted – a collection of thatched mud huts, of curiously familiar design, situated in the middle of a sun-drenched clearing. Ringed by palm trees bearing coconuts as big as Johan's head, the village certainly looked idyllic. The tinkling burble of fresh, flowing water sounded from behind the furthest hut, and the only other sounds came from the jungle.

Stepping around the pile of skulls, which on close inspection seemed to belong to an assortment of creatures of all shapes and sizes, Johan peered at the dwellings laid out before him. Squinting in the harsh sunlight, the tatters of his sweat-soaked shirt sticking uncomfortably to his back, he stood stock still and watched for any sign of movement.

Having wisely discarded his scarlet blouse, Jiriki was a shadow amongst shadows. The last Johan had seen of him the elf had been

somewhere to the left, behind a cluster of wooden, shed-like buildings. That had been at least ten minutes ago. Of Keanu there was no
sign at all.

'Come on then, lad, no point in hanging about when there's beer
to be drunk,' Grimcrag said cheerily. ''Sides, there's obviously no one
at home.' With that, the dwarf strode into the village, his heavy boots
kicking up little dust motes in the clearing. Somewhat more hesitantly, Johan followed in his footsteps.

In the centre of the cluster of huts, a small and overgrown pyramid
thrust uncertainly towards the sky. Overhead, the palm trees which
ringed the clearing sent branches scurrying as if to try and close off the
immodest gap carved in the jungle canopy. Johan approached the structure for a closer look. He was troubled by the red-brown stains which
marked the age-worn stone. Nonetheless, he tugged at the covering of
lianas and vines, a twisted mat of root and leaf which conspired to convince the casual observer that this pyramid was, in fact, simply a strangely
shaped bush or tree. Undeterred, the envoy pressed on, ripping and tugging at the tenacious growth. Johan had spotted something which he
thought be of considerable interest, and wasn't to be put off easily.

So had Grimcrag, pulling aside a hastily thrown-together shield of
palm fronds from alongside of one of the buildings. What he saw
positioned in the cool dark of the side alley made the old dwarf gasp
in surprise.

At that moment, a commotion on the far side of the clearing
announced Jiriki's arrival, as the elf marched a captive lizard-creature
into the clearing.

'Writing on stone!'

'Gentlemen, we have a captive.'

'Beer!'

The three adventurers all exclaimed at the same time. Jiriki's prisoner took advantage of the confusion by trying to scuttle off to the
safety of a pond on the edge of the clearing. The elf hauled it back
quickly with a tug on the rope which he had tied around its stomach.
The creature sank down onto its haunches beside the elf, looking disconsolate. A long tongue shot out to grab a passing fly, but after a
moment the bizarre reptile-man sat still, blinking its big eyes in the
harsh sunlight.

'Not so fast, froggie. Stay where you are!' The elf tied the other end
of the rope around a sturdy post which supported one of the huts,
then turned to the others. 'Now, what did you say?'

'Writing!' Johan shouted, scraping furiously at the pyramid.

'Beer!' Grimcrag exclaimed, gesturing at the unmistakable shape of
a large vat sitting in the cool shadows of the side alley. The dwarf had
found a supply of hollowed coconut shells that obviously served as

mugs, and held one beneath a cork bung on the side of the wooden vat. Removing the bung, the dwarf was showered in a dark brown liquid. A hoppy smell filled the warm and humid air. Filling the shell, he replaced the stopper, grinning happily.

'See, beer!' Grunsonn chuckled, downing the shell full in one capacious gulp. 'Good too, but maybe could have done with standing f'ra bit longer.'

'Never mind that, come and look at this lot!' Johan was beside himself. He had climbed almost to the very top of the pyramid, where a large clump of vines concealed some kind of ornate stonework.

The others walked over, Grimcrag slurping beer. The elf shook a warning finger at the lizard thing, which had crawled into the shade offered by the canopy of a nearby hut.

'Rik!' The creature gave a croaking burp, but made no attempt to untie itself, apparently resigned to its fate.

'Did that thing call you "Rick"?' Grimcrag asked, throwing the empty coconut shell away. The dwarf stood at the base of the pyramid, clenched fists on hips, staring belligerently up at the young man atop the construction. Bits of vine and moss floated down towards the dwarf. 'Wotcha doing, Anstein? This thing doesn't look too safe!'

'Rik! LsssRik!' said the lizard.

'And you can shut up n'all.'

Jiriki was peering intently at the base of the pyramid, where Johan had uncovered a patch of bare stone. Using a silk kerchief, the elf dusted some smaller fragments away from the surface, peered for a moment, then stood back in surprise. A clod of earth hit the elf on the head, but he made no indication of noticing.

'How?' Jiriki began, brows furrowing in surprise and consternation. 'What?'

'See, I told you, and that's just the start!' Johan's voice wavered with excitement.

'LsssRIK! LSSSRIKK!' In the shelter of the hut, the lizard thing was getting quite animated.

'Wot?' Grimcrag called, stomping over to where the elf stood mesmerised. The dwarf peered at the stonework. 'Wot is all the fuss ab–eh?' The dwarf stood as if frozen, a thick and stubby finger repeatedly tracing a carved line in the exposed stonework.

'RIKKRIKKRIKK!! LSSSRIKKK!'

'I... vill... Return...' whispered Grimcrag, reading the words inscribed on the base of the pyramid. A large clump of vines descended upon him, and he looked up, the spell broken. 'Unh?' grunted the dwarf, dropping his axe in surprise.

Jiriki was staring, mouth open, pointing at the top of the structure with a slender finger.

Johan Ansteln, ex-imperial envoy, was kneeling unmoving in front of the statue he had revealed at the very pinnacle of the pyramid.

'I'll be blowed!' declared the dwarf. 'Looks like a statue of one of them Norsey types.' He scratched his head, puzzled, leaving streaks of soil smeared across his brow. 'How'd that get 'ere then?'

Staring down at them from atop the small pyramid was the unmistakable form of a Norseman.

'Actually,' Johan began, 'don't you think it looks a little like–'

A spear thumped into the ground inches from Jiriki's boot, making the elf jump in shocked surprise.

'LSSSRIK! LSSSRIK! LSSSRIK!' This time, the croak was a chorus of many voices.

Very slowly, the Marauders turned round. They were completely surrounded by perhaps a hundred angry and agitated lizard creatures, all wielding spears, bows or blowpipes.

'Poisoned, like as not,' Grimcrag exclaimed, reaching for Old Slaughterer. A cruelly barbed arrow shot into the sand, a mere hair's breadth away from the dwarf's reaching fingers. He hurriedly snatched his hand back, and a glassy grin crept over his face. For the first time in years, Grimcrag Grunsonn faced a multitude of foes without his trusty axe in his hand. In his heart of hearts, Grimcrag knew that this did nothing good for their odds of winning. It also made him horribly embarrassed. Caught short, he flushed bright red.

The lizards advanced, hissing noisily and brandishing their impressively sharp-looking weapons.

'Don't worry, Grimcrag, I won't tell anyone… even if this whole tragic mess is your fault!' Jiriki whispered, nodding at the dwarf's axe.

Their captive lizard nodded knowledgeably and burped almost to itself. 'S'Rikkitiz!'

INEXORABLY THE MARAUDERS were being forced up to the top of the pyramid, where Johan stood swaying in the intense heat of the sun. Grimcrag could see his axe at the base of the pyramid, apparently of little interest to the lizard creatures which ringed the pyramid, gesturing with their spears and bows. Their hissed chanting was all but deafening. The Marauders glanced nervously about them, hoping to spy some way out of their hopeless predicament.

'A pretty pickle you've got us into, lad, and no mistake,' Grunsonn grumbled, sitting down on the top step. 'And us with no weapons 'n'all.'

Johan gasped in indignant surprise. 'What do you mean, Grimcrag? It was you who said the place was deserted. It was you that drank their beer.' The young man pointed at the axe the dwarf clutched. 'And what do you call that thing, a toothpick?'

Grimcrag was clutching his spare axe, Orcflayer, in one scarred paw, but his miserable countenance spoke volumes. 'It's not the same. Just don't feel right. It's all in the runes, y'see.' The dwarf gestured vaguely with the deadly looking axe at the throng of lizards before them. 'If them things kill me while I'm not using Ole Slaughterer, I'll, I'll…' His voice choked, and a tear crept into the old dwarf's eye. Grimcrag cast a shamefaced gaze at his boots. When he spoke again, it was with a small and tremulous voice. 'Well, I'll just never live it down.'

Jiriki slapped the dwarf on the back of his head, knocking his helm down over his eyes. 'Stop being so pathetic, Grunsonn; we've been through worse that this, just.' The elf stood steely-eyed beside young Anstein, an arrow nocked in his fine elven bow.

At that moment, their attention was drawn to a commotion on the edge of the clearing. A huge lizardman, bigger than the others and bedecked in all manner of feathers, bones and other dubious finery, strode towards the pyramid. The creature had almost blue-black skin, and in one scaly clawed hand it wielded a long staff. As the Marauders watched, lightning-blue flames glittered balefully around its tip.

'Uh oh, they've got magic.' Johan manoeuvred himself behind the statue.

A crackling bolt of blue energy surged towards them, but even though it was lying at the base of the pyramid, the potent runes on Old Slaughterer drew and earthed the seething forces emanating from the shaman's staff. After a moment, the lizardman stopped trying to immolate the Marauders and stood nonplussed, its head cocked on one side like a bird. It studied them intently for a minute or so, then squawked something at its fawning retinue. They scuttled off and returned moments later, bearing some heavy-duty nets. The Shaman nodded up at the warriors, and licked its thin lips expectantly.

On top of the pyramid, Grimcrag stood up and set his lips in a stern pout. 'Ain't going in no net. Sharn't. Ain't no fish!' The dwarf looked at Johan and Jiriki, and grinned his familiar grin. 'Dunno what came over me, lads!.' Setting his helm to its correct angle, he whispered quietly to himself. 'Me old dad always said "It's not the axe as makes the dwarf", and 'appen he was right.'

'I hear you, my friend. Now is not the time for carping,' Jiriki agreed. 'Let's do it!'

'Oh heavens, there are hundreds of them, with magic and nets. We're bound to die now, aren't we?' muttered Johan, more in anger than fear. The deathly confidence exuded by Grimcrag and Jiriki was strangely infectious, and the two older Marauders were heartened by the sound of Johan's sword scraping clear from its scabbard.

At the base of the pyramid, twenty feet of very steep steps below them, the lizard things gathered. Looking up, they obviously weren't too keen to climb the steps, nets or no, not into the waiting blades of three belligerent warriors who had such an obvious height advantage over them. They rasped and burped amongst themselves, and a few launched arrows up to skitter and skip on the flagstones of the pyramid.

'Come on then, frog spawn!' Johan shouted. 'Come and get your legs chopped.' He turned to Grimcrag. 'Shame old Grail-mad Pierre isn't here, he loves frogs' legs.'

Grimcrag guffawed. Jiriki smirked.

'LSSSRIKK!' the lizards croaked as one, but they did not advance. The shaman reached the bottom of the pyramid with bounding steps, and squinted up at the warriors. 'Nrsssssssss?' it hissed angrily at them, then rounded on its cowardly compatriots. After a few minutes of frantic hissing and croaking, the black lizard threw off its headdress in apparent disgust, and shook its mottled head resignedly. It shrugged its shoulders and pointed up beyond the pyramid top. The other lizards followed its gaze, and immediately went into a frenzy of excitement, hopping up and down and hissing enthusiastically.

Atop the pyramid, the Marauders watched, transfixed.

'Now what?' Grimcrag grunted.

'They seem excited about something,' Johan muttered, confused.

Jiriki turned to face the way the lizards were looking. 'Sun's going down. They'll wait for the dark.'

The others turned and looked. There was no denying the fact that the sun was sinking fast. Already its ruddy red globe fondly touched the top most branches of the trees, and soon it would drop out of sight completely.

'It sinks so fast in these climes,' began Johan.

'No wonder neither, it puts such an effort in all day. It's prob'ly 'zausted.'

'So what shall we do?' the elf asked.

'Do?' Grimcrag snorted. 'What d'ya think we're going to do?'

'Well,' began Johan, 'I, for one do not intend being butchered in the dark.'

'That's the spirit, young 'un. Let's go get 'em, eh?'

'Yes, well… oh hell, why not!'

Drawing themselves to their full respective heights, the Marauders prepared for battle.

At the base of the pyramid, the lizards realised that something was about to happen, and they began to form formal ranks of shield, spear and bow.

If still undecided in their hearts (and not one of them would ever admit that such was the case) the Marauders atop the pyramid had their minds made up by a familiar heavily-muscled figure who appeared in the dusk light around the path to the village. His voice reached them as a heavily accented bellow.

'Vot you vaitink for – Marauders or Mauses?' The barbarian was already at a run towards the lizards, the glitter of his sword a deadly sliver of malice in the dying rays of the sun.

'CHAAARGE!!!!' roared Grimcrag, leaping down towards the waiting lizard horde. He didn't even turn to see if the others were following. Battle cries to the fore and now to their rear threw the lizards into total panic. Despite the entreaties of their shaman, Anstein saw them turn to flee. Their path was blocked by a charging barbarian. A barbarian who wielded a two handed sword in his right hand and a heavily scarred iron shield on his left arm. A barbarian who howled like a wolf as he charged towards the assembled hordes of reptiledom with no apparent concern for his own safety.

Tumbling down the pyramid towards the lizards' backs, Anstein could see that this was going to get very bloody very fast. They obviously didn't take very well to surprises.

Then something very strange happened.

SEEING THE CHARGING barbarian, the lizards flung their weapons aside, dropped to their knees and buried their heads in the sand.

Grimcrag, Jiriki and Johan came to a halt at the bottom of the pyramid. A carpet of lizard backs stretched away from them.

Grimcrag shrugged and raised his axe. 'Hardly seems fair! Still, never look a gift coin and all that.' he grunted, decapitating three lizards in one blow. Jiriki stopped the slaughter by adroitly tripping the dwarf over. Black blood was splattered everywhere, but the remaining lizards sat motionless.

'Oi!' exclaimed the dwarf, dragging himself to his feet. He made for the security of Old Slaughterer.

'Leave it, Grimcrag,' Johan hissed. 'Something's happening.'

Berserk, Keanu charged onwards, dimly wondering where the enemy had gone and why the floor was all lumpy. He slowed to a loping trot, then a walk, then finally stopped. He could see Jiriki, Grimcrag and Anstein all right, but he could have sworn that there was a whole horde of... Jiriki was gesturing at his boots.

'Vot?' he bellowed, still partly berserk, peering down. He was standing on the chest of a large lizard creature, a black-skinned one bedecked in feathers and bone. He raised his sword to strike.

The lizard's eyes bulged, but it managed to croak loudly. Keanu dropped his sword in surprise; the other Marauders did likewise. They all clearly heard the lizard shaman speak words – understandable words.

'Velkomsss God LosssErikkk. Long haff ve Vaited innit yessssss.'

The living carpet whispered at Keanu with the rustling, hissing squeak of a hundred lizard voices: 'LSSSRIKKK! LSSSSSRIKKK! LSSSS-RIKKK!'

Grimcrag patted Johan on the shoulder. 'I'll be blowed! Maybe this isn't going to be so bad after all!'

SIX MONTHS IN paradise was probably enough for anyone. It was certainly enough for Johan Anstein. Much as he enjoyed lying on a beach being feted as a god by proxy – just knowing Keanu seemed to be enough to get you in the club – Johan knew that there was a whole world out there over the horizon, just waiting for the unique influence of Grunsonn's Marauders.

Still, he had had time to write up their adventures in his journal, the food was good, the natives friendly (except for the odd hostile glare from the extended families of those accidentally killed by Grimcrag and Keanu) and the weather beyond compare. As he curled his toes lazily in the warm sand, Johan pondered on his companions.

Grimcrag, certainly, was unusually happy, what with his beer and the cave full of gold which the dwarf was lovingly transferring to their patched-up and extended rowing boat in his secret cove. Johan sighed contentedly.

Only Jiriki was unhappy with the situation, his wanderlust frustrated by the confines of the small island. The elf had become quite solitary of late, taking to long sojourns along the cliff-tops on the lookout for ships. He had even built some warning beacons out of dead brushwood. He had meticulously timed the tides, how long it took to get a fire going, run to the boat and get out to sea. Johan really couldn't see the point, and hoped that Jiriki would perhaps relax a little when he realised that they truly were in the lap of the gods regarding rescue. They had not had so much as a sniff of a sail since their arrival six months ago.

Still, it was sunny and warm every day of the week… maybe they could stay awhile longer yet. Actually, it wasn't as if they had any real choice in the matter. Jiriki should jolly well wake up and–

His thoughts were interrupted by a familiar rasping voice.

'Ansssstein, 'vake?' The voice was that of Froggo, Johan's adopted lizard man. The young creature – apparently they called themselves 'skinkz' in their native tongue – followed Anstein everywhere, eager to learn as much as it could of the big, wide world beyond its island home.

'Yes, Froggo, me lad, I'm awake. Just musing.' Johan turned to look at the skink, which as usual sat a respectful distance away from its adopted mentor. On matters of gender, when pressed, the creatures had been ambiguous to say the least, and Johan was none too sure if

Froggo was in fact a boy or a girl, or even whether they made such distinctions. Johan had pigeon-holed Froggo (he had quickly realised that he had no way in this world of being able to pronounce the creature's real name, which sounded like a cistern being flushed) as being a boy, for neatness' sake more than anything else.

'Musink?' the skink enquired, blinking its toad-like eyes and scratching a leathery patch of skin under its long chin. 'Vot meaninksss?'

'Another word for thinking, sort of... You know, your accent is terrible, Froggo; abominable, in fact!' Johan turned over and lazily threw a small stick at the reptile, which dodged nimbly out of the way. In return, it cheekily threw a small pebble which hit Johan square on the forehead.

'But better zan yoursss in my ssspeaks yessssss?' the lizard creature quipped, making the loud hissing noise in the back of its throat that Johan had learned passed for laughter in skink.

Johan jumped to his feet and chased the small scampering creature back to the village. It was nearly time for lunch.

Behind them, on the furthest visible reach of the ocean, the small black speck of a sail hove into view over the horizon. On a nearby cliff-top, a thin plume of black smoke clawed its way upwards into the heavy air.

IN HIS CAVE, Grimcrag worked tirelessly, piling yet more gold artefacts into the boat and tying them securely down. As he worked, he endlessly muttered to himself under his breath: 'Can't last, got to be a catch. Can't last, got to be a catch.'

The dwarf's arms and armour were stacked neatly to one side of the cave, glittering from the sparkling reflections cast by the clear water. The mouth of the cave was perhaps a hundred feet distant, a patch of white heat against the shadowy black of the cave. The slap-slap of water kept a constant rhythm by which the dwarf worked, stacking the gold items one at a time in a strange looking boat which was moored beside a natural stone jetty.

The boat was an odd mongrel contraption, new wood gleaming against older, more battered timbers. Its prow bore a proud dragon head, and there was provision for a small mast. Four old and rusted shields lined each side of the vessel, one to protect each of the oars which dipped into the cool waters of the cave. A bigger, steering oar was mounted at the higher stern, and the boat looked to be just what it was – a mix between the wreck of their rowing boat and a much older Norse longboat.

The soft pattering of booted feet disturbed the dwarf, and he instinctively reached for his trusty axe. A moment later and Jiriki's sun-tanned face peered into the cave. The elf had taken the most naturally to the tropical climate, and now looked healthier than the dwarf had ever seen him. 'Grimcrag?' he called, and from his tone, the dwarf knew that something was of grave concern. He stepped from the shadows.

'Here, Jiriki – what's up, old friend?'

The elf strode into the cave, grinning at the boat despite himself. He pointed at Grimcrag's construction and tapped a foot impatiently. 'Will that thing really float out of there?' The elf nodded towards the cave mouth. 'Weighed down by so much gold?'

Grimcrag spat on the floor, disgusted by the temerity of such a question. 'Course it will! What do you take me for?' The dwarf stomped up to the elf and prodded him with a stubby callused finger. 'While you lot've bin living it up with yer froggy friends,' Grimcrag's arm swept around the cave as evidence of his industry, 'some of us 'ave bin working blimming hard!'

The elf clapped Grimcrag on the shoulder and smiled. 'Splendid, my industrious friend, splendid. You know that, of all of us, I am least happy with our predicament, and now, we may have... an opportunity.' Jiriki headed back to the rear entrance to the cave, before turning once more to face the bemused dwarf. 'Come on, Grimcrag. We'll be using that boat of yours sooner than you'd imagine, I'll wager!'

'What do you mean?' Grimcrag began. 'I'm not using it for fishing, nor joyrides neither – look what happened last time...'

Jiriki winked conspiratorially as he stepped out into the daylight. His lilting voice drifted back into the cave. 'Come on, Grimcrag, grab your axe too – the tide's rising, the beacon's lit. By my estimation we have no more than an hour!'

'It's the sun, isn't it?' The dwarf frowned as he grabbed his axe. 'That, and all the time you've spent moping around those cliff-tops.'

But Jiriki was off and running. His last words, echoing around the cavern, persuaded the old dwarf that something important was happening: 'I've spied a sail. We have company!'

KEANU SAT ON his bamboo throne, two skinks fanning him with the feathers of some particularly large and gaudily-plumaged bird. Swathed in garlands of exotic flowers, the barbarian drank warm beer from his helmet; his feet rested in a bowl of cool water, which was replenished regularly by more scurrying minions. He faced out onto the village square, where the now spotlessly clean pyramid reared up into the sky.

On top of the pyramid, Keanu's likeness, or something approaching it, stared back at the barbarian. If he squinted hard, the entire village had a distinctly Norse look. Keanu sighed contentedly. If only it were nice and cold.

The Reaver burped loudly. 'Fang, da Legend vunce more, f'ya pleez.' Keanu gestured languidly at the black-skinned shaman, who stood in his ceremonial place beside the throne. He had named all the skinks in his 'hearth-guard' after his wolf hounds back home in Norsca.

Keanu fondly thought of the band of heavily-armed reptilian warriors as his very own Berserkers, although none of them had, as yet, betrayed any leanings towards going berserk at all. 'Not got the temperament fer it,' Grimcrag had explained at the last banquet, whilst Jiriki maintained that it was something to do with their blood being cold, or some such typical elf nonsense.

On a cue from Fang the shaman, a bigger lizard creature, stripped down to a loincloth, banged heartily on a brass gong strung up on sturdy wooden poles beside the throne.

Within minutes, the clearing was alive with skinks, all jostling for places from where they could hear the story again. Being a Norse barbarian himself, Keanu appreciated good tales. In his consideration, like a good wine, they improved with age. Not that any wine which came Keanu's way got the chance to enjoy its autumn years, but the principle was, he felt, a sound one.

After a while, the hubbub in the small square died down. Fang cleared his throat to speak the story on which the skink island civilisation was founded. With an imperious wave of his massive arms, Keanu bade Fang be silent. Standing, the barbarian addressed the assembled throng. Agog, they listened intently.

'Today,' Keanu began, his eyes sweeping the appreciative crowd, 'today I'm tellink da Saga, ja?'

'Ya, yesssss, ya!' the lizards chorused, rocking backwards and forward in delight. Fang smiled benignly and nodded his crested head.

'I'm keepink 'im short, koz nearly Dinna time,' the barbarian continued, striding to the front of the crowd. Already, a bunch of skinks stood ready to perform the odd ritualistic actions which always accompanied the story.

Keanu grinned: what a stupid bunch of lizards. He'd heard the story enough times that he knew it off by heart, almost felt it was of his doing. He'd give them a story to remember. He began, his voice echoing loud and strong across the clearing.

'Und so beginz da Saga of da Voyage of Erik da Lost, Great God Warrior of Norsca, und how he brought Kulture und Beer to Paradise.'

The miming lizards were ahead of Keanu already, making rowing actions as they envisaged the ship of Eric the Lost ploughing across the mighty oceans to this small island. Looking around, Keanu could see that the majority of the lizards had their eyes closed, broad grins of contentment splitting their leathery faces.

And so, at least for a few minutes, Keanu escaped from the real world of reaving and death, as he told the age-old story of Eric, great warrior king, and his voyage across the sea. He told of mighty storms and huge sea monsters (several mimers became carried away and bit each other at this point), of treacherous rocks and wicked pirates. He told of strange lands populated by strange creatures, of mighty heroes and deeds of wonder. And he told of how, after many years of travelling, Eric arrived at this fair land, which he took to be the fabled land of Lustria, and named it Ericland.

Keanu looked around the band of skinks and almost laughed aloud. He still couldn't really believe the next part of the story himself, although there was proof enough for anyone. The skinks doing the actions were confused by Keanu's expression: normally the story didn't stop here, and they were repeatedly miming planting a flag in the earth. Keanu hastily drew a breath and continued.

Eric and his wise heroes had stormed the island, killing all of the great lizard monsters who had once lived here. (Fang had showed Keanu the cave full of bones, and the barbarian had been truly impressed – Eric had certainly known how to fight judging by the size of some of the skeletons.) He liberated the skinks to true civilisation: true speech, freedom… and beer.

The next part of the story almost stuck in the barbarian's throat, such was the enormity of the lie. Now he told of how Eric and his noble followers had revealed the true horror of that evil and glittering substance known as 'Golt', and how those brave and selfless Norsemen had liberated the skinks from the horrid material of which they had so much, and hidden it in a far distant cave, never to trouble their idyllic lives again.

And finally, Keanu told of how the day dawned when Eric and his band of warriors had proven the true depths of their selfless love, by setting sail away from the island in their ship full of the hated gold, simply to get rid of it once and for all. Several of the skinks were weeping great salty tears at this part of the story, and not for the first time, Keanu marvelled at their gullible nature.

'Ja, but too much Golt was there for vun Schip, so as he vent avay, Eric was makink da Promise, ja?' Keanu shouted the words at the throng. They were all staring, a hundred pairs of unblinking eyes fixed on his face, hanging on every syllable. 'Und vot was dat Promise?' Keanu implored, secretly pleased with his performance.

As one voice, the skinks shrieked the words which ended the story every time it was told. Their voices echoed around the jungle, and several flocks of multi coloured birds took flight in terror. 'I VILL BE BACK FOR DA GOLD – SSSO DON'T TOUCH, JA?'

Exhausted, the assembly fell silent, and Keanu fell back onto his throne, gesturing for beer. The crowd abruptly erupted into applause, as they hooted and hissed and slapped their tails on the ground.

Fang smiled. His prophecies over the years had been borne out. He was the true priest of Erikkk. Everyone now knew that Eric had kept his promise, even if his warriors had changed a bit over the years. Especially the short, grubby, bearded one.

At that moment, the spell was broken as Johan, Froggo, Jiriki and Grimcrag rushed into the village square, panting and out of breath.

'Kean– Eric!' Johan shouted. 'We've got to go!'

'Vot? Going vere?'

'Forty-five minutes now!' Jiriki added.

The skinks were somewhat agitated, for they were not used to such an abrupt ending. Usually, when Fang was telling it, they got a good hour's sun bathing after such an energetic story, or at last half an hour in the cool water of the pond.

Jiriki ran over to the bemused barbarian, and whispered in his ear. The effect was electrifying. Like a scalded cat, Keanu was on his feet, weapons grabbed and running across the clearing in one fluid motion. The throng of skinks blinked and hissed uncertainly. Fang frowned, unsure as to what his lord was doing.

Jiriki ran after Keanu, shoving him in the back to keep him moving. Grimcrag and the others had already vanished down the path to the cave, the dwarf showing a surprising turn of speed.

Shaking himself free of the elf's grasp, Keanu glared at Jiriki and turned to face his villagers. 'Not Vurryink,' he hissed at Jiriki, before turning and bellowing at the hundred or so lizards. 'Now is da Time!' he began, raising his sword to the air. 'My Berserkers – Volf pack, Bear soldiers, Schnow Leopards, now is your Time to fight!'

The most inappropriately named groups of skinks scuttled off to collect weapons, growling and snapping at each other. A nimbus of blue fire already played around the tip of Fang's ceremonial staff.

'What are you doing?' Jiriki snapped, dancing agitatedly from foot to foot. 'We don't have time for this.' Keanu pushed the elf away and faced the skinks again.

'Now ve must be goink!' Keanu stabbed himself in the chest with his forefinger. 'Me, Erik, und my Varriors!' He grinned, showing sharp white teeth. The lizards were starting to look crestfallen. 'But not to be Vorryink! No! Ve take all da nasti Golt vith us to da land beyont da sea!'

At this, the skinks looked mightily relieved, and his 'Berserkers' started to look worried that there might be nothing to fight about after all. Keanu put them right, as he backed slowly away from them down the trail.

'A ship full of evil men is Komink, friends of, er, da big dead Lizart Monsters,' the barbarian improvised magnificently. 'Ya! S'right! Lizart friends komink to take you away! You stop them, ja? Stop them, my friend Fank! Lead skinkz to victor, ja?'

At this, Jiriki and Keanu turned tail and fled along the jungle path, heading to the boat and hopefully a slim chance at escape. Behind them, they heard growing chanting and shouting as the skinks prepared to fight for their island.

'You certainly got them going,' Jiriki gasped as they plunged down the muddy trail, vines whipping their faces as they ran.

'I'm makink da Divershun – they'll have to get everyvun ashore from da ship for da fight!' Keanu answered. 'Vot's da Hurri?'

'Diversion? Excellent plan!' Jiriki abruptly darted down a side trail. 'This way, Keanu. Tide's rising fast and we still have to get the boat out of the cave!'

A few minutes later and they burst onto the stony path which led to the cave. Hearts pounding, they had covered the distance to the mooring harbour in a scant five minutes. Ahead, Jiriki could see Johan dashing into the entry tunnel, and he knew it was a fair bet that Grimcrag was there already. Despite his bulk and shape, the dwarf could put on a ferocious burst of speed when need be. Particularly if time was of the essence, and the reward might be escape to freedom with a vast fortune in pure gold.

They plunged into the darkness of the cave, and headed for the heavily loaded boat. If Jiriki was right, and if they were very lucky, six months of not too arduous captivity were shortly about to end.

'AVAST THAT BILGE, mister mate. Bring the mains'l forr'ard and mainbrace the spinnaker!' Looking through the fine bronze telescope with his one good eye, Hook Black Pugh could see the plume of smoke rising from the island. As he studied the idyllic looking landscape, he shouted his orders over his braid-encrusted shoulder. As usual, old Yin-Tuan, first mate and veteran of a hundred such voyages, sighed resignedly and did nothing of the sort. Instead, the hulking first mate gave out a string of clipped, near-intelligible orders to the cut-throats who leaned eagerly over the port bulwark. As if already stung by the barbed whip hanging at Yin-Tuan's belt, the pirates brought the vessel around with a speed and efficiency which belied their ragged looks.

Pugh turned to his second officer, 'Teachy' Bligh, and sighed loudly. 'Aaargh, Bligh me lad, as fine an island fer a-plunderin as I ever did see!'

Bligh, hailing from Sartosa, was a nasty piece of work, all muscle and psychopathic intent. A grim smile split his normally emotionless face, and a familiar glitter came to his black eyes. 'Only island we've seen this past six month, sir. Lads need a bit of pillagin'.' He half-pulled his cutlass from its orcskin scabbard and looked around as if intending to pillage something right here, right now.

Pugh grabbed Bligh's hand and tutted. 'Now, now, Teachy boy, there baint none o'them Cathay slaves left to a-play with, you've bin and pillaged 'em all.' The pirate captain held his hook under Pugh's nose. The spike glittered menacingly in the sunlight. 'Yer don't want to go a-makin' me cross again, does yer?' Hook Black made a thrusting, twisting action with the hook. 'Or it might be spiky time fer you again!'

Bligh blanched visibly and clenched his legs tightly together. With a disconsolate grunt, he pushed his cutlass back into its scabbard. 'Okay boss, okay. I din't mean nowt. S'just...' Bligh's voice died away and a cunning animal gleam came into his black, dead eyes. 'The lads needs a good pillage, is all – they say it's bad luck as kept us away from land or plunder for the past six month, bad luck of that there Bretonnian gold we stole!'

Bligh stepped back, ready to make a run for it. After a moment's silence, however, his captain began rocking to and fro, giggling to himself merrily. The braid on his salt-stained jacket swayed with his rocking, and the faded medals on his once-red sash jangled in the sunshine. Throwing his black bearded head backwards, the pirate captain gave out a huge bellow of laugher.

'Curse o'the Grunsonns, is it?' he guffawed.

'Yer, that's right!' Bligh affirmed, looking around the rest of the crew for moral support. None was to be had: they all seemed to be busy swabbing decks or preparing cannons. A good few of them had climbed the rigging of the mainmast and were studiously making long needed repairs to the tattered expanse of a hundred bits of ancient stitched canvas that passed for the sail on the Dirty Dog.

Pugh's laughter abruptly stopped, and he stomped his iron tipped peg leg hard on the wooden planking of his bridge. When next he spoke, it was with the deathly calm he usually reserved for the last words his victim was destined to hear. He pointed his hook down at Bligh, who grinned nervously and held up his hands in something approaching an attitude of apology.

'Lissen, Mister Bligh, and lissen good!' Hook Black Pugh pulled his shabby tricorn down over his forehead, and glowered the length of the ship. 'And that goes double fer you lot of scurvy blaggards. Even you, Mr Yin-Tin-Tong or whatever y'name is!' He swept the fearful crew with his steely eye. 'You might be better sailors than I'll ever be...'

The pirates all exchanged confused looks at this frank admission, most unlike their hated captain.

'But!' Pugh turned back to face his crew, and there was fire in his voice. "Tis my ship! My letter of marque from our Tilean Lords–' at this, all the pirates, including Pugh, made elaborate mock bows to one another, '–and my leadership what's got us an 'old full o'gold to take 'ome.'

Pugh paused to let the truth sink in. 'And now, me hearties, we have discovered a new island for our gracious lords.' (More mock bowing.) Pugh shook his right hand at the island, fast hoving into full view, his filthy lace cuffs dropping crumbs of bread and other detritus onto the floor.

'So break out the rum, me lads, and make it a double, fer today we makes our fortunes from our proud and noble patrons!' This time the pirates' bows were most sincere. Pugh held a finger to his lips as the cheers began to swell. 'ain't finished yet.'

He turned and pointed once more at the island. 'We'll call it Pughland, and it'll be a most profitable watering 'ole and stop off point for the fleets of Tilea, Bretonnia, Estalia, maybe even the Empire toffs.' He closed his eyes and a blissful smile split his raggedly bearded chin. 'Oh yes, me lads, and a bounty we will collect from each and every one. So no more bloody yellow talk of bad luck! That dwarf is dead and gone this six month back!'

The ship erupted into cheers and whoops as the avaricious gang envisioned the glories and riches to come. Bligh smiled menacingly and wondered how he could get rid of Pugh for good.

At that moment, the foppish voice of keen-eye Dando in the crow's nest rang out: 'War canoes, loads of 'em... and they're full o'bloomin' frogs!'

As one, the pirates rushed to the side of the ship and peered towards the island. Sure enough, a score or more slender canoes were heading straight for them. As Pugh focused on the lead vessel, he could make out a dozen or so fiercely betoothed lizards working hard at the paddles. Standing in the prow of the boat was a mean looking black-skinned lizard, wielding a large staff, about which a nimbus of light flickered ominously.

Hook Black Pugh snapped his telescope closed and turned to face his crew. He grinned maliciously. 'Tides a'risin' fast! Yin-Tin, turn her about. Grog-boy, open the gun ports. Teachy, get ready fer boardin'. Looks like we got us a fight!'

Like a well oiled machine, the pirates went straight to battle stations, the Dirty Dog heeling around so that her port guns faced the oncoming canoes. In short order, the barrels were run out of the gun ports, ten lethal iron-cast eyes staring grimly out at the frail craft of the lizardmen.

Pugh raised his scimitar, sunlight glinting off the oiled blade. On the foredeck, Yin-Tuan frowned and gestured with a brawny arm.

'Cap'n–'

'Not now, Yin-Tin!'

'But the elevation–'

'FIRE!' Pugh's blade swept down, and the world erupted in a roaring cloud of smoke and fire, as ten cannon balls hurtled towards the hapless lizardmen. Already several canoes were turning about to head back towards the relative safety of the cove.

They need not have worried. As the wily Yin-Tuan had realised, the small canoes were already inside the arc of fire of the great cannons, and their deadly cargo crashed over the heads of the desperately paddling skinks to turn the sea beyond into a welter of threshing foam.

'Fire lower, you idiots!' Pugh screamed, but the great cannons were already at their lowest elevation.

'Cap'n, no need to waste any more shot – the toads is runnin' away!' Yin-Tuan grinned toothlessly, his scrawny arm gesticulating excitedly over the side of the ship.

Pugh spun around, telescope raised to his eye. 'Aaargh, it be so!' The captain continued staring down the tube, scratching his beard with his hook. 'And they be putting a fair old distance between us and them 'n'all... are we a-driftin' with the tide, Mr Mate?'

With a timeworn sigh, Yin-Tuan gently prised his captain's fingers from the telescope and turned the brass tube around. Pugh visibly started, and his hat fell off, revealing a balding pate surrounded by a scraggy mop of stringy black hair.

'Aaargh! We can catch the scurvy frogs!' Pugh folded the telescope and secreted it in the voluminous folds of his jacket. Grabbing hold of a bell rope, he gestured with his hook over the port side of the galleon. As the action stations bell rang loud and clear over the still waters of the lagoon, Pugh squinted at the receding canoes. The manic glint which normally preceded grand slaughter was in the pirate's eye, and his thin lips were wet with spittle. 'Aaargh, me brave lads! Lower the boats, drop anchor, boarding all crew, women and children first, take no prisoners!' His cut-throat crew made for the boats, carrying marlin spikes, muskets and cutlasses.

Pugh shoved with a spur-booted foot to encourage any laggards to embark in the boats. 'Last one ashore is the lily-livered son of a toothless bar-crone from Marienburg!'

'So you'll be last aboard then, sir – shall I save you a seat?'

'Less of that, me lad or you'll feel the business end of me 'ook!'

'Err, are we all going?' Yin-Tuan frowned.

'Aaargh! That be so – not fair to deny some of me fine crew the pillagin' they deserve!' Pugh grinned, showing surprisingly white teeth.

'But all of–'

'Don't be so wet, Yin-Tong, it's not like the Bretonnian navy is about to show up, is it?' Pugh made a great show of scanning the horizon with his telescope. 'We ain't seen another sail for months!'

'But—'

'Get in that there boat NOW!'

Moments later and the long rowing boats splashed down into the warm, clear waters. Moments after that, some fifty cut-throats were rowing hard for the beach amidst much shouting and jeering. In the lead boat, Pugh could see that the lizard things had already disembarked, and the last few were disappearing into the jungle, leaving their canoes on the beach.

'Lily-livered sons of frogs!' he shouted 'We'll be eating thee afore sundown!' Turning to face his crew, he grinned maliciously at Belly Fat Dave, the ship's cook, his tongue licking his lips in eager anticipation. 'I hope you've got that there Tilean mustard you're so keen on, Mr Cook. I foretell a grand feast in a few hours' time!'

The fat and sweating cook was already sharpening several deadly-looking cleavers on a whetstone he always carried with him. 'Cap'n, theys going to taste bootiful!'

The pirates' boats surged towards the prey, like hunting dogs hot on the scent of a wounded beast. In Pugh's estimation, the isle was not so large, and once the lizards' canoes were burnt, the things would have nowhere to go, except into the pirates' waiting cooking pot.

'Faster, me lads, faster – I'll warrant there's gold an' jewels fer the pickin' too!' As one voice, Hook Black Pugh's scurvy crew cheered lustily and pulled harder on the oars. A few moments later, the prow of the lead boat ground against the soft sand of the beach, and a dozen hard-bitten pirates leapt eagerly ashore. They were confident that their great captain was going to deliver booty, treasure and grog in abundance to the dark holds of the Dirty Dog. He always did.

One way or another.

'AnSSstein, sssssstop!' A sibilant hissing filled the cave as the Marauders rushed into the welcoming darkness, Johan in front and just a little out of breath. He almost ran into a spear in the darkness, and they skidded to an abrupt halt, scant twenty paces from their boat.

'Go easy!' Grimcrag grunted, nearly tripping over his axe. 'Is that our friendly reptile?'

'Froggo?' Johan asked, confused by the flinty point which dug sharply at his chest. 'What's all this about?'

As his eyes grew accustomed the dark, Johan could make out perhaps a dozen shadowy figures, dappled reflections flickering on the wall in the dim light from the cave mouth. Lizardmen, hand-picked 'Berserkers' by the look of it – wielding spears and other dangerous-looking weapons. This felt an odd time for a goodbye committee, and the lizards' general demeanour suggested agitation.

'Maybe quarter of an hour left, Anstein. Look at the water level: the cave mouth will soon be impassable!' Jiriki's silky voice was edged with impatience, sounding like it was emerging despite clenched jaw and grated teeth. 'I – will – not – miss – this – chance!' The threat in the elf's voice was clear.

'Well, Froggo?' Johan demanded, trying to size up the situation. Glancing ahead, he could see that the rising tide had indeed already ensured that it would be a tight fit getting their outlandish boat out of the cave; in a few minutes the task would be impossible. He knew that they had very little time if they wanted their plan to work, otherwise they would be stuck on the island in the middle of a war between pirates and lizards, with no means of escape. The clock was ticking, and Johan knew that the last thing they could afford now was an unexpected run in with their lizard 'subjects' over some misinformed breach of tribal etiquette. Johan could see that the other Marauders had already made their decisions, and were imperceptibly moving into full combat readiness. More hissing and angry spear-gesturing, however, stopped them in their tracks.

From the shadows, Froggo stepped forward, with what passed for a sinister grin on his reptilian features. 'Ansstein, you teach too well. I lissssten yessss, lissssten welll…' The creature bared sharp teeth and brought up its spear to point accusingly at the Marauders.

'What's it mean, Johan?' Grimcrag demanded gruffly. 'We haven't time for this…'

'SSSSHUTTUP!!' one of the Berserkers barked at the dwarf, whose stubby fingers were already twisting restlessly at the haft of his axe.

Froggo upended his spear and prodded Johan hard in the chest with the haft. 'Not godsssss no!' He prodded again for emphasis and Johan stepped back a pace. 'Not freindssss no! Not LossRikk no!'

A faint ripple of 'Losssrikklosssrikk' echoed around the cave. Froggo nodded and continued.

'Robbersss yes! Liarssss yes! Thieves yesssss!' the lizard man hissed, pointing at the boat. 'Gold! Richessss in ressst of world!'

Johan rubbed his chest and sighed. 'Look Froggo, you really don't understand–'

'Yessssss, do underssssstand!' the creature interrupted, tongue flicking rapidly in and out. 'Undersssstand too well!' Froggo took a step forwards and gestured towards the Marauders. His fellows shuffled forwards after their leader, not looking too sure of themselves but taking comfort in their superior numbers. Spears and dart guns were levelled at the Marauders, and a dozen pairs of reptilian eyes stared with unblinking ferocity.

The tide rose implacably in the watery cave. The atmosphere of urgency was almost tangible in the cool damp air.

Johan instinctively knew that this could get very nasty, very fast. Even under the situation, he briefly marvelled to himself that a few months ago he wouldn't have known anything instinctively at all, except perhaps how to serve wine to a visiting burgomeister or Tilean ambassador. Danger is a marvellous teacher, and Johan had recently been undergoing some very practical remedial tuition at one of the most infamous cramming schools around.

'Now, Froggo,' he began, backing leisurely in the direction of what looked to be a fairly safe alcove in the cave wall, arms raised in supplication. 'Don't do anything rash…'

'Noo, Anssssstein, this isss the time of Firssst Lord Froggo!' The lizard expanded its throat sac and croaked emphatically. If lizards are capable of a mad glint in their eyes, Johan rather fancied that he could see one right at this moment. 'King Frogggo!' the skink croaked, raising its spear above its head as the others nodded and bobbed enthusiastically.

'Eh?' Grimcrag muttered, axe half-raised.

'Vot?' scowled Keanu, his sword somehow mysteriously out of its scabbard.

Jiriki seemed to have vanished completely, to the surprise of the lizards. Maybe the cold of the cave was getting to them, but compared to the lithe movements of the Marauders, they seemed to be distinctly slow. Then again, Grunsonn's Marauders in action did seem to have the ability to make time run like treacle. Whatever, there were a dozen of the enemy, so Johan decided to take no chances and quietly slid behind the rocks in his alcove.

'Yesss! You go! Now! Leave disss boat! Go and fight piiiratessss!'

Froggo seemed to be getting quite agitated, and Grimcrag seemed to be getting the drift of what the skink was suggesting.

'You what?' the dwarf grunted, a dangerous edge creeping into his voice. Clearly Froggo wasn't listening too carefully.

'Leave now and live, meeesssssta Grimcrag,' he hissed, and his retinue prodded angry spears towards the dwarf's rock solid and disconcertingly squat frame. 'You go! We takessss da gold and ssship, and ssssail away yesss!'

The lizards hissed and burped appreciatively, clearly pleased at the prospect of sailing the high seas in their new found ship full of gold.

'What?' Grimcrag bellowed. 'Did I hear you right? Did you say "take the gold"?'

Blinded by his recently acquired confidence, Froggo nodded and licked his lips. 'Yesss!'

A moment's silence descended upon the cave, broken only by an urgent elf voice whispering, 'Do them, do them now!'

The skinks shuffled in the sand. Grimcrag looked like he might be about to explode. Johan peered at the scene through his fingers, almost daring not to look. Beyond the gaggle of lizardmen, the cave mouth looked awfully small. Water was lapping over the top of the jetty, and Johan doubted whether the bow or stern of the boat would clear the entrance already.

'We're going to be too late,' he mumbled to himself, aghast, 'and it's all my fault!'

In the event, Froggo decided the matter. The lizard hissed at Grimcrag and pointed to the tunnel at the back of the cave. 'You are not ssso tough! Take your beard and go!'

'Right, that's enough of that! That's enough of that! That's fighting talk and I'm your dwarf!'

The cave abruptly exploded into violent and bloody action, largely composed of a swinging axe, a lunging sword, a flurry of deadly arrows and a dozen screaming lizard men.

Johan closed his eyes tightly, and covered his ears too, just for good measure. This of course meant that he completely missed the arrival of another twenty or so hand-picked and heavily armed lizardmen via the back tunnel to the cave.

'GO EASY, LADS, they'll be around here somewhere.' The pirates edged through the jungle, following the path from the beach. So far they had quickly despatched the few lizard creatures who they had caught. They hadn't had it all their own way, though, three of their number falling to poisoned darts, and one being dragged into the jungle by something big which roared and hissed as it carried the screaming man away into the undergrowth. Four dead pirates for a half dozen dead lizards seemed poor trade to Pugh's boys, used as they were to attacking ships carrying nothing more hostile than a few easily-bribed guards and a hold full of shackled slaves. They were getting nervous. They knew the island wasn't very big, yet they had been marching for what seemed like hours. And they had left their ship completely deserted in their bravado and eagerness to kill.

Pugh recognised the restlessness amongst his men, and knew that he had to think of something fast. He knew that his lads weren't above following his own past example of slitting the captain's throat and making a quick getaway, no doubt led by a new leader rapidly self-promoted from the ranks. Pugh licked his lips and fidgeted with his hook, beady eyes scouring the jungle for signs of life. The path was well trodden, that was sure enough, but whether it actually went anywhere...

'Cap'n, here!' Yin-Tuan's excited voice broke the oppressive silence. Pugh spat on the sand and smiled, wiping a grimy cuff across his sweaty brow. He hurried up to where the first mate and 'Teachy' Bligh stood at a bend in the path with swords drawn and wolfish grins. A small stream could be heard running over rocks somewhere close by, and a pile of skulls indicated some kind of warning. The pirates ignored it, staring ahead around the bend.

'Aaargh!' exclaimed Pugh, beaming roundly and slapping his first mate on the back. Yin-Tuan coughed and swallowed a chunk of chewing tobacco, grimacing at the vile taste. 'Aaargh! Didn't I say as how we would catch em?'

Yin-Tuan and Bligh nodded, raising cruel swords as their captain gestured for the rest of the pirates to catch up. Soon a gaggle of cruel-eyed thieves and cut-throats peered around the corner, grinning and chuckling at the sight of the lizard man village laid out undefended before them. The pyramid in the centre of the village did not attract a second glance as the pirates spread out to begin the looting.

'Lets burn it to the ground, boys!' shouted Pugh. 'That'll bring the newts a-runnin', I'll warrant!'

Within a few minutes the first huts were burning, black smoke rising straight into the still dead air, no wind to disperse or blow it away. A few minutes later, the pirates discovered the beer vat, to evil cheers of great delight.

Amidst the carnage, Pugh stood on the bottom step of the pyramid with Yin-Tuan and Bligh. 'Very good, me lads, this'll do nicely! Reckon they'll be back any minute now, eh?'

Bligh just grinned wickedly and held up a razor-sharp cutlass until its silver blade glinted in the sunlight, reflecting the warm blue of the sea behind them through a break in the jungle canopy. Something caught his eye, and he suddenly looked away, across the clearing. 'What the–' he began, well-honed murderous instincts immediately to the fore, but his fears were quashed as a multi-coloured bird broke cover with a raucous atonal squawk which belied its beautiful red plumage. It fluttered and flapped clumsily to another tree, where it perched nervously on a topmost branch, obviously readying itself for more prolonged flight.

'Losing yer nerve, Mr Bligh?' Pugh enquired, and all the pirates in earshot laughed appreciatively. Pugh secretly thought that perhaps Mr Bligh was getting a little too big for his stolen gentry boots, and it wouldn't hurt if they were one less officer when they rejoined the ship. He grinned condescendingly at his second officer, who scowled back at him. Hook Black Pugh was happy. Things looked to be turning out just right after all.

JOHAN DUCKED DOWN, both so that his head would not scrape against the roof, and also to avoid the slashing blade of the sword wielded by a lizard who was frothing at the mouth with uncontrolled rage. Keanu had taught the skinks only too well 'Da Vay off da Berzerka'. The boat rocked alarmingly, and Johan grabbed at the bulwark to stop himself going overboard into the cold water.

The hissing groans of dead and dying lizards reverberated chillingly around the cave as the Marauders desperately tried to cast off. Blow-darts, spears and arrows hissed through the air all around them, and several struck the boat with dull thunks as they splintered the wood.

Grimcrag held the stern, his axe carving a glittering figure of eight in the damp air, an arc which no lizard man had so far stepped into and survived. Jiriki was at the dragon prow, shooting with deadly precision into the mass of reptiles which heaved around the small dock where the boat's stern was still tethered. Every so often, the elf turned and squinted at the diminishing arch of light which was the cave mouth.

'Cast off, for pity's sake, Keanu, cast off now!' Jiriki screamed, loosing another arrow into the throng. 'I have few arrows left, and we have no time at all!'

In the stern, ducking to avoid spears and darts, Keanu fumbled with the knot with which Grimcrag had secured the boat. 'Left unta Right und through… nyet, dammit! Right ova Left und bak… Nyet!'

Glancing down from his position at the stern, Grimcrag sighed as he saw the mess Keanu was making. 'For heavens sake, meathead, it's a simple bendshank!' The dwarf tried swinging his axe one-handed and leaning back to undo the rope, but his gnarled and stubby fingers could not quite reach. As the dwarf looked away, momentarily distracted, the skinks took their chances and swarmed towards the stern. Three were instantly decapitated, the glowing runes on Old Slaughterer hissing and flashing as the awful blade did its bloody work. The blade snagged on bone deep in the fourth lizardman's body, and Grimcrag almost toppled over as his momentum was abruptly stopped. Blood boiled from the lizardman's mouth as it collapsed on the killing blade.

'Bugger!'

'Kill them yessssss!' the lizards screamed as they swarmed up the side of the boat. There were so many of them now that they threatened to overturn the small craft, overloaded as it was with carefully boxed-up gold and jewels.

Grimcrag tried desperately to fend them off from his kneeling position in the bilges, as Keanu redoubled his efforts with the knots. The fight was now too close in for arrow work, and Jiriki's blade was a cold streak in the dappled light.

'By all the gods let's go!'

'Unnh! These floorboards ain't well made, them's all splinters. Not so quick, frogface!'

'Left unda Right unda back unda dammit dammit DAMMIT!'

Without really thinking what he was doing, Johan plunged into the fray, sword stabbing to left and right. Needle teeth snapped at him, scant inches from his face, and he seemed to be surrounded by a wall of steel and claws and sharpened stone axe-heads. The sharp smell of lizard washed over him, a mix of rubber and fish-heads, and scaly arms reached out to drag him from the boat.

Not to be stopped, Johan stabbed and thrust, peering into the gloom until he saw what he sought – the rope at the point where it passed over the rim of the boat side. His sword raised over his head before descending in a flashing arc. A burly lizardman blinked in comprehension and tried to stop the wicked blade, only to have his arm severed cleanly below the elbow. Black-blue blood fountained over Johan. The sword parted the rope and thwacked into the bulwark with such force that it was stuck fast. Even with a two-handed grip, Johan could not drag it free.

All around him, lizards hung onto the boat to prevent it drifting into the cave, and cold eyes stared at the ex-Imperial envoy. A forest of blades inclined towards him, and time slowed to a standstill. A face he recognised grinned evilly, twisted into a malevolent parody of the creature he had once counted as a friend. It wielded a spear in both hands, and as it thrust forward, Johan saw his death in the glittering black orbs of its eyes.

'Froggo, nooooo!'

'Anssssssstein oh yesssssss!'

At the last moment, Johan felt himself thrown backwards by the scruff of the neck by what could only be described as heavily muscled fingers. A massive sword cleaved the air, barely slowing as it cleaved Froggo too. In the same gracefully deadly movement, and with barely a shift in his stance, Keanu reversed the blade and swept its razor edge along the side of the boat. A great hissing wail resounded, and a moment later the boat began to drift into the middle of the cave. Sitting up in the bilges, Johan was almost sick as he saw the row of perhaps a dozen clawed lizard paws still clutching the side of the boat like the broken sutures of a macabre wound.

'Get rowing!' Jiriki yelled, and Johan grabbed vaguely at an oar. Grimcrag was already pulling with a vengeance, and the heavily laden boat surged gamely towards the rapidly diminishing entrance. Even Johan could see that the water in the cave was almost at the high tide mark, and he doubted whether there was already any room for the miniature Norse longboat to clear the cave.

A rasping, scraping grinding sound assured him that he was right, when the proud dragon prow caught on the craggy rock of the cave roof. The boat ground to a halt immediately, throwing Keanu hard onto a heavy crate and ripping the oar from Jiriki's hands.

The elf lowered his head and closed his eyes. 'We've lost!' he whispered 'We're really stuck here now… and even we can't beat all the lizards on this forsaken island.'

Johan looked around wildly. Jiriki was right, there was no way that the boat was going any further. The cave roof sloped down towards the entrance, and their boat was firmly wedged in place by the ornate dragon headed prow. Glancing shoreward, he could see that the water was boiling as the lizardmen hurled themselves into the water and began swimming towards their frail craft. Johan knew in his heart what the skinks intended: they would turn the boat over and drown the Marauders by sheer weight of numbers and their superior aquatic fighting skills.

'It can't end like this!' Johan shouted, looking around for some way of escape. there was none. Despair clutched at his heart.

'Unngh!' grunted Keanu, clutching weakly at his sword, the wind knocked from his lungs by the impact with the heavy crate.

'Heads down, everyone!' Grimcrag shouted cheerfully, leaving barely a second for the Marauders to act on his sage advice, as once more Old Slaughterer was pulled back for a mighty swing. As he dove for the deck, Johan could see the sheer, grim, bloody minded expression which belied the dwarfs easy words. As the blade swung back, Johan could have sworn that he caught the words, 'Shan't – have – me – gold!' expelled through gritted dwarf teeth, and then the axe was hurtling towards its target. And Johan understood Grimcrag's intent the split second before the axe ripped through the proud dragon prow, sundering four feet of very solid and seasoned wood as though it was the pulpy flesh of an overripe fruit.

From his position on the crate, Keanu could only gulp appreciatively, heaving air into his lungs as he recovered his breath.

'That'll do nicely, eh?' Grimcrag gasped, gesturing over his shoulder with a callused thumb. 'Now we'd best get a move on, as we have company on the way!'

Johan and Jiriki needed no second bidding, and were already at their oars, pulling for all their might. Together, their efforts just matched those of Keanu, who heaved mightily on the opposite oar, corded muscles standing out on his neck and shoulders. Freed from the grip of the rocky roof, the boat leapt forwards almost eagerly, and Johan reckoned that with their lower profile, they might make it after all. Just. If they ducked.

'Pity; that figurehead was the best bit of the boat I reckon, good solid timber crafted by a skilled carpenter!' Grimcrag's voice drifted wistfully across the cave.

'Shut up and grab an oar!' came the chorus back.

* * *

'AAARGH! YES, ME lads!' Hook Black Pugh beamed, surveying the burning village 'This'll do very nicely indeed!' Well satisfied with the pillaging so far, Pugh grinned broadly, scratching at his stubbled chin with the business end of his hook.

A few yards away, invisibly merged with the jungle, several hundred skinks looked on with murder in their cold eyes. Sharp daggers, spears, bows and poisoned darts awaited the signal, for they were determined that none would escape. 'When red bird flysssss away...' a feather-bedecked lizard man with blue-black skin hissed ominously.

If Bligh had not been so distracted by the flight of the brightly coloured bird, he might have noticed movement in the reflection in his highly polished blade. But even if he had seen it, he would probably have thought he was seeing things. For who could believe a smallish, makeshift mongrel boat, piled up with crates and so low in the water that it looked near to sinking... or the tiny reflection of the dwarf waving rudely at him from the tiller?

As it was, he saw nothing but an ugly red bird which caused his mates to laugh at him. And if there was one thing he hated, it was being made fun of. So he just stood at the base of the pyramid and fomented murderous plans for his captain. 'No one makes fun of Arbuthnot Bligh,' he muttered, and death was in his eyes.

With an ungainly flapping of scarlet wings, the strange bird took flight.

'YOU KNOW,' BEGAN Grimcrag, lounging on a hammock strung up on the poop deck of what was up until very recently an abandoned pirate ship, 'I don't think this could have worked out much better if I'd planned it.'

'You mean you didn't?' Jiriki chided in mock surprise, from his place in the shade of the mainmast.

Grimcrag ignored the elf and continued ticking off their successes on the callused fingers of his left hand. 'We've got a ship, lizard gold, our Bretonnian gold back, had a holiday...' The dwarf glanced around the poop deck. 'Have I forgotten anything?'

'Vot 'bout da Frogmeat stew?' Keanu shouted from the crow's nest. 'Dat vas gut!'

'I still can't believe you actually cooked him,' Johan muttered sulk-ily. 'Just 'cos he tried to force you to crew the ship with lizards.'

'You saw what he was going to do with that there spear, lad, let's not forget, eh?' He wagged a finger remonstratively at the ex-Imperial envoy. 'Him or us lad, him or us. And you do like a bit of crackling as much as the next man!'

Johan brightened up a little at the mention of crackling, and looked over the stern of the vessel. The sun glittered on the wake of the ship, and seagulls danced in the air, no doubt hoping for any detritus from the Marauders' last meal. 'You won't find any crackling!' Johan shouted through cupped hands, but his voice was lost in the wind in the sails.

The Dirty Dog sailed serenely away from the island into the setting sun, and a new chapter in the legend that is Grunsonn's Marauders drew to a close. Well, almost...

On top of the small pyramid, grouped around the noble statue, Hook Black Pugh and the remaining pirates nervously eyed the throng of angry lizard kind gathered menacingly below them. To the pirates' consternation, the leading lizards were wearing what looked like Norse helmets. At least one of them was frothing at the mouth and rolling its eyes in its scaly head. A disconcerting bellowing and hooting reached the ears of the beleaguered pirates, as arrows clattered about the pirates' booted feet.

'Getting dark.'

'They're... berserks, ain'ts they?'

'Carn't be – can they?'

'Remember, their arrers is poisoned.'

'Looks like that one's got some kind of magic.'

'We're doomed and no mistake.'

'Aaargh! I'm sorry, me lads, looks like me luck's run its course this time.

'Hold on, what's this 'ere statue?' Pugh's deafening shout of pure frustration and despair echoed across the clearing.

'I don't believe it! It's that accursed barbarian! I knew THEY had to be at the bottom of this somewhere! Aaaaargh!'

NIGHT TOO LONG

James Wallis

'Two BEERS, Frau Kolner, and a kiss for Hexensnacht!' He swooped at her, arms outstretched. She dodged around him, laughing, a tray of tankards held level with a polished skill of avoiding amorous drunks.

'Sit down, Herr Johansen, and I'll bring your ale presently.'

'And the kiss?'

'Hexensnacht's tomorrow night. And no kisses till you finish finding those poor missing women, and pay off your ale bill.' She swept away towards the bar. Johansen watched her go, then ran his hand over his short-cropped dark hair, smoothing it into place, and sat back down next to his companion, Dirk Grenner.

'She's great, isn't she?' he said.

'She's a short, penny-pinching shrew with a half-wit for a brother and a string of suitors as long as the Great North Road,' Grenner said. 'I don't understand what you see in her.'

Johansen looked across the plain wood of the inn table with incomprehension on his face. 'She's a blonde widow who owns a pub,' he said.

'So you say, too often,' Grenner said. 'The landlady of the famous Black Goat Inn. What makes you think she'd go for someone like you?'

211

'Me? A high-ranking officer in the prestigious Palisades, charged with protecting the Emperor and his Elector Counts?' Johansen puffed out his chest. 'I'm a fine catch.'

'You're an overworked, underpaid captain in a small division most people have never heard of. You've got a humourless tyrant for a boss–'

'A sarcastic ex-Watch sergeant for a partner,' Johansen said and reached for his tankard.

'–you don't wear a smart uniform most days, and you spend your time watching Kislevite insurrectionists or Bretonnian spies. Or, Sigmar help us, seconded to the city Watch, who couldn't find their arses if a horse bit them.'

'They're not doing much better with our help,' Johansen said. 'Four women missing in two weeks. It's not good.'

'And while we were fooling around, Schmidt gets himself killed.'

'His own fault. He knew they suspected he was watching them.'

'Bretonnians,' Grenner said with vehemence. 'Sons of bitches. Killing him is one thing, but stuffing his mouth with his–'

'Here's to his memory,' Johnsen said. They raised their beer-mugs, drank, and were still. Grenner broke the moment.

'Still, Hexensnacht tomorrow and Hexenstag the day after. Things should be quiet. The city's practically deserted.' He pulled his tankard closer and inspected it, thinking.

A deep boom echoed from outside. The building shook, sending ripples across the beer.

'What was that?' Grenner said.

'You tempting fate,' Johansen said. 'Gunpowder. A lot of it. About half a mile.'

'Not magic?'

Johansen shook his head. 'No, the echoes were wrong. Come on.' He was on his feet. Grenner stood up, staggered and leaned on the table. 'Are you sure we're on duty?' he asked.

'We're always on duty,' Johansen reminded him.

'I'm too drunk to be on duty,' Grenner protested.

'Dunk your head in the horse-trough,' Johansen said.

They staggered to the door. Outside, flames lit the night sky above the wide empty space of the Königplatz. Altdorf, capital of the Empire, lay still and cold under a blanket of thin snow and stars, the streets lightened by the eerie light of the two moons, one crescent and the other a day from full. Tomorrow would be Hexensnacht, witches' night, the last night of the year.

THE SEVEN STARS Inn was ruined and ablaze. The fire raged against the cold, its leaping heat forcing back the crowd of gawping citizens. Stirrup-pumps forced futile jets of water into the inferno and nearby buildings were being emptied in case the flames spread.

Grenner gazed at the blaze. Almost nothing was left except the ground floor. Nobody could have escaped this cataclysm, but he couldn't work out why someone would blow up a prosperous merchant-inn at one of the few times of the year when it was almost empty.

He saw Johansen moving through the crowd, circling the building. The man had studied pyrotechnics when he was in the army; he'd be able to tell where the charge had been set and how large it was. Grenner's speciality was less technical and more dangerous. He was a student of human nature.

'So, Grenner, what's the situation?' The voice jolted him from his thoughts, made abrupt by its strong northern accent. Grenner didn't have to turn to know General Hoffmann, the leader of the Palisades and the only man whose orders he respected, had arrived.

'Probably nine dead, sir,' he said. 'No survivors found so far, nor witnesses. No reports of threats or recent trouble.'

'A hundred and fifty pounds of gunpowder in the cellar,' Johansen added as he joined them. 'Blast went straight up, killing everyone inside. Very effective. Good evening sir, you're up late.'

'Hard to sleep with so many disturbances,' Hoffmann said, his eyes dark against the flames.

'Don't give us that,' said Grenner. 'Something's up or you wouldn't be here. Why this inn, and why tonight?'

Hoffmann held his stare for a moment. 'You're on the ball for a man who's been drinking all evening, Grenner. Yes, this is no routine tavern-bombing. Grand Prince Valmir von Raukov, Elector Count of Ostland, is known to share a room with a female associate here late at night. We've warned him it's a security risk, but...'

'Was he inside?' Johansen wanted to know.

'He was but he left earlier, luckily for us. Someone just tried to kill a senior officer of the Empire, and in a very public way. I need to know who and why, and I need them stopped. Your job.'

Johansen looked mock-aghast, Grenner dismayed. 'Can't you put someone else on it?' he said.

'There isn't anybody else. It's almost Hexenstag. Everyone's out of the city or on leave, except the Meer twins who are working incognito and Schmidt, who I don't need to remind you is dead. Get to work.'

'We'll start first thing,' Grenner said.

Hoffmann's face was in shadow, the raging fire behind him. 'Someone's trying to kill an Elector, you don't wait till morning. Start now, and don't stop till their bodies are in jail or cold.'

Johansen groaned. 'When do we sleep?'

'Perhaps the explosion deafened your ears.' The general's voice was ice. 'You don't stop until they're jailed or dead.'

Chains of people passed buckets of water to watchmen who flung them at the burning inn. The inferno consumed the water and blazed on, turning the sky above the city red.

THE KÖNIGPLATZ IS the wide market-square separating the University of Altdorf from the merchant district. By day it is crowded with traders, peddlers, goodwives looking for a bargain, street-thieves looking for unguarded purses, pilgrims, soldiers and messengers, gawkers staring at the huge statues of past emperors that dominate the square with the hundred foot-tall figure of Sigmar, the founder and patron of the Empire, towering over them.

By night the square is quieter, the market-barrows left stacked and bare at the side of the cobbles. On cold nights between the midwinter feasts of Mondstille and Hexenstag, when the river Reik flows through the city slow and sluggish like thick blood in the veins of old tramps huddled in warehouse doors, Altdorf's streets are deserted apart from a few drunken revellers, a few Watch patrols, those who prefer not to go home or who have no homes, stray dogs, and rats scurrying in the garbage. Those with more clandestine business stick to less well-let areas.

'Gunpowder in the cellar,' Grenner said as they headed across the square towards the Black Goat. 'How did it get there?'

'Probably a barrel,' said Johansen. 'Who'd notice an extra barrel in a beer-cellar?'

'The cellarman would. And they'd have to get it down there. First thing, we check out the Seven Star's regular brewers, wine-sellers, anyone who might supply them with casks. Find witnesses. Find out who's got a grievance against the prince.'

'A lot of work,' Johansen said, 'for just two of us.'

Grenner groaned. 'I know. And I've got a fitting at my tailor.'

'Oh yes?'

'Couple of shirts and a new short-cloak. Dark blue, Tilean style.'

'Very nice. Big evening?'

Grenner gave him a scathing look. 'Hexensnacht. In case you'd forgotten.'

'Oh yes. Let's hope we're done by then.' Johansen, distracted, glanced across the empty square. 'Wait, what's that?' He pointed into the maze of shadows among the bases of the emperors' statues.

It was a pile of displaced paving-stones, the bare earth beside them rude and frosted. Grenner and Johansen regarded them.

'Odd,' Johansen said. 'I didn't see that earlier.'

'Maybe you weren't looking. Maybe it wasn't here. We can check on it in the morning.'

Johansen looked up as if realising where he was for the first time. 'Why are we back here?'

'Because we need to do some planning. And the best place for that is over a mug of mulled wine, with the chance Frau Kolner's still around to bring it to you.'

Johansen grinned. 'Let's get planning.'

IT WAS A long night. For an hour they talked and thought and speculated over hot wine brought by Frau Kolner's idiot brother who was less interesting to look at than the landlady, but who understood instructions and did not sleep. Then they left the inn again, into the biting cold of the night to bang on the doors of informants, rousing them to answer questions in exchange for a few silver coins, a promise of future favours, leniency for relatives or associates in jail, or a stare that said nothing but threatened much. Grenner did the talking. Johansen stifled yawns, fingered his sword and blocked the escape routes.

As six bells sounded across the city, the sky still dark, they found themselves in the merchant district a few streets away from the Königplatz, hammering on a door that didn't respond. Johansen looked at Grenner.

'Probably spending Hexenstag in the country,' he said.

'Wish I was.' Grenner gave the door a kick and stepped away. 'Enough for now. Breakfast at the Goat?'

'You're on.' They began to walk back to the square, Grenner slapping his hands to ward off the frost.

'And what has this wasted night taught us?' he said, only partly to his partner. 'That the prince has a lot of enemies. The Bretonnians and Kislevites hate him because of his trade-treaties with Norsca, his neighbours in the north hate him because his army drove a greenskin force into their lands last year, the Chaos-worshippers hate him because the witch-hunters run freely in his province, and even his own people hate him because he left the church of Ulric and became a Sigmarite. All of which we already knew. None of them have agents working in the city, as far as we know, and he's not annoyed anyone for at least two months. We have nothing.'

'Perhaps he wasn't the target after all,' Johansen said.

Grenner looked at him with eyes smarting from the cold. 'If he wasn't then it stops being our problem.'

'He left the inn. Perhaps he was in on the scheme.' Johansen paused, peering ahead. 'Hang on. They've started early.'

In the Königplatz market-traders were setting out their stalls, but Johansen's attention was on the crew of workmen among the emperors' statues at the centre of the square. He tapped Grenner on the shoulder, but Grenner was looking elsewhere.

'You go. Shout if you need help,' he said and walked away. Johansen shrugged, rubbed tiredness from his eyes and walked across to the crew of masons and apprentices, working with shovels and picks, digging a trench among the forest of plinths. One stopped and watched him approach, arms folded, his thin red hair a dash of colour against his sombre clothes and the dullness of the morning.

'Cold day for working,' Johansen said, raising a hand in greeting. 'You the foreman?'

The man nodded, lips tight and eyes guarded.

'You're starting early,' Johansen said.

'Aye.' The mason's northern accent was thick as porridge. 'Work's got to be done by t'night.'

Johansen nodded, looking at the work crew. 'Are all your men members of the stonemasons' guild?' he asked. 'They don't like it when–'

'Affiliate members. From Wolfenburg,' the foreman said. 'It's rush work. Base subsidence. No local masons to do it.'

'You've got a guild certificate?'

'Not here.' The foreman turned his head, his eyes suspicious. 'Who's asking? Are you from the masons? Checking on us?'

'Just a concerned citizen,' Johansen said, and walked across the square to where Grenner was.

GRENNER RAPPED THE side of the cask on the cart. 'All the way from Bretonnia?' he asked. 'Why? We make wine in the Empire.'

The diminutive wineseller looked mock-shocked. 'Not like zis!' he exclaimed. 'Zis, she is grown under zer sun of Bordeleaux, the vines viz no frost, no fungus – ze finest wine, rich and complex, a subtle bouquet viz afternotes of cherries and oak...'

Grenner held up a hand to stop him. 'I meant transport's expensive. How can you make money on one cartload?'

The Bretonnian shook his head sadly. 'Monsieur, I do not know eizzer. My buyer, who supplies ze houses of Bretonnians in Altdorf, I find 'e is dead of the plague since four months. I cannot find my customers, so I must sell in ze market like a– a– a peddler.'

Grenner nodded, studying the casks, turning thoughts over in his mind. There had been trouble with Bretonnians the summer before, and rumours said there might be more trouble next year. Not to mention the business with Schmidt. He thumped one of the barrels and it shook solidly. 'Open it. I want to check.'

'Check?' The merchant looked puzzled. 'Check what?'

'That there's wine inside, not something else.'

The man's eyes narrowed. 'What?'

'Just open it.'

'But zat would ruin ze wine!' The short man's hands were raised beseechingly. There was silence for a moment. 'Maybe I draw you off a cup?' he suggested.

Grenner shrugged acceptance, and the Bretonnian filled a metal beaker from the spigot at the base of the barrel. The liquid flowed deep and red. Grenner took it, sniffed and swigged, looked contemplative.

'Well?' The little man's eyebrows raised into questions.

Grenner looked at him. 'You say this is the finest wine in Bretonnia?'

'Oui, m'sieur.'

'Stick to making cheese and seducing married women. This stuff's swill.' He put down the cup, to greet Johansen as he walked over. 'You get anything?'

'Non-guild workers doing repairs.'

'Suspicious?'

Johansen scratched his unshaved chin. 'Maybe. If the work's urgent there may be no guild men available, given the time of year. But the order must have come from the city council, and the local guilds get all those contracts.'

Grenner pushed open the door of the Black Goat. 'The Königsplatz will be packed with people this evening. If the statues are unsafe and there aren't any local masons to do the work, then...' He let the sentence trail off as he slumped into a seat by his regular table. Johansen pulled out a chair and sat.

'What did you get?' he asked.

'Bretonnian with a flimsy story, selling what he said was expensive wine from a market-stall. Big barrels of the stuff.'

'Barrels, right. Did you see the wine?'

'I tried a cup. It tasted like fruity tar. Ho, Frau Kolner, how are you this morning?'

'As concerned about the size of your bar-bill as I was last night,' the landlady said. 'Don't settle yourselves. I have a letter for you.'

Johansen reached out but she gave it to Grenner, who smirked at his colleague as he snapped the seal and unfolded the paper.

'What is it?' Johansen asked.

'Hoffmann. He guessed we'd come back here. Breakfast is cancelled, we're to get back on the streets. Hunger sharpens the mind, he says.'

'Sarcastic old sod.'

'There's more. We report to him at noon. Alchemics should have analysed the explosion by then. And meanwhile he's got us an interview with the Elector.'

'When?'

'Now.'

'So much for your appointment with your tailor.' Johansen swiped a half-finished mug of beer from a neighbouring table and swigged it. 'Let's go.'

* * *

GRAND PRINCE VALMIR VON Raukov, the Elector Count of Ostland, sat upright in his four-poster bed. A tray lay beside him, hot breakfast scents rising from it: sausages and kippers. In a chair on the other side of the bed a tall man in the grand prince's house uniform sat, not saying a word, his hand never leaving the pommel of his sword.

'Can you think of anyone who'd want you dead, your Highness?' Grenner asked from where he and Johansen stood at the end of the bed. He knew how scruffy and tired they must look compared to the opulence of the prince's bedroom. They ought to be in dress uniform, scrubbed and shaved, answering questions instead of asking them.

'Of course people want me dead. I'm an Elector, for Sigmar's sake. It's not my job to be liked. You know that.' The prince regarded them from under bushy eyebrows and chewed bacon. 'No, nobody has threatened me lately beyond the usual cranks – correct, Alexis?' The man in the chair nodded, his eyes never leaving the Palisades officers.

'So you know of no reason why–'

The prince raised a hand. 'Captain, if I knew anything useful I would tell you now. I'm not oblivious to danger, I have people like Alexis who monitor my enemies' activities. If we knew anything we would tell you.'

Grenner stared ahead, but in the corner of his eye he saw Alexis move, shifting position. Perhaps, he thought, he's uncomfortable at his master's words. He wanted to ask more, but knew better than to pose heavy-handed questions of an Elector.

'Perhaps,' the prince continued, 'what you should be asking is why the Seven Stars was blown up if I wasn't there? The assassins would surely have checked I was in the building before they set the fuse.'

'Why would they have thought you would be there?' Grenner asked.

'Because that is my habit,' the prince said. 'I usually stay till morning. Last night I returned home early because I received word my wife was ill. Yet they blew up the inn all the same. Captain, either I wasn't the intended victim, or the bombers had an informant who misled them, by accident or on purpose. There's the next piece of your puzzle.'

'Thank you, your highness. We'll look into it.' Grenner felt disdain but masked it. He hated it when officials did his job for him, particularly when they did it better. 'Can you tell us who your companion was?'

The prince shrugged. 'Her privacy makes few odds now. Her name was Anastasia Kuster. I met her in the Street of a Hundred Taverns a few months ago, when I was – I was dressed plainly, let's just say that. She's an honest girl, works in a glove-shop. A little scatterbrained but works hard. She's originally from Ostland, a northerner like myself. When I'm in Altdorf we meet once or twice a week.'

'Might your wife have had something to do with the explosion?'

'My wife?' The prince snorted. 'If I die, she loses everything: her title, her status, her palace, her income, the lot. She's terrified by the thought of my death. Her relatives too, they all ride on my coat-tails. None of them would do anything to harm me.'

'Hell has no fury like a scorned woman,' Johansen said.

'Scorned? She doesn't love me. We married because it was politically advantageous to link our families. If I want warmth and emotion and life in a woman, I'll go to – I went to Anastasia.'

'Yet you returned home because your wife was ill,' Grenner said.

'She is heavy with my son. It would not have been seemly for the boy to be born while I was away from the house.'

'Are you sure it's a boy, your highness?' Johansen said. Grenner flinched. It was a flip remark, inappropriate and irreverent. Such things were dangerous.

The prince regarded them from under heavy brows, and did not smile. 'It had better be.' His tone was cold.

Grenner's heart dropped. Lower ranks should know their place, and Johansen's remark had crossed the line. They'd get no more useful information here. 'Thank you for your time, your highness,' he said. 'We will report anything–'

The prince's cough stopped him. 'Not so fast. I have questions too. Were any bodies recovered?'

Grenner snapped back to attention. 'No, sir. The place was an inferno. It's almost certain that everybody was cremated in seconds.'

'Not everybody,' the prince said. 'The inn's cellarman survived.'

'What?' said Grenner. 'We weren't told.'

Across the room, Alexis sat forward in his chair. 'Hans Kellerman was in the stableyard,' he said. 'The blast blew him twenty feet and broke his every bone.'

'He's alive?' Johansen asked.

'No, he died three hours later. But I was able to ask him some questions first. The Shallyan priests had given him herbs to numb the pain and he was almost coherent.'

'What did he say?'

Alexis glanced at the prince, who gave a slight nod. He turned back. 'A few things. He told me there were four other people staying in the inn, but nobody of consequence. Just before the explosion he heard someone leave the inn, but didn't see who. And one of the cellar keys had gone missing a few days earlier, and he suspected Anastasia, who had taken things bef–'

The prince coughed and Alexis stopped talking abruptly, sliding back in his chair under his master's glare. The prince turned to the Palisades officers.

'That will be all,' he said.

'Thank you for your time, your highness,' Grenner said, bowed and backed out of the room, Johansen beside him. He made sure they were twenty feet down the empty corridor before speaking. 'I hate dealing with nobs,' he said. 'Humourless sods.'

'This one not as stuck-up as most, though,' Johansen said. 'What do you reckon? Did he get his mistress up the spout, she was blackmailing him, and he hired someone to blow up the inn to get rid of her?'

'I know you can be thick as a brick sometimes,' Grenner said, 'and that may explain why you never get anywhere with Frau Kolner, but did you really not notice?'

'Notice what?'

Grenner let out a sigh. 'He didn't kill her. He was in love with her.'

'You should have pushed him for more information about the girl.'

Grenner turned on him. 'Don't tell me how to ask questions. That's my job. You almost got us thrown out of an audience with an Elector with your ridiculous...' He stopped, pressing a hand against his eyes. 'Sorry. Sorry, Karl. I didn't mean that. It's just... I'm tired and stressed.'

Johansen put a hand on his friend's shoulder. 'That goes for both of us. And it'll get worse before it gets better. Still, come midnight we'll be laughing about this and toasting the new year, eh?'

'I bloody hope so.' Grenner said dryly. 'Right. How many glove-shops are there in Altdorf?'

THERE WERE SIX, but they got lucky with the second one. Anastasia hadn't come to work that day, the glove-maker's wife told them, and hadn't sent word that she was ill. But it had happened before, and besides it was Hexensnacht, so they weren't worried. Grenner turned on his charm and got the girl's address in two minutes.

'Fast work,' Johansen observed as they left the shop.

'New personal best,' Grenner said. Inside he felt distant, distracted, as if there was a layer of wool between his thoughts and his actions. The bright cold sunlight made him feel cold, reminding him of too much beer and not enough rest the night before. His feet were heavy. He hoped there'd be no need for fast reactions or swordplay today.

The girl's lodgings were close to the city's north wall, decorated with the fripperies a rich lover buys for his fancy, or a girl not used to luxury buys for herself. Anastasia wasn't there and the bed had not been slept in. They searched the place with a swift thoroughness born of long practice.

'She was an Ulrican,' Johansen said, holding up a silver wolf-head.

'Interesting. She could read, too,' Grenner said, holding up a ragged, leather-bound book. He leafed through the pages.

'Any good?'

'Hardly Detlef Sierck. What's that?' A piece of paper fluttered down from between the pages. Grenner picked it up. 'Address.'

'One she wanted to hide.'

'Wouldn't she memorise it?'

'The prince said she was scatterbrained.'

'Oh yeah.' Grenner peered at the scrawled writing. 'It's in the docks. Warehouse district.'

'Probably a glove wholesaler, knowing your luck.'

'My luck?' Grenner looked askance. 'Explain that to me on the way there, Herr Not-been-kissed-for-a-month.'

THE WAREHOUSE ON Weidendamm was old but the lock on its wide doors was new. Grenner tested its inner workings with a bent piece of metal while Johansen kept watch. Technically, as Palisades officers, they could enter and search any building, but dockers' understanding of the finer points of the law was often shockingly bad.

'So we're here because we found this address in the effects of an Elector's mistress, right?' Johansen said.

'Right.'

'Why do we think this is a good lead?'

Grenner stopped his picking and looked up. 'It's our only lead. Plus we're seeing Hoffmann in an hour and he'll want to know what we've been doing.'

'That's what I'm afraid of.'

'Shut up. I'm concentrating.'

'We could claim addled wits from lack of sleep.'

'Shut up.'

'Face it, this is half-arsed.'

Grenner stood up, put the lockpick back in his pocket, and kicked the door hard. The wood around the lock splintered and the door swung inwards.

'Subtle,' Johansen said.

'Subtlety is over-rated. Come on.'

The air inside was cold and dark and their breath hung in the faint shafts of sunlight. The floor underfoot was hard earth. A figure lay slumped and twisted a few feet in front of the door. The rest of the warehouse was bare.

Grenner went to the body. 'Girl. Twenties. Pretty. Last night's party frock. Neck broken. Want to bet she's Anastasia?'

Johansen peered at the dead girl's face. 'Does she remind you of anyone?'

'No,' Grenner said, squinting. 'Who were you thinking of?'

'I don't know.' Johansen studied the corpse for a moment, then squatted and ran his hands over the ground, gathering a thin powder onto his fingertips. He sniffed them. 'Gunpowder,' he said. 'There's the imprint of a barrel in the earth too.'

'Just one?'

Johansen blinked, letting his eyes adjust till he could make out the faint outlines on the floor. 'Eight. No, twelve. More if they were stacked.'

'How many of that size would have blown up the Seven Stars?' Grenner asked.

'Three at most.'

'Damn!' He stood and prowled. 'So... assume the prince's mistress is feeding information to the assassins. Maybe she knows their motive, probably not. Last night she has a lucky escape and realises that they'd kill her too if necessary. So she comes to confront them... why?'

'Scatterbrained,' Johansen said.

'They do kill her. So they were here between the explosion and now, probably clearing the warehouse. But we still don't know who they are.'

'My money's on Ulrican fanatics. We could look for witnesses,' Johansen suggested.

'It's the docks. Nobody ever admits seeing anything here.' Grenner thumped the wall. 'It's going to be a city records job, get a clerk to dig out the old ledgers and find who owns this place. The cargo records too, where it came from.'

'I'm more worried about where it's gone. Cart tracks here.' Johansen pointed to the floor.

'Cart. Barrels,' Grenner said. 'You thinking what I'm thinking?'

'A good way to get gunpowder into an inn cellar. You?'

'I was thinking about a Bretonnian wineseller.'

Johansen stood, brushing dirt from his knees. 'We're late for Hoffmann. And I'm hungry for lunch.'

Grenner took a length of twine from his pocket to tie the warehouse doors shut. 'Lunch? Some of us are still starving for breakfast.'

FROM THE WINDOW of General Hoffmann's room on the top floor of the Palisades building, the thin plumes of smoke still rising from the site of the Seven Stars were faint dark columns against the cold blue sky. Hoffmann stared out over the city, his back to his two agents.

'Twelve hours,' he said, 'and all you've got for me is an empty warehouse and a dead girl.'

'An Elector's mistress. That's got to be worth something,' Grenner said.

Hoffmann shook his head. 'She can't tell us what's going on, who these people are or where they'll strike next. So who's behind this?'

'Ulrican extremists,' Johansen said.

'Bretonnians,' Grenner said.

Hoffmann turned his stare to them. 'Make your minds up,' he said. 'The city's in uproar, every noble is screaming for protection, we've got a report of skaven in the sewers, and on top of it another woman's disappeared. The last thing I need is you two following a wrong lead.' He paused. 'You do have more leads?'

The agents exchanged a tired look. 'Can you send someone to the city records office, to find out who owns that warehouse?' Grenner asked.

'And the customs records, to see if there's anything on who brought the barrels to the city,' Johansen said.

'Who do you suggest I send?' Hoffmann asked. 'There isn't anyone else. Get the records clerks to do it.'

'You think there'll be any records clerks there on Hexensnacht?'

'Then you do it. I've got my hands full.' Hoffmann turned back to the window. 'We got the explosion report from Alchemics,' he said. 'Inconclusive. The sulphur in the gunpowder was Tilean, the saltpeter was gathered near Wolfenburg and the charcoal could be from anywhere. The ingredient ratio suggests a Middenheim-trained alchemist, but that means nothing.'

'Couldn't you send someone from Alchemics to the records office?' Johansen asked.

Hoffmann snorted. 'Nobody's going to do your book-work for you. And don't dare fall asleep over them, or I'll have your guts for garters. Go on, get out.'

The street outside the Palisades was quiet. A cat padded silently down the gutter. Grenner watched it go, yawned and flexed stiff muscles.

'If we're going to the records office,' he said, 'can we go by Weberstrasse?'

'What's in Weberstrasse?'

'My tailor.'

'You and your clothes, I swear–' Johansen said, but Grenner wasn't listening. Movement had caught his eye: a laden cart moving past the end of the street. He ran after it.

He was right: it was the Bretonnian's cart, still piled high with barrels. The short man was staring straight ahead, as if deep in thought. Grenner overtook him and stood in the road, hand raised.

'Stop,' he said. 'Where are you going?'

The Bretonnian reined in his horse. 'Ah, m'sieur,' he said. 'You have come to buy some wine? Ze aftertaste of cinnamon, she has lingered on your tongue...'

'Where are you going?'

The wineseller shrugged. 'The market is finished. I go to find some taverns, maybe zey buy.'

'Where were you last night?'

'I put my cart in an alley, I sleep zere.' The little man raised his hands in supplication. 'M'sieur, I have no money. I am–'

'You're under arrest. I want you off the streets.' The Bretonnian turned white. He grabbed for his whip and swiped it across the horse's rump. It started forward, towards Grenner, who ducked sideways and groped in his jerkin for a throwing-knife. A hand landed on his arm, restraining him. He turned. It was Johansen.

'What the hell are you doing?' he asked.

'I'm arresting this man.' The cart was rattling away behind him.

'It's not him.'

'How do you know?' Grenner demanded, turning to give chase. Johansen gripped harder.

'It's not him. It's Ulrican extremists, trying to kill their Elector.'

'I think he's working with them.'

'Why?'

'Because...' The cart was gaining speed. 'Look, he's up to something or he wouldn't be running.'

'Not our problem,' Johansen said. 'Electors in peril, the safety of the Empire to protect, that's us, remember? Leave him for your friends in the Watch. Besides,' he added, 'if I was stopped by someone looking like you, I'd run too.'

'What do you mean?' Grenner ran a hand through his blond hair.

'You're unkempt. Not to mention unshaved, haggard and smelling of last night's beer.'

'Visiting my tailor would let me–'

Johansen laughed, a short humourless bark. 'Forget it. We've got records to check.'

THEY WENT TO three breweries, to ask about beer deliveries to the Seven Stars. Nobody knew about anything unusual.

They knocked on the doors of the houses around the remains of the Seven Stars to see if anyone had been awake before the explosion, or had heard or seen anything. Nobody had.

They spoke to a couple of winesellers about the Seven Stars, but the inn had only taken small casks. Grenner asked about a Bretonnian wineseller dying of plague four months ago, but they didn't know of anyone. Grenner looked at Johansen significantly. Johansen raised his eyes to the ceiling.

They walked through the Königplatz. The market-stalls had closed up early for the day, clearing the space for the evening's celebrations. There was no sign of the stoneworkers who had been there earlier.

They went to Grenner's tailor, who fitted his new clothes and wanted to know how the search for the missing women was going. Even wearing a new shirt and stylish short-cloak, Grenner still looked unkempt and sleepless.

After several hours, after putting it off for as long as possible, they went to the city records office, in the basement of the council-hall. There was one clerk on duty, but after he showed them the section of leatherbound warehouse and tax records that they needed, he excused himself and they didn't see him again.

'Typical work-shy civil servant,' Johansen said.

'Not very civil either,' Grenner observed.

The books were cold, wide, dry and dusty. Their parchment pages were filled with tightly written records of who owned everything in Altdorf, who had sold it to them, and what percentage of the sale the tax collectors had taken. It was slow, tedious work.

Johansen yawned and picked up the fifth ledger in the pile beside him. It was hard to stay awake: the cold air and the candlelight were soporific, and outside the narrow window daylight had fled hours ago. Across the table, Grenner echoed his yawn.

'We're doing this the wrong way,' he said.

'What?'

'We're looking for where they've been. We should be working out where they're going. Who they're going to target next.'

'Oh yeah?' Johansen raised a weary eyebrow. 'How do we do that, a crystal ball? You know what Hoffmann thinks about that scryer the Watch uses.'

Grenner passed a hand over his face, trying to wipe tiredness away. 'It was just an idea.'

Footsteps weaved through the racks of records towards them. Johansen raised his head to look. It was Alexis, the prince's bodyguard.

'Sigmar's teeth, you two are hard men to track down,' he said.

Johansen thought of a snappy response, but swallowed it. It was too late and he was too tired. 'What's this about?'

Alexis leaned on the edge of the table. 'Anastasia.'

'You know we found her body?' Grenner said.

Alexis nodded. 'We heard.' He paused. 'The prince lied to you. He sends apologies but he was trying to protect her.'

Johansen was suddenly very alert. Across the table, Grenner pushed his chair back.

'What was the lie?' he asked.

'His wife wasn't ill. He was going to stay the night at the Seven Stars, but Anastasia told him he was in danger and he should leave.'

'So she was the person the cellarman heard leaving a few minutes later,' Grenner said. Alexis nodded.

Johansen absorbed the information, fitting it together. 'She wasn't an innocent,' he said, 'she knew what the Ulricans' plan was. But she couldn't go through with it. She may even have lit the fuse, knowing the prince had left. And they killed her for that.' He looked up at Alexis. 'When you learned the prince was seeing Anastasia you checked her background, had her followed, right?'

The bodyguard nodded. 'We didn't find any links to known troublemakers.'

'What other northerners did she meet regularly? Friends? Associates?'

'Her brother's in the city.'

'What does he do?' Grenner asked.

'He's a stonemason.'

Johansen exhaled sharply. 'Grenner,' he said, 'remember I said the dead girl reminded me of someone?'

'Yeah?'

'The stoneworkers' foreman in the Königplatz this morning.'

Grenner stared at him, horror across his face. No words were needed. They sprinted from the records room, out of the council building, heading towards the Königplatz.

IT WAS LATER than they had realised and the darkened streets were thronged with revellers. Johansen let Grenner take the lead, following the former Watch sergeant move through narrow alleys and through short-cuts, avoiding the crowds. After five years in Altdorf he still couldn't understand why people celebrated Hexensnacht, the night of witches. Back home in the south his family would be around the fire tonight, doors locked and windows shuttered. Bad things happened on Hexensnacht.

Above them the two moons sat, one thin and one fat in a sky that flashed with bursts from fireworks, their explosions echoing off the buildings. It was not a good omen. As he ran, Johansen clenched his fists and made a silent prayer to Sigmar that he was wrong.

They burst into the Königplatz. The square was a sea of people and movement, lit by flickering braziers on poles. Johansen leaped onto a market-barrow to scan the crowd.

'The statues,' he shouted to Grenner over the hubbub, and began pushing his way to where he had seen the work-crew. They had been digging a trench, he recalled, deep enough for several barrels.

A knot of merrymaking students blocked his way. 'Clear a path! Imperial officers!' he bellowed, shoving through them. Ahead a red-haired figure turned sharply, slapped someone on the shoulder and

raced away through the crowd, towards the base of the statue of Sig-
mai. Johansen felt a rising dread, and gave chase. They'd spent the day
assuming an Elector was in danger. They hadn't thought about symbols of the Empire.

If the Ulricans had buried gunpowder, he thought, there would be
a way of lighting it, some kind of fuse. As if on cue a firework went off
behind him, throwing colours over the crowd. The red-headed man
ducked between the bases of the outermost statues. It was darker in
there and the crowd was thinner. Johansen saw Grenner to his left
and gestured towards the maze of stonework. Grenner nodded. That
was all the plan they needed: they knew how each other worked.

Johansen drew his hand-crossbow from its holster and stepped into
the shadows, heading for the statue of Sigmar. He surprised an
entwined couple between the feet of the Empress Magritta, and sent
a black-lotus peddler scurrying away from under Ludwig the Fat.
Around the plinth of Leopold I, he could see where the Ulricans had
been working that morning. Above, Sigmar's mighty hammer
eclipsed the moons, and in its shadow he could see the red-haired
man kneeling on freshly laid paving-stones, crouched over something. A spark. It was a tinderbox.

Johansen knew he was out of time. He rushed forward, his crossbow raised, shouting, 'Drop it!'

The man didn't turn as he'd hoped, but crouched lower, blowing on
something that glowed. Johansen charged in, firing as he ran. The
bolt hit the Ulrican in the arm and the tinderbox went flying. The
man twisted, his face maddened with rage, and Johansen kicked him
in the teeth. He went backwards, his skull hitting the base of the
statue with a crack.

Johansen's eyes searched the ground. A white cord lay between two
flagstones, one end raised and singed. He grabbed it, pulling it with
both hands. It came free, about three feet of fuse. He dangled it in
front of the man's eyes.

'Happy Hexensnacht,' he said.

The man grinned through broken teeth and raised something in
one hand, smashing it down onto the stones. Shards of clay splintered and a liquid spread, covering the ground, seeping between the
flagstones into the soil below. Johansen punched the Ulrican in the
side of the head, then dipped a finger and smelled it. Oil.

'Johansen!' Grenner yelled and he jerked his head up. A man was
running out of the shadows, carrying a torch. It was the man the Ulrican had slapped in the crowd. A back-up. From the other direction
Grenner's throwing knife spun and sunk into the new man's chest, a
second into his eye. He fell. The torch went up, curving a bright path
towards Johansen.

He jumped to catch it, and his foot slipped on the oil. It bounced through his hands and hit the flagstones. The oil burst into flames.

He stared for an instant.

'Run!' Grenner was bellowing. 'Run!'

He ran, roaring warnings, grabbing people and pushing them ahead of him. As he ran past the Empress and out into the crowd, he thought he might be safe.

Then the world picked him up and flung him across the square, filling his senses with bright loud disaster. He ducked and rolled, bruised and breathless, clambering back onto his feet, running through the panicked, screaming crowd to get away. There was a second explosion. People were knocking each other down, trampling over bodies, desperate to get away.

The statues were falling like trees in a gale, crashing into each other. Stone limbs dropped, torsos cracked, heads fell and exploded. Leopold collapsed into the Empress Magritta, her hollow bronze frame booming like a bell across the stampede in the square. She crumpled down into the crowd, crushing – Johansen didn't want to think how many people. He could see bodies impaled on the spikes of her crown. He felt sick.

Above the mayhem, the mighty figure of Sigmar stood firm, warhammer raised against the sky, the symbol of the Empire. Johansen, swept away by the crowd, tried to keep his eyes on it. Could it have survived the blast? Would it stand? Then he saw the first crack appear in its right leg. Pieces of stone fell. The crack grew. The leg shattered. The stone warhammer moved against the sky, slowly but unstoppably.

Johansen watched, not caring about the people streaming and screaming past him, as the first emperor fell from his plinth like a god falling from the heavens, smashing its hundred-foot length across the flagstones and crowds of the Königplatz, splintering into uncountable pieces. The head of the warhammer, ten feet across and solid granite, bounced once, rolled and crashed into the Black Goat Inn. Beams fell, tiles cascaded off the roof into the crowd below, and part of the front wall collapsed.

Johansen felt a hand grip his forearm and turned to see Grenner. His partner's face was gaunt and covered in dust, his clothes torn, his face bleeding where it had been cut by flying stones. They stared at each other and at the devastation around them. Grenner raised an arm and pointed at the wreckage of the inn.

'You know,' he shouted above the tumult and chaos, 'that's hurt your chances of getting a snog tonight.'

Johansen almost hit him. Instead after a second he said, 'Give me your cloak.' Grenner passed it and Johansen tore it into strips. Together they knelt and began bandaging the wounded.

* * *

'GET SOME SLEEP,' Hoffmann said.

It was four hours later. Altdorf was in shock. The Königplatz lay in chaos, corpses still strewn amidst the rubble of two thousand years of history, everything covered with a layer of powdered stone, made ghostly by the flames of a hundred torches, lighting the rescuers' efforts to find more wounded. The temples and hospices were full, and the cold stone slabs in the temples of Mórr too. Messengers had already ridden out from the city to carry the news across the Empire, like a rock dropped in a frozen pond, the news fracturing and rippling out across the land.

That, Johansen thought, was what the Ulricans had wanted, what they were prepared to give their lives to achieve. In the north of the Empire, in Ostland and beyond, the fall of Sigmar would be a rallying-cry. Come the spring, there might even be civil war.

He sat in Hoffmann's office, drinking hot spiced wine, Grenner beside him. The three had spent the night lifting rocks, carrying bodies and comforting the wounded and the grieving until they were utterly exhausted. Logically, he thought, they should have been searching for the other Ulricans. But this was more important.

'Sorry we didn't stop them, sir,' he said for the fifth time. Across the room, Hoffmann shook his head. The leather of his chair creaked with the movement.

'Not your fault. You did everything you could. We didn't have the manpower, it was as simple as that.' He looked contemplative. 'Get some sleep.'

'Shouldn't we find the rest of them, sir?'

'They're probably miles outside the city by now,' Hoffmann said, 'heading north. But don't forget the two of you are on duty at seven bells.'

'You're bloody joking,' Grenner blurted out.

'I'll overlook that insolence, Grenner, given the circumstances. Hexenstag dawn: the Emperor will be at the cathedral service for the blessing of the new year. We attend him. Plain clothes, not uniform. And shave, for Sigmar's sake.'

'Won't it be cancelled?' Grenner asked. 'Under the circumstances?'

Hoffmann shook his head. 'The Emperor's determined to show his people that Sigmar's Empire and its faith are still strong – and to mourn the dead as well. He's adamant. He's instructed all the Electors in Altdorf to be there too.'

'Oh Sigmar,' Johansen said quietly.

'What, Johansen?' Hoffmann asked.

'Don't you see?' His mind was exhausted; perhaps that was how he could understand the Ulrican fanatics, the way they thought, the depths of their madness and the extremes they'd go to. He remembered the eyes of the red-haired mason, a man who knew he was going to die and didn't care. 'It's not over. The cathedral with the Emperor and the Electors, all the nobility of Altdorf... that's the next target. They're not settling for sending a signal, they want to start the war. Today.'

Hoffmann stared at him. 'Sigmar's balls, man, didn't they use all their gunpowder this evening?'

'No.' His neck ached. 'The crater in the Königplatz wasn't deep enough. I reckon they've got four or five hundred pounds left.'

Hoffmann stared across the dark room. 'An hour's sleep,' he said. 'No more. Then we search the cathedral from top to bottom.'

SOMETHING CLANGED, AND Grenner was instantly awake. It knelled again and he realised what he was hearing: the great bell of the cathedral, ringing to summon the faithful to worship. Light streamed through the windows. He threw off his blanket and shook Johansen on the next bed.

'We've overslept! We've bloody overslept!'

Johansen was alert in a second. 'What happened to Hoffmann? He was going to wake us.'

'No idea.'

Johansen began throwing on his torn and filthy clothes. 'You know he's an Ulrican?'

'Who?'

'Hoffmann.'

'What are you saying?' Grenner stared at him.

'Nothing. Just an observation.'

'I hope you're right.' They rushed downstairs and out into the street. Nobody turned to look at them: there were too many ragged, haggard people in the city that morning. Thin grey dust coated everything. Two horses stood at a hitching-post outside a building opposite. Grenner caught Johansen's eye. A moment later they were on horseback, galloping towards the great cathedral of Sigmar.

'How would they have got barrels of gunpowder into the cathedral?' Grenner shouted above the clatter of hoofs on cobbles.

Johansen gestured with one hand. 'Bribery. Concealment. The powder may not be in barrels any more. Where the hell's Hoffmann?'

'How should I know?'

Ahead, they could see a crowd around the cathedral's high doors. Many people had come to worship alongside the Empire's greatest citizens today, to mourn loved ones, or ask for divine retribution on their killers. Grenner could see armoured guards by the doors, swords drawn.

'Stop,' he shouted. Johansen reined in his horse.

'Why?' he said.

'We need to think about this.'

'Every second counts.'

'They're not going to let us into the cathedral looking like this.' He paused. 'How much gunpowder did you say the Ulricans had left? Enough to bring down the building?'

'Enough to make a hole in it, maybe.'

'They want more than that.' Grenner grimaced, thinking. 'Maybe they're going to crash a Bretonnian wineseller's cart stuffed with gunpowder through the doors and blow themselves up.'

'Not funny.'

'I wasn't joking.' Grenner wiped his brow and stared up at the huge building, its buttresses rearing up into the sky around the peaked slates of the pitched roof. Between their stone arms, hanging over the high crenellated wall around the top of the building, a scarlet flag was blowing in the wind.

'What would five hundred pounds of gunpowder do to the roof?' he asked.

Johansen furrowed his brow. 'You could collapse the whole thing.' He raised an eyebrow. 'Why do you think they're up there?'

Grenner pointed at the flag that had caught his eye. 'Recognise that?'

'No.'

'You should pay more attention to fashion. That's Hoffmann's cloak.'

Johansen was silent for a second. Then: 'How do we get up there?'

Grenner grinned. 'Follow my lead.' He dug his heels into his horse and galloped down the street, heading for the crowd around the cathedral doors, Johansen hard on his heels. Heads turned as people heard their approaching hoofbeats, there were shouts, and a path opened. Grenner rode down it, heading for the doorway, holding his reins tight to keep the horse straight.

The guards tried to block them with their swords but they weren't fast enough and their blades weren't long enough: Grenner thanked the gods that they hadn't been pikemen. He flashed past them and into the cathedral's antechamber, glanced back to check Johansen was still behind him, then crouched low as the horse plunged through the smaller arch into the vaulted expanse of the long nave.

People in the pews either side leaped to their feet as the two horses galloped down the cathedral's central aisle. There were shouts of surprise and anger. Grenner ignored them. He knew a stairway in the south-east transept; it led up past the gallery where the Elector Counts sat to watch the service, then spiralled upwards to the roof. That was their way up.

He galloped past the choir. Almost there. People behind them were chasing on foot, but he was well ahead of them. The horse cantered into the shadows of the transept, Grenner leaped from its saddle, drew his sword and ran to the stairs, taking them three at a time. Johansen was right behind him.

A wall of armed men blocked their way.

Oh Sigmar, he thought. The Electors' guards. There was no way through. He twisted round, to see more soldiers behind him. No way out either. Trapped.

There was a strange hush in the cathedral at this invasion of a holy place. Off to one side Grenner could see the open gallery where the Electors were seated. He recognised faces among them. He'd saved some of their lives, but they wouldn't know him.

No, he thought, one would. Grand Prince Valmir von Raukov, Elector Count of Ostland.

'Prince Valmir,' he shouted. 'The men who killed Anastasia are on the roof.'

The Elector's head jerked up and he stared at the Palisades officers as if woken from a dream. He looked surprised and alarmed. Startled, Grenner thought, to hear his mistress's name echo across the cathedral. It was a risk. If the prince was a typical cold-blooded noble he could ignore them and the guards would cut them down. But if, as Grenner had guessed, he had really loved the girl...

The prince stood. 'Let them pass,' he said.

The guards moved aside. Grenner pushed between them and headed up. Behind him, Johansen paused to take a loaded crossbow from one of the soldiers. 'I'll borrow that,' he said, and followed his partner.

THE DOOR AT the top of the stairs was closed. Grenner shoulder-charged it and it flew open with a crash. Outside, in the narrow trough between the low wall of battlements and the steep pitch of the roof, three men looked up. One grabbed for a lit lantern, one for a bow, and one did not move because he was bound hand and foot, gagged and leant against the wall with his cloak flapping in the cold wind. Hoffmann.

Grenner dived to one side. Behind him, Johansen raised his borrowed weapon and shot the other bowman in the head. He fell.

The second man, dark and heavily built, ducked behind Hoffmann, wrapping an arm round his neck, using him as a shield. 'You cannot win,' he shouted. 'This is Ulric's year! The false god Sigmar has been destroyed and his temple and priests shall perish too! It is ordained!' His voice had a northern accent and the hectoring tone of a true believer.

'Morning, sir,' Johansen said, looking at the network of oil-soaked cords running over the roof, doubtless leading to caches of gunpowder. Grenner had been right: they were planning to bring the roof down on the worshippers below.

'Don't move, or the nobleman dies!' the Ulrican shouted, pulling Hoffmann with him. The fuses were joined into a single twist of cord, Johansen saw. So they were all linked. Any fuse lit would ignite the others. Thirty feet away the Ulrican was moving towards the cords, lantern in one hand, Hoffmann in the other.

Johansen slowly raised his hands. 'Don't kill the nobleman,' he said.

'It'd look bad on our records if you did,' said Grenner from behind him. 'Sorry about this, sir.' A throwing-knife flashed from his hand and embedded itself in Hoffmann's thigh. The general's leg gave way and he collapsed. Johansen was already drawing his small crossbow from its shoulder-holster and firing, running forwards.

The Ulrican took the bolt in the temple and fell, throwing the lantern at the cords. It struck the stonework of the gutter at an angle and rolled, the oil inside blazing up.

Johansen sprinted and kicked it as hard as he could, away from the fuses. Glass shattered and glistening liquid sprayed out as the lantern soared away over the battlements and down into the city below. He didn't hear a crash.

He turned. Grenner was crouched beside Hoffmann, cutting his bonds. Johansen made an abrupt gesture and Grenner stopped.

'What?'

'Remember last night?'

Grenner's eyes widened. 'Back-up guy.'

'Where?' There was no sign of anyone else. Johansen took a few paces, checking around the exit to the stairway.

There was a scream from the top of the roof and a figure hurtled down the steep slope full-tilt, a lantern in one hand, a sword in the other.

The sword slashed at Johansen's arm. He dodged sideways, grabbing for the man's jerkin, lifting him as he ran, using his momentum to throw him over the wall.

The man screamed all the way down.

'I CAN'T BELIEVE Hoffmann went to start the search on his own,' Grenner said as they walked away from the cathedral, leaving the oblivious crowds behind them. 'He must have known the Ulricans would have left people on guard.'

'Why didn't they kill him when they caught him?'

'They wanted him to distract people like us. They only needed a few seconds.'

'They almost got them.' Johansen looked around. 'Where are you taking me?'

'Since the Black Goat is out of commission,' Grenner said, 'I thought I'd treat you to Hexenstag breakfast at a place I know by the west gate.'

'I'd rather have a wash and get some sleep.'

'You'll sleep better with a full stomach.' Grenner paused. 'Have you noticed that nobody thanked us?'

'Hoffmann did.'

'Hoffmann is deducting his surgeon's bill from my wages. That's hardly thanks.'

There was silence as the two men walked on through the city. Some things didn't need to be said out loud. The watery sun was warm on their skin and the light breeze helped them forget how dirty and tired they both were.

There was a queue of carts, wagons and pedestrians at the west gate, waiting to leave the city. Already security had been tightened after the Königplatz explosion, and every guard wanted to be seen doing his job. Grenner felt Johansen's elbow dig into his ribs and looked up. His partner was pointing at a familiar cart in the queue. 'You owe someone an apology,' he said.

Grenner gave him a long look, then sighed and walked up to the cart, its cargo of wide barrels stacked upright and roped together for travel. He reached up a hand in greeting.

'It is Hexenstag morning, a time of goodwill, monsieur,' he said, 'and I owe you an apology.'

The Bretonnian wineseller in the driver's seat looked startled and scared. He groped for his reins to jolt his horses into motion. Grenner stepped back, raising his hands in appeasement.

'We were looking for the men who caused the explosion last night. I thought you might be involved. I was wrong. So,' he added, 'you're leaving Altdorf.'

The short man nodded sourly. 'Zis city, she is not friendly to strangers, you know? And zis thing last night, very bad. I go home.'

'Did you sell your wine in the end?'

The Bretonnian nodded. 'Oui. In the end.'

'Well, that's something. Travel safely.' Grenner nodded farewell and walked away from the cart and back to Johansen.

'Stop looking so smug,' he said.

Johansen grinned. '"Hexenstag morning, a time of goodwill",' he said. 'You hate admitting you're wrong, that's your problem. You should keep some goodwill in your heart the rest of the... What?'

Grenner was staring at the back of the Bretonnian's head. 'If he's sold his wine,' he said, 'why's he still got the barrels on his cart?'

Johansen turned to look. 'I don't know,' he said. 'Do you want to ask?'

'You do it.'

The queue of carts had moved and the Bretonnian was almost at the gatehouse. Grenner waited as Johansen walked up to the cart, then went to its rear, climbed up and stood between the upright casks. He drew his sword, turned it and smashed the hilt down on the lid. It cracked and splintered. A female face, gagged and bound, terrified, streaked with tears, stared up at him from inside. The Bretonnian leaped from his seat and ran for the gate, but the guards were ready for him. They caught him, holding his arms as he struggled and hissed.

Five barrels on the cart. Five missing women. And he'd known there had been something strange about the wineseller from the moment he'd met him. Johansen hadn't believed him, but he'd known. The man was a kidnapper, a slaver or something worse.

From the ground, Johansen looked up at him. 'Result?'

Grenner nodded. 'Happy Hexenstag,' he said. He stared up at the sun, letting its warmth massage the weariness from his body. 'The nights start getting shorter now.'

'They'll get longer again soon enough.'

'I know. So enjoy them while you can.' He tugged the rest of the barrel lid away and reached in to help the woman inside to her feet. 'I know you're not much use at handling women, but I could use some help here.'

They set to work.

GRUNSONN'S MARAUDERS

Andy Jones

'GENTLEMEN, THE DEAL is done. Your honour, sorry, *our* honour is at stake!'

The young man stood defiantly in front of the rough wooden table, around which three travel-worn characters played cards and drank from battered tankards. Two tankards were full of frothy ale in which suspicious shapes surfaced now and then. The other held a liquid golden glitter, which the owner refilled from a delicate bottle every so often.

'Raise yer ten, and throw in me spare dagger of wotsit slaying.' The gruff voice was that of a dwarf of indeterminate age and very few teeth. His black beard was streaked with silver grey (and gravy stains), his face a mass of scars from old wounds, weather-beaten and rugged. His armour was dented and scratched, and two fingers were missing from his left hand. A huge, rune-encrusted axe leaned against the table next to him. Unlike everything else about the dwarf, the axe gleamed and shone, even in the fuggy gloom of Ye Broken Bones Inne. Grimcrag Grunsonn peered at his cards through beady black eyes.

'Ach, Grimcrak, ven to admit Defeat! Dat Kard is nozzink bot a Seven.' The heavily-accented growl came from the lips of a wolfish barbarian sitting opposite the dwarf. Heavily muscled, with a bearskin draped across his broad shoulders, the barbarian glanced at Johan Anstein and grinned, showing white teeth. 'I got 'im now, ja?'

Johan threw his eyes heavenwards and tapped an impatient foot on the worn floorboards. 'Look, we've been sitting around for weeks now. So I've sorted us a job out, and–'

'What sort of a job, lad? More wet-nursing ladies on the way to court? You know what happened last time! Hah! Wet-nurses!' Jiriki the elf laughed quietly, a knowing look shining in his eyes.

Keanu the Reaver, the fur-clad barbarian, emitted something halfway between a belch and a throaty guffaw. 'Vet-nurse! Ha! Zome joke dat, eh, Grimcrak?'

The dwarf stared stony-faced at his cards. 'Weren't no fault of mine. Should've had good dwarf buckets 'stead of them shoddy things.'

Johan winced at the memory, but pressed on bravely. 'No, a proper job. You know, underground – with monsters and danger and stuff, a real quest.' The young would-be hero looked dreamily across the bar, already envisaging the many brave and daring deeds awaiting them.

The others ignored him. They'd heard it all before; Johan's pipe-dreams rarely came to anything.

'Okey-dokey, Grimcrak, da dagger it is.' The Reaver held his cards to his massive chest in a conspiratorial fashion.

'It's a wizard, see, lives here in town, wants us to find a long-lost magical item.'

'They all do, lad, they all do,' Grimcrag muttered. 'Let's see you, then.'

'Funf tenz!' proclaimed the barbarian.

'Damn!'

'Ja!' Keanu grinned viciously. 'I vin! I vin! Da dagger, if ya pleez…'

Johan drew in a deep breath and threw a sizeable bag down on the table. It clinked with an instantly recognisable metallic sound. 'He's given me a down-payment.'

Expecting a row for dubious tactics, Keanu was more than a little surprised when Grimcrag handed over the dagger, but the Barbarian did notice that a familiar glazed look had come over the dwarf's craggy features. Even as Grimcrag's left hand passed over the weapon, his right sidled of its own accord towards the bag, giving it a nudge. The bag jingled again.

'It's–' Johan began.

'Shush now, lad, I knows what this is.' Grimcrag's features had taken on a look of rapturous awe. 'Bretonnian gold, brought back from the new lands of Luscitara.'

'Lustria actually,' Jiriki corrected. 'And you only had to ask; we've known about the humid, swampy, jungle infested place for…'

'Never mind that. Their gold is second to none.' Grimcrag felt the bag again. After a few more investigative pokes, a secretive, greedy look came over the dwarf's craggy face, and he paused, before continuing in a disappointed tone.

'Actually, on second thoughts, I'm wrong y'know.' He dragged the bag towards him across the table.

'Vot meanink?' Keanu asked, his razor-sharp intuition picking up the change in the dwarf's manner.

'He's gone all goldsome on us. They all go like that,' the elf sighed. 'He'll be alright in a minute or two.'

'Can we get on with it? The wizard is waiting.' Johan was getting more exasperated by the second. 'You've got... sorry, we've got the gold. It's just a down-payment; we've got to meet him at his tower within the hour.'

Grimcrag shook his head, a sly look in his eye. Jiriki gave a short barking laugh and drew his dagger. From past experience, the elf knew what was about to happen.

'You've bin done, lad,' the dwarf said, peering inside the bag. 'Yup, just as I thought: brass and copper, brass and copper – just enough to pay back what you owes me for the sword and stuff I gave you.' Tutting disappointedly to himself, Grimcrag made to put the bag into his pack, moving with startling speed – but the elf and barbarian proved faster.

Keanu held Grimcrag's wrist while Jiriki split the bag open with one lightning-swift stroke of his dagger. Gold coins spilled across the table, glinting and gleaming in the light.

'Koppa?'

'Brass my–' Jiriki began.

'Sorcery!' exclaimed the dwarf, looking sheepish, 'It was all brass a moment ago, I swear.' Johan could have sworn that the dwarf was shaking, and had tears in his eyes, but he put it down to the smoke which filled the air of the gloomy inn.

The young man drew a deep breath and gave it one more try. He was one of the Marauders now, so they had to listen to him. Johan tried to look stern and authoritative, copying a look he'd seen Grimcrag use to good effect a number of times – usually when confronting ogres or trolls and addressing them as if they were naughty children who deserved spanking.

'Ahem!' Johan frowned for effect. 'AHEM!'

Keanu shot the ex-Imperial envoy a glance and involuntarily spat beer across the table.

'Vot's up, jung 'un? Konstipatid?'

Grimcrag was dabbing his eyes with a dirty cloth, whilst trying to regain his composure. Jiriki was putting the last coin away in his pack to be shared out later, but he looked up and grinned at Johan's posturing.

'Not bad, lad, not bad – now, what's the story again?'

Seizing his chance, Johan closed his eyes and took a very deep breath, before rattling off as many of the details as he could remember of his chance encounter with the cowled wizard with the twinkling eyes.

'Err… He wants us to rescue a magic item of some sort from the clutches of the monsters – that's undead and suchlike – from some caves under the Grey Mountains. He's been after it for years, and it's all he wants. He has lots of gold and treasure, and the bag is a down-payment. He lives in the big tower on the outskirts of town, and says that if we bring the artefact back, we can keep all the other loot from the dungeon – all he wants is the thing itself!' Panting, Johan finished his monologue and opened his eyes, proud of his powers of recall.

He was sitting on his own at the table. A few regulars stared at him as if he was mad, or had the plague perhaps.

Flushing a bright red, Johan picked up his pack and stumbled for the door, making his excuses as he fled. 'Damn them all to hell!' he muttered, buckling on his sword belt and setting off after his com-panions. He could just make out Grimcrag's stumpy figure running off at the end of the street.

'Wait for me, you callous bunch of thugs!'

Johan set off in hot pursuit. Well, he knew where they going. As he tore round the corner, he heard the unmistakable voice of an enraged innkeeper.

'Wretched Marauders! Who's payin' for all this beer?'

Johan Anstein wasn't stopping. This was his quest, and he was going to be in on it whether the others liked it or not.

THE GREY-COWLED wizard had obviously been expecting them, since he was waiting by the door to his tower. It was a run-down building, perhaps a hundred feet high and little more than twenty feet in diam-eter. Weeds grew in thick clumps around its base, and ivy crawled up the lichen-encrusted brickwork. No windows looked out any lower than a good thirty feet up the walls, giving the tower obvious defen-sive capabilities.

From the top, Johan imagined, you could see for miles and miles, at least as far as the Grey Mountains, far off to the north. He also noticed that although the tower looked decrepit in places, the front door was very impressive indeed. Ten feet tall, five feet broad, its dark black timbers and heavy iron surround suggested indomitable strength and near indestructibility. It had so many locks and bolts that in places it was hard to see the wood at all.

'Spose that's magic-locked too?' Grimcrag had asked with grudging admiration.

'Not at all, not all,' the twinkly-eyed wizard beamed from deep inside his grey hood. 'You can't beat a good set of locks and a strong door. In my experience, ostentatious displays of magic just seem to make the wrong sort... inquisitive, if you know what I mean.' With that, and the jangling of a hefty bunch of keys, they were in.

The tower was gloomy and dusty inside, betraying the fact that it had not really been occupied for some time now. Most of the doors up to the fifth floor were boarded over and nailed shut, and Johan couldn't help being intrigued and curious. He'd never been in a wizard's den before, not a real one.

Keanu had stayed outside 'To be keeping Guard' but Johan knew that, for all his muscles, the hulking barbarian didn't much trust the powers of magic, and stayed well clear unless he couldn't help it. If the stories were to be believed, the only way Keanu liked to deal with wizards was with a sharp blade. However, gold was gold, a job was a job, so the Reaver was 'Votchink for Troubles' outside.

'A wizard's tower, eh, Grimcrag, Jiriki?' Johan's voice was a muted, awe-struck whisper.

'Poor decor, very dusty, not much of a colour scheme,' the elf muttered, mostly to himself.

'Badly built, needs repointing, I've knocked down better,' Grimcrag added from up ahead. 'Hold on a minute – how come Keanu had five tens anyway?'

'Yes, but still... oh, never mind!'

Eventually they had reached the top level and emerged breathless into the wizard's chamber. There, seated amidst the bubbling vats, stuffed animals, astrolabes, ancient books and all the other accoutrements of his trade, the wizard had explained the mission.

It seemed that he had spent his whole life searching for the Finger of Life, a powerful magical artefact, crafted when the world was young and death but a dream.

'Read that somewhere,' Grimcrag interjected at that point. 'Go on.'

The wizard explained that this item was a power to heal, to restore, and unspecified Dark Forces had conspired for years to keep it from his grasp. Now he had pinpointed where it rested, yet he was too old to go and wrest it from the powers of darkness. He needed heroes, mighty warriors of great renown, to go and retrieve the Finger of Life for him. He had heard of the great deeds of Grunsonn's Marauders, and knew that it was Fate which had brought them to this small backwater, south of the Grey Mountains.

'The way will be hard, but think of the greater good! Think of the children to be healed, the starving to be fed!'

'It's really that good, is it?' Jiriki inquired languidly as he peered out of the window in the tower. 'Hey, Grimcrag, I can see into young Miss Epstan's boudoir from here.'

'That good and better, young man!' exclaimed the kindly old wizard, ignoring the elf and concentrating on Johan. 'You see these boxes?' He threw a stout chest open, so that sunlight glinted on the contents within. Johan gasped: he'd never seen so much gold all in one place. The wizard noticed his shock and grinned. 'All as nothing compared to the Finger of Life, believe me.'

Grimcrag coughed and tried to maintain his composure, but when he spoke his voice shook a little. 'Take it off your hands if you like, I can see it's, erm, cluttering the place, and filling all your nice boxes too. If you like, that is…' His voice trailed off as the wizard flung open another chest containing a myriad assortment of gemstones. 'Gggn-ngh…'

'A pretty speech, Grimcrag, but motivated by gold-lust rather than concern for my storage facilities I fear, eh?' The old man laughed at the dwarf's obvious discomfort.

'Well, I just thought–'

The wizard swept his arm dismissively around the chamber. 'The Finger sits in such company as makes this little lot worthless, and you, my friends, may have it all. All I want is the Finger.'

'Lots of treasure then?' Grimcrag had that pensive look that usually preceded a new adventure. Johan crossed his fingers behind his back. It looked as if Grimcrag was on board at least. The wizard nodded.

'Plenty of orcs and other hellspawn to test the mettle of my Ulthuan-crafted blade?' Jiriki leant out of the window, looking straight downwards, his words a careless whisper. The wizard nodded. Johan exhaled with relief; he'd thought that the elf would be the hardest to convince. Jiriki looked over his shoulder, staring the wizard straight in the eye. The old man nodded again. After a moment, the elf shrugged and looked out of the window once more. This time he shouted: 'Hey, Keanu, can you hear me down there?'

'Ja! Vot's happenink?' The unmistakable voice drifted faintly upwards 'Is jung Anstein turning into a Toad yet?'

'No, my friend. We just wondered if you fancied liberating a fortune in jewels and gold from some of the greenskins you hate so much?'

There was a brief pause.

'Ja! Of course! Vot schtupid Qvestion!'

THE MINOTAUR BELLOWED and roared as it charged down the narrow underground passageway. Johan backed away fast, holding his sword in front of him. During his years of schooling to be an Imperial Envoy, he'd obviously missed the 'Minotaurs: Etiquette and Handling Thereof' lessons. His sword looked ridiculously puny, even to himself. Still, if he was going to die, he might as well go down in a way worthy of one of Grunsonn's Marauders.

'Come on then, come on then!' he shouted, inwardly preparing for a painful demise.

The minotaur grunted and slowed to a stop. Its head swung slowly to and fro as it sniffed the air warily. Its teeth were still bared, but it obviously wasn't quite so keen to face Johan as a few seconds previously.

Anstein blinked, and regarded his sword with new respect. Perhaps Grimcrag had given him a magic one by mistake. He waved it at the minotaur again for good effect. 'You want some? YOU WANT SOME?'

The minotaur growled loudly and backed off towards the darkness from where it had emerged scant seconds earlier. To the young adventurer, it already seemed as if hours had passed since he'd first seen the beast. Time moved like glue.

'Um... you craven coward, come taste my blade!' Johan took a step forward, much emboldened.

This was obviously too much for the massive beast, as it turned tail and fled into the darkness. Johan heard its cloven hoofs beating a rapid tattoo on the rough stone floor. He was just sheathing his sword, in pride and relief, when Grimcrag, Jiriki and Keanu came hurtling around the corridor.

'Hey, did you see that, I just...' Johan's voice tailed off in terror.

The Marauders were looking at him with open horror and revulsion, and Johan could see what was coming – these were trained warriors who reacted first and regretted their actions later. Well, sometimes.

'No, it's all right. It's me – Johan!' he shrieked, wondering if somehow he had been enchanted to look like a fearsome creature. This was crazy. It was also much too late. As if in slow motion, Johan saw two arrows flash from Jiriki's bow, even as Keanu hurled a wickedly barbed spear, and Grimcrag's massive axe hurtled through the air. Even under the circumstances, Johan had to admire their reactions.

Still in slow motion, he backed away, dropping his sword in abject terror. The missiles crossed the short space between them. Johan mouthed silent curses. The axe glinted in the air.

Johan's improvised escape stopped abruptly as he backed into something big and hard. Something that growled. Something whose foetid breath touched him for a split second. Something whose beady red eyes regarded him balefully in the instant before it was simultaneously decapitated by a large axe, pinioned by a spear and spitted by two arrows to its black heart.

With a growling gurgle and a fountain of viscous black blood, the immense troll collapsed and died, one viciously clawed hand dragging Johan down with it. His desperately flailing arms caught a knobbly projection of rock, which came away in his hand. Hitting his head hard on the granite floor, the last thing Johan heard was a dull grating, rumbling sound. Even as he passed out it occurred to him that they may well all be about to die.

A BOOTED FOOT prodded Johan Anstein in the ribs. Callused fingers tugged roughly at his jerkin. Foul, caustic liquid was forced down his throat. A harsh voice shouted at him in a barely understandable tongue, as powerful and (from the smell) none-too-recently washed arms wrenched him moaning to his feet. Even in his groggy haze, and with his head smarting badly, Johan knew that something awful was about to happen. Maybe everyone else was dead. Maybe he was the last of the Marauders.

He blinked and tried to stand unaided, swaying dizzily but determined not to give his captors the satisfaction of seeing his weakness.

'Vot you think, Grimcrak, not holt his Liquor?'

'He'll be alright, had a nasty knock on the head. Go easy on the lad,' Jiriki said.

'Knock some sense into him perhaps.'

'Now now, Grimcrag, the lad's done fine by us so far, give him credit,' the elf chided. 'We'd not have found the concealed door otherwise.'

Waving away another slug of the noxious brew Grimcrag was toting, Anstein looked slowly about him. He quickly ran his hands over his bruised body, checking that nothing was missing. Apparently not. A thought trickled sluggishly through his battered brain. It eventually came to rest.

'What concealed door?'

As one, the Marauders stepped aside to reveal a large portal, where before there had been only a rock wall. Evidently the piece of stone Johan had grabbed as he fell had been some kind of hidden trigger mechanism.

'Are you sure it's the right one?' Anstein asked nervously. 'I've seen what happens when you lot go poking around for treasure behind secret doors.'

'You've got the map, young 'un,' Grimcrag grunted, still affronted that Johan didn't want any of his beer, 'and all the other stuff from the wizard too.'

'Let's just open da verdamten Door, ja?' Keanu enthused, drawing his sword.

Grimcrag began to smile, and a split-second later he had his savage axe firmly gripped in both hands. 'OK! Let's maraud!'

'Hold it, hold it!' The elven voice cut the air. 'Johan's right for once.' Jiriki was squinting at the inscriptions on the doorway. 'These are very old and powerful runes, and we don't want to break them without good reason.' He traced their shapes with a slender finger. 'Very good reason indeed.'

Grimcrag peered at the symbols, muttering under his breath. 'Good workmanship this. Old. Powerful.' The dwarf turned to Johan. 'OK, young 'un, get the stuff out, let's be 'aving you. Who knows what'll be along in a minute?'

'Ja, Monsters, Dragonz even!' the Reaver chipped in enthusiastically, looking at the dark recesses in the narrow passage, perhaps to spot any lurking behemoths they had missed earlier.

Johan reached into his backpack and pulled out a selection of objects given them by the wizard. One was an old map, which Johan rolled out on the stone floor and weighted down with some bits of troll. The warriors hunched over the map, illuminated by the flickering light of their torch.

JOHAN CAREFULLY PACKED the objects away again one at a time. He had a bag to hold the Finger of Life when they found it. There was also a simulacrum of the artefact, to be placed exactly in the spot where the Finger rested. Apparently it contained enough power to paralyse the guardians whilst the Marauders made their getaway. This bit had worried Johan a great deal, nervous as he was about powerful artefacts and cursed guardians, but he feared to say anything as the other warriors had taken the announcement in their stride.

Johan had also been given a magical talisman, which would re-seal the runes on the doorway – if the accompanying instructions were closely followed. That bit had worried him too, but the others had pointed out that if push came to shove even Grimcrag could run pretty fast. Finally, there was the agreement signed by the wizard that any other treasure they liberated was theirs to keep: all he wanted was the Finger.

'OK, this is definitely the place, I've got the gear. Let's do it.'

'Vot's da plan then?'

Grimcrag scratched his bearded chin thoughtfully. 'Well, in my experience, places with secret doors – ones which are magically locked by old and powerful runes, mind – spell two things.' He paused a moment and counted on his stubby fingers. 'The main one is treasure. Gold.' At the thought, his eyes closed wistfully for a few moments.

'And the second?' Johan prompted.

'Ah, the second...' Grimcrag scowled and looked fierce. 'That'll be all the hideous monsters defending the gold, all destined to die by my blade!'

'Und mine also!'

Jiriki looked heavenwards, arms folded. He tapped his foot impatiently. 'And the plan is?'

Grimcrag beamed. Jiriki began to grin. The Reaver's barking laugh cut the dank air.

'We all know the plan, don't we? It's the same one we've always used,' Grimcrag said politely, before lowering his voice to a rumbling, menacing rasp. 'We goes in, we kills 'em all, we takes the loot, we legs it. Gottit?'

'Clear as a bell, my friend.'

'Ja, Kunnink!'

Johan blanched in terror. 'Is that it? Shouldn't we at least–'

But it was too late. Grimcrag and Keanu rolled back the great stone doors, ready to rush the inevitable horde of monsters. Jiriki had an arrow nocked, the string on his fine elf bow pulled taut.

A moment later and they were all reeling back in shocked surprise. Rather than the expected flood of zombies, Chaos creatures, orcs or worse, they were completely blinded by a burst of pure white light. The brightness threw the tunnel into stark whiteness, and the Marauders fell to their knees, their hands covering their eyes. The torches they carried were dropped, to gutter and die on the floor, but no one noticed, such was the intensity of the light streaming from the long-sealed cavern.

Johan hurled himself to one side of the stone doorway, where he lay panting in terror. After a moment he found that he was, surprisingly, still alive.

Johan blinked. 'It's just light!' he called out, standing up warily and dusting himself down. Shielding his eyes and peering around the doorway, he saw the others walking into the light, black silhouettes against the brightness.

'Get in here, manling, sharpish!'

Johan staggered forwards, tentatively entering a chamber where the air was crisp and sweet, and the sound of soft breathing resonated peacefully. As his eyes grew accustomed to the glare, Johan gasped in astonishment. They were in a low roofed, circular chamber at least thirty feet in diameter. The walls were bright white, and radiated the light which had assailed them.

This was not what had caused Johan to gasp. In a circle around the walls of the cavern there was a ring of stone slabs, perhaps twenty in all. On each, bedecked in the finery of princes, was an elf warrior of such beauty and nobility that it was almost painful to look upon them. They slept, and theirs was the soft breathing which filled the air. Each was in full war gear, each held an elaborately styled sword to his chest. Each looked to be a king.

'Ancient elf lords, livery of Tiranoc, the sunken kingdom,' Jiriki spoke softly, his voice tinged with awe.

But even this was not what had caused Johan to gasp. At the centre of the chamber, surrounded by the sleeping elf lords, was a plain yet elegant plinth. elf and dwarf runes were inscribed in its surfaces, the spidery grandeur of the elven sigils contrasting with the powerful majesty of the dwarf work.

Atop the plinth sat a finger. A black, wizened finger. A wrinkled, mostly decayed, scabrous thing of great antiquity. Despite its obvious age, Johan was under no illusions that this was what these princely lords were here to protect.

Grimcrag looked over at Johan and laughed. 'Don't be taken in, boy, one false move and these charming lads will be revealed in their true shape. Vampires, I wouldn't wonder. Daemons even. Don't touch 'em.'

Johan paused; doubt assailed him. Then, with trembling steps, he made for the central dais. Jiriki was already there. The elf stood by the plinth, reading the inscriptions as best he could. 'These are beyond me, but they are probably powerful runes of protection akin to those on the doorway.'

'Vot Treasure?' Ever down to earth, the barbarian was scouting the chamber, looking for secret compartments where the great treasure trove might be found. 'Nothink here. Not vun think.'

The dwarf looked around and sniffed the air, shaking his head in evident disgust. 'Good point, meathead. We've been done!'

'Never mind that now,' whispered Johan. 'Let's get the Finger and get out of here – we can sort out payment later, when we get back.' Once more, he was sure that something awful was about to happen. Sweat beaded on his forehead.

They converged on the central dais. The Reaver's sword weaved, testing the air, and his eyes darted nervously about the chamber. Grimcrag stood close by, legs apart for balance, his axe held firmly in both hands. Jiriki reached out for the finger – as he touched it, the breathing of the sleepers faltered in its regular rhythm.

'Leave it, Jiriki!' Johan screeched. 'Remember the instructions: the simulacrum!'

The elf recoiled from the finger as if struck. He nodded to Johan, eyes wide. Grimcrag guffawed, a nervous cough of a laugh.

Johan carefully unwrapped the simulacrum from his pack. It looked little like the blackened stump on the plinth, but the wizard had assured them that it held magic properties enough to contain the guardians for a while at least. Johan reached carefully with his left hand for the aged finger, his right simultaneously manoeuvring the simulacrum into place. As he grasped the finger, a shudder went through the sleepers. Quick though Johan was to remove the artefact, one of the lords abruptly awoke, sitting upright and reaching for his sword.

'WHO DARES–' he began, but his voice was cut short as Grim-crag's axe removed his noble head from his elegant body. Jiriki winced. Johan placed the simulacrum on the dais. The sleepers resumed their slumber, although now their breathing was dis-turbed, and they fidgeted restlessly in their sleep, as if in the throes of nightmares.

'Goddit, ja?' Keanu asked.

Johan nodded.

'Let's go,' growled Grimcrag.

They made for the door, half expecting a hideous trap to be sprung as they left. Jiriki paused by the defiled slab, his forehead furrowed by lines of uncertainty.

'Come on, Jiriki, it was him or us,' Grimcrag said softly from the doorway. 'If I'm wrong, at least it's not you 'as been kin-slaying, and I'll owe someone due reparation.'

Hesitantly Jiriki joined them outside the chamber. 'We're all in this together, my friend. Let's hope we're right.'

In the passageway, Keanu had a torch re-lit, and the warriors care-fully closed the stone door behind them, shutting out the white light and plunging themselves into gloom once again. Johan handed the magical talisman to Jiriki, who passed it around the doorway, realign-ing the broken runes once more.

'There you are, see!' Grimcrag exclaimed. 'That wizard knows what he's up to all right – all bar the treasure, that is…' His gruff voice trailed off, and he spat on the floor.

'Somvun get da Treasure first?' Keanu suggested, striding off along the corridor with lantern held high.

'Mebbe so,' grunted the dwarf. 'And wait for us!' Johan and the griz-zled dwarf followed the barbarian.

Jiriki joined them a moment later, a puzzled frown still on his face. 'The problem is, if we think for a moment, that the chamber had lain undisturbed for ages. We found it as it was sealed, runes unbroken. No one has been there before us.'

'And that means–' Johan added after the required moment's thought.

'No treasure!' Grimcrag scowled even more ferociously than usual. 'As I thought, that wizard has some explaining to do once he's got 'is precious Finger back!'

Dispirited, the adventurers made their way to the surface and the long trek back to civilisation. It seemed that the quest was, at least from their own point of view, a failure.

'At least ve're gettink da Finga,' Keanu commented, attempting a glimmer of cheer as they trudged out of the broken down cave entrance 'Und ve can see da Daylicht vunce more.'

Grimcrag looked around the desolate hillside. It was starting to snow again. 'What good's that to us, eh? Daylight won't keep us warm, nor pay our expenses neither.'

Jiriki laughed. The situation had tickled his elvish humour. 'And all for a mummified bit of man-flesh that is worth nothing to anyone except our misguided patron. We can't even sell it to anyone else.'

Grimcrag snorted and stomped off into the snow, followed by the barbarian, now wrapped tightly in his bearskin. The dwarf's gruff voice floated back towards the elf, who was stowing his bow to avoid the string being ruined by the damp air. 'Not funny. Not funny at all!'

Bursting into a bright and spirit-raising melody, the elf ran lightly after his companions, leaving Johan shivering in the entrance. A plan was growing in Anstein's mind, a plan so devious that it might just work.

'Hold on you lot! Hold on!' he shouted, rushing off down the hill-side after the vanishing figures. In a few minutes he caught them, waiting for him in the lee of a large boulder which offered a little shelter from the elements.

'Make it quick, lad,' Grimcrag said through gritted teeth.

'Yes, yes, but listen to this idea,' Johan began, hopping from foot to foot.

'Ideas, pah!' spat Keanu, his breath steaming in the cold. He stabbed Johan in the chest with an iron hard finger. 'Dis hole grosses Dizazta ist 'coz of your verdamten Planen.' Johan had noticed before that the barbarian's accent thickened to near-incomprehensibility when he got angry.

Even Jiriki shook his head wearily. 'I think you've got us in enough of a mess already with your pipe-dreams, lad. Leave it alone, eh?'

As the three Marauders turned to go, Johan jumped in front of them, eyes gleaming.

'Listen, you miserable beggars. We've got the Finger, right?'

'Ja, so vot?'

'The Vizard, sorry, the wizard wants it, right?'

'Yesss, go on…' Grimcrag was interested. He could see the glimmerings of a plan happening, a plan which might involve some gold.

Johan seized his chance and blurted out the whole scheme. 'We get old Gerry the butcher to make us a finger just like the real one. After all, the wizard has never seen it.' Johan counted the points off on his fingers. 'Then we take the real finger and bury it somewhere secret nearby.' Jiriki was nodding in approval. Johan held up another finger. 'We take the fake finger to the wizard and try and get an explanation from him. He won't let us in the tower if we don't have something to wave at him.'

'Klevva lad. Be Kontinuing.'

'Well, as I see it, once we're in the tower, he'll either spin us a yarn, or offer us some gold by way of apology. If we get some treasure, we go back and get the real finger for him. Otherwise, we tell him he's got a fake and sell him the real one. Simple! We can't lose!' Pleased with himself, Johan swelled up with pride.

The others, standing by the boulder on the desolate hillside, assessed the plan.

'Butcher, ja?'

'A simulacrum of a simulacrum, I like that.'

'Treasure and gold after all!'

'Well?' enquired Johan after a minute or so. 'What do you think?'

Grimcrag grabbed him by the shoulders, staring sternly into Johan's eyes. The dwarf's black eyes gleamed ferociously. Johan thought perhaps now something awful was going to happen after all. The others crowded round, looking over Grimcrag's shoulders to see what was going on. Johan felt his back meet the cold stone of the boulder. He gulped.

'Manling,' Grimcrag began, speaking slowly and with deliberation. 'Of all your harebrained schemes...' He stopped, and Johan cringed inwardly at what was to follow. 'This... is the best so far!' With a whoop of joy, Grimcrag threw his helmet into the air, caught it again and set off down the hillside at the nearest he was ever going to get to a sprightly jog.

Jiriki grinned. 'This is going to work, lad – he's even singing his favourite song!' Punching Johan cheerfully in the chest, the elf set off after the dwarf.

'What song?' Johan shouted, wincing from the blow.

'Komst, lad, let's go.' The Barbarian sprang catlike down the hillside.

Still smirking with satisfaction, Johan began picking his way down the treacherous slope. Even though he was concentrating hard on not falling over, his ears caught the unmistakable sound of the Marauders in full song as they descended the hill. After a moment's hesitation, Johan threw caution to the wind. Well, no one from the Empire was around to hear him.

'Gold gold gold gold!
Gold gold gold gold!
Wonderful gold!
Delectable gold...'

It was all going to be all right after all. Probably.

THE WIZARD WAS pleased to see them, skipping excitedly as he undid the myriad locks and bolts to his tower.

'You have it, you have it?' he fussed, leading them by torch light up the steps 'Of course you have, I saw it from the window.' The wizard turned around on the steps and reached out a bony hand. Johan thought he saw a rather greedy glint in the eyes which peered out from the shadows of the heavy cowl. 'I'll carry it from here on now, shall I?'

His eyes were mesmerising, and Johan felt his hand reaching unintentionally into his back pack. 'You can carry it now,' he intoned dully. Johan was barged aside by a sturdy armoured figure, who broke the spell with a characteristically gruff outburst.

'Not till the tower, that was the deal. We deliver it to the top of the tower. Always does things to the letter, we does. We've got honour!' Grimcrag's voice was laden with sarcasm, but if the wizard noticed he did a good job of not showing it, running off cheerfully up the steps.

'Very well, my friends. Hurry along, hurry along, I have a kettle on for a nice hot drink.'

'Hrrumph!' Grimcrag added, but they followed the excited sorcerer up to his den nonetheless. Five minutes later and they were sitting around his table, glasses of a hot, mead-like drink steaming before them. None of them touched a drop.

'Come along now,' the wizard chided, rubbing his hands together gleefully 'Drink up, we have much to celebrate!'

Johan smiled glassily and made to take up his glass, but the Reaver stopped him with an iron hard forearm. 'Njet drinking!'

'We always keep clear heads when concluding business. Nothing personal, you understand.' Jiriki's silky steel voice decided the issue.

'Of course. You are… professionals.'

Shaking his head to clear what felt like a thick fog, Johan thought he caught the edge of a snarl in the wizard's voice. The Marauders made no move. There was a heavy silence.

'Well?' the wizard exclaimed after a moment, and there was no mistaking the impatience in his tone now. 'Where is it?'

Grimcrag turned to Johan and winked. He was enjoying this immensely, although the canny dwarf had noticed that there were no treasure chests lying around this time. 'Where's all the treasure then?' he enquired of the wizard, as politely as a hard bitten dwarf who has been dragged to the perilous ends of the world for absolutely nothing could manage. 'Where's the gold?'

The wizard waved a hand dismissively and smiled. 'I took your advice and moved it. It was a lot of worthless clutter. All locked away safely downstairs, never fear.' He patted the large ring of keys under his cloak. They jangled comfortingly. 'Now, if I might insist, the Finger of Life, power of goodness, please, as agreed. I have waited long enough, and we do have a deal!'

'Ahem!' The dwarf cleared his throat after a moment's thought. 'Johan, the Finger if you please!'

All eyes were on the table as Johan Anstein, ex-Imperial envoy and latest accidental addition to Grunsonn's Marauders, unwrapped the prize for which they had fought so hard.

The wizard gasped. Johan thought that they'd been tumbled. But no, the wizard was enraptured by the burned and charred chicken leg that sat before him. 'May I take it?' he whispered, reaching out a scrawny hand. 'Oh, it's a beauty!'

Privately doubting his aesthetic judgement, the Marauders nevertheless nodded in concert. The wizard was almost in their trap. So far so good.

Then, with a speedy move which they would not have dreamed of witnessing from one so apparently old, the ancient wizard swept aloft the 'Finger' and simultaneously gave a loud and triumphantly sinister laugh.

'Mine, it is mine at last!' he roared, holding the chicken leg above his head. As the Marauders looked on in shocked disbelief, the old sorcerer leapt onto the table, scattering maps, charts and wizardly tomes onto the floor of the tower. Discarding his grey robe with a dramatic flourish, the wizard was revealed in a jet black gown, covered in unmistakably necromantic symbols.

'Vot?' Keanu began, backing away. It had taken enough beer to get the Barbarian into the wizard's tower in the first place, and seeing their patron revealed as a foul necromancer did nothing for his nerves.

Fully aware that the evil wizard was wielding anything but a potent magical item, Grimcrag and Jiriki remained seated, grinning to themselves. Johan, a little unnerved, tried to follow their example, and managed an idiotic teeth-clamping grimace.

With a face like thunder, the dark wizard looked down at them. He regarded them balefully. 'Idiots!' he hissed. 'Now you see the truth!' Glancing at the Finger, the sorcerer grinned wickedly. Snake-like eyes glittered in his long, bony face.

'This,' he continued, 'this is one of the long-lost fingers of the Dread King, foul lieutenant of Nagash himself.' He capered in delight on the tabletop. Johan recognised insanity when he saw it, and by anyone's book this was a whole chapter to itself.

'You doubt me?' shrieked the sorcerer, regarding their placid expressions. 'Why should I lie? I have searched for this for ages. I am old beyond my mortal span, and now, with this, I gain ultimate power and immortality!' Spittle flew from his foam-flecked lips as he ranted.

'Why didn't you retrieve it yourself, old man?' Jiriki asked quietly. 'You've obviously known about it for years.'

The sorcerer threw back his head and cackled maniacally. 'That's the joke, you see, that's the joke.' Doubled up in laughter, tears rolled down his hollow cheeks. Suddenly his squawking laughter stopped, and he stood straight, regarding the warriors with a baleful glare. Pointing at Jiriki, he laughed derisively. 'Your kin, ages past, locked the claw away beyond my reach. Sealed it so that none like me could enter the chamber. Guarded it with twelve mighty elf lords for all eternity.' He spat on the floor to mark his disgust. 'But I waited. Oh yes, I was patient. I tracked the resting place of the Finger and I plotted and planned. Many tried and failed whilst I brooded long in my tower. Then you arrived and all was clear. I needed you as pawns to do my bidding, just as my great undead armies will do!'

He studied the warriors as if they were mindless vermin, all but unworthy of his gaze. 'I needed you to go, unwitting, where I could not. You would unknowingly breach the defences set up by your own kind, and retrieve that which was rightfully mine.' The sorcerer laughed. 'Your lot ever was to be lured by greed and avarice.'

'And now?' Grimcrag asked, nodding for the others to stand up. 'What happens now?'

The sorcerer paused for a moment, head cocked to one side. 'Ah yes, what happens now...' He coughed to clear his throat, and solemnly adjusted his robe about his scrawny body.

'Now I must kill you all. You have been a great help, and it is a great shame of course, but really you have to die!' The wizard chuckled ruefully, and brought the claw down to point at the Marauders. 'Doubtless you will later join my hordes of undeath which will march across the world, but now YOU – MUST – DIE!'

As he finished his speech, he closed his eyes, and portentously threw out his arms, waving the claw at Grimcrag and the Marauders.

Despite knowing the impotence of the device, Johan found himself flinching. He need not have worried.

The sorcerer opened his eyes and frowned, puzzled. The Marauders watched him, transfixed by his performance. The wizard drew in a deep breath and tried the ending again: 'MUST... DIEEEEE!'

When this didn't work, and he noticed the grins on the warriors' faces, he began to suspect that all was not well. Tapping the claw on the palm of his other hand, he jumped off the table and quickly found himself backed up against the turret wall. 'Die...?' he whimpered feebly.

'We weren't born yesterday, mate!' Grimcrag grunted. 'Eh, Johan?'

The Marauders closed in on the pathetic, misguided and evil old man.

THE WHITE RADIANCE faded and vanished as the great stone door slid into place once more. This time around, the Marauders had taken the precaution of bringing two other long-standing sorcerous acquaintances to supervise the resealing of the runes protecting the vault, and to work out how the secret door could be brought back into place. Then, and only then, could they really forget about the whole affair.

There wasn't much Johan could do except stand by with a torch and a sword. Keanu was doing the same: torch to illuminate the others' work, sword to deter any would-be intruders. Johan was mightily relieved that no monsters of any description had turned up yet. In contrast, the barbarian was staring intently down the rough hewn passageway, and Johan was sure that the Reaver did not share his sentiments.

The two wizards – one bald and portly with fiery red gown and ruddy cheeks, the other tall and gaunt with flowing and sombre purple robes – stood back from the doors to admire their handiwork. After a few minor runic readjustments, they proclaimed their task completed.

Jiriki had already declared that the elf sigils were largely unbroken, and should stand the test of another few thousand years without any strain.

Grimcrag had enquired, checking over the dwarf runes on the portal, if that was really the best that could be expected from shoddy elf work? 'Aha!' he declared, stubby fingers probing the recesses around the stone-wrought door frame. 'I've found the catch to young Anstein's secret portal.' As far as his stout build would allow, Grimcrag pressed himself flat to the surface of the door, and reached his hand into a dark crack at one side. His eyes were closed to mere slits and his tongue protruded from between his compressed lips in concentration.

'Votch for Skorpion, Grimcrak!' Keanu whispered, all too familiar with the sorts of creatures to be found simply by probing one's fingers into the myriad small nooks and crannies to be found in any hostile dungeon.

'Thanks, musclehead, that's just what I don't need to hear!' grunted Grimcrag. 'This thing was built by dwarfs, so it must be set up to… ahhh, that'll do it!'

With a muted grating sound, a sheet of roughly surfaced rock began to slide slowly down over the rune-encrusted doorway. In a few minutes the secret chamber would be invisible to all but the keenest search. As they stood and watched the monumental slab descend, they all heard the unmistakable sound of scrabbling coming from within.

'Ee's Voken up then,' the barbarian stated impassionately.

'Looks that way,' Grimcrag added.

A barely discernible voice reached them through the stone door, which was already at least halfway covered by the descending slab. Grimcrag strode forward and listened to catch the words.

'Don't leave me here… The light it pains me so… My powers are nothing in here… Please, I implore you!'

Grimcrag rapped on the stone door. 'Hush now, you'll wake 'em up – and I'll wager you don't want that!'

The scrabbling redoubled, but was soon blocked out as the massive slab slotted into its final resting place with a solid booming thud and a cloud of dust.

When the air cleared, they were standing in a nondescript and gloomy passage once more.

Grimcrag rubbed his hands together. 'There now, a job well done.'

'Many thanks to you, Marius, Hollochi,' Jiriki added gracefully, bowing to the two wizards.

'Least we could do after that nasty business with the Crown of Implacable Woe,' replied the Bright wizard cheerily, whilst the Amethyst mage simply gave a single, sombre inclination of his head.

'Ja, tanks a lot!' the Reaver added. 'Now ve're getting to da Alehaus.'

Without further ado, the party of adventurers set off towards daylight and a well-earned tankard or two.

Grimcrag hung behind and walked alongside Johan, filling the latest addition to the Marauders with pride. 'Well, lad, it could've turned out worse,' the dwarf stated. 'At least we've done a good service to folk hereabouts.'

'Oh yes, Grimcrag, all-told a jolly successful quest, eh?' Johan agreed happily.

'Well, I wouldn't go that far. We're not dead, and he–' Grimcrag cocked a grubby thumb over his shoulder. 'He's locked up for good'n'all, but…' The dwarf sighed sadly. 'Not even a snifter of any gold.' His shoulders sagged as far as his battered armour would allow.

Johan grinned and reached into his pack, retrieving a large bundle of keys. They jangled comfortably.

'Oh I don't know about that, Grimcrag. Whilst you lot were busy bundling him up, I took the liberty of borrowing these.'

Recognising the keys, the dwarf's jaw dropped in surprise. 'I'll be blowed!' he exclaimed. Further up the passageway, heads turned to see what the commotion was about.

Johan lifted up the keys and jangled them merrily above his head. 'It's a big tower, I know, but somewhere there's a heck of a lot of gold going begging – and the way I see it, he still owes us for the job!'

Relieved and uproarious laughter filled the dingy tunnel. In a moment the buoyant adventurers burst into song, Grimcrag leading and the others taking up the refrain:

'Gold gold gold gold!
Gold gold gold gold!
Wonderful gold!
Delectable gold…'

As they marched along, Grimcrag patted Johan paternally on the shoulder. 'Yer one of us now, lad,' he said between verses. 'Ain't it grand when a brilliant plan of mine comes together!'

THE MAN WHO STABBED LUTHER VAN GROOT

Sandy Mitchell

IF SAM WARBLE had anything which might be described as a philosophy of life, it could best be summed up as 'Don't go looking for trouble.' Not that he had any need to; trouble had a habit of looking for him, which, on the whole, he was prepared to tolerate. Other people's trouble tended to be lucrative, and his own even more so. Like most halflings he had a strong affinity for life's little comforts, and prising him away from them was an expensive undertaking for anyone wishing to engage his somewhat specialised services.

This evening, however, trouble seemed conspicuous by its absence. Sam was settled comfortably in his favourite seat in Esmeralda's Apron, a halfling-owned tavern on the fringes of Marienburg's elven quarter, quietly contemplating the remains of a light seven-course supper, the most pressing matter on his mind the one of whether to order a Bretonnian brandy or Kislevan aquavit to wash it down with. The food in the Apron was widely renowned, so it wasn't that uncommon to see human customers squeezing themselves uncomfortably onto the halfling-sized benches, but he was mildly surprised when one of them approached his table and sat down opposite, staring at him morosely between a pair of knees clad in crimson hose.

'Alfons. It's been a while.' He nodded a cordial greeting, and gestured to the serving maid who'd been hovering nearby, flirting with a party of customers from the Kleinmoot. He might as well order the

brandy, as it looked like someone else would be paying. 'Or am I supposed to call you Mineer de Wit now you're an alderman?' He looked
thoughtful for a moment. 'You're a long way from the Winkelmarkt,
so I'm guessing this isn't a social call.'

'I thought I might find you here,' the man confirmed, ordering a second brandy for himself. He waited until it had arrived, and sipped
appreciatively at it before continuing. 'I have a problem. One better
discussed away from home.'

'I see.' Sam nodded thoughtfully, savouring his own drink. It was
smooth and fragrant, and knowing the proprietor of the Apron,
undoubtedly smuggled into the city to evade the excise duty. 'So
who's blackmailing you?'

'What makes you say that?' de Wit asked, a little too casually, and
Sam nodded, his guess confirmed.

'You're a politician. With a lot of goodwill in your home ward, after
that business with Luther van Groot, and that means influence.'
Which in Marienburg meant the chance to make money; here in the
mercantile capital of the Old World, wealth and power were almost
synonymous. 'A little fish tells me you're in line for a seat in the Burgerhof too.'

'People say these things,' de Wit said, his air of modesty about as
convincing as a streetwalker's protestations of virginity. Sam nodded
again. The Stadsraad, Marienburg's parliament, was little more than a
puppet show put on by the cabal of merchant houses which really
took all the policy decisions, but a seat in the lower house would
open up all kinds of valuable contacts to a man as ambitious as de
Wit.

'So I'm guessing someone wants their own slice of the pie, and
thinks you're just the man to get it for them. With the right induce-
ment, of course.'

'That's just it,' de Wit said. 'They haven't made any demands yet.' He
pushed a folded scrap of paper across the tabletop. 'Just veiled
threats.' Sam unfolded it.

We know the truth about you and van Groot, he read. *You'll hear from
us again soon.*

'Short and to the point.' He shrugged, and finished his drink. 'Luckily for you, so am I. Thirty guilders a day, plus expenses.' He half
expected de Wit to argue, but the alderman merely nodded.

'Don't take all week. I don't have a bottomless purse, you know.' He
counted out thirty gold coins, and tucked the now empty bag back
into his belt. 'The first day's fee up front, as usual?'

'That'll do fine,' Sam said, slipping the money into his own purse and
calling for another round of brandies. He glanced at the slip of paper
again, folded it, and handed it back. 'What do you think it means?'

'It seems to imply that I was involved in van Groot's criminal activities,' de Wit said at once. 'Which is ridiculous, of course. I was the only man in the entire ward with the guts to stand up to him.'

'He's not exactly been missed,' Sam conceded. The death of their leader had broken the back of van Groot's gang, and although his lieutenants had carved up most of his illegal enterprises between them, their activities since his demise had been on a far smaller scale. De Wit had been quick to capitalise on the gratitude of his fellow tradesmen to run for office, and both his political and financial affairs had begun to prosper as a result. Sam waited until de Wit had climbed laboriously to his feet, banging his head against one of the rafters in the process, before asking his final question. 'By the way, and just between the two of us, were you doing any business with van Groot before he died?' The alderman flushed.

'If you really believe that, I'll have my thirty guilders back right now,' he said. Sam shrugged.

'For thirty guilders I'll believe anything you ask me to,' he replied cheerfully.

WITH HIS PURSE now considerably heavier, and several of the finest restaurants in Marienburg within easy walking distance, Sam saw little need to hurry home. Not that he had one in the conventional sense; he rented half a dozen rooms in different districts, moving between them as the mood took him, or his current job dictated. One happened to be in the heart of Alfons's home ward, so he decided to sleep there that night, hailing a water coach and crossing the Reikmouth the easy way rather than taking the circuitous route across the single mighty bridge which linked the two halves of the maritime city. The boatman dropped him in the heart of the Winkelmarkt, navigating skilfully through the maze of narrow canals which threaded the island chain, leaving him on one of the innumerable landing stages which could be found within a few hundred yards of almost anywhere in the city if you knew where to look.

Waiting a moment to let his eyes adjust to the darkness, Sam climbed the rickety wooden stairs to the alleyway above, hardly needing to see his way at all. His lodgings were only a couple of streets away, and he'd used this landing stage so often he could have found his way home from there blindfolded; or at least blind drunk, which he had done on several occasions. Tonight, though, he was still sober, despite the amount of drink he'd taken on board, ballasted as it had been by enough fine food to have sunk a small carrack.

The alleyway seemed deserted at first, no surprise at this time of night, and he quickened his pace towards the flare of torchlight marking the wider street which crossed it. As he did so one of the patches of shadow ahead of him seemed to move, detaching itself from the darkness of a doorway. Sam glanced behind, seeing another flicker of motion cutting off any possible line of retreat down the alleyway. Fine, he'd just have to keep going forwards then. Breaking into a run, he drew a dagger from his belt.

If the man waiting for him was surprised by this, he gave no sign of the fact, simply walking forward in an unhurried fashion and bracing himself to meet the halfling's attack. If anything he seemed amused at the idea of his prey being able to mount any effective resistance. Well, the cemeteries were full of humans who'd underestimated a halfling opponent, Sam knew, having put a fair number of them there himself over the years.

As he closed with his assailant, a faint thread of unease began to prickle behind his scalp. The man stood as though he was holding a weapon, but his hands were empty, and something didn't seem quite right about them.

Almost at the last minute Sam realised what was wrong. Though the would-be assassin's hands were bare, his arms showing pale where they emerged from his enveloping cape, their outlines were blurred, a haze of darkness hovering about them, swallowing the light that oozed into the alleyway from the street beyond. A clear sign of sorcery.

Forewarned in the nick of time, Sam ducked under the reaching hand, and rolled, trying to ignore the hardness of the cobbles and the thin coating of filth which adhered to his jerkin. A jolt of pain seared through his shoulder as the groping fingers brushed against it, failing to close in time, and then he crashed into the shins of the black-robed assassin. With a yell of surprise the man fell, and Sam slashed at his throat with the dagger in his hand. A spray of blood, almost as black as the shadows in the distant torchlight, fountained, drenching the halfling in warm, sticky fluid.

Almost retching with revulsion Sam clambered to his feet, already searching for the other man he'd seen, but the wizard's confederate had obviously had second thoughts despite the drawn sword gripped tightly in his hand. With one look at the furious, blood-drenched halfling, he turned and fled.

Sam hesitated, considered going after him, and dismissed the idea. Whoever he was, the fellow had a good start, and he'd never be able to catch up with him now. Instead he began to search the body, hoping to find some indication of who wanted him dead so badly.

'You! Shortarse! Stop right there!' A clattering of boots rang on the filth-slick cobblestones, and the narrow alley was abruptly full of lamplight. Sam stood slowly, and smiled without humour.

'Sergeant Rijgen. Who says there's never a watchman around when you need one?'

'Oh, it's you.' Rijgen took in the blood matting Sam's hair and jerkin, and the crimson-stained dagger in his hand. 'Self defence again, was it?'

'That's right.' Sam nodded. 'Two of them jumped me. The other one ran off towards van der Decken's boatyard.'

'Can you describe him?' Rijgen asked. After a moment of silence he shrugged. 'Thought not. Anything on the body?'

Sam shook his head.

'What did you expect? A strange tattoo, or a mysterious medallion? You've seen too many melodramas.'

'What I expect is a bit of co-operation,' Rijgen said, then sighed. 'You do realise I should take you in, don't you? But what would be the point? You're not going to tell me what this is all about anyway, and Captain Marcus would never let me hear the last of it.' He sighed again. 'Bugger off, while I clean up the mess. It's what I'm paid for, after all.'

'IT SOUNDS LIKE sorcery, all right.' Kris nodded thoughtfully, and took a long pull at his ale tankard. After cleaning up as best he could, Sam had sought out the young magician in the taproom of the Dancing Pirate, a local tavern where they habitually met. He'd made use of Kris's talents before, and trusted his judgement where magic was concerned. 'The bad kind too, pure Chaos.' He looked at Sam appraisingly over the rim of his tankard. 'Lucky you're a halfling. A man would have been crippled by that spell, at the very least. It wouldn't have taken them long to finish you off after that.'

Sam nodded thoughtfully. It wasn't the first time he'd had cause to be grateful for his kind's innate immunity to magic, and he doubted that it would be the last.

'Do you know anyone who might be dabbling in that sort of thing?' Kris shook his head.

'I wouldn't want to,' he said, although he didn't take offence at the question. Unlike the Colleges of Magic in the Empire, the great university in Marienburg taught elements of all the magical traditions in a fairly piecemeal fashion, although it shared their abhorrence of Chaos; however, the line between legitimate and forbidden thaumaturgy was rather more blurred here, and it wasn't always easy to tell when someone had crossed it. 'I'll ask around, see if anyone's been taking an unhealthy interest in the forbidden stuff lately.'

'I'd appreciate it.' Sam emptied his own tankard. 'You know how to find me if you hear anything.'

WHOEVER IT WAS behind the assassination attempt, Sam thought, they'd be unlikely to try again so soon; nevertheless he kept his eyes open as he made his way home, and didn't really relax until his door was closed and firmly barred behind him. After that he slept perfectly soundly until the following day, when the familiar sounds of the laundry below opening for business accompanied the hearty breakfast his landlady brought up the stairs for him. She sighed as she picked up his discarded clothing.

'You should have put these in to soak, Master Warble. I don't know how many times I've told you, cold water's the best thing for blood.' She tutted under her breath, and turned his shirt over, assessing the damage with a professional eye. 'I'll do the best I can with it, but I'm not promising anything.'

'I have complete confidence in you, Frau Gutenburg.' Sam bit into a fresh herring sausage with undisguised relish. 'Your powers as a laundress are exceeded only by your talents in the kitchen.'

'Get away with you.' Mollified as always by his appreciation of her cooking, the middle-aged woman hesitated in the doorway. 'There isn't going to be any trouble around here now, is there? Things have been going really well since that nice Mineer de Wit got rid of van Groot. We wouldn't want that sort of element getting a foothold in the Winkelmarkt again, would we?'

'We certainly wouldn't,' Sam agreed, and went off to look for the nearest example of that sort of element he could find. The task was hardly difficult. Van Groot had operated out of a small fish smokery, which his chief lieutenant, Jan Alten, had inherited along with a low-grade smuggling ring and a brisk traffic in stolen goods. A bordello catering mostly to the local merchants had passed to the late crime lord's other trusted confederate, Karin van Meeren, and so far neither had shown much overt interest in moving in on the other's business; which hadn't stopped them from circling one another like sharks, alert for the first sign of weakness. Van Groot's other main money-making enterprise, a far from subtle but nonetheless effective protection racket, had been allowed to quietly wither away by both his heirs, at least for the time being; neither seemed willing to risk the wrath of the local tradesmen, who might just follow de Wit's example and refuse to cave in, with lethal consequences for the would-be extortionists.

'Sam. Come in.' Alten looked up from behind a battered wooden desk in the sparsely-furnished office he clearly liked to think gave the impression that he was running a legitimate business. 'What can I do for you?'

'You can talk to me.' Sam stepped over the groaning thug who had tried to bar the door. 'Your snotling here didn't believe I had an appointment.'

'Mineer Warble always has an appointment,' Alten told the chastened guard, who climbed slowly to his feet and closed the door with a venomous look at the halfling as he did so. The racketeer sat back in his chair, his relaxed posture at odds with the unease in his eyes that he couldn't quite conceal. 'What do you want to talk about?'

'Someone tried to kill me last night,' Sam said. He shrugged. 'Petty-minded of me I know, but I tend to resent that kind of thing.'

'That was nothing to do with me,' Alten said hastily. It was precisely what Sam would have expected him to say, but he let it go for now. 'Can you think of anyone who might want you dead?' Sam shrugged again.

'How long have you got?' he asked rhetorically. It was true that there were plenty of people with power and influence who might sleep a little easier knowing he was at the bottom of the Doodkanal, but there were just as many who valued his services, and most of them were the same individuals. 'But the chances are it has something to do with the job I'm on.'

'I see.' Alten nodded. He hadn't risen to his current position of eminence in the League of Gentlemen Entrepreneurs by being stupid. 'And this job involves...'

'Your old boss,' Sam told him. 'Luther van Groot.'

'Luther's dead,' Alten said flatly, with a trace of unease. 'That scrawny little baker stabbed him. Everyone knows that.' He shook his head. 'Never would have thought he had the guts. Just goes to show, you should never underestimate people.'

'Sound advice,' Sam said dryly. It had been a couple of hours since breakfast, and the smell of smoked fish was making him feel hungry again. 'And speaking of de Wit, do you know if he had any sort of dealings with van Groot before he killed him?'

'Only the usual,' Alten said. 'Luther sent a couple of the boys round to talk about fire insurance, avoidable accidents, that kind of thing. When they came back empty-handed he went himself.' A reminiscent smile ghosted across his face. 'One thing you can say for Luther, he never minded getting his hands dirty.'

'Not if there was money in it,' Sam agreed. 'Know many magicians, did he?'

'Magicians?' Alten looked blank for a moment. 'I don't think so. But then he never talked much about his personal life.'

'I didn't know he had one,' Sam said.

'You'd have to ask Karin about that. He used to borrow girls from the knocking shop now and again.' He glanced at Sam, with a surprisingly prudish expression. 'Nothing sordid, mind you. Just escorts for those dinners he used to go to.'

'Dinners?' Sam said, trying to ignore the growling of his stomach. Alten nodded.

'Luther was going up in the world. He'd been asked to join this dining club.' An expression of puzzlement crossed his face for a moment.

'Ranald knows why, they didn't seem like his sort of people at all. Guild masters, aldermen, people from the university; maybe one of them owed him money, and put him up for membership to pay off the debt. But they all seemed to like him.'

'When did they meet?' Sam asked. Alten shrugged.

'Couldn't tell you. It seemed to change from month to month. They never had a fixed date for it that I could see.'

'Did the venue change too?' Sam asked. Alten shook his head.

'They met at some house in Zweibrugstraat. That's all I know.'

'Thank you.' Sam nodded, and dropped a shilling on the counter. 'I'll take a couple of your mackerel on my way out.'

As HE'D EXPECTED, Karin van Meeren was no more happy to see him than her business rival had been, but greeted him anyway with the practiced smile of a professional hostess.

'Sam, my dear. This is an unexpected pleasure.' She gestured to the nearest of the blank-eyed young women lounging around the over-decorated parlour with an air of apprehensive boredom. 'Liserle, get some refreshment for our guest.' Then she turned back to Sam. 'I assume you want to talk in private?'

'I assume you do,' Sam said, following her through a door into a more comfortably appointed room. After a moment Liserle appeared with a decanter of indifferent wine and a plate of pastries which looked a couple of days old at least. At a look from Karin she put them down hastily on an occasional table and fled, closing the door behind her.

'Luther van Groot,' Sam said, as the wooden panel clicked into its frame. 'I hear he used to dine out in the Zweibrugstraat from time to time.'

'Then you'll have heard he used to take one of the girls with him,' Karin said, draping herself across an overstuffed chaise, which brought her overstuffed bodice down to the halfling's eye level.

Sam blinked, and tried to concentrate. 'The same one every time?'

Karin shook her head. 'No, just whoever happened to be around. I could have done without it, to be honest.'

'Why's that?' Sam asked.

Karin shrugged. 'I've got a business to run. All right, it was his at the time, but I was the one taking care of everything. The customers expect things to be nice around here. It doesn't help if the girls are get-ting upset.'

'Upset?' Sam took a small bite from the nearest pastry, and replaced it hastily on the plate. 'I'd have thought they'd enjoy an evening out.'

'So would I,' said Karin. 'But they came back spooked. They thought some of the guests were a bit strange. I mean, you get all sorts in a place like this, don't get me wrong, but this was something else. And then one of them never came back at all. Luther said she'd hit it off with some rich merchant from the Oudgeldwijk and gone off with him, but she never sent for her stuff.'

'When was this?' Sam asked. Karin shrugged again.

'A couple of days before he died.'

'I see.' Sam considered trying the wine for a moment, then decided against it. 'Do you know where this dining club met?'

Karin nodded. 'I can give you the address if you like.'

'I'd appreciate it. And a list of the dates too, if that's no trouble.'

'I can remember a few,' Karin said, dipping a quill into an inkstand carved to resemble a pair of feminine buttocks. She scribbled for a moment, and handed Sam a slip of paper. 'Those nights, I think. And that's the address.'

Sam scanned it briefly. 'Thanks,' he said. 'That's all I needed to know.'

'YOU WERE RIGHT,' Kris said, glancing up from the slip of paper. 'These were all nights when Morrslieb was in the ascendant.' He tapped the last date speculatively. 'And it was full the night the girl disappeared.' His chubby face seemed unusually pale, even in the shaft of sunlight striking through the shutters of the Dancing Pirate. 'You think she was sacrificed by a Chaos cult?' Sam nodded grimly.

'It's possible,' he said. 'The man who attacked me last night was using dark magic, you said so yourself. And where there's one witch there's often a whole coven of them.' Kris nodded too. 'Got any leads on who he might be?'

'I might.' The portly young mage said. 'There's a research student at the university who's got a reputation for unorthodox theories. Nothing to get the Temple Court excited, he's too discreet for that, but rumour has it he's been looking into things better left alone.' He looked narrowly at Sam. 'And no one's seen him since last night.'

'Haven't they?' Sam drained his ale tankard thoughtfully, and pushed aside the plate which had once held a fish stew. 'Is that unusual?'

'Not really. He often disappears for a day or two, especially if he's been to some dining club he belongs to.' Kris looked narrowly at the halfling. 'What? What have I just said?'

'WHAT EXACTLY ARE we doing here?' de Wit asked, huddling a little more deeply inside the doorway where he and Sam had taken refuge from the thin blanket of drizzle enveloping the Zweibrugstraat. Sam shrugged.

'Waiting for the show to begin.' Dusk was falling, and so far he'd counted twelve people entering the house Karin had named. De Wit made a small sound of exasperation as a trickle of water slithered from the brim of his hat down the neck of his shirt.

'If you've got nothing new to tell me, I'm going home.'

'The note was sent by Karin van Meeren,' Sam said. 'I got another sample of her handwriting earlier today, and the match was perfect.'

'Van Meeren?' De Wit shook his head slowly. 'How does she fit into all this?'

'Because she was waiting for van Groot outside your shop the night he died,' Sam said. 'She wanted answers about one of her girls who'd disappeared, and she knew he was going there to threaten you in person. He had to. If one man stood up to him, everybody would, and his whole protection racket would crumble.' He glanced up at the white-faced alderman. 'The only thing I don't understand is why you'd take a risk like that. No offence, Alfons, but you never struck me as the heroic type before.'

'I wasn't,' De Wit nodded sombrely. 'I was terrified. But I just didn't have the money. Business had been so bad the past few months I was on the verge of going bankrupt.'

'So let me guess. You saw him coming, and slipped out the back.

De Wit nodded. 'That's exactly what happened. But I wasn't quick enough.' De Wit paled a little in the flickering torchlight, the memory of his old terror still uncomfortably fresh. 'He came after me, and cornered me in the blind alley behind the slaughterhouse. I thought I was done for, then he suddenly dropped. Someone else had stabbed him from behind.'

'But you didn't see who,' Sam said flatly.

De Wit shook his head. 'No, just a flicker of movement in the shadows.'

The halfling nodded, and de Wit went on. 'I went over to make sure he was dead, and the next thing I know I'm surrounded by people, all cheering and calling me a hero.' He looked beseechingly at Sam. 'I couldn't just turn my back on that. It's the sort of opportunity that only comes along once in a lifetime.'

'Unfortunately van Meeren knows the truth,' Sam said. 'She must have seen you checking the body, and realised that someone else killed him.'

De Wit nodded, and made a valiant attempt to match Sam's businesslike tone. 'Any idea of what she wants?'

Sam nodded. 'She's been eyeing Jan Alten's little empire for some time, my guess is she'll want you to keep official attention looking the other way when she decides to make her move. Once you get your seat in the Burgerhof, though, she'll start to get more ambitious, you can bet on that.'

'I see.' De Wit took a deep breath. 'And if I don't agree to her demands, she'll denounce me as a fraud. It'll all be over.'

'Maybe not,' Sam said. 'Who are people going to believe, a hero like you or a lowlife like her?'

A flicker of hope appeared in de Wit's eyes as he considered this. 'Especially after your reputation gets another boost. By this time tomorrow you'll be feted throughout the city, not just the Winkel-markt.'

'How do you mean?' de Wit asked, clearly out of his depth again. Sam gestured in the direction of a party of grim-faced men approaching them, all armed. Most wore the floppy black hats which marked them out as members of the city watch, and the exceptions were clad in the blue tunics of templar marines.

'Luther van Groot was a member of a Chaos cult, which meets in that house over there under the guise of an innocent dining club. When they heard I was investigating van Groot's affairs for you they tried to kill me, which wasn't the brightest thing they could have done, all they did was bring themselves to my attention.' He shrugged, and indicated the men leading the group as they approached. 'May I introduce Brother Josephus from the Temple Court? Sergeant Rijgen I'm sure you already know.'

'Alderman de Wit,' Rijgen said. 'It seems we owe you our thanks again.'

'Indeed.' Josephus echoed the gesture. 'Master Warble told us it was you who pointed him in the direction of these heretic scum.' He drew his sword, while a couple of the burlier Black Caps kicked open the door of the house. With a final nod of acknowledgement he led the templars inside, most of the watchmen perfectly happy to let them go first.

'Why did you give me the credit?' de Wit asked, his face bewildered, as hoarse shouts and the sound of clashing blades began to echo through the street.

Sam shrugged. 'Because you're an honest man, at least by the standards of this place, and you just might do some good with the influence you've gained. If Karin's still stupid enough to try black-mailing you now, all you have to do is point out that she's a known associate of a Chaos cultist, and you have the ear of the witch hunters.'

'That ought to keep her mouth shut.' A bemused smile spread across the alderman's face. 'There's only one thing I still don't understand. Who did kill Luther van Groot?'

Sam shrugged, remembering the expression of shock and surprise on the racketeer's face as he'd died. The man had been stupid as well as brutal, the city authorities would turn a blind eye to a certain amount of smuggling, so long as the appropriate bribes were paid, but attempting to deal directly with agents of the Empire intent on breaking Marienburg's stranglehold on foreign trade had been tantamount to suicide. Given de Wit's known defiance of van Groot's protection racket, all Sam had needed to do to collect a generous bounty on the traitor's head was find a dark alley near the baker's shop and wait. Joining the gathering crowd of onlookers had been easy, and getting them to applaud the accidental hero had been the perfect cover for a neat and profitable assassination.

'Some things are best left a mystery,' he suggested, his attention suddenly shifting to the house across the road. A number of cowed and battered cultists were being escorted from the building, and he'd just recognised the second man who'd tried to kill him the night before. 'If you'll excuse me, that fellow still has his purse, and the son of a goblin owes me a new shirt.'

TALES OF
REVENGE & BETRAYAL

THE FAITHFUL SERVANT
Gav Thorpe

THE SKY WAS filled with the beating of black wings and the screeches of ravens, crows and buzzards. The odour of decay was strong in the air as the flock circled in the warm thermals that rippled above the burning Kislevite town. Brought from many miles around by the rotting scent of food, the huge black birds circled lower, seeking the source.

Below them, Gorlensk was a scene of carnage and wanton destruction. Many of the buildings were little more than heaps of smoking ash, and all of those that still stood bore signs of the slaughter that had occurred. Bodies were piled haphazardly where clusters of men, women and children had been cut down where they cowered by their psychopathic attackers. However, the flickering flames and billowing smoke deterred the hungry scavengers, until the chill wind brought a much stronger scent of death. The flock moved onwards and downwards, seeking out the larger feast it promised.

The scene outside the town walls was no better than inside. The shadowy shapes of the scavengers skimmed low, using the trail of dismembered bodies to trace a gory path to the main battlefield, a mile or so north of Gorlensk.

The flock's excitement grew as the rotting stench of death grew stronger. Their cries becoming more raucous, the hungry birds scattered into smaller groups that flapped low over the battlefield, each picking out a tasty-looking target. Here the potential banquet would sate the hunger of even this massive flock. The armoured bodies of knights lay next to the gouged and hacked corpses of their steeds. The blocks of infantry had been run down as they fled, and the piles of their carcasses blocked the road and the scattered farmsteads they had tried to defend.

There were more than human bodies littering the field. The feasters of the dead cawed in alarm and avoided the unnatural corpses of Chaos warriors and half-animal beastmen which lay heaped by the dozen in some areas, their armour rent by massive blows. The ground was red with drying blood, a crimson testament to the ferocity of the battle. Rats scurried everywhere, their sleek bodies matted with dried gore, as they weaved through the carnage, disturbing lazy clouds of fat, blue flies. The heavy, bloated sun was perhaps an hour from dusk, giving the scene of death and decay an even bloodier cast.

Picking out the pile where the press of corpses was greatest, the birds plunged down amid raucous skrawks and the heavy beating of wings. The bulk of the flock had just settled down to picking at the body of a brilliant white horse and the tangle of bodies around it when something stirred next to them from the midst of the dead. One of the corpses, clad in what was once a white robe now stained with swathes of dried blood, shivered slightly and an arm shot upwards to grip thin air. A plaintive cry wailed across the field, sending the scavengers flapping into the air again.

Markus rose to consciousness with a shriek, awakening from a nightmare filled with hoarse battle cries and blood-chilling screams. His heart hammered on the anvil of his chest, and his breathing was laboured and heavy. His head reeled and a feeling of utter horror swept through him. Not daring to open his eyes for a moment, unsure of what might await him, Markus paused to take a deep breath and fumble the sweat from his brow with his aching arm. His sleeve was ragged and damp, and left a warm smear upon his forehead.

As his stomach settled and his nausea subsided, Markus opened his eyes slowly, terrified that the visions from which he had woken would be true. His attention was immediately drawn to the corpses scattered all around him and he knew that his nightmare was real. The crows had returned and he watched in disgusted fascination as they gnawed at bones and pecked at tender eyes and other soft delicacies. Markus felt his stomach heave at the sight, but as he retched nothing but bile rose up, burning his throat and leaving an acrid taste in his mouth.

Markus turned his head to take in the huge white shape lying alongside him and he groaned aloud. His beautiful war-horse had been a gift from a captain of the Tzarina's Winged Lancers, given to him in grateful thanks for the many blessings he had bestowed upon the captain's warriors. The white mare lay still, legs stiff and lifeless eyes open, a gaping, leaking wound in her side providing a feast for a swarm of vermin.

As he tried to rise, Markus whispered to his four-legged companion, though she would never hear his words. 'Farewell, faithful Alayma...'

As he sat, pain lanced through Markus's left leg, making him fall back, a startled cry ripped from his lips. The pain brought back a flash of memory.

THE HIDEOUS WAR cries of the beastmen surrounded Markus on all sides. A rust-edged halberd blade thrust out of the swirling melee engulfing him and caught a glancing blow on his armoured shoulder. There was a movement in the press, like a wave coming towards him. The swordsmen all around him were being pushed back as an enormous bestial figure, a brutal mace gripped in its clawed hands, strode forward, crazed eyes fixed solely on the priest. Markus raised his hammer in defiance, but his heart quivered as he looked into that monstrous, bull-like face.

Then Alayma took over, his mount more highly trained in war than Markus himself. Rearing high on her back legs, her steel-shod hooves flailed into the beastman's face, smashing it to a pulp. Twisting slightly as she landed again, the mare bucked, kicking out behind her with her powerful legs to send another mutant foe sprawling to the ground, its chest crushed. Without waiting for guidance the mare turned and leapt through the newly created gap, carrying Markus clear. As he dared a glance over his shoulder, he saw the last of the Imperial swordsmen falling beneath the blades of the Chaos beastmen and, as he had done so many times, silently thanked Alayma for saving his life.

MORE GINGERLY THIS time, Markus managed to raise himself up on his elbows and noticed for the first time the extent of his predicament. In her death throes, Alayma had rolled onto his leg, crushing it beneath her weight. The grim truth slowly dawned on him and he whispered a prayer to Sigmar.

He was all alone on this blighted field of death, trapped beneath the heavy body of the war-horse – and easy prey for whatever creatures the fast-approaching night would bring. The thought that Alayma, who had saved his life, would now be the cause of his death, lay bitterly at the back of Markus's mind. With a sigh of despair, the priest of Sigmar tried to recall what twists of fate had brought him to such an unlikely end.

It had been a fine spring day when Markus had joined the Emperor's glorious army. For weeks before there had been increasing rumours of a large enemy force marauding through the northern reaches of Kislev. Stories abounded of the depraved Chaos horde, emphasising its merciless butchering and unholy acts of destruction.

Word came through that the Tzarina herself had requested aid of the Emperor, and shortly after came the messengers of Elector Count von Raukov announcing the mustering of an army. The recruiters came to Stefheim a week later, calling upon all able-bodied men to join in this righteous fight.

Markus had not been drawn in by the well-crafted speeches, drafted to stir men's hearts and make them feel honoured and courageous beyond their normal bounds. However, as he had watched the congregations of his sermons daily swell in size, and noticed the fervent look in his followers' eyes, he felt his own faith in Sigmar strengthening. The sacrifice of the normally peaceful townsfolk and farmers stirred Markus far more than any amount of fiery rhetoric. The humble peasants had looked to Sigmar for guidance and protection, and Markus had felt beholden to help them.

Before the newly-recruited soldiers of the Empire marched off to war in their ill-fitting new uniforms, Markus sent a message to Altdorf notifying his superiors that a replacement would be needed. When the tramp of marching feet reverberated through the hills of Ostland, Markus's tread had sounded with it.

A SUDDEN MOVEMENT close by made Markus snap out of his reverie. A fat, black rat, well-gorged on flesh and slick with the fluids of corpses, had tugged at his robe and was now attempting to gnaw at his shattered leg. The priest looked around for some form of weapon, but could find nothing close at hand. Flinging his arms about him, Markus shouted hoarsely.

'Begone! Feast upon the dead. I'm still alive, you vermin!'

Startled, the rat scuttled under the broken neck of Alayma in search of a quieter feast. Seeing his mare's neck so strangely angled brought back another rush of memory to Markus.

WITH A ROUSING blare of horns sounding the attack, the Knights Panther and Tzarina's Winged Lancers charged the vile black-clad horde, spitting hundreds of deformed adversaries on their lances within a few minutes. As the impetus of the knights' charge was spent, the crazed enemy army surged back. A wave of deformed creatures bellowing in bizarre tongues smashed into the Empire and Kislev's finest cavalry and a sprawling melee erupted.

To Markus, things looked grim, as they were assailed from all sides by the demented followers of the Dark Gods. However, the armour of the knights was holding out and they smashed and thrust at the enemy with their swords or the butts of lances, holding the sudden onslaught.

Then something unimaginably ancient and terrible rose up amongst the ranks of Chaos warriors and beastmen. The hideous creation, born of the darkest nightmares, stood thrice the height of a man and bellowed orders in some arcane tongue that did not need to be understood to strike fear into the hearts of all who heard it.

'Blood of Sigmar...' whispered the leader of the halberdiers deployed to Markus's right.

The priest turned in his saddle and scowled at the hoary veteran. 'Watch your tongue, sir! This unholiness has nothing to do with Sigmar, but is the spawn of depraved and mindless enemies.'

The daemon's massive horns gouged armour apart while its clawtipped hands wreaked a red swathe through all who tried to stand before it. The almost tangible aura of violence and malevolence that preceded it caused the Knights to retreat rather than face its unnatural vigour and savagery.

Faced with such unholy wrath, the men of the Empire began to give ground. As the monstrosity continued to carve a bloodied path of destruction through the ranks, the retreat turned into a rout and the brave soldiers turned to flee. Markus stood up in his stirrups and tried to rally the desperate men with prayers of courage and steadfastness. He had sworn to Sigmar that he would face these foes, and even if all around him was anarchy he would fight on, alone if he must.

'Hold fast!' he cried. 'As your lord and protector, Sigmar will see you through this carnage!'

It was to no avail and the panicked horde swept around him, embroiling him in a tumult of screams and pressing bodies. As the crying mass of men packed tighter and tighter, Alayma panicked and tried to force a way free, but there was no line of retreat.

Suddenly hands were grabbing at the reins and desperate faces lunged out of the throng, intent on stealing what they thought was the only route to safety – Markus's steed. Gnarled fingers closed around the priest's robes and tugged at him, and he felt himself falling. Markus kicked out at a bearded face and it disappeared into the crowd. He tried one last attempt to restore sanity.

'Hold! Sigmar is with us! These abominations cannot harm us if our faith is strong. Victory to the Empire! Attack!'

Markus's last words were drowned out by an unearthly bellowing and the screams of the dying came ever closer. Over the heads of the Empire soldiers he glimpsed the scaled form of the daemon prince. Its massive eyes were pits of darkness and a pile of battered bodies was heaped around it. It was so close now that Markus could smell the fear that crept before it.

A blade caught Alayma and she reared, whinnying. Knocked off balance by the press of fleeing soldiers, she toppled to the ground, crushing men beneath her weight. Markus heard a cracking sound, audible even over the hoarse cries of the panicked mass. He was scrabbling about in the blood-soaked mud when a boot struck his forehead. Darkness descended beneath unseen trampling feet.

WITH A START, Markus realised that the blow that had torn a rent in his horse's side must have come much later, when the victors spilled across the battlefield, hacking and ripping at everything they could find. Sigmar had been merciful and somehow he had avoided a killing blow while he lay oblivious to the world. At that moment, though, the baying of wolves reverberated across the surrounding hills and Markus corrected himself – he was not safe yet.

A shadow crossed him as something blotted out the setting sun. Turning his head in surprise, the priest saw a bulky figure silhouetted against the western sky, picking its way through the carnage. Markus's throat was too dry to call out but he managed a croak and lifted his arm to wave at the approaching figure, silhouetted against the deep red glare.

'Over here, friend!' he called. 'Thank Sigmar, I thought none alive but myself.'

The man turned abruptly and strode towards Markus. However, far from relaxing, the priest tensed as the figure came closer. He walked directly towards Markus with a determined stride that unnerved the priest. Markus thought that anyone wandering this blighted place would surely be wary of more Chaos followers lurking nearby.

As the shadowy figure came closer, the priest could pick out more details. The man was clad in thick armour and a horned helmet, and all about him were hung dire symbols of power, sigils of the Ruinous Powers proclaiming his status and allegiances. Otherworldly runes were engraved into the black enamelled chest-plate, inscriptions of protection and power that writhed with their own energy, written in a language no normal mortal could speak. It was plain the newcomer was no saviour.

Markus's heart fluttered and he struggled frantically to pull himself clear from Alayma's heavy corpse. Pain lanced through Markus's leg again and he collapsed on his back, whimpering despite himself.

Muttering entreaties to Sigmar, Markus tried to calm his ragged breathing and studied the approaching figure, who was just ten strides from him. He tried to speak, but his throat, dry with fear, just made a cracked, croaking noise. The dark warrior now stood perhaps three paces away, not moving at all. Dark eyes glittered inside the helm's strangely shaped visor, staring at the priest with unblinking intensity.

As his own eyes took in the immense scabbard hanging at the warrior's waist, Markus recoiled in fear, expecting a deathblow to come swinging down with every thunderous beat of his heart.

Markus flinched when the warrior reached up with a gauntlet-covered hand, but the death blow did not fall. The stranger gripped the single horn protruding from the forehead of his helmet, then wrenched the helm free and let it drop to the ground.

Markus blinked in disbelief. The man in the bizarre armour was startlingly normal. His chin and nose possessed an aristocratic line, his dark eyes more amused than menacing without the confinement of the helmet's visor. The warrior looked straight into Markus's eyes and smiled. An icy shiver of fear ran through the priest. That seemingly benign expression terrified him more than the slaughter that had occurred earlier, or even the horrifying carnage wrought by the daemon prince.

The terror he felt was wholly unjustified and unnatural, and his spine tingled with agonising horror, though Markus could not fathom why the warrior was so frightening. This was no vile daemon from the *Liber Malificorum*, but a normal man. For some reason, this just increased Markus's panic and his whole body trembled with every shallow breath he managed to gasp.

When the Chaos warrior spoke, he found himself listening carefully and – despite the awful predicament he was in – trying to place the man's accent. He thought it might be from the Reikland, but the intonation and phrasing of the stranger's words seemed slightly mispronounced and somehow archaic.

'Are you afeared?' the sinister figure began. 'Does your blood coldly run with the sight of myself?'

Markus swallowed hard, and tried to look as defiant as possible. 'You don't scare me, foul lapdog of evil! My master protects me from the ravages of your desperate gods.'

The dark warrior laughed, a deep, disturbing sound. 'But of course you must have divine protection.' He looked around himself extravagantly. 'Amongst this slaughter you alone lie alive and breathing, spared the fate ordained for your countrymen. However, could it not be that someone other than your master has stayed the hands of your attackers?' The warrior lowered one knee into the crimson-stained earth and leaned forward to whisper in Markus's ear. 'Is your master so strong he could hide your presence from the gaze of the Lords of Chaos?'

This time it was Markus who laughed coldly, shaking his head in disbelief. 'Sigmar watches over his faithful followers; he loves them now as he loved them in life. Of course it is Sigmar who has spared me from death. My soul is pure. Your loathsome gods have no hold on me.'

The warrior laughed in mockery and stood up, wiping the filth from his armour with a rag torn from a corpse's jerkin. Markus ignored the disbelieving look directed at him.

'Sigmar provides my life and soul with every contentment they desire,' he spluttered bravely. 'There is nothing I want from your dark masters.'

The stranger moved across to Alayma's corpse, kicking at the rats that scurried underfoot. With a sweeping gesture, the Chaos warrior unhooked his dark blue cloak and laid it across the wide curve of the dead horse's body. After smoothing out a few creases, he sat down on the carcass, causing it to shift slightly and send more pain roaring along Markus's leg. The priest gasped. When his tear-misted eyes focused on the warrior once more, the strangely armoured man was still staring straight at Markus, with the same amused, almost playful look in his eyes, his mouth twisted in a slightly crooked smile.

'Did that hurt?' he said in a low voice. 'Or did mighty Sigmar prevent your mind exploding with agony for a moment? They say pain focuses one's mind. In my long experience, however, I have found pain to be a constant distraction, whether in the suffering or the infliction. You say your soul is pure – yet you have had doubts, no?'

Markus shifted uneasily, trying not to move his leg. As he looked away from the warrior's constant stare, the man laughed shortly, an unpleasant noise like the yap of a small dog.

'Was it pain or guilt that averted your gaze from mine?' the Chaos warrior continued smoothly. 'I once heard a philosopher say that life was a constant series of questions, with each answer merely leading to more questions, and only death provided the final answer to which there were no more questions.' The warrior paused and his brow briefly knitted in thought.

'Jacques Viereaux of Brionnes, I think.' He waved a dismissive hand. 'It doesn't matter. I have many such questions, and I expect you have even more. Shall we live a little, and exchange our questions for yet a little more of life? How come you here, Sir Priest? You are ageing. Nearing forty? Why would a slightly overweight, peaceful priest be found lying as a casualty on this forsaken field? What brought you forth from your shiny temple?'

Markus was confused; the stranger's words were baffling his pain-numbed mind. Gritting his teeth, he felt compelled to ask the questions burning in his mind. 'Just who are you, foul-spawned deviant? Why not kill me now? What do you want with me?'

The warrior's eyes almost glowed with triumph, the setting sun reflected in those dark orbs. 'Now you see! Questions and answers, answers and questions! This is life!' The warrior laughed again, slapping his hands on his knees. He calmed himself and his face took on a veneer of sincerity. 'I am called Estebar. My followers know me as the Master of Slaughter, and I have a Dark Name which you would not be able to pronounce, so "Estebar" will suffice.

'As for my being here? I have come for your soul!'

Lord Sigmar, Father of the Empire, Shield of Mankind, protect me from evil…' That chilling horror Markus had felt when first seeing Estebar returned with even greater strength and he whispered a prayer to Sigmar, asking for guidance again and again.

As the desperate litany spilled from the priest's lips, the warrior bent closer, his voice a savage whisper.

'Your god will not hear you.' His arm swept back, taking in the expansion of death and destruction that spread for miles in every direction. 'Around this battlefield, my masters laugh and scream in triumph. The Dark Gods' power is strong here and your prayers will go unanswered. If you want salvation, you had best ask for it of other entities than your weak lord.'

Markus tried to spit in disgust, but the thin dribble of saliva merely dripped down his chin, making him feel foolish rather than defiant. 'I would rather be torn apart by wild creatures than to ask your insane gods for aid. If that is the best you have to offer, I think my soul is very safe. Just strike me down now, and stop wasting my time!'

'Strike you down? As you wish!'

Estebar stood up abruptly, unsheathing his sword and holding it high in one clean motion. Markus flinched involuntarily and shrank back from its glowing blade. The Chaos warrior appeared to be scowling and his dark eyes burned intensely.

'See, you still want life!' Estebar sighed as he lowered the sword slowly, then slid it back carefully into its black sheath. 'You have not the conviction you would like to believe you possess. I would not strike you down, you who I barely know and yet who intrigues me so much.' He shook his head and fixed Markus with a twisted grin. 'Your faith is uncertain, so what makes you think you really have Sigmar's protection?'

'My faith is certain; be sure of that, hellspawn!'

Markus surprised himself with the vehemence of his words. The priest wanted this strange conversation to end. This was not the threat of Chaos he had been brought up, and then taught, to fight. How could one fight an enemy who tried to defeat you with words alone, spoken by a voice which seemed to hover inside one's very mind. Markus did not want to answer Estebar's inquiry, but the warrior's voice seemed to reach into his head and pull the answers from his lips.

'Sigmar has saved me before,' Markus started before he knew what he was saying, his eyes glinting with defiance. Estebar looked at him quizzically, one eyebrow raised. That one simple gesture seemed to have a world of meaning and Markus felt a tug at his consciousness, pulling the story from the depths of his memory.

'I grew up in a small village near to the World's Edge Mountains. I was the son of a miller and fully believed that I would continue running the mill after he was dead or retired.' Markus's eyes were drawn to Estebar's. Those midnight orbs were like a bottomless gulf, pulling everything into them, sucking Markus ever deeper. The words came tumbling from the priest's mouth, despair overwhelming his heavy heart.

'Then one day, in the spring, the beastmen came. They attacked without warning: the militia had no time to assemble. I saw my father and younger brother cut down by their wicked blades, and I watched as they chased my mother and sister into the foothills. I had been delivering our monthly tithe of flour, four half-sacks of the finest, to the shrine of Sigmar when they stormed out of the dark forests. They did not enter the shrine – they couldn't, it was too holy a place for their kind – but they had other plans. They were clever; they brought torches and stole oil from the store house and set light to the chapel while we were still inside.'

Markus's voice cracked and tears welled up in his eyes at the memory. The other man's black orbs continued to stare intently, as if sucking the information out of Markus. Wiping the tears from his bloodstained cheeks, the priest felt compelled to continue.

'The old priest, Franko, soon fell to the smoke and fumes and I hid in the crypt. The smoke and flames followed me, though, and I thought I was trapped and would certainly die. Even if I could get past the flames the beastmen would cut me down as soon as they saw me. Then another's voice was in my head, talking to me. It was Sigmar, you see,' Markus insisted, 'guiding me, directing me, telling me an escape route. One of the tombs was false; pressing a hidden lever I opened the secret doorway within and stumbled down a long tunnel which took me away from the village.'

Estebar's face was a blank mask, but the priest pressed on in eager confession. 'When I hit the open air again I ran and ran, and almost died of exhaustion before I came to the count's castle. He sent an army of his men to harry the foul raiders while his daughter tended to my health. She was sweet and I would have loved her... had I not heard another's calling even stronger.'

Markus remembered that feeling, of salvation from the flames, and how his own faith had been fanned from a flickering spark into the raging fire of belief. Looking at Estebar he felt his fears subsiding.

'From that day on I swore I would return Sigmar's grace. I took up the robe and hammer in his name. That is the root of my faith and though I may flinch at your blows, it is still strong enough to thwart your masters.'

MARKUS STARED AT the dark warrior, the defiance rekindled in his eyes, expecting some petty retort that would seek to belittle his convictions again. None came. Estebar sat looking thoughtful for a moment, his hand toying absently with the sculpted pommel of his sword. The warrior looked around him again at the carnage, then cocked his head to one side a moment before the howl of wolves, closer this time, echoed through the heavy air. He looked to the west and frowned.

'Sundown is nearly upon us, and the time is fast approaching. Shall I tell you of saviours and debts? Of divine deliverance and holy missions?'

As he saw the longing in the Chaos warrior's eyes, Markus's lips formed a sneer. 'I do not need to hear your tale of treachery and weakness. You are less than nothing to me!'

Estebar waved dismissively, as if Markus was little more than an irritating insect, and sighed. 'Whatever.' He looked up at the rapidly darkening sky, his memory lost in a dim, distant time.

'My faith started much younger than yours, and I had not the choice you were offered. I was the eldest son of a wealthy merchant family in Nuln. I had a good education, lots of friends and powerful allies, and all this before I had seen fifteen summers! Life was good – probably too good, my later experiences have taught me. Chaos was the bane of my family too. I can see why you were brought to me now; we have at least that much in common. Behind the strong walls of Nuln we were safe from marauding beastmen, but another peril, one much more loathsome and insidious, awaited us.'

The warrior's dark eyes were sad, though a faint glimmer of a smile played about his lips for a moment and then faded. He sat down on Alayma again, more gently this time, and stared at the ground. Absentmindedly, he began to pull off his heavy gauntlets.

'A cult, dedicated to the Lord of Pleasure, enticed us into a trap. For all we knew, it was just another magnificent party, another event in a busy social calendar. However, they locked the doors after we had entered, and then the sacrifices began. I will not say what perverse fascinations went on there, for it would take too long and I have no wish to be found alone on this field when the stalkers of the night come running. However, let me say simply that one by one the guests were sacrificed to Slaanesh, until only a few of us, the youngest, remained. Obviously we were highly prized. Fate had other plans for me, though, and when the Reiksguard broke down the doors and smashed through the windows I thought I was saved. They slew the cultists and freed us, but I was never truly free again.'

The Chaos warrior fell silent for a moment, his gaze fixed on the withered, blood-soaked grass between his boots. Then he gave Markus a crooked smile.

'Slaanesh, Prince of Chaos, had already caught my soul without even asking for it! The warpstone incense burnt during the long ceremony took a grip on me. Slowly at first, I remember, my senses grew more powerful. I could see minute details on plants and animals, I could hear the whispers of my neighbours like the thunderclaps of a storm and the feel of the silken clothes in my wardrobe against my skin approached ecstasy.' Estebar stroked a hand through dead Alayma's flowing mane and shuddered, his lip quivering and his eyes rolled up for a moment. Then he snatched his hand back, as if taking control of himself, and his eyes narrowed dangerously.

Markus could see that the memories were not as pleasant as Estebar would like him to believe. Who could tell how much the young man had endured, half-possessed by an ancient, evil god, forced to follow the ways of darkness. Perhaps, Markus considered, Estebar was longing for an end to his curse. Mind whirling, the priest started formulating a plan that would save them both from damnation.

'There is no need for this agony to continue. Come with me and I will teach you the old path of Faith. You will learn again what it means to have your freedom,' he insisted.

Estebar did not seem to hear or want to listen; he was wholly wrapped up in his own past. Regaining his composure, he carried on with his tale.

'That was not all. My mind expanded also, giving me a prescience, a foresight into the future. Combined with everything else, my life was full of pleasure. I endured the moment to every extent and could see the later pleasures that would follow at the same time. I wasted these skills at first, taking pleasure in women and feasting and drinking. I used my foresight to amass a fortune at the gambling tables.

'When the rich society had been exhausted, a conquest of perhaps seven or eight years, I looked to lower quarters for my entertainment. Slaanesh had me in its grip and every night for years I frequented the dockside taverns, challenging death with cut-throats and other scum for the sheer excitement and rush of blood.' The Chaos warrior sighed again.

'Then suddenly I was bored again. A wanderlust filled me, and I travelled wide, revelling in every new experience; a night under the stars, the feel of a hearty farmhouse daughter, the taste of exotic foods. Slowly, but with a subtle determination, I made my way northwards, through Kislev, and a few elegant dances at the Tzarina's court, up into the Troll country, ever onwards to the realm of the Lost and the Damned. I was Slaanesh's pawn and loved it. I travelled those nightmare regions until I stood before the Great Gate itself and begged Slaanesh to allow me to enter into the beautiful paradise that lies beyond.' Estebar looked up, his face made of steel. 'I was flung back far, scorned and ridiculed for my impudence. Entrance into that plane was not to be given lightly. I would have to buy my way in.'

Markus was shocked. The implication of the other's words were clear. 'You seek no redemption, you truly are happy in your chains. You are a greater fool than I realised to be held by such a weak lure. The only eternity worthwhile to strive for is in the embrace of Sigmar, not some unholy hell forged from a mad god's whims!' Then another realisation dawned on Markus and he eyed Estebar with renewed suspicion.

'Souls. You must pay a number of souls to the Ruinous Powers before they let you cross over, isn't that it?'

Estebar laughed loudly and for a long time. With an enthusiastic grin he nodded. 'Yes, yes! My dear Markus – but of course I know your name; how sharply your wits are honed!' The Chaos warrior smiled benevolently. 'But not any souls. Oh no, that would be far too easy. The souls I have claimed for Chaos, for I forswore Slaanesh as my sole patron, have been men of high standing, strong of courage and moral fibre like yourself.'

Markus was shocked. 'How can anybody willingly give themselves to Chaos? Even you are not guilty of that stupidity!'

Then another thought occurred to him: they hadn't gone willingly at all, they had been used and perverted by the same subtle power that Estebar was using on him right now. In the twilight, the Chaos lord seemed to swell. An aura played about his body, spilling through the air like a vapour. As Estebar spoke, Markus fancied he could feel the insubstantial tendrils of that vile aura reaching out to wrap around him too.

'Lord Sigmar, Father of the Empire, Shield of Mankind, protect me from evil…'

Estebar seemed to grow angry, his face twisted in a sneer, eyes boring deep into Markus's head. 'You will be my last soul! You will be mine! Guided by the Lord Tzeentch, I have slaughtered thousands just to bring you here. My precognition has waxed powerful over the years and I saw this day long ago. It is the day of my ultimate triumph. I could kill you now, swifter than a blink of your clouded eye, but only you can vouch your soul to my cause. Your soul will be given over to my lordly masters. As you take my place and serve them in this world, I, Estebar, the Master of Slaughter, bringer of despair to a hundred towns, will ascend to the glories of the Otherworld. It is written in my destiny. It will be so!'

* * *

ESTEBAR RELAXED HIS hands, which had been gripped in fists so tight a trickle of blood dripped from his palms where his nails had dug deep into the flesh. Taking a deep breath, he calmed himself.

'And yet, at the last, you still have a choice. Renounce your faith in Sigmar and I will depart to greater glories. Without me at its head, my army will fragment and scatter and the Empire will be safe. If you defy me, I will burn, torture and defile every man, woman and child between here and Altdorf searching for another who will fall before my grace.' He sighed. 'There is no point resisting, I will have another soul, so make it yours and you can save thousands of lives, end the torment and suffering and earn your own salvation. Just a simple nod or word is all I need.

'What does it feel like to be the saviour of the Empire, Markus?'

'Lord Sigmar, Father of the Empire, Shield of Mankind, protect me from evil…' the priest groaned.

Markus's prayers brought no solace. The fiend's subtle words were playing tricks with his mind. The bargain sounded so simple, and he did not doubt the truth of Estebar's pledge. Markus was confused, his mind travelling in circles. How could he tell if it was truly Sigmar who had saved him from the fire in the chapel? Could it have been the twisted Chaos Gods who had freed him so many years ago simply so that he would be here now? No doubt the plans of the Dark Powers were bold and only the test of time would see their fruition. Plans within plans, wheels within wheels spun in Markus's terrified mind. Summoning his mental strength he spat out his defiance, wrenching each word from the depths of his soul.

'I will… not… betray… my… lord!'

Estebar spoke again, his voice at its most subtle, sliding into Markus's consciousness and leaving its indelible mark. 'Thousands will live or die by your choice, yourself included. Whether you listen to your heart or your head, you have no real choice. Perhaps one day you will come to join me in Dark Paradise.'

Doubt crept into Markus's mind like an assassin. Perhaps he could claim his abandonment of Sigmar and thus save the Empire from the ravages of this madman, but in his heart remain true to his faith. Maybe Sigmar had been his saviour, for the very same reason that he alone could avert this catastrophe. Either way, the priest's past life took on a whole new meaning and many mysteries were now explained to him.

But what if that was but the first chink in the armour of his faith? Could he truly lie about what he believed? Was this the same path trodden by Estebar's past victims, believing themselves safe until they realised that they had lied one time too many and they were now damned? Could faith ever be feigned and would Estebar realise Markus's lack of sincerity?

As Markus wracked his brains for the right answer, the agonised yowling of some forest creature's final moments sounded across the darkness, followed by a series of monstrous roars. Estebar stood up and gazed towards the forest in the distance, pulling on his gloves.

'Make your choice quickly, priest. Other creatures more fell than wolves stalk this night. That is the cry of Khorne's hunters, the flesh hounds. I will make the choice simple for you. Even if you could free yourself you might not escape the swift chase of those daemon stalkers. You must have a symbol of your new allegiance to protect you from their ripping claws and savage jaws.'

Estebar stood and drew his sword from its scabbard once again. Startled, Markus was transfixed by the ill-forged blade. It was of the blackest metal, inscribed with golden runes that writhed under his gaze. For a brief moment, though, Markus could understand them; he could decipher the dire spells of cleaving and maiming that they embodied. The moment passed and they turned into evil but non-sensical sigils once again. Estebar thrust the sword blade down into the ground a foot to Markus's right, within easy reach. He plucked his cloak off the cold body of Markus's horse.

'Cut yourself free, priest, and you and thousands of your countrymen will live. Fulfil your destiny and take up the sword! Do not deny this; it has been written in fate since the stars were formed and the cursed sun first burned. Now I will leave you with your thoughts. Don't take too long or the choice will be made for you.'

With a bow of his head and one last regarding look, Estebar fastened his cloak again and strode away into the looming darkness of the early night.

For a long time Markus did not move, but lay with his eyes closed and listened to his own ragged breathing. There was no one else to convince but himself and he could not lie to his own heart, even if his head could be betrayed. Could he wield that twisted blade at all, even to cut himself free and still remain faithful to Sigmar? There was no guarantee that the sword would let him wield it without first swearing his allegiance to Chaos. There were tales of holy weapons that would burn the hands of the impure if they held them. Perhaps similar unholy weapons existed to test the faith of the impure. Markus was lost inside his own arguments.

A howl split the silence, and Markus imagined he could feel the padding of many huge clawed feet across the ground. The sound of bestial panting came out of the darkness. Markus opened his eyes.

The moon of Morrslieb, harbinger of Chaos, was rising over the night-shrouded forest. Silhouetted against that baneful orb was the grip of Estebar's sword. In the unearthly green glow of the Chaos moon, it looked to Markus for all the world like a hand reaching out to take him into the darkness.

THE SOUND
WHICH WAKES YOU
Ben Chessell

You NEVER HEAR the sound which wakes you. It remains in the realm of sleep while you enter the world of wakefulness.

Tomas sat up like a bending board and willed his eyes to open. He slept on the smooth, black stones beside the forge; a good place to sleep, especially when the winter chills rolled down like waves from the Grey Mountains, leaving a coating of frosty brine come morning. One night a spark from the forge had spat out and ignited his bed of grass and bracken while he slept but, unlike his father, Tomas was not a heavy sleeper.

His father! Pierro was smith to the people who lived in the village of Montreuil, under the jagged shadow of the Grey Mountains, in the north of Bretonnia. Tomas came to the realisation, as he did every morning, that the sound which had woken him must have been that of his father's first hammer stroke for the day, which was closely followed, with mechanic inevitability, by the second.

Each blow of the hammer bid Tomas an ungentle good morning, before departing the smithy to wake the creatures of the forest, and reminded him sternly of the amount of brandy he and Luc had consumed the previous evening. Tomas prised open his eyes and, through the narrow slit which he managed in his visor of sleep, located his smock and boots.

Manoeuvering around his father, Tomas began slowly to dress. Neither acknowledged the other. Tomas pulled his smock over his head and squeezed into his boots while Pierro bent over the forge, puffing great blasts of air from his lungs with every swing of his hammer: a set of human bellows. Tomas's father worked hard and never left the smithy, unless it was to tend to the grove of ancient oaks which stood at the edge of the forest beyond the common pasture land.

It had been his father's responsibility, and so on down to the very roots of the family tree. One day, Tomas supposed, it would be his. Tomas left the smithy as soon as he was ready, as he did every morning.

In the doorway he met Marc, who was Pierro's apprentice and had held the post ever since Pietre. Tomas's elder brother had been the most promising young smith Montreuil had seen since the brighter days of Pierro's youth and the old regime. Marc was capable enough in his own steady way, and he and Tomas were friendly, accounting for the fact that Marc held the job which might have been thought most rightly to belong to Tomas. When his time had come, Tomas had refused to take up the position as his father's apprentice and it was only because of the prayers of his mother who had lost one son already, that Tomas was permitted to continue to live under Pierro's roof. Tomas brought in a little money to the family through different jobs for farmers in the district and Marc became the smith's apprentice. The two exchanged a polite greeting and Tomas plunged into the bright, grey world.

MANY IN THE forest-edge village saw fit to comment about the estranged family, wondering whether it was Tomas who refused to meet his inherited responsibilities or Pierro who refused to fulfil his parental ones. Whatever the facts of the matter (and actually it was both), it was fortunate for Montreuil that young Marc, whose father had perished in the cells of the Marquis, could step in and fill the need.

These things wandered through Tomas's mind as he rounded the back of the smithy and stuffed his head and torso into the barrel of ice and water. Tomas practiced this routine every morning almost as though it might harden him as his father tempered a glowing blade. Tomas had need of the hardness of iron, if he was going to rid Montreuil of Gilbert: Gilbert de la Roserie, Marquis, holder of the King's commission – and tyrant.

Montreuil was a political enigma, a political embarrassment. Squeezed like a stone between the toes of a giant, the village lay in the foothills of the northern Grey Mountains. Further north even than the great spa city of Couronne, Montreuil had almost no value to the thriving rural heart of Bretonnia many days to the south.

The King, however, who wielded the complicated feudal system like a well-weighted blade, had found a use for Montreuil. He made a grant of land there to one of his lords whose outspoken militaristic opinions had become unfashionable in these times of détente. This commission, this putting out to pasture, had been bestowed on Gilbert Helene, who had become the Marquis Gilbert de la Roserie more than thirty years ago, after he had served the king faithfully, if a little bloodily, in the wars of their youth.

Most of the villagers guessed, quite rightly, that the King had entirely forgotten about the existence of Montreuil and the man who ruled there. Marquis Gilbert certainly behaved as if the village was his own private kingdom and the troop of border guards – a dozen aging career soldiers and petty officers – was his royal army.

THIS WAS THE sad situation that Tomas was determined to upset. Approaching his twentieth year, Tomas was brimming with the rebelliousness of youth and the sense of invincibility which comes with it. He dreamed constantly of calling the hundred or so villagers to arms and ousting the tyrant with his twenty men. There were practical problems of course. The soldiers, called 'sergeants' by the villagers because most of them had held at least that rank in the national army before their ambition had got the better of them, were the only armed folk in the village. One of the Marquis's many laws prevented the villagers from owning anything more warlike than a bow for hunting and a knife for cutting meat.

What made this restriction all the more unbearable for Tomas was the fact that his own father forged the swords and spears with which Gilbert's men enforced his laws. Every helmet, every breastplate had begun life in the forge at the end of Tomas's house, beside which he slept each night and yet not one blade remained there.

This alone would have been enough to estrange father and son but the situation was aggravated for Tomas by the fact that his own father, Pierro, refused to talk about any aspect of his work with Tomas since Tomas had declined to become his apprentice. Pierro was a talented smith and on Gilbert's own hip hung a rapier, hilted in fine gold set with uncut topaz, made by Tomas's father. Besides which, the villagers of Montreuil were an infuriatingly peaceful people and took each new injustice as simply another trial to be borne in silence.

Lost in such thoughts, Tomas broke free of the woods and began the climb up the slope above the village. Sheep and goats picked among the scree for the meagre spring grasses, having only recently made the trek from their winter quarters themselves. Tomas headed toward the shepherd's hut, made from dark pine logs lashed with the innards of stock unfortunate enough to be chosen for the table.

Tomas knew that, after last night's drinking episode, Luc would still be sleeping while his sheep strayed where they chose, unprotected from wolves, bears or rustlers.

The brandy had hit Luc a little harder than it had Tomas and besides, Luc loathed to leave his bed without the strongest provocation. He was just like any other villager, Tomas reflected as he chose a large stone with which to announce his arrival: happier sleeping, but waiting for the right signal to rouse him. Tomas heaved the stone overarm and watched with satisfaction as it bounced from the side of the hut with a loud thump. He sat on a rock to wait.

Luc stumbled out soon enough and, having realised how seriously he had overslept, looked about frantically for the source of the danger. Tomas sent another, smaller rock sailing in a graceful arc toward the younger boy. It struck him on the hip and he spun to discover his laughing assailant. His relief was clear to see and it occurred to Tomas that Luc was more worried that he might have to confront one of the owners of the sheep, come to check the flock, than a wolf come to eat it.

Luc was a simple enough lad as far as Tomas was concerned though there was something about him the older boy could never quite grasp. The two breakfasted together among the stones and picked up their conversation of the previous evening. The plans they had made seemed less practical in the grey light of morning than they had by the lively dance of the fire the night before.

'Firelight makes all things seem possible, Tomas'.

'But did we not agree that all that is needed to begin this thing is for the right spark to be set to the tinder?'

'Tomas we did, but we had the confidence of the brandy then', Luc paused to consume a piece of bread, 'and besides we do not know how to set that fire, where to place the spark.'

'I hear you, I hear you', Tomas gestured, stabbing the air twice with his piece of bread, 'but what if I told you I had discovered where the spark should be set, what if I told you I will not wait any longer?'

'I would not believe you, and I would say you were still drunk.'

'But we do nothing! Even when my brother is killed my father does nothing. He accepts the blows of fate with the meekness of one of your sheep, in the jaws of a wolf.'

'Tomas, your brother killed a sergeant...'

'Who killed his lover...'

'Who poured wine over his head and threw him from the tavern...'

'This is senseless Luc, what matters is that nobody here does anything but work, eat and sleep. And I will be different.'

'Well that is what I want too Tomas, but...'

'Good, then bring your flint.'

'Now?'

Luc stopped chewing as the conversation which he had had many times with Tomas became something else altogether. 'Now.'

'But my sheep–'

'The sheep can see to themselves, we have a more important flock to tend.'

Tomas leading, Luc following, the pair descended from the mountainside down the path to Montreuil. The view afforded by the summer pastures mapped out the tiny village, clustered around a green common from which a tree-lined avenue led to the manor. The large house, more in some ways a small castle, was surrounded by a thick hedge of briar and roses, thus 'The Roserie'. The hedge was more decorative than defensive, although it would take a determined attacker to hack through its thorns, and in spring, as it now was, it bore a crop of white and pink roses of notable beauty.

It was forbidden for any villager to pick a rose with which to adorn their own dwelling, or to make a cutting from the ancient tangle. Occasionally the Marquis would make a gift of a small bunch of the blooms to some young woman of the district he had chosen for his amusement, but otherwise he enjoyed his exclusive hold on beauty. It was towards this hedge, and the dwelling it concealed, that Tomas led an increasingly dubious Luc.

Although there would be no guard set at this time of day, Luc pulled Tomas up behind the last copse of trees before the rose hedge. Luc said nothing but looked hard at Tomas, perhaps willing him to reconsider, perhaps something else. Tomas returned the stare, expecting to find uncertainty, and saw instead a testing glance, questioning. Whatever the truth of it, Luc solemnly handed over his flint and tinder and climbed up into the oak to observe the crime.

'If you are not back in half an hour I will come looking.'

Tomas nodded, watched him climb in silence, and then turned toward his objective. A large brown arm descended from the tree and signalled to Tomas. Sufficiently comforted, Tomas sprang into a low run. There was a part of the hedge at the back corner of the manor which was particularly wild and Tomas headed for that now. It concealed the beginning of a tunnel which led through the vicious thicket and which was a dangerous children's challenge in Montreuil. Tomas had made the run many times as a youth, winning ale, sweets or merely admiration. The punishment if caught depended on which of the sergeants found you, and how drunk they were on that particular day. Having never been caught, Tomas had become something of a village champion at the game and in his later years had taken to making the trip around the hedge for his own sake, seeking no accolades. Today those journeys of childish rebellion seemed like the memories of another boy.

He found the entrance to the tunnel with little difficulty though it had been some years since he had last been here. Indeed the architecture of the place had changed as does the shape of any childhood haunt when revisited. The dimensions shift, not just because the viewer is taller, but also because of the years spent away from the place. Certain things were more important to Tomas now than when last he had navigated the spine-wrought passageway and these things changed the very shape of the tunnel through the hedge.

He crawled in and lay still. The sounds of the manor drifted across the lawns which lay in between. Marquis Gilbert would still be asleep, but the maids and gardeners were at work. The sergeants slept in a long, low barracks on the other side of the house and Tomas wasn't sure how many of them would be awake. A few maintained notions of martial excellence and practised drills regularly with his father's swords upon the well-cut lawns which ringed the manor like a bright, green moat. Tomas listened hard for the sound of metal on metal, one the smith's son knew very well, but heard nothing. He began his work.

The driest fuel in the hedge was high in the branches but the best place to set a fire is low to the ground so Tomas set himself the task of fetching some down.

Climbing up through the hedge was a process best undertaken slowly and carefully, and ensured a certain amount of scratching nonetheless. After four trips up and back and about a half an hour's work, Tomas had a pile of kindling which reached his waist, topped by an old bird's nest.

At this point he paused and sat, sucking his arm where a thorn like a doornail had dug deep. With his other hand he took out the sheepskin pouch which contained Luc's flint and laid it on the mat of thorns and leaves which formed the floor of the rose-hedge.

Certain actions, certain distances are, when it is you that must travel them, very much greater than they appear. Such was the tiny fall which the sparks made to the tinder as Tomas struck steel against grey stone. He had set many fires in his time, every night before bed until the age of fifteen, but none so hot as this.

At first he thought it wasn't going to catch. The fuel was dew-laden and in some cases had been lying for a long time, but it did begin to burn. Tomas nursed his fire to the fulcrum point, beyond which it could take care of itself, coaxing it with small twigs and grass from the nest. In a final poetic gesture he pulled a hair from his head and added it to the blaze, watching it curl and snarl, the acrid smell lost in the sweet aroma of burning rosewood. Tomas accepted several deep scratches on his arms and cheeks as he made his way forcefully from the hedge, already breathing smoke, his eyes seeping tears. The final part of the plan was simply to run, low and quick, and climb the hill to watch the drama unfold.

Tomas began his run, flat and hard, toward the tree where he had left Luc. He heard his name called. Luc's voice, not from in front but from behind. Tomas spun and fell, rolled and regained his feet. Looking back he was first struck by how quickly his work was taking effect. The fire had moved quickly upward and fifteen foot high flames now claimed the top reaches of the hedge. Rose blooms dropped to the ground in a burning rain as the upper limbs of the hedge bent, snapped and plunged backwards into the hungry blaze. Then Tomas saw Luc.

It is often something totally simple and yet totally unpredictable which undoes a great plan, or even a modest one and Tomas watched in horror as Luc stood as near as he could to the base of the blaze and called 'Tomas!'.

Tomas hesitated. The sergeants, were any awake, would be at the fire any moment and Luc would be seen. He ran back, driving the ground with his legs, and felt the intense heat of the fire. He dared not call Luc's name in case the sergeants heard. That Luc had called his could not now be helped, both of them need not be revealed.

The younger boy was almost blinded by the fire and would not see Tomas until he was close. Coughing out the smoke which invaded his lungs with each breath, Tomas watched the manor gate as he reached Luc. Two sergeants ran out, buckling their belts and fanning smoke away in order to better gauge the extent of the blaze.

Tomas shouldered Luc in the back and both hit the ground hard. The two rolled away from the fire, Luc following Tomas, and rounded the corner of the hedge. There they stood and sprinted for the relative safety of the woods which backed the manor. Reaching the trees they crouched and Tomas wiped black tears from his eyes while striving to regain his breath.

Luc lay in the bracken and looked up at Tomas. 'I'm sorry. I was scared. There were men in the grounds. I came to warn you.'

Tomas did not look at Luc when he spoke but instead kept his gaze fixed on the fire, which now consumed the entire east corner of the hedge and was almost at the gate. He bit down hard on his lip and said nothing.

Above the gate, a span of almost twenty feet, there was a thin archway of hedge fronds and thorn-bush. The fire snaked out one end of the span while one of the sergeants tried to hack it down with his sword. The work was too much and the heat too great and as he fell back the fire made the journey across the bridge and the entire hedge was doomed.

Tomas had seen enough and took Luc's hand to lead him away. He was surprised to hear himself accuse, 'Luc, you said my name.'

* * *

BY THE TIME the two parted company the news was all through the village. So was the smoke. Tomas joined the steady stream of spectators
walking cautiously up to the manor to see the fire and soon most of
the inhabitants of Montreuil stood by as the rose-hedge collapsed
inwards into a pile of coals and ash. At one point the blaze threatened
the manor itself but a few of the younger sergeants managed to keep
it at bay, filling buckets from the stream. Noon came, grey and dull;
the show was over and the talk had begun.

Tomas mingled and listened with satisfaction to the rumours as
they evolved. Some said it was out-of-towners, others that it was
one the many lovers Gilbert had jilted and a third tale conjured
enemies from the Marquis's past. Tomas joined some of the conversations enthusiastically, encouraging whatever theory held
sway. He was relieved to hear no mention of his own name on anybody's lips.

As the crowd dispersed Tomas turned to leave – and walked directly
into the leather apron which his father wore, dawn until sleep, at
work or abroad. He did not know how long Pierro had stood there,
his face golden in the glow from the hedge. Tomas's name was on his
father's lips and Pierro's hand was firmly on the boy's shoulder.
'Tomas, come with me. Now.'

His father propelled Tomas away from the crowd which had begun
to disperse and marched him back to the smithy. Tomas felt no fear
from what was about to happen. He had more serious concerns than
familiar discipline, and besides, the actions of the early morning had
hardened him to the point where his father's leather belt was no more
than a light switch of rush grasses. Pierro pulled the hide across the
door of the smithy and turned around. Tomas cocked his head to one
side and planted his hands on his hips. He waited for his father to
unbuckle his belt and administer the punishment. Instead Pierro
looked at his son, long and deep. Tomas found himself able to meet
the gaze but the beginnings of confusion stirred in his stomach. His
father had not looked at him in such a way before.

When Pierro finally spoke it was not with the tone, nor indeed the
words, that Tomas expected. 'Go and say farewell to your mother.'

'My mother?'

'Did you not hear me, Tomas?' Normally his father called him 'boy'.
'She is mourning your loss already.'

'What loss?'

'They will be here soon.'

'How do you know? How could you know that?' Tomas's anger
came from fear but also from losing control of the conversation.

'I have friends among the sergeants.' His father's calm certainty
frightened Tomas even more. He hit back.

'Because you are their friend, because you help them to hurt all who live in Montreuil, because you are a traitor even to your own family!'

Pierro sighed, his apron rising and falling with his bellows lungs. 'No, Tomas. Because an uprising such as the one of which you dream must be planned properly and with patience, otherwise good people have to die.'

Tomas tried to grasp the meaning of this last and very unexpected answer. He failed, drowning in uncertainty, and waited desperately for his father to throw him a rope.

'Did you think, Tomas, that I bore this injustice willingly, that I befriended tyrants for my own betterment?' Tomas's head was suddenly light and he leant against the forge, warm clay against his back.

'The blood which flows in your veins, my son, was my blood before it was yours. That is the reason that I cannot be quite as angry as I might. In some ways, Lady forgive me, I am proud.'

Pierro stopped as they both heard voices from outside the smithy. The smith peered through a hole in the hide door and turned back to Tomas with a grave expression. Without saying anything he picked up his son and placed him on top of the forge like he had many times when Tomas had been a young lad, to warm the soles of his feet on winter mornings. He removed his leather gloves and handed them over. Tomas put them on without understanding why.

'Go to the grove and wait for me there. I must think what is best to do.'

The sound of several riders dismounting could be heard clearly from outside. Pierro looked hard into Tomas's eyes and then, touching the hot metal pipe which was the chimney of the forge, said one word: 'Climb.'

Tomas watched the ensuing scene from the thatched roof of the house in which he had spent his entire life. The events which occurred seemed even more unreal framed by this most normal of settings. The surprise Tomas might have expected when his father produced a sword from underneath a stack of raw iron ingots and bundled it with the apron in his right hand, never occurred. Neither did the shock register when the Marquis himself, with four of his men, stood in Tomas's front yard. He wriggled to the apex of the roof, where he himself had knitted the thatching together and saw his father approach the men. By the time the exchange began he felt himself ready to witness anything and remain unsurprised. He was wrong.

Tomas could not hear the conversation in detail and voices reached him only when they were raised. His father faced away, leather apron folded and hanging from his right hand. Tomas could hear none of Pierro's words.

The Marquis remained mounted, untouchable on his black perch, while his men spread out, their hands never far from their sword hilts. They were clearly looking for Tomas. How they knew, with such certainty, that he was responsible for the rose-scented smoke which still clung to the valley, he could never be sure. Perhaps they had heard Luc's cry; maybe Tomas had made one too many drunken speeches on sunny festival afternoons. Whatever their source of information they were only angered by his father's denials. The Marquis stabbed the air with his gloved hand and early in the exchange augmented his gesturing by drawing the rapier which Pierro had made for him. The blade was dull in the grey light but Tomas knew that the edge would be well honed. His fingers clutched handfuls of straw and he breathed moss and dust as he watched the scene unfold. Two of the men entered the house while the others kept Pierro from following.

The Marquis rested his blade on the smith's chest and pushed to emphasize a heated point he was making. Pierro stepped back, between the two sergeants who crushed him between their shoulders. The others returned from the house, having failed to find Tomas. Both had their blades drawn; one also carried a red-hot iron from the forge. Tomas strangled a squeal.

WHEN RELATING THE details of his father's last moments, as he later had to do many times, Tomas could never exactly account for what happened.

At the Marquis's signal, the two men behind Pierro grabbed his arms and, with some effort, pulled them from his side. The apron fell to the ground, revealing Pierro's sword. Gilbert shrieked hysterically and pointed with his own blade. The sergeants looked with open mouths and one pounced to retrieve the blade. He was rewarded with Pierro's boot in his face and he rolled backwards into the Marquis's horse. Tomas's father swung his huge arms in front of him and his captors crashed together, bone on bone. He twisted his hands from theirs and sprang back, claiming his sword and apron from the dirt. Pierro backed cautiously toward his house, and the sergeant who remained uninjured followed up hard. Gilbert's man crouched and stretched his arms, willing them to remember the long lost training grounds and infantry manoeuvres of his youth. He lunged and Pierro beat the attack away with his left hand, wrapped in the heavy leather apron. With a booming cry Tomas had never heard his father utter before, the smith covered his attacker's head with his apron and smashed his knee out and away. The man fell and Pierro looked up to consider his options.

The Marquis sat safely on his horse behind his men who moved slowly forward, trapping Pierro against the wall of the smithy. Tomas crept further up the roof as his father retreated under the eaves. He couldn't see him anymore, only the expressions on the faces of his foes. At a command from the Marquis the three rushed Pierro in an unsophisticated charge. All combatants disappeared from Tomas's view and all he could see now was Gilbert's face wearing a feral snarl. One sergeant reappeared immediately, one hand grasping the other to stem the wellspring of blood which gushed there. Tomas didn't see his father die – but he heard it.

As he slid off the roof behind the house he tasted blood and realised he had bitten down on his tongue. The sound of his father dying was still in his ears, the cry and the unholy punctuation of the body meeting the ground. Tomas dropped from the straw eaves and set off for the woods at a barely controlled scamper.

Tomas wasn't sure whether they had heard him or not and he didn't care. He kept running, weaving between the trees like a fox before the chase. He rested only when he reached the grove of oaks, heavy and dark in the late afternoon sun. Tomas propped his back against the largest of the trees and slid to the ground, the shadow of the canopy reaching down and embracing him in its lattice. Tomas cried then. He sat and cried and watched the shadow grow and twist and finally fade as the pale sun faltered. He thought about his father. He thought about their final conversation and the sound his father had made as he fell to the ground. He felt like a little boy. Tomas decided what he had to do and only then could he fall asleep.

He woke in the pre-dawn hour when the deep-green canopy of the oaks gathered the mist and distilled it into crystal drops. A drop landed on Tomas's nose and rolled down, pooling between his lips. He opened his eyes and adjusted slowly to the flat, grey light. Standing at the other end of the grove, barely visible through the curtain of fog, were four figures. Tomas drew breath. He lay still and examined the group. They did not appear to be sergeants; the outlines were too slim and lacked weapons. They were talking quietly to each other and occasionally one would glance in Tomas's direction. He lay still, nestled between the bony roots of the oak. The figures knew he was there but not that he was awake. He determined to lie still until he could learn who they were.

The four became six with the arrival of a pair from the direction of the village. The two newcomers came in at a run and spoke to the others in breathless tones. Their message was clearly urgent though Tomas could catch none of its detail. The smaller of the arrivals grabbed the shirt of the figure he addressed with both fists to add emphasis to his news. Tomas studied the silhouette of the messenger against the growing dawn. He recognized the shape of the shoulders and neck and wondered hard what it was that had roused Luc from his bed before the sun itself. By the time dawn was undeniably upon them the six had become nine, and then twelve, and Tomas could see who they were: men from the village, men he knew, farmers, shepherds and Ludo the tavern keeper. They were deep in discussion. Suddenly a decision was reached and all turned their faces toward the tree at whose feet Tomas lay.

'Tomas, wake up.'

Tomas stood slowly and looked around the group. Their faces were grim and not altogether friendly. They seemed to be sizing him up.

'That you have done this thing you have done is brave, we acknowledge.' The speaker was Paul, a lean farmer and a friend of Tomas's father.

'What we need to know is how brave you will be now.' The group seemed to move closer to Tomas, blocking the morning sun.

'What does it matter what I do?'

'It matters a great deal.'

'I don't understand any of this. I am the one who must run and hide. It is my father who is dead, Lady watch over him.'

'Did you speak with him before he gave his life to save you? Have you opened your eyes just a little?' Now Tomas was addressed by a younger man, whose anger was palpable. Gerni the miller pressed his questioning further. 'Did he give you his blessing?'

'He told me to come here.'

There was a general murmur concerning what this might mean. Some thought that Pierro's last request was of great significance and that the smith had intended and foreseen the conversation which was taking place. Others were more skeptical, citing the less than perfect relationship between father and son. Tomas was almost forgotten for a moment.

Luc stepped from the huddle and asked him in a low voice. 'What will you do?' Tomas looked at him, hard.

'Have you always been part of... part of whatever this is?'

'Don't be angry, Tomas. Your father always wanted to know what you were thinking, what you were saying.'

'And you told him?'

'Everything.'

'What was my father to these people?'

'He was our leader.'

'He was what?'

'From the very beginning.'

'Leader, leader in what?'

'Are you so very blind, Tomas?'

'What is this meeting? What are you here for?'

'To decide what should be done.' Luc looked away. He might have been about to say more but Paul turned back to Tomas.

'What would you have us do, boy? What would you do?'

No response of Tomas's would have satisfied the group. Their expectations were based on their respect for and memory of a dead man, and their palpable disappointment with his replacement.

'I am going to the manor to kill the Marquis, or I will join my brave father, that is all.'

The men thought for a moment. Before one of the more senior figures could respond, Luc spoke up.

'We could come with you. Perhaps you need not die.'

'That would mean war. We can't fight soldiers with sticks, Luc.'

'The village is already full of sergeants, looking for us, and besides...'

Gerni choked a little laugh and walked past Tomas to the oak under which he had slept. The miller reached up into a hole near the bole of the tree and his hand returned with a large hessian sack, sewn shut at both ends. He lay the bundle heavily at his feet and cut a careful, longitudinal slash with his knife.

Tomas still could not understand what he was seeing as the bright blades spilled onto the grass. Something about the simple, elegant ironwork was familiar but a part of him still refused to understand. 'Where did these come from?'

'Your father, boy. Pierro forged these over years of crafty, secret work. An ingot of iron here, a few spare hours there. Paid for by the Marquis and crafted by his own smith. Intended for his downfall. There aren't quite enough but we will have to make do. That is, unless you have a better idea.' The bitterness in Paul's speech cut Tomas and his eyes stung with salt.

'My father?'

'Your father.'

The men distributed the weapons and made final repairs to the leather handles. They sharpened the blades on stones among the trees which seemed to be too well placed in the grove to have lain there by chance. Others spent the day practicing, or preparing a meal for the group. By nightfall they were ready. There had been no discussion, no decision and there was no plan, but a general consensus had spread through the group that they would move at night. It was agreed that the sergeants would know something was up but would not be anywhere close to ready for exactly what was. Tomas felt unable to claim a sword when others were without them, and he gripped his knife as if someone was trying to wrest it from his grasp.

* * *

THE FIRES WERE well and truly out around the manor and the huge house lay strangely naked in the moonlight when the mob arrived. They hid at the edge of the woods and watched for long enough to establish that four sergeants were out in the grounds, patrolling, and that fires burned in many of the manor's hearths. What they didn't know was how many of the sergeants remained in the village and how many were in the barracks. Facing all the armed men at once they would be fatally outnumbered. Their only hope was to deal with their enemy piecemeal. The distance between the forest and the manor, only about a third of a mile, seemed an uncrossable chasm of open ground.

Tomas heard himself give what sounded like an order and thought only later about how easily it had come to him. 'This way. Follow me.'

Tomas, Paul, Gerni and Luc went ahead, the others waiting in the woods for their signal. The four scouts crept as far as the scar of the hedge and hit the ground. Nothing remained but a few twisted black bones of the great growth and a two-foot deep ditch of coals and ash. Tomas felt the warmth of it on his face, even now, and took some comfort from that. They waited for two of the sergeants to pass further away and then Tomas demonstrated his idea. He found a deep pile of ashes and took a double handful. With this he painted his face and clothes black and grey and almost disappeared into the background of the burnt hedge. The others followed suit and the four crept up the hedge-line, keeping low, almost invisible towards the main gate where the two men stood guard. The gates looked forlorn and foolish with their stone gateposts standing alone and no hedge to justify them.

Tomas, Paul, Gerni and Luc crept as close as they dared and halted again, looking briefly into each other's eyes and waiting for what must come next. Tomas looked at Luc's blackened face and saw his brown eyes brighter than the ash, wide and fearful. Gerni wriggled over to Tomas, making too much noise for Tomas's liking.

'What's your plan now, boy?'

Tomas didn't like the diminutive but could only agree that the doubt on the older man's part was justified. He thought quickly.

'I will gain their attention while you and Paul rush them from behind.' A sound enough plan.

'What about me?' Luc whispered.

'You can go back and bring the others to the hedge, what's left of it.' Luc was clearly relieved by this job. He pulled his sword quietly from his belt.

'Give me your knife, Tomas. You will have more need of this.'

Tomas took the sword and felt its cool weight. He looked briefly at the simple, sturdy ironwork in the moonlight and thought of his father. 'Not now', he told himself, 'not now.'

They watched Luc crawl away down the hedge-line and melt into the black scar, one more grey lump, and turned to their allotted task. Paul looked up at the moon.

'Time to move, Tomas.' Tomas was grateful not to be called 'boy' this one time. 'How do you mean to get their attention?'

'Be ready and you will know soon enough.' Tomas wished he had a better answer but he did not. Paul, however, took his brusqueness as evidence that he had everything under control. Paul and Gerni moved quietly into position.

Tomas crept toward the front of the hedge and the gate. He could see the two men clearly now, he even thought he knew one of their names. Alain, an older sergeant, had come to the smithy more than once to have his armour adjusted to suit his expanding girth. Tomas willed a clever idea to come into his head but none did, so he fell back on the only notion he had. He stood up, walked several steps away from the hedge and began to stroll toward the gate. He tried to whistle but his mouth was shaking so much that he couldn't form the proper shape.

ALAIN AND HIS colleague didn't see him until he was quite close. 'Who's there?'

'It's me, Tomas, I've come to see the Marquis.'

'You've what?'

'Gilbert. I've come to pay him a visit.' The soldiers peered into the night to ascertain whether Tomas was alone. Alain stepped forward a little and peered at the boy in the darkness.

'Let me get this right. You've come to see the Marquis. We've been looking for you all the last night and day, and you waltz up here, bold as you please, asking to see the boss?'

'That's right.'

'Well you got balls on you, boy, even if you don't have brains.' In a strange and somewhat terrifying development to Tomas, he was beginning to enjoy himself.

'Please don't call me "boy". My name is Tomas.' He hoped Paul and Gerni would not take too much longer and his ears were rewarded with the sound of a stealthy footfall. If he could just hold the attention of the guards for a moment longer… Alain's companion joined the conversation.

'Well, boy, the Marquis will be very pleased to see you, but not with that sword at your hip. Where did you get it?' Tomas had forgotten the weapon stuffed through the rope which held his trews up. Tomas still couldn't see Paul or Gerni but decided that if they didn't arrive soon he was in serious trouble anyway.

'This sword?' One last stall.

'Yeah, boy, that sword. What are you going to do with it?'

'I'm going to stick this sword into Gilbert's soft belly and watch his bright blood spill out.'

The men stopped for a second and looked at each other. They reached for their own blades and Tomas dragged his from his belt. For a brief moment he found himself facing two experienced fighters with a weapon he had never wielded before. He bit his tongue and opened the wound from the day before, tasting iron.

Had Paul and Gerni synchronised their attacks a little better it would have been over instantly. As it was, the younger sergeant went down under a double handed stroke to his neck, not pretty swordplay by any means but brutally effective. Alain had a breath after this had happened to turn and put his arm in the way of Gerni's upward thrust. The tip of the blade pierced his much repaired chain-mail vest at the bottom of the ribcage and both men fell to the ground. Alain was a big man and had taken wounds before, though not for many years. He punched Gerni in the mouth with a mailed glove and the miller rolled away spitting blood and teeth.

Paul was still engaged and so Tomas grabbed his weapon tightly and approached the panting Alain. The fat soldier was having trouble getting his sword out of its scabbard which had fallen underneath him and he was concentrating on this task when Tomas arrived. He looked up at Tomas's face. 'Now, boy…'

Tomas stamped hard on his sword hand and kicked at his face. Looking down at the older man, cradling his broken fingers against his bleeding face Tomas paused, but he quickly realised he had come much too far for remorse. He reversed the sword in both hands and struck downward as hard as he could. The brief battle was over and the three men fought to regain their breaths.

Hardly had they drawn three lungfulls each when they heard Luc cry, 'Tomas!'

The distance and the dark made it hard to discern the situation but this is how it seemed to the three at the gate. Luc must have run into the other patrol and now fled across the open ground toward the forest with the two sergeants on his heels. The unarmoured Luc was faster but was done for if the soldiers caught him.

Paul grabbed Tomas, 'Quickly! We must help.' Tomas was torn.

'No, wait.'

'There will be more men.'

'We knew we'd have to fight. Wait.'

LUC ALMOST REACHED the eaves of the forest before he fell. He rolled and tried to stand but he had hurt his leg or his ankle and he pitched forward again. The men were on him. From the trees which offered

him safety came a roar and eight villagers sprang out, charging toward
the soldiers who stood over Luc. The sergeants did a quick head count
and attempted a rapid about face. The farmers caught them and
Tomas lost the details in a whirl of bodies and blades. He counted
eight men standing at the end of it and that seemed to be a comforting thing. He couldn't tell if any of them were Luc. A door at the end
of the house burst open and six armed sergeants carrying torches ran
out and down the hill towards the forest. Paul gripped Tomas's arm
again.

'They need us. Them's trained soldiers.' The door stood open and
firelight spilled out.

'We'll never get a better chance to get inside the house.' Tomas heard
the sound of raised voices from the barracks on the other side of the
manor.

'They'll be cut to pieces.'

'It's now or never.'

In the end Paul ran back to help the others and Tomas and Gerni
made a dash for the house.

They ran hard, bent double, and plunged without hesitation into
the fire-lit kitchen whose door stood open. Tomas led and Gerni followed. Had they stopped to think at the door Tomas might never
have found the courage to go in at all. The kitchen was empty as they
discovered after picking themselves up off the wooden floor. Gerni
had slid all the way under the table and stopped against a sack of
flour. A cloud of white snow settled in his hair. Tomas's elbow caught
on the door frame and sent him spinning against the stone trough in
the corner. He splashed his face and combed a handful of water
through his hair with his fingers. If he strained his ears Tomas could
hear the sounds of a battle from outside in the grounds. Inside the
house it was silent. Gerni and Tomas shared a 'you first' look before
gripping their swords and going further into the house.

Heavy carpets lay on the floor and hung on the walls eating the
sound of their footfalls so that Tomas and Gerni rounded a corner
and found themselves almost seated at a table with two sergeants
before either group was aware of the other. One of the men was
almost asleep and the other strained to read by the guttering stub of
a candle. A bottle lay on its side, resting against the book. Their position stood sentry over the main staircase of the house which swept up
to the private apartments of the Marquis. The four men looked at
each other, unsure of what might happen next.

Had Gerni or Tomas been a competent assassin the outcome would
have been simple and quick but the struggle in the dark at the gate
had not prepared them for striking in cold blood. The sergeant with
the book, a young man with reading spectacles, woke the other with

one hand while folding his spectacles and replacing them with his sword in the other. The sleeper stirred and made an inquisitive snort as his eyes opened. He grasped the situation quite speedily and stood, clearing space as he drew his blade.

Tomas and Gerni circled away from each other a little and exchanged a nervous glance. The odds were hardly even. The sergeants were veterans and the older one wore armour, Tomas and Gerni were farmers with weapons they had never, until recently, even held in their hands. Neither side seemed willing to make the first move. Tomas realised that the sergeants had everything to gain by waiting, and he much to lose. It was unlikely the battle outside would go his way and soon more soldiers would return to the house. Tomas swallowed the urge to run and hide. An indistinct shout made its way in from outside and he could wait no longer. The soldiers continued to stand at the table, blocking the stairs. Gerni hung back, the point of his sword wandering aimlessly in front of his face.

In what he was sure would be his last and most foolish action, Tomas leapt forward with his sword in front of him, almost closing his eyes in silent supplication to the memory of his father.

You NEVER HEAR the sound which wakes you. He was fairly sure something was amiss in his house, however, and so Marquis Gilbert sat up, letting the satin sheet slide down his naked, hairless chest. He heard something then, a thud and a crash from outside his room. He dressed quickly but clumsily, missing the aid of his dresser who had left for the evening. In the polished silver mirror he frowned at his paunch as he did every morning. He had to admit to himself that he was not the lean and dangerous man he had once been, but there wasn't much that could conceivably be in his house which could cause him to raise a sweat. He buckled on his rapier, which hadn't struck a blow in all its elegant life, and composed himself, risking one more glance in the looking glass before unbolting the door and walking onto the landing.

At the top of the stairs stood two boys. One, the elder of the two, was bleeding seriously from a cut in his cheek. Gilbert looked to the bottom of the staircase. Two of his men lay there, probably dead, certainly on the way. On the table the stub of a candle illuminated one of his books, some spectacles and an empty bottle which would once have contained port, his port.

He snorted. His useless soldiers spent more time drunk than sober. Gilbert's eyes climbed the stairs and settled again on the boys. They held swords in their hands. They held them far from their bodies, as if the blood on the blades might poison them. A good swordsman loved his blade, especially when bloody. Gilbert walked quietly towards the pair. One of them, the younger one, yelled something indistinct and charged along the balcony toward him. The other, the bleeding one, stayed put. Gilbert sank into a fencing stance and waited patiently. The charger realised he was alone about three quarters of the way to his objective and spun around, exposing his back. The older boy was clearly too scared to charge; clever boy.

Gilbert lunged forward, hopping on his back foot first for extra distance, and whipped his blade across the younger boy's back. It raised a welt from waist to shoulder and the lad fell, screaming. Gilbert gently broke his nose by stepping on the back of his head with his boot heel and walked over to attend to the frightened one.

He seemed to find a morsel of courage as he squared up and faced the Marquis rather than run down the stairs as he clearly wanted to. Gilbert feinted low and the boy followed like a trout to a fly. The Marquis's knee connected with his face and the lad cart-wheeled backward and down the stairs, taking every third one as if he were eager to reach the bottom. He lay still and Gilbert turned around.

The young boy had got up again. Bravo. Gilbert assumed a dueling stance with all of the proper flourishes and detail, and signaled as was proper that his opponent might begin when he was ready. As the boy looked into his eyes, with some anger it must be said, Gilbert noted with amusement that it was the wretch they had all been looking for. How fitting that he might kill him here, with the sword made by his own father. Gilbert doubted that the child would appreciate the irony.

The Marquis set about playing with his victim a little. He stepped out of the way of the increasingly desperate attacks, spinning and pirouetting like a dancer. In between each of the boy's sorties he gave him a little cut, on the face or the arm, with the tip of the blade. Eventually Gilbert tired of the game and it occurred to him he should find out if there were other intruders in his house. He imagined with a certain amount of grim glee the retribution he would exact from whoever was responsible for this little insurrection. He turned to his opponent.

The boy lunged, straight and unimaginative, slow and clumsy. Gilbert was an enthusiastic user of the stop-hit, a manoeuvre in which one fencer, instead of parrying his opponent's offence, attacks instead, hitting before the original blow lands. He employed it now, bringing his blade inside the boy's, and placing the tip accurately at the base of his ribcage. The golden-hilted rapier cut the boy a little, bent – and then snapped.

Gilbert had a brief, very brief, moment to comprehend his mortal danger before the boy's sword penetrated deep into his stomach. Both fell to the floor and blood poured from two wounds. Only the boy managed to stand, however.

It occurred to Gilbert, only in his very last moment, that in truth he had never fully trusted the smith, and had been unsurprised when he had discovered that the smith's son was a troublemaker.

Like father, like son, he thought, as he died.

THE AFTERMATH OF the battle at the manor was a sad time in Montreuil. The surviving sergeants, which turned out to be most of them, drifted away when it was discovered that the Marquis would no longer be paying their wages. One stayed on and married a village girl, when their affair was made public, and another downed his weapons and installed himself at the mill, now that Gerni was gone.

Tomas didn't stay long in Montreuil and not all were sad when he left. Though nobody was sorry to see the end of the Marquis, many thought that the cost in lives was too steep, and that things had been bearable as they were. Tomas didn't say where he was going, though perhaps he told his mother.

The manor house stood mostly empty at one end of the village and fell quickly into disrepair. It became custom in Montreuil, when a roof was leaking, or a hinge fell off a door, for the villager in need to make a trip to the manor and to take what he sought to make the repair.

The rose hedge slowly grew back, but was kept to a modest height, perhaps the waist of a tall man, and on festival days in honour of the Lady the village was covered in a garland of roses.

It was purely speculation on the behalf of some villagers that the new flowers were brighter and more fragrant than those which had grown there before.

THE SLEEP OF THE DEAD

Darius Hinks

COUNT ROTHENBURG FINISHED his gruesome tale with a wry smile and leant back into the comfortable leather of his chair. As he viewed us over the rim of his wineglass, the light of the fire glinted in his vivid blue eyes, and he gave a mischievous laugh.

'Well? Have I stunned you all into silence?'

There was a round of manly coughs and laughter, as we attempted to dispel the sombre mood he had created. '*Bored* us into silence maybe,' chortled one gentleman. 'I've heard that story several times before, and at least once from your own lips!'

'Aye,' said another, with an exaggerated yawn. 'I think maybe you've been enjoying a little too much of your own hospitality.'

With some difficulty I managed to rise from my chair and wander unsteadily over to the window. The count's cellar was stocked beyond the wildest dreams of most of Nuln's citizens, and we had spent the better part of the evening attempting to make a small dent in it. As I gazed drunkenly out into the moonlit splendour of Rothenburg's ornamental garden, I struggled to remove the more unpleasant details of his story from my memory.

Tales of unspeakable horrors and strange happenings seemed to have become the mainstay of our conversation whenever we met. I doubt any of us could pinpoint the exact genesis of this morbid tradition, but it seemed now that every gathering was simply an excuse to plumb to new depths of absurd fantasy.

I shivered.

Bravado insisted that we make light of even the most shocking yarns, but I could not help wondering where it might all lead. This passionate desire to outdo each other made me somehow nervous.

Stories sometimes have a way of returning to haunt you.

'I have a tale,' murmured a voice from behind me, 'though... though I am not sure it is right that... that I should share it.'

A ripple of derisory laughter filled the room.

'Ho!' exclaimed the count, leaning forward in his chair, 'what a coy temptress you are, Gormont! "Not sure it is right" you say! What a tease! Do you take us for a bunch of prudes?'

I turned from the window and saw that the Gormont in question was a small, anonymous-looking youth I had not previously noticed. He was sat away from the light of the fire, in the shadows by the door, and was obviously very drunk. As the party turned their attention towards him, he retreated back into the folds of his huge chair like a cornered rat, and seemed to regret having spoken.

'Well?' demanded our host, obviously intrigued, 'what have you to share with us, nephew?'

'I'm not totally sure – not sure I should...' he whispered, shuffling nervously in his seat.

There was an expectant silence, as we all waited for him to continue.

'I have brought something with me, you see...'

There was another chorus of laughter, and one of the guests began slapping his thighs dramatically. 'He has something with him! He has something with him! Speak, boy! We demand entertainment!'

I peered through the smoky gloom to get a clearer view. There was a manic quality to the boy's expression that seemed to go beyond mere drunkenness; he was obviously torn between an eagerness to impress his audience, and fear.

For several more moments he prevaricated and evaded, and soon the haranguing of the group reached such a deafening volume that even the servants began to look nervous.

'Very well,' he shouted finally over the din, looking somehow triumphant and terrified at the same time, 'I will speak!'

A grin spread across the count's handsome face and the room grew quiet. I looked around at the circle of rapt faces. The combined effect of the wine and the glow of the fire gave us the appearance of hungry daemons, leering over a defenceless prey. I knew all too well the urbane derision that would greet the conclusion of the boy's tale, yet we were all, to a man, desperate to hear it relayed.

'I must beg of you that this go no further!' hissed Gormont dramatically.

The count rolled his eyes as this cheap showmanship, but shooed his servants from the room nevertheless.

Gormont cleared his throat nervously and began. 'My family has employed the same physician for decades,' he said, turning away from us to rummage in a bag. 'Gustav Insel. You may have heard of him?' He turned to face us questioningly, holding up a few scraps of paper. 'This is his journal. Well, some of his journal, that is. Do you swear to secrecy gentlemen?'

'Get on with it boy!' cried the count in an imperious tone, which caused Gormont to flinch.

'Very... very well,' he stammered. 'I'm sure we all understand these matters require discretion.'

We nodded impatiently, without the slightest idea what he was talking about.

'Yes, Gustav Insel. When I was a child he treated me for every imaginable ailment, and has bled my family regularly for almost every year of my life. Every year, that is, until last year. We heard rumours that he had gone abroad, or been killed even, and my father was forced – at some inconvenience – to find another doctor. However, just a few months back, he returned and the change in him was awful to behold.' An expression of almost comical dismay came over the boy's face. 'That a man can be so altered, in the space of a year is hard to comprehend.

'I would not have given any credence to this,' he continued, holding up the papers, 'were it not for the fact that some of the incidents mentioned seem to have a basis in actual facts. Ships' records and the like seem to concur; and the baron he describes is no fictional character – I have made some enquiries, and not only did he exist, but also he did indeed disappear in a most mysterious fashion. And the foreigner – Mansoul – I have discovered that he also exists.'

'I cannot bear this!' exclaimed the count, striding across the room and snatching the papers from Gormont. 'We'll all be in our grave by the time you start the first paragraph! Let me read the thing myself!'

Gormont seemed too shocked – or too inebriated – to resist, and Rothenburg marched back to his seat with the journal. He turned the papers over in his hands a few times, and then began to read: 'It is only as a warning to others that I tell this morbid tale...'

IT IS ONLY as a warning to others that I tell this morbid tale. For myself, I would wish nothing more than to wipe the whole tragic affair from my memory. However, my duty is clear, and I could not, in all conscience, allow these terrible facts to go unrecorded. Even now, only months after my return to the south, those events which have so haunted my every waking moment are already becoming indistinct and hazy. It is almost as though such terrible visions are too much for a mortal mind to comprehend; like worms they writhe and twist in my thoughts – elusive and serpentine, eager to avoid a closer inspection. But I will pin them to these pages with my quill. My tale must be told.

We set sail from Erengrad on the good ship *Heldenhammer* in the year 2325. As ship's surgeon, and close friend of our intrepid employer, Baron Fallon von Kelspar, I was blessed with a cabin that was merely unpleasant rather than uninhabitable. The damp seeped through the bed linen and the rats nested in my clothes, but to have a bed of any sort was enough to earn the enmity of our swarthy Kislevite crew. They eyed me resentfully from within their fur-lined hoods.

Still, if it is possible for me to remember any stage of that doomed expedition with fondness, it would be those first few days. The baron wore the air of a man possessed, and his enthusiasm was infectious. Even the Kislevites seemed affected by it. The whole ship's company was charged with his fervour.

There were, however, rumours of a scandal following closely on his heels, and I heard it said that his journey to the north was one of convenience as much as discovery. Certainly it was true that he seemed to show scant regard for the family estates he had abandoned so suddenly, and he politely evaded any enquiries about the baroness; but nevertheless, I could not doubt him. Seeing him stood at the prow of the ship, leaning forward impatiently into the bitterly cold wind, I found it impossible to harbour any suspicions as to his character. In fact, with the ice freezing in his beard and the snow settling on his broad shoulders, he looked more worthy of trust than any man I have ever served. My faith in him was absolute.

We HAD MADE good headway around the coast of Norsca, but were in the midst of a five-day gale when the first of many disasters struck. I was up in the slings of the foreyard, struggling to hang on as the ship rolled and lurched, when out across the churning black sea I spied a jagged shape rearing up from the horizon.

'Land,' I called down to the deck where our captain, Hausenblas, was busily bailing water with the rest of the crew, 'to starboard!'

He rushed to the prow of the ship, and shielded his eyes from the snow. Even from my perch up in the swaying spars, I saw the colour drain from his face and, as he hurried back to his cabin, I clambered down the rigging with fear already tightening in my stomach.

Moments later, the baron and I watched helplessly as he pored over his maps and charts with increasing desperation. 'Clar Karond?' he muttered.

'Can we be that far west? It cannot be!' Although the name meant nothing to me, my fear continued to grow, and as I watched him wading through map after map, filling the cabin with a storm of papers, I wondered what it was that I had seen out there across the waves. What could have driven Hausenblas into such a frenzy?

Finally, as his muttered curses seemed on the verge of hysteria, Kelspar stepped forward and calmly placed a hand on his shoulder. 'Captain,' he said, 'is there something you would like to share with us?'

Hausenblas whirled around to face the baron. Kelspar's composed tone seemed to calm him a little, but there was a wild look in his eyes and, as he replied, he could not disguise the tremor in his voice. 'North of the Empire all is damnation and ruin, baron, but a sailor of my years can – with the good will of Manaann – avoid the worst of the dangers…' His voice trailed off into silence, and he looked distractedly out of the porthole.

'Yes?' prompted Kelspar after a few moments.

Hausenblas grabbed a crumpled piece of parchment and thrust it at the baron. 'It's the Clar Karond peninsular!' he barked. 'The storm has taken us too far west! We've entered the Land of Chill, where the foul corrupted elves dwell!'

I gasped involuntarily. The ship's carpenter had told me many tales and legends concerning that cruel, mysterious race, and the look of fear in the captain's eyes banished any doubt I may have held about their existence.

'They'll be on us like dogs within hours,' wailed Hausenblas, dropping heavily into a chair. 'We don't stand a chance.'

Kelspar stood in silence for a few moments, seemingly lost in thought, then he nodded and strode out into the raging storm.

WITH EVERY OUNCE of his skill and experience, our captain tried to steer the *Heldenhammer* away from the coast I had spied, but Manaann's thoughts must have been elsewhere that day and within hours, sinister silhouettes began looming out of the tempest like ghosts. At first, as I peered out through the falling snow, I thought we were being surrounded by great living creatures – terrible leviathans of the deep, with brutal slender claws and arched ragged wings; but as they grew nearer, I realised to my amazement that they were ships.

They were like no ships I had ever seen before.

Their design seemed the work of some strange, incomprehensible mind; but despite their hideousness, I could not deny that was also a perverse beauty to them. The twisted curves and cruel lines were strangely sensuous, and graceful.

The charismatic baron had a way of making the impossible seem achievable, and whatever the scheme, his men would leap to realise his every whim and fancy. They were not fools, however. An expedition into the unforgiving north, from whence few men had returned was something that required the necessary tools, and from the bowels of the ship emerged an armoury fit to defend a small city: swords, slings, muskets and the like were soon arrayed along the taffrail in their dozens as the men prepared to engage the enemy. Beside them stood all of the crew that could be spared – these were men used to hardship and war, living so far north, and they would not give up their livelihood, or their lives, easily.

The *Heldenhammer* was no warship, however, and there was little that could be done to prevent the dark elves boarding us. After a brief game of cat and mouse, their grappling hooks and ropes began sailing over the deck, and I finally saw with my own eyes the terrifying nature of our foe. In terms of physical proportions they were not so different from men; but there the similarity ended. Their screaming elongated faces froze my blood in a way that the even the icy temperatures had failed to do, and the twisted, ornate curves of their armour left me gasping with fear – what possible hope could we have against such a foul corruption of nature? I saw in an instant that there was no hope for us against such inhuman opponents.

From out of the dazzling whirling snow they came, falling on us like daemons. Cruel blades glinted in the cold light as the elves hacked and lunged. Frozen fingers fought to grip the hafts of weapons, and warm blood washed over the icy deck. I fought blind, with the snow in my eyes, and in my fear I struck wildly at every shape that came near me. Sigmar preserve me, but in those moments of panic I knew not what, nor whom I struck with my clumsy blows. The battle was not the epic struggle for glory I had so often read about; but rather it was a brutal, ignoble farce with men slipping about on the ice and blood, while others fell clumsily on their own blades.

It was with something akin to relief that I felt a blow against the back of my head; and as I collapsed into the welcoming oblivion of death, I felt as though I had cheated fate in escaping the fight so early on.

In the frozen wastelands of the north, strange sinews of light flicker in the heavens, fitfully illuminating the blasted landscape; but all else, as far as the eye can see, is darkness.

I did not perish on the rolling deck of the *Heldenhammer*, but as I stumbled on through the endless night of Har Ganeth – the bleak, frozen tundra that lies far to the north of our glorious Empire – I wondered if that was such a blessing. Certainly with the benefit of hindsight, knowing all that I now know, it would have been a kindness to have died then, innocent of the horrors that were to follow.

It had been the baron himself who plucked me from beneath the mound of corpses, and as I watched him striding through the knee-deep snow, just a few yards ahead of me, I wondered at his fortitude. The battle against the elves had been a grim, brutal affair, and whilst the victory had been ours, it had been hard won. Few of the baron's men had made it off the *Heldenhammer* alive – it was a pitiful group who remained to set foot on the packed ice of that forbidding waste-land – yet Kelspar seemed utterly undaunted.

As for the rest of us, it was the white heat of our own avarice that drove us onwards through the plummeting temperatures. I remembered all too well the cheery warmth of the baron's drawing room, and the passion with which he had told me his story. It was a tale of the Hung: fierce, nomadic wild-men who roamed the barren north, worshipping foul ancient gods, and feasting on the flesh of their own fallen. It was a tale of frozen lands and unexplored realms; but most of all, it was a tale of gold.

I had seen with my own eyes some of the strange guests entertained by Kelspar over the years: many of them travellers from the east, with gifts of exotic spices and lurid poetry, who regaled the wide-eyed baron with tales of uncountable wealth in the vast steppes of the north. I had heard one man in particular – a small, twitching seer named Mansoul – tell the baron in hushed tones of a great city called Yin-Chi, deep in the realms of the Hung. He whispered of great towers of ivory and gold rising out of the ice-capped mountains, and streets littered with the accumulated wealth of generations of the barbarians. As I turned away to pour the baron and his guest another glass of Carcassonne brandy, I had seen in the cut crystal a sinister fractured image of the room behind me, in which Mansoul discretely leant towards the baron and slipped him a crumpled map. From that moment, my interest was piqued – and my fate sealed.

All the remaining members of our party now shared this vision of riches, and to a man we were consumed with greed.

There were seven of us in all, plus dogs, a sledge, food supplies and other items, including a mysterious chest the baron claimed would guarantee our entry into the fabled city. From his hints I deduced it contained gunpowder, or mage-fire of some sort, with which he presumably intended to create a distraction. In truth, I had not pressed him too hard as to the details of his plan – I knew he had one and, in my fevered lust for wealth, that was enough.

I THOUGHT I had known the meaning of cold before we set foot in that cursed realm... but I was wrong.

It is the nights that I remember the most. As the wind howled outside the tents, we cowered inside, sleepless on bedding too frozen to crawl into, and with terrible cramps in our stomachs from the fat-laden food we were forced to eat.

Then, with no dawn to guide us, we would rise at some arbitrary hour and attempt to don our packs; but by this time our robes were like plate-armour, and our hoods had become soldered to our faces. We would lumber off like a group of bloated revenants, limping and stumbling through the powdery whiteness. Our breath froze and cracked painfully in our beards, and beneath all the layers of coats and tunics, our own sweat became ice. Without the kernel of avarice glowing deep in my thoughts, I think I would have simply lay down in the soft embrace of the snow, and lost myself in the peaceful sleep of the dead.

But, even then I had not experienced a fraction of the horror that was in store for me.

Despite the horrors we had already endured, it was not until the twenty-first day of our slow, tortuous trek that we discovered the true face of terror. It was the dogs that first alerted us to the fact that we were no longer alone in the snow. At first they seemed merely nervous, barking more than usual and hesitating where they had previously been sure-footed. In the pale light of the moon, the all-encompassing whiteness felt smothering and claustrophobic, and the agitation of the animals quickly filled us all with a nameless dread. The younger members of the party began flinching at imagined shapes in the drifting banks of snow, and even the baron seemed to quicken his pace a little.

Soon the dogs became utterly impossible to control. They howled and yelped, seemingly in mortal terror for their lives, and however much the baron cursed and kicked them, they would go no further. The barking sounded alien and muffled in the blizzard, and my mouth grew dry with fear.

Then, suddenly, the noise dropped. The dogs crouched low to the ground with their hackles raised and began emitting a low, pitiful whining sound that seemed horribly ominous.

We all waited.

The sound of my heart thudded so loudly in my ears that I felt certain the others must surely hear it.

I looked over at Kelspar, and saw that his hands were resting nervously on his two long sabres. Something glittered in his eyes. Was it fear or merely impatience? I could discern nothing clearly through my ice-encrusted hood.

Silence reigned, and I sensed the muscles of every man near me tensing with expectation. I felt I might scream just to break the awful quiet.

Then, out of the snow, came the creature from my darkest childhood dreams. My mind split like a shattered glass as I beheld a sight that in one cruel stroke tore apart my every conception of all that was logical and natural in the world. It loomed out of the whiteness like a mighty tree crashing down on us. Its size was immense – ten feet tall at least; but it was not the scale of the thing that tore screams of abject horror from me, it was its form: a shifting writhing mass of muscle and teeth that had no right to exist in an ordered world. Bestial faces howled and moaned in its blood-red flesh, before twisting into other indescribably awful shapes, and cruel weapons appeared from nowhere in claws that had previously not existed.

I'm afraid any greater detail is impossible for me to relate; my mind seemed as incapable of grasping the being's true nature as my hands would be to grasp falling snow. To my shame, my legs gave way completely in the face of such a monstrous assault on my senses and I fell to the floor.

Fortunately, the others somehow retained the strength of their limbs and drew weapons to strike. A burly Middenheimer near to me swung an ice pick at the heaving, thrashing creature, but its muscles seemed to slip effortlessly out of the way of his weapon. As we all looked on in horror the man was lifted up into the air by several pairs of arms, and, with a sound like the ripping of wet cloth, torn clean in half. Another man leapt at the beast with a terrified howl, swinging his hammer at what seemed to be a face, but the creature tore him open like ripe fruit and his remains fell steaming onto the snow.

I saw then that our expedition was over, and that our end had come. I prepared myself for the pain.

The baron had other ideas, however. With a look of determination that seemed absurd in the face of such an unholy apparition, he strode purposefully towards the creature with his musket drawn, and before the lumbering, howling brute had registered his presence, he unloaded his buckshot straight into what currently appeared to be its face.

The pitch of the thing's voice suddenly rose to a high-pitched keening, and for a split second, as a torrent of gore rushed from its head, the beast's form became fixed and solid. The baron seized his chance and, as we all looked on, paralysed with fear, he drew both his sabres, stepped calmly forward, and thrust them straight through the creature's gelatinous eyes.

There was an explosion of noise and blood as the thing reared up in pain, and at that moment, spurred on by their leader's fearlessness, the other men rushed forward and plunged their weapons into its still unchanging form.

This seemed more than it could bear, and with a deafening roar of impotent rage and a spray of blood and viscera, it lurched back into the shadows from whence it came.

'Bloodbeast,' said the baron calmly, wiping the gore from his swords and face.

FROM THAT TIME on, I fear I became something of a burden to the others. My mind seemed irreparably torn and I found even the smallest tasks arduous. The best I could do was to shuffle along behind the others like a simpleton, muttering to myself and flinching constantly at imagined apparitions.

Strangely, little was said of the attack over the following days. The bodies of the dead men were placed in rudimentary graves, and we marched on in silence. It seemed too awful a subject to broach; and what good could come of raising it? We were alone in the wilderness. What could we do? Other than his enigmatic statement after the beast had fled, the baron had said nought else on the subject.

Bloodbeast. What could such a word mean? It festered in my fractured thoughts like a canker. How was it that the baron could put a name to such a monstrosity? What foul tomes had he pored over to discover such a phrase? I itched to interrogate him on the matter; but I feared that what would start as rational speech would descend into the wailing gibberish of a madman. So I simply acted out the mechanics of life and waited for the violent death that I felt was waiting for me out there in the snow.

In the fourth week of our journey we perceived a change in the landscape. We appeared to be crossing a great plateau and occasionally, through gaps in the constant downpour, we spied what might be the distant crowns of a mountain range. The Baron's determination seemed not to have waned one jot and, if anything, at the sight of those peaks, I noticed a quickening of his pace. He began checking Mansoul's map more frequently, and I detected a new urgency in his voice when he spurred us on. Could we be getting near, I wondered, and, like a long forgotten tune my greed returned to me. I felt a new resolve harden in me and I put aside my idle thoughts of lying down to sleep on the crisp white bed of snow.

The turn around in my spirits was, however, short lived. On the morning of the thirty-first day of that journey into despair, I awoke to a nightmare. As the baron and I lurched awkwardly from our tent to raise the others, we saw their tent slashed and flapping in the wind, and their equally torn bodies strewn across the bloodstained snow.

All three were dead.

The scene was too much for me and I retched dryly as I beheld it. Their remains were barely recognisable: it was unmistakably the work of the creature Kelspar had named Bloodbeast.

I searched for hours, but could not find their heads.

* * *

MY DESCENT INTO lunacy now seemed complete. I was nothing but a gibbering wretch. I lay on the ground and called out for the beast to come and take me. I begged for death.

I was, however, all that the baron had left by way of a companion and, slapping me firmly across the face, he insisted that I take hold of myself and remember that I was not some raving savage, but a gentleman of the Empire. Through fear of his rage, rather than any real self-control, I managed to make a show of calming myself.

Fortunately, the dogs were miraculously unharmed and I begged the baron to consider returning to the coast. We had a rendezvous arranged with Hausenblas and the *Heldenhammer*, and if we made good speed we might still evade horrors that waited for us in the snow.

'What?' cried Kelspar, his eyes flashing in the dark. 'You would return now? When we have come so far?' Suddenly I feared him almost as much as anything else in that frozen netherworld. There was a barely checked hatred in his voice as he grasped my jacket and pulled my face to his. 'Are you mad? Only days away from treasures you could not even comprehend and you would turn back?' He hurled me to the ground, and rested a hand on the butt of his pistol. 'We go on, Gustav,' he growled. 'We go on.'

From then on I became little more than a beast of burden to the baron. His dislike for me was painfully apparent, and it seemed I was there simply to lug around the box of explosives and the other luggage, while the baron plotted our course.

WAS IT THE madness and carnage I had endured, or the lack of food? Or was it – as certainly it seemed – the very air that began to warp my senses? My mind seemed gradually to be growing strange to me. Alien thoughts, of no apparent sense, gripped me as we rushed over the snow on the sledge. Scenes of violence and power only to be replaced just as quickly by a grovelling awe of what lay ahead. Now when I saw those mountains through a gap in the blizzard, they seemed near and strangely ominous. Something in their make-up seemed not the stuff of reality, but rather the ethereal matter of dreams and visions.

The shifting, capricious nature of my mind began to distort even my memory. The details of my life leading up to that point would sometimes slip away and be replaced by darker memories filled with blood, and a lust for war. I fear my reason was truly gone by this time and I can only accept that my description of what followed cannot be considered the product of a completely rational mind.

Desire seemed to grow in the baron as we neared the peaks. He seemed now almost unrecognisable as the cultured, urbane gentleman I had met all those years ago in Nuln. His face was now a frozen mask of greed and lust. I could not meet his eye and, as the days went by, I grew to fear him greatly.

I KNOW NOT WHAT day nor week it was, but finally the awful contortions of my mind reached a crisis point. Whenever I saw the mountains now they seemed of no fixed shape, but instead they had become a shifting mass – much in the manner of the foul creature that had attacked us. The stone seemed in some places to be formed into monstrous screaming skulls, whilst in others it became impossibly tall towers, whose sinister shapes reared up into the darkness like claws. I even fancied that I saw the faces of beings too hideous and incomprehensible for me to describe, looming above the peaks and beckoning us on.

Finally I could take no more. I knew that the baron was leading me not to wealth and glory, but death and madness. Sigmar forgive me, I began plotting his murder.

The state of my ruptured mind, however, meant that while I had intended to contrive some subtle plan with which I would safely kill my erstwhile protector, I instead leapt on him clumsily with my knife at the first sight of him looking distracted. He was in the process of lifting the heavy chest of explosives from the sled when I attacked, and sent him, the box and myself all tumbling down a steep drift of snow.

We spun and tumbled silently in the soft powdery whiteness, and when we came to a stop I noticed two things: firstly, the baron's leg was lying at a hideously unnatural angle to the rest of his body, obviously broken, and secondly: the baron's wooden chest had split open during the fall, spreading its contents over the snow.

I froze in shock.

Rather than the gunpowder I had been expecting to see, I saw instead the severed, and by now quite frozen, heads of our three murdered companions.

'It was you?' I gasped through a parched throat. 'You killed them?'

'Of course,' snapped the baron impatiently, trying to rise on his one good leg. 'How else does one buy entry into the kingdom of the Blood God, but with skulls?'

My mind reeled. In a heartbeat I saw that Kelspar had never intended to simply plunder some mythical city like a common thief, but rather he wished nothing less than to offer his fealty to the Dark Gods themselves. His years of research into the peoples of the north must have corrupted his mind. The man was a heretic!

I lurched towards him through the snow, raising my knife to strike, but he was quicker, and even balanced on one leg he managed to aim his pistol at my head.

'Fool,' he said, with a bitter laugh, 'you could have joined me in paradise.' And with that he pulled the trigger.

I flinched, but felt no pain.

Looking down I saw no blood, and so I raised my eyes to the baron in confusion.

By the look of rage and frustration on his face, I guessed what had happened – the hammer of his weapon had frozen fast.

I took my chance, kicked away his one good leg, and thrust my blade deep into his chest.

I stepped back in horror as he thrashed furiously around with the weapon still protruding from his coat. His cries and curses were too terrible to bear and I covered my ears as I staggered away.

As I turned the sledge around and headed back south, I could still hear his cries echoing weirdly through the darkness – even after several hours had passed, the hideous noise was still there, shaming me with every cry of rage and pain.

As I sit here now, by the warmth of my fire, I question all that I once felt so sure about. I question even my opinion of the baron. Maybe he had intended to simply find his treasure and return to the south; maybe it was only after we entered that forsaken realm that his thoughts turned to madness and the unspeakable gods of the north. The one thing I *am* sure of is that it was no city of the Hung he was leading me towards; if I had followed him over those forbidding mountains, I believe I would have entered another realm completely. Sigmar forgive me, but since my desperate flight to the coast, and my rendezvous with the *Heldenhammer*, I cannot stop my thoughts straying back to those mountains, and wondering what I may have discovered on the other side.

I find myself sleeping more than is natural, and in my dreams the baron still calls to me; but his cries are no longer full of rage and pain, they are the words of a man who has found a great prize and simply wishes to share it. When I awake, my sheets damp with sweat, his voice still echoes through my thoughts: 'You could have joined me in paradise' he calls.

As the days crawl by, all that was once so dear to me seems chaff, and I find it harder and harder to resist his call.

There was a long silence which even Count Rothenburg seemed reluctant to break.

Finally, after several awkward minutes had passed, he spoke, but his voice did not carry the ring of confidence I was used to. 'How did you come by this journal?'

Gormont smiled conspiratorially, obviously revelling in the tense atmosphere his tale had engendered. 'My father's study,' he replied smugly. 'He thinks it secure in his safe, but he has few secrets I am not aware of.'

The count stared at him.

'And where is this "Gustav" now?'

'Well,' said Gormont, rising from his chair, and beginning to stroll cockily around the room, 'when he came to us, he was obviously in a very bad way, and so my father took him in out of pity; but he soon regretted it. The man had obviously lost his reason – we would hear him wailing like a lame dog in the middle of the night, and his presence in the house was beginning to play havoc with my poor mother's nerves. Then, thankfully, two nights ago he disappeared as suddenly as he arrived, leaving behind all his possessions – including the journal.'

I had never seen it before, and I never saw it again, but the count was lost for words. He gaped at Gormont as though the lad were suddenly a stranger to him. There was a terrible ring of truth to the tale that had finally silenced us all, and even the count seemed incapable of making light of his nephew's story. He began to reread the journal in silence – seeming to forget that he still had company – and as he pored over the words, a frown of deep concentration settled over his face.

Soon, the guests began to depart, pulling on their great coats in an uncomfortable silence, and disappearing one by one into the cold winter's night.

A little while later, as I stood in the hall buttoning my own coat, I noticed the count leading Gormont away towards his private chambers. As they turned a corner and disappeared from view, I heard a brief snatch of their conversation.

At the time the words seemed of no importance, but since Rothenburg's mysterious disappearance, they have begun to haunt my thoughts. In fact, they have circled my mind now so many times, that I doubt I will ever forget them.

'Tell me again,' I heard the count say to his nephew, 'what you know of the map and the man called Mansoul.'

PATH OF WARRIORS

Neil McIntosh

A CHILL WIND drove in across the sea, churning the water into great crests, steel grey flecked with white. A storm was coming. Change was coming. A finger of cold, plucked from the sea, entered the boy's heart and pierced it like a dagger. Change was coming, and things would never be the same again.

Stefan looked up towards his father, standing like a statue at his side. His father did not return his glance, but kept his stare fixed beyond the raging waters, out towards the far horizon where the sun was a deep orange globe sinking into the sea. Fedor Kumansky was waiting. Waiting for the change.

Questions formed upon the boy's lips and faded away, unspoken. A feeling, one that he barely yet knew as fear, was growing inside him. On either side of them, the huge sugar-ice cliffs that marked the shores of Mother Kislev stretched away into the distance. Before them, the boundless ocean besieged the shore.

They were standing on the edge of the world. It was the world Stefan had known all of his life, but this unknowing fear that swelled like the sea in the pit of his stomach was something that he had not felt before in all his eleven years.

He tightened his grip upon his father's hand, pinching with his fingernails until they bit deep into the tough, leathery skin until, at last, his father looked down at him. Fedor Kumansky smiled for his son, and Stefan saw that the smile was a mask.

'What is going to happen, father?'

By way of answer, Fedor Kumansky extended an arm out to sea. There, where moments before there had been only the jagged line separating sky and ocean, tiny black specks now peppered the horizon.

The ships were too far distant for Stefan to make them out, but it was a common enough sight. Here, where the mighty Sea of Claws funnelled down into the estuary that became the River Lynsk, the traffic of ships was ceaseless. Fishermen, traders, merchants ferrying their wares to and from the great city of Erengrad and beyond. Stefan found the sight of the ships almost comforting. Except that the tiny masted vessels gathering on the horizon seemed to be multiplying by the moment. There were too many of them.

'So many ships,' Stefan said, quietly. 'Perhaps they have sailed all the way from Marienburg, or even from L'Anguille, to trade with us?'

His father shook his head, slowly, and in that movement Stefan knew that the small branch of comfort he clung to was gone.

'I have waited for sight of these ships,' his father said. 'Waited, through waking hours and times of sleep. Waited in the hope that they would never come. But last night the gods spoke to me through my dreams. They told me of the dark clouds about to gather.' He drew his son to him.

'No,' Fedor said at last. 'I don't think they come from Marienburg, nor from L'Anguille or anywhere to the west.' He drew his cloak tighter round him to fend off the biting cold of the wind. 'I think they come from the north. And I fear they have no wish to trade with us.'

North. Stefan turned the word over in his mind. North was not a place; he had never seen the north nor met any man or woman from his village who had been there. But he had heard of 'north', and knew it as the thing that had seeded the fear that turned his stomach. North was the savage lands of Norsca, or worse; the savage, nameless lands whose ships set sail upon the seas of his dreams, his nightmares.

The salt air stung Stefan's face and tears prickled in the corners of his eyes. He looked to his father for some sign of what he was feeling, but Fedor's face was blank. The time of his waiting was over. The dark shapes were more numerous now, and larger. Stefan could make out the outline of the sails billowing full-blown upon tall masts. Fedor Kumansky laid his arm gently across his son's shoulders, and turned him away from the sea.

'The time has come,' he told Stefan, softly. 'And we have work to do.'

Father and son retraced their steps upon the flint path that led from the cliffs back towards their village, into the heart of Odensk. Their pace was brisk but not hurried; a good sort of pace for a crisp, cold day at the beginning of spring. Stefan sensed no panic in his father's measured strides across the headland, but at each timbered house along the path into the village Fedor stopped, and rapped hard upon the door with his staff.

Calm, sombre faces appeared in doorways. Strong, upright men with proud, weather-beaten faces much like his father's. Fedor clasped each one of them by the hand, but this was not a time for greetings. To each of his kinsmen, the same words, clear, spoken almost without emotion: 'The time has come.'

Where there had been one man and his son soon there were a hundred, moving through the streets of Odensk, the same message passing from mouth to mouth. Each repetition met with the same response. Knives that had only seen service gutting fish were cleaned ready for a grimmer purpose. Broadswords tarnished with the rust of peaceful years were brought down and polished with oil. Staffs became clubs in the hands of men who had spent their lives at peace. And from out of an underground store, long-disused and fastened with padlocks, two small cannons were removed and wheeled slowly towards the cove where the seas broke hard upon the shore.

The sleepy afternoon quiet of the fishing port had been broken, the people roused to a level and kind of activity that Stefan had never seen before. Half running at his father's side, he watched as the village transformed itself into something new, something frightening. Tools of life turned to weapons of war; men hardened by work stood ready to become warriors. Homesteads became fortresses.

By the time Stefan and his father reached the low thatched building that was their own home, the sun had gone and a chill twilight was settling over Odensk. Stefan tried to imagine the fleet of ships as they closed upon the coast; tried to imagine the construction of the masts, the shape and position of the sails; tried to picture the faces of the men, on deck or climbing in the rigging, hoping that somehow they looked no different to his father and the men of Odensk. Most of all he tried to imagine the ships turning away before they entered the mouth of the cove, hoping against hope that their intentions were not, after all, warlike.

But in his young heart he knew that there was no hope. His father's expression, and the calm, repeated mantra at each door along the way told him that. The time had come, and there would be no returning.

Mikhal was still in the salting sheds, helping the women clean and gut the fish ready for market. He looked up expectantly as he saw his father enter. Stefan ran to his younger brother and embraced him, hugging his body tight against his own.

Their father moved to the centre of the long room and called for quiet.

'The time for work is over now,' he said. 'All of you go home. And may the gods watch over us all.' There was a moment of silence, and then the women began to collect together their bundles of food and belongings. A few celebrated the working day ending prematurely, others looked curious or suspicious. The elder women amongst them stayed quiet, but gathered their things together and left as quickly as they could.

Fedor Kumansky led the two boys across the courtyard to the house. He turned down the wick on the single oil lamp until the room was lit only by a faint amber glow. Then he drew the heavy curtain across the narrow window, closing out the last of the fading twilight. The embers of a fire still burned low in the hearth, and the room was suffused with a smoky warmth. For a moment Stefan felt safe again, comforted by this familiar world.

'Listen to me.' Fedor gripped him tightly by the shoulders. 'Soon I must leave you. You and Mikhal must stay here, where you will be safe. After I've gone you will lock all of the doors and bar the shutters across the windows. Open them to no one, no one, until I get back. And whatever happens, Stefan, you must look after your brother. You understand that?'

Stefan nodded. He understood, and he did not understand. He understood that his childhood was ending, understood that the time of his being a man was beginning. Understood that he was Mikhal's protector now, no longer his playmate. But he did not understand why. He took his brother's hand.

'But you will return, father, won't you?'

Fedor bent down and removed the silver chain from around his neck. He showed the boys the locket he held in his hand, an oval tablet inscribed with the likeness of Shallya, the Goddess of Healing. 'This was your mother's,' he told the boys. 'She gave it to me just before she died. It became my pledge to her that I would always care for you, our sons.' Stefan touched the locket, and a picture of his mother, faint in his memory, came back to him. He pressed the silver tablet into his brother's palm.

'It feels cold,' said Mikhal.

'I'm giving this to you now,' Fedor told Stefan. 'Keep it safe for me, just as I will keep my pledge to your mother.'

'Why do you have to go?' Mikhal asked. Tears ran down his cheeks, and he was shivering despite the warmth from the fire. Stefan drew a protective arm around his brother, as his father had so often done with him.

'The time has come for me to fight,' Fedor said. His voice was grave but calm, and Stefan suddenly realised that his father had been preparing for this night for a very long time. He hugged Mikhal tightly but his shivering would not stop.

'Why do you have to fight?' he implored. 'Stay here with us!'

'Bad people are coming,' their father said. 'And we must fight them, or they will destroy us.' He smiled, trying to soften the message in his words. Standing in the yellow glow of the oil lamp he looked very tall, very strong. It seemed inconceivable that anyone, or anything, could defeat him. 'Don't worry,' he said. 'We're ready for them.'

Stefan's mouth felt dry and tight as he spoke. 'We can fight too,' he said. 'We can fight by your side.'

His father shook his head. 'No, you must show your bravery by staying here. And staying safe. Look after your little brother. That is your duty now.'

Stefan looked down at the icon of the goddess, and twisted the braided silver chain around his fingers.

'I'll keep us safe until you return,' he said at last.

His father bent and placed a kiss on the forehead of each son. 'Keep faith in the goddess. She'll watch over you always.'

Fedor Kumansky unlocked a cupboard by the side of the hearth and reached inside. Stefan looked in awe at the sword in its scabbard fastened to the stiff leather harness. Fedor drew the harness around his waist and secured it tightly. Then he took two short daggers from the cupboard, and stuck one inside his belt. He hesitated, turning the second knife over in his hands, then laid it upon the table in front of the boys, and nodded.

'Stefan, my cloak,' he said gently.

Mikhal had stopped shivering now. Either that, or Stefan was holding him so tightly that he could no longer shiver. Both boys were transfixed by the sight of their father with the sword. Their father, the warrior.

'Are the bad ones going to come into the village?' Mikhal asked.

'No,' his father said. 'We're going to stop them before they get that far'

Stefan could feel his heart beating faster and faster. The sick fear in his stomach had returned. 'But,' he said, 'you'll come back for us, you promise?'

Fedor Kumansky paused, one hand outstretched towards the heavy oak door, the other held out to his children. His gaze was fixed upon the ground, but at last he looked up and met Stefan's eye.

'Keep your brother safe,' he said. 'I'll come back. I promise.'

Stefan felt something inside him about to burst. He wanted to sob, to cling to his father, stop him leaving the house. Then they would all be safe. But he knew that was not possible. Another Stefan was starting to emerge from the child that had woken that morning, a Stefan who knew that could not be. But still he needed something, some words of reassurance from his father that he could cling to.

'Father,' he said. Fedor Kumansky had the door half-open. He turned and looked back sadly at his sons.

'Is this how things must be now?' Stefan asked. 'Will it always be like this, forever?'

'No,' his father said, quietly. 'Nothing lasts forever.'

FEDOR WAS ONE of the last to arrive at the cove. The beachhead was in total darkness, but from the voices audible above the roar of the waves, Fedor knew that the men from the village were there in force. As he drew closer, bodies and faces became visible. They must have numbered nearly a hundred, men armed with swords, knives, staves, anything that would deliver a blow. At each end of the bay, the two cannons sat primed and ready to fire. Set against the enormity of the ocean, they looked puny and useless.

Fedor scanned the faces of the men around him. He had known many of them since he himself had been a child. Daily they risked their lives together on the ocean, trawling for fish with their nets, pitting their strength against the cruel power of the Sea of Claws. These were brave men all, Fedor knew. His trust of them was no less than the trust they placed in him. For a moment his heart lifted; they might yet prevail.

The gathering storm that he watched from the cliff-tops that afternoon had not abated. The sea boiled in great plumes around the rocks and crashed down upon the shore. Only a fool would contemplate landing a boat in weather like this. A fool, or a madman. He looked around at his kinsmen, and guessed many of them had the same idea. Perhaps the storm would save them.

He joined a group of villagers who were studying the sea with a spyglass.

'How many ships?' he asked them.

Jan Scherensky lowered the glass and handed it to Fedor. 'A dozen, maybe more,' he replied. 'Not all are bearing lights, so it's hard to be sure.'

Fedor took the glass and looked out into the channel. A spread of lights bobbed up and down upon the water line, sometimes dipping below the towering waves, but moving ever closer to shore. It might almost have been the fishing fleet, returning to port after the long night at sea. But these were no honest fishermen.

'Well,' he said at last. 'They're headed in towards the mouth of the estuary, that's for sure.'

Heads around him nodded solemnly. The older ones amongst them remembered the last time, when the Reavers had visited bloody slaughter upon their homes. Maybe this time it wasn't the Reavers, but one thing was certain: few travelled this way from the north in friendship or for trade.

'They'll be headed up river,' Jakob Kolb muttered. 'Maybe they even fancy a crack at Erengrad itself.'

Fedor nodded. It was possible. History had it that raiders had got that far before. 'The question is,' he said, 'whether they've a mind to stop off here first.' He knew in his own mind what the answer to that question was.

Andrei Markarov took the glass from Fedor and put it to his eye. He was a young man, well over six foot tall, and one of the strongest in the village. And yet Fedor marked the fear in his eyes as he took the glass. A young wife and three small children at home. Fedor knew exactly where that fear came from.

'All the lights in the village are doused,' Andrei said. 'Maybe they won't even know we're here.'

'Maybe,' Jakob agreed. 'And maybe not.'

'At any rate,' Jan Scherensky added, 'it would be madness to try and land their boats in this storm.'

Madness indeed, Fedor thought. He fell to wondering what form that madness might take. Very soon, one way or another, they would find out.

Within a matter of minutes, the dark shapes of the ships themselves were visible through the gloom, and voices from the men on deck were drifting in to shore. Fedor motioned his men back to take cover behind the shelter of the rocks lining the bay. Nothing must give their presence away; they must stay silent as the grave, and wait.

Jakob Kolb crouched down behind a crag of rock beside his friend. 'Small ships,' he observed. 'Small enough to navigate the channels of the Lynsk.'

Fedor nodded. 'And big enough to cause us plenty of trouble. How many do you make now?'

Jakob raised the glass above the rim of rock. 'Fourteen.' he said at last. 'Men on deck of most of them. High in the water; no cargo aboard. They mean to carry back more than they bring.'

Fedor felt the muscles in his stomach tighten. 'Pray to the gods they keep going,' he said, then added: 'Gods forgive me that I should wish misfortune on others.'

The wind suddenly dropped, smoothing the waves. Far above them, the moon Mannslieb emerged from behind the clouds. Silver light washed over the bay, picking out the black fleet in the water below.

The lead ship reached the entrance to the bay, then tacked away from the beachhead towards the mouth of the Lynsk. The second and third ships in the convoy made to follow. Fedor's heart gave a leap; he shook Jacob's arm in early celebration. 'Keep sailing,' he muttered, 'keep sailing.'

Then a voice nearby said: 'Oh no!'

The fourth boat was turning in mid-stream, back towards the shallows of the bay.

'Not this way,' Fedor found himself whispering. 'Not this way, not this way.'

Shouts broke out amongst the men on the fourth boat. Moments later, a burning flare, flew up from the deck of the ship, lighting the night sky a vivid scarlet.

'What have they seen?' someone shouted. 'Why are they stopping?'

Fedor watched the leading vessels sway and churn in the water. He knew that could mean only one thing: they were turning around.

A second and third flare spiralled skywards. Now every one of the ships in the fleet seemed to be ablaze with lights. Voices screamed commands in a language that bore no resemblance to any tongue of man that Fedor had heard before.

Several splashes in the water, almost simultaneously. They're dropping anchor, he realised. He lifted the glass to his eyes once more and saw the rowing boats being lowered into the water from the decks of at least three of the ships.

Fedor Kumansky rose from behind the rock and drew himself up to his full height. His throat felt parched and tight; his voice, when he spoke seemed small and insignificant, but he forced it out, summoning all the power he could muster to carry his commands above the sounds of the invaders closing on the shore.

'Aim the cannon!' he shouted. 'Be ready to fight for your lives.'

FOR A LONG time after their father had gone, there had been only silence. The two boys sat cross-legged by the fire, the only other light the dim glow of the oil-lamp which they had been forbidden to turn any higher. To distract his younger brother from his fears, Stefan had told stories: imaginary tales of the lands beyond Kislev; the princes of Bretonnia, of the magicians that wove their spells across the vast lands of the Empire. And he told Mikhal of the brave warriors of Kislev, the strong, upright men like their own father, men who would never be defeated, not by any foe.

The light from the lamp guttered and died. The only light and warmth in the room now came from the embers in the hearth.

'It's dark,' Mikhal protested. 'Light a candle, Stefan.'

'We mustn't,' Stefan said, firmly. 'Not until father's back. We have to wait.'

'How long?' Mikhal demanded. Stefan made no reply; he wanted the question answered too, and suddenly he wished he had a big brother of his own to protect him and answer his questions. Most of all, like Mikhal, he wished their father would return.

He crept to the window and levered open the shutter far enough to allow him to peer out into the night. It was a sight he had never seen before: the village in total darkness. Not a single light burned in any of the windows of the houses spread around the edge of the square. The streets were empty, the temple bells stilled. Even the birds that settled after dark in the trees beyond the house had fallen silent.

For a moment the thought leapt into Stefan's mind that they had been abandoned, that he and Mikhal were the only ones left in the whole village of Odensk. But that was stupid, just a child's imagination. There must be others, people in every one of the houses, perhaps even now looking out from their windows, like him. In the dark he just couldn't see them, that was all.

But suddenly the darkness was no longer total. At the very far end of the street, along the path that led down to the bay, he could see the orange flicker of a lamp or torch being carried up the hill. The silence was no longer total either; Stefan could hear voices following behind the light, though he couldn't yet make out any of the words. A surge of excitement filled Stefan's body. He closed his eyes and made a wish, wished that the news was good, that, in a few moments, the door would be flung open and their father would be standing on the step in front of them, his arms spread as wide as the grin upon his face.

'Mikhal,' Stefan called to his brother, remembering moments later he had promised to keep his voice low. 'Mikhal,' he repeated in a whisper. 'Come here and see.'

Mikhal joined his brother at the window, elbowing Stefan aside to get a better view. The single lamp had become a procession, the voices swollen to the sound of a large crowd. The air rang with the clatter of footsteps, marching up the hill that led towards the centre of the village.

A wave of relief rushed over Stefan. It was over. His father and the others were coming back. He reached up to unfasten the window, ready to call out to his father as he spied him approaching the house.

His hand fastened upon the latch and then froze. Maybe it was the sound of heavy boots upon the cobble stone – too loud, or too many. Or maybe it was something in the building cacophony of voices, voices singing songs his childhood had never taught him, in a tongue he still could not recognise. Without thinking, Stefan found himself reaching out towards Mikhal, but his younger brother had slipped away from the window.

He turned and saw Mikhal tugging hard upon the door.

'I'm going outside!' Mikhal shouted. 'Find father!'

'No!' The intensity in Stefan's voice frightened them both. But the bolts were already drawn back; the door was open.

* * *

FEDOR KUMANSKY GAZED at the bloody carnage all around him and
wept. The men of Odensk had been prepared. They were strong, and
though they had lived for peace, they were ready to fight fearlessly to
protect their homesteads. It had made no difference.

He brushed away tears with a hand stained red with blood whilst
he rested upon his sword to draw precious breath. All around, his
brothers of the sea lay dead or dying, slaughtered by creatures driven
by a single purpose; to destroy every living thing that lay in their path.

At first, the battle had gone well. The invaders hadn't seen Fedor's
men lying in wait behind the rocks, and each of the cannons had
found their mark. The two boats that had been lowered from the
ships at anchor were destroyed, the men inside killed or thrown into
the heavy swell of the sea.

But even as the first boats sank, three more were in the water, then
five, then six. Within minutes the mouth of the bay was clogged with
oared vessels being rowed hard towards the shoreline.

The cannons were reloaded and fired a second, a third time, but the
men of Odensk might as well have tried to hold back the tide itself.
The invaders made no attempt to rescue those who had been pitched
into the water. They were left to die as the next wave of boats
ploughed onwards, relentless.

Fedor drew the sword from its scabbard and held it high above his
head. Moonlight glinted off the newly-polished steel.

'Rise up!' he called to his men. 'We'll send them back wherever
they've sailed from, and make them rue they ever made the voyage
south!'

Cheers rang out from the rocks around and behind him. Men
emerged in their dozens, no longer fishermen, but warriors. Andrei
Markarov appeared at his side, his face flushed and excited. 'Don't
worry,' he told Fedor. 'We're all ready for this.'

'I know,' Fedor replied quietly. 'I know we are.'

Andrei turned and urged his comrades forward. 'Come on!' he
yelled, stabbing down at the beach with his sword. 'This barren strip
of land will be their first and last taste of Mother Kislev! Let us make
them pay dearly for each yard!'

The leading boats had run aground in the shallows of the bay. Now
the men of Odensk would come face to face with those who would
take their land, their living, their lives.

As one the villagers rose up to form a human shield. Together they
would drive the invaders back into the sea, and the waters would run
red with their blood.

Figures were in the water, ploughing through the waves towards the
beach. Fedor tried to take stock of their numbers and quickly lost
count. Tens, dozens, it might be hundreds. The air around him sang

with the sound of arrows being loosed, as all those nearby who carried bows launched the next attack into the swirling waters of the bay. Fedor saw several of the advancing figures stumble and fall beneath the onslaught. Countless other arrows found their mark, but seemingly made no impact. The invaders strode on through the waters oblivious to the arrow shafts lodged in their flesh, or tore out the wooden shafts from their bodies and tossed them aside as if they were no more than irritations.

Any hope that the invaders could be forced back before they had got as far as the beach died there and then. Fedor Kumansky said his prayers to the gods and stepped forward towards the water's edge. He thought about the life he was about to set behind him, a hard life of peaceful struggle and simple reward. He thought about his wife, lain six years in the cold ground. And he thought about his sons, Stefan and Mikhal, waiting on his safe return at home. He begged the Goddess Shallya for her vigilance in protecting them.

He looked into the faces of his attackers. Surely they, too, must be men like he, men with homes and loved ones that they longed to see again. Surely some sense could still intervene before the madness engulfed them all.

But Fedor Kumansky saw nothing of the kind. The faces that stared back at him had long ago been leeched of any vestige of humanity as he understood it. In fact, he was not certain if many of them were human at all. Most wore the coarse fur jerkins and horned steel caps of the Norse hordes, but on some the marks of mutation were clear. Stretched jaws gaped open to display rows of yellowed rodents teeth. Horns grown out of bone jutted through ruptured faces and foreheads. Skin sparkled with the chill lustre of the serpent's scales. But one thing they had in common, every one: their eyes, vacant, almost unseeing, empty of compassion. They offered him no hope, no respite. This would be unto death.

The opposing forces met where surf crashed upon the shore. Fedor stood at the edge of his world, and cast a last glance inland towards the village. The invaders were shouting orders at each other in a harsh, guttural tongue, their rough voices obliterating even the sounds of the waves. Tall figures dressed in dark, foul-smelling skins were advancing on him on three sides. Fedor picked a target at random, and attacked.

As he ran towards the thick-set figure he had marked out, it struck Fedor Kumansky that he had not fought another being for more than six years. His opponent turned towards him almost in slow-motion, and he aimed his first blow. There was a moment that seemed to last forever as Fedor looked at the man; his milk-white face and fair hair poking out from beneath the rounded iron cap upon his head; the small scars pocking the baby-smooth skin on his face. The sly, hungry grin that spread over his features as he met Fedor's eyes.

Fedor swung his sword, and felt it judder as it struck home, cutting through leather, cloth, or bone – he couldn't tell. His opponent tottered as though slightly drunk, but did not fall. Fedor saw the man's sword arm swinging up towards him. All of a sudden, Fedor found himself possessed by a furious frenzy. He pulled back his sword, parried the blow aimed towards him then struck again and again, hacking at the other's man's body as he might cleave meat from a bone. Blood sprayed out of a deep cut through the man's neck as, finally, he toppled into the shallow water lapping the beach.

Fedor experienced a moment of pure horror, looking down upon a scene from the very pit of Morr. Then he felt something cut through the cloth of his shirt, cold metal grazing the skin below his ribs. He spun round to find a huge figure bearing down on him, knives in both of its hands, the same insane, blind bloodlust in its eyes. Fedor took his sword in both hands, stepped back and swung a blow directly into the Norse's face, the blade paring flesh away from bone.

He wasn't seeing men, or even mutants, any longer. Fedor Kumansky's existence had become distilled into one simple equation: kill or be killed. And he went about that business with every ounce of his being.

But, even as he fought, Fedor was aware that they were being pushed back up the beach, on to the path that would lead eventually to the village. He saw Jacob Kolb on his knees, trying to fend off the blows raining down upon him from a Norscan wielding a fierce-looking, double-headed axe. Fedor cut a path through the battleground with his sword, his desperation to reach his friend endowing him with the strength of two men. He lunged with his sword, slicing through a Norse arm, severing it above the elbow.

'Get up, old friend! Get up!' He lifted Jakob's face towards his own and wiped away the filth crusting his friend's face. But Jakob was already dead, he had seen the last light of this world. Fedor had barely a moment to mark his grief before something landed heavily upon his back, sending him sprawling face-down. Long fingers ending in sharpened talons fastened a grip around his neck. Fedor felt as though the very life was being squeezed from him. Then, just as suddenly, the pressure eased and the weight was lifted off his back. Fedor turned to see Andrei freeing his sword from the mutant's body with the help of his boot. Andrei's face was caked with blood. He stretched out a hand and helped Fedor to his feet.

All around him Fedor saw the dead and the dying. Friends, brothers he had toiled with very working day of his life. Men who would not be beaten by anything had given their all, given their lives. And it was not enough.

'We must re-group,' Fedor said, fighting for his breath. 'Pull back to the village. They'll destroy us out here.'

'But–'

'No buts, Andrei. This is not glory. This is survival. Survival of our loved ones. Gather whoever you can. We pull back, to the village. We must defend our homes.'

STEFAN'S HEART POUNDED hard inside his chest. Mikhal had either not heard, or not heeded him. By the time Stefan had reached the door of the house his brother had gone. Now he stood in the empty village square, calling Mikhal's name. His breath came in short, tight bursts, frosting the cold night air. The surrounding houses were still wrapped in darkness, but in the distance street a house at the edge of the village was on fire. Orange flames licked the night sky, and thick coils of suffocating smoke rolled up the hill towards Stefan.

Moments later a figure emerged from the smoke, staggering wildly from one side of the road to the other. The man was clutching the side of his stomach with one hand and cradling his head in the other. His face looked wet, and red.

Stefan felt his body tense. His hand was inside the pocket of his jerkin, clutching the handle of the short knife as though his life depended upon it. The man slowed his pace as he got closer to the centre of the village and looked up at Stefan.

Stefan recognised him. It was Jan Scherensky, one of the men who worked the nets on his father's boats. His son was a friend of Stefan's; they had played together only a day or so ago. It all seemed a lifetime away now.

Stefan stared at the man in shock. As well as his face, one side of his body seemed to be have been drenched in blood. Something thick and dark oozed from a hole that had opened up beneath Jan's ribs. Scherensky noticed Stefan standing by the side of the road and limped towards him.

'In the name of the gods, Stefan,' he shouted, 'save yourself.'

Stefan was stunned. It was a while before he could reply

'I can't,' he said at last. 'I have to find Mikhal.'

Jan Scherensky knelt upon the ground as though he had been overcome by tiredness. He held out a hand towards Stefan and Stefan took it in his own. He didn't know what else to do.

'Jan,' Stefan said, 'what's happened to my father?'

Other figures were starting to emerge from the smoke and flames at the end of the village. Men carrying torches, marching towards them. Scherensky looked back down the street then turned back to Stefan, his eyes bright with fear.

'Save yourself,' he repeated. 'Save yourself.'

He slipped forward, his forehead cracking hard against the cobble-stones. Stefan shook Scherensky's body in desperation, trying to stir him back to life. He hadn't said anything about his father. He needed to be told that his father was safe.

But Scherensky wasn't going to tell him anything now, and eventually Stefan let go, and left him lying in the road. The marching men hadn't yet reached as far as the village square. They were stopping at every house along the way, Stefan realised. The air was filled with the sounds of wooden doors being broken down, glass being smashed. And the sound of the screaming.

The sky flared orange as more and more homes were lit by the flames that danced along the wood-slatted sides of the houses and across their straw-thatched roofs. Soon the whole village would be engulfed.

Stefan saw something move in the shadows on the far side of the square. A tiny figure, huddled in fear by the side of the road. Stefan ran towards him, calling his brother's name above the rising crescendo of destruction all around them. As he reached the centre of the square, he saw the men coming. Two men, taller than any he had seen before, rushed towards him. One was carrying a blazing torch and a heavy axe, the other had something swinging from his hand, a ball or a bundle of some kind.

Stefan froze. He looked into the faces of the men. They were laugh-ing. Their soldiers' clothes were matted with filth and blood. Stefan saw now what it was that the second man was carrying. His fist was clenched around the hair of a severed head.

Stefan found he was paralysed, rooted to the spot. He wanted to reach Mikhal and the safety of the shadows, but could not move. The men kept running. For a moment it seemed that they would run straight past him. Their eyes seemed to look through Stefan as though he wasn't there. Then, at the last moment, the second man pulled up short. The dead villager's head swung from side to side in his bloody hand. Stefan recognised a face. Sickness forced its way up from the pit of his stomach into his mouth.

The Norse tossed his trophy to the ground and turned towards Ste-fan. He was young, probably little more than a boy himself. His features looked human but his eyes were the colour of blood, set like dark red stones in his smooth, white face. His face broke into an leer-ing grin, exposing a row of sharpened teeth like those of a wild dog or a wolf. He said something to Stefan that Stefan didn't understand, and reached out to touch him. Stefan flinched away in terror and a voice called out: 'Leave him alone!'

Both Norse turned at the sound of the small, frightened voice. Mikhal tried to scramble away out of sight but it was too late. The white-faced monster laughed evilly, and pulled a short knife from his belt. The first man moved round behind Mikhal to cut off his escape. He was whistling.

Stefan heard his father's voice in his head. His fear dissolved, and with it the ice that had frozen his limbs. Suddenly he was running, desperately running to put himself between Mikhal and the Norse. The knife lying in his pocket chafed against his skin as he ran

He was no longer thinking. Every movement of his body was driven by instinct alone. The younger of the two men appeared not to notice him. His attention was fixed upon Mikhal now, like a snake mesmerising its prey. The Norse crouched down and beckoned Mikhal towards him. His companion was laughing a cruel, hoarse laugh.

At the last moment the Norseman saw Stefan. As he turned towards him, Stefan lashed out with his feet, kicking the man in the guts. Mikhal darted forward, escaping the clumsy lunge of the other man.

'Run!' Stefan yelled at his brother. The younger man uttered a curse and grabbed wildly at Stefan. Stefan fended him off, hardly realising he had the knife in his hand. He heard the Norse scream. He caught a brief glimpse of the man's face; saw the socket running red with blood where the ruby eye had been gouged out. The Norseman screamed with pain and rage, and struck out blindly. Stefan felt a cold spike of pain shoot up through his arm.

Then he was running, running with his brother, away from the square, towards their home, the heat of the flames scorching the skin at the back of his neck, the voices of the pursuing Norsemen rising above the screams from the village. A sweet smell of burning wood mixed with the stench of the butcher's slab.

Mikhal dashed ahead of Stefan, towards the door of the house that still lay open to the night. Stefan clutched his younger brother by the hand and hauled him along in his wake.

'Our house,' Mikhal shouted. 'Our house is over there!'

'No,' he said, fighting for breath. 'Not there. They're burning the houses.'

'But I want to go back,' Mikhal protested. 'I want to go home, Stefan.'

Stefan charged on past the house, dragging Mikhal behind him. He knew that their lives depended on them keeping going. 'We can't go there again,' he repeated. 'We can't go back.'

'But father–'

'Father will know where we've gone.'

His mind was racing, trying to sift the sounds rushing through his ears. He could no longer hear the voices of the Norse behind them. He begun to hope that, for the moment at least, they had lost their pursuers. The dark outline of the salting house loomed up in front of them; the oddly comforting scents of the sea mingled with the smell of smoke and carnage.

'In here,' he gasped, tugging his brother's arm. 'Hurry, Mikhal!'

The air inside the thick stone walls of the salting house felt still and cool. Moonlight creeping through the narrow slats across the window was mirrored in the silver scales of the gutted fish that lay motionless in their hundreds, row upon row spread out to dry upon the shelves.

Stefan stopped still and held Mikhal to him. He placed a hand across his brother's mouth.

'Quiet.'

Some way in the distance they heard the sound of footsteps approaching the shed. Stefan looked around in desperation for somewhere to hide themselves. Stefan walked between the salting trays to the large open vat at the end of the room where the guts from the cleaned fish were collected, and lifted himself up onto the lip of the vessel. A familiar stench of rotting entrails filled his nostrils. The vat was almost full.

Stefan swallowed hard and called Mikhal over. There was no other choice if they wanted to stay alive.

'I can't,' Mikhal said, horrified.

Secretly, Stefan agreed. 'Yes, you can,' he told him. He took a firm grip on his brother and lifted him up onto the edge of the vat.

'Take a deep breath,' he told Mikhal. Take a deep breath and pray.'

Stefan lifted a leg over the edge of the vat so that he was balanced over the mass of stinking entrails. Part of him could not believe he was about to do this. The other part of him told him that he had to.

Mikhal looked at him in horror and disgust. 'I know,' Stefan said. 'But I promised. I promised father.'

He pushed Mikhal backwards into the slippery mass, then followed on, trying not to crush Mikhal beneath him. His eyes, nose and mouth filled with a cold oily pulp that stank beyond belief. Stefan choked and gagged, fighting to draw breath. The darkness enveloping them was total. After a while Stefan pushed an arm upwards until it broke through the surface of the vat. A little light and air leaked in.

Stefan spat out the vile tasting scraps that had forced their way into his mouth. He whispered Mikhal's name quietly and heard his brother sob a muted reply.

'How long?' his brother whimpered.

'Hush...' Stefan felt for Mikhal's hand in the oily mess and tried to take a grip upon it. 'We must wait,' he said.

At first there was only the silence, and the distant sounds of fighting in the village. Then Stefan thought he heard another sound, closer at hand. The sound of the door being opened. Not kicked apart, like the other houses in the village, but eased open gently, as though someone were playing a game of hide and seek.

He listened carefully, tracking the muffled footsteps around the interior of the salting shed. Stefan felt his body begin to tremble. The footsteps completed a half-circuit of the room and then stopped. For a full minute the silence was absolute.

Stefan held his breath. The urge to look outside and see what was happening was overwhelming.

Then a voice spoke somewhere in the darkness. It was the voice of the white-faced Norseman, the man that he had wounded, speaking in Stefan's mother tongue.

'Boys,' he drawled, slowly, slurring his speech around the foreign words. 'You come out now, be good. You be safe with us. You see.'

Stefan clamped a hand tight over Mikhal's mouth. His heart was pounding so hard in his chest he was sure it could be heard all round the room.

'Boys! You do a bad thing with knife. You got to say sorry now!'

Then a second voice. Stefan couldn't tell what the second man was saying, but his tone sounded harsh, impatient. Outside there was a sudden explosion, and light flashed through the window-slats. Shouts rang out, some in Norse, some in Kislevite.

The first voice cursed in Norse, then shouted out again Stefan's own language: 'I find you, one day. I find you, I promise.' Then Stefan heard the sound of the door being thrown open, and footsteps retreating into the distance.

More than anything else, Stefan wanted to climb out from the vat. His body was chilled through and soaked in cloying, stinking oil that covered him from head to foot. His wrist throbbed savagely from the encounter with the norse. Yet he understood that the only possibly safe place for the two of them was right there. Somehow he did not think the norse would be back.

He tried his best to hug Mikhal and give him some reassurance. He did his best to find some way of getting comfortable and the confines of the cold, filthy tank.

And he waited, waited for he knew not what.

The faint messages from the world outside changed as the night wore on. At first the sounds of battle had intensified; the clash of steel and inhuman screams of triumph or pain seemed at one point to be ringing the building itself. It was impossible to tell which way the battle was going. He could only hope that, somehow, his father had prevailed and the invaders had been destroyed.

Gradually the sounds receded, fading into the background as the fighting either drew farther away, or simply ended. Perhaps, Stefan thought, the Norsemen had given up. Or perhaps there was no one left to fight. He pushed the thought away, and waited. Miraculously, Mikhal had fallen into an uneasy sleep, punctuated by moans and, sometimes, yelps of pain. But Stefan had not the heart to wake him. Who knew what the new day was to bring for either of them?

STEFAN CAME TO with a jolt, shocked by the realisation that he, too, had fallen asleep. He had no idea how long now they lad lain hidden, but faint grey light had begun to creep through the windows of the salting house. Dawn had come.

He listened. Now there was no sound at all, above the steady whisper of Mikhal's breathing. Nothing. Even the birds were silent.

His body ached with stiffness and cold, and his wrist throbbed with incessant pain. Stefan raised his left hand and looked at it. A broad red gash had been carved across the palm. The salty slurry had served to staunch the flow of blood, but the wound was deep, and would take a long time to heal.

He found he had lost most of his sense of taste and smell, which was probably just as well, for he surely stank. Stefan stood up slowly until he was able to rest his arms on the lip of the vat and look out across the salting house floor.

Sooner or later, he knew, they would have to find the courage to venture out. And it might as well be now. He doubted anyhow that he could bear hiding in the stinking vat of entrails any longer.

Everything was exactly as it was the day before, or a thousand days before that. And it was quiet, peaceful even. Just for a moment Stefan allowed himself the childish hope that, somehow, all of that dark night had been just a dream. He stifled the thought quickly and stirred his brother.

'We can get out now. Go and find father.'

'Are you all right?' Mikhal asked him.

'Yes, I'm fine,' Stefan said. In fact he could not remember ever feeling worse. He hoped that once he started walking his limbs would return to normal. He took a few steps forward, trying to ignore the pains and the revolting filth that covered every inch of his body.

The door of the salting house hung open, flapping to and fro in a gentle breeze. Stefan was just able to make out the faint scent of burning wood that hung still on the air, reminding him of bonfires on the Feast Days. He took Mikhal's hand, and led him outside.

The sun had not yet risen over Odensk. The light was cold and grey, misted with the smoke from dying fires. But even in this half-light Stefan could see enough to realise that the village he knew had gone.

His first thought was of the fire in the hearth when he and his father got up at first light. All around him, fires smouldered and cooled.

The village was no more. Where wooden buildings had stood, only blackened piles of debris remained. Only those few buildings made from brick or stone had survived. The wind swept dunes of pale grey ash along the street.

Stefan searched with his brother through a cold new land. Up the path that led from the salting house, towards the square in the centre of what once had been the village of Odensk.

Around a bend in the path their search came to an end.

Stefan grabbed at Mikhal to hold him back, but he was too slow.

'He kept his promise!' Mikhal shouted. 'He promised to come back!'

Even before Mikhal's shouts of joy had turned to howling despair, Stefan knew what they had found. He knew, too, that the door that led back to his old life, his child's life in Odensk had shut forever; that in a moment he would have no choice but to step through a door into another life altogether. The grey dawn was giving birth to a cruel new world.

Stefan advanced a few more steps and sank to his knees in front of the figure lying outstretched before them. Mikhal was sobbing now, pounding the hard ground with his little fists in grief and rage, but, for the moment, Stefan did not hear him.

He had seen death before, seen it reflected in the glass-beaded eyes of the fish spread in rows across the wooden slats. But this was different.

'You're right,' he whispered to Mikhal. 'He kept his promise to come back.'

Stefan's fingers closed upon the silver icon clutched in his hand, but the goddess had no comfort to offer him. He looked to the sky, the pitiless grey sky stretching out above them, and said a silent prayer.

He looked again at death, and death looked back at him through his father's eyes.

Nothing in his life, not even the horror of that last, long night, had prepared Stefan for this. He wanted to understand how this could be, how the world that had kept him safe from harm through all his years could now have dealt so savage a blow.

He wanted to howl with rage, to beat against the cruel earth like Mikhal had done; but that belonged on the other side of the door that had closed behind him. And he wanted revenge, desperate bloody revenge, upon the men, the monsters, that had destroyed his life. But that lay beyond the door through which he had yet to pass.

He lifted Mikhal gently to his feet. Gradually the convulsions racking his brother's body subsided.

'Stefan,' he said, his voice choked with tears. 'Will things always be like this?'

'No,' Stefan replied at last. He took his brother's hand and held it tight inside his own. His wound hurt, a burning, stabbing pain. But Stefan knew that he must bear it, for pain would be his companion now.

'Things won't always be like this,' he whispered. He held Mikhal within his arms, rocking his little brother to and fro as their father used to do. 'Nothing lasts forever.'

'Where will we go now?' Mikhal demanded of him, his voice beseeching. Stefan shook his head, slowly. He did not know where they would go, but he knew that he alone would have to decide. Gently, he pulled his brother away from their father's body and started back towards what once had been their home. After only a few moments he realised it was futile. Their home was gone; it lay with childhood in a place that existed only in the past. Now they must walk the path that led to the future. Now they must walk the path of warriors.

Stefan Kumansky stopped and looked around him. To the north lay the sea, and the cruel lands from whence the tide of death had swept through their village. That would not be their path; not yet, at least. He turned away from the sea, away from the ruins of Odensk, and faced inland.

'Come on,' he said gently, taking Mikhal's hand. 'It's time.'

Together the two boys took the first steps along the road that lead to the place that Stefan still knew only as the World. The first steps along the long road that would lead to vengeance.

RAT TRAP

Robert Earl

HOFFMAN CUT AN impressive figure. His boots glowed with a deep polish and his baggy trousers were of smoothly brushed moleskin. An embroidered tabard encased the barrel of his chest, and although the sleeves of his shirt were fashionably loose, there was no mistaking the slabbed muscle beneath.

As well as his tailor, the swordsman was obviously a friend to his barber too. Only careful work could have made such a proud shape to his beard, and his scalp was shaved as smooth as wax with barely a nick to be seen.

Yet, for all that, Hoffman was no fop. Far from it. His eyes were alive with a restless intelligence and he wore his sword like a workman's tool.

'Herr Hoffman?' Reinhard asked as he approached his table.

Hoffman looked up to study the newcomer. He wasn't much to look at. Just one of the thousand flabby merchants that thronged the streets of Nuln.

Hoffman took his pipe out of his mouth and blew a smoke ring. 'And what if I am Hoffman?' he asked as the smoke dissipated. His eyes had become cold, evaluating, and it occurred to Reinhard this was a truly dangerous man.

At least, that was what he had been told.

'My name is Reinhard. Reinhard Bosse. Somebody said that I might find you here and… Well, look, let's have a drink, shall we?'

Hoffman nodded. He watched the merchant hail a serving wench, his features smooth with disdain.

'Thank you,' Reinhard said as the girl brought over two flagons of wine. He seized one and drank thirstily. When he had finished he banged it down and wiped his mouth with a velvet sleeve.

'So,' Hoffman said, his own drink untouched before him. 'To what do I owe the honour, Herr Bosse?'

'Oh, call me Reinhard. Everybody does.'

Apart from me, Hoffman's frown said.

'Yes, well. You see, it's like this. My family are in the tanning business. Maybe you've heard of us. The Bosses of Gunwald? No? Well, no matter. The thing is, my sister has always been quite jumpy. You know, afraid of the dark, screaming when one of the servants drops a pot, things like that. And servants will break pots. It's amazing how they get through them, really. You know, I don't think I've ever dropped a pot in my life. Although, to be fair, I don't suppose I've carried as many as…'

'Herr Bosse,' Hoffman's voice was quiet. 'Why have you come to see me?'

'Oh, yes. Right. Sorry. It's just that I haven't been sleeping very well lately and… Right. So this is why I've come to see you.'

Reinhard broke off and took a long, gurgling swig of wine. He sighed as it hit the spot. Then he saw the expression on Hoffman's face, and quickly started to explain.

'It all began about a month ago. My sister was in the courtyard, drawing up a bucket of water from a well, when she dropped the bucket and started screaming. I'd never heard anything like it. I mean, I told you she shrieks when she's surprised, but not like this. It was horrible.'

Reinhard broke off and finished his flagon of wine. His eyes slipped towards Hoffman's full one and the swordsman, curious in spite of himself, slid it across the table.

'Thanks,' Reinhard said, a guilty look in his eyes.

'What,' Hoffman asked as his host drank again, 'did she see?'

'Oh, it was nothing. Nothing. You know how women are. It must have just been her reflection in the water at the bottom of the well. Maybe a mouse or something. But what she thought she saw… well, it's ridiculous.'

'What did she *think* she saw?' Hoffman's tone had become as cold as the steel he wore on his belt.

'Well,' Reinhard lowered his voice and looked embarrassed. 'A monster. Something from one of the nursery rhymes our grandma used to tell us. These things, I can't remember what she called them, they were like rats. Only as big as men. And as cunning. Just stories to frighten us when we were naughty, you know the kind of things.'

'Yes,' Hoffman said. He stared through the merchant and into the world of memory. 'Yes, I know the sort of things.'

'Of course it's all ridiculous. We told her so, too. Mother even lost her temper in the end, shouted at her to stop being so silly. So then she started sobbing. It all gave me such a terrible headache. In fact I've still got one now, a little. I can feel it right there, just between my eyes. It's all too much, really it is. I've got to think about prices, markets, wages. And now this.'

Hoffman watched Reinhard pinch the bridge of his nose and blink back tears. Pathetic. 'So what did you do about this thing she thought she saw?'

'Do? Well, nothing. What can you do? Bertha's just highly strung, that's all. We all are. Our late father's artistic temperament coming out, I'm afraid.'

Reinhard smiled wanly.

Hoffman regarded him with ill-concealed contempt. 'He was a tanner *and* an artist?' the swordsman asked.

'In a way,' Reinhard nodded. 'In a way. You should have seen him in action, Herr Hoffman. He could sell anything to anybody. I remember once, there was this countess...'

'Is this relevant?'

'What? Oh. No. No, I suppose not. Anyway, where was I?'

Hoffman felt his patience beginning to crack.

'Oh yes, that was it. So anyway, Bertha wouldn't listen to reason. So she started living in her chambers, refusing to drink water out of the well, arguing with mother. Terrible arguments. But then, as if that wasn't bad enough, one of our servants got the idea that she'd seen one of the things as well. Oh, Sigmar, after that the whole household started to collapse. And now the men are refusing to use the well to get the water for the tanning pits. Say they're afraid of the monsters. I told them, I said if there were human-sized rats with teeth like chisels lurking in the shadows don't you think somebody would have seen them by now?'

'Were they reassured?' Hoffman wanted to know.

Reinhard shook his head miserably. 'No. See, there were a couple of fellows have gone off over the past month or so. Just upped and deserted us. The tanning business isn't for everyone. But all of a sudden everybody seems to have decided that they were eaten by Bertha's ratfolk. I tell you, I've reached my wits' end. Constant arguing in the house, nobody to cook the dinner or do the laundry, and now even the business is in peril.'

Reinhard drained the last of Hoffman's wine and signalled for more.

'I can see you're upset,' Hoffman told him as a girl brought more drinks over.

'I am, Herr Hoffman, I am. Anyway, that's why I've come to see you. Schilburg the baker said that you helped him out once when he had a problem. Something about some merchant who he had a disagreement with?'

'Ah yes,' Hoffman smiled. 'Him.'

For the first time the mercenary picked up his drink. Somehow Reinhard knew that it wasn't to celebrate anyone's good health.

'Well then,' Reinhard continued. 'What I was thinking was that, if you were to come back and climb down into the well, you could reassure everybody that there are no monsters down there. No tunnels leading away from the well shaft or anything.'

Hoffman put his tankard back down and looked into it thoughtfully. 'That's all?'

'Yes. Oh yes. I'm sure that that will be enough to put everyone's mind at rest. It will be a quick and easy job for you, too. Just pop down a rope ladder with a lantern, then come back up again.'

'If it's so easy, why ask me?' the swordsman wanted to know. 'Why not do it yourself?'

'Oh, well. You know.' Reinhard looked shifty, and fiddled with his goblet. 'I'm not as fit as I was. And anyway, if there was something down there, not that there is, I mean, but if there was...' He trailed off and hid his embarrassment behind a swig of wine.

Hoffman looked at him with the easy contempt of the strong for the weak.

'I see,' he said. 'Very well, I think that I can accept this contract. However, it will cost you. Monsters or no, my clothes will have to be replaced after splashing around in a well. And as well as that, of course, we will have to agree on a bounty for anything that I do find down there.'

'Yes, of course,' Reinhard said, relief lightening his face. 'Of course. We'll pay you a fair wage for popping down and having a look. In fact, I doubt if even twelve coppers would be too generous.'

'Ha!' Hoffman barked with false laughter. 'Twelve crowns, more like.'

The two men ordered more wine and settled down to haggle.

THE NEXT MORNING Hoffman rose with the sun. Blinking in the light that flooded his attic room, he pulled on his breeches, and staggered down into the courtyard of the inn. He plunged his head into a barrel of icy water to clear his hangover, then looked around the yard.

To his surprise, Reinhard was already there. The merchant stood by the stables, nervously wringing his felt hat.

'Good morning,' he said when he caught the swordsman's eye.

Hoffman just grunted. 'Got the money?' he asked.

'Oh yes. It's all here.' The merchant lifted up a leather purse. It clinked reassuringly. 'Shall we make a start now, Menheer Hoffman?'

'You're keen.'

'Sooner this is over with the better,' Reinhard said.

Hoffman shrugged. He had intended to call on a couple of friends of his, men with whom he'd worked in the past. But now that he thought about it, why bother? In the clear light of day all this talk of fairy tale monsters seemed even more ridiculous. Better just to do this coward's work for him, take the money, and find a decent cookhouse for breakfast.

'Wait here,' he told Reinhard. 'I'll get my weapons and be down in a moment.'

The merchant nodded and shifted from foot to foot as the swordsmen went to fetch his gear. When he returned he was armed with half a dozen scabbarded blades, the belts fastened over a sleeveless leather jerkin.

'Come on then,' he told Reinhard. 'Let's go.'

The merchant looked impressed as he set off, leading the mercenary through the twisting streets and gathering crowds of Nuln. In the distance the first series of booms from the gunnery school started to drift through the chill morning air, and the smells of frying sausage and freshly baked bread began to weave through the stink of the night soil. Then the smell changed, growing acrid as the two men entered the tanners' quarter.

'What is that stuff you use?' Hoffman asked, his nose wrinkling.

'Oh, all sorts,' Reinhard said. 'Mainly bark and fermented urine.'

Hoffman adjusted his leather jerkin and wished he hadn't asked.

The smell grew stronger until they reached the merchant's workshops. They went through a door that led off the street and into a courtyard beyond. Sheds stood on three sides, and on the fourth a wood-beamed house rose up above the complex. Between it and the gate stood the well.

'So this is it?' Hoffman asked as he prowled towards the circle of masonry. A timber frame stood above it, and the winch for the sunken bucket was fastened on one side. The swordsman peered cautiously into the depths of the well. There seemed to be nothing down there but cold and the faint glitter of water.

Reinhard joined him, looking nervously over his shoulder.

'Shall I winch you down, or do you want a ladder?' the merchant asked.

Hoffman blinked with surprise. 'Don't you want to wait for your men to turn up?' he asked, glancing around the deserted yard.

'No, I can do it. And anyway,' Reinhard continued, a certain bitterness creeping into his tone, 'none of them will come back until you've gone down and come back up again.'

Hoffman snorted. 'Just fasten the winch handle and I'll shin down the rope,' he said. 'Quicker we get this over with the quicker I can eat. And just to remind you, it was six crowns we agreed on, wasn't it?'

'Oh yes,' Reinhard nodded, his eyes never leaving the blackness of the well. 'Six crowns. It's all here.' He jingled the coin pouch reassuringly.

'Good.' Hoffman leapt nimbly onto the wall that edged the well and watched the merchant fasten the winch handle. When it was secure he took the rope in one hand, tested it, then swung out over and into the darkness below. He caught the rope between his heels and shinned easily down into the depths.

As soon as he entered the darkness, a chill of captured night bit at him. He shivered, and the bare flesh of his arms was soon stubbled with goose bumps.

When he was about half way down he stopped, dangling on the rope as easily as a spider on a thread, and listened. Below him the only sound was that of moisture dripping down into the well. He looked down at the glimmering liquid beneath his feet, then gazed up at the circle of sky that lay above. It was a perfect O, broken only by the silhouette of Reinhard.

Hoffman was about to carry on down when something about that silhouette made him look up again. A sudden jolt of fear flashed through him as he saw what was wrong with it. The arm that reached out to the rope wasn't there to steady it. On the contrary. As Hoffman squinted up, he could clearly see the glittering blade of a knife lying across the hemp.

'What are you doing, you damned fool?' he roared, the stone-lined sides of the well turning his voice to thunder.

By comparison, Reinhard's voice was little more than a squeak. 'Justice,' he said.

Hoffman, deciding that the merchant had cracked up, began to quickly shinny back up the rope.

'Don't move or I'll cut it!' Reinhard snapped.

Hoffman stopped, his hands gripping the hemp as he glared up at the silhouetted figure above. 'Alright,' he said, trying to keep the rage out of his voice. 'No problem. You can keep the coin. There's no sign of anything down here anyway.'

Reinhard laughed, a shrill sound that soon turned to sobbing.

Hoffman, so gently that the rope barely moved, began to slide surreptitiously back up towards him.

'This isn't about the coin, you fool,' Reinhard shouted down. 'This is about my father. You murdered him. You and that bastard Schilburg. And all for what? A few lousy barrels of tannin.'

Hoffman crept further up the rope, pausing every time he thought that Reinhard might be paying attention. It was damned lucky that the man's insanity had taken the form of hysterics.

'You're wrong, Menheer Reinhard,' Hoffman shouted up. 'I have never killed any of your family. The man Schilburg paid me to... to talk to was called Klumper. Otto Klumper.'

'That is my name too,' Reinhard said, suddenly sounding very tired. 'Just as it was the name of the man you murdered. So you see,' he smiled a death's head grin, 'there *are* vermin in the well after all.'

And with that he sliced through the last of the rope. Hoffman screamed as he fell, although not for long. There was a booming splash as he hit the water, and then the churning desperation of an armed man trying to tread water.

The man who had called himself Reinhard looked down into the darkness. Hoffman, it seemed, wasn't above begging for his life, but soon his pleading turned to gurgling as, weighed down by the tools of his trade, he sank into the icy embrace of the water.

The merchant sat in the silence that remained until the eleven o'clock cannon boomed out from the gunnery school. Then he roused himself, took a final look into the still depths of the well, and went back out into the street.

It was a fine day and, for the first time in a long time, he had one hell of an appetite.

TALES OF
DECEIT & OBSESSION

ROTTEN FRUIT

Nathan Long

IT ISN'T OFTEN a man gets to witness his own hanging, but Reiner Hetsau was being given the privilege. He didn't much care for it.

It was a week after the battle of Nordbergbusche, where Reiner and his companions had helped Count Manfred Valdenheim reclaim his family castle from the Kurgan who had occupied it since the Chaos invasion. This despite the fact that Manfred's younger brother Albrecht had turned on him, attacking him with two thousand troops, all under the spell of the cursed banner Valnir's Bane, which had turned them into bloodthirsty automatons. If Reiner and his companions hadn't slain Albrecht and destroyed the banner, the day would have been lost. And for this great service to Manfred and the Empire, Reiner and his companions were to hang. At least it was to appear.

'Poor damn butcher lambs,' said Giano, the Tilean mercenary, as he peered through the slats of the louvre-windowed coach Reiner shared with his fellow condemned. Pavel, the scrawny pikeman, swallowed and blinked his one good eye. 'There but for the grace of Sigmar...'

Reiner nodded, squinting at the scene outside. The coach sat amidst Manfred's retinue of twenty knights in the square before the Middenheim gaol. A great crowd surrounded them, all looking towards the gallows in the centre – a gallows that could hang five at once. The crowd was in a cheerful mood. There was nothing like a hanging to break up the monotony of rubble clearing and rebuilding that had become the daily life of Middenheim, the site of the final battle of Archaon's aborted invasion. Sellers of pinwheels and sweetmeats wound through the crowds, while on the gallows, five frightened men with passing resemblances to Reiner and his companions were about to dance on air.

'Why do I feel guilty it isn't us up there?' asked Franka, a dark-haired archer who only Reiner knew was not the boy she pretended to be.

'Because yer a soft-hearted fool,' said Hals, a bald, jut-bearded pike-man. 'They're villains. They'll be guilty of something.'

'But not guilty of what they're to hang for,' Franka pressed. 'They're being hanged for looking like us.'

'They're being hanged because Manfred doesn't want his family name besmirched by his brother's infamy,' said Reiner. He affected Manfred's statesmanlike tones: '"It would not do for the citizenry to believe their betters could be corrupted as Albrecht was."' Reiner snorted. 'I'm sure if Albrecht were someone else's brother, Manfred wouldn't be so concerned with the morale of the citizenry.'

A drum roll began. The crowd fell silent. Reiner and his companions stared through the narrow louvres.

On the gallows, Middenheim's chief magistrate read the charges as Manfred and a host of dignitaries looked solemnly on. 'Reiner Het-sau, Hals Kiir, Pavel Voss, Giano Ostini, Franz Shoentag, you are charged with the foul murder of Baron Albrecht Valdenheim; of bewitching his troops by means of heathen sorcery; causing them to attack his brother, Count Manfred Valdenheim, thereby bringing about the deaths of countless innocent men. For these and sundry other bestial crimes you are to be hanged by the neck until dead. May Sigmar have mercy on your souls.'

As the hangman pulled sacks over the condemned men's heads, Reiner looked at the man chosen to be his replacement, a debauched-looking villain with a pencil-thin moustache. Reiner wasn't flattered by the comparison.

Beside him, Franka sobbed. 'He's only a boy.'

Reiner looked at the lad who had been picked to die for her. It was doubtful he'd seen sixteen summers. He wouldn't see seventeen.

The drums stopped. The trap banged open and the five men dropped and jerked at the end of their ropes until the hangman's apprentices jumped up and hung from their knees. The crowd cheered.

'There's another five deaths on our consciences,' sighed Pavel.

'Speak for yourself,' said Hals. 'I put 'em square on Manfred. He's the one ordered 'em hung.'

But why he'd hung them instead of us, thought Reiner, is that we're too damned clever for our own good. Manfred had gone to the trouble of all this subterfuge because he had been impressed by the guile Reiner's companions had demonstrated in their defeat of Albrecht, and wanted to employ it for himself. As he'd told them, winning battles was not the only way the Empire stayed strong. There were less honourable deeds that had to be done to keep the citizenry safe, deeds no true-hearted knight could undertake, deeds only blackhearts could stomach. Reiner and his companions were those 'Blackhearts'.

So Manfred was having them 'executed' so that they would be invisible men – perfect spies who did not exist in the eyes of the world. But because he also feared they might abandon their new duties at their earliest opportunity, the count had insured their cooperation by magical means.

'We are just as much hanged men as those poor devils,' said Reiner. 'For the cursed poison Manfred put into our blood is a noose around our necks – and he could drop the trap at any time.'

Outside they heard Strieger, the captain of Manfred's retinue, call 'Forward!' and the coach lurched into motion. As they rode out of the square Reiner took a last look at the five hooded bodies swaying in the breeze.

THEY WERE TRAVELLING to Altdorf, where Manfred had a townhouse and where he advised the Emperor on matters of state. Locked in the louvred coach, the Blackhearts saw the passing world as dim light, shadow and sound. At least they were alone, with no one to overhear them, and this allowed them to plot their escape, however fruitlessly.

'Why not we kill the mage who know the poison spell?' suggested Giano.

'Manfred would get another, and have *him* unleash the poison,' said Reiner.

'What if we broke the mage's fingers until he removed the poison?' asked Hals.

'And if he said the spell that killed us instead of the spell that freed us, would you know the difference?' countered Reiner.

Pavel folded his arms, 'Alright then, captain, what do we do? Let us poke holes in yer ideas for once.'

'Well,' said Reiner, leaning back, 'perhaps we could pay a hedge witch to remove the poison.'

'If we could find one, and that would require a lot of gold,' said Franka. 'Something we are sorely lacking.'

Reiner nodded. 'True. But fortunes change. While helping Manfred we may find opportunity to help ourselves.'

'But a hedge witch could cheat us as well,' said Hals. 'He could spout any sort of mumbo jumbo and we wouldn't know if he'd removed the poison until we tried to run and fell dead on the spot.'

And on and on it went, an endless circle of argument as monotonous as the sound of the wheels rolling below them. Only occasionally would the monotony be broken when Reiner would look up to find Franka's eyes hot upon him. She and he had first shared that look after they had killed Albrecht. Since then, each time they locked eyes, visions of Franka's lithe body stripped of her boyish trappings danced through Reiner's head. But even these pleasant dreams led to frustration, for none of the others knew Franka was a woman, so their desire could not be acted upon, and the cycle of lust stirred followed by lust denied became as grinding and dull as everything else.

THE AGONY CONTINUED for three days, with the Blackhearts only let out of the coach when the company made camp. Then, on the third afternoon, the sudden booming of the coach wheels rolling over wood woke them from their stupor.

All five crowded to the slatted windows. The narrow view told them little more than they were crossing over a drawbridge into the courtyard of a castle. After a moment the coach came to a stop amid hails and responses from Manfred's retinue and the house guards.

One voice rose above the rest. 'Count Manfred! Well met, my lord.'

'And you, Groff,' came Manfred's voice. 'I see you survived the troubles.'

'Barely, my lord. Only barely.'

The coach door was unlocked and the guard in charge of the Blackhearts' transport, a sour veteran named Klaus, swung it open. 'Fall out, vermin,' he growled. 'And no nonsense. We're staying with quality tonight.'

'We'll be on our best behaviour,' said Reiner stepping out. 'Lay out my finest suit and ruff, won't you, Klaus?'

'That's just the sort of thing I'm talking about,' snarled Klaus.

'We were hit very hard, my lord,' Groff was saying. He was a short, dark-haired man with a flabby, careworn face. 'We held supplies for Baron Hegel's cannon, and somehow the devils got wind of it. Tried for three days to get in before Boecher's garrison came up and chased them off, by the grace of Sigmar. But by then three-quarters of my men died, and as you can see...'

Groff gestured around at his castle, which was in terrible disrepair. Crews of peasants laboured to close up holes in the outer walls that one could have led a company of lancers through, but they were making little progress. The roof of the stables had burned, and one of the turrets of the keep had collapsed, and now lay across the courtyard like the corpse of a dragon.

'But we seem to have bested one evil only to have another spring up. Indeed, I am glad you have graced us with your presence, m'lord, for something's brewing in the forest that I would have you warn Altdorf about.'

Manfred looked up. 'Remnants of the Chaos horde?'

Groff shrugged. 'Something in there is carrying off the villagers and driving the woodsmen mad. And they're getting bolder. I'd appreciate you asking Altdorf to send reinforcements. We're in no state to face any–'

'Right, you lot,' said Klaus at Reiner's side. 'We've got your lodgings sorted. This way.'

But before they could follow, there was a clatter of hooves at the gate and everyone turned to face the potential threat. It was a single horseman, a flush-faced youth in black and silver with fevered excitement in his bright blue eyes.

'Father!' he cried as he reined his horse to a halt. 'Father, I saw a white stag in the woods just now. It was beautiful. You should hunt it with me.'

Manfred's knights relaxed. Their hands dropped from their hilts.

Groff looked embarrassed. 'Udo, pay your respects to Count Valdenheim. My lord, may I introduce my son, Udo.'

Udo dismounted and bowed distractedly to Manfred. 'My lord count. Welcome to our humble house.' He turned back to his father. 'So, may we have a hunt, father?'

As Klaus led the Blackhearts away, Reiner looked back to see Lord Groff bowing Count Manfred towards the main door and shooting angry looks at his son. Udo seemed oblivious. He followed his father into the keep with a far-away smile on his too-red lips. It looked like he had been eating cherries.

THAT EVENING, REINER and his companions ate in silence with Klaus and the castle's servants, more interested in hot food than conversation after their claustrophobic journey. The servants talked enough for all of them anyway.

'Hans the baker disappeared last night,' said a serving maid. 'Third this month.'

The groom snorted. 'Disappeared? Everyone knows where he's gone. Off into the woods.'

The cook nodded. 'His woman said he woke up from a dead sleep sayin' he heard music, and ran off, naked.'

Reiner was busy trying to think of a way to be alone with Franka that night. They would be back in the coach on the morrow and he had no idea how they would be lodged in Altdorf. Tonight could be their only chance at intimacy – their only chance even to speak privately.

'Tain't funny, young Grig,' said a burly huntsman to a giggling young footman. 'Those fools are dangerous as well as mad. They'd eat you as soon as look at you. And the wood ain't the same neither. The trees are changing. Honest Drakwald oaks growing thorns and...' he made a face, 'fat purple plums. It ain't natural.'

'If there's a danger in the forest,' asked Hals, his garrulous nature surfacing, 'why are yer walls still all a jumble?'

'There's not many left to build 'em, sir,' said the footman. 'The war took so many. The village was nearly deserted even before this business in the woods begun. Now–'

'Even the bandits what used to steal our sheep are leaving,' said the cook.

'And what with m'lord's lady taken away by fever,' said the groom. 'And young master Udo taking on so queer...'

'There's nothing wrong with master Udo,' barked a long-faced fellow who hadn't spoken before. Then he chuckled, trying to smooth over his outburst. 'The boy's moon-eyed over a girl in the village is all.' He winked. 'She wears him out.'

'He don't go to the village, Stier,' said the groom. 'He goes to the woods.'

'Don't talk of what you don't know, boy,' Stier snapped. 'I'm his manservant. I think I should know what he does.' He stood, stiff. 'It will be time to serve the port. Come, Burgo.'

The footman wiped his lips and joined Stier as he unlocked the wine cabinet. They selected a few bottles, and went upstairs.

Reiner stared at the cabinet. They had left it open. He smiled.

'YOU LOT ARE lucky they ain't got a full complement of servants,' said Klaus as he herded them into a below-stairs dormitory. 'You'd be sleeping in the stables else.' He turned on Reiner. 'And I'll be right outside the door, you, so no sneaking out windows, no sneaking in serving girls, no gambling with the grooms. We're on our best behaviour. Understand?'

Reiner looked suddenly contrite. 'Actually, sergeant, if I might have a word alone, I have a confession to make.'

Klaus sighed and beckoned him into the hall, then closed the door behind them. 'What is it now, Hetsau?'

Reiner slipped a bottle of wine from under his jacket. 'Well...'

'What's this?' asked Klaus suspiciously. 'You trying to bribe me?'

'Bribe you?' said Reiner, astonished. 'Sergeant, bribery was the furthest thing from my mind, I assure you.'

'Then...?'

'I, er, well, I nicked this to share with the lads, but your admonitions have shamed me, and I want you to return it to its rightful place. I don't want to embarrass Manfred with any bad behaviour.'

Klaus looked longingly at the bottle. 'Why, that's damned decent of ye, Hetsau. I'll put in a good word for you with Count Manfred for this.'

Reiner gave Klaus the bottle. 'I was just hoping you wouldn't report me.'

'No fear,' said Klaus, not taking his eyes off the bottle. 'No fear.'

LATER, AFTER THE other Blackhearts had gone to sleep, Reiner slipped out of his cot and peeked into the hall. He was gratified to see Klaus sprawled in his chair snoring like a lumber mill, the wine bottle empty beside him. Reiner tip-toed to Franka's bed and shook her gently. Like a good soldier, Franka came awake without a murmur, merely opening her eyes and reaching for her dagger – which she didn't have, as Manfred had disarmed them.

Reiner put his finger to his lips and nodded towards the door. Franka looked around, frowning when she saw the other Blackhearts still asleep.

'What's this foolishness?' she mouthed.

He winked and motioned to the door again. Franka hesitated, then, with a shrug, swung out of bed and joined him at the door. They eased out together.

Reiner led Franka quietly through the dark hallways and twisting stairs of the silent castle until he found the musicians' gallery above the main hall. He pulled her in and crushed him to her, kissing her passionately. She resisted at first, surprised, but after a moment the tension went out of her arms and her lips parted. They melted into each other, as if the boundaries between them were blurring. Franka moaned in her throat and her hands ran down Reiner's back. Reiner gripped her hips and pulled her into him.

'Wait.' Franka was suddenly pushing back, her hands on his chest.

'Wait?' asked Reiner, baffled. 'Why?'

'My lord, please. I cannot.'

'You cannot? But you just did!'

'You surprised me. But we must not continue.'

Reiner's brow furrowed. 'But then why did you come away with me? Why...?'

'I came so that we might speak of... all this.'

'Speak? You want to waste these few precious moments we have speaking?'

'Hist!' said Franka, turning. 'I heard a noise.'

'None of your tricks,' said Reiner, but now he heard it too: a shuffling and bumping. He and Franka stepped to the lattice.

Moving somnolently through the great hall below, dressed only in his night shirt, was Udo. His eyes were open but he moved through the room like a blind man pulled by some invisible rope.

'He sleepwalks,' murmured Reiner.

'We should make sure he doesn't do himself a mischief,' whispered Franka, and turned towards the door.

'But...' Reiner sighed. She was already in the hall. He followed.

As they started down the stairs to the hall, they saw Udo coming up. They backed around a corner until he topped the stairs and walked away down the hall.

They started after him. Reiner cursed. He had felt Franka's desire. It would only have been a matter of time before she succumbed. Now who knew when they could come to grips again.

Udo turned a corner. When Reiner and Franka reached it, Franka peeked around, then pulled quickly back.

'What is it?' asked Reiner.

'A... a woman,' said Franka, frowning.

'What?' Reiner eased his head around the corner.

At the end of a short hallway, open doors revealed a scene from some old romantic painting – a couple embracing on an ivy-covered balcony, the lovers haloed softly in the moonlight – except in the painting, the man would undoubtedly have worn breeches.

The woman was shockingly beautiful, a voluptuous succubus in a plum velvet dress, with glossy black hair and a full-lipped, heart-shaped face. Udo was fully under her spell, trying to close with her like a lust-crazed schoolboy while she held him off.

'Later, beloved,' she was saying. 'We must speak of other things first.'

The scene felt familiar, but Reiner was so beglamoured by the woman's beauty he couldn't remember why.

A hand pulled him roughly back. 'Do you want them to see you?' hissed Franka.

'I was, er, well...'

Franka rolled her eyes.

The woman's voice floated around the corner: a throaty contralto. 'No, beloved. First you must tell me what was said at dinner. Why is Valdenheim here? Does he mean to destroy us?'

Reiner and Franka froze at the mention of Manfred's name.

'Dinner be damned,' whined Udo. 'You don't understand how much I need you. I ache for you.'

'I know exactly how much you need me, silly boy. Now tell me or I shall leave.'

Udo yelped. 'No! You mustn't! I will tell! Though they said little enough. Father begged Valdenheim for help fighting the "horror" in the forest, but Valdenheim put him off, saying the Empire hasn't the resources.'

'So he hasn't come to hunt us down?'

'No. He's only passing through. Taking spies to be questioned in Altdorf, he said.'

Reiner and Franka heard the woman's relieved sigh. 'Very good. Now did you tell your father of the white stag as I asked? Has he agreed to the hunt?'

'I told him, but... but, beloved, is it really necessary to kill him?'

'He will never consent to our union, my sweet. Or to the kingdom of pleasure we hope to found here. It is best...' She stopped suddenly, then murmured something Reiner and Franka couldn't hear.

'What?' said Udo loudly. 'Overheard?'

Reiner and Franka began backing hastily away, but before they could take three steps Udo was around the corner, swinging his fists wildly. 'Assassins!' he cried. 'Spies!'

'Hush, beloved!' hissed the woman, following him. 'You'll wake the house.'

Reiner and Franka dropped Udo with a few well-placed fists and knees, and he rolled away, groaning. The woman was another matter. She flashed towards them like an oiled shadow, stiletto glinting in her hand. Reiner and Franka dropped their hands to their belts, forgetting again that they had no daggers.

The woman lunged at Reiner, her blade seeking his neck. He grabbed her wrist, trying to force it back. It was like trying to bend iron. He looked in her eyes. They shone with a weird light. His mind began to swim. Franka kicked the woman in the stomach. The beauty snarled and backhanded her, breaking eye-contact with Reiner. Franka flew back, head bouncing off the wall, and she slid to the floor.

Reiner caught the woman's arm as she stabbed again, this time averting his eyes, but even using his whole body to hold the stiletto away, still it inched towards his neck.

Sounds of doors opening echoed down the hall.

'Unhand her, villain!' cried Udo, staggering up. Franka grabbed his legs. He kicked her in the face.

'Idiot child!' hissed the beauty. 'Be silent!'

Udo pummelled Reiner. His blows were weak, but a lucky punch to the kidney made Reiner's knees buckle and the witch's stiletto jerked forward, gashing his collar bone.

With a look of triumph, she ripped her arm free of Reiner's grip and raised the stiletto, but feet were running towards them and they heard the scrape of unsheathing swords. The beauty looked up, cursing. Reiner kicked her in the stomach. She stumbled back, eyes flashing angrily at Udo. 'Fool! I told you to be silent.' With a frustrated hiss, she ran to the balcony and leapt over. Reiner half expected her to fly away like some bird of prey, but she dropped out of sight and was gone.

Udo's fist caught Reiner on the cheekbone. 'Spoilsport! You've chased her away!'

Reiner ducked back and grabbed Udo's arms. Franka lurched up and caught Udo's collar from behind, pulling his shirt down over his shoulders to trap his arms. Reiner was about to head butt the youth when he saw a livid mark on Udo's exposed chest. A small puncture wound, purple-black with infection, rose directly over his heart. It looked like a third nipple.

'Ware,' muttered Franka, looking past Reiner. 'Manfred and our host.'

Reiner looked back. Manfred and Groff were hurrying towards them in robes and nightshirts, swords drawn, leading a handful of knights and house guards.

Udo shoved Reiner back and pulled his shirt closed. 'Father,' he cried. 'These men have assaulted me! Arrest them!'

'What is the meaning of this?' demanded Groff, bustling up. 'Manfred, aren't these your prisoners?'

'They are,' said Manfred. 'And I promise a reckoning when I discover who let them out.'

'My lords,' said Reiner quickly, 'there is greater evil afoot here than our petty truancy. Your house is infiltrated, Lord Groff. There is a witch on your grounds. She came to meet your son and just now leapt over the balcony. If you hurry...'

'What nonsense is this?' barked Groff. 'You try to draw attention from your crimes by accusing my son of witchcraft? Manfred, slay these insolent...'

'But 'tis the truth, my lord,' said Reiner. 'She has marked him. You have only to look at his...'

'Enough,' said Manfred. 'What are you doing out of quarters, and who let you out?'

'My lord,' said Franka, imploring. 'She is getting away.'

'Answer my question, curse you!'

Reiner ground his teeth. 'Here's your answer, y'damned fools.' And before anyone could stop him, he grabbed Udo's collar and ripped his nightshirt clean off.

Groff jumped forward, shouting and swinging his sword as Reiner dodged back. 'He assaults my son before my eyes! Stand, villain, I will...'

But Manfred was staring at Udo, who stood dumbly, with the unclean wound exposed for all to see. Groff followed his gaze and choked as he saw it.

'Groff,' Manfred said quietly. 'Lock up your son. He has been tainted and cannot be trusted.' He turned to one of his knights. 'Strieger, rouse the others and make ready. And lock the prisoners in the carriage. We ride within the hour.'

'You're not leaving?' exclaimed Lord Groff. 'Not now?'

'We must,' said Manfred. 'This was obviously an attempt to corrupt your house from the inside, but now that they know we know of their existence and their intent, they will try to stop us from warning Altdorf. We must be away before they surround us.'

'But they'll slaughter us!' cried Groff.

'Twenty knights would do nothing to change that outcome,' said Manfred, striding down the hall. 'We will pass Boecher's garrison on our way south. I will ask them to send reinforcements.'

Groff trotted after Manfred, mewling his distress, as Manfred's knights took Reiner and Franka in tow while Groff's guards did the same with Udo.

'But my lady doesn't wish to hurt anyone,' whined Udo. 'She wants us all to live only for pleasure.'

A HALF HOUR later, the Blackhearts were back in the cramped coach, bouncing and jolting uncomfortably as they raced down the rough track that led to the main Altdorf road. The thunder of Manfred's knights riding at full gallop drowned out all other sound and made conversation impossible.

A quarter of an hour out, there came a cry of 'Ware, bandits!' and the Blackhearts heard the knights draw steel.

Reiner and the others crowded to the slatted windows. On both sides of the road was a large, hastily made camp. Bandits caught in the act of raising tents and starting fires were backing towards the woods as they gaped at Manfred's retinue. Others were snatching up weapons and preparing to fight. But when it became clear that the knights didn't intend to stop, some of the bandits waved their arms and called out after them.

'What they say?' asked Giano.

Pavel swallowed, nervous. 'They said, "Turn back".'

ONLY A FEW minutes later there was another cry from the knights, and the coach reined to a sudden, slewing stop. Reiner and his companions again pressed to the windows. It was impossible for them to see forward, but they heard anxious muttering from the knights, and on both sides of the coach the forest crowded too close to the road.

'It's blocked,' said a knight.

The forest was changed as well. Choking the tall pines and stout oaks were twisted vines, black of leaf, and heavy with purple, pendulous fruit that gave off a cloying odour.

'The vines,' whispered Giano. 'They move.'

'Dortman!' came Manfred's voice. 'See if a way can be cut.'

'Yes, my lord.'

Hooves trotted forward and the Blackhearts heard a thwacking of sword on vine. 'It is very thick, my lord. I can see no end to...'

His words were cut off by a whistling thud, and a crash of armour hitting hard-packed dirt.

'Archers!' cried a knight, and suddenly the air was hissing with arrows. They thudded and rattled off the coach and the Blackhearts jerked back from the windows and dropped to the floor in a frightened pile.

'Fall back!' cried Manfred. 'Back to the castle!'

As the coach lurched around awkwardly, arrow heads splintered through the back wall. They glistened with green putrescence.

Hals hissed. 'Poison.'

THREE KNIGHTS DIED in the ambush, and two more were dying from cuts that barely bled, screaming in agony as poison burned through their veins. The coachman too had died. Klaus had manned the reins in their headlong flight to the castle.

Now Manfred conferred again with Groff in the courtyard while his knights stood by, and the Blackhearts, who waited with Klaus.

'How many men do you have?' asked Manfred.

'Sixteen knights, my lord,' said Groff. 'And forty foot, most with bows and spears, And I've pressed the staff into service, though they've to make do with pitchforks and fire-irons. Isn't much, I'm afraid.'

Reiner followed Manfred's gaze as the count surveyed the broken walls, where a collection of peasant conscripts, cooks and pot-boys made an inadequate defence. Groff's 'knights' – beardless youths pressed into armour after their older brothers had died in the recent conflict – guarded the widest, most easily breached gaps in the walls. They were spread very thin. Manfred looked grim. Reiner wanted to throw up.

'Pull half those boys off the wall,' Manfred said, 'and set them to tearing apart that scaffolding. Sharpen the ends of the poles and plant them at an angle before the gaps in the walls. Next, use the wood of the stables to make bonfires fifty yards from the walls in all directions so we may see the enemy before they're at our throats. Pour all the lamp oil you have into the moat and be ready to light it when they attempt to cross. It will not be enough. We will die, but at least we will take as many with us as...'

'My lord,' said Reiner. 'Might I make a suggestion?'

'You may not,' snapped Manfred.

'A suggestion that may allow us to win, my lord.'

Manfred turned on him, glaring. 'What is it?'

'The bandits, my lord. They are trained men, armed with bow and sword. If...'

'Absolutely not,' said Manfred. 'They are deserters. We cannot count on their loyalty, or their courage.'

'They are trapped just as we are, my lord. They have little choice but...'

'Silence! I have said no.'

'STIFF-NECKED FOOL,' said Reiner, furious. 'His righteousness will get us killed.'

The Blackhearts sat on a pile of rubble in a gap in the north wall.

'Don't know why he cares,' said Hals. 'He doesn't have a problem using us, and I'll lay odds we're a nastier lot than them bandits.'

'Aye,' said Reiner. 'But he doesn't have the leash around their necks he has around ours.'

Reiner looked below them where Groff's conscripts were wedging sharpened poles into the rubble. Beyond the moat, a wagon full of scrap lumber and brush was crossing the field as more conscripts built bonfires at regular intervals.

'I no want to die,' said Giano. 'Not for foolishnesses.'

'Nor do I,' growled Hals.

Reiner sighed. 'I think it's up to us to save ourselves, lads. What do you say we go find those bandits? It's a poor chance, but it's better than sitting here waiting for death.'

The others shot nervous glances at Klaus, then leaned in.

'I'm in,' whispered Hals. 'If you've a way.'

'Won't Manfred unleash the poison?' asked Franka.

'Not until he knows we're gone,' said Reiner. 'And when the battle begins, he'll be too busy to check on us.'

'But we'll have to dispose of him,' said Hals, nodding at Klaus.

'Kill him?' asked Franka uneasily.

Reiner smirked. 'No need to go so far. Plenty of places in all this mess to hide him until we get back.' He looked up. 'Hoy, sergeant. I seem to have cut myself. I don't think I can participate in forthcoming conflict.'

'Hey?' cried Klaus. 'Not participate? Damned if you won't. Let me see this *cut* of yours.'

Hals grinned and balled his fists as Klaus climbed down to them.

'STAND WHERE YOU ARE, dead men!'

The Blackhearts raised their arms as a score of spears and five times as many arrows pointed their way.

After binding and gagging Klaus and tucking him behind a fall of rubble, then crossing the moat with the help of a scaffolding ladder, they had stolen one of the wagons which had been building the bonfires, and rode towards the bandit camp. Now, having found it, Reiner was having second thoughts.

A huge, broad-chested villain with matted grey hair and a filthy beard stepped through the outlaws, a scrawny boy at his side with the swaying gait and roving eye of an idiot.

'Brother,' said Reiner. 'We come...'

'Shut yer gob!' said the giant. He urged the boy forward. 'Sniff 'em out, Ludo. See if they've the taint.'

The boy wove to the Blackhearts' wagon like a dreamer and reached out limp hands. Reiner recoiled. Giano made the sign of Shallya, but they dared not move. The idiot sniffed and fondled them like a dog with hands, then with a whimpering sigh lay his head on Reiner's leg. At this the outlaws relaxed a little.

'Well,' said the giant. 'Yer not touched ones at any rate. What do y'want?'

'We come to ask a boon,' said Reiner, trying not flinch from the idiot's fawning. 'The touched ones, as you call them, mount an attack on Lord Groff's castle, which is grievously undermanned. He and Count Manfred need your help.'

The outlaws roared with laugher.

'Groff needs *our* help?' asked the leader. 'Groff, who hangs us for hunting the deer of the forest. And another jagger who's no doubt just as bad? Why should we help the likes of them?'

'Because the alternative is worse.'

'Yer mad. I'll dance a jig when Groff is dead.'

'Would you rather the touched ones ruled here in Groff's stead?' asked Reiner. 'Where would you be then?'

The outlaws were silent.

'Groff may hang you now and then,' Reiner continued, 'but at least that death comes quick. How many have you lost to the dark lady's seduction? Good men gone rotten, running naked in the woods, stealing your children to sacrifice to their daemon masters. Is that what you want?'

The outlaws muttered among themselves.

The giant crossed his arms. 'Nobody wants that. But we don't care to walk into a noose either. What's our guarantee that Groff, or this Manfred, won't turn around and hang us after we've saved their worthless hides?'

'I can offer you no guarantee,' said Reiner, 'but I have some sway with Manfred at least, and I will do what I can. Count Manfred is an honourable man. He may even reward you.'

Franka shot him a look at that. Reiner shrugged. He hoped it wasn't a lie, but he had to say something.

After a moment's conversation with his lieutenants, the big man turned back to Reiner. He nodded. 'Alright, silver-tongue, you've convinced us. Lead on.'

A RED GLOW above the trees as the Blackhearts and the bandits approached the castle gave evidence that battle had already been joined. The noise came next. The clash of steel on steel, the cries of men and the screams of horses. When they reached the fields, Manfred's bonfires illuminated a grim scene. The massed cultists – one couldn't call them an army – attacked the ruined castle from all sides, undisciplined but bloodthirsty. They had bridged the moat with tree-trunks, and pressed Groff's meagre forces and Manfred's few knights fiercely at every gap in the walls.

Hals gaped when he saw them. 'The madmen! What're they about?'

Franka giggled.

Reiner grimaced. 'Some things are better covered by darkness.'

The cultists, despite the cold of the spring night, were naked, their only covering swirls of purple and red, which looked more like smeared fruit and blood than paint. But, though naked, they were armed. Men and women, young and old, wielded swords and spears and clubs and bows, and though many seemed unlearned in their use, there were so many of them, and they were so frenzied in their unholy ecstasy that even alone they might have carried the day. Unfortunately they were not alone.

Leading them were troops of a different calibre altogether. Fighting at the wall were immense warriors in black and purple armour, while, further out, purple-clad bowmen cut down defenders with impossible accuracy. 'Northmens,' whispered Giano.

'We fought that sort at Brozny,' said Pavel, shuddering. 'Their swords had spikes in the hilts which pierce their own hands as they fight.'

Hals nodded. 'Pain was like drink to them. They loved it.'

'Well,' said Reiner. 'There ain't enough of them to take the castle without their followers. If we can drive them off we'll at least give Groff a fighting chance.'

Loche, the bandit leader, smiled. 'You leave that to me.'

LOCHE BROUGHT HIS men to the wood's edge and spread them out.

'You'll never hit them from here,' said Reiner, priming his handgun.

'No,' said the bandit. 'Groff's cut the woods back two bow shots for that very reason. We'll have to come up to the first hedgerow.'

He signalled his men forward and they and the Blackhearts advanced at a jog. Fortunately the cultists, expecting no reinforcements, had posted no real guard. The bandits reached the hedgerow with no alarm raised.

'Ready boys?' asked Loche.

The bandits put arrows to strings and flexed their bows. Franka did as well. Reiner and Giano raised their handguns. Hals and Pavel, pikemen with no skill with a bow, stood by with second guns, ready to reload while Reiner and Giano fired.

'Fire.'

With a thrum like a hundred guitars, the bandits loosed their shafts. Reiner's and Giano's guns cracked like snare drums. The arrows disappeared into the night, but reappeared as if by magic in the bare flesh of the cultists, who screamed and fell by the score.

It took the madmen a moment to understand their plight, and by then, more feathered shafts were cutting them down. A wave of panic overcame them and they ran in all directions, dropping their weapons. Reiner wondered that men so frenzied that they stormed a castle naked would lose courage under fire, but facing an enemy you can see is very different from invisible death speeding from the night.

'Don't waste arrows on the runners, boys,' said Loche. 'Let's circle and...'

But suddenly it was the bandits who were falling and screaming as feathered death whistled among them. Worse, even those only scratched were falling and writhing in agony, clawing at their wounds as if they were on fire.

Reiner looked at the arrows. They were the same that had riddled the coach on their flight from the ambush.

'The purple archers,' growled Loche, as his men pressed into the hedgerow. 'Concentrate yer fire, boys.'

Reiner sited along his gun barrel as the bandits nocked fresh arrows, but something behind the purple archers caught his eye. Below the north wall, a handful of Northmen, their black armour flashing red in the light of the bonfires, crossed the moat on a plank and crept toward the postern gate. There were no troops to stop them. Most of the fighting was on the far side of the castle. If this little force could somehow break down the iron-bound door...

Reiner checked as the postern gate swung suddenly open. What treachery was this? Reiner squinted, trying to identify the shadowed figure who let the warriors into the castle. It was impossible. He cursed. The Blackhearts looked around.

Reiner pointed. 'Our efforts may be for naught. Someone lets the Northers in by the back gate.'

Loche looked up. 'Hey?' He peered forward.

'We'll have to stop them,' said Franka. 'Unless we wish to die in this cursed wood.'

Reiner glared at the girl. She was right, but the last thing he wanted to do was hunt through dark corridors after Northern marauders. He'd faced their like before, and nearly died of it. 'It'll take more than the five of us to bring those monsters down. Loche, we...'

'Not to worry,' said the big man. 'I ran from them once. And won my coward's brand for it. I'll not run again. Murgen, Aeloff, pick ten men and come with me.'

'Ten and five.' Hals swallowed, nervous. 'I hope it is enough.'

REINER AND LOCHE and their men entered the open postern gate and peered into the empty kitchen garden. Sounds of the battle echoed around the bulk of the keep, but it was quiet here.

'Where are they?' whispered Pavel.

'Shhh!' hissed Giano, cupping his ear.

They held their breath. From over the garden wall they heard a closing door.

The party started cautiously forward, but Franka slipped quickly ahead. 'I'll keep 'em in sight,' she said.

'Frank... Franz! Wait!' called Reiner, but the girl had already slipped into the garden.

'Come on,' growled Reiner.

As they entered the kitchen they saw Franka waving them towards the cellar stairs. They followed, and caught up with her at the door to the dungeon.

'What are they doing down here?' asked Reiner.

'Forcing a cell door,' replied Franka.

'Ah. Udo.'

The sound of steel biting into wood echoed down the narrow hall. Lantern light flickered from a door at the end. Franka started ahead. Reiner stopped her and went forward himself. She gave him a dirty look.

Reiner peered into a low-ceilinged guard room with stout oak doors on each wall. The Northmen had just broken the lock of one and were swinging it open. Udo stepped out and embraced the smallest warrior, who Reiner suddenly realized was the sorceress, dressed in black armour of barbaric splendour. Her six companions wore black and purple as well, and disturbingly, though they were as fiercely bearded as any Northman, were as rouged and painted as Marienberg streetwalkers. Udo's manservant, Stier, stood with them, holding a lantern. It was he, Reiner realized, who had let them in.

After receiving Udo's enthusiastic kiss, the sorceress stepped back. 'It is time, beloved, to seize your destiny. Are you ready?'

The boy nodded, unable to look away from her eyes. 'I am ready.'

The beauty removed a jewelled broach from her cloak. The pin was covered in black crust. 'Then take this and go to your father. A mere scratch and he will fall. When Manfred and his knights turn to assist him, prick as many of them as you can. We will be nearby, ready to protect you from any survivors.'

Udo hesitated, looking at the broach. 'Will it be... painful?'

'Worry not, my sweet,' said the witch, caressing his cheek. 'Your father will not suffer. In fact he will die of an excess of pleasure.'

She turned towards the door with Udo. Her men fell in around her. Reiner backed down the corridor to the waiting bandits.

'Bows out,' he hissed. 'Pin 'em inside the room.'

He and Giano shouldered their guns as the others raised bows. Two warriors filled the door, eclipsing the room behind them with their bulk.

'Fire!'

The warriors bellowed as the barrage battered them. Most of the arrows glanced off the ebony armour, but a few hit more, and Reiner and Giano's shot smashed through brains and bone. The Northmen fell. Behind them, Udo stared at an arrow sticking from his arm.

'I... I am... hit!'

The sorceress snatched him back into the room as one of her warriors leapt forward, sword drawn, and the last three backed up, protecting her.

'Fire!'

Reiner dropped his handgun and fired his pistol as the bandits' bowstrings thrummed in his ears. The massive warrior took the ball and a thicket of arrows full on. He kept coming, eyes blazing with ecstatic fury.

'Fire!'

But the Northman was on them before they could reload. Pavel and Hals shouldered Reiner and Giano aside and jammed their spears into the warrior's chest just as he reached their line. The force of his charge drove them skidding back, but at last he stopped, blood erupting from his painted mouth as he fell.

'Die hard, don't they?' said Loche.

'Aye,' agreed Hals.

A noise returned their attention to the guard room. The bandits flexed their bows again. Reiner aimed his pistol, but no berserk warriors spewed forth. Instead, stepping into the hall was the sorceress, arms raised... and naked.

'Hold,' she said. 'I would parlay.'

Reiner and the Blackhearts and the bandits stared, open-mouthed, as she paced forward, her ripe curves swaying with every step. 'You wouldn't shoot an unarmed woman, would you?'

Reiner began forming a joke about the woman being better armed than most armies, but it died in his throat as a delicious scent reached his nose. It wafted from her like musk: vanilla and jasmine, and drifted into his brain like fog.

He tried to tell the others to shoot her before she ensorcelled them all, but found himself unable to speak or raise his gun. The others seemed similarly affected.

The sorceress continued forward, smiling sweetly. 'In fact, you would kill any man who tried to harm me, wouldn't you? You would defend me to the death.'

She stopped in front of them. Reiner fought to free his mind, but her beauty was all-consuming. He couldn't tear his eyes away. He would do anything for her – die for her, if she would only take him into her arms. He heard bows and guns clatter to the floor as they fell from slack hands.

'You, boy,' she said, pointing at Franka. 'Your captain raised his gun to me. Will you protect me? Will you cut his throat?'

Franka nodded and wove towards him, drawing her dagger, glassy-eyed. Reiner raised his chin obligingly. It was true. He had tried to kill the sorceress. He deserved to die.

Franka raised her dagger.

The sorceress licked her lips. 'Of course you will,' she said. 'No man can resist me.'

But suddenly Franka spun and stabbed her in the throat. The witch stared, more shocked at Franka's disobedience than at the dagger in her neck.

Franka smirked. 'Fortunately, I am no man.'

The woman fell, blood pouring down over her alabaster breasts. The spell was broken. Reiner shook his head. The others did the same, cursing and groaning.

'No! Beloved!'

Reiner looked up. Udo was racing at them, sword above his head. 'Murderers!' he cried. 'Savages!'

Behind him came the three remaining Northmen.

Reiner fired but missed. The bandits were still picking up their dropped weapons and got off only a few shots. Reiner drew frantically, and met Udo sword on sword as Pavel and Hals thrust their spears at the Northmen and the bandits rushed to back them up.

'Foul defiler!' shrieked Udo. 'To kill such a gentle–'

Reiner ran him through. The boy curled in on himself and fell. Reiner felt strangely guilty.

Around him, the Blackhearts and the bandits were beating on the Northmen with all their might, but the corridor was too narrow and too crowded to make a good swing, and the warriors' armour was too strong. The men could hardly dent it.

The warriors, on the other hand, swung mailed fists and axes held high on the haft. Reiner saw Pavel reeling back from a fist to the shoulder. An axe sheared off a bandit's arm at the elbow.

'Fall back!' shouted Reiner.

The Blackhearts and the bandits ran up the stairs, leaving their dead and wounded behind, the Northmen hot on their heels. A bandit went down, his skull crushed as he turned to flee.

As they burst out of the castle into the yard, Reiner was momentarily afraid that they had run into more Northmen. The garden was full of men in blood-caked armour. But then he recognized Manfred and Groff in the chaos. The knights raised a shout as the Northmen roared out of the kitchen, and a fierce battle erupted as the two sides slammed together.

Reiner was happy to observe from the sidelines, as were the bandits and the Blackhearts, who sucked in deep breaths and mopped at their wounds.

After it became certain that the knights would be victorious, Hals turned to Franka and gave her a curious look.

'What meant ye,' he asked, 'when y'said "fortunately you wasn't a man"?'

'What?' said Franka. Reiner swallowed nervously. The girl was turning bright red. 'I... er, I, well, I merely meant that I am but a boy.'

Hals scowled. 'When I was your age, laddie, I was twice as likely to fall for a woman's wiles.'

But before he could pursue the question further, the last of the Northmen fell and Manfred was striding their way, glaring.

'Hetsau, what is the meaning of this?'

'My lord,' said Reiner as he thought how to answer. 'We are most glad...'

'Never mind that, villain. I...'

Behind the count, Groff suddenly raised a cry. All turned. Servants were carrying Udo's body into the garden. Groff hurried forward and took the boy in his arms. 'Who has done this?' he cried. 'Who has slain my son?'

Manfred glared at Reiner. 'Hetsau?'

'My lord, you wound me.' said Reiner. He crossed to Groff. 'Lord Groff, the sorceress came to free your son so he might assassinate you, but he refused. They slew him for it.'

Groff looked at him with grateful eyes. 'He resisted then?'

'Yes, my lord. I only regret we were not able to stop them.'

Manfred gave Reiner a cool look. 'Regrettable indeed. And who are these gentlemen with you, who were yet not enough to save Lord Groff's son?'

Reiner swallowed. 'My lord, this is Captain Loche, leader of the noble woodsmen who helped you hold the castle this night.'

Loche touched his forelock to Manfred. 'M'lord.'

'A leader of bandits, you mean,' said Manfred, ignoring Loche. 'Who you recruited against my orders.'

'I thought your lordship might be pleased to find yourself alive at the outcome.'

'I am never pleased to be disobeyed.' He turned to the captain of his retinue. 'Strieger, arrest these outlaws, and all who have remained on the field.'

'What?' said Loche, surprised.

'But, my lord,' cried Reiner as the knights began to surround the surviving bandits. 'They have saved your life. You must admit that. You would be dead if not for their help.'

'That may be,' said Manfred, 'but certainly they aided us not out of any loyalty to the Empire, but only to save their own skins. They are still outlaws. They must still hang.'

'Hang? My lord!' Reiner was sweating now. 'My lord, it took all my gifts to convince these men to come to your aid. I promised them that you would be grateful – that you might even reward them for their service.'

Manfred raised an eyebrow. 'Ah. Then they have no one to blame for their fate but you, who promised things it was beyond your power to grant.' He motioned to Strieger. 'Take them. In these troubled times the laws of the Empire must be firmly upheld.'

As the knights took the bandits in tow, Loche shot a look at Reiner that pierced him to his soul. 'Y'dirty liar,' he rasped. 'I hope y'rot.' He spat on Reiner's boots. The knights jerked him forward and marched the bandits out of the garden.

Reiner hung his head, more ashamed than he'd ever been. He felt like a trained rat who had led his wild brethren into a trap. He wanted to tear Manfred's throat out, but – more shame – he was too much of a coward. He valued his life too much.

Franka put a hand on his arm. It didn't help.

THE NEXT MORNING the Blackhearts were locked back into their coach and Manfred and his knights continued south to Altdorf. As they rode from Groff's castle Reiner and the others peered back through the slotted windows. Hanging from the battlements were scores of bandits and cultists, mixed together as if the hangmen had made no distinction between them – rotting fruit hanging from a stone tree.

Reiner's heart clenched when he saw Loche's massive body swaying among them. He closed his eyes, then sank back in his seat. 'And that, my lads,' he sighed, 'is fair warning of how Lord Valdenheim will deal with us when he no longer finds us useful.'

Pavel nodded. 'The swine.'

Giano shook his head. 'We dead soldiers, hey?'

'There must be a way out,' said Franka.

'But how?' asked Hals.

And so the endless conversation began again, all the way to Altdorf.

FAITH

Robert Earl

'WHAT ABOUT THIS one?' Claude the retainer asked with poorly disguised irritation, holding up the bloody prize.

'As I've already told you,' his master replied sharply, 'that is not good enough. I want something... more.'

Claude shrugged and dropped the blood-spattered head back into the dust. The orc's rictus grin leered up at him insolently, but he resisted the urge to give it a kick. Knights had funny ideas about things like that. But then, knights had funny ideas about a lot of things.

With a grunt of disgust Claude turned his back on the grisly trophy and stalked off to collect the evening's firewood. As he reached the tree-line he heard the sibilant hiss of whetstone against steel. It was the first of the evening's hundred sweeps, the ritual that kept the knight's sword sharper than any tooth or fang in this wilderness.

In spite of himself, Claude felt the sound cutting through his ill humour. This de Moreaux, Gilles, the third of his line to rely upon the old retainer's good offices, was the first to have taken care of his own weapons. And when Claude's rheumatism had bitten deep, curling and crippling his hands, Sir Gilles himself had ordered the older man to rest whilst he foraged and rooted for the herbs needed for a cure. Not many knights would have lowered themselves so far as to serve a servant.

On the other hand, not many knights would still be traipsing around the Massif Orcal at this time of year for any reason, let alone an apparently never-ending quest for a trophy large and impressive enough to return with.

Claude, stooping to lift a dry twist of wood from the debris that littered the forest, grimaced at the thought. True, the sun was still warm on the leathered skin at the nape of his neck, and even this mild exercise of bundling firewood was beginning to dampen his brow. But despite the comfortable heat the leaves on the trees of this valley were already beginning to redden with an autumnal fire. A thousand traceries of red and gold raced and tumbled through the green sweeps of their boughs, a final explosion of colour before the skeletal days to come. He knew that in a fortnight, a month at the most, those leaves would be gone, mulch beneath the ice and rain of winter.

He also knew that in a fortnight, a month at the most, the rheumatism would be back. Claude's fingers twitched at the thought. If he were still out here when the ice came there would be no escape from the pain. It would eat into his bones with a fervour beyond the powers of any poultice to soothe. Every movement would become an agony, every joint would ache like shattered glass. It was too much.

Still muttering to himself, the old man claimed a length of splintered branch to complete his load then turned back towards their makeshift camp. He found Sir Gilles sitting cross-legged by the edge of the clearing. Apart from the repetitive whisper of the sharpening stone along the blade of his sword, the young knight remained as upright and as silent as one of the Lady's stained glass saints.

Claude surreptitiously watched the blank mask of his master's face as he built their fire. Not the slightest hint or ripple of emotion stirred the even symmetry of his dark Bretonnian features, yet still the old man knew what lay behind the shuttered windows of the youngster's eyes. He knew, and in knowing despaired of a return to their demesne before winter's misery began.

It was all the fault of Gilles's brother, Leon. Leon the brave. Leon the fair. Leon who, after a scant two weeks of questing, had returned with a massive troll's head the size of a cartwheel and the blessing of the Lady.

If only Sir Gilles had found a prize to match that, Claude thought unhappily, we'd be home by now.

He struck a shower of sparks into the tinder heart of the fire and stooped to blow them into life, his sigh lost in the operation. A few tiny flames leapt up and Claude tended them, fed them, watched them grow. After a few moments the kindling was a fist of fire, bright even in the light of the setting sun. He imprisoned the blaze within a latticework of thicker sticks and swung the pot containing the evening's stew into the heat. Only then did he realise that the sound of the whetstone had ceased. He glanced up at his master. The knight had sheathed his sword and slipped into that deep breathless trance that seemed to be the mark of his kind.

Knights! Claude shook his head resignedly. Thirty-four years as an equerry and his masters still remained a mystery to him. Perhaps it was because the Lady asked so much of them. Perhaps it was because they truly were a different breed. Who knew?

Claude shrugged and turned his attention back to the pot. As he stirred the glutinous soup, a sudden gust of wind sprinted down the valley, rustling through the falling leaves with a thousand chill fingers. One more harbinger of winter. Silently cursing the fate that seemed set to keep him here, the old man pulled up his collar and waited for the stew to boil.

'THE LADY IS beauteous indeed,' breathed Sir Gilles.

The quiet intensity of the statement twisted Claude around in his saddle to follow the knight's gaze. But a quick glance around was enough to still the sudden, startling burst of hope that had flared within his chest. The Lady had not appeared. All that could be seen from the eyrie of this valley pass was the usual panorama of the Massif Orcal. Claude pulled the tattered blanket that now served him as a cloak around his scrawny shoulders and studied the scene.

Beyond the distant heights, the slopes were shot through with a thousand shades of wintry dawn sunlight, the colours a sharp contrast to the depths of the valley floor, now a grey sea of morning mist. Claude pulled his threadbare blanket tighter around his shoulders and yawned.

'If you don't mind me saying so, sire–' he began.

'We should make the most of the fine weather remaining to us,' Sir Gilles completed for him. The look of rapture faded from his face and he turned to regard his old retainer. 'You are correct, of course, Claude. First, though, I will sit a while in this place. I feel her presence here, I'm sure of it. Why don't you wait for me over the slope, and perhaps brew some of that filthy Empire tea of which you are so fond?'

This last was with a smile, the first crack in the knight's iron mask for days. The expression was as fleeting as the rise of a trout, yet in that brief moment Claude had read the lines of frustration and exhaustion that his master's composure had so well concealed. For a moment the old man felt his own worries swamped in a swell of sympathy.

'I'll wait as you say, sire,' he assented, turning to lead their horses over the crest of the ridge. Behind him Sir Gilles sank to his knees, hands clasped together in silent prayer before the upright hilt of his sword. As he set to beside the fire once more, Claude snatched a quick glance at the tableaux. He felt a sudden burst of affection and shook his head.

'You're getting sentimental in your old age,' he scolded himself in a mutter as he split the kindling sticks needed to boil his water. 'Too sentimental by half.'

The ripe globe of the autumnal sun climbed into the cloud streaked depths of the sky. Claude sat and drank his tea. When he had done that, he lay back and let the warmth of it sink into him.

Sharp-edged shadows stalked across distant slopes and valleys as the sun began to rise higher. The light was bright but unnatural, thin and brittle like before a storm. Claude was watching a hawk spiral overhead on the first of the day's thermals when a furtive movement from below snatched his attention. He lowered his gaze to where a grove of stunted bushes below rustled and moved jerkily against the wind.

Claude froze and watched the undergrowth for any further sign. Perhaps it was just a trapped deer, or some sort of mountain hare. He didn't want to disturb his master for such a–

With a sudden snap the bushes burst apart and a ragged creature sprang out.

'Sire!' the old man bellowed, leaping to his feet with adrenaline-fuelled agility. He fumbled at his belt for his dagger, struggling to unsheathe it in time, and snatched a glance at the tattered form that even now approached him. Only then did he realise that beneath the layers of dirt and bracken it was human, a man. He found himself fumbling for words of greeting or warning but, before he could find either weapon or challenge, Sir Gilles arrived.

His appearance was silent, marked only by a sudden rush of displaced air. Gone was the man, the youngster Claude had known since his swaddling days. Gone was the tiredness, the yearning. Gone was the humanity. All that remained of Sir Gilles now was the knight, the steel-clad killing machine. The dark stormcloud of his cloak whipped around him, driven either by the wind or by the corona of terrible energy that radiated from him. Claude, without even noticing that he was doing so, flinched away from his own master.

Despite the layers of metal which encased his form, Sir Gilles bounded forward with all the grace and poise of a big cat. With the hiss of steel slicing through air, his sword was in his hand as he leapt towards the newcomer.

'Thank the gods!' the man said, his features wild with a confusion of fear and happiness. After a moment's hesitation he threw himself to his knees. 'Our prayers have been answered.'

The knight hefted the length of his sword, flicking it upwards in an effortless arc that sent a wink of sunlight flashing along the edge. And for a moment, just one moment, Claude was certain that the blade was about to guillotine down across the newcomer's shoulders. But of course it did not. The Lady, bless and protect her, would not have allowed it.

Yet how would it be, the old retainer suddenly found himself wondering, if the knights of Bretonnia should lose their respect for the Lady?

Claude shuddered, suddenly cold, and switched his attention to the stranger who still knelt before Sir Gilles.

'...prayed for you to come for weeks. It's become too much, far too much,' the man continued to babble, tears glinting unashamedly in the corners of his eyes. 'None of us can sleep at night, none of us can work. Where are they going, where? One more and we're leaving, I swear it.'

The man's voice was beginning to edge upwards into the realms of hysteria. Seeming to realise it, he paused and took a deep breath. Then turned his red-rimmed eyes back to the knight.

'You will help us, sire, won't you?'

Sir Gilles, who until now had remained poised for combat, suddenly relaxed. He sheathed the wicked length of his sword and raised his visor to reveal a hungry, wolfish smile.

'Have no fear. I am sworn to help men such as yourself,' he reassured the peasant, whose grubby features split open into a wide grin of relief. 'How far is this village of yours?'

'In the next valley, sire. If you have horses it will take a few hours at the most.'

'Yes, we have horses. Perhaps you can help Claude here saddle up... ah, how are you called?'

'Jacques, sire, Jacques de Celliers. And thank you.'

Sir Gilles waved away the man's gratitude and turned to face the bright rays of the mid morning sun. Claude led the newcomer to the horses. It took them a few minutes to saddle the beasts and lead them back to where the knight still stood.

Somehow Claude was not surprised to find his master's head bowed and his lips moving in a silent prayer of gratitude.

THE INN WAS packed.

Even with the trestle tables pushed back into the shadows there hardly seemed room to breathe. Claude had even considered slipping back outside, away from the choke of this room, but somehow the tension of hope and fear that sawed through the smoke-filled air kept him still. That and the presence of Sir Gilles, of course.

The knight sat comfortably within an almost tangible sphere of personal aura that none seemed willing to invade. He looked as calm and serene as always as he chatted to those around him about their crops, their children, the first signs of change in the season.

Claude saw the awe that washed across the features of those being spoken to, watched it being reflected on the faces of their neighbours. In a gesture that he would have denied even under torture he straightened his back and smiled with pride. Sir Gilles was, after all, his knight.

Not until François, the village elder, made his entrance did the meeting come to some sort of order. The inn door was thrown open by a burst of cold, eastern wind and the old man stalked into the warmth of the room. He had hooked one claw-like hand onto the shoulder of his nephew for support or perhaps guidance through the chill darkness that now laid siege to the building. Favouring Sir Gilles with what could just about have been taken for a half-bow, he then studied the depths of his guest's face with yellowing eyes as puffy as poached eggs. For several long moments the two men regarded each other until, with a grunt of satisfaction, François lowered himself onto one knee. Claude could almost hear his bones creaking.

'Please,' Sir Gilles said earnestly, 'there is no need to kneel, especially for one as steeped in the grey hairs of wisdom as yourself.'

'Thank you, lord,' François said curtly. His nephew helped him back to his feet and led him to the cutaway oak barrel that served as the old man's seat of office. Knight and elder faced each other across the few feet of swept earth which lay between them and, in place of any common currency of small talk, smiled.

'I thank you for coming to our aid,' François began. 'I only wish I could tell you what we need that aid against.'

The knight shifted in his chair, eyes beginning to sparkle with a quickening interest.

'Your man Jacques here told me something of your dilemma,' he said, gesturing towards the peasant. Jacques, who had become something of a local hero since his return this afternoon, puffed himself up with pride at the mention. 'Perhaps, though, you could tell me the full history of these, ah, events.'

François nodded and sighed. Staring past the knight's head into some invisible point beyond the inn wall he began to speak, the years seeming to weigh down on him as he did so.

'It began after the first of the year's harvests, just after the festival of the summer corn,' he started, his voice dull and hopeless. 'This year we took a goodly crop, thanks to the brightness of the sun and the depths of the rains. In fact, after we had filled the granaries we had a surplus. We felt rich so, for the first time in years, we stopped the river trader and exchanged a few bushels for gold. At first I thought – we all thought – that was what had led to Pierre's disappearance.'

'How so?' the knight demanded. He leant forward eagerly, elbow rested on one knee and eyes locked on the elder's tragic countenance. His right hand, seemingly of its own accord, had stolen down to brush against the hilt of his sword. Claude regarded his master with a wry smile. Now that action beckoned he looked more warrior than gentleman, and more wolf than either.

François, though, seemed oblivious to this change in his guest's character. His attention had wandered far beyond the present murky depths of this world and into the past. He sighed and, with an obvious effort, dragged himself back to the here and now.

'How so? Well, because when a man has gold in his pocket and the sun is warming the stone of the high passes it's only natural for him to consider straying. Especially when…'

François eyes flickered upwards with a sudden guilty start and he broke off in consternation. Claude wondered what had caused his host's evident discomfiture until, from behind him, a woman's voice rang out.

'Especially when he's married to such a shrew. Isn't that what you were going to say, François de Tarn?'

Claude turned to regard the speaker. She was, he thought charitably, a solidly built woman. The black cloth of her smock looked hard-pressed to contain the bulk of her hips and chest. Despite her impressive girth, though, her face look pinched, sharp and hard even in the dull glow of the rush lights.

Shrew-like indeed, thought Claude sadly, and felt pity welling up inside of him. He could guess how it must have been for this woman when she tried to tell her neighbours of her husband's disappearance. How they must have frowned and talked of search parties in public whilst privately wishing the runaway all good speed.

'No, Celine, I wasn't going to say that,' the elder rallied, cutting through the thread of Claude's speculation. 'I was going to say that when a husband and wife have problems… well, you know.'

'Yes, I know,' the widow sighed, suddenly deflated. François shrugged uncomfortably and ploughed on.

'Anyway, about a week after Pierre was taken we lost Charles. Then Alain the smith. Then Bastien. Then Fredric and Sullier right afterwards. And then… then the children, Sophie and Louise…' His voice trailed off into nothingness and he swallowed painfully.

As the old man had recited the terrible litany of the lost it had been punctuated by choked sobs or low, miserable moans from the assembled villagers. Claude shifted uncomfortably. The air felt greasy with the grief and fear that was tearing this small community apart. The tension, almost unbearable, crushed down on his chest.

But if the weight of their misery had made any impression on Sir Gilles he wasn't showing it. The only emotion visible on the knight's face was a terrible hunger, an eagerness that reminded Claude of boar hounds straining at the leash. For the second time in as many days the old retainer faced the gulf that lay between them and shivered.

'So,' the knight said, his tones crisp and oblivious to the pain around him. 'What sort of intervals are we talking about between disappearances?'

'It varies.' François shrugged his shoulders. 'Between Pierre and Charles ten days. Between Sophie and Louise only three.'

'The children. Not as much meat on them, I suppose,' Sir Gilles mused aloud.

Behind him Claude heard a stifled cry and a rush of feet to the door.

'And you found no sign of a struggle? No smashed doors, no cries in the night?'

'No.' The elder paused for a moment, his eyes flickering over the assembly before he continued. 'Charles was taken from his very bed whilst his wife lay sleeping beside him.'

Sir Gilles nodded. One moment crawled slowly into the next, the time marked only by the rise and fall of the wind outside and the spluttering hiss of the rush lights within. When the knight finally spoke it was with a cry that sent those nearest to him lurching backwards.

'Of course! Where do you bury your dead?'

'In the crypt behind the shrine,' the elder replied, puzzlement adding a fresh tide of wrinkles to his brow. 'Why do you ask, lord?'

'And tell me, do you have a store of garlic here?' the knight continued uninterrupted.

'Of course, my lord. What kitchen doesn't?'

Claude shared the old man's confusion until, with a sudden flash of inspiration, he remembered a tale from one of the castle grimoires. A tale of nocturnal vanishings and blood black in the light of the moon. A tale of strange weapons, garlic and water and…

'The only other things you'll need are sharpened staves.' Sir Gilles rubbed his hands together and sighed with satisfaction. He looked, thought Claude with a touch of awe, like a man contemplating a feast or a day's hunting.

'Well,' the knight prompted his host after a moment or two, 'could you find such staves of which I speak?'

François, the bafflement which marked his liver-spotted features reflected in the faces of the rest of the assembly, nodded slowly.

'We can certainly make some, and that within the hour. But, my lord, Charles and Pierre were woodsman, with woodsman's axes. If their weapons failed them, what use will sticks be to us?'

Claude watched a touch of irritation flicker across the brown depths of the knight's eyes before he answered.

'Using steel against the thing which now preys upon you is like try-ing to drown a fish. No, don't ask me why. Only the Lady knows how these things gain their terrible strengths. All I know is that against the vampire the peasant's only weapon is wood, his only shield garlic.'

'The... vampire?' François asked, eyes widening in horror. A chorus of whimpers and low curses rushed through his fellows, the sound as soft and insistent as the chill wind that even now tried the locks and hinges of the inn.

Claude felt the hairs raise themselves one by one along the back of his neck as he moved unthinkingly with the press of bodies that hud-dled closer to the knight. As the crowd around him shifted with the restrained panic of a herd of cattle before a storm, he noticed the furtive glances they cast towards the shadowy corners of the inn and the rattling shutters of the windows.

Vampire! It was a name to chill the hardest of hearts, a name to con-jure up a thousand half-remembered terrors from the darkest nights of childhood. Claude was suddenly very grateful for the claustropho-bic mass of warm bodies that were packed so tightly around him.

'Am I right in thinking, my lord,' François began with all the cau-tion of a man taking the first step out onto a tightrope, 'that you intend to lead us against this beast?'

'No, I don't think so,' Sir Gilles replied. There was a sudden, angry murmur of protest from the crowd and, for the first time, the knight seemed to notice them. He looked up and the granite wall of his gaze cut off their protests with a guillotine's speed.

'I won't be leading you good people anywhere,' he continued, turn-ing back to François as if there had been no interruption. 'I will go now to await this monstrosity in the crypt you mentioned. Such things are usually tied to their burial grounds, making a mockery of these resting places with their filthy presence. Meanwhile, you'll bring everyone back here tonight and arm yourselves against the creature's attack.'

A thoughtful silence descended upon the villagers. Claude could almost taste their relief.

'Any further questions?' the knight asked.

'I don't think so, sire.' François shook his head. 'But is there naught we can do for you?'

Sir Gilles looked into the old man's eyes and smiled, the expression cold and humourless. 'Yes. Make sure that nobody goes anywhere on their own until this is finished.'

'Even to the latrines?'

A ripple of nervous laughter spread through the confines of the room at this. Sir Gilles was pleased to hear it. Better foolish catcalls than blind terror.

'Even to the latrines,' he replied presently. 'Now, who will show us to this sepulchre?'

IT WAS DARK and, despite the bulk of Claude's borrowed blankets, cold. He could smell the thin, metallic scent of rain on the wind and feel the choking weight of cloud that blocked out even the scant light of moon and stars. Only the guttering red fire of their rush lights gave the two figures any trace of light by which to keep their lonely vigil.

They sat like mismatched bookends on either side of the burial pit, these two, their very presence defying the hungry shadows of the sepulchre's maw. Claude glanced across at his master, a little awed as always by the man's inexhaustible capacity for stillness.

Only the silvery glitter of the knight's hooded eyes gave any indication that he was awake, or even alive. That same glitter was reflected in the straight-edged length of steel which lay across his begreaved knees. Sir Gilles had been strapped into his full armour as he had given the villagers their last instructions.

'Stay together. Even if it breaks in, don't panic. Stand shoulder to shoulder and call for me. But don't pursue it. Remember, stay together.'

Claude, remembering the earnestness of the young knight's expression and the terrified eyes of the villagers, smiled. Had Sir Gilles really believed any of that frightened herd would have charged a vampire, a drinker of souls?

The old retainer's grin faded as he studied the reassuring lines of his master's face. The steel dome of his helmet was gone, a concession against the near-blinding darkness that enveloped them, and even in the flickering half-light of their peasant torches Claude could see the look of peace which had fallen across Sir Gilles's trail-hardened features. The expression reminded him of the knight's father. He had had the same look about him on the night before the Battle of Ducroix. It was only at times like these, whilst sat in the very eye of the storm, that the Lady's chosen warriors seemed to find true peace.

A sudden burst of wind whistled around his ears and the old man shrank down further into his blankets. It had started to warm up within this little cocoon. Claude yawned and stretched, luxuriating in the rare feeling of comfort. Gradually, little by little, his thoughts melted away into dreams.

He jerked back into wakefulness with a guilty start, eyes springing open like traps. It was too late. Sir Gilles was regarding him with the tolerant composure that the older man found so irritating. Claude opened his mouth, fumbling for an apology, but the knight silenced him with a gesture.

'Try to sleep, Claude. I will need your wits about me in the morning.'

'Sire, I said I would share your watch and I will.'

'And I said there was no need. Sleep. If I have need of you I will wake you, have no fear of that.'

'Well…' Claude begin, then stopped and shrugged. The heavy droop of his eyelids weighed more than any arguments. And, at his age, what did he have left to prove?

'Thank you, sire.'

Sir Gilles nodded, the gesture almost imperceptible amongst the wind-chased shadows of the night, and returned to his silent meditation.

A few moments later Claude began to snore. The wind, as if in response to the old man's guttural breathing, blew harder. It screeched through the draughty eaves of the burial pit, groping with icy fingers at the chinks and hinges of the knight's armour and setting the forest-lined slopes of the valley aroar. The distant trees rushed and splintered as though some mighty beast had been set loose amongst them.

Sir Gilles, unmoved by the rising tumult, sat and waited. Soon even the rise and fall of his servant's breath was drowned beneath the howls of the wind, but this hardly concerned him. And when the rush lights started to die, one by one, he merely smiled at the memory of how darkness had frightened him as a child. That fear was gone now. It had gone the way of all other fears during his training as a knight.

All other fears but one, of course, the last and the greatest. And with the Lady's help that final fear would be vanquished tonight.

The last of the torches died, its flame strangled by a sudden gust. In the blinding depths of the darkness that remained, Sir Gilles sat and awaited his destiny, a murmur of thanks on his lips.

If he survived this night's trial he knew that he would be blessed indeed. If he survived this night all would know that the blood of his line ran true in his veins and that his faith in the Lady was true. Yes, all would know it. Even himself.

He just hoped that the vampire, when it came, would be the equal of its reputation.

CLAUDE AWOKE TO dew-soaked blankets and tingling joints. His knuckles felt hot and swollen, blistered from within. There was no real pain, not yet, but in the vulnerability of the single unguarded moment that separates sleep from wakefulness he made a mistake. He thought about what might be going on beneath his reddening skin.

He imagined the gristle in his fingers swelling, choking off the blood. He imagined the nerve endings rasping and sawing against granite-edged bone, fraying like lengths of twine. He imagined a colony of rat-headed creatures eating into the very stuff of him, their burrows growing deeper and more painful by the minute.

With a low moan he clenched his fists, damning the first sparks of pain the movement ignited. The cold, he knew, would fan those first few sparks, tend them and feed them until they twisted his hands into crippled, burning claws.

Well, to the hells with it. If he had need of his hands the Lady would unclench them. And if the pain became unbearable the Lady would take it away. In one way or another, She would take it away.

The old man sighed and opened his eyes. The dawn sky above him was as sombre and cheerless as a shroud, lacking even a smear of cumulus to cut through its grey monotonous weight. Claude shrugged indifferently and climbed to his feet. At least it wasn't raining. He wrapped his blankets around his thin shoulders and yawned. Time to start on breakfast. Now where had he left those damn horses?

He coughed, more out of habit than anything else, and swept the camp with his gaze. It wasn't until he noticed the dark bulk of the sepulchre that remembrance hit him with an impact as dizzying as vertigo.

This was no trail camp, no woodland clearing or rocky overhang. There would be no quiet breakfast routine here, no wistful meditations. This was Celliers, the village where Sir Gilles had finally found a monster worth killing.

But Sir Gilles was nowhere to be seen.

'Sire?' Claude called, his voice cracked with sleep and uncertainty.

'Sire?' he called again, louder this time against the dumbing curtain of fine mist that had begun to dampen the air.

There was no reply. Claude wrapped the roll of blankets tighter around the frail stalk of his neck and studied the ground. A deep depression still marked the spot where the knight must have kept his vigil last night, although some of the crumpled blades of grass had already sprung defiantly back. The old man shook his head and hissed. His master must have been gone a fair while.

'Sire?'

No reply.

He looked further and studied the semi-circle of burnt out torches that surrounded the spot. Their black stumps jutted out of the damp earth like a jaw full of bad teeth. None of them, it seemed, had been disturbed.

'Si–?' Claude began, and then froze. He listened, straining his ears against the blanket of drizzle that had begun to fall. For a while there was nothing more than the muffled sounds of a damp and dreary morning and the distant croak of pheasant. One minute crawled towards the next, then the next. Finally the old man began to relax. His ears must have been playing tricks on him, he decided.

Then he heard it again.

The low moan drifted as softly as a dandelion seed on the morning's breeze. Claude listened cautiously as the cry faded back into nothingness and shivered suddenly as it ceased. His fingers, arthritis forgotten, clenched tightly around the heft of his stake.

Surely that weak and inhuman keening couldn't be from a man, he told himself, let alone a knight.

Yet where was Sir Gilles?

Once more the cry came floating through the haze, raising the wiry hairs on the back of Claude's neck. He waited until the fell voice began to wane and then, with a blasphemous combination of curses and prayers, the old retainer lurched forwards towards the sound.

He left the burial pit behind him and stomped past the dripping grey bulk of the village shrine and the first of the houses. The village seemed as desolate and empty as any ghost town. There were no scurrying children or scolding women or singing artisans. All that moved here was the drizzle, its silent rain weighing down on an atmosphere already leaden with dread.

The moan came again, louder this time. Louder and closer. In fact, Claude decided as he shivered the weight of blankets off his shoulders, whatever was making the noise seemed to be around the next corner.

A ghostly reflection of his master's wolverine smile played around the old man's lips, a nervous reaction as he plucked the dagger from his belt with his free hand. Then, with a last murmured prayer to the Lady, he stepped around the corner.

And froze.

Sir Gilles was there, the centrepiece of the huddled mob of peasants. The sight of his broad armoured shoulders shook a delighted bark of laughter from Claude, who allowed the wavering point of his stave to drop.

'Sire! You're all right?'

'Yes, of course,' the knight replied, a pair of puzzled lines marking his brow as he turned. 'Why shouldn't I be?'

Claude shrugged, still smiling with relief. Then the plaintive wail that had brought him here rang out again and for the first time he noticed the girl.

She squatted in the cold and damp of the earth, supported on either side by two solidly built village women. They flanked her protectively, like two mother hens with a single chick, but she obviously drew scant comfort from their presence. The girl herself was pitifully thin, the bundled rags she wore incapable of hiding the frailty of her frame. Every shuddering breath she took seemed to rattle down the knuckles of her vertebrae, every choking sob seemed ripe to burst the tight cage of her chest.

Claude felt obscurely glad that her face was turned away from him. He had heard such misery before, of course. From battlefields and deathbeds and scaffolds he had become familiar with the sound of the human heart torn and bleeding. Yet had he ever heard such horror mixed in with the grief?

Without giving himself time to think the old man pushed forward into the mass of cringing villagers who encircled the girl. He looked over her shoulder to the... the shape that lay upon the crimson turf.

Just think of it as meat, he told himself. It's not human. Not now.

But the signs of the thing's humanity were still horribly plain to see. Almost half of its face had been left, the exposed tendons and drained flesh conspiring to lock the man's face into a final eternal scream. Some of its fingers also remained. They were as rigid and gnawed as the branches of autumnal trees and even more dead. Claude studied the savaged expanses of the man's forearms, shoulders and neck. The frenzy of half-moon bite marks somehow reminded him of a head of corn.

Biting back a sudden rush of bile, the old man looked away and studied the faces of the villagers whilst composing himself. He read the disgust and frightened rage he had expected, the emotions as clear as any sculpture could ever make them. But there was something else there too, something that skulked guiltily behind their horror like rats behind a skirting board.

It took Claude a moment to recognise it as relief. The realisation snared his revulsion, gave it a target. Selfish swines! Relieved for their own worthless skins even with this child choking her heart out over the corpse of her father. His lips drawn back in a silent snarl, he turned to François, the village elder.

'I thought you were told not to let anybody go out on their own,' he spat.

But if François heard the anger in Claude's voice he gave no sign of it. 'We didn't let anyone go out on their own. Jules here, Lady guide and protect him, went out with Jacques. Jacques whose absence from the village stopped the killings. And whose return brought them back.'

Claude stepped back and dug thumbs into his forehead in an effort to stop the turmoil of his thoughts.

'Look at the wounds on Jules,' François added. 'What beast leaves marks like that?'

Claude gazed steely eyed at the carcass. It was the same as a hundred others he had witnessed. His career had led him through many valleys a lot more death-illed than this one. He had seen savaged bodies abandoned by all manner of wild beasts. Aye, he thought grimly, and ones trained to it too. Yet something about this one was different.

'Of course!' he finally cried out, voice thick with horrid realisation. 'The teeth. The bite marks. They're like mine. I mean like any human's,' he added hurriedly – even this far from the border, Sigmar's hungry witch hunters had ears – and daggers. 'So Jacques was the vampire?'

'No, he's no vampire,' Sir Gilles cut in with a sigh. 'He only has human teeth. He's just a man. A sick man.'

'Sick?'

'Yes, sick of mind. Or Chaos-tainted perhaps. It matters not. My cousin told us of it the last time he returned from the Empire. There they call it the madness of Morrslieb, the contagion that flows from the Blood Moon when it's at its zenith. That is when your problems began, isn't it?'

This last was addressed to François. The old man shrugged vaguely, then nodded.

'Madness indeed,' Claude muttered, taking a last look at the corpse which lay congealing in front of its daughter. 'Shall I prepare the horses, sire?'

'Yes. Light tack. Against this pitiful creature we'll need speed more than power. François, are there any hounds here?'

As Claude turned to ready their horses, he heard the bitterness of the disappointment that edged his master's words. But he realised that above the sobs that still wove through the mist he alone had heard it, and for that he was thankful.

THE DAY'S HUNT was a futile affair. The only hounds to be found in the village were a trio of aged boar hounds, gaunt beasts whose stiff movements and swollen joints made Claude wince in sympathy. Sir Gilles, still hiding his disappointment behind a flawlessly polite mask, had decided to leave the motley pack behind, overruling François's attempts to press the dogs into service by explaining that speed of horse and clarity of vision would suffice to hunt down the fugitive.

It had proved to be a foolish boast. The beast of Celliers, although only a man and a crazed one at that, had vanished with all the ingenuity and cunning of any other animal. As Claude followed Sir Gilles out of the village the impossibility of their task struck him. What chance did they stand of finding the fugitive in the mighty swathe of forests and crevasses that covered this, his native territory?

By the time they had cleared the fields and broken into a canter the old man had begun to wonder why the same thought hadn't occurred to his master. It wasn't until Sir Gilles, with a wild cry that ignited frustration into exhilaration, closed spurs that Claude finally understood.

Their task here was complete. Jacques was gone. They might catch him, they probably wouldn't. Either way it made little difference to the lunatic. Alone and unarmed against the predators and dark races of this savage land he wouldn't last long.

He gave his own horse its head, allowing it to race along behind the knight's charger. Holding on to his mount with aching knees, branches slashing over his head and the wind stinging his eyes, Claude listened to the rolling thunder of their horses' hooves and felt a rush of excitement course through him.

By the Lady this was the life! Ahead of him, pulling away as swiftly and as surely as a stag from a drunken orc, Sir Gilles crested a low hill. By the time Claude had reached the spot the knight was already disappearing into the arms of the wood that lay beyond. Just before he was lost to sight the armoured figure turned in the saddle and called back.

'The pass. Meet me at the pass.'

'Aye, sire, the pass it is.' Claude bellowed his reply as Sir Gilles vanished. As if sensing that the race was lost Claude's horse slackened its pace from gallop to canter to brisk walk.

'Lazy beast,' he muttered affectionately as they plodded along. The blood was still racing briskly through his veins after the impromptu charge and, despite the continuing grey dampness of the day, his spirits were high. And why not? Celliers's problems had been resolved, the beast had been vanquished. Even if he did return to the village, the madman, now that he had been unmasked, would find little chance of repeating his atrocities. For the people of this valley, at least, the winter would hold no more than the usual dangers. For himself and his master, though…

Claude sighed, his high spirits draining away at the thought of the coming months. 'I'm too old for this,' he told nobody in particular and spurred his mount into a canter.

By the time he reached the high saddle of the pass, Sir Gilles's horse was already grazing contentedly. The knight himself sat perched atop a boulder, dark eyes scanning the valley below. His aquiline nose and deep, predatory stare made him look a little like a beast himself, Claude thought as he toiled up the final approaches to the pass.

'It seems the king has more than one hippogriff,' he muttered to himself, the words lost beneath the clatter of scree underfoot.

'I'll take that as a compliment,' Sir Gilles called out as his man approached. Claude bit back on the expression of mortification he knew had crept treacherously across his weathered features and shrugged.

'And how else would I have meant it, sire?' he asked ingenuously.

Sir Gilles barked with laughter and jumped lightly from the boulder. The tension of the preceding days seemed to have melted away leaving the young man full of fresh energy. It was almost as if the conclusion of Celliers's problems, bloody and seedy as it had been, had lifted a weight from his shoulders – almost as if his task had been accomplished.

Claude hardly dared to ask, but the sudden rush of hope within his chest was too much to be denied.

'Sire…' he began, then hesitated, not quite knowing how to put the question. A moment's confusion passed before he shrugged and ploughed on: 'Is our quest complete?'

The knight's brows shot up in amazement as he studied his old retainer.

'No, of course not. Why should it be?'

'You seem… rejuvenated,' Claude explained, trying to keep the weight of disappointment out of his voice, out of his posture. It was hard work.

'I thought maybe you had seen the Lady after, you know, saving the village,' he continued with another shrug.

Sir Gilles's brow cleared with sudden realisation.

'I understand,' he nodded. 'But no, I have done nothing yet. And yet I do feel as if a burden has been lifted. I've come to a decision. I'm going to exchange greaves and bucklers and lances for furs and push on into the heart of these mountains. It is only there that I can be sure of proving the strength of my belief in the Lady and continue slaying the evil that would devour her people.'

Claude felt a moment's unease as he watched the features of the knight harden, straightening into a mask of fanaticism stronger than any steel. Even after all these years this transformation of his masters from men into something… something *more*… still sent a cold shiver racing down his spine.

But then his master was once more just Sir Gilles. His expression softened as he turned his attention from the jagged spikes of distant mountains to his faithful old retainer. 'The other decision I've made is that you'll stay in Celliers until I return. Or until the summer, whichever comes first. I'll leave you gold and a letter of safe conduct in case I am found, um, wanting.'

Now it was Claude's turn to look amazed. 'Sire, I will not leave you. I am sworn to follow you on this quest. My honour is at stake as much as yours.'

'You are sworn to *obey!*' the knight snapped, his tones suddenly harsh. 'And by the Lady you will! I'll not take any ill man into the ice and snow of mountains in the winter. And I'll certainly not throw your life away.'

In a gesture that looked strangely guilty Claude thrust his reddening knuckles behind his back.

'Sire, I–'

* * *

'You'll obey my orders,' Sir Gilles cut him off. 'Apart from anything else I don't want to waste one of my father's best men. You will stay here.'

The old man, who suddenly looked much, much older, dropped his eyes and slumped his shoulders. Without another word he turned back to his horse.

With a last resentful look towards his master Claude led his mount down the shifting carpet of scree and tried not to let his anger get the better of him. To be cast aside now, left in safety like a woman whilst his knight rode off into bitter danger! Was he an idiot or a cripple to be left on the roadside like a piece of useless baggage? It was an outrage.

What made it even more difficult to bear was the treacherous sense of relief that even now buoyed up his steps. But that, at least, proved to be short-lived.

'What do you mean you're leaving? Are you mad?' Sir Gilles barely controlled his exasperation, but at a cost. His wind-rouged cheeks reddened further and a small vein began to pulse a warning above his brow. If the village elder noticed these small chinks in his guest's composure he gave no sign of it.

Without taking his eyes off the two men who continued to over-burden his haywain, François sighed and shook his head. 'No, we're not mad. Madness would be to stay.

'We found something after you went, ah, hunting this morning.' The elder flicked a glance almost contemptuously over the mud flecked flanks of the knight's horse. Her mighty chest heaving in great lungfuls of air and the heavy organic smell of horse sweat radiated off her in waves. After Claude had returned, his foul temper buried under consternation at the sight of Celliers packing up to go, Sir Gilles had ridden back here as hard as he could, sparing neither his horse nor himself.

'What did you find?' the knight finally asked, successfully keeping the irritation to himself.

'Jacques.' François said the word softly, almost reverently, and Sir Gilles wondered at his tones. What terrible ven-geance must these vil-lagers, his erstwhile comrades and erstwhile prey, have meted out to make them now sound so compassionate about the lunatic?

'Oh. Well, that's good. I take it he's dead?'

The pained expression on François face deepened and Gilles could almost imagine that tears glinted beneath the craggy overhang of the elder's brow.

'How did the village execute him?' the knight asked gently, choosing his words now with the care of a surgeon choosing his instruments. A vil-lage execution. How clean that sounded. How impersonal.

François, however, had obviously being pushed beyond the niceties of not just diplomacy but even common sense. With a sudden start he wheeled on the knight, the fury in his eyes no longer hidden.

'Nobody *executed* him,' the elder hissed, lips drawn back in a snarl as he pronounced the word. 'He was murdered, horribly murdered, just like all the rest.'

The sudden vehemence of the elder's words sent Sir Gilles stepping automatically backwards into a defensive stance. His hand fell to the hilt of his sword before he realised what he was doing. He dropped his empty fist guiltily, but it was too late. François had already seen the gesture. The elder laughed bitterly, hopelessly.

'Oh yes, the protection of your knightly virtues,' he sneered mockingly, pulling himself to his feet and lurching towards the armoured man who towered above him. One of the lads who had been loading the cart appeared at his elbow to offer a supporting hand. The elder shook him off angrily as he stalked towards Sir Gilles.

'The only difference you've made is to double the number of this cursed thing's kills,' he said, the anger in his voice twisting into an accusation. Once more the youth, with a terrified glance at the knight, grabbed the elder's arm and tried to pull him away. Once more the old man shook the anxious hand off, this time turning his ire on the youngster who hovered nervously at his grandfather's side.

'Get away. What's the great knight going to do? Kill me? Ha!' He spat a gob of contemptuous phlegm onto the ground an inch away from Sir Gilles's boots, then turned away with a grunt of disgust.

Claude had watched his master flush beneath the old peasant's tirade, the vitriolic fusion of shame and rage burning on his cheeks. Now, as the villagers went on with their wary preparations, Claude saw the colour drain away from Sir Gilles's face, leaving him pale and shaking with emotion. The retainer opened his mouth to say something, anything, that might be of comfort to the stricken young knight. But before he could think of a single thing to say it was too late.

The muscles in Sir Gilles's jaw bulged with sudden determination and he strode forward after François. The old man's hunched back was still turned towards his guest. He must have seen something reflected in his grandson's widening eyes, though, for he turned when the knight had approached to within a dozen paces. Claude saw the rigid mask of defiance still etched across the elder's features. There would be no apology, of that he was sure, no more bowing. And behind the stubborn old fool a dozen of his sons and grandsons had noticed events unfolding.

As the steel giant closed in on their ancestor they fumbled for knives, hoes and pitchforks. In their shaking hands and round eyes Claude saw the same desperate courage that will drive a ewe to attack the wolf pack that has cornered her lambs. He felt his heart plummet at the tragedy he knew was about to unfold.

Sir Gilles, reaching out one gauntleted hand towards the old man, seemed oblivious to all this. His whole attention was focused on the elder. As the mailed fist fell towards him the old man's only response was the small straightening of posture that was all an aged skeleton would allow. The first of the villagers lowered his pitchfork and started forward. Claude, mind frozen by the speed of events, wished futilely that what was going to happen wouldn't.

Then the metalled talon of Sir Gilles's hand swept past his host's neck and landed gently upon his shoulder.

Bowing down to peer into the astonished elder's eyes the knight said: 'I am truly sorry to have so failed you. I am sorry that you are frightened enough to leave your village. I have failed in my duty to the Lady and to you, her people. My father would not have failed. Nor would my brother, Leon. But I have and I have no excuse.'

Suspicion chased astonishment off François's wizened features. By the time the knight had finished his apology the sincerity of the words had melted away even that.

'No, no, lord. I should apologise to you,' he replied warily, voice softened now with grudging compassion. 'I had no call to blame you. Since the black hail fell on these hills in my grandfather's day much has happened here, much that has proved beyond man's power to change.'

'Yet I would be more than a man,' Sir Gilles smiled bitterly. 'And perhaps I still can be. All I ask is that you give me one more night. Give me one more chance to find the monster that would prey upon the Lady's people.'

François hesitated for barely a moment before giving the shallowest of nods and turning to address his flock.

'We'll leave tomorrow,' he told them. Then, with a stiff bow towards Sir Gilles, he turned and hobbled back into his hut. The knight returned the bow and walked stiffly back to his horse.

'What will we do now, sire?' Claude asked, hurrying to catch up.

'I go to beg for the Lady's aid. There was a pool a little way into the woods we rode through this morning. It seemed like a goodly place.'

'And will I come with you?'

'No, you'll stay here. I want you to organise these people into three regiments and make sure they stay in them. I leave you in charge of the details.'

'Yes, sire, of course.' Claude bowed subserviently whilst his master climbed back into the saddle and cantered back out of the village. He waited until Sir Gilles was out of sight before crossing to François's hut. He ducked below the heavy oaken lintel of the door and instructed the elder.

'I want you to organise your people into three groups,' he told the old man urgently. 'All of them are to carry their weapons at all times. None of them are to leave their groups for any reason. Any that break these rules are to be fined half of their wealth. Do you understand?'

As soon as François had grumbled his assent Claude took his leave and went to fetch his horse. He had carried out his orders. Now he would go to watch his knight's back, as was proper for an equerry. There was nothing underhanded about that, he thought, as he carefully scanned the horizon. Nothing underhanded at all.

Sir Gilles was not difficult to follow, especially to one as skilled at reading the land as Claude. He had followed the path of crushed moss and snapped twigs through the forest just as easily as he had followed the great crescents of the charger's hoofs through the mud of the road.

He had tethered his own mount some way back and continued stealthily on foot beneath the great damp overhangs of beech and birch and twisted ancient oak. The undergrowth was thick here, heavy with moisture and dying brown leaves. As Claude pushed through it his nose wrinkled at the acrid smell of decay. In most parts of Bretonnia, he reflected, such a bulk of vegetation would have been cropped back by deer or boar, but here it seemed untouched.

And come to think of it the forest did seem strangely quiet, almost as if it had been cleared of life by something, perhaps even something that left human bite marks in the raw flesh of its prey. The thought sent a sliver of ice down the old man's spine and he found himself walking faster.

'Don't be such an old woman,' he scolded himself, consciously slowing his pace. 'A small wood in a small valley is easily over-hunted. There's nought more mysterious here than greedy peasants.'

Even so he was more than a little relieved when he finally reached Sir Gilles. Only the fact that the knight was so obviously immersed in prayer stilled the cry of greeting that rose to his retainer's lips.

Sir Gilles knelt silently before a wide pool, his attention lost in its cool depths.

Overarching trees shone and glimmered in the calm surface, one world reflected by another, and around the banks rushes swayed gently to some ancient and inaudible rhythm.

Claude sank to his haunches at the edge of the clearing, lulled by the peace of the scene. The only real movement was the light fall of autumn browned leaves. He watched one as it spiralled down onto the placid mirror of the water and began to float away, pulled by some invisible current.

Leaning back against the bole of a willow, the old man half-closed his eyes. In his imagination the leaf became a ship, bound for distant Cathay or even mythical Lustria. The stem became a mast, the withered edges the gunwales. And when the first splash of water sent thick ripples rolling towards the little craft he saw only waves riding before a storm.

A moment later he began to wonder what had caused such a disturbance in the water. Surely this pool was too isolated to contain trout to rise and leap. He looked up with a frown. For a moment he saw nothing but the enveloping mass of trees and shadows that encircled them, and the stooped form of his master's back.

Then he saw her and his heart leapt.

It was *her*, there could be no doubt of that. How many times had he seen her form, revered in stone or glass or on parchment? How many times had men whispered of her in the depths of the night or called upon her in the midst of battle? He'd even met her before in dreams and amongst the labyrinths of his imagination and felt her sacred presence, a comforting hand in the depths of hardship or a playful ripple of light on the water.

Yes, it was her. As she glided through the pool Claude's eyes caressed the skin that glowed paler and more precious than Araby pearl. Her hair cascaded down onto her shoulders, framing a face both girlish and ancient, wise and forgiving. And her eyes! How they sparkled and shone with a healing warmth of green fire.

Claude felt a moment's dizziness and realised that he had been holding his breath. He managed to tear his eyes away from the Lady for long enough to glance at Sir Gilles.

The knight still sat slumped in prayer, lips moving silently even as his goddess approached. The light gossamer of her dresses flowed around her, shining with a ghostly luminescence against the dark backdrop of rotten forest. For a moment Claude considered calling out to his master, of heralding her approach, but somehow he lacked the courage. In the presence of such divine beauty he felt too unworthy to speak. Instead he gazed upon her and let every detail of her magnificence burn itself into his memory.

She had almost reached Sir Gilles before he looked up. He rose to his feet, then started as though stung. The Lady smiled at his astonishment, a beatific expression of love and compassion speeding slowly across her face, and he sank back down to his knees.

'My Lady...' he whispered as she approached, arms opening and hands outstretched in benediction. Sir Gilles, head bowed, watched her glide through the last few feet of water and step onto the bank. He saw the water dripping from the hem of her dress, the white of it now speckled with the green of pond weed.

'My Lady...' he repeated breathlessly as she laid a perfect hand on his shoulder and stooped down to brush cold lips across his brow. She smiled again, revealing teeth as white and hard as bones and lowered her lips to kiss his neck.

'*My Lady!*' he said a third time, his voice suddenly full of fire as he sprang backwards. With an evil hiss of steel against leather, his sword was free of its scabbard, the burnished metal of the blade dull despite the divine light that surrounded the goddess. Then, before the enormity of the knight's actions could penetrate through Claude's shock, he watched his master slice his sword backhanded across the smooth, cream-coloured flesh of her neck.

It was a killing stroke. The blade spat out a bright plume of blood as it sawed effortlessly through the cords and tendons of her neck, almost decapitating her where she stood.

Claude watched as she crumpled backwards into the mud and filth of the forest floor. After a moment he walked numbly over to where the body lay and gazed down stonily at the ruined flesh that had once lived, once breathed… had once been a goddess. Now it was no more than meat cooling on the forest floor.

And bad meat at that. He watched as the flowing silk of its hair withered and died, shrinking back into a malformed skull. Already the supple grace of her frame had collapsed into something ruined and hunched, the skeleton twisted out of shape by who-knew-what dark sorcery?

Claude shivered and hugged himself as the fair pigment of her skin darkened and mottled, turning into a sickly grey leather before his very eyes. Even worse was the thing's face. How could those evil and wizened features have resembled anything even the least bit fair? Only the colour of the eyes remained unchanged, but the green now seemed rotten and cancerous and so very cold.

He remembered the expression she had worn. He remembered how beautiful it had been, how alluring. Suddenly, for the first time since the brooding of his first battle, Claude's stomach clenched itself into a fist that doubled him up with nausea. With hardly a backwards glance he stumbled away into the undergrowth, leaving Sir Gilles still standing pale and trembling over his foe.

THE NEXT MORNING they crested the pass above Celliers for the last time. Below them the valley was laid out like a map. Claude turned in his saddle to take a last look at the village, the forest, the smoke from the great bonfire upon which the beast's body had been burned so gleefully the night before.

Where had it come from, he wondered for the dozenth, the hundredth time. Had it been made, or born, or ensorcelled by Chaos? And how long had it lived here, silently haunting the edges and dark places of this land before hunger drove it in to the village and the addictive taste of man-flesh?

Claude found his gaze shifting from the valley floor to the distant rock spires that were the heart of the Massif Orcal. Beyond them, peering from between the granite peaks, towering clouds waited blue and heavy with the year's first snow.

The old retainer shivered and thankfully turned his back on them. By the time they caught up with him he would be back beside the great fireplace of Castle Moreaux, a horn of spiced wine steaming in his hand.

Only one thing still bothered him. It hung in a leather bag from Sir Gilles's saddle, a diminutive, evil smelling lump that still sweated a disgusting grey slime. It had no scales, this head, no savage teeth or needle-sharp fangs. Its jaws were weak, lacking even the knots of muscle any man might boast. In fact when it had been cleaned the thing would be scarcely bigger than two clenched fists.

'Well, sire,' Claude began, knowing that he would have to broach the subject before they went much further. 'I'm sure we'll be able to pick up that boulder of an orc's head tomorrow afternoon. I lashed it to a lone pine tree for the birds to clean. It should look good mounted in the great hall, don't you think?'

'What do you mean?' the knight asked, turning in his saddle to regard his servant. 'I have my trophy here.'

'Yes, of course. Your real trophy. But for the family gibbet...'

'This is for the family gibbet. This thing is the beast that tested my faith to the utmost. It is this that will hang amongst the rest of my family's great trophies.'

Claude, sensing the strength of purpose that lay behind his master's words, sighed as he realised it would be pointless to continue.

'How... how could you be so sure that thing wasn't the Lady?' he dared to ask, changing the subject.

Sir Gilles smiled wistfully for a moment before he replied.

'The eyes,' he said at length. 'In the old tales she is always dark, a real Bretonnian woman. Brown hair. Brown eyes.'

'Tales, yes,' Claude nodded. 'But when your brother saw her she had green eyes. As green as your mother's, he said.'

'Yes,' Sir Gilles nodded, 'I know.'

Then, for no apparent reason, he began to laugh until his sides shook and tears glinted in his eyes.

Claude lapsed back into silence and shook his head. *Knights!* He would never understand them.

PORTRAIT OF
MY UNDYING LADY
Gordon Rennie

'A COMMISSION, YOU say? What kind of commission?' Giovanni Gottio leaned across the table, wine slopping from the cheap copper goblet in his hand. It would soon be replenished, he knew, in just the same way as his new-found friend sitting opposite had been steadily refilling Giovanni's goblet all night.

'A portrait,' answered his new-found friend. 'In oils. My employer will pay you well for your time.'

Giovanni snorted, spilling more wine. Absent-mindedly he dabbed one grimy finger in the spilled mess, painting imaginary brush strokes on the rough surface of the bar table. Faces. Faces had always been his speciality. Strangely, though, he had been sitting with the man for hours, drinking his wine and spending his money, but if the stranger got up and left this minute, Giovanni would have been unable to say what exactly he looked like. His was more a blurred impressionistic sketch of a face – eyes cold and cruel, mouth weak and arrogant – than any kind of finished work. The most memorable thing about him in Giovanni's mind was the way the emerald ring on his finger caught and held even the dim candlelight of this grimy back street taverna.

'Haven't you heard?' Giovanni slurred, becoming gradually aware that he was far more drunk than he should be this early in the night, even after those three pitchers of wine the stranger had bought for him. 'The great Gottio doesn't do portraits any more. He is an artist, and artists are supposed to show truth in their work. The trouble is, people don't want the truth. They don't like it. That fool Lorenzo Lupo certainly didn't, when he commissioned the great Gottio to paint a portrait of his wife.'

Giovanni realised he was shouting now, that he was drawing sniggering glances from the other regular patrons of the taverna. Not caring, he reached out to angrily refill his goblet once more.

'Did you see it, my portrait of that famed beauty, the wife of the Merchant Prince of Luccini? Not many people did, for her husband had it destroyed as quickly as he could. Still, those few that did see it said that it captured the woman perfectly, not just in its reflection of her exquisite beauty but even more so in the way it brought out all the charm, grace and personality of the hungry mountain wolf that lurked beneath that fair skin.'

Giovanni drained his goblet and slammed it down, stumbling as he got up to leave. This drunk after only three pitchers, he thought. The great Gottio truly has lost his touch…

'So, thank you for your hospitality, sir, but the great Gottio no longer paints portraits any more. He paints only the truth, a quality which would sadly seem to be in little fashion amongst this world's lords and masters.'

Mocking laughter followed him out of the taverna. Outside, he staggered along the alleyway, leaning against a wall for support. Shallya's mercy. That cheap Pavonan wine certainly had a kick to it!

A welcome night breeze sprang up, carrying with it the strong scent of the fruit orchards that grew on the slopes of the Trantine Hills overlooking the city, and Giovanni took several deep breaths, trying to clear his head. From behind, he heard quick, decisive footsteps following him out of the taverna; clearly his new-found friend wasn't a man prepared to take 'no' for an answer.

Giovanni turned to greet his persistent new friend for the night, but instead of the ingratiating smile he expected, he saw a snarl of anger. A hand reached out, grasping him by the throat and lifting him off his feet. Claws sprang out where there had only been fingernails before, and Giovanni felt their sharp edges dig into the skin of his exposed throat. The hand held him there for long seconds as he struggled, unable to draw breath, never mind cry for help. And then it suddenly released him. Senses dimming, Giovanni fell to the ground, only half-conscious as his supposed friend effortlessly dragged him through the shadows towards a nearby waiting coach. There was the sound of a coach door opening, and a face as bright and terrible in its unearthly beauty as that of the Chaos moon of Morrslieb looked down at him as Giovanni finally slipped into unconsciousness.

'No matter, Mariato,' he heard it speak in a voice as cold as glacial ice. 'This way will do just as well...'

GIOVANNI AWAKENED, IMMEDIATELY recognising in the pain throbbing behind his eyes the all-too-familiar signs of the previous night's excesses. Mind still numbed by the copious quantities of wine he had no doubt cheerfully downed, it took him several seconds to register the fact that this was not the hovel-like garret that the recent down-turn in his fortunes had reduced him to calling home. Nor were his clothes – a shirt of finest Cathay silk and breeches of pure Estalian calfskin – the same threadbare and patchy garments that he had put on the previous morning.

Previous morning? he thought suddenly realising that it was still night, a silver sliver of the waxing Morrslieb moon visible through the barred window above his bed. He ran a hand to his face, feeling the rough stubble of what felt like two days' beard growth that had not been there earlier. Shallya's mercy. How long had he been unconscious?

There was a rattle of keys at the only door into the room. Giovanni tensed, ready to... what, he wondered. Fight? Overpower his gaolers and try to escape? Half a head smaller than his average countryman – the stature, or more precisely lack of it, of the inhabitants of the Tilean peninsula was the basis of many jokes amongst the other nations of the Old World – and with something of a paunch that the long months of penury since his fall from grace had still so far mostly failed to diminish. Giovanni knew that he was hardly the stuff that dashing dogs of war mercenary hero legends were made of. The only wound he had ever suffered was a broken nose inflicted during a heated taverna dispute with some fop of a Bretonnian poet over the favours of a young and curvaceous follower of the arts. The only blade he had ever wielded was a small knife used to sharpen the charcoal pencil nubs he sketched with.

The heavy door swung open, revealing two black-robed figures standing in the corridor outside. Faceless under their hooded robes, it was impossible to determine anything about them. A hand, pale and skeletal thin, appeared from within the folds of one of the robes, gesturing for the artist to rise and come with them. Shrugging with an attempted air of casual nonchalance that he wished he truly felt, Giovanni did as commanded.

He found himself in a wide, stone-walled corridor, falling into step between his faceless gaolers. Stars shone through breaks in the wood-raftered ceiling, and, glancing up, Giovanni saw the shattered ruins of a burned-out upper storey above him. The floor at his feet had been hurriedly swept clean, with piles of rubble and ancient fire debris piled up at its sides, and Giovanni could just make out blackened and faded frescoes under the grime and soot on the corridor walls. They showed nymphs and satyrs at play and were of a pastoral style that went out of fashion over a century ago. The night breeze drifted in through the breaks in the ruined ceiling, and Giovanni caught the faint but familiar scent of distant fruit groves.

With a shock of recognition, he realised that he was probably in one of the abandoned villas that dotted the countryside hills above Trantio. There were many such ruins, Giovanni knew, for in safer and more prosperous times it had been the fashion amongst the city's wealthy merchant families to build such palaces in the surrounding countryside, as both an ostentatious display of wealth and a retreat from the squalor of the city. A downturn in mercantile fortunes and the steadily increasing numbers of greenskin savages stealing over the Apuccini Mountains had brought an abrupt end to the such rural idylls, and the survivors abandoned their countryside retreats and fled back to the comfort of their counting houses and the safety of high and well-guarded city walls. Since then, the abandoned villas had become notorious as lairs for the predators that hid out in the wilderness areas beyond the limits of the Trantine city guard's horseback patrols.

Predators such as bandit gangs, or orc warbands, or–

Or what? Giovanni wondered with a shudder, his lively artist's imagination painting a series of vivid nightmare images of all the things bad enough to scare bandits and even orcs away from such a place.

Something rustled at Giovanni's feet and he jumped back as a large rat scampered out of a hole in the floor and ran across the corridor, running right over the top of his booted feet. There was a blur of movement from behind him, followed instantly by a harsh squeal of pain and an abrupt wet tearing sound. Giovanni turned, catching a glimpse of the scene beneath the hooded cloaks behind him – long skeletal fingers crammed something squealing and still alive between jaws distended horribly wide open – before a warning hiss from his other gaoler urged him to keep moving. Suitably inspired, Giovanni's imagination mentally erased the previous portfolio of nightmare images and began work on a new gallery of even greater horrors.

The corridor ended in an open doorway, soft light spilling out from the open doorway there. Urged on by a low angry grunt from one of the gaoler creatures, Giovanni gingerly stepped forward into the room beyond.

The chamber was how he imagined the villa would have looked in its heyday. It was opulently furnished, and his gaze passed over a tempting platter of fruit and a crystal decanter of wine laid out on a nearby table – did his captors seek to trick him into poisoning himself after having him at their mercy for at least a day as he lay insensible in his cell, he wondered? – and also the oddly disquieting sight of a painting easel with a blank canvas upon it. But it was the paintings on the walls all around that drew his immediate attention.

There were a full dozen of them, and they were by far the greatest collection of art that Giovanni had ever seen.

There he recognised the brushwork of the legendary da Venzio, whose monumental frescoes decorating the ceiling of the great Temple of Shallya in Remas were still one of the great wonders of the Old World. And beside it was a canvas bearing the distinctive Chaos-tainted style of the mad Estalian genius Dari, whose work had been condemned as heretical two hundred years ago and was still banned throughout the Empire to this day. Hanging on the wall opposite the Dari was a work bearing all the hallmarks of the work of Fra' Litti. There were only eight known Litti paintings still in existence, all of them in the possession of the richest merchant princes of Tilea who competed with each other in bitterly fought bidding wars to purchase only the rarest and most exquisite works of art. If this really was a ninth and until now unknown Litti, then its potential value was truly incalculable.

Giovanni's senses continued to reel at the wealth of artistic riches that surrounded him. Over here a work by Bardovo, whose epic depiction of Marco Columbo's discovery of Lustria spawned a whole school of lesser talented imitators. Beside it hung a canvas bearing the disturbing scratch-mark signature of the mysterious Il Ratzo, who some historians now whispered may not even have been fully human.

It was only then, as he reached out to touch the da Venzio canvas, his fingers reverently tracing the maestro's brushstroke patterns, that an even greater and more profound realisation about all the paintings collected here occurred to him.

They were all portraits, and they were all of the same subject: an alabaster-skinned noblewoman of striking but glacial beauty.

Giovanni gazed from portrait to portrait, his eyes confirming what his mind would not yet accept. No matter the artist, no matter the difference in their individual styles, each had painted the same subject, and from life too, if the telltale details in each painting were to be believed. Here he saw the same glint of forbidden promise in the dark pools of her eyes, there the same hint of unspoken secrets behind the faint mocking smile on her lips. But while each artist had found the same qualities in their subject, each also found in her something different. In da Venzio's portrait she was a beguiling angel of darkness, his painting a blasphemous twin piece to the images of the blessed goddess of mercy on the temple ceiling in Remas. Bardovo's work showed her as a lonely spectral figure standing against a backdrop of a corpse-strewn battlefield.

How could this be, Giovanni wondered? Da Venzio had lived three hundred years ago, Bardovo more than a thousand and Fra' Litti and one or two others even longer than that.

A faint breeze passed through the air of the room, sending flickering shadows over the faces of the portraits as it disturbed the flames of the many candles which lit the chamber.

'How could artists that lived centuries apart all come to have painted the same subject?' said a voice from somewhere close behind Giovanni, completing the thought that his mind dared not yet ask itself.

He turned to face the figure reclining on the couch behind him, a figure who had not been there moments ago, he was sure. She was even more beautiful in person, he thought. More beautiful and more terrible than any portrait – even one by the great da Venzio himself – could ever do full justice to. Her eyes were endless pools of mystery that drank in everything, surrendering nothing in return. Her blood-red lips were full and of the same colour as the burning scarlet rubies which hung at her plunging neckline, revealing flawless skin that glowed like soft moonlight, skin that had not felt the kiss of sunlight in centuries.

'I am the Lady Khemalla of Lahmia,' she said in a voice that whispered like the shifting desert sands of her long-dead homeland. 'I bid you welcome to my home.'

'Then I am not a prisoner here?' asked Giovanni, surprised at his directness of his own question.

'You are my guest,' she smiled. 'And, while you are my guest, it pleases me for you to paint my portrait.' She gestured at the paintings around them. 'As you can see, I have a taste for art. And occasionally for artists too.'

She smiled at this last comment, blood-red lips curling back to show the subtle points of concealed fangs.

'Why me?' asked Giovanni, pouring himself a generous measure of wine from the decanter. Doomed as he was, he saw no need to deny himself a few final pleasures.

'If you know what I am, then you must understand that it has been many years since I have gazed upon my own face in the glass of any mirror. To never again see the features of your reflection, to live so long that you perhaps forget the image of your own face, can you begin to imagine what that might be like, mortal? Is it any wonder that so many of my kind give themselves fully over to madness and cruelty when they have nothing left to remind them of their own humanity? I can only see myself through the eyes of others, and so I choose to do so only through the eyes of the greatest artists of each age.'

She paused, favouring him with a look from the deep desert oases of her eyes as she again gestured at the paintings hanging on the walls around them. 'You should be honoured, little mortal. After all, consider the company I am including you in here.'

'You know that I have a reputation for only painting the truth as I see it.' Nervous, he reached to refill his already empty glass, concentrating hard to quell the involuntary tremor in his hands. 'It is a trait of mine that found little favour with my previous patrons. I have discovered to my cost that people wish only to have their own flattering self-image of themselves reflected back at them.'

She smiled at his show of bravado. 'I chose you because of your reputation. You say you only paint the truth, the true soul of your subject. Very well, then that is what I want, brave little mortal. The truth. Look at me and paint what you see. To try and capture on canvas the soul of one of my kind; what greater challenge could there be for an artist?'

'And afterwards, when the work is complete? You will let me leave?'

'You will be free to refuse my hospitality when you have gifted me something that I deem worthy of your talents. If your work pleases me you will be well rewarded for your troubles, I promise you.'

'And if it does not, what then?'

The question hung unanswered in the air between them.

Giovanni set down his goblet and went over to the easel and blank canvas set up nearby. As he had expected, there was a palette of every imaginable kind of artist's materials. He rummaged amongst them, selecting a charcoal pencil for sketching and a knife to sharpen it with. A challenge, she had called it, and so it was. To paint the soul of a creature of the darkness, an age-old liche-thing, and yet to paint only the truth of what lay beneath that perfect ageless skin while still producing something that would please this most demanding of patrons. This would either be the greatest work of his life, he thought, or merely his last.

He turned back to his waiting subject, his practised eye seeing her at this earliest stage as merely a vexing collection of surfaces, angles, lines and subtle blends of light and shadow. The fine detail, in which lay those crucial insubstantial elements that would determine whether he lived or died here, would come later.

'Shall we begin?' he said.

LIKE THE VILLA's other inhabitants, he worked only at night now and slept by day. Each night after sundown they came for him, and each night she sat for him. She talked while he worked – he always encouraged his subjects to talk, the better to understand them and their lives, for a portrait should speak of far more than its subject's mere outward physical appearance – and as he worked he heard tales of her homeland. Tales of gods, heroes and villains whose names and deeds are remembered now by none other than those of her kind; tales of mighty cities and impregnable fortresses now reduced to a few ancient crumbling ruins buried and forgotten beneath the desert sands.

Some nights they did not come for him. On those nights, she sent apologies for her absence, and gifts of fine wines and food, and books to let him pass the time in his cell more easily. The books, usually works of history or philosophy, fascinated him. Several of them were written in languages completely unknown to Giovanni – the languages of legendary and far Cathay or Nippon, he thought – while one was composed of thin leafs of hammer-beaten copper and inlaid with a queer hieroglyphic script which he doubted was even human in origin.

He knew that there were other occupants of the villa, although besides his silent faceless gaolers and his patron herself he had seen none of them. But as he lay in his cell reading on those work-free nights, he heard much activity going on around him. Each night brought visitors to the place. He heard the clatter of rider's hooves and the rumble of coach wheels and the jangle of pack team harnesses, and once he thought he heard the beating of heavy leather wings and perhaps even saw the fleeting shadow of something vast and bat-like momentarily blotting out the moonlit window above his bed.

There were other sounds too – screams and sobs and once the unmistakable cry of an infant child – from the cellars deep beneath his feet. At such times Giovanni buried his face into the mattress of his bedding or read aloud from the book in his hand until either the sounds had ceased or he had convinced himself that he could no longer hear them.

ONE NIGHT HE awoke in his room. The sitting had been cut short that night. One of the black-cloaked servant things had entered and fearfully handed its mistress a sealed scroll tube. As she read it her face had changed – transformed, Giovanni thought – and for a second he saw something of the savage and cruel creature of darkness that lay beneath the human mask she presented to him. The news was both urgent and unwelcome and she had abruptly ended the night's session, issuing curt orders for him to be escorted back to his room. He had fallen asleep as soon as he lay down on the bedding, exhausted by the continued effort of keeping up with the night-time schedule of his new employer.

Again, he heard the sound that had awoken him. There was someone in the room with him.

A face detached itself from the shadowy gloom of the cell, leaning over the bed and glared angrily down angrily at him. Jagged teeth, too many of them for any human mouth, crowded out from snarling lips. It was her servant, Mariato, the one that had approached him in the tavern that night. He had obviously just fed, and his breath was thick with the slaughterhouse reek of blood.

'Scheherazade. That is what I shall call you,' the vampire growled, glaring down at him with eyes full of hate and the madness of blood-lust. 'Do you know the name, little painter? It is a name from her homeland, a storyteller who prolonged her life for a thousand and one nights by entertaining her master with tales and fables.'

The vampire raised one bristle-covered hand, pointing at the half-face of Mannslieb in the sky above. The ring on his finger flashed green in the moonlight.

'How many nights do you think you have left, my Scheherazade? Her enemies are close, and by the time Mannslieb's face shines full again, we will be gone from here. Will your precious painting be finished by then? I think not, for such things take great time and care, do they not?'

He paused, leaning in closer, hissing into Giovanni's face, stifling him with the sour reek of his carrion breath.

'She will not take you with us, and she cannot leave you here alive for our enemies to find. So what is she to do with you then, my Scheherazade?'

The vampire melted back into the shadows, its voice a whispering promise from out of the darkness.

'When Mannslieb's face shines full again, then you will be mine.'

'YOUR SERVANT MARIATO, he doesn't like me.' She looked up with inter-est. This was the first time he had dared speak to her without permission. She lay reclining on the couch in the position that he had first seen her in. A bowl of strange dark-skinned fruit lay on the floor before her. The main composition of the piece was complete, and all he needed to concentrate on now was the detail of the face.

'He is jealous,' she answered. 'He is afraid that I will grow bored with him and seek to make another my favourite in his stead.' She looked at him sharply. 'Has he disturbed you? Has he said or done anything to interrupt your work?'

Giovanni kept his eyes on his work, unwilling to meet her keen gaze. 'Has he a right to be jealous?'

She smiled, favouring him with a look of secret amusement. 'Per-haps,' she mused. 'His kind always have their place at my side, but they are always dull and unimaginative. Perhaps I will take a new con-sort, not a warrior or a nobleman this time. Perhaps this time an artist? What do you think, little mortal? Shall I make you my new paramour and grant you the gift of eternal life in darkness?'

She laughed, picking up a fruit from the bowl and biting deep into it, enjoying the taste of his fear. Thick juice, obscenely scarlet in colour, bled out of the fruit as she ate it.

Giovanni studied the lines and contours of the painted face on the canvas in front of him. A few brushstrokes, a subtle touch of shading, and he had added an extra element of sardonic cruelty to the line of her smile.

THE NEXT NIGHT he returned to his cell at dawn to find a small tied leather pouch sitting on his bed. He opened it, pouring out a quantity of powdered ash. Puzzled, Giovanni ran his fingers through the stuff, finding it strangely unpleasant to the touch. There was something amongst it. Giovanni gingerly picked it up, discovering it to be a ring. He held it up, the light of the rising sun catching the familiar emerald stone set upon it.

It seemed that Mariato no longer occupied the same position amongst his mistress's favours as he had once done.

GIOVANNI KNEW THAT their time together was coming to an end. Mannslieb hung high in the night sky, almost full, and for the last few nights there had been more activity than usual in the villa. He heard the sound of heavy boxes – earth-filled coffins, he supposed – being dragged up from the cellars and loaded into wagons. He worked in daylight hours too now; foregoing sleep and working on the painting alone in his cell, making changes so subtle that he doubted anyone other than he would notice the difference. Adding new details and taking away others. Revising. Reworking. Perfecting. He was haggard and gaunt, exhausted from too little food and sleep, looking more like one of her pale ghoul-thing servants than the portly florid-faced drunk who had been brought here just scant weeks ago.

All that mattered now was the painting itself. The greatest work of his life, that is what he had said he would have to produce, and that is what he had done. After that, he discovered to his surprise, nothing else really mattered.

SHE SENT FOR him the next night, with Mannslieb shining full-faced in the night sky. The painting too, was now complete.

She stood looking at it. The room had been stripped almost bare, and the easel that the canvas stood on was the most significant item left in it. There were faint outlines on the walls where her portraits had hung.

'You are leaving?' he said, more in statement than question.

'We have many enemies, my kind. Not just the witch hunters with their silver and fire. We wage war amongst ourselves, fighting over sovereignty of the night. It has become too dangerous to remain here.'

She gestured towards the painting. 'It is beautiful, master Gottio. I thank you for your gift. What do you call it?'

'*Unchanging Beauty*,' he answered, joining her to look at his masterpiece. It showed her standing regally against a backdrop of palatial splendour. Giovanni's talent had captured all her cruel and terrible beauty as the others before him had also done, but the real artistry was in the detail of the trappings around her. Look closer and the eye was drawn to the tarnished gold of the throne behind her, the subtle patterns of mildew creeping across the wall tapestries, the broken pinnacles of the palace towers seen through the window in the far background. It was a world where everything other than her was subject to change and decay. Only she was unchanging. Only she was forever.

'Then my task here is done. I am free to leave now?' He looked at her, half in hope, half in dread.

'I had thought to keep you here with me as an new diversion to replace poor Mariato.' She looked at him, trying to gauge his reaction, toying with him yet again.

'But, no, you would make a poor vampire, master Gottio,' she reassured him, relishing one last taste of his fear. 'There is something in our nature that destroys any creative ability we may have had in our mortal lives, and I would not deny the world the great works still within you. So, yes, you are free to go.'

'And my reward?'

She gestured towards a small open casket nearby. Giovanni glanced at it, silently toting up the value of the gold and precious stones it contained and coming to a figure comparable with a minor merchant prince's ransom. When he looked back, she was holding a goblet of wine out to him.

'What is it?' he asked, suspecting one final cruel jest.

'A little wine mixed with a sleeping draught, the same one that Mariato tried to lull you with. Call it a final precaution, for your own safety. When you awaken, you will be safe and in familiar surroundings, I promise you. I could compel you to drink it, but this way is easier.'

He took it, raising it to his lips and drinking. She watched him intently as he did so. The wine was excellent, as he expected, but mixed in with it, the taste of something else, not any kind of potion or sleeping draught. Something dark and rich, something that rose up to overwhelm his senses.

'An extra gift,' she said, seeing the reaction in his eyes. 'With your painting, you have given me a part of yourself. It only seemed fair that I give you something equally valuable in return. Farewell, little mortal, I look forward to seeing what uses you will put my gift to.'

She reached out with preternatural reflexes to catch him as he fell, as the darkness rushed in to envelop his numbed senses…

HE AWOKE IN blinding daylight, crying out in pain as the unaccustomed sunlight stabbed into his eyes. When he recovered, he realised that he was in the pauper's attic garret he called home. The precious casket lay on the floor beside him.

It took him several hours to realise the nature of the additional gift she had given him.

He sat inspecting his reflection in the small cracked looking glass he had finally managed to find amongst the jumble of his possessions. Days ago he had been a haggard wreck, now there was not a trace of the ordeal left upon him, none of the exhaustion of the last few weeks. He looked and felt better than he had in years. In fact…

Shallya's mercy, he thought, studying the reflection of his face in the mirror. *I look ten years younger!*

He thought of certain legends about her kind, about the gifts they granted to their loyal mortal servants and about the restorative powers of…

Of vampire blood. Only the smallest portion, but he could feel it flowing in his veins, feel her inside him. Her life-force added to his own. Had she done this with the others, he wondered, and then he remembered that the da Venzio had been reputed to have lived to over a century in age – blessed by the mercy goddess, they said, in reward for the work he had done in her great temple in Remas – and of how Bardovo had lived long enough to paint not just the portrait of the Marco Columbo but also that of the legendary explorer's merchant prince great-grandson.

He wondered how long he, Giovanni Gottio, had, and about how he would put his time to best use.

He looked around his squalid attic, seeing only the detritus of his former miserable life: smashed wine bottles and pieces of cheap parchment torn up in anger and thrown in crumpled balls across the room. He picked one up, smoothing it out and recognising it as the abandoned portrait sketch of a local tavern girl. The workmanship was poor and he could see why he had so quickly abandoned the piece, but looking at it with fresh vision he could see possibilities in its line and form that had not been there to him before.

He found his drawing board and pinned the parchment to it, sitting looking at it in quiet contemplation. After a while, he searched amongst the debris on the floor and found the broken end of a charcoal pencil.

And with it, he began to draw.

SEVENTH BOON

Mitchel Scanlon

IT WAS LATE and, given the hour, the draughty expanse of the orphanage's dining hall seemed hardly warmer than the wintry night outside. Yet despite having been roused blearily from their beds, a dozen barefoot children filed across the cold flagstone floor without complaint. Quiet and dutiful, they came to where Sister Altruda stood with the visitors and formed a line facing them, heads up and spines held straight like diminutive soldiers summoned to a parade ground muster. Then, seeing one of the visitors step forward to inspect them, twelve small faces grew bright with sudden hope – only for those hopes to be abruptly dashed as, finishing her inspection, the young woman turned to Sister Altruda to deliver a terse and crushing verdict.

'No,' Frau Forst said, 'none of these will do.'

As one, twelve faces fell. Watching it, Sister Altruda felt a familiar sadness to see twelve childish hearts hardened a little more against hope by the pain of rejection. It could not be helped. As priestess to the goddess of mercy, Sister Altruda's own heart went out to them. But, as director of the Orphanage of Our Lady Shallya of the Blessed Heart, she was a realist. Marienburg manufactured so many unwanted children and if she could find even one a new home tonight it would be a triumph. Though, given that her visitors had spent the better part of an hour viewing dozens of children now without finding one to please them, presently even that small victory seemed beyond her.

411

Sighing inwardly, Sister Altruda beckoned to the novitiate Saskia to lead the children from the room. Then, summoning her most diplomatic tone, she turned to her visitors once more.

'You must understand,' she said, 'there are hundreds of children here. Perhaps if we were to discuss more fully your criteria in choosing the child you wish to adopt, we might speed the selection.'

'Criteria?' Frau Forst replied, as though vaguely bewildered by the term. 'There are no criteria, sister. It is simply a matter of finding a child my husband and I can love as our own. A child we can share our lives with. We will know him when we see him. Isn't that right, Gunther?'

Behind her, Herr Forst gave a single silent nod. They made a strange couple. Frau Forst seemed no more than twenty-odd years of age: a vivacious butterfly of a girl shrouded in colourful silks and velvet furs. A woman whose prettiness, to Sister Altruda's eyes, was only slightly marred by an over-enthusiastic application of rouge to her lips. In contrast, her husband looked more than twenty years her senior. Trim and well-preserved perhaps, with broad shoulders and none of the heaviness of waist common to men of his years and position. But his dark hair and well-groomed beard were flecked with streaks of grey, while his shrewd, quiet eyes spoke of a man who had seen enough of life to always be wary.

A moth to his wife's butterfly, Herr Forst dressed in sombre greys and blacks, his only ornament an amulet on a heavy gold chain around his neck announcing his membership in one of Marienburg's innumerable mercantile orders. Given their disparities, Sister Altruda could not help but suspect that Frau Forst had come here on a whim, intent on choosing herself a trophy child in the same manner as her husband had evidently chosen himself a trophy wife. Still, it was none of her concern. Whatever their motives, she did not doubt that any child would be happier living with the Forsts than in the dreary and overcrowded confines of the orphanage. And besides, the good character of Herr Forst himself was beyond question.

Where others who might consider themselves among the 'great-and-good' of Marienburg seemed content to let the city's flotsam children be condemned to the streets, over the last five years Gunther Forst had been the orphanage's single most generous private benefactor. He had his eccentricities though and if after five years of distant benevolence he had come to adopt a child outside the orphanage's usual hours of business then so be it. Sister Altruda would no more reject a reasonable request from Herr Forst than she would the High Priestess in Couronne. No matter how difficult Frau Forst was to please, no matter how nebulous her requirements or exacting her standards, her position as the wife of Gunther Forst placed her beyond reproach. If need be, Sister Altruda would rouse every child in the orphanage and spend the next six hours trooping them past Frau Forst until she found one that pleased her.

Though, given how late it was already, she sincerely hoped it would not come to that.

Hearing the door open once more, Sister Altruda turned to see Saskia leading another group of a dozen children into the room. Lining up as the others had before them, the children waited patiently as Frau Forst stepped forward to examine them. This time though, instead of glancing briefly over the line, Frau Forst paused two-thirds of the way along to gaze down at a sandy-haired boy of about eight whose features seemed almost angelic in their perfection. Guilelessly, the boy lifted his own eyes to stare back and for long moments the woman and the child stood there with eyes locked as though entranced – only for the spell to be broken as, abruptly, Herr Forst cleared his throat. Hearing it, Frau Forst turned to look at her husband for a moment, before turning back to the silent boy before her.

'And what is your name, my little prince?' she cooed at him.

'The boy does not speak,' Sister Altruda said.

'He is mute, then?' Frau Forst asked, raising a quizzical eyebrow towards her.

'No. We examined him when he was brought here and could find no sign of any physical defect. It may be that some shock has caused him to temporarily lose the ability to speak. It is difficult to say. He was found wandering the streets some days ago and we know nothing of his background. Given time, we can only hope his voice returns to him.'

'I see,' Frau Forst said, turning to coo at the boy once more. 'If you ask me, my little prince, all you need is a nice loving home. A warm, safe place with toys and dogs and all the things a boy could want. Why, once you come home with us, I'm sure we'll have you talking ten-to-the-dozen in no time.'

With that, Frau Forst held out her hand, smiling in delight as she saw the boy raise his own hand to meet it. It seemed, finally, she had made her choice. And, privately, Sister Altruda found herself forced to admit the search had been worth it. There was indeed something different about this one. There was something about his eyes, a sense of pure and untarnished innocence. If that was what Frau Forst had been looking for all this time, no wonder it had taken her so long to find it.

It was rare, after all, to find much that was innocent on the streets of Marienburg.

* * *

A FTERWARDS, SITTING WITHIN the shuttered comfort of his coach as it sped away from the orphanage into the night, Gunther Forst allowed himself the luxury of a small moment of satisfaction. It had gone better than he could ever have dared hope. The efforts he had invested over the last several years – all the donations, the grand and charitable gestures – had finally paid a handsome dividend. There had been no resistance, no awkward questions; the priestess and her novitiate had given him the boy gladly. And though he might have only a few scant hours left in which to put the rest of his plan in motion, if it proceeded half as smoothly as matters had at the orphanage he should achieve his wider aims with ease.

'My, but you're a quiet one aren't you, boy? I don't know, we save you from that nasty orphanage and not even a word of thanks. What's the matter, my little prince? Cat got your tongue?'

It was the woman. His erstwhile 'wife'. Evidently bored, she produced a small golden heart on a string of teardrop-shaped garnet beads from within her glove and began to dangle it in front of the face of the silent boy beside her, teasing him.

'Surely you can tell us your name at least,' she cooed. 'Every boy has a name. Tell me yours and perhaps I will give you this pretty thing as a gift. You would like that, wouldn't you?'

Looking at the ruby light jumping from the dancing beads, the boy said nothing. Grimly, Gunther recognised them as the same set of Shallyan prayer beads he had seen on Sister Altruda's wrist earlier. It seemed the dubious talents of the woman opposite him went beyond the obvious. Though it had seemed a masterstroke when he had conceived the idea of hiring a courtesan to accompany him to the orphanage and play the part of his wife now he was beginning to find her tiresome. Granted, she had lent a veneer of legitimacy to his attempts to adopt the child, but now the woman had served her purpose, her presence here was at best an irrelevance, at worst an irritation.

'Leave the boy alone,' he told her.

Pausing, the woman turned to look at him as though trying to read the limits of his patience in the lines of his face. Then, turning back to the boy once more, she began again in the same idiot tone.

'Did you hear that, little prince?' she purred. 'Poppa sounds cross. Do you think he is angry because you won't tell us your name?'

'Far from it,' Gunther said, enough of an edge to his voice to let her know she was trying his temper. 'I have long counted silence as a virtue, in both children and harlots alike.'

At that, the woman fell quiet. Crossing her arms, she turned to face the lowered shade of the coach window with her mouth set in a sulky line. But if the boy felt any gratitude towards Gunther for his intervention, he gave no sign of it. Instead, seemingly interested in nothing in particular, he continued to sit in wide-eyed silence. Looking at him, Gunther found himself struck once more by the child's manner. The boy seemed possessed of a flawless, almost otherworldly aura of innocence. Seeing it, Gunther felt a rising feeling of hope. The vital task of finding someone possessed of a perfect and utter purity had always seemed the hardest part of his plan.

Now he had the boy, the rest should fall into place.

The coach lurched to a halt. Hearing the coach roof above him creak as the driver left his seat, Gunther waited for the door to be opened. But when it was, instead of the coachman he saw a dark figure appear in the open doorway with a black kerchief tied around the lower half of his face, though of more immediate concern was the loaded handbow the man aimed at Gunther's heart.

'My apologies for the inconvenience, mein herr,' the interloper said. 'But I would count it a personal favour if you and the boy would step down from your compartment. Oh, and you will be careful to keep your hands where I can see them, won't you? I would hate for either of you to have to suffer a misfortune.'

Doing as he was told, careful to keep himself between the handbow and the boy, Gunther stepped down from the coach with the boy behind him. Once outside, he saw the coach had stopped in a refuse-strewn alleyway the uncobbled surface of which declared it to be among one of the city's more isolated and disreputable thorough-fares. A second kerchief-masked footpad stood behind the first, a short wooden cudgel in his hands, while to their side the coachman lurked nervously beside his horses. Seeing the coachman unharmed and apparently unguarded, Gunther realised at once that he was part of it. Just as he realised, outnumbered three-to-one and with the added distraction of having to protect the boy, he would have to weigh his options carefully.

Having long feared the twin evils of disease and violent death, Gunther had devoted no small number of years to learning the skills necessary to defend against the latter. He was an excellent shot, and hidden out of sight beneath his cloak were a pair of duelling pistols purchased some years past from the grieving widow of hot-headed nobleman whose passion for honour had been exceeded only by the incompetence of his marksmanship. But for all the finely-crafted elegance and accuracy, the pistols were loud and clumsy weapons. And, even in this isolated spot, the sound of shots might serve to draw the attention of the Watch.

It would have to be the knife.

'Here,' he said, lifting the chain from around his neck, 'I will give you anything you want so long as you let the boy and I go in peace.'

'A most commendable attitude,' the handbowman said. 'Really, mein herr, your clear-sighted grasp of the situation does you credit.'

'Not at all,' Gunther replied, holding the chain out in his right hand and watching as the man took two steps towards it. 'I am simply a pragmatist. All the same, I must confess to some surprise. I would have thought a handbow far too expensive a weapon for the purse of a pimp.'

Abruptly, the advancing figure stopped, his eyes above his mask grown suddenly hard and tight.

'He knows, Ruprecht,' the one with the cudgel said, breaking the ugly silence. 'He knows who you are.'

'Well, if he didn't before, Oskar, he certainly does now,' the other replied, pulling his mask down to reveal a sallow yet handsome face. As Gunther suspected, it was the woman's pimp. 'Bravo, Herr Forst. You are right about the handbow, of course. It came into my possession in the wake of a financial dispute with one of Greta's gentleman clients. But, tell me, how did you know it was me?'

'You let the woman stay in the coach,' Gunther said. 'No matter the tales of the gallantry of highwaymen, it seemed unlikely you would leave her possessions unmolested unless they were effectively yours already. That alone was enough to make it clear you were her pimp come to rob me.'

'I am afraid you overrate your value to us, Herr Forst,' the pimp sneered. 'Robbing you was never anything more than an afterthought. It is the child we want. To the right buyer, a boy like that is a valuable piece of merchandise. And, I assure you, I make it my business to know all the right buyers.'

'Now,' the pimp said, taking a step forward as he raised his handbow to fire, 'seeing as you have been so helpful as to make us aware you know who we are, it would seem foolish to leave you alive to tell of it.'

With a sudden twist of his wrist, Gunther threw the amulet at the pimp, the chain hit the man in the face just as his finger tightened on the trigger. As the bolt flew wild over his shoulder, Gunther stepped forward, pulling his knife from its hidden sheath with his left hand and thrusting it deep into Ruprecht's side. Eyes startled with pain, the pimp tried to scream, the sound emerged as a wet gurgle as, dying, his body pitched forward towards the ground. But Gunther was past him already. Seeing the other footpad lift his cudgel and charge forward to attack, Gunther tossed the knife from left hand to right with a fluid motion, raising his left arm to block the descending wrist holding the cudgel while, with his right, he slid the knife between the man's ribs and into his heart.

Pulling the knife free as the second man collapsed, Gunther turned to see the coachman still standing beside his horses. Holding the butt

of his coachwhip before him as an improvised weapon, the coachman seemed glued to the spot, caught between the urge to attack and
the fear Gunther would dispose of him as easily as the others.

'All I want is to go in peace with the boy,' Gunther told him. 'And I
want the coach. Run now, and I will let you live.'

For a moment, the coachman stood staring in disbelief. Then, the
prospect of escape overcoming his distrust, he turned and ran. Only
for Gunther to throw his knife the instant the man turned his back,
taking the coachman high in the neck and dropping him before he
had gone three steps.

Striding forward to pull his knife from the dead man's neck, Gunther's first thoughts were for the safety of the boy. Turning to look
behind him, he was relieved to see the still strangely silent child
standing, uninjured, beside the coach where he had left him.

'Get into the coach, boy,' Gunther said, stooping to pull his knife
free. 'We are leaving.'

Instead of moving, the boy turned his wide eyes to stare at something on the coach, before looking back at Gunther once more.
Noticing for the first time a slumped figure hanging halfway through
the window of the coach door, Gunther stepped forward to investigate and saw something which soon had him silently cursing his luck.

It was the woman. She was dead: the flight of her pimp's errant
bolt jutting from a wound in her neck. Evidently she had been
standing watching the confrontation through the window when it
struck her. But what concerned Gunther more was the woman's
blood. It was everywhere, staining the side of the coach and the running board beneath it. The coach was next to useless to him now. He
could not afford the chance some over-eager watchman would see
the blood and be moved to ask questions Gunther would rather not
answer. Nor could he simply clean the blood away – even had a suitable supply of water been at hand, it would take too long. And
tonight, more so than at any other point in Gunther's life, time was
of the essence.

His decision made, Gunther opened the coach door, stepping to
one side to let the woman's body fall past him. Being careful not to
get any more blood on his clothes, he retrieved his belongings from
inside the coach before stepping outside once more to take one of the
night-lanterns hanging from the coach's side and fashion a makeshift
carrying handle for it from a piece of cloth. Ready at last, he turned to
the boy. For better or worse, if they were to reach their destination in
good time tonight, they would have to walk.

Or one of them would at least.

'Get onto my shoulders, boy,' Gunther said. 'We are going to play
piggy-on-my-back.'

Silently, the boy did as he was told. Getting to his feet with the boy clinging to his shoulders, Gunther started on a brisk walk headed southwards. At best estimation they were at least a mile and a half from their destination. He would have to walk fast: the confrontation with the pimp and the others had cost him too much time already. No matter what else happened tonight, all his preparations needed to be ready by midnight.

If not, there would be hell to pay.

HE WAS SWEATING by the time he got to the docks. And when he reached the outside of the burnt-out tavern in an alleyway just off a deserted wharf, the weight of the boy on his shoulders seemed to have grown so much it was as though he had an adult perched upon his back. Relieved to have arrived at his destination at last, Gunther sank down to his knees to let the boy climb off. Then, rising to his feet and pleased to see no sign of life anywhere along the alley, he made his way toward the tavern with the boy behind him.

It had a history, this place. In its heyday the Six Crowns had been the nexus for much that was illicit and illegal in Marienburg; a place where deals could be struck and bargains made with no questions asked. Most recently, it had served as de facto headquarters for the Vanderhecht Organisation, a ruthless gang of smugglers whose leader had lived a double life as one of the most respected merchants in the city. But Hugo Vanderhecht was dead, killed by a bounty hunter after fleeing to the marshes, while the Six Crowns had been gutted a year ago in an unexplained fire, rumoured to have been set by the gang's second-in-command in an attempt to hide his identity from the Watch. Still, it hardly mattered to Gunther who had set the fire. Whoever had done it, he owed them a debt of thanks. His work tonight needed privacy, and the derelict, ramshackle building before him would suit his purpose admirably.

Besides, he had his own history with this place. Years ago, it had served as the backdrop to an event which had changed the course of his life. And now that life had come full circle and brought him to the Six Crowns once more.

Advancing towards the fire-blackened doorway, Gunther found himself briefly troubled by thoughts of his own mortality. Something of the tavern's current state, the crumbling plaster of its walls and the gaping heat-warped windows, brought to mind unpleasant echoes. For a moment he felt the weight of every one of his years bearing down upon him, greater even than the weight of the silent boy who now walked beside him. Perhaps it was nostalgia, or the last spasms of conscience of the man he had once been, but he suddenly felt a sadness he had not known in years. Then, shaking his head to clear it, he put sentiment behind him and pushed the door aside to enter the tavern.

'Come on, boy,' Gunther said, seeing the child hanging back at the threshold. 'There is nothing here to harm you.'

Once past its deceptively ruined outer shell, the tavern's interior was surprisingly intact. Picking carefully through a hallway choked with fallen timbers and ash-strewn debris, Gunther made his way towards what had once been the smaller of the inn's two public bar rooms. Then, checking to see the boy was still behind him, he stepped inside the room, lifting his lantern to inspect the surroundings.

It was exactly as he left it. Thanks to several hours' worth of heavy labour when he had visited the tavern earlier in the evening, Gunther had cleared the floor of the bar room of its dust and detritus. Happy to see no sign of the room having been disturbed since, Gunther crossed the floor to the ruined bar. Then, stepping behind it, he stooped to pull away some of the fractured casks beneath, revealing the shape of the small wooden chest he had hidden there earlier. Relieved to see it undamaged and its lock intact, he lifted it onto the bar. As he took the key from the thong around his neck, Gunther noticed the boy leaning on the bar, craning his neck expectantly to watch the chest being opened. Pausing, Gunther put his hand inside his cloak to retrieve one of the small cloth purses hanging from his belt before, pulling open the drawstring, he took a bag of waxed paper from within it.

'Here, boy,' he said, giving it to the child. 'Inside there are dried apricots and sugared almonds. You may have as many as you want, so long as you sit in the corner there and keep quiet.'

Accepting the offering, the boy jumped down from the bar, hastening to sit cross-legged in a distant corner and begin eating the sweets. For a moment Gunther watched him. Then, satisfied the boy was occupied, he twisted the key in the lock and opened the chest, checking a mental inventory as he arranged the contents on the bar beside him. It was all here: brazier, mortar, pestle, verbena leaves, mandrake root, man-tallow candles, wyrdstone fragments, vials of beastman urine and two dozen other things besides. Coming to the bottom of the chest, Gunther lifted out a long object wrapped in cloth, before pulling the edges of the cloth aside to reveal the bladed iron tube of the trocar. Staring at the thumb's-width notch set halfway along its length, his hand strayed unconsciously to the small, round object nestling safely within a hidden pocket inside his vest. For a moment he cupped it in his hand, feeling the comfortable weight and hardness of it through the cloth. He had everything he needed. Now, it was simply a matter of putting his plan in motion.

Opening a jar containing the crushed fingerbones of a martyred Sigmarite saint, Gunther put them in the bowl of the mortar, adding a quantity of chalk and powdered dragon tooth before grinding it together with the pestle. Then, being careful to leave no gaps, he used the mixture to draw a circle of binding on the floor around the bar. To give the circle power he would have to chant the warding spell. But that would come later. He must see to the tripwires first, then draw a pentagram within the binding circle, centred on the bar. After that, there were candles to be lit, incenses to be burned, an altar to be arranged. A dozen different tasks awaited him before he could begin the ritual, and a single moment's carelessness in any of them would spell disaster. But he was confident, all the same. He had prepared for this night's work for decades. Years spent carefully considering all that might go amiss, shaping and reshaping his design, planning everything down to the smallest detail. But he had needed to; the stakes were high. So high, not one man in ten thousand times ten thousand would have ever dared risk what he would tonight. But no matter the risks, no matter the dangers, the prize would be worth it. Come what may, tonight he would play a devil's gambit.

And he would play to win.

DIMLY, THROUGH THE walls of the tavern, Gunther heard a bell tolling in the distance. The harbourmaster was calling time. Ten bells. Two hours to midnight. He would have to work fast. As he hurried to the contents of the chest once more to resume his preparations, Gunther was struck by the irony of it. The course of the life he had set upon in the backroom of the Six Crowns when Marienburg was still part of the Empire would be decided in the selfsame tavern in two hours time. Despite all the groundwork and the decades of planning, all his life came down to in the end was a mere two hours. No, not even that. Like all men, ultimately the course of his life would be decided in a single moment – a moment for him that would come when the bell tolled midnight. But he could hardly complain. Where most men stumbled blindly towards the defining instants of their lives, he had been forewarned of his decades ago. It was not as though the moment had caught him unawares; he had been gifted with many years in which to make ready. Years more than three times past the normal span of man.

Exactly one hundred and fifty years, to be precise.

IT WAS BUSY in the *Six Crowns* that night and, as he edged his way through a crowd of hard-faced men towards the bar, it came as no surprise to Gunther to see that the tavern's reputation as a den of thieves and cutthroats seemed well-deserved. He saw men who wore the scars of branding, others with clipped ears or penal tattoos, even a man with a rope scar around his neck. More than half the men there had been marked in one way or another by the city fathers' justice. Though, to Gunther's mind, that was all to the good. His business here tonight was a private matter. And, whatever their other vices, criminals at least could usually be relied upon to keep themselves to themselves.

Coming to the bar at last, Gunther signalled to the barman, dropping a guilder on the counter by way of enticement.

'Can I help you, mein herr?' the barman asked, lifting the coin to his mouth to test it with his teeth.

'I am here to meet someone,' Gunther told him. 'In the backroom. It has all been arranged.'

Saying nothing, the barman looked Gunther up and down with ill-disguised suspicion. Then, right hand wandering beneath the bar before him, he spoke once more.

'You were given a token?' he asked, eyes dark with distrust.

Fumbling in his vest, Gunther produced another coin, a six-sided silver one that had been delivered to his house by messenger three days earlier, and handed it to the barman. Rather than bite this one, the barman stood studying it in his hand, looking first at the embossed motif of a serpent coiled around a piece of fruit on one side, before turning it over to see Six Crowns arranged in a circle on the reverse.

'Six crowns, mein herr,' the barman said, offering a hard, humourless smile as he handed the coin back to him. 'Quite a coincidence, don't you think?'

Lifting the hinged flap at the end of the counter, the barman nodded for Gunther to step behind the bar. Then, leading him through a curtained doorway, he ushered him into a hallway stacked on either side with empty beer casks and crates of bottles, before pointing towards a door at its end.

'The backroom is down there, mein herr,' the barman said. 'No need to knock. You are expected.'

With that, he was gone, stepping back behind the curtain towards the bar and his patrons. Alone now, Gunther found himself strangely paralysed by the weight of his own expectations. He could hardly believe it could be so simple. Where he had expected blood sacrifice or elaborate rituals, there was only a short walk down an ordinary corridor towards a perfectly nondescript door. A door through which, he hoped, lay the answer to an ambition he had pursued for more than twenty years.

Summoning his will at last, Gunther advanced down the corridor and lifted his hand to the doorknob. Doing his best to keep it from shaking, he pushed the door open.

'You must be Gunther,' a smoothly spoken voice said from within the room. 'Please, come in. I assure you, there is nothing here to harm you.'

Stepping inside the dingy backroom, Gunther found his expectations con-founded for the second time in as many minutes. Ahead of him at a table at the centre of the room sat a blond-haired man in the clothes of a gentleman, a sardonic smile twitching at the corner of his lips as he raised a wineglass in languid greeting.

'You were expecting horns, perhaps?' the figure said as though reading his thoughts. 'Cloven hooves? A barbed tail, even? I hope you are not disappointed. Given the unfortunate tendency of mortals to soil themselves when confronted with my true form, I thought it better to dress down for our meeting. Frankly, the floor of this room seemed filthy enough already.'

The smile on his lips grew even broader. Stunned, his mind reeling, Gunther gawped at him for a moment, before stammering a reply.

'You are the Silver Tongue, Daemon Prince and First among the Infernal Legions of the god Slaanesh?' he said, voice cracking as he said the last word aloud.

'Generally, I prefer the name Samael,' the other purred. 'But really, Gunther, you know all this already. Otherwise you would never have come here to meet me.'

'You know my name?' Gunther asked, regretting how foolish the question made him sound the second it left his lips.

'Of course I do, Gunther,' Samael replied, sliding an opened bottle of wine and spare wineglass across the table towards him. 'When a man comes to bargain with me, I make it a point to learn all I can of him. But we can discuss that later. First though, I suggest you take a chair and try to re-gather your wits. Oh, and help yourself to the wine. Whatever its other faults, this tavern possesses a surprisingly inoffensive cellar.'

Sitting down warily to face the daemon, Gunther picked up the bottle, only to pause halfway through filling his glass at the thought of a sudden, fearful premonition.

'You may drink freely, my friend,' the daemon said, seeming to read his thoughts again. 'Even if I had the slightest intention of killing you tonight, I need hardly resort to anything so tiresome as poison.'

Feeling vaguely embarrassed, Gunther finished filling the glass, then took a healthy draught of what soon proved to be an agreeable, if not quite vintage, red Bordeleaux. Despite his best efforts to hide it, he was sure his nervousness was entirely obvious to the creature before him. Just as it was similarly obvious to him that the daemon's pleasant appearance – the easy charm, handsome good looks and fashionable frills and ribbons of his clothing – were no more than a mask. No matter how convivial his host, Gunther did not for a minute doubt that he was in presence of an ancient evil. With that thought there came a rising tide of barely suppressed panic as suddenly he was struck by the sheer enormity of what he had come here to do tonight. But this was no time for second thoughts. For better or worse, he had set himself on this course willingly. And even here, in the face of damnation, he would not waver.

'Now, where were we?' the daemon mused, apparently convinced Gunther had settled himself enough to begin their business. 'Ah yes. I was commenting on how well I know you. And I do know you, Gunther, better than anyone else in the world, I'd wager. For example, unlike your mercantile peers, I know you have spent the last twenty years of your life obtaining and studying a wide variety of magical, alchemical and heretical texts. You have read the works of Van Hal, von Juntz, Krischan Donn, Ralfs, even the tedious prose of the Rat-men-obsessed Leiber. And all of it with the aim of achieving a single burning ambition. But it was only recently, after a visit to Marienburg's Unseen Library to read Hollseher's *Liber Malefic*, that you finally discovered a means by which to achieve your aim. Now, you have come here to me in the hope that I can give you what your books could not. Well, happily, I can help you, Gunther. But there are rules in these matters. And, if you want me to grant your wish, you must first speak the words of it aloud.'

It was true, all of it. But, before he moved his mouth to frame the words, Gunther reminded himself he must be wary. It went without saying that the daemon would try to trick him. But in the end, the selling of a man's soul was a business matter like any other. If he was to get what he wanted in return, Gunther must simply be careful when it came to negotiating the contract.

'I want you to make it so that I will not age and will live forever,' Gunther said.

For a moment, the daemon stared at him in amusement, the smile at the corner of his lips growing several notches wider. In the days leading up to the meeting Gunther had practised this scene in his mind many times, but despite all those rehearsals he had never expected to hear the answer Samael gave him now.

'No,' the daemon said with a smile.

Gunther sat open-mouthed, gaping at the smug daemon in disbelief. He had come to sell his soul – how could Samael refuse him?

'You must try and see it from my point of view, Gunther,' Samael said, fingers pressed together in a curiously human gesture. 'What use is it, after all, for a daemon to be pledged the soul of a man who is going to live forever? How would I ever collect the debt? No, I am sorry, my friend, but I am afraid I must reject your proposal.'

Stunned, Gunther sat in uneasy and despairing silence. Twenty years, he thought. Twenty years, and I am no closer to my objective.

'Of course, I do have a counter-proposal,' the daemon said mildly, as though unaware of the effect his words had on Gunther's desperate heart. 'Absolute immortality may be out of the question. But there seems no reason I couldn't keep you from aging and grant you longevity enough to extend your life beyond the normal span of man. And in return all I ask for – aside from your soul, of course – is that you perform a limited number of tasks on my behalf. Shall we say seven? Give me seven boons, Gunther, and I will give you a part of your wish at least.'

'Seven boons?' Gunther said, still barely able to comprehend how quickly his horizons had been diminished. 'And who is to decide what the nature of these boons will be?'

'I will,' the daemon replied. 'I promise you they will all be well within the scope of your abilities. Nor would I insult your intelligence by demanding that you give me all seven boons at once. You need only perform one boon now and I will stop you from aging and guarantee you another twenty years of life. Then, when those twenty years are done, you will perform a second boon in return for another twenty years, and so on, until all the boons are done. Think of it, Gunther, perform all seven boons and you can have another one hundred and forty years of life without aging a single day. Naturally, our agreement would not extend to protecting you from disease or violent death – even my powers are not limitless in that regard. But really, I think I am being fair enough already. As I'm sure you'll agree, one-hundred-and-forty years is a long time for a daemon to wait to claim his due.'

Letting his words hang in the air a moment, the daemon sipped his wine as Gunther wrestled with a thousand silent thoughts and fears. Then, seeing Gunther's discomfort, the daemon leaned forward once more with the smile of a huntsman who knows his trap is sprung.

'Of course,' he said, 'if you do not like the terms of my offer, you can always say no.'

He had said yes, of course. Granted, he had bargained for better terms, ultimately persuading Samael to extend the period of guaranteed longevity between each boon to twenty-five years. But, beyond that small concession, he had had little choice but to accept the daemon's terms. In the end, the daemon Samael had every cause to be smug; his was the only bargain on the table.

Now, as he hurried to complete the preparations for his ritual in the shell of the ruined inn where he had met Samael all those years ago, Gunther found his thoughts turning towards the six boons he had completed on the daemon's behalf already. Some had been relatively straightforward: arranging the disgrace and murder of a high-ranking nobleman, or the theft of a holy relic – a cup – from the Temple of Sigmar the Merciful in Stirland. Others had been both more complicated and time-consuming. Take the six years he had spent working as a humble lay gardener in the grounds of a temple of Shallya in Ostermark, corrupting the priestesses and their novitiates one-by-one until he had turned them all to the worship of Slaanesh. He could still remember the look of outrage on the mother superior's face turning to delight when she had finally yielded. And, while Samael's motives in requesting some of the boons had been obvious at once, others had been more obscure, only becoming clearer with time. Take the sixth boon for example, when he had been called upon to ensure the progression of a young Sigmarite cleric called Johann Esmer. But, no matter how strange or onerous the tasks he had been called upon to perform, he had completed them regardless. And with each completed boon Samael had kept his own side of their bargain: Gunther had not aged a day in one-hundred-and-fifty years.

Tonight though, the seventh boon was due.

Two days earlier, a messenger had arrived bearing Samael's instructions to meet him here in the Six Crowns at midnight. But, for all the successes of their arrangement thus far, Gunther was not so foolish a man as to trust a daemon to his word. He had always known Samael would try to cheat him. And Gunther had seen the loophole in their bargain a century and a half earlier when Samael told him he would not be protected against disease or violent death. Once the seventh boon was done and his value was at an end, Gunther fully expected the daemon to kill him. Why should Samael be willing to wait another twenty-five years for his soul after all, when it was within his power to kill him and take it at once? There could be no doubt, the daemon was going to try and cheat him.

Unless, of course, Gunther cheated the daemon first.

From the very beginning he had been playing his own double game, only agreeing to Samael's terms to give him the time he needed to find a method by which to cheat the daemon of his due so that he might live forever. And now, after one hundred and fifty years of planning and preparation, the final movements of that game were almost upon him. The pieces were all in place. Soon, Gunther would play his devil's gambit.

There was only one last thing.

Turning towards the corner of the room, Gunther saw the boy lying slumped and asleep on the floor, surrounded by the spilled contents of the bag he had given him earlier. Seeing the sedative he had put in the sweets had done its work, Gunther allowed himself the luxury of another moment of satisfaction.

He really had thought of everything.

* * *

BY THE TIME the first peals sounded from the harbourmaster's bell calling midnight, all the preparations were in place. At the five corners of the pentagram the man-tallow candles had been lit, thin plumes of acrid smoke rising to join the sickly-sweet haze of incense hanging above them. At its centre, a section of the counter of the ruined bar had been set out as a makeshift altar with the unconscious boy bound and spread-eagled on top of it. Beside it, Gunther stood stoking a burning brazier, chanting the words of the final ritual.

Then, as the bell pealed its last, he heard the door to the room open and saw the blond-haired figure of Samael arrive with cloak flowing behind him in a gentlemanly flourish.

Careful not to allow his eyes to meet the daemon's gaze, Gunther continued his chant. From the corner of his eye he saw Samael advancing towards him. Coming to the binding circle the daemon stopped, raising his hand to press palm-outwards on the invisible barrier before him, testing its power.

'A binding circle? Impressive, Gunther, if ultimately pointless. After all, you can hardly stay within your circle forever, can you?' Then, hearing the sound of lapping water, the daemon finally looked behind him.

The trap had been surprisingly easy to build. Set to be triggered by a tripwire when the door to the room swung shut, a hidden mechanism had caused a gourd to tip, releasing a steady flow of water which, even now, fed a shallow circular channel encompassing the entire outer circumference of the room. Of course, the real power of the trap lay not in channel, but in the nature of the water that flowed through it.

'Holy water?' the daemon said, eyebrows raised in sardonic amusement. 'It seems I am caught in the space between two impenetrable circles. Really, Gunther, you are full of surprises tonight. But tell me: now you have me where you want me, what do you intend to do with me next?'

On top of the counter, close to his right hand, one of Gunther's pistols lay primed and powdered, needing only a bullet to give it lethal force. And, glowing white-hot within the flames of the brazier, the bullet was almost ready.

It had taken fifty years spent in the study of forbidden texts to learn how Samael's bargains worked. Fifty years, in which he had slowly come to understand that when they had entered into their contract, Samael had lent him a tiny fragment of his own daemonic essence. A fragment so small that Samael would never miss it, but still powerful enough to stop Gunther from aging. Hence the time limit built into their bargain – as small as that fragment was, the daemon was not about to give up a part of himself forever. But at the same time,

Gunther had learned this essence would not naturally flow back to Samael. It had to be taken.

And, if Gunther could kill Samael first, he could keep it forever.

Of course, killing a daemon was no easy thing. But, gifted with great wealth and a century in which to search for the answer, Gunther had finally discovered a method. In the brazier before him was a bullet forged from meteoric iron and covered in sigils which Gunther had paid a down-on-his-luck dwarf craftsman a small fortune to create. One of dozens of savants Gunther had paid to help him over the years without any of them ever knowing the true nature of his project. All of them working unknowingly towards the creation of a bullet ensorcelled to act as a bane to daemon flesh.

A bullet to kill a daemon.

Taking a pair of tongs, Gunther retrieved the glowing bullet from the fire and slotted it into the notch set in the side of the trocar. Even now, with his own life in the balance, he could not be sure whether it was possible to kill a creature like Samael forever. At the very least though, killing the daemon here and now would banish him back to the daemon realms for a thousand years – more than long enough for Gunther to find a more permanent solution. But before the bullet could be used, the ritual demanded that it be tempered in the heart's-blood of a sacrificial victim. As to the nature of this victim, the terms of the ritual were very precise: Only someone possessed of a perfect and utter purity would do.

Abruptly, eyelids fluttering, the boy on the altar began to stir. But Gunther had come too far and risked too much to give in to squeamishness now. Besides, whether the boy died asleep or awake hardly mattered. Lifting the trocar above his head, Gunther stepped forward to complete the sacrifice. Only to see the boy's features suddenly seem to shift and blur, growing bigger. In an instant the boy was gone.

Staring in amazement at the alabaster-skinned female figure that had replaced him, Gunther found himself strangely attracted to the swelling curve of her hips, the sharp-toothed seductiveness of her smile and the jagged perfection of her horns. Then, as the writhing goddess before him lashed out with a scythe-like claw, Gunther found the growing warmth of his desire displaced by a more primal sensation.

Pain.

AFTERWARDS, WATCHING THE daemonette flaying the flesh from Gunther's dead bones, Samael found himself wondering briefly if he should punish her for her excesses. He had so wanted to see that last look of despair in the man's eyes when he realised his long life was finally over and torment awaited him. But, lost in her enjoyment, the daemonette had killed him too quickly. Though, on balance, Samael decided to let the matter pass – it must have been difficult for her, after all, to have had to walk beside the mortal all night without tearing him apart. And, besides, the daemonette's purpose here was not yet done.

In her abandon, the daemonette had knocked over one of the pentagram's candles, breaching the binding circle. Approaching the altar, Samael saw the trocar lying on the floor where Gunther had dropped it and he stooped to pick it up. Inside, the bullet was still hot, the magical energies released by Gunther's ritual still waiting latent within it.

Turning towards the daemonette, Samael saw her pause in her mutilations to lick the blood, cat-like, from her talon. Looking into the amber irises of her eyes, Samael saw a perfect and utter purity, untainted by conscience or thoughts of compassion. Then, savouring that thought for a moment, he took the trocar and stabbed her in the chest.

'Why?' the daemonette asked him in Darktongue, her accent like the mewling of scalded cats.

'Because it would be a shame to let Gunther's work go to waste,' he told her, pushing the blade deeper into her heart. 'Especially when I spent so very long covertly guiding that dull-witted mortal on his quest.'

Strength fading, her heart's-blood ichor flowing down the tube of the trocar to temper the bullet inside it, the daemonette looked at him in incomprehension. Then, the memories of thousands of years' worth of sensations dying with her, her heart grew still.

Letting her body fall as he pulled the trocar from it, Samael was pleased to feel the stirring of painful energies emanating from within the bullet. In the end, the whole affair had come to a most satisfactory conclusion. After one-hundred-and-fifty years, the ritual – and the seventh boon – had finally been completed. The bullet was ready now. A bullet to kill a daemon.

One could never know when a thing like that might prove useful.

RATTENKRIEG

Robert Earl

THE SCRATCHING HAD started again. Freda lay huddled in the darkness, cold sweat gluing her nightdress to her trembling body. In the light of the day it was a pretty thing, this nightdress. She'd chosen it because of the rabbit pattern sewn into the hem. Tonight, with the pattern hidden by darkness, it felt like a shroud.

Her knuckles were already bruised, but she carried on gnawing at them anyway, like a rat with a bone. Even when her sharp, little teeth tore through the skin and her mouth filled with the bitter, hot, copper taste of blood, she couldn't stop.

Tonight there were more things to worry about than cuts and bruises. Horrible things.

Beneath the weight of her terror, Freda struggled to remember the words of a prayer, any prayer that might make the scratching stop. But she struggled in vain. All she could think of was the thing in the cupboard and how far away her father was.

Then the sound stopped. The pause lasted for a second, then a dozen, and then a dozen more. Freda held her breath, willing the silence to last. At length she felt the first tiny flicker of relief and took her fist out of her mouth. Slowly, with as much courage as a warrior entering a dragon's lair, she raised her head from beneath the covers and peered towards the cupboard.

A loud impact banged against its doors.

With a shriek, Freda leapt from her bed, ran from the room and raced down the stairs. Her feet pounded on the floorboards, like a drummer sounding the retreat, the noise of her flight making her run all the faster.

'Daddy!' she screamed, as she fled down the short hall to his study, the rabbits on her nightdress snapping about her heels.

'Daddy!' She flung open the heavy wooden door and burst inside. Magretta, the house maid, sprang up from her place on Freda's father's knee, her cheeks burning. The old man himself also seemed a little flushed.

But Freda didn't care if they both had the flu. She just wanted to be with her daddy. With a leap she flung herself into his arms.

'What is it?' he asked, his tone a kaleidoscope of embarrassment, anger and concern. 'Nightmares?' He stroked her hair, feeling the sweat that had turned her beautiful mane of golden hair into dank rats' tails.

'You're trembling,' he said.

'It was the thing in the cupboard again,' she whined, clinging to him. He exchanged a glance with Magretta and shrugged.

'Oh,' her father said, and sighed. 'Well, let's go and have a look, then.'

'No!'

'Yes. It's just your imagination.'

Taking the lantern from the table, he swung her onto his hip and carried her back upstairs. He grimaced a little at her weight. She seemed to be getting bigger by the day now, and he was no longer a young man. But Freda was oblivious to the effort the climb cost him. She stared into the shadows ahead, her expression as grim as a convict climbing the gallows.

'Look,' her father said, lifting the lantern to chase the shadows back behind the tumbled mess of her bed. 'No monsters.'

'The cupboard,' she whispered, edging around behind him.

With a grunt, he lowered her to the floor and walked over to the twin mahogany doors. He opened them with a theatrical flourish. Inside a wall of hanging clothes hid the camphor wood rear of the cupboard, and for a moment he thought about pulling them aside and pretending to find something behind them. But, with the suspicion that such a joke might backfire and the knowledge that Magretta was waiting for him downstairs, he decided against it.

'There, you see?' he said. 'Just clothes. Very pretty clothes for a very pretty girl. And perhaps some mice, but you're too big to be scared of little mice, aren't you?'

Freda nodded doubtfully.

'Good girl. Now, hop into bed. I'll leave the lamp and send Magretta up to check on you later.'

'Why not now?'

'Because she's, ah, busy.'

With a little sigh, Freda climbed back into her bed. At least he was leaving her the light. Daddy lent down and kissed her on the forehead, his whiskers tickling her skin, then he turned and left her, closing the door behind him as she pulled the blankets up to her chin.

The thing in the cupboard waited until he had returned to his study before it started scratching again. It was soft but insistent, like the throbbing of a rotten tooth, but this time she fought against the fear. The lamp helped. Even though Daddy had turned it down it still bathed the room in a warm light that somehow seemed to hold the noise at bay.

'It's just mice,' she whispered to herself as the scratching was replaced by a series of sharp, crunching sounds.

'Shoo!' she said loudly. To her immense relief, the noises stopped.

'You're just mice,' she told the cupboard triumphantly. She raised her head farther up out of the eiderdown, like an archer peeing over a castle wall. The sweet, glorious silence remained unbroken and a sense of triumph began to steal over her.

For a while she savoured her triumph and drifted off towards sleep. It was almost a shame that she had frightened the mice away. They were funny and sweet. And she always impressed daddy by being such a brave girl when they appeared. Not like silly Margetta who screamed and jumped onto chairs. Maybe tomorrow night she would leave out some cheese and see if…

The cupboard door swung silently open. Freda stopped breathing.

'Daddy must have left the latch off,' she told herself. 'He must have.'

But before she could finish the thought, the monsters rushed out. There weren't just one of them but two, four, a dozen. They swarmed over Freda in a single great mass, their filthy, black hair scratching her smooth skin, their jagged claws gripping her arms and legs like sprung steel rat traps. Freda, almost insane with terror, opened her mouth to scream, to vomit out this paralyzing horror, but a slimy paw thrust itself into her mouth. She gagged at the taste of the rotten skin and was choking as they bound her with thongs of rough leather.

And all the while, the lamp burned upon the table, it's light still and even. The monsters had stirred no more breeze than they had noise. Their tails thrashed excitedly above their writhing bodies like scaly whips.

Within seconds their work was done and they left as noiselessly as they had arrived, slipping through the hole they had so painstakingly chewed through the back of Freda's cupboard.

So it was, that when Magretta came to check on her a few hours later, all that remained of the little girl was a torn scrap of her nightdress: an embroidered rabbit torn in two.

* * *

THE SHRINE WAS so old that it looked more like a thing grown than a thing built. Centuries of winter storms and harvest suns had rounded off the sharp edges of its masonry, leaving its granite bulk as smooth and featureless as a river washed boulder.

The centuries had blanketed the shrine with ivy, the greenery growing as thick as an old man's beard. Within its rustling depths were many families of birds, the creatures living out their entire span amongst the foliage. In ages past, some of the shrine's keepers had scoured the ivy from the walls because of them. Perhaps they had feared that those whom they were sworn to protect might be disturbed by the constant irreverence of the birdsong.

But the present incumbent had no such delusions. The dead, he knew, were dead. It would take more than a few chattering sparrows to disturb their sleep.

Besides, he liked to watch the birds flitting about the graveyard. Some of them had even grown enough trust to perch on his hunched shoulders as he worked. They'd watch with cocked heads as he chopped wood, drew water, scythed down the grass that poked up like green fingers from between the graves that huddled around the shrine.

And they did huddle, these graves, clustering around the ancient building like lambs around an ewe, nervous lambs that could smell the scent of a wolf. It was a fanciful notion, but the shrine's keeper knew it to be an accurate one. The black depths of the forest that lay beyond his walls were alive with those who sought to enslave the dead. Kings and citadels had fallen beneath the onslaught of these abominations. Armies had been slaughtered. Great walls crumbled to dust.

Yet where they had fallen the shrine had stood, the neatly trimmed hedges that enclosed it remaining inviolate.

Morr, after all, was a powerful god.

The shrine's keeper smiled contentedly at the thought and decided that he'd worked enough for one day. He stood up, pressed his bony thumbs into the knots that had formed in his back and returned to his chamber. There he swapped his scythe for a jug of water, a crust of bread and a handful of small, wrinkled apples.

He sat on one of the gravestones as he ate and watched the sun setting over the forest. He enjoyed the sight as he munched his way through the fruit and scattered his bread to the birds that had flocked to his side. In the light of the setting sun their plumage shone and their shadows were dagger sharp. The priest found himself smiling again.

Despite the pain and the suffering, this world was a beautiful place. It was understandable that some men clung to it in defiance of their preordained span. Unforgivable, but understandable.

With a sigh, the old man glanced down at the liver spots on the back of his hands, the mottled skin there as creased as last month's apples.

'It won't be long before Morr greets me,' he told one of his fluttering friends. As if in silent confirmation, the sun dipped below the horizon and the breeze turned chilly.

As day turned to night, the priest dispersed the last of his bread and hobbled back to the shrine.

HE'D BEEN DREAMING of wide, open grassland, an ocean of green, above which clouds as big as galleys sailed lazily past. In the distance, an old limestone wall stretched across the horizon. Sun-gilded lichen covered every inch of it, except for the single oak door. As he approached, the wood started to shake with the impact of a hard knocking. The sound was as loud as thunder and as relentless as a funeral bell.

It was also absolutely terrifying.

All the same, the keeper ground his teeth together and carried on marching towards the shaking door. A second later he was stood in front of it. His fingers closed around the handle and he pulled, swinging it effortlessly open to reveal...

With a suffocated scream the old man sat bolt upright on his cot, his skin washed with sweat and his bony chest heaving as he gasped for air.

Wide eyed in the darkness of his chamber, he ran his fingertips against the rough stone of the wall. He pulled the covers back and swung his feet onto the floor. The tiles were cold, cold enough to send a welcome chill of reality through his befuddled thoughts.

With a long, shuddering breath, he shook off the last scraps of the dream and ran a trembling hand across the damp skin of his scalp.

Although the dream had gone, the knocking continued. For a moment the priest sat and listened to it, as it rattled against his door with a desperate, knuckle scraping urgency. There was a mute terror in the sound, as though the visitor was living in a nightmare of his own and for a split second the shrine's keeper considered ignoring the summons. But he extinguished that traitorous thought as soon as it appeared. Above all things, he was a priest of Morr. It was his duty to make sure that the dying didn't slip away unshriven, and after sixty years of service his duty was as much a part of him as his bones.

Another volley of impacts rang out. Clenching his jaw, the keeper got painfully to his feet and stumbled blindly over towards the cell's ancient fireplace.

'Have a second's patience,' he called out to his unwelcome guest as he knelt down, knees popping, in front of the fire's charred remains. 'I'm making light.'

The knocking paused for a moment. Then it started again with a renewed urgency.

'Wait,' the priest snapped, then drew in a deep breath and blew. Ash flurried up into the darkness like grey snow, revealing glowing embers beneath. 'I'm coming.'

The priest, ignoring a sudden fit of dizziness, took another breath and blew again. This time a tiny flame burst into life amongst the fire's remains. After the darkness of the unlit cell, the light was painfully bright and the priest wiped a tear from his eye as he fed the fire with tinder.

Only when the fireplace was once more crackling did he turn to the door. Suppressing an edgy sense of déjà vu, he made himself walk over to it and lifted the bar.

He closed his fingers around the latch and pulled, swinging it effortlessly open to reveal…

Without a word of warning the door was slammed backwards in a rush of movement and cold night air. Even as the tortured hinges squeaked in protest, a huge figure, shapeless and shadowed in the flaring firelight, burst into the room. The guttering flame revealed it to be a hideous confusion of feathers, and furs and wild, staring eyes.

The shrine's keeper moved with a speed that would have amazed his parishioners. Leaping back as easily as a man half his age, he seized the scythe from its place in the corner. Hefting its bulk upon his bony hip he turned, ready to throw his weight beneath the sweep of the blade. But before he could, the apparition swept the bedraggled mass of felt and feathers off of its head and bowed stiffly, chin to chest in the northern manner.

The priest recovered his wits quickly as he studied the man who stood before him. 'Come in,' he said, his voice level with a soothing calm that he'd practiced on generations of grieving relatives. 'Take a seat.'

His guest watched him return the scythe to its corner. Beneath the filth encrusted mop of his hair and the singed remains of his beard, his face was deathly pale and hard with suspicion. Only when satisfied that the priest wasn't going to attack him did he look away, his eyes flitting about the bare walls of the cell, as though he expected them to spring open in some trap.

'Here, take a seat by the fire,' the priest repeated, hastening to bar the door against the quickening wind. But when he turned around, the man was still in the centre of the room, sniffing the air suspiciously.

The priest sniffed too and immediately wished that he hadn't. The filth that stained his guest's rags also greased the air with a foul, sickly sweet stench. The odour had great intensity and reminded the old man of some of his riper charges.

None but a lunatic could live with such an odour, the priest decided unhappily. Then, as cautious as a man testing the heat of a stove, he placed a hand on the madman's shoulder and steered him towards a stool.

'We'll take a drink,' he said soothingly. 'Then you can tell me what brings you here.'

After a moment's hesitation, the foul smelling stranger grunted his agreement and slung something from his back. At first the priest had taken it to be a beggar's bedroll, but now he could see that it was a weapon.

At least he assumed that it was a weapon. What else could it be? The great polished lump of stained timber that served as a stock looked to belong to a crossbow, its smooth curves designed to rest easily against a man's shoulder. On the top of this familiar shape, though, taking the place of the crossbows arms, there was nothing but a simple barrel of blue steel. As long and as thick as a man's thigh it glinted dangerously in the firelight, its muzzle flared open in a toothless snarl.

It had a strange smell, too. An acrid, sulphur smell that was even sharp enough to cut through the rank stench of its owner.

'Here,' the priest said, pulling the threadbare blanket from his cot and throwing it to his guest. 'Sit you down.'

'Thanks,' he muttered, his accent harsh and guttural. 'And why not, hey? Why not be comfortable for the last few hours?'

'Why not, indeed?' the priest agreed, studiously ignoring the emotion in his guest's voice. At least the man was talking.

Deciding to take the risk of turning his back on him, he went to rummage in the cell's single cupboard, listening to the squeak of his stool beneath the stranger's weight all the while.

'Ha! Here it is.' A smile eased the spare lines of the old man's face as he produced a fat bottle of glazed clay and two pots. He poured out two generous measures, passed one across to his guest and took a seat.

'Drink,' he said.

Again the man grunted his thanks. He drained the cup in one deep draught, lowered it and peered into the dregs that remained. Gradually, as if in response to something he'd seen there, a glistening tear slid down a pale scar and disappeared into the bristles of his moustache.

'Give me your pot,' the priest said. He poured another measure and waited until his guest took it. 'You did well to survive the trap.'

For a split second the stranger froze, his drink held halfway to his lips. Then, in an explosion of movement that sent his stool spinning away and the cup rolling across the table he was on his feet, a dagger sprouting downwards from his left fist.

'What do you know about it?' he snarled, baring strong yellow teeth as he edged forward.

The priest slowed his breathing, unclenched his fists. For a second he watched the patterns the fire made in the razor sharp steel that quivered beneath his chin. He forced himself to look away, to look instead into the crazed eyes of his tormentor.

A lunatic, a beast at bay, he thought, not without a touch of pity.

'I know only what I see,' he said, marshalling his words as carefully as a surgeon would his tools. 'With those weapons and those scars you'd find it hard to pass for a civilian. Your obviously a gentleman of fortune. You're garb's worth more gold than I see in a year.'

'Perhaps. But...'

'And you've recently been set upon,' the priest hurriedly continued. 'That much is obvious. A man whose bearing and profession speaks of a proud nature wandering the night dressed in those rags? No. I'll wager that two days ago those tatters were good enough to wear in any court.'

The soldier lowered his knife uncertainly as his host pressed home his advantage.

'As for the trap, well, what bandit would run into the jaws of that weapon of yours? It must have been a trap. Anyway, there have been no battles hereabouts of late.'

'Haven't there?' the man asked contemptuously.

Then, as suddenly as it had come, the mad energy deserted him. The rage bled away from his features, leaving in its place a terrible exhaustion. Sheathing his dagger, the man recovered his stool and sat back down with a sigh.

'My apologies,' he muttered half-heartedly, and shrugged.

'Accepted,' the priest nodded. He recovered his guest's pot and refilled it. 'Why don't you tell me your name?'

'Otto van Delft,' he said, a trace of pride straightening his back. The priest wasn't surprised to find that he had one of Karl Franz's subjects on his hands. That would explain his manners.

'And what brings you to the shrine?' he asked warily. 'You're healthy, strong. What do you want of Morr?'

'I'll tell you,' Otto said.

He peered into the depths of the fire, the flames burnishing his grimy features with a dozen shades of light and darkness. For a while he was silent, listening to the crackle of wood settling in the fireplace and the muted complaints of the rising wind that now lay siege outside.

Finally he took a deep drink and began. 'What do you know of the ratvolk?'

'Ratvolk?' 'Yes, the ratvolk. The skaven.' Otto turned his attention from the fire to the priest and saw him shiver, a reflex that had nothing to do with the draft that slunk around the stone of the old walls.

'So you do know of them.' The soldier smiled grimly. 'Of course you do. Everyone does.'

The priest merely nodded and poured another measure from the jug. This time it was for himself.

'Tell me everything,' he said, and took a drink.

'I have been hunting the vermin all my life. In sewers, swamps, forests. In catacombs of brick and living stone, in lands of fire and ice and skin rotting dampness. And why? Because...'

Otto paused, his brows meeting in sudden suspicion as he studied his host. The priest's slight nod seemed to reassure him.

'Because,' he continued heavily, 'they're part of me, part of all of us. They're the evil that we try to hold at bay, with law and discipline. And I hate them.'

A log, settling in the fireplace, snapped open in a shower of sparks. The two men watched the sudden flare of light for a moment. Only when it had died down did Otto continue.

'I have a reputation. I am a – what did you call it? – a gentleman of fortune. Yes. And like a thousand other gentlemen of fortune, I haggle like a whore for the best price, then throw the money away on ale and women. But unlike them,' he said, leaning forward with a sudden intensity, 'I do what I'm paid for. I keep the battle moving forward. Believe me, priest, that's no easy thing.'

The older man nodded.

'Reputation,' the mercenary sneered, injecting a whole world of contempt into the word. As if in further comment he coughed, hawking up a gob of phlegm that he spat with unerring accuracy into the fire. It hissed and sizzled as he continued.

'Reputation is what you need in my business more than in any other. Wealth I have, but I needed more than one man's gold for what I had in mind. There are rumours, you see, rumours of a city in the south, the heartland of the skaven, the womb of their race. I wanted backers. I wanted enough men to sweep down into those swamps and tear out the guts of the enemy.'

Otto, his pupils narrowing into twin pinpricks of fanaticism, spat the words out. 'I needed one more war to make that happen. I came so close. Ever heard of Magdeburg?'

'Yes,' the priest said. 'I knew a merchant from there. He made a contribution to the shrine.'

'He wasn't called Gottlieb, was he?'

'No. Why?'

'Gottlieb was the man who hired me. He was the mayor of Magdeburg. Poor bastard.'

Once more Otto drained his pot, once more his host refilled it. This spirit, White Fire the donor had called it, was proving to be very effective at loosening tongues.

'Forty crowns a week,' the mercenary said, 'plus another fifty for a pelt. I let the lads keep the pelt money. That's always the best way. Krinvaller skimmed a little off the top, of course, but not too much.' The mercenary snorted. 'Krinvaller! What an idiot. Still, I liked him. Everyone did. He'd made a great watch captain, lazy and kind hearted. Then Gottlieb launched the rattenkrieg and turned him from a good watch captain into a terrible colonel.'

'The rattenkrieg,' the priest ventured uncertainly, 'is a war against the skaven?'

'That's it. Gottlieb's daughter was taken, you see. She was a pretty girl, by all accounts, apart from a strawberry birthmark on her cheek. Not that that matters. A man's child is his child and always beautiful to him. When she began to wail late one night about things hiding inside her closet, Gottlieb just thought she was having nightmares. Then, one morning… well, there was nothing left of her, just crumpled sheets and a torn scrap of nightdress. The skaven had gnawed their way from the sewers, up between the walls and through the back of her wardrobe. Their tracks were everywhere in the room.'

Van Delft paused, looked reflectively into the fire.

'So Gottlieb went to war. He was winning it, too, even before I got there. I should have known something was wrong. A halfwit doesn't lead a couple of dozen vagabonds down into the deeps and come back victorious. He doesn't come back at all.'

'Oh, gods, I should have known.' Van Delft; face crumpled into a mask of pain and he smacked his palm against his forehead. 'I should have known.'

The priest, his own features carefully composed, wondered if the mercenary was going to break down altogether. But after a few tense moments, he took a long, deep shuddering breath, pulled his hands reluctantly from his face and continued.

'The information we were getting was very good. Before every mission Gottlieb would call us in and give us numbers, deployment, even these maps. Look.' Van Delft reached inside the ruined cloth of his tunic and pulled out a roll of parchments. Even in the uncertain firelight, the wealth of detail remained crystal clear. As well as the multi-coloured inks, which distinguished each tangled strand from its neighbours, each of the cobwebbed lines was beaded with its own peculiar series of dots and dashes. The priest held one up to the flame to admire the workmanship.

'Why are they made of leather?' he asked, rubbing the material between his fingers.

'Because parchment tears.' The mercenary, seized by a sudden fit of shivering, wrapped the blanket tighter across his shoulders. 'I'd never worked with such information before. Usually underground all you have is instinct, smell, hearing. Fear. But with these,' he waved a hand towards the maps, 'we had depths, scale, everything. I should have known.'

'Known what?' the priest blurted out in spite of himself, and immediately regretted his lapse of patience.

His guest noticed the slip and smiled wearily. 'This potcheen of yours seems to be loosening both of our tongues.'

'We'd better take some more then. Give me your pot.' As he poured, he watched his guest's expression harden and guessed that his thoughts were falling back into the depths of the past.

'Ever heard of warpstone?' Otto asked.

The deepening gurgle of a filling cup faltered.

'Yes. When I was a younger man–' he broke off. 'Yes, I've heard of it.'

'You know of its value then?' Otto asked curiously.

'I know of its value to some.'

'So do I. And beneath Magdeburg I saw enough to buy a city. Although no sane man would risk trying to get it.'

'At first,' he continued, 'I thought that the stuff must have been something else, some kind of mould or fungus. I was leading a gang down to a cut-off point when I first saw it, a great twisting seam threading itself through the walls like an artery through a corpse. And that light, that sickly green light! I swear it was pulsing, beating like the heart of some living thing. That light, it made our faces look like...'

He stopped, eyes blank and unseeing, his drink forgotten in his hand.

'It made them look like daemons,' he finished and drained his pot. 'Such wealth was before us. For a moment, a second, I thought that here I'd found my key to the south. Madness of course, the idea of selling the enemy power in order to raise an army against him is insane. Then another thought hit me. Stuck down there, beneath countless tons of rock, with nothing between myself and the darkness except a single flame, I realised what sort of skaven pack must own this territory and just how powerful they must have been. If I'd have had time, I'd have retreated back up and thought things through.'

'You didn't have time?' The priest nudged his guest out of a brief reverie.

'No. That's when the first attack came.'

Wordlessly he held his pot out and wordlessly the priest refilled it.

'It's always the same in the beginning, especially underground. There's always that terrible moment when you realise that you're not imagining things anymore, that what you're hearing is actually real. That's when the air seems to turn to liquid, heavy and tough to breath, even before the stink hits you. The noise is always the same too: the hiss of fur against stone, the scrape of claws, the pattering of feet and the squeals of pain. Even in the seconds before battle those filthy things are snapping and biting at their own kin.'

Van Delft sneered into the depths of the fireplace, his bared teeth gleaming as sharp as a terrier's beneath his moustache. 'They even hate each other.'

This time, when he paused, the priest said nothing and merely sat transfixed.

'The weakest always come first, the slaves and the vanquished. Pathetic creatures these, but crazed with a fear of what's behind more than what is in front. I waited for them to come. I felt fear twisting into terror, felt terror twisting into madness. We waited some more. I thought of the lads behind me and tried to take strength from them. They didn't have it to give, though. All I got was the sound of sobbing and the smell of piss. If their fear hadn't frozen them I've no doubt they would have fled at the first alarm. As it was, they waited until we could see the lice crawling on the enemy. Then I fired Gudrun.'

He reached over to the weapon and ran his fingertips lovingly down from its muzzle to its breech.

'She punched a hole straight through them, stopped the charge with a single smack of blood and shrapnel.'

Van Delft smiled gently and drew the firearm to his chest like a favourite dog. The priest half expected him to pat it.

He did.

'Yes, she cut through them. That's pretty much all I remember. In that battle Sigmar blessed me with the madness.'

The priest, who could well believe it, nodded and said nothing for a long while.

'And was the pack as strong as you feared?'

'No. No, they were nothing. Most of them were crippled with old injuries or disease. The rest were only half grown, or so old that they were toothless. There were even some females. The only one of them that was up to anything was the leader. Now he was something.' The soldier nodded approvingly. 'A great beast, at least as tall as a man, his pelt was almost pure black where it wasn't riven through with scar tissue. And from the tip of his snout to his left ear there was nothing but shiny, pink flesh, studded with a lump of warpstone in the place of his eye. How it flared when we'd cornered him!'

A strange smile lifted the mercenary's moustache. It looked almost nostalgic, as if he were telling the story of nothing more than a boar hunt or a particularly wild party.

'That pelt I took myself. His clan marking – a burning paw – was new to me. I brought him down with nets, put a spear through the arteries in his neck and stood back. Time was I'd have gone in with a knife, but I'm not as young as I was.'

'Taking it easy in your old age,' the priest replied, deadpan.

'Patience wins,' van Delft shrugged, oblivious to the irony. 'I just wished I'd paid heed to him. He must have spent at least five minutes biting at the wire of the mesh, splashing around in his own blood, and all the while shrieking about traitors to the race. I thought he was just trying to curse me, like they do, but…'

Van Delft ran his fingers through his hair and then clutched at his temples. He sighed, the sound barely audible over the distant thrashing of the forest beneath the night winds.

'That was the first of a dozen sweeps. The maps were always right, the numbers were always correct. And all we ever met were the dregs of three different clans. They were sickly things, not the least because they had all been cursed with some sort of fire. It seemed to have swept over them like a plague, leaving the survivors with withered limbs and scorched pelts. I had the idea that they'd pretty much wiped each other out before we'd arrived. I thought I had it all worked out. Then, three nights ago, I realised that I hadn't.'

The bitter snap of his laughter slapped against the stonework, briefly cutting through the distant hiss of the troubled forest. The priest, who had began to guess at the holocaust that had brought his guest here, shifted uneasily in his seat.

'It was supposed to be one of the easiest patrols yet, just a slash and burn against some breeding chambers. I'd decided to let one of the corporals take over command for this one. Gunter, he was called. He was sharp, canny and not afraid to use his authority, but not reveling in it either. He'd have made a good leader.'

Van Delft's eyebrows furrowed into a deep ravine of sadness. The priest found himself wondering if the mercenary had ever had a family, children of his own. He supposed not.

'Gunter was leading the column to a rendezvous point,' he continued. 'We were dispersed into small groups. It's tough to stop people bunching up for protection, especially underground. All that fear, all that darkness. But I could see that the lads were making an effort. They knew that Gunter was being tested and they wanted him to succeed. In fact, as soon as I saw that, I knew he had succeeded.'

The soldier looked up and saw the question in his host's eyes.

'I needed to know if they'd work for him. That was the test. That was all we were really down there for. I knew there'd be no sort of fight that night. Thought I knew, anyway.' He shrugged miserably. 'After all we'd swept through most of these catacombs already. The first I knew of what was to befall us was when Krinvaller fell into our midst. We were supposed to be linking up with his party, but he had no men with him now. Nor did he have any weapons and his clothes, all that silk and brocade and gilding that he was so fond of, had been shredded into rags.'

Van Delfts picked absent-mindedly at the ruins of his clothes. 'Hell, at first I didn't even recognise him. I thought he must have been some madman who'd wandered down. It wasn't until he cried out my name that I realised who it was, and even then I wasn't sure. All that bonhomie, that soft arrogance that had flowered in the safety of the light above was gone, bled away by the reality of the deeps. I pitied him, then, a weak man in a terrible place. But before I could reach out to him and reassure him, the enemy struck. The enemy! This time they truly were skaven. Compared to these two, the weak and crippled vermin we'd hunted up until then were nothing.'

'Only two?' the priest asked, uncertainly.

'Yes, only two. And if anything they were even smaller than average, wiry little twists of things. You could see that even beneath the black strips of their camouflage. It didn't matter. They had that energy, you see, that manic sort of power that can gnaw through stone or bend the bars from an asylum window.'

'I'd seen their like a few times before. Usually just a glimpse, a shadow, a chill running down the back of your neck.'

Van Delft lifted the pot to his lips and didn't seem to notice that it was empty. The priest, eyes reflecting the candle light in twin circles of fascination, made no move to refill it.

'Down there, though, they'd thrown off their caution. Desperation had made them drop it, I suppose, the same as they'd dropped everything else that might have slowed them down. The only steel they carried sparkled in their paws. They'd dropped swords, bandoliers, nets, globes, everything. Sigmar alone knows how Krinvaller had made it this far.'

'They hit him a second after he'd appeared. I was close enough to hear the thud of weapons burying themselves between his ribs. He fell to one knee, his face already twisted with pain from the poison, and reached out towards me. He looked so… surprised.'

A log snapped in the stove and the priest's heart leapt. He silently scolded himself and refilled the two pots.

'I pulled back Gudrun's hammer, but the assassins were already gone, quicker than screams from a nightmare. Then I looked down and realised that Krinvaller was still breathing.'

The mercenary's face hardened and he took a drink.

'I almost finished him there and then. The poison the enemy use, it's truly horrible. The first tears of blood were already flowing from his eyes and nose, and the tremors were flopping him around on the cold stone of the floor, like a fish on the quayside. I'd seen it before, I knew how bad it would get. So I bent down and found the sweet spot beneath his jaw with my knife. But before I could strike it home, he spoke.

'It wasn't easy for him. Even in the dimness of the lantern light, I could see the muscles in his neck cramping, and when he spoke you could see the soup of his lungs beginning to gurgle up over his teeth.'

The priest grimaced. He asked a question, as much to take his mind off the image van Delft had conjured up as anything.

'What did he say?'

'He said to tell Gottlieb it had all been in vain. But for Sigmar's sake, don't let him look at the maps. He managed to thrust a roll of the damn things into my hands before the final seizure took him.'

'At first I didn't understand what he meant. Delirium, I thought, or the beginnings of insanity. But then I started to wonder again about the excellence of our information and the detail of our maps. Who'd made them? No human, that was for sure. And who was the "she" Krinvaller had been, talking about? Who else could it have been but the girl whose disappearance had sparked this whole damn war?'

Suddenly van Delft sprang to his feet, kicked back his stool and started to pace the room.

'I should have known!' he cried. 'After so many years of cunning and deceit, a lifetime of traps and stratagems. I thought myself so clever! Yet here I was working for the enemy. That's when the true owners of that terrible domain fell upon us. We'd exterminated the last of their rivals, you see. They'd given us those cursed maps and used us as a weapon against the other clans. And now it was our turn. We were already deep into the catacombs by then. Every few yards the passageways split, tangling across each other like tubes in offal. There were so many conduits, that even at that depth, we could feel a faint, moldy breeze. It brought us the first rumours of our doom, this breeze, a secret, whispering sound started to emerge. It seemed to come from everywhere at once, as soft and insistent as a far off ocean.'

'I remember Gunter looking at me, his eyes bright with terror in the darkness, and I knew that it was time to withdraw. Krinvaller was dead, his patrol annihilated and our plans were betrayed. There was nothing to be gained from throwing our own bodies into the jaws of the enemy too. So I sent Gunter down the line to lead the retreat. But before he'd gone a dozen paces the enemy attacked.

'They spewed out in a great boiling swarm from every passageway, every narrow crevasse, every crack and rat hole that bit into our line. I gave the order to hold, to stand our ground. I think most of the groups heard. Some even obeyed. Most of them just broke and fled. I was beyond caring, by then. In the deeps there are no elegant manoeuvers or set piece formations. No bright uniforms or distant hill tops from which to signal your troops. There is only rage and terror and the will to win.'

Van Delft's teeth ground together beneath a tight smile as he absent-mindedly tested the spring on his gun's hammer. The priest could hardly believe the expression of savage joy that now seemed to mark his companions grimy features, but neither could he mistake it for anything else.

Van Delft was obviously a man who loved his job.

'Gudrun here smashed through the first ragged mob that fell upon us,' he continued, oblivious to the priest's stark appraisal. 'And, with the flare of her muzzle flash still blooming in my eyes, I led a charge into the gap she'd opened for us. I hoped to punch through the trap, then turn and fall on their rear. But this time things weren't so easy. This time, when we'd sliced through the front runners, we found stormvermin.'

The mercenary eased the hammer back down and peered thoughtfully into the fireplace. A gust of wind rattled its way beneath the door and sent a brief plume of flames flaring upwards.

'Black they were, and massive. They had teeth like carpenter's chisels and carried heavy, iron bound spears. The blades were clotted with rust and blood, but the edges were sharp enough. They were too much for my lads. As soon as the first of the beasts leapt into the glow of our lamplight, I felt them break behind me, could almost hear their nerves shattering. I dropped a litter of caltrops and bolted after them, vaulting the dead, kicking away the hands of the dying. Thank Sigmar for those poor bastards. If the skaven hadn't stopped to play with them, I wouldn't be here now.'

Van Delft lifted his pot and took a hefty swig. The priest recognised it as a toast, a tribute to those who'd paid so dearly for their captain's freedom. There was no guilt in the gesture, only a sort of red-eyed celebration.

Morr would have approved.

'There's a real joy to running away. I felt it for the first time as I overtook first one straggler then the next. We were winding blindly through the labyrinth now, recoiling from passageways held by the enemy, cutting through them when we had to. In the haste and the darkness, tripping over the still warm corpses of our comrades or hurtling blindly into sudden, vicious skirmishes, I knew that we were being driven, like sheep to the butcher's. Deeper and deeper we fled, sinking beneath levels not shown on any map. The air became thick and suffocating, so much so that the flames within our lanterns started to choke out. By the time we reached the skaven's slaughterhouse we had only the pulsing green glow of warpstone to guide us.'

'Their slaughterhouse?' the priest asked, leaning forward and pouring them both another drink. He had a feeling they'd need it.

'Yes,' the mercenary muttered, staring for a moment longer into the bright heart of the fire. 'It was a chamber, as round the cathedral at Quierms. And huge, perhaps a quarter-of-a-mile across.

'I recognised it for what it was as soon as we reached it. It was the bones that gave it away. They covered the floor as far as the eye could see, a great crunching carpet of them. There were bats there, too, fluttering around amongst the stalactites. I didn't look at them too closely. The warpstone seemed to have done something to them. Something horrible. The last of the survivors stumbled in behind me, and we started off across the bone yard. But we had nowhere to go. There was only one entrance, and every minute more skaven poured through it, as thick as sewage from a pipe.'

'I called the lads while we were still in range, reloaded Gudrun, and took aim. At that, the ratvolk started to scurry away, the great mass of them opening up before Gudrun's gaze. I thought that it was because of their cowardice, but I was wrong. They weren't fleeing from me. They were fleeing from the things that were approaching from behind them. At first, the monsters hardly seemed to be skaven at all. They seemed too bulky, for one thing. They were wearing masks, too. Great leather things with brass muzzles and round glass eyes.' He took another swig of drink.

'Then, glinting in the warplight, I noticed the tangle of pipes and tubes that the first members of this bizarre procession carried and a new terror of something far worse than death gripped me. I'd seen these weapons before. I remembered the hunched bearers, spines bent beneath great tarred barrels that carried liquid death. I remembered the tubes and steel snouts that splayed outwards from the fuel tanks. And I remembered the burning horror.'

The storyteller shuddered, and snatched for his pot. He drank deeply, then met his host's eyes. Almost defiantly, he said: 'I know that this sounds like madness, priest, but some of the skaven have learned how to torture fire into a horrible new form. Green, it is, and closer to liquid than the honest blaze in your grate. I've seen it leap and flow, surging forward from their infernal contraptions like water from a hose. I've seen it feasting upon skin, then flesh, and then bone. I've seen it melt armour and stone, or slip cunningly between them to seek out the soft flesh beyond. And I've seen men devoured inch by inch, driven insane by the agony.'

'Down there, in the killing pen in which we'd been cornered, I knew that I couldn't face that horror again. I raised Gudrun's cold muzzle to the hollow beneath my chin and tightened my finger on the trigger. The ratvolk saw it and rushed to ignite their weapons. One of them produced a flaring sulphur match from its filthy rags and held it warily in front of the nozzle. I pressed harder on the trigger, but still the hammer remained locked. The first faint mist started to roll from the burnt black muzzle of the fire thrower, and I pulled harder. Still, no matter how I pulled on the trigger, Gudrun wouldn't fire.'

'I glanced down to check the mechanism but then, with a hiss of frying air, the skaven's weapon blossomed into hideous life. A great ball of writhing flame belched out of the machine and rolled towards me, towards us all. But it never arrived. Instead there was a metallic shriek and the fire was sucked back into the very contraption that had given birth to it. By the gods, you should have heard the ratvolk squeal when they saw what was happening. Some of them turned to run but got jammed in the passageway, others tried to swat out the flame with their paws and when they caught light... well, lets just say it was a glorious moment.'

Van Delft smiled at the priest. He seemed not to notice that the old man wasn't smiling back.

'It only lasted for a moment, though,' he continued. 'As the enemy's fire turned upon itself, the cavern erupted into a flash of light and darkness. I can still see it now, when I close my eyes. The thousands of fangs bared in terror, the thousands of widening eyes gleaming as bright as stars, then melting like wax. Then the very earth shifted uneasily, as if disturbed by the foul beasts that crawled within its depths and I heard the first rumble of falling stone. And then... and then nothing.'

Van Delft ground to a halt. The priest studied his haggard features, the pallor of his skin. The two high red blotches on the sharp angles of his cheekbones had little to do with the jug of potcheen they'd drunk. The mercenary looked exhausted, stretched to his limits. But for all that, the madness that had gleamed in his eyes when he'd arrived seemed to have passed. Perhaps the telling of his tale had been the cure he'd needed.

The priest had seen it happen before. Sometimes words could drain the poison from a man's soul, just as leeches could sometimes drain infection from a wound.

The old man poured the last of the potcheen into his guest's pot and sat back. He noticed that the first grey fingers of dawn were creeping between the timbers of his door.

'That was two days ago, maybe more, maybe less,' van Delft shrugged. ' As far as I know, I alone survived the holocaust. And now I am finished. My reputation is in tatters. My dreams died with the corpses I left behind me. There's not a man in this land who'll give me a command after Magdeburg.'

'What will you do?' the priest asked softly.

'I will finish my contract. I still have gold for black powder, snares and nets. I'll go to Magdeburg, eat and sleep for a final few days. Then return to the deeps. Amongst such rivers of warpstone the enemy will never be far from reach.'

'Ah. Now I understand your errand, I think. But you can't be shriven now. I can only offer Morr's blessing to those who near his realm, and you aren't, not really. I can't.'

'No. Not me. Them,' van Delft said, gesturing to the bed where the priest had thrown the maps, 'Them.'

'I don't know about that,' he said, duty warring with caution, as he considered what a grisly treasure hunt that would be. 'Anyway, I thought that you said the bodies were buried beneath...'

The squeak of the opening door distracted the priest from his dilemma and he looked up to see that van Delft had let himself out. Gathering his robe about him, the old man followed him out into the chill grey light of the dawn.

'Where are you going? Stay here and rest, eat.'

Van Delft, who'd already reached the liche gate, stopped and turned back. He looked suddenly younger. Perhaps it was no more than a trick of the morning light.

'No. I have work to do. As do you. But Priest?'

'Aye?'

'Thank you.'

And with that he was gone.

The older man watched him disappear into the mist. Then, with a shiver, he returned to the warmth of his cell.

He threw another log into the stove, straightened the chair and rolled his blankets up. Then he picked up the maps van Delft had left him. The columns and lines that tattooed the soft leather remained clear and untouched by the hell their owner had been through, the leather still supple and well oiled. The priest picked up one at random, smoothing it out on the flat of his thigh. Although the square of its shape was slightly misshapen the texture was smooth, finer than any leather he'd worn before. The priest held it up to the light that spilled in through the doorway, tilting it this way and that against the shadows that still haunted the room.

The detail really was incredible. But now that he looked, there was one flaw. It was a single, strawberry shaped smudge on the corner of one of them. The priest picked up the next one and found another imperfection. This one consisted of an arc of little curled hairs, golden blonde in the gathering sunlight.

The next one was marred by a little indentation in the centre. An inverted button of leather, perhaps as big as his fingertips, the skin within had been compacted into swirls.

The priest ran his thumb over it, wondering what it reminded him off.

A rose, perhaps.

No. No, that wasn't it. It was something less fragile.

Ah yes, of course. It was just like a belly button.

Just like a…

The potcheen soured in his stomach. His hands began to shake. Reluctantly the old man looked back at the unusual leather of these maps.

Looked at the belly button that marked one.

The birthmark that blemished another.

The eyebrows that furred one edge of a third.

And he realised that van Delft had brought him the remains of a body to be shriven, after all.

OUTSIDE, THE MIST gave way to drizzle, which in turn gave way to the warmth of the sun. It warmed the fields and the cemetery and the stones of the shrine. It shone golden on the wet ivy and sent flights of sparrows wheeling up into the sky, born aloft by the joy of their lives.

The priest, the rites of death completed, watched them. They scattered across the blue vault of the sky, tiny little sparks of happiness born up the warm, southerly wind that whispered gently through the greens of the forest below. He took a deep breath of clean air, only slightly scented now with the smoke of the funeral pyre and smiled as the first of the sparrows descended, drawn by the sight of the bread in his hand.

'Yes, little friend,' he told it as it hopped forwards. 'This world is a beautiful place.'

He pursed his lips as it flew away. Then softly, as if he didn't want the bird to hear him, the priest added the single word:

'Sometimes.'

TALES OF
TRAGEDY & DARKNESS

MORMACAR'S LAMENT

Chris Pramas

MORMACAR WAS DROWNING in a sea of agony. Although he longed to surrender to the undertow and let the pain consume him, he continued to struggle towards consciousness. Far off he could hear voices but he couldn't understand what they were saying. He strove to listen, to somehow bring the voices nearer. After a torturous struggle, the sea calmed, the voices became clear and Mormacar opened his eyes.

'He's awake,' a gruff voice said, 'bring him some water.'

Suddenly a cup was at his lips and water coursed down his throat. Although it was warm and stale, the water tasted sweet beyond words. He looked up into the scarred face of an old elf with tangled hair and only one ear, and asked in a cracked voice, 'Where am I?'

The old warrior looked down on him, pity on his face, and whispered, 'I'm sorry, son, but you're in Hag Graef.'

Mormacar groaned and grabbed his throbbing head. He had thought it couldn't get any worse. How wrong he was. Hag Graef was the most notorious of the dark elf slave cities, a city of doom and death where untold prisoners were worked to death and from which no one had ever escaped. He began to wish he had simply been slain in battle, along with the rest of his Shadow Warrior band. The Forsworn, however, missed no opportunity for cruelty, especially against their hated foes from Ulthuan.

Sitting up, Mormacar looked about him. He was in a dark cell of crude stone, its floor covered with rank straw. He shared the cramped room with a dozen other prisoners, many elves like himself, but also some humans and dwarfs. All of his fellow prisoners looked dirty and weary and many bore bruises and welts, plainly gifts from their dark elf tormentors. A stout door closed them in and one sputtering torch added the smell of smoke to the stink of the windowless cell.

'Rest now,' the old elf said. 'You won't get another chance.'

'Thank you, brother,' the Shadow Warrior replied. 'May the Everqueen bless you. I am Mormacar of the Night Stalkers. May I ask your name?'

'Galaher,' the man said tersely.

'Galaher?' Mormacar cried. 'Surely not Galaher Swiftblade?'

'Some used to call me that,' the scowling elf hissed. 'Now I am just Galaher, a slave like you. Leave me be.'

Mormacar was momentarily stunned and could not speak. Galaher Swiftblade alive! The Shadow Warriors had produced few greater heroes and he was long thought dead. Mastering himself, Mormacar reached out and grabbed Galaher's arm. 'Please forgive me if I offended you, Galaher, but everyone on Ulthuan thought you perished on Eltharion's raid on Naggarond. With you alive, our escape is assured.'

Galaher knocked Mormacar's hand from his arm. 'There is no escape from Hag Graef save death,' the old fighter replied, his voice hollow, 'and only fools seek death.'

Mormacar could hardly believe this was the same Galaher from the stories. His shock must have been plain, for Galaher's face softened a little.

'Be strong. Endure,' the elf continued. 'And hope that Tyrion brings an army here and razes this place to the ground.' Galaher looked away, as if he searched his own soul for the dying embers of a long-held dream. 'Any other course is pure foolishness.'

Mormacar stared incredulously at the old elf. 'I can't believe you, of all people, are telling me to submit to the lackeys of the Witch King. Never! I will try to escape from Hag Graef, with or without your help!'

'Then you'll die,' Galaher said simply. Without a further word, the scarred warrior turned his back on Mormacar and crossed the cell.

The young Shadow Warrior lay back, a storm of emotions coursing through him. It pained him to see one of the great heroes of his people dead of spirit, but he could not take Galaher's advice. It was the duty of every elf to escape if captured by their ancient foes. Why couldn't Galaher see that?

Mormacar was so wrapped in thought that he didn't notice another presence until a deep voice jarred him back to his senses. 'The old elf's fire died out long ago. Don't waste your breath on him, elfling.'

Mormacar slowly got to his feet, grimacing in pain as he drew himself up to his full height. 'Who dares to insult Lord Galaher Swiftblade?' he said icily.

Facing him was heavily-muscled human, who stood a head above the defiant elf and whose dirty face was framed by thick braids. 'I am Einar Volundson of Jaederland,' the giant boomed, his Norse accent thick, 'and I insult every member of your gutless race!'

Before Mormacar could reply, one of the other prisoners near the door hissed, 'Be silent, they are coming!'

Everyone in the cell quieted. The Shadow Warrior and the Norseman stared at each other, their antagonism wordless yet potent. Outside, the thump of heavy boots echoed in the hallway. When the pounding advance stopped, the air was rent with the screech of grinding metal as a distant door opened. Then the screaming started.

The Shadow Warrior looked at his cellmates, seeing the terror etched on their faces. He would die, he resolved, before he would live in fear of the dark elves. The heavy footsteps continued, at last stopping in front of their door of the cell. The prisoners looked at each other as keys clattered outside, but if they sought solace than they found none.

The fear in the cramped room was palpable as the heavy portal swung open slowly to reveal three cruel-eyed dark elves. Their leader, a tall woman clad head to toe in black leather, feigned demureness as one of her henchman mopped fresh blood from the front of her leather vest. She could have been beautiful, but her raven hair and striking features were ruined by the twisted sneer on her pale face. Her gloved hands lovingly cradled a long whip, which seemed to writhe with a life of its own under her expert caress.

Her henchmen, two lithe, heavily mailed guardsmen armed with ornate maces and wicked blades, barked in unison, 'On your knees for the Lady Bela, scum!'

The witch elf watched with pleasure as the prisoners fell to their knees. Mormacar hesitated for a moment, but complied when he saw even the cursed Norseman obey.

Lady Bela walked slowly around the small cell, her boots clicking on the rough stone. She stopped in front of Mormacar, who met her stare with one of his own. 'What have we here?' she purred as she stroked Mormacar's face with a slender hand. 'This one is still defiant.'

'One of the new batch, mistress,' offered one of the guards. 'We'll break him soon enough.'

Lady Bela stared at Mormacar, drinking up the hatred in his eyes. His skin crawled as her hand continued to caress his cheek. 'Oh yes, I like this one. He's got spirit.' Entwining her whip around his head, she tugged him closer. 'Tell me, slave, what is your name?'

'You'll get nothing from me, you murdering bitch!' Mormacar shouted and spat in her face.

The dark elf guards rushed forward, maces raised, but Lady Bela waved them away. Still holding the high elf with her whip, she pulled a long pin out of her hair and jabbed Mormacar lightly in the side of his neck. The Shadow Warrior jerked as his body was swept by a burning sensation. Then all feeling went dead and he could not move a muscle. Lady Bela smiled lasciviously and pulled a small blade from her belt. Seeing the blade, Mormacar strove to move, to knock it from her hand, but his body let him down and he remained as still as a statue.

'That's much better, isn't it?' she asked, wiping the saliva off her face. 'I must say I do have a weakness for the lively ones.' Her blade flashed out and slashed Mormacar's chest. 'They provide much better sport than these others, don't you think, Rorga?' Again the blade swept down, this time cutting Mormacar's ear. Her grin widened as she tightened the whip around his neck and pulled him closer still.

'Yes, my lady, great sport indeed,' said one of the dark elf guards, staring meaningfully at the other prisoners. 'Will he be the one then?'

'A fair question, Rorga,' Lady Bela replied, pausing as if in contemplation before turning once again to her motionless prey. 'What do you think, slave?' she asked Mormacar, with a cruel smile. The Shadow Warrior tried to speak, tried to scream out his defiance, but the witch elf's poison was too potent and he could only gurgle in response. Lady Bela laughed. 'Oh yes, slave, I agree completely.'

The cruel witch elf knelt to inspect her handiwork. As the blood welled in the wound on Mormacar's chest, she closed her mouth over it and drank greedily. Then she stood, smacking her lips contentedly. 'It is always refreshing to drink blood that isn't tainted by fear. A rare treat, Rorga, especially here at Hag Graef. I think I'll keep this one awhile.' Lady Bela regarded Mormacar afresh and her eyes lit up with excitement. 'In fact, dear Rorga, I think this noble elf is perfect for my plans. Victory must be assured, after all, and I fear I can't count on Galaher any more.'

'As you wish, mistress. Who's it to be then?'

Lady Bela turned her attention away from the paralysed Shadow Warrior and looked over the rest of the prisoners, tapping her chin with a finger. She stared long at old Galaher. 'You'd like to die now, wouldn't you, sweet Galaher?' The old elf stared vacantly, and remained silent. 'But no. While it is a tempting thought, one cannot be too careful where the gods are concerned.' She turned around. Elf, man, and dwarf shrank under her gaze, all trying to avoid catching her attention. Finally, her eyes settled on a swarthy human whose numerous tattoos bespoke years of piracy. 'That one will do. Take him to Khaine's altar.'

The guards moved forward and seized the frightened prisoner. He began to scream and struggle but a few blows from the dark elves quietened him and he was dragged unconscious from the cell. Lady Bela once again regarded Mormacar, at last unlashing her whip from his unmoving form. Stroking his face as if he were a beloved pet, she purred, 'I'll be seeing you again.' Then she turned and strode from the cell.

The other prisoners stared at Mormacar as if he were already dead.

MORMACAR WORKED IN the mines, as he had every day for the past two weeks. As a pair of overseers looked on, the wretched slaves toiled in the near-dark, scrabbling out ore in the humid tunnels for the anvils of Hag Graef. Those prisoners who dropped from exhaustion and refused to rise had their throats slit by the dark elves. The lesson was not lost on the other prisoners. Nor could they help but notice that the prisoners' ranks grew thinner each day, as more and more of their number were dragged off by the Lady Bela's minions. Death hung like a pall over the squalid prisoners of Hag Graef, and most had become resigned to their fate.

Mormacar refused to give in. His muscles quivered with hatred as he swung his pick into the hard rock, imagining that the unyielding stone was the soft flesh of the Lady Bela. Every day another prisoner was taken to Khaine's altar. At night he saw their faces and heard their screams, but even in his dreams he was powerless to help them.

But now his grim endurance was to prove its worth. While the Lady Bela had been engaged in her deadly work, Mormacar had slowly cut away at one of the support beams at his end of the long tunnel. This passage had been dug in haste, and the supports groaned under the weight of the rock overhead. Now one good blow would smash the weakened support beam and hopefully cause a cave-in.

Mormacar swung his pick into the rock again, but scarcely paid attention to what he was doing. His attention was fixed on the hated overseers, who even now were striding down the tunnel to inspect the work. Out of the corner of his eye he saw the cursed Norseman working across the way and resolved to watch him closely. Humans were never to be trusted. Galaher, despite what he had said back in the cell, Mormacar knew he could trust. The old elf would come through in the end. He could feel it.

When the overseers were scant feet away, Mormacar hefted his pick and smashed it into the weakened support beam. The beam shuddered from the blow and dust fell from the ceiling. Mormacar's heart leapt, but his elation was short lived. The beam held.

The overseers whipped their swords free of their scabbards. One of them spat, 'That was your last mistake, slave,' and strode forward, blade at the ready. Mormacar hefted his pick, determined at least to die a warrior's death.

The other overseer followed his compatriot, but hissed, 'Remember the Lady Bela's orders!'

'Damn that witch!' snapped the first dark elf, his voice hot with bloodlust. 'This wretch is mine!'

The tunnel was eerily quiet. All of the other prisoners had stopped their work, watching the unfolding drama with dumb fascination. Mormacar looked down the tunnel, hoping to see Galaher coming to stand at his side. But the old elf just stood and stared, his pick dangling from his weathered hands. Suddenly the silence was pierced by a echoing crack. Glancing to his right, Mormacar saw that the Norseman had smashed the weakened support beam on the other side of the tunnel. The beam shuddered and fell, loosing a rain of falling rocks.

Mormacar instinctively leapt out of the way, but the dark elves, surprised by the falling debris, were knocked to the ground. Before they could rise, the Norseman and the Shadow Warrior were upon them. Mormacar smashed in the head of one of the dark elves, while Einar swung at the other, pinning him to the floor. The Norseman hurriedly stripped the dying elf of his sword and dagger.

Above them the ceiling groaned menacingly. As uncounted tons of rock shifted and slid, dust and debris fell in streams. Mormacar turned to the stunned prisoners, most of whom still stood at their work stations. 'Get out of here!' he yelled furiously.

That was enough for most of them, who dropped their tools and ran up the tunnel. Mormacar and Einar followed them, grabbing torches from their wall brackets along the way. They ran desperately, hearts pounding, until at last they came to an intersection, where the ramshackle band halted to rest. A dull roar echoed up the tunnel, as more of the ceiling caved in behind them.

The two warriors exchanged looks of grim satisfaction, pleased with their handiwork. Looking around at the other fugitives, the Norseman asked, 'What now, elfling? Is this as far as your plan goes?'

The Shadow Warrior answered without hesitation, 'Now we follow the tunnels down and look for a way out.'

'What do you mean "down"?' Galaher spoke up. 'There's naught down there but cold ones and endless tunnels. The best you can hope for is to starve to death. We must go up and try to find an escape route there.'

'I know it sounds crazy,' Mormacar said, looking around at the desperate throng, 'but I've thought this through. You yourself said there was no way out, Galaher. Now we've all seen dark elf war parties in the tunnels, haven't we? Well where do they go? I think the Forsworn have an underground way through the mountains and I mean to find it. ' His compatriots looked dubious, and shifted uncomfortably in the gloom. 'Above are countless soldiers, thick walls and stout gates,' Mormacar continued, speaking quickly, as if he could feel the crowd slipping from him. 'If you go up, you'll surely die. My way we have a chance.'

Chaos erupted as all of the fugitives began to talk at once. Mormacar tried to break in, tried to calm their fears and make them see sense, but had little chance as the panic-stricken fugitives babbled about what to do.

Eventually, the Norseman lost his temper. 'Shut up, all of you!' he bellowed, his angry words bringing immediate silence. 'You're acting like children. There are only two choices, up or down.' Einar pointed to Mormacar. 'The elf and I go down. Who will join us?'

Mormacar looked at the others, sure that they would see sense. If the oafish Norseman was convinced, surely his elven brethren would join him. He was shocked when not one voice rose up in support.

'I'm sorry, lad,' said Galaher gravely, 'we know what we must do.' The others nodded in agreement and clustered around the old elf.

The Shadow Warrior could scarcely believe his ears. It seemed the former slaves were prisoners still, if only in their minds. He started to speak but Einar cut him off.

'Don't waste your breath, Mormacar,' spat the Norseman in disgust. 'Let's go.' Spinning on his heels, the furious giant stomped down the tunnel.

Mormacar hesitated, hoping even now that someone would join them. None stepped forward. With sadness in his heart, he approached Galaher and pressed a sword into his hand. 'You'll need this, brother,' the Shadow Warrior said quietly. Then he turned away and followed Einar down the passage.

MANY HOURS LATER, the two warriors stood in a large cavern which was dimly illuminated by glowing fungi. Peering intently down the three passages that descended further into darkness, Einar, for once sounding hesitant, asked, 'Well, which way now?'

Mormacar considered each of the tunnels carefully before answering. 'I think we must follow the right-hand path.' He indicated barely discernible marks. 'See all the bootprints there? It is clearly frequently used.'

'Which makes it that much more likely we'll run into some of the dark elf scum,' Einar said, grinning as he ran his fingers up and down his blade.

'True, but remember that we are trying to escape, not to settle the score,' Mormacar said levelly, 'That can wait for another day. Agreed?'

'Cease your prattle, elfling,' Einar scoffed. 'The blood of berserkers runs in my veins. I do what I must.'

'Fine,' the elf said curtly, suppressing an urge to comment on the apparent foolishness of all Norsemen. 'Let's go.'

By Mormacar's estimate, the two warriors were already several leagues underground. After leaving the other prisoners behind, they had hurried down a cavernous tunnel that shot through the bowels of the earth, turning neither right or left. The sounds of the other fugitives had soon been lost as the two warriors continued their descent. Wary of both pursuers and whatever unknown dangers might lie ahead, they had nonetheless set a quick pace. Eventually they had come to this large cavern. Now, as they made their way down the right-hand passage, they were quickly confronted with more choices, as passages split, caverns multiplied, and tracks became ever harder to identify.

Shadow Warrior and Norseman pressed on urgently, stopping only to drink from the few streams and stagnant pools they happened across in their wanderings. Eventually, after what must have been many hours, sheer exhaustion dictated that they stop and rest, and the two collapsed next to a evil smelling pool. They sat in silence, breathing heavily and occasionally drinking the scum-covered water at their side. The weeks of overwork and under-nourishment at the hands of the dark elves were taking their toll. And now that they were deep under the earth, the icy chill made a mockery of their ragged clothing.

'Perhaps the others were right after all,' Mormacar ventured, shivering as he choked back some of the vile water. Suppressing the urge to retch, he sprawled on the ground, his muscles aching with every movement.

The Norseman snorted. 'The others are surely dead already,' he replied. 'At least we are still alive.'

Mormacar accepted this assessment without comment; he knew Einar was right. Sighing, he added, 'I never expected to end my days like this, wandering under the Land of Chill. Curse the day those hellspawn captured me!'

'The day I was caught was a dark one as well,' Einar said softly, his face betraying shame and despair. His voice trailed off. Abruptly, he shook his head as if to clear it, and stared at Mormacar. 'Tell me, how did you come to be in hellish mines of Hag Graef?'

A black look crossed over Mormacar's face as he remembered his last day of true freedom. By his own estimate, it was probably no more than two months since his capture, but it seemed so long ago. 'I was travelling with a band of my brethren, the Night Stalkers of the Shadow Warriors. We've been fighting the thrice-damned dark elves for centuries on Ulthuan and it's a war that never ends.' As Mormacar talked, he held his head high and his exhausted slump became a proud pose. 'While other of my kin live in shining cities and try to forget the Witch King's bloody hordes, my folk scour the Shadowlands for invaders and bring red death to the Forsworn defilers.'

Thoughts of what the dark elves had done to his homeland filled his mind, and Mormacar strove to push down the hatred that welled-up in his heart. Consumed by his own emotions, he failed to notice the grin of approval break out on the Norseman's face. 'In any case,' he continued, 'my brethren and I set an ambush for a raiding party. We thought to trap them, but fell into a trap ourselves.' His voice grew quieter 'While we rained death on the Forsworn below, another group of them surprised us from behind. Before I could even unsheathe my sword, one of the cowards struck me from behind.' He spat in disgust. 'The next thing I knew, I awoke in Hag Graef.'

Einar nodded, having heard many similar tales in the slave pits. 'Those evil scum do not fight with honour,' he noted. 'Poison, foul magic and tricks are not the weapons of true warriors.'

Mormacar could not but agree. Strangely curious about this barbaric human, the Shadow Warrior asked, 'What of you? How did you come to be so far from frozen Norsca?'

'That is a tale worthy of the skalds, elfling,' the Norseman replied, 'although I doubt any lived to take the story back to Norsca.' He shook his head as he continued, 'Ah, a black day it was indeed. I was sailing with Grimnir Ogre-kin, as fierce a reaver as ever prowled the Sea of Claws.' Einar settled back, as if the two of them were drinking mead in front of the hearth. 'We'd just raided an Empire merchant fleet and our holds were heavy with booty. Then a great storm blew out of the east, like the breath of the gods themselves.' Mormacar cracked a smile. Storytelling came easily to the Norseman. 'My ship was separated from Grimnir's and we tossed on the seas for three days. When the storm finally blew its last, we were adrift and mastless.' Einar shook his head and dropped his gaze to the ground. 'It was then that the dark elves found us. It was a fearsome sight, a castle that floats on the sea, filled with sea serpents and worse. Truly an abomination sent by Mistress of the Damned herself.' The Norseman crossed his arms in front of him, making an ancient ward against evil. 'Seeing its towering walls and countless warriors, I knew that we would soon be dead.'

'It was a black ark that you beheld,' Mormacar said. 'None can stand against them.'

Einar nodded but he was talking quickly now, his blood racing as he was caught up in remembrance. 'I swore a vow to the Father of Battle to die before surrendering. Soon the murderers boarded my ship and we fought like berserkers that day.' Suddenly, Einar was on his feet, braids flying wildly as he shook his head back and forth. 'I wish the skalds could sing of the deeds of Halfdan Wolfclaw, Skragg the Grim and Canute Shield-breaker, for few have equalled their skill at arms. One by one, though, all were slain, pierced by bolts, hacked down by swords or felled by black magic.' He stood there, shaking his fist at unseen foes while Mormacar looked on, wondering if the Norseman had lost his mind. 'My heart cried out for vengeance as more and more of the dragon-cloaked corsairs boarded my ship. At last, only I was left alive.'

Mormacar could see that guilt stained the Norseman, guilt at not dying with his shipmates like a good captain should.

'I lay about me with my axe, slicing and cleaving, but I could not kill them all. When the bodies were piled up high around me, one of their foul wizards ensorcelled me.' Einar slammed his fist into cavern wall and howled in frustration. 'Instead of letting me die with my crew, the captain of that evil vessel took me to Hag Graef in chains. When we escape, I will hunt him down and feed him his own heart. Only then will my comrades be avenged.' Story finished, Einar slumped to the floor in despair. His hand, now bloody and torn, was still clenched tight as he continued to relive that fateful day.

Mormacar stared at the Norseman, impressed despite himself. 'I think you may have missed your calling, Einar. You should have been a storyteller yourself.'

Einar chuckled a little at this and Mormacar joined him. For a short while, they forgot the mistrust between elf and man and enjoyed the laughter together. But the moment ended quickly, as the harsh reality of their situation intruded upon them once more. An uncomfortable silence descended on the two fugitives and Mormacar feared that Volundson would sink back into his guilty despair. But then Einar forced another laugh to break the silence. 'If you liked that tale,' the Norseman said, 'let me tell you of the battle at Brienne. Grimnir's wrath was something to behold that day–'

'Einar, shut up,' whispered Mormacar, squinting in obvious concentration. The Norseman bristled, but Mormacar's insistent gesture silenced him. 'Do you hear that?' asked the elf.

'Hear what?'

'Listen closely, I heard something.' The Shadow Warrior stood up silently and crept over to one of the passages.

Volundson followed, listening intently.

After a minute, the Norseman said, 'I don't hear anything, elfling. Have your wits left you?'

'Follow me, you oaf,' Mormacar hissed, yanking his dagger free from his belt. 'And be quiet.'

* * *

THE ELF PADDED silently through the dank and gloomy passages, followed clumsily by the big Norseman. At each intersection, the Shadow Warrior would stop, listen, and then pick a new direction. After a few minutes, even Einar could hear the clash of metal and the shouts of combat.

'What now?' Einar asked. 'Who knows what lurks this far under the earth?'

'Whoever it is,' the elf whispered, 'let's hope they know a way out of here. This way, and try harder to be quiet.'

A gruff belch was all he got by way of a reply. The two fugitives set off again, easily able to follow the echoing cacophony. The minutes passed slowly, as each warrior wondered what lay ahead. They were concentrating so much on the noises that they all but tripped over the body of a dark elf lying in the passage. His head had been ripped from his shoulders and was nowhere in sight. Mormacar stuck his dagger in his belt and took the dead elf's sword. Slowly, silently, the two warriors inched ahead.

Finally, they came to a large cavern, whose circular shape and smooth walls made it seem man-made. Peering inside, they beheld a furious conflict. Battle cries, howls of pain and triumph, and the sound of clashing steel filled the air. Around a dozen dark elves were locked in combat with savage lizard creatures. These green and black scaled monsters walked on two legs and wielded crude spears and clubs with considerable skill, although Mormacar and Einar did not fail to notice that they used their razor-sharp teeth at every opportunity. The cavern was already littered with corpses, both elf and lizardman, and the fight had clearly become a grim battle of attrition. Most of the smaller lizard creatures were dead already, but their larger cousins were putting up quite a fight.

Two in particular towered above the battle, their huge spears smashing in elf skulls with unmatched strength. As the fugitives watched, one of these gargantuan lizardmen was felled by a savage attack from a frenzied witch elf. Her twin blades danced over the slow-moving reptile, slicing scales and driving deep into the monster's vitals. With a bellowing death scream, the creature fell backward, crushing a dark elf warrior beneath its ponderous bulk. Jumping onto the monster's carcass, the witch elf beheaded the monster with one blow and a rapturous howl of 'Blood for Khaine!'

Mormacar, utterly transfixed by this titanic clash, suddenly realised that he looked into the twisted face of Lady Bela. The Shadow Warrior's blood turned cold, and he was so full of loathing at the sight of her that he almost didn't notice that the battle was coming to him. One of the Forsworn had broken and was running right towards the hidden fugitives. A small, crested lizardman and the other hulking giant chased the fleeing warrior. Einar and Mormacar fell back down the passage and waited in a small alcove. Mormacar could feel the cold, hard, rock against his back but the sword felt good in his hands. Presently the terrified dark elf ran around the corner. Before he even realised that he faced a new foe, the Forsworn found Mormacar's cold steel in his belly. Face to face with his enemy, Mormacar watched the life drain from his victim's eyes. Stepping back, he let the body slide off his sword and fall to the ground.

Overcome by all-consuming hatred, he hadn't even noticed that Einar had split the crested lizardman nearly in two. There was no time to celebrate, however, as the crash of clawed feet and an ominous bellowing reminded both of them of the other imminent threat.

The huge lizardman, a mighty spear grasped in its clawed hands, stalked around the corner, roaring fiercely. Einar and Mormacar looked at each other, then jumped forward to attack. Although slow to react, the beast had scales as tough as hardened steel and the two warriors found that their blows were all but ineffectual. The raging beast hissed angrily and smashed Einar to the ground with the butt of his spear. In the same movement, its heavy tail snaked out and slammed down on the Norseman's chest, knocking the wind of him.

While the beast was momentarily fixated on Einar, Mormacar seized his chance. Balancing lightly on the balls of his feet, he took his dagger in his right hand, steadied himself, and then threw the wicked blade at the scaly monstrosity. The beast reared back in agony as Mormacar's dagger flew straight and true into its eye. The Shadow Warrior grasped his sword in both hands and drove it into the creature's exposed throat. Black blood gushed from the wound, showering the elf and causing him to lose his grip on the blade. The lizard creature, two blades buried in its flesh, stood there stupefied for a few moments, then fell forward with a ground-jarring crash.

Einar sat up, looked at the Shadow Warrior, and marvelled, 'Truly a feat for the sagas. The Father of Battle has blessed you today.'

Mormacar motioned him to be silent. The elf quietly recovered his weapons and did his best to clean the blood off their hilts. No new foes ventured down their passage and eventually the sounds of battle began to fade. Soon all was quiet.

AS THE TWO warriors crouched in the passage, wondering who had won the brutal battle, animalistic howls of 'Khaine' grimly answered their question. Then they heard the Lady Bela, her usually icy voice hot with the joy of bloodletting. 'We leave in ten minutes,' she said simply. 'Be ready.'

'But lady,' one of her warriors objected, 'what of the wounded and the missing?'

Even from where they sat, the two fugitives could hear the ferocious slap Lady Bela delivered to her soldier. 'You insubordinate wretch, if you ever question me again your entire family will go to the altar of Khaine! Anyone too wounded to travel is to be killed, as are all these lizardmen who yet offend me with their breathing. Now, move! It's a long way to Arnhaim and we wouldn't want to disappoint our high elf brothers.'

The remaining dark elves did their work quickly and soon the whole band marched off in the darkness.

'Faster,' the Lady Bela urged, her voice now distant, 'we've got a prediction of victory to deliver.'

When their footsteps could no longer be heard, Einar boomed, 'That was refreshing. It's been too long since my last battle. I would have preferred dark elves to lizardmen, but a fight's a fight.'

'You are familiar with those things?' Mormacar asked, gazing down at the corpses at his feet.

'Only by reputation,' the Norseman replied. 'I've heard stories of these creatures but I never believed they truly existed.' They walked carefully into the cavern but found nothing but the slain. 'Leaving aside the question of what these lizardmen were doing under Naggaroth, what are we going to do now?'

The Shadow Warrior considered the question and decided quickly. 'I think we should try to follow the dark elves.'

'I see,' the Norseman sneered, 'you miss your girlfriend already.'

Mormacar glared back at him. 'No, you brainless oaf, but if anyone knows the ways out of these caverns, it's the Lady Bela. Did you not hear her say they were heading to Arnhaim?'

'Aye, I did,' Volundson said, 'but I've never heard of it.'

'It's a high elf bastion south of Naggaroth – but it must be a thousand miles away. I don't know what Lady Bela's plans are, but she must be stopped.'

'Speculate later, elfling. If we're going to follow them, we should do so quickly.' Looking about the cavern, Einar's eyes lit up. 'But not before availing ourselves of the opportunity for booty.'

'How can think of treasure at a time like this,' Mormacar asked incredulously.

Einar, already sifting through the backpack of a dead elf, pulled out a parcel. 'If you're not interested in treasure, I suppose I'll have to eat all this food by myself.'

Mormacar nodded approvingly. 'Perhaps you are not such a fool after all, Einar Volundson.'

After gathering up all the food, clothing and weapons they could carry, the two warriors set out after Lady Bela. If they looked ridiculous in the ill-fitting clothing of their former tormentors, they did not care. They were warm, they had food in their bellies for the first time in days, and they were still free. And they intended to stay that way.

THE FOLLOWING WEEK was a hellish one for the two fugitives as they trailed their former tormentors through the labyrinth of caves far beneath Hag Graef. They had to stay near enough to Lady Bela's band to follow their tracks but far enough away to avoid detection. They ensured that one of them was always awake, keeping watch and wak-fire, lest they draw unwanted attention to themselves, so they continued to navigate by the eerie light of the fungi.

The Lady Bela travelled at a terrific pace and rarely sent out scouts. Indeed all her attention seemed fixated on some distant goal, although neither of the two fugitives could say what that might be. Despite their fatigue and the darkness, man and elf would not be left behind. The followed the Forsworn with a manic single-mindedness, so desperate were they to see the light of day again. As the days passed, uncharted by sun or moon, Mormacar and Einar dropped into a monotonous, numbing routine. Conversation had died out after only a few days. It was all they could do to keep going.

When the dark elves finally did stop, the two fugitives, tired and dazed, nearly stumbled into the large cavern occupied by their foes. But the Norseman saw the glint of steel in the gloom and pulled his companion back down the tunnel in silence until they found a small cavern full of dripping stalactites. Despite the slimy floor, Mormacar flung himself down and immediately fell asleep.

The elf awoke to the sound of drums, and at first thought he was back in fair Ulthuan. But a quick look at Einar, who looked nearly dead as he sat on watch, brought his dreaming mind crashing back to reality. 'Einar,' he whispered, 'what's going on?'ensured that one of them was always awake, keeping watch and wakThe Norseman slid back a few paces, but kept his eye on the passage ahead. 'It sounds like a foul ritual of some sort,' replied Einar, his voice full of loathing. 'You slept through the chanting, but it's been going for at least an hour by my reckoning.'

Mormacar nodded, and rubbed the sleep from his eyes. Gathering up his few possessions, he asked, 'Shall we pay a visit to the Lady Bela?'

The Norseman grinned. 'I was hoping you'd say that, elfling. If I sit here any longer, I may well turn to stone.'

The two warriors crept forward. Mormacar still cringed at what the Norseman considered to be 'moving quietly', but the drumming and chanting drowned out even his blundering. After a few minutes they approached an enormous cavern lit up brilliantly with dozens of flaming torches. The bright illumination was almost too much to bear, so used were they to the dim light of the caves. A few minutes of blinking and quiet cursing and their eyes had adjusted enough to see into the chamber beyond. They crept closer still, and it was then that Mormacar spotted a jagged column of black rock that thrust up from the floor. Signalling Einar with his eyes, Mormacar dashed the few yards to the column, followed quickly, if not gracefully, by Einar. Safely obscured, they crouched behind the rock and peered inside.

At the far end of the cavern was a tall altar of glassy black stone carved with evil runes and darkly stained. A hooded figure lay chained to this hideous slab, his frantic straining useless against the strong steel of the manacles. Surrounding the altar were four mighty stalagmites, and upon each of these was chained another hooded form. Below the altar, dark elf warriors beat wildly on a dozen drums while half-clad witch elves danced around the cavern singing the praises of Khaine, god of murder. Presiding over this scene, her face glowing with ecstasy in the torch light, was the Lady Bela.

'This is truly a place of evil,' whispered Einar, his gaze transfixed on the spectacle before him.

Mormacar nodded in response. This is what Ulthuan would be like without the constant vigilance of the Shadow Warriors, he thought grimly. But even his brethren were but a breaker against the dark tide of Naggaroth.

The wailing of the witch Elves reached a fevered pitch, and Lady Bela began to dance around the altar, lashing about with her whip in a fit of rapture. As she passed each of the stalagmites, she tore the mask from the face of the bound victim. Mormacar's heart caught in his throat as he recognised all four as prisoners from his cell who had gone upward with Galaher to try to escape. Seeing the terror on their faces, there was no comfort in knowing that he had chosen the right path.

Now all the assembled dark elves began to chant, 'Khaine! Khaine! Khaine!'

Lady Bela pulled a jagged blade from her belt, threw her head back, and howled like an animal. 'Lord Khaine,' she intoned, her voice hot with passion, 'accept this sacrifice!' With that, her blade swept down and plunged into the chest of a screaming victim. Mormacar could watch no more and he turned away, his heart heavy. He could hear the laughter of Lady Bela, and the scuffling of her minions as they fought over the crimson prize he knew she had thrown them.

But realising this was no ordinary ritual, Mormacar steeled himself and turned his head back to watch. And as the last heart was torn from the last victim, a dark mist began to rise around the altar. It seemed that Lord Khaine was listening.

Einar dropped down behind the rock they were hiding behind, and pulled Mormacar down with him. 'Haven't you seen enough?' he said, his voice full of disgust. 'Or are you waiting for Khaine himself to appear?'

Mormacar knocked the Norseman's hand away. 'This ritual is important, Einar, and we must find out why. If it's too much for you cover your eyes!'

The Norseman bristled, and anger flashed in his eyes. Standing slowly, he spat, 'I've seen more blood than any gutless elf. Pray you never know how much!' Then he turned his gaze away from the Shadow Warrior, and once again looked down on the Lady Bela.

Mormacar, cursing fate for throwing him together with this lout of a Norseman, did the same.

During their heated exchange, the black mist had surrounded the altar and now Lady Bela seemed to be adrift in clouds of inky darkness. She swayed back and forth above the altar, running the flat of her blade over the still-hooded form bound there. 'Lord Khaine,' she shouted, 'I ask for your favour in exchange for one final gift!' She grasped the hood and tore it free. 'See!' she growled. 'Galaher Swiftblade!'

Mormacar froze in horror as the hood came free. There was poor Galaher, beneath the knife of the murderous Lady Bela. Instinctively, he pulled his blade free and made to leap over the rock, but strong hands restrained him.

'Don't do it, elfling!' Einar hissed urgently. 'You'll get us both killed!'

'Let me go, Volundson! It's Galaher down there!' Mormacar strained against Einar's arms but couldn't break free.

'Remember your own words,' the Norseman whispered in his ear, as he struggled to hold back to writhing elf. 'We will have our vengeance later. Now, we must escape.'

Mormacar struggled half-heartedly but his body slowly relaxed. As much as he hated it, he knew the Norseman was right. But Galaher! What of Galaher?

As if in answer to his unspoken question, Lady Bela's voice echoed through the chamber. 'Lord Khaine, even now our armies are on the march. Accept the blood of this elf Lord as a sacrifice fitting your dark majesty!'

Once again the chants rose high, and the Lady Bela's knife plunged down. If she had hoped for a howl of fear, she was disappointed. Galaher had long ago become resigned to his fate, and the sharp blade brought him the eternal rest he craved.

Mormacar wept silently as Lady Bela sacrificed Galaher Swiftblade to her dark god. Einar held him but there was no need; Mormacar knew what he had to do.

Lady Bela dropped her knife, so she could hold the elf's heart in both hands. 'Lord Khaine, this heart is yours!' she intoned. 'In return,

I ask only one question. Will it burn with the fire of victory, or shrivel with the decay of defeat? Hear your humble servant and know that victory will bring hundreds more to your bloody altars!' Gripping the heart tightly, she tore it free from Galaher's body. Holding it high, she shouted, 'For you, Lord Khaine, and victory!'

'For Khaine and victory!' howled the assembled witch Elves. Every eye in the cavern was fixed on the pulsing heart. No one moved, no one breathed – and then the heart exploded in black flame that licked up and down Lady Bela's arms. She embraced the flame like a sister, and shouted one word with indescribable joy: 'Victory!'

The dark elves screamed with delight. Lady Bela lowered the heart and looked with pride on her savage minions. Smiling her cruel smile, she tossed the flaming heart into the boiling mist below the altar. The black flame ignited the unnatural mist, and the heart exploded to form a vortex of swirling energy.

Lady Bela mounted the altar and with a shout of, 'To Arnhaim and victory!' she dove into the vortex and disappeared. One by one, her minions followed her lead.

Soon, Mormacar and Einar were alone in the great chamber with the bodies of the slain. As the two dumbfounded warriors looked on, the vortex began to shimmer and shrink. Mormacar quickly regained his senses and shouted, 'Quickly, Einar, we must follow them!'

The Norseman, eyes wild, said, 'Are you insane?'

'If you want to live, follow me!' Mormacar yelled. With that, he vaulted the rock and ran towards the shrinking vortex. Einar hesitated for a moment and then barrelled after him. Without a word, Mormacar dove into the endless blackness that hung over the floor.

Einar shouted, 'The gods love a fool!' and flung himself after the elf as the vortex winked out of existence.

Mormacar landed hard on cold stone. A few seconds later, Einar appeared from nowhere and nearly fell on top of him. From the expression on the Norseman's face, he seemed entirely surprised to be alive. Warding himself against evil, the superstitious Norseman asked, 'In the name of all the gods, what was that?'

Mormacar stood up and listened intently. Mindful of the chanting and howling of the dark elves, which could still be heard from a nearby tunnel, he whispered, 'That was the darkest of magics.' Mormacar could feel the taint on him, and he brushed furiously on his ragged clothing in a vain attempt to wipe himself clean. 'It must have been some kind of gate. We could be anywhere now.'

'Then we have little choice,' Einar replied, at last rising from the cold floor. 'We must follow Lady Bela before her trail is lost.' Mormacar nodded in agreement. Their path was clear.

So the two warriors wearily resumed their previous routine. They followed Lady Bela and her minions, keeping their distance as best they could. Her pace had once again accelerated, and they pushed themselves hard to keep up. Two days later, the tunnels took a definite upward turn. This small victory gave the two fugitives a renewed burst of energy.

Early the following day, Mormacar stopped without warning, and Einar crashed into him, sending them both to the ground. 'Mind yourself, elfling,' the angry Norseman whispered. 'I've killed men for less.'

'Forget bloodletting for a single moment and smell,' Mormacar said insistently.

'Smell? I think you've eaten too many strange mushrooms these past few days.'

Mormacar grabbed the Norseman and shook him. 'Use your senses! Can't you smell the fresh air?'

Einar drew his hand back to strike the agitated elf, but paused and then broke into a toothy grin. 'Aye, I can smell it. Fresh air, elfling! It can't be far now.'

The two pressed on through the day, noting excitedly the widening of the tunnel. Then, without warning, they simply emerged above ground. It was night, so they had not seen light ahead, but there was no mistaking the stars above. The two warriors looked at each other and could not speak. What words could describe their feelings after such an ordeal? They simply clasped hands and laughed. They laughed at their fate, laughed at their luck, and laughed at the stars. And the laughter was real because it was theirs and they were free.

Looking about, they saw that they had emerged in the shadows of a imposing chain of mountains. Jagged spires reached for the heavens, towering above the exhausted fugitives. Below them stretched a valley, perhaps once fertile but now full of withered trees and blasted earth. Still, Einar and Mormacar could not help but find the sight full of beauty. Compared to the mines of Hag Graef and the terror of the underworld, this place was paradise.

Warily now, lest a wrong step end their journey in tragedy, elf and man crept down into the valley spread out below them. They searched amongst the withered trees for a sign of their foes, but found none. When they were sure it was safe, the fugitives made camp and then slept.

They awoke the next day refreshed, but their eyes burned in the dawning sunlight. It suddenly seemed so bright, so used had they become to the darkness below. Walking under the barren trees of the forest, Mormacar and Einar slowly regained their eyesight.

That night, Mormacar consulted the stars and tried to figure out where they were. 'I don't know how the Lady Bela did it, Einar, but we are only about two hundred miles from Arnhaim. We could make it there in nine days if we push ourselves, twelve if we don't.'

The Norseman chuckled, scratching at his ragged beard. 'Something tells me, elfling, that you want us to push on ahead.'

'You are no fool,' Mormacar said. 'I don't know what Lady Bela has planned, but we must stop her.'

'So be it. We can rest behind the walls of your bastion.'

Without further discussion, the two warriors continued their great trek through the wilderness, leaving the vast Black Spine Mountains behind. Of Lady Bela and her dark elves, they saw no sign. It was as if the witch elf and her minions had been swallowed alive by the ancient forest.

Einar and Mormacar spent the days travelling and the evenings swapping tales. They were pleased to find that the further east they travelled, the greener the land became. They soon left the blasted forest behind and entered a region of wild grass broken up with copses of trees. The crossbows they had looted from the dark elves allowed them to hunt some game. The Norseman turned out to be a fine trapper, which more than made up for his lack of aim. And thanks to Mormacar's ability to build a nearly smokeless fire, they were able to enjoy their first hot meals in memory. By the week's end they had shaken the worst effects of their imprisonment in Hag Graef.

At the end of the seventh day's march, Mormacar spotted a wispy plume of smoke to the east, where a series of low hills rose above a forest of pine. Cautiously, the two warriors headed towards it, hoping to find a friendly settlement of some kind. Coming to a gentle hill, Einar and Mormacar quickly climbed it. Dropping to the ground, they crawled the last few feet to the top and then peered below. Bile came to Mormacar's throat as he realised what they had stumbled upon.

Beneath them lay an entire dark elf army. Mormacar looked in horror at the spectacle before him. The plains below were covered with the tents of the Forsworn, and the once-green grassland had been turned brown and lifeless beneath thousands of boots. It seemed all of Naggaroth was going to war, and the elaborate tents flew the shrieking banners of the dread cities of the dark elves.

Hundreds upon hundreds of warriors swarmed across the camp, united in their hatred of their high elf kin. The executioners of Har Ganeth, fearsome in the billowing black cloaks, strode amongst the crowd, their brutal axes sharpened and ready. Savage witch elves danced lewdly around a great cauldron of blood. Black armoured knights whipped their reptilian steeds into readiness for the battle ahead and engineers worked feverishly to build more of their dreaded repeating bolt-throwers. It was as if the Witch King himself had vomited forth a black stain onto the green lands below.

'Einar,' Mormacar whispered, 'they mean to attack Arnhaim!' His heart sank when he thought of his kin in the unsuspecting city.

'Aye, elfling, the words of Lady Bela now ring true.' Einar looked into his companion's eyes and, seeing the fire that burned there, knew their ordeal wasn't yet finished.

'We must reach Arnhaim first and warn my people,' the Shadow Warrior said, his voice strained. 'The Forsworn must be stopped.'

'You know I have no love for your folk, Mormacar,' the Norseman replied, 'but to thwart the dark elf scum I will gladly help you and your kin.'

Mormacar gripped Einar's hand. They had fought and bled together, their fates bound inextricably together. The Shadow Warrior stood, then turned to make his way down the hill. His keen eyes quickly picked out the skulking forms of two dark elf scouts who were silently making their way up towards them.

'Einar!' he yelled, unloading a bolt at the nearest scout.

The Norseman turned about as a speeding dark elf bolt pierced his left leg. Mormacar's missile also found its mark, burying itself in the scout's chest. Norseman and dark elf both fell to the ground, as the two remaining combatants closed. Mormacar drew his sword but kept the repeating crossbow hanging loosely in his left hand. The scout smiled wickedly, unsheathed his own blade, and charged up the hill. Mormacar parried a brutal overhead blow, brought up his crossbow, and fired it point blank into his enemy's stomach. The scout fell back with a grunt and rolled down the hill. The Shadow Warrior ran to finish off his foe, but could not plunged his sword home before the wounded scout had screamed long and loudly.

'Einar, let's get out of here!' the elf shouted, his eyes picking out the shadows of more enemy scouts.

'I'm not going anywhere on this leg,' the Norseman said gravely. 'Leave me and go warn your people.'

Only now did Mormacar see the Norseman's wound. Einar had tugged the bolt free and tied off the bleeding, but he could hardly walk. 'Einar, I can't just leave you here! Not after what we've been though.'

'Yes, you can, because you must. Together, we'll never make it, but alone you just might.' The Norseman smiled grimly. 'Perhaps now I can make an end for myself worthy of a saga. I'll hold them here as long as I can. Now, go!'

Mormacar embraced the big Norseman. 'Einar Volundson, I swear this oath before all the gods: the skalds will sing of your bravery this day.'

* * *

WITH A LEADEN heart, Mormacar turned and ran down the hill. He wanted to turn back, to stay until the bitter end, but he knew that he couldn't desert the people of Arnhaim. Even now, he could see dark elf soldiers rushing towards Einar. The Shadow Warrior doubled his speed, determined to make his friend's sacrifice meaningful. Einar stood alone on the hill, a sword in either hand and death in his eyes. His life would not be sold cheaply.

The Shadow Warrior made it to the forest, and already he was breathing heavily. Diving behind a fallen tree trunk, he stopped to scan for pursuers. There were none yet. The dark elves' attention was fixed on Einar, who lay about him with mighty strokes and sent his foes reeling down the hill. Mormacar tore his eyes from Einar and, moving quickly, plunged into the forest and headed east. He needed to skirt the enemy camp if he was going to make it to the plains beyond. As he ran, he could hear the bloodthirsty howls of the frenzied Norseman. The Father of Battles was surely proud that day.

Mormacar had been reared in the wild expanses of the Shadowlands, and spent his life waging a merciless war on the Forsworn. Now he used every iota of his instinct and his training to slip through the woods unnoticed. He could hear the pounding of hooves and the shouts of the search parties, but he was a ghost in the shadows. Striving to keep his pace steady, Mormacar darted from tree to tree, his passing silent and leaving no sign. It took him nearly two hours to circle the dark elf army and he could now see the plains beyond. He was close, and the hated enemy was almost behind him.

Suddenly, the quiet was shattered by the thunderous approach of a Forsworn war party. Heart pounding, Mormacar threw himself flat and crawled into a tangled bush. The sharp branches cut his face and hands but he uttered no sound. Sitting perfectly still, he waited as the dark elves approached. The horses had slowed their pace as they entered the forest, and now Mormacar could only hear the gentle clip-clop of hooves and the jangling of harnesses. The sounds got louder as the Witch King's minions approached, and Mormacar gripped his crossbow tightly with his sweaty palms.

The dark elves broke out of cover, and the Shadow Warrior could see the wiry forms of three dark riders atop their midnight steeds. They circled the area slowly, scanning the ground for some sign of their quarry. When the riders found nothing, they regrouped and began to ride deeper into the forest.

But a chance glance from the last of the retreating horsemen aroused his suspicion. This rider broke off from his companions and cantered toward the concealed elf. Mormacar noticed too late that a piece of his cloak had torn off and was now clearly visible, hanging in the branches of the bush. Cursing himself for his carelessness, Mormacar readied himself as the dark elf approached.

The remaining horsemen now turned their steeds and galloped towards the hidden high elf, skilfully guiding their horses around the intervening trees. The foremost rider, spear extended, moved ever closer.

Mormacar launched himself out of the bushes with a yell. The evil steed reared in surprise, its rider dropping his spear while seeking desperately to calm his snorting mount. Mormacar stepped to the side of the stomping beast, and levelled his crossbow at the other two dark riders. With cold precision, he fired the crossbow twice in quick succession at the approaching horsemen, the infernal mechanism of the Forsworn weapon now turned against its masters. Both bolts found their mark, and the stunned dark elves fell from their saddles, wounded or slain. The last of the dark elves had regained enough control of his mount to leap from the saddle and tackle the weary Shadow Warrior. Both elves fell to the ground and the Forsworn smiled cruelly as he felt Mormacar's bones crunch beneath his weight.

Mormacar felt the breath knocked out of his body, and could only struggle as the dark elf rained blows down on him. The dark rider pulled a gleaming dagger from his belt, his other hand at Mormacar's throat. The Shadow Warrior thrashed desperately, trying with all his might to wrench the blade free. As the two mortal foes struggled, Mormacar's empty hand closed around a rock. Smiling grimly, the Shadow Warrior shifted his weight, and smashed the jagged rock into the skull of his foe, caving it in with one great blow.

The dark elf crumpled to the ground and Mormacar struggled to his feet. He grabbed the reins of the dark elf's mount and swung himself into the saddle. Nothing would stop him from reaching Arnhaim. Nothing!

Leaving the dead and dying behind, Mormacar raced out onto the plains and kept on riding. He could almost feel the hot breath of Lady Bela on his neck, and whipped the horse furiously to coax every ounce of speed out of the swift beast. Even though he rode at a full gallop, he would turn to look for dark riders every few minutes, but the crucial first hours saw no pursuit. All too aware of the power of dark magic, however, the Shadow Warrior rode on as if Khaine himself was in pursuit.

For the better part of a day, Mormacar stayed in the saddle and drove the horse on. Finally, the dark steed could take no more: it threw the Shadow Warrior from the saddle and collapsed. The huge steed rolled in the tall grass, whinnying in pain.

Mormacar lay in the grass, agony shooting through his shoulder. For minutes, or maybe it was hours, he drifted in and out of consciousness. He could tell that his arm was broken and his body seemed to be one big bruise. Gods, but he was wrecked. Perhaps he should surrender to the screaming pleas of his body and rest? But what of Arnhaim?

He could still hear the horse screaming in pain. It thrashed in the grass, surely dying. And its howls took him back to the altar of the Khaine. Once again he was in dark temple at Hag Graef, prisoner of the Lady Bela, forced to watch his kinsmen fall under her knife. And he could not decide if the screams of the dying horse reminded him more of the victims of Lady Bela, or of her bestial witch elf minions. But he did know that he would gladly give his life to spare his brethren in Arnhaim such a fate. There was no more time to waste. He had to push on.

So steeling himself, Mormacar rose, every joint and bone straining with the pressure. But he staggered forward... east, always east towards Arnhaim. As he crossed icy streams and tore his way through obstructing brambles, he lost track of time completely. It was all he could do to put one foot in front of the other, to ignore the pain in his shoulder and cover those final miles. When his body threatened to fail him, he thought of those who had already fallen in the struggle. The faces of his dead friends seemed to hang before him, urging him on. He saw his Shadow Warrior brethren, slain in foul ambush. He saw the prisoners of Hag Graef and Galaher Swiftblade, ruthlessly sacrificed by the Lady Bela. And he saw Einar Volundson, now surely dead. For all of them, and his kin yet living in Arnhaim, he forced himself on.

So Mormacar passed the night, stumbling in the dark in a desperate bid to bring salvation to the last high elf bastion outside of Ulthuan. As the morning haze evaporated under the burning sun, he saw it. In the distance, rising above the well-ordered fields of the outlying farms, a shining tower of pure white, surrounded by stout battlements and sharp elven steel. Arnhaim! Arnhaim at last!

He stopped, overcome with emotion, all his pain forgotten for that one instant. He had done it. He had escaped from Hag Graef and come in time to warn his kin of the impending attack. He looked forward to watching Lady Bela wither under a crushing defeat, and hoped he could face in her the battle to come. Only when his blade clove her in twain would justice be served.

Eyes closed, Mormacar smiled then, thinking of his sweet revenge, and failed to notice the tell-tale hiss of a speeding missile. His head jerked up as it struck his throat and pain shot through him like fire. He fell to his knees, blood oozing from the terrible wound. He reached out to the horizon, reached for the tower of Arnhaim but his hand grasped at nothing. His life ebbing away, Mormacar tried to cry out, to warn his brethren in Arnhaim that doom approached. But no sound emerged from his ruined throat, and he fell forward in a heap.

'Forgive me,' Mormacar thought, his head full of visions of Einar, Galaher, and his kin, 'I have failed you all.' Then he surrendered to the pain, and it consumed him utterly.

'HE'S DOWN!' AN icy voice shouted. 'Let's take a look.' Three figures rose from the tall grass and walked over to the body of the fallen elf. They looked him over silently, poking the body to make sure the arrow had done its work. Seeing his haggard form, bloody and dressed in a ragged dark elf uniform, their faces filled with disdain.

'Look at this Forsworn scum, he's filthier than a pig,' a disgusted voice said.

'What was a lone dark elf doing so close to Arnhaim?' said a second.

'You can tell by the state of him,' the icy voice said, 'he's clearly a fugitive. We get these strays now and again. Throw him in that ditch and let's continue our patrol.'

'But sir, shouldn't we alert the garrison, just in case.'

'There's no need to rush, brother. We'll report in at the end of the day, as usual. What could happen by sunset anyway?'

THE CHAOS BENEATH
Mark Brendan

IN THE DANK, subterranean depths of the Marienburg Grand Sewer network, more than effluent was being carried along the crumbling, cavernous conduits. The stark glare of the flaming torches held aloft by four sinister, robed figures projected dancing shadows upon the tortured frame of a man dragged along the waste channel between them.

The captive was clad in fine, black leather britches and riding boots. Above the waist he had been stripped, revealing a gaudy patchwork of lurid bruises and angry red weals where a lash had bitten him, and most disturbing of all a mass of blisters and scabs which traced an unearthly, sinuous pattern where he had recently been branded on his breast. The cluster of sores formed a circular hub, from which a broad point projected from the bottom left quadrant, and a lithe tail twisted away from the top right to form a design as strangely fluid as the flames which had imprinted it onto the victim's flesh. A sack of purple velvet covered the man's head and was securely knotted around his throat, so that he was forced to stumble along, being shoved, kicked and whipped in the correct direction.

Passing beyond the grand arches of the main channel, they entered a little-used part of the system, where the walls once more narrowed about them like the jaws of a great serpent. It was here that they came upon a bizarre little iron bound door and the journey came to its end as the cultist bearing the lash unlocked the portal and the group passed into the dim glow beyond.

The room within was of a comfortable size to accommodate perhaps twenty or more people and had a high, vaulted ceiling. Low swirls of thick, choking incense from braziers situated around the walls carpeted the tiled floor. The central area of this floor was dominated by a huge mosaic, with a pattern delineated in slivers of coloured glass, marble and shell which bore a strong resemblance to the brand seared on to the prisoner's torso. At the centre of the design, four shackles anchored to the floor by thick steel chains awaited a victim.

On the opposite side of the chamber from the door was a slightly raised platform, upon which stood a large throne of twisted black wood and purple velvet. A tall, feminine silhouette rose from this throne and came down from the platform to stand before the circle. Like the other cultists she wore a long, deep purple robe, but rather than being belted by a simple cord, hers was a thick leather belt with a large, wrought-iron skull for a clasp. Also, there were long vents up to her hips in the sides of the robes, beneath which she wore fine purple velvet trousers and soft, doeskin boots. The tall figure wore her hood down, in contrast to the other disciples, and her face was concealed by an ornate black ballroom mask shaped like a raven. Delicate mother-of-pearl inlay chased around the eye slits of the mask, behind which blazed violet irises, and edged the elegant beak too, whilst a spectacular spray of midnight black feathers held soft golden hair back from her temples.

'Let the offering be brought forward to the circle,' she announced in a clear, cultured voice. At her behest, the four cultists thrust their prisoner forward into the circle and more robed figures hurried forth from the shadows to spread-eagle him in the centre of the mosaic. Only once he was securely shackled to the floor was the bag removed from the prisoner's head. His face bore none of the marks of the torment his body had suffered in the cultists' care, and for the briefest of instants his clear grey eyes locked upon the dreamy violet orbits of the figure looming over him, before he closed his eyelids in despair and submission. His jaw was clean shaven, and his features lean and predatory, with a suggestion of strong lineage in both his high forehead, with its sweeping collar-length black hair, and in the long, straight line of his nasal bridge.

'Well, well, well,' the woman mocked. 'Obediah Cain, second lieutenant of the Church of Sigmar's Holy Inquisition in Marienburg. You are welcome as our very special guest of honour. Indeed, you might even say that we need you.'

'Do what you will with me, witch!' groaned the man on the floor. 'Remember that when judgement comes, it is final!'

'It is good that you have given up all notion of redemption, and you are now looking to history for vindication,' the masked woman spat. 'For when M'Loch T'Chort, Weaver of the Ways, High Daemonic Prince of Twisted Destiny and Misguided Fate, comes to seize possession of your miserable skin, the last thing he needs is some lost soul contesting his right to it.'

With that, she delivered a stinging kick to his ribs, causing him to whimper as the scabs on his brand cracked with the force.

'It's such a shame that we have to inflict punishment on your earthly clay before our lord can take up residence within it, but as you witch hunters are always so fond of demonstrating, the prisoner's co-operation isn't adequate grounds to carry on to the next stage of the procedure. You, more than anyone, should appreciate what is required to ensure the veracity of any actions or claims made by a prisoner, because, after all, their co-operation might be a falsehood to avoid torture. Isn't that the option presented to your victims, witch hunter?' she asked, bending down so that her face was close to his own pained visage. 'Isn't it, you pious worm?' she howled when he did not answer, and dug the points of her gauntleted fingers into the weeping wound on his chest.

'Yes! Yes it is, damn you!' sobbed the broken man squirming on the floor.

'Very good,' she said evenly, and stood up once more. 'Then let us begin the rite.'

The dozen or so cultists in the room took up positions around the circle and began to sway rhythmically, chanting in alien, melodious tongues an otherworldly mantra of damnation which rose up from the strange vaulted room and out into the still night beyond, inviting a thing which should not be into the realm of living men.

Led on by the strange, powerful sorceress, the cultists' performance became more frenetic, their exhortations more desperate, and a singular change began to take place within the eerily lit room. The heavy clouds of incense drifting languidly at waist height coalesced in the centre of the chamber, above the recumbent witch hunter, and then spiralled upwards into a point like some grotesque, ectoplasmic worm rearing its swollen bulk out of the foetid soil. The tip of the apparition dipped towards the unconscious man's face and infiltrated his mouth and nostrils, feeding itself, coil after coil into his twitching, choking body.

The ritual's leader suddenly ceased her rapturous chanting to command, 'It is time. Let the sacrifice be brought forth for the Sanguinary Binding!'

From a curtained alcove in the shadowy chamber, a night-spawned abomination of uncommon vileness shambled into the circle. It was a man in stature but, through constant exposure to the warping malignancy of the Chaos lord, Tzeentch, his head had puckered and inflated like an over-ripe fruit, the skin thick, wrinkled and lurid pink in hue, his mouth a broad, grinning slash filled with row after row of sharp, blackened fangs and his scalp studded with starfish's suckers in place of hair. His left arm, too, had become severely mutated and was grossly elongated and jointed in four places, covered in tough pink skin like his face, while the hand on the end of the offensive limb had grown to absurd proportions and its eight thick fingers were hollow tubes. In the daemonic limb he held a struggling lamb, while in his other, human hand he carried a large sacrificial knife. Taking up position over the witch hunter, the mutant prepared to complete the ceremony with a blood sacrifice.

Despite everything that Obediah Cain had been through, some spark of his original consciousness yet remained untainted by the invading entity, and the unacceptable presence of a Chaos mutant hovering over him stirred that faint ember into scintillating action. Cain did the only thing he could under the circumstances – he brought his knee up sharply, as far as the chains would permit, into the creature's shin. It was enough to cause the mutant's leg to buckle and deposit him in a heap on top of the witch hunter. The sacrificial lamb scurried free and gambolled around the room, adding to the confusion.

When the mutant picked himself up from the witch hunter's body, ready to give the prisoner one final taste of pain before the ritual erased his soul forever, pain and shock registered upon his grotesquely leering visage. Others, too, had noticed the unthinkable thing which had befallen their great plan and began gasping and crying out in fear and dismay.

'You fool! What have you done?' shrieked the sorceress.

The mutant backed away, shaking his bloated head, his eyes never leaving the terrible sight in the centre of the circle. The sacrificial knife jutted from beneath the chin of their prisoner – but worse than that an ephemeral glow was intensifying within Cain's open mouth and his cheeks were beginning to bulge with warp-born energies. Then the coruscating wash of power seemed to contract in upon itself.

The cultists eyed one another with deep trepidation. The mutant continued to back off, still shaking his head in pained denial.

Suddenly a brilliant, prismatic cascade of light erupted from the corpse's hideously stretched mouth, an otherworldly illumination which seemed to siphon the flesh from the cultists' bodies where it touched them, drawing out their substance in little lumps which evaporated within the searing beams. In the space of a minute, the screaming and pleading was done. A dozen charred skeletons clattered to the stone floor.

Obediah Cain's body writhed and jerked with unholy vigour, then sat bolt upright tearing the steel bonds from their fittings as though they were a child's paper chains. With an impatient gesture he yanked the knife from his throat and cast it aside. After a deep, gurgling cough, he clamped a hand over the hole in his voice box and uttered in a horrible, reedy, burbling timbre, 'Nec-ro-mancer! I must find a necromancer!'

'I'M SORRY, DE la Lune, but after careful consideration the Guild's senior tutors have concluded that you are simply not possessed of the finer skills of meditation and concentration required to make the grade as a qualified Wizard in this academy.'

Michael de la Lune perched on the edge of a comfortable leather chair in the opulent office of Paracelsus van der Groot, the Marien-burg College of Magic's master of apprentices. Across the magnificent teak table, strewn with arcane trinkets and scrolls, van der Groot was telling him the awful, unbearable news that he had failed his appren-ticeship. De la Lune was a slight man, who had witnessed the passing of no more than twenty summers, and his boyish, Bretonnian face wore an expression of crestfallen astonishment. A lock of dark, wavy hair fell across his forehead as he hung his head in defeat.

'But don't take on so, lad,' continued the corpulent van der Groot, toying with one of his enormous rings in embarrassment, 'There are plenty of careers wanting for resourceful, educated fellows like your-self. Have you considered perhaps something in one of the mercantile professions – they're always looking for accountants and administra-tors. Or if you still want to work with magic, how about the Alchemists' Guild? I know a few people there and everything they do is academic. Not quite so esoteric as our stuff, eh?

'I could get in touch with–'

Against all the protocols, the young man dared to interrupt one of the masters and spoke for the first time since entering the office. 'Please sir? By your leave, I think I'd just like to collect my belongings and be gone.'

'Yes, yes. I understand lad,' van der Groot said breezily. 'I know it's a sore blow to you young ones to be told that you've failed, but only a few ever succeed. There's no shame in it, so you stay in touch and–'

There was the sound of the door shutting.

Michael strode down the tangled web of corridors which burrowed through the great edifice that was the Marienburg College of Magic. He kept his head down on the way to his private quarters, ignoring the greet-ings of other wizards of his acquaintance along the route. His head was a whirl of confusion and resentment. What had he done to fail the test? He had thought this establishment to be an enlightened one. After all, hadn't they offered him a second chance after he had failed the entrance exam to the exalted Altdorf college. Though he had long suspected that entrance to Altdorf's college had more to do with money than ability, and he reasoned that his Bretonnian lineage being of freeman stock, rather than the aristocracy who more usually gained admittance there, was the real reason that he failed the exam. However, he couldn't understand why the establishment which had eventually permitted him entry to the field of his beloved magical research would now turn their backs on him. Their reasoning seemed to be beyond him.

Michael reached his spartan quarters and began packing such meagre possessions as he owned into the sling bag which had accompanied him from his home city of Lyonesse four years earlier. What would become of him now? It was a bitter irony that he had travelled so far, learning two new languages in his pursuit of magical expertise and the Classical script employed in conjuration, just to seemingly have to return to Bretonnia with nothing to show for it but a couple of apprentices' parlour tricks. Oh, he might stay in Marienburg as van der Groot had suggested, but that would be taking an almighty risk with his dwindling funds. If he couldn't find some way to sustain himself here then he might end up a beggar or worse, and he was in no mood for taking chances at present. It would be much more sensible, he reasoned, to use what money he had left to buy passage back to his homeland whereupon he could take up employment in his father's textile trade, much though the idea pained him. On the face of things, however, he didn't see any other reasonable options open to him.

'Damn it! Everything is a mess. Damn magic and damn merchants too!' he muttered, swinging the heavy satchel over his shoulder. With that, he left the little room he had inhabited for the past four years for the final time and headed out of the building.

BLINKING OWLISHLY IN the light of day, Michael passed beyond the portals and out into Guilderstraase, pausing briefly to hand his room keys over to the gatekeeper. Eyes which burned with intent unknown marked him as he proceeded down the broad thoroughfare, then a dark figure hurried from the alley whence it had observed him so that it might intercept the youth before he passed from sight.

Michael was still in a condition of shock, his thoughts lost in fanciful notions of how he would spend the rest of his life, when a hand clapped down heavily upon his shoulder. Michael almost leapt clean out of his skin at the sudden contact and whirled to face whoever it was that presumed to be so familiar.

It was a tall man, garbed in the traditional attire of the religious puritans who made the vanquishing of heretics their lives' work:

wide-brimmed hat, leather britches and high riding boots, a half cloak worn over a blouson shirt, and a burnished steel gorget to protect his neck from Vampires. At his belt he wore a long, heavy bladed sabre and a fine duelling pistol, along with pouches for powder and shot.

'Forgive me,' wheezed the stranger in a voice curiously thin and consumptive for one so impressive of stature. 'It was not my intention to startle you.'

A witch hunter! Michael's heart dropped into the pit of his stomach. Just when he thought things could get no worse, along came the practitioner of wizardry's worst nightmare. These religious zealots were notoriously indiscriminate in their inquisitions, and many an innocent whose only crime was an interest in sorcery had suffered torture and death under their regime. It would be a bitter irony indeed if he were to get into trouble for practising magic now of all times, and he briefly wondered if the gods were having sport with him.

'What can I do for you?' asked the young man guardedly.

'Please. You have nothing to fear from me,' continued the witch hunter in his unhealthy tone of voice, 'My name is Obediah Cain. Would I be correct in assuming that you have come from the College of Magic?'

'Well, yes, but I won't be going back there. My apprenticeship came to an end today, and I shan't be going on to indoctrination in the higher mysteries.'

'Ah. I am sorry to hear that,' answered the man, his eyebrow and the corner of his mouth raising a little in unison. 'Despite that, I should still very much like to talk with you concerning your days at the college. If you can spare me the time over a drink that is?'

'Alas, it seems that I have all the time in the world now, and a drink would be most welcome at this juncture.'

THE TULIP WAS a ribald establishment in a side street off Guilderstraase, patronised mainly by labourers and menial workers. Cain had suggested it so that they were not likely to encounter any of Michael's erstwhile colleagues, and any reservations the youth had about entering such a bawdy house in his academian attire were dispelled when he saw how the presence of the witch hunter discouraged the clientele from even a cursory glance in their direction.

Cain himself refused to drink with Michael, proclaiming that his religious ascetism would not permit him to partake of alcohol, but he generously provided the youth with a jug of foaming table beer from which he could refill his tankard.

'So what's this all about then?' enquired Michael once he had properly introduced himself to the sinister witch hunter. He was eager, he realised, to get this encounter over with, since he instinctively mistrusted this strange man. But at the same time a resentment for the world of magic and wizards which had so cruelly rejected him was beginning to fester in the undertow of his shattered emotions – a resentment which was stirring up faint notions of respect for the work of such men as Cain, even as he spoke.

'As you can imagine, where I am involved it is about heresy, blasphemy and cult activity!' Obediah Cain smiled.

'You surely can't think that I–' Michael blurted, but he was silenced by an impatient wave from the witch hunter.

'No, no, no, lad! Of course I don't think a failed apprentice is involved. But answer me this: why do you think capable young men like yourself fail at that academy all the time?'

'Well, I mean, the course is very rigorous, isn't it? It takes a high degree of spiritual fortitude as well as academic prowess. They told me that only rare individuals are cut out for such a challenge,' Michael answered carefully, not yet prepared to damn his erstwhile colleagues, but somewhere deep inside he was starting to entertain the notion that damnation was perhaps their lot.

'Ha!' Cain spat. 'And do you suppose that all those bloated old men up at the college are possessed of such purity? Don't you believe it, lad! Why, you can reckon the sins of the flesh on their fat carcasses like the bites on that serving wench's neck. They haven't the moral fibre to do what they ask of you young apprentices who fail, but they'll happily take your money. No, the easy route to arcane power is the path trodden by their well-shod soles, and that means bargains with daemonic powers. Dark magic and necromancy, pacts with Chaos daemons is their mystical currency, you mark my words.

'Now listen well, young Michael de la Lune. I have it, from an unimpeachable source, that there are ancient books of necromancy, and the unguents used in the mummification rituals of distant Araby, in the college libraries.'

'No, it's surely impossible,' Michael gasped, shaking his head to clear the ale fumes, aghast at the enormity of what he was hearing. 'I spent four years in that place. I would have known.'

'Do you think that such a well-established secret society would reveal itself to a mere apprentice? Even one under their own roof? Now I'm not saying that everyone at the college who isn't an apprentice is in on this. That would be madness.' Cain smiled enigmatically. 'But certainly the top echelon of the guild are guilty of the vilest crimes against the Church. I'm appealing to you now to perform a deed that could save countless souls. You're the only one who can do it Michael. I can't go in there, so I want you to go and steal the books and the oils and give us solid evidence to bring these blackguards to trial.'

It all seemed to make sense to Michael in some awful, surreal sort of way. He prayed earnestly that the witch hunter with the strange voice was labouring under a gross misapprehension, but now that those things had been said, he knew he had to find out whether it was true for his own peace of mind. He had spent such a large part of his life within those walls, under the tutelage of those implicated, that he must discover the truth. And if the truth should prove as the witch hunter would have it? Then damn all practitioners of magic! He would name every last one of them to clear the taint of their sorcery from his soul. He must keep reminding himself that he was no longer a wizard, and the only thing of any consequence now was the pursuit of truth. He had been lied to for long enough; although Michael knew not what was to become of him in the years to come, he determined that honesty would characterise it.

'How will I know?' Michael asked quietly, 'You said yourself that such a society, if it exists, has kept its secrets well hidden.'

Cain smirked triumphantly and reached down inside his boot.

'I have a map.'

MICHAEL EMERGED FROM his hiding place in one of the smaller, and lesser-used libraries of the Marienburg College of Magic. It was a strange twist of circumstance indeed which had caused him to return to this building the very next day after he had been evicted from it.

Obediah Cain had remained with Michael during the previous day, and had provided for the youth's comfort generously, paying from his own purse for both their lodgings. The next morning Cain had instructed him on using the map and drilled him thoroughly on the need for secrecy in the mission he was about to perform for the good of the Old World. Cain had also provided him with a curious little serpentine charm of blackest obsidian, hung upon a pendant of brass. The witch hunter assured him that the talisman would negate the power of any wards he might encounter in liberating the evidence he sought, but also warned him that whilst wearing it he should be quite unable to use any of his own magical powers, such as they were.

As to what pretences Michael would employ to gain access to the college, Cain left him to his own devices. So Michael had simply used Paracelsus van der Groot's invitation to keep in touch in order to convince the gatekeeper to permit him access.

Following the spidery lines traced upon the parchment map, the young man crept stealthily through the familiar halls. Although it was late at night, he knew there would still be many powerful Wizards awake within these ancient walls.

After a fraught journey, he eventually arrived at the location of his quest. The Library of Forbidden Mysteries was on a floor which had always been deemed off-limits to apprentices and it was a part of the building he had never before visited, since he was an obedient student. Although the room was unlocked, various magical alarms and warding devices existed to discourage the excessively curious. Those who had tried in the past to gain unwarranted access to this place had paid the price of their folly by expulsion from the academy, or worse in some cases.

The atmosphere within was one of timeless serenity, and thus far the power of the witch hunter's talisman seemed to be holding out. Most of the dusty volumes on the creaking shelves seemed to be historical texts warning of the dark side of magic, texts which chronicled and cautioned the unwary against the machinations of Chaos and evil rather than actually instructed one in the Dark Ways. Nevertheless, even the knowledge that such practices existed at all was deemed too unsafe to reveal to impressionable apprentices.

According to the parchment given to him by Cain, the things he sought were in a safe behind the large portrait of the rather stern-looking founder of the college, Zun Mandragore, that hung upon the back wall. Perspiration pricked Michael's forehead as he tremulously reached his hand out to the heavy frame of the picture. Gently sliding the portrait to one side the map proved true, for sure enough a bulky steel safe was embedded in the wall.

But before he could react, a previously invisible rune on the metal safe door blazed with arcane power. There was no time to react: a brilliant bolt of cerulean lightning arced from the rune at his hand… only to fizzle into harmless ozone an instant before he betrayed himself with a scream. Gingerly Michael shook his head as the coppery tang of blood wet his tongue where he had bitten his lip in alarm, and then resumed his task with vigour, desiring only to be free of this oppressive place. The world of Magic had turned upon him so quickly and profoundly now that he no longer experienced wonder and awe in its presence, just fear and revulsion.

Feverishly Michael dialled the combination provided with the parchment, vague questions about how such a map had come into existence subsumed by his excitement. The door swung open without a sound. Before him lay an enormous volume, bound in what seemed to be very soft, thin leather, entitled *Liber Nagash vol. III*, together with six stoppered vials of brackish liquid. He quickly stuffed the contents of the safe into his satchel and fled the room.

'BOUND IN THE skin flayed from the backs of living men,' Obediah Cain breathed almost reverentially. A small table set before him in their small upstairs room in the Tulip inn was dominated by the hulking tome. It was a Classical translation, the witch hunter had been explaining, of one of the original nine treatises on necromancy penned by the Supreme Lord of the Living Dead, Nagash of Nagashizzar himself. 'And here too, the sacred preserving fluids of the ancient Tomb Kings,' continued Cain in a sort of distant rapture. 'Natron, imbued with the dust of cadavers, to bind a spirit to empty, dead flesh, and protect the carnal vessel from the ravages of time.

'However, I grow weary now, young Michael, and I must rest. Know that there is yet one more thing I would ask of you on the morrow before you shall be properly compensated for your service. A dangerous thing in which we both must share but, before all that, I would urge you to read... here for example...' A slender finger tapped the dry parchment page. 'The binding ritual used to create mummified undead creatures such as the Tomb Kings themselves. Read this and drink deeply of the corruption and easy power with which your former tutors dabble. Fore-warned is, after all, fore-armed.'

With that, Cain swung his legs up onto his bunk and passed immediately into such a deep stupor that it almost seemed to Michael that he was not breathing at all.

It seemed odd to Michael, who in his own estimation might be a touch naive but certainly wasn't gullible, that this champion of holiness, this supposed paladin of temperance, should encourage him, a young disgruntled practitioner of magic denied the way to naturally progress his art, to read forbidden texts. As far as Michael knew, one could be burned at the stake for simply having seen such a work as *Liber Nagash*, never mind actually having read it. The young man suddenly grew very suspicious and deeply afraid of his strange new mentor.

However, he determined to read the extract, as Cain had decreed, in order to perhaps gain a clue as to what was going on, but no more. He would have to play along for the time being, until he found out what Cain's game was and then act in whatever small way he could. He was scared, but a sudden determination not to mess this up, as he had done the rest of his life, steeled him and prevented him from bolting from the room that instant and catching the first stagecoach to Bretonnia. Eyes darting sideways, as if he dared not the read the words he was even now taking in, Michael began to read.

IF ANYTHING, DESPITE his long rest, the witch hunter seemed even wearier the next day. Michael himself didn't exactly feel in the peak of condition himself, and noted the deep black rings under his own eyes whilst shaving his downy chin in the tiny silver mirror he carried. It was afternoon, Michael having spent most of the night poring over the crumbling pages of *Liber Nagash*'s mummification ritual. Abhorrent lore permeated his mind, but unlike weaker men, Michael had no desire to exploit this easy power, which he knew would only lead to self-serving evil. Nevertheless, a part of his innocence had gone forever with the knowledge that vast earthly gain could be bought for the meagre price of one's soul. His optimistic idealism, already damaged by rejection from the college, was further undermined with the realisation that in these dark times there would be no shortage of desperate people prepared to pay such a price. Somewhere deep within his soul, a vow to set this bitter world of greed and opportunism to rights was starting to take shape.

For his daemonic part, M'Loch T'Chort could feel the hold he had over Cain's body growing weaker by the hour. He knew that he did not have much time left to salvage his diabolic plot. He was pleased to note the taint of horror on the boy, and could sense a nascent treachery flowering in him. Although the daemon prince could not read the minds of men, he was possessed of certain intuitions for the darkness in their hearts, and he felt assured that Michael's corruption was now advanced enough to offer the young man a daemonic bargain. Until that time came, he must conserve his energy.

Michael found the witch hunter to be uncommunicative for the remainder of the day, and noted how he had never once seen the man eat or drink anything. When Michael suggested they dine, Cain grunted non-commitally and tossed a few coppers in the youngster's direction, but did not stir from his bunk when Michael left the room and descended the stairs to the bar alone.

WHEN THE EVENING finally drew around, the witch hunter was suddenly galvanised into action. The cadaverous figure rushed around, collecting up his belongings and instructing Michael to bring the oils and the book. Michael hurried to comply, fear of Cain and curiosity about his intent blending in equal measure to bring about his obedience. The witch hunter was obviously in a hurry to be away from the Tulip, and Michael almost had to run in order to keep pace as Cain strode out of the premises.

'Where are we going now?' Michael enquired guardedly as they left the inn.

Cain smiled in a paternal way. 'To the sewers, lad. There is to be a ritual this very night and I need you with me.'

'Why don't you just inform the authorities and let them deal with it? It sounds terribly dangerous.'

'Ah,' said Cain with a snort, 'we prefer to work independently of such institutions, and I want you to positively identify the participants. We'll observe quietly and bring them to trial later, so I can guarantee your safety.'

This explanation rang false to Michael but, with no one else to turn to, he knew he had to rely on his own resources to get to the bottom of this mystery. So it came to pass that he found himself scurrying along behind the bobbing lantern of the witch hunter on the slippery walkways of Marienburg's sewer network. They had entered through a disguised door in the cellar of a silent, shuttered town house. Before descending, Cain had slipped away for a moment before returning bearing long robes of purple velvet. They were a disguise, Cain explained, that would allow them to get close to the ritual.

After slogging through the foul, dank underground for what seemed like hours, eventually they came to the threshold over which, only scant days before, the cultists had dragged the tortured body of the second lieutenant of the Church of Sigmar's Holy Inquisition. M'Loch T'Chort, struggling to maintain a grip on the dead body of Cain, went about the room, igniting flambeaux held in sconces to illuminate the scene for a plainly shocked Michael.

Grey traces of ash delineated the skeletons of those whom the daemon prince had consumed in panic, in order to fuel the strength he had needed to hold on to the rapidly expiring body of the witch hunter. In one corner of the chamber, a lamb stood tethered, contentedly munching on a bale of hay. M'Loch T'Chort had clearly made some preparations for his salvation before ascending to the surface of Marienburg.

'What– what is going on?' Michael asked slowly.

'You are,' the witch hunter hissed. 'To better things!' He leapt up to the throne and snatched up a parchment.

'You see this?' he continued in a wild voice. 'This is a contract I have prepared for the one who would solve my dilemma. This contract holds the keys to the greatest magical mysteries of the age! Its clauses have been set down in the name of the unchallenged master of magic, Lord Tzeentch himself! Aid me now and sorceries beyond your wildest imaginations shall be yours to command, if you but dedicate yourself to the service of the Changer of the Ways!'

Michael stood open mouthed in astonishment. He had expected some sort of elaborate con trick, but nothing of this magnitude. 'So you're not a real witch hunter then?' was the best he could manage in that frozen moment.

Ignoring the young man, Cain's face become deadly serious and his hand grasped the hilt of his sabre. 'I am the High Daemonic Prince of Twisted Fate and Misguided Destiny, from the nethermost planes of the Void!' he hissed. 'Do you accept these terms?'

Michael's mind raced. He was terrified, but also strangely thrilled. Temptation was before him, or death. What would he do?

'I– I accept,' he announced, struggling to keep a level tone of voice. 'What is your dilemma?'

'Excellent!' Cain wheezed. 'I will talk plainly. I am a spirit from beyond this world, and the body I have acquired is dead. It cannot be brought back to life, and I do not have the energy to sustain it much longer. However, the necromantic process of mummification will preserve the corpse and allow a spirit to control it. I believe you are now familiar with that ritual.

'I want you to carry out such a ritual and then spill the lamb's blood over me, a requirement I have as a daemon to indefinitely exist upon this realm, for reasons too complex to explain to you just yet. I will now prepare.'

Cain hastily stripped off his clothes and lay in the circle on the floor. Michael saw now the hideous wound that was the source of the witch hunter's speech impediment, and no doubt the demise of the real Obediah Cain. He wondered briefly how the great man had come to such a tragic end, then falteringly began the rite. He poured the natron potion over the body before him in the prescribed fashion, enunciating the words from the pages of *Liber Nagash*, using the vocal techniques he learned at the college to craft the phrases into vibrations of mystical power.

Within moments, dark energy gathered in the room, its easy, exhilarating flow threatening to consume the boy with more and greater secrets yet. There was the scent of lightning in the air, and death.

When he completed the mummification process, Michael untethered the lamb and fetched it across to the ritual circle. Then, taking a deep breath, he reached down for the sacrificial knife. Now would come the part of the ritual which completed the binding.

However, instead of picking up the dagger, at the very last moment Michael swept up the witch hunter's sabre instead. Its wicked steel blade incised the still, dark air with a hissing silver arc as it plunged towards the form on the floor. For the second time in its short existence, the lamb had a narrow escape and skipped away unharmed as Obediah Cain's blood poured out onto the mosaic. There was no redemption for the daemon prince this time. The ex-apprentice had totally severed Cain's head. The glassy eyes blinked once in astonishment before expiring forever.

'Never underestimate humans, daemon filth!' Michael gasped, still clutching the sword in both hands, his whole body heaving in uncontrollable spasms.

M'Loch T'Chort's grasp upon the Earthly Plane had not totally loosened yet, however. Tendrils of vapour began to emanate from the corpse's neck, rapidly ballooning into a twisted, ropy tentacle. Behind the tentacle a burgeoning cloud of foul gases pumped out of the awful, headless body. As it formed, howling, enraged mouths manifested across its horrendous surface. It was a dank, nebulous obscenity which writhed and billowed before Michael's panic-stricken eyes with an oozing, hypnotic plasticity.

It reared up before the young man as a towering column of smoking, stinking Chaos, its absolute horror profoundly changing his outlook on the world forever, and turning his luxuriant black locks snow white in the passing of but an instant in its unholy presence.

'Innn-ssect!' sputtered the ephemeral nightmare. 'I sshaall crussshh you!'

And then the most intolerable of all the violations of nature, beyond anything Michael ever dreamt possible, unfolded before him. For the headless body of Cain rose jerkily to its feet. It groped towards him, the dank cloud of daemonic essence dancing above it, whispering its vengeance in grossly distorted tongues. It was all too much and Michael turned and fled for the door, sick with the knowledge that humanity could never stand against abomination of this magnitude.

Before he could make good his escape, though, M'Loch T'Chort reached out purposefully with Cain's hand, making a curious sign with the fingers, and the door slammed shut with such force that the brickwork of its frame cracked from the impact.

'Now, boy!' wheezed the daemon. 'I will flay the meat from your bones and eat your very soul!'

In panic, Michael shrunk against the wall, trying to steel himself for the inevitable end and turned his eyes away. White hot light burst all around him. Michael was shocked rigid and, blinking his eyes seconds later, he wondered if he was in the Halls of Morr.

But no, he was still in the chamber and had somehow survived the daemon's magical assault. Not three paces from him, he saw to his horror, the last wisps of M'Loch T'Chort slithered free from Cain's ruined neck and the witch-hunter's corpse slumped, almost gratefully it seemed, to the ground.

The daemon was yet abroad, though, hovering like a wrathful thunderhead of pure magical essence in the centre of the room, swelling rapidly as hatred and rage fuelled its murderous purpose. Knowing that it had to be the end for him this time, Michael's mind, which had been feverishly calculating ways to survive this ordeal quite simply overloaded, and pure instinct took over. Rolling himself into a tight ball on the floor, he unconsciously clutched the amulet at his neck and prayed over and over to Sigmar as the hell-begotten daemon cloud washed over him. There was an awful, agonised wailing like the lament of a legion of tortured spirits... then nothing.

After a moment, Michael risked opening his eyes again, just in time to watch the last flickering trails of M'Loch T'Chort's magical form disappearing between his fingers, into the curious little obsidian talisman he wore at his throat – the very talisman that the fiend had given him.

* * *

'SO THAT WAS a daemon,' Michael said to himself.

He looked thoughtfully at the remains of Cain, who had given his life in the battle against these plagues and vexations of decent folk, and reached for the sword with which the witch hunter had set out to right such wrongs. Hefting the sabre and picking up the pistol from the floor, he gauged the weight of them both. They felt good. He had carried on Cain's good work, ensuring that the heretic-slayer's death had not been in vain.

It had been the first thing he had done right in his entire life, he reflected

'Truth? Inquisition? Balance?' he muttered, donning the wide-brimmed hat that Obediah Cain would definitely be needing no longer, and scooping up the other belongings of the late witch hunter.

'Work to be done,' Michael de la Lune, one-time apprentice sorcerer, said in a stronger, more determined voice as he left behind the carnage of the small cultist's chamber. As he strode through the sewers, a strange gleam shone in his eye and he clutched the witch hunter's sabre in his white-knuckled fist.

WOLF IN THE FOLD
Ben Chessell

THE LIGHT IN the temple at night had been reduced to two iron braziers in deference to lean times. The stone pillars leapt into the
resulting darkness, supporting a vaulted roof of pure midnight. An
insistent drip of water had found its way through the tiles above and
hissed into one of the braziers, as regular and relentless as a torturer's
whip.

Magnus, named for 'The Pious', straightened from where he was
squatting to cover his sandals with his robe, his sole meagre defence
against the cold, and resumed scrubbing the altar. Chores were performed at night by the boys. Sigmar's altar must never be touched by
an untrained hand and yet it must shine like a looking glass come
morning. Magnus wondered if his namesake had ever considered this
paradox, or indeed polished the altar. Certainly the Arch-Lector did
not do so now, cocooned in his velvet sheets with a concubine like as
not, his privacy enforced by gates and blades.

The knock on the huge doors caused Magnus to drop his bucket and
spill water and sand on the piecemeal image of a rampant Heldenhammer which adorned the knave of the Nuln temple. The mosaic, picked
out in tiles of blue, white and gold, made little sense to a viewer as close
as Magnus. Six tiles comprised the hero's nose which only took on a convincing curvature with some distance and a fair amount of latitude on
the behalf of the observer. Biting a curse sufficient to have him expelled

from the seminary, Magnus circumnavigated his pond and made his way down the aisle, inhabiting for a moment the scoured footsteps of countless processions of now-dead priests. The knock was repeated: three sharp cracks made with a heavy object. Magnus conjured the image of the leaden pommel of a sword until he remembered the hammer, cast in bronze, that was fixed to the left-hand door.

The boy straightened his shoulders before he drew back the heavy bolt. A wet cloak knocked him to the cold floor. The body rolled off him and lay still as the storm beat its way into the temple. Magnus struggled to his feet and put all his weight against the door.

By the time he had forced the bolt into place, the man had dragged himself to one of the huge pillars and was leaning against its massive carved base. He was a tall man, with all detail of form muffled by the sodden cloak, perhaps more than one, which he wore like a shroud. His breathing was heavy and Magnus could see the man was not well. Both of his hands grasped his stomach as if he had eaten very poorly and in the second pond made on the floor of the temple that night Magnus saw curling fronds of blood.

The man spoke, with obvious difficulty, his voice fine wine in a rough wooden mug. 'Kaslain.' The name of the arch-lector.

'Arch-Lector Kaslain sleeps, as do all the priests. Might I find you a cot in which you could rest until they awaken?' Magnus was a good student and his lessons served him well on this occasion.

The man straightened himself a little and a flash of pain stained his features.

'I doubt,' a nobleman's voice, Magnus was sure now, 'I will see the dawn.' The boy could not deny that, from the size of the stream of blood, which was nosing its way to a drain beneath the altar, the man was unlikely to wake from sleep.

'Perhaps,' Magnus took a step forward so the man could hear him without straining, 'I might wake one of the other priests to give you audience?'

The expression might have been a smile. 'My last words, the confession of the sins of my life, are fit only for the ears of the arch-lector.'

Magnus searched for the textbook reply but was interrupted.

'Perhaps it might help you, boy, if I told you who I was. You have heard, I presume, of Hadrian Samoracci?' The guarded but blank stare by way of reply convinced the man that he had not.

The man sighed and a licked a fleck of blood from the corner of his lip. The taste wasn't enough to carve an expression from the hard muscles of the man's face. He continued, the names coming out with the measured curiosity of a man more used to hearing them than speaking them: 'The Tilean Wasp? The Thousand Faces from Magritta? The Coffin Builder? There are other names.'

Ah, recognition.

'You are he?'

'I am.' A pause. 'And I wish, before I go kicking and screaming into Morr's blessed company, to purify my soul of the stains which are upon it. Can you be sure any lesser priest is so enamoured of your god that he can grant me that absolution? And, boy, are you the one to deny the arch-lector the greatest confession your cult has taken in his lifetime?'

There is a certain dignity, lent to a man, even a dying man, who asks questions which cannot be answered. Magnus walked quickly from the knave of the chapel and followed a route which he knew well but seldom traversed.

One must pause for thought, to find resolve for action, before waking the arch-lector of the Temple of Sigmar at Nuln. Magnus waited for several long moments with his small fist cocked before the door. The distance it had to cross was hardly the length of his forearm but any distance crossed for the first time is a journey in darkness. Magnus had to knock twice before a voice came from inside.

'Your holiness, a man is here.' The reply was predictably scathing and Magnus waited politely for it to play itself out. 'Your worship, it is a man of great import who asks for you by name. Even now his heartblood spills on the temple floor.' Over-poetic, perhaps, but Kaslain had a penchant for that kind of language in his sermons and Magnus took a gamble. The next response would decide the issue.

'Who is this man?'

Victory. Of a kind.

TWO LESSER PRIESTS came to carry the Tilean Wasp to Kaslain's chamber. The killer had drawn his hood over his face and Magnus's imagination couldn't help but conjure up the expression on the face which had looked on death so many times as he now went to face it.

As the almost funereal procession passed Magnus, the dark head lolled towards him and the faceless hole studied him. Magnus found something pressing to examine in the pattern of the marble. He had looked at this pattern many times, head bowed in prayer, and imagined grape vines, clouds, fish netting. Now he saw veins, like the pale cheeks of an elderly man.

Left to himself in the dying hours of the night, Magnus began to sponge the man's blood from the stones. Some had stained the mortar and Magnus scrubbed hard, removing most of it. His last act before retiring at dawn – he would be allowed to sleep until mid-morning devotions – was to open the temple doors to greet the rising sun. He stepped out onto the wide stone platform and fastened the doors to the walls by means of their hooks. Solid oaken doors.

Magnus was about to enter the temple and go to his few allowed hours of sleep when he was stopped by what he saw on the doors. The bronze hammers, usually fixed to each door had been removed, taken for polishing so Sigmar's temple would show no tarnish. He remembered the sound of the stranger's insistent banging on the door. He dropped the sponge and walked carefully back down the corridor to the Arch-Lector's private chambers.

KASLAIN PREPARED HIMSELF, but not as he would for any common final confession. The cult of Sigmar often received last testaments from dying men, promising them Sigmar's blessings on their journey to the land of Morr.

The ceremony was relatively simple but often the man receiving the blessing had travelled too far on that journey to understand much of what was said. Sometimes he had something he needed to say, a long-held secret which had ceased to be important to anybody but its bearer: an evil deed, perhaps, a disloyal act or a petty criminal doing. Whatever the exact nature of the event, each man amputated the memory and gave it into the keeping of the priest so the doing would not accompany him into the next life.

Kaslain had heard many sordid and foul acts recounted to him in this manner but they seldom made an impression on the ageing priest. He had too many such tales of his own to be impressed by the petty wrong-doings of some mud-spattered farmer or bloodstained soldier.

This man he prepared to see, however, was neither of those. What reckonings had he to make with Sigmar? Kaslain, dressed in his ceremonial garb and ready to receive his dying visitor, reviewed what he knew about the man.

The Tilean Wasp, so called because of a supposed mastery of the vile arts of brewing and administering poisons. The Wolf in the Fold, or the Thousand Faces of Magritta – he had these names apparently because of an ability to disguise himself with consummate skill and infiltrate his victim's camp.

For this he was perhaps most famous and there were numerous stories of his duping this guard or that official. The stories were often recounted as humorous rhymes, idle entertainment, and each ended with a corpulent public official having his throat cut or his belly stuck. One could make jokes out of the death of fattened bureaucrats as few cared for them, but Kaslain knew the truth was more grisly than such tales allowed.

Another name this man had acquired was the Coffin Builder, because of the sheer volume of murders attributed to him in a career which spanned almost twenty years. Everything known about this assassin was premised with 'perhaps' or 'supposedly' and almost nothing was held to be indisputable fact. No one knew his real name and nobody could recognise his face for what it was.

That, thought the priest, was about to change.

The boys carried the man into Kaslain's private suite and laid him on a divan. The couch had been covered with a canvas curtain to protect it from the blood which stained the boy's white robes and bare arms in generous brushstrokes.

Kaslain, not normally one for humorous comment, was unusually buoyant, commenting that the two boys were perhaps alone in having received wounds from the Tilean Wasp and lived to tell the tale. There was little laughter as the boys retreated and Kaslain pushed the heavy door closed.

The man spoke before the last echoes of iron and wood had been swallowed by the woollen mats and velvet curtains. 'Father, I have come to make my peace.' The voice had a sheathed edge about it.

Kaslain steadied his own voice. 'You can find here what you seek.'

'I know it to be true. It cannot be given by any man. You alone, father, can give me peace.' The man's words were chosen carefully.

'You are a man surrounded by much evil but perhaps we need not speak of it all. What would you have my ears hear and my heart absolve?' Kaslain repeated the ritualised phrases with no greater conviction than was usual, but his body was taut.

'Father, I wish to tell you of how I came to kill a priest.'

Kaslain's intake of breath was audible and abrasive, the extra air stabbing at his lungs. A priest! He would have to deal very carefully with the dying legend on the divan.

The legend coughed and opened his eyes. The blood staining his shaven chin underlined the eyes which stared at Kaslain. So devoid were they of any feeling that Kaslain thought the man was already dead. The priest froze in mid-gesture, as if his slightest movement might push the assassin over the edge before the all-important absolution.

The man called the Thousand Faces of Magritta struggled onto one elbow and looked straight at his audience. 'My name is Hadrian Samoracci.'

Kaslain raised an eyebrow. If the man was who he said he was, that made him the son and heir of one of the powerful merchant-noble families of northern Tilea.

'My name is Hadrian Samoracci and I have been twice bereft. The first time was long ago and does not concern the matter of which I crave absolution, except in so much as it made me what I am today. The second time, however, the second time occurred in the autumn which is only now dying. Dying as I am.'

* * *

AT FIRST I thought her to be a farmer's daughter. A simple farmer's daughter covered with earth, testament to her daily exertions in the field. She had hair the colour of the chaff she spread before the swine on the manor estate of the man who owned her. I saw her beside the road as I rode up to the manor for the first time and she fixed me with a stare which I did not understand – though I understand it now. Like knows like. Like knows like, and now she is dead. Such is the way of things and few think much about it. Just as the hawk preys on the hare and it is never the other way about, so the peasant works for the lord…

But I have not come here to waste my last breath on politics, and in truth, she was no hare. I have come here to use my last breath on the things that matter, at least to me. I have come here to spend my last breath talking of love and death.

I am a seller of death, almost a merchant you might say, or an artisan, or even a whore whose body is her only ware. I am all these things. My work takes me to strange places and I often have cause to touch the lives of the noble, wealthy and fortunate. Few men pay gold for the blood of a cobbler or silver to have a blacksmith's apprentice quietly drowned in the Reik.

The Count of Pfeildorf, a pole-cat of a man, maintained a manor house outside of the town of that name, for which he had nominal responsibility. A man had found me, found one of my men in Nuln and got a message to me: twelve ingots of Black Mountains gold for the death of the count. The gold safely in my vault, for I never extend the privilege of credit, I travelled to Pfeildorf, adopting the guise of a trapper of wolves – a subject I knew very little about, though I was to learn more.

Once in Pfeildorf, I took up residence in a boarding house of roaches and wenches and went to work. It was a simple enough matter to steal a horse and ride out to the estate each night. The count's personal security was extensive – a pole-cat but a paranoid one. His underlings were more accessible, however.

The count's chief man, castellan and gamekeeper, was a greasy pudding named Hugo. The count's flocks strayed on the hillside while Hugo plotted to increase his consumption of Bretonnian cakes, or pursued some similar activity.

For four nights I crept close to the flock, stealing a lamb. I would wrap the struggling creature in my cloak and carry it away so its noise wouldn't wake the dogs. Here my plan almost faltered for I could not bring myself to slaughter the animals with their fleece still yellow from their birthing. They were guilty of nothing. All my victims are guilty of something. Whatever you may say, you choose to be a killer's victim.

I left the lambs in my rank room where they consumed the straw mattress and soiled the floor, similar behaviour to most of the patrons of the establishment. Each morning I stood on a crate in the market and plied my new trade. A wolf trapper I was, on the trail of a rogue female, a killer from the north, a huge brute of a creature which had taken halflings from out of their houses. I made the creature into a fearsome scourge for the whole district. Many farmer's woes were no doubt erroneously blamed on this fictitious blight and some even sought to hire me to rid them of it. My fee was correspondingly high, high enough that the poor shepherds could not afford my services. You may imagine that I found the work tiring but there is an easy calm in playing out my strategies and I find great delight in the invention of tantalising detail.

Eventually it happened. Hugo waddled into the square escorted by one of the count's men. The duo approached me and, after a brief haggle over the price, which I pointedly refused to drop, engaged me to kill the wolf which had been taking their lambs.

I was given lodging in the servant's quarters on the estate, a pallet on an earthen floor. I have slept in worse places and I have lain between silken sheets. My unique profession has given me the opportunity to learn about the way others live their lives, miserable and bleak, often before I take those very lives. Take them and break them. But I am not without compassion, as you will see. As I have said, I saw the girl as I rode in and her face stayed with me, though I did not know why.

My plan was simple: to range the estate making a show of setting snares during the day and to scout by night, and decide on the best way in which to gain entrance to the count's wing. I was to be there three days, no more. Once I have devised a plan I do not like to be distracted. Thus it was that I was angered by Hugo's rousing me early on the second morning and demanding that I explain the two missing lambs, taken the night before. All of my snares lay empty and yet the animals were gone. Hurrying because I feared my mock snares would not stand close examination, I dressed and followed the track up to the flock just as the count was being served fig and pheasant breakfast in his feather bed.

I have some skill in reading prints in the ground and what I saw surprised me. In the mud near the stream where the flock drank I found signs of the abduction: here were drag marks to indicate the demise of the lambs, here a little wool caught on a thorn, here the prints of the shepherds arriving late on the scene – and everywhere were the indentations of a large wolf. The wind, already cold along the stream bed developed a cutting chill. I followed the prints until they crossed and re-crossed the stream; a smart wolf, this killer I had supposedly created. A smart wolf manifested from thin air and imagination. I could do little but wait for the night which is usually my friend.

I am not a man who frightens easily, nor one who is used to fear. As the night settled over me, as it fell gently to earth and blanketed the greens in a cobweb shroud, a bead of sweat found the scar at the base of my neck and settled there. Most foolish of all, this man, this killer who is scared of nothing, was frightened of a beast of his own creation. After a brief discussion with the shepherds, who informed me they had had this wolf problem for some months, and who, gratifyingly, were more scared than I was, I positioned myself in the low branches of a large oak which spread itself over the flock like a priest blessing the multitudes.

There was no question of my falling asleep. Such vigils are common in my profession and besides, the perch was religiously uncomfortable. I watched as the moon traversed the sky, describing a pearly slice through the low western horizon. Morning was only a few hours hence and I had long ceased jumping at the shadows of the dogs, shaggy brown brutes from kennels in Averheim. It was one of these mutts who saw her first, however, or more likely smelt her. Even though she came from downwind, we could all smell her stench. It was a smell I have smelled before, many times. When a man is about to die, when he knows he stares death in the face, he has a certain smell. It is in his breath, or comes from his skin, I don't know, I am no physician. I smelt that smell that night on the wind. When I looked down from my perch she was there.

I have seen wolves before, but only in cages, rolling, barred wagons in the streets or in fairgrounds: 'Come bait the ferocious wolf, feed a mad killer with yer own hand!' She was a killer all right, but far from being mad. She moved with determination and poise. I slithered lower in the tree, silent as she, hunters both. Her approach put me downwind of her and I was almost overpowered by the stench of death which was her musk. As in an old Kislev folk tale, I had made a lariat from heavy twine and I balanced on the low bough, watching her. She was fascinating, huge certainly, but agile and sure-footed. I imagined her yellow eyes as I watched the muscles shift beneath her flanks.

She moved quietly towards the flock. One of the dogs found the source of the smell and loped over. The well-trained mongrel bared its teeth and crouched on its forequarters, a language that the she-wolf would surely understand. As soon as she turned I was ready to spring my trap. She did not sway from her purpose, however, ignoring the dog's threat, and I detected something strange in her gait. She was hungry like a wolf, certainly, but she did not crouch low as a hunter would, walking rather at her full height past the snarling dog.

This was too much for the mongrel which threw itself at her throat, a studded collar wrapped about his own. She turned, acknowledging the brutal assault. With a flick of her neck, which might equally have been contemptuous or desperate, she flipped the attacking dog and snapped its spine against the hard ground. Her unfortunate assailant yelped and rolled away trying to straighten a body which would never be right. I say 'contemptuous or desperate' because I could not read this strange creature, I had not the language. I should have sprung then and there but I waited, crouching in the darkness, in what could equally have been curiosity or fear.

The shepherds came then, with the other dogs. No doubt they wondered why I had done nothing, had not sprung my trap. Three young, strong men of Averland, armed with stout staves picked clean of bark during long, all-night vigils. Two more dogs, angry and frightened after the scream of their pack-mate. They would drive her off, perhaps before she took a lamb; anything else was unthinkable.

At the last minute I knew it would not be so, something in the way she moved, something in the unreadable curve of her ribs. I almost shouted a warning, but then I am no stranger to death, and these men were nothing to me. Besides, they outnumbered her. I have, I must confess, a sentimental attachment to the underdog, the lone wolf.

What followed was a lesson for a killer in killing. Again she waited until the last instant, turning as the two dogs came crashing in with their heavy skulls set in a charge. She rolled to the side and opened a gash on the flanks of the closest one with her bottom jaw, sending her victim in a scything skid down the stream bank. Before the other dog could recover she was on her feet and charging herself. She ducked under its guard and clamped her maw about its neck, spinning the animal in the air and crashing it sideways into a rock. The dog coughed once and lay still. The shepherds paused, fear and anger competing for their countenances. Anger won, as it so often does with younger men. They gripped their sticks tightly and strode in. The lariat hung loose in my hand.

She turned to look at the men and to my surprise she cowed. She looked away and lowered her tail, which flickered like a flame above her hind legs. The men rushed her and I read the signs an only instant before her ruse was revealed. The first shepherd was on his back with her paws on his chest before the second caught his brother's hand with a wild blow of his stick. The brother screamed and dropped his weapon. He brought his hand to his mouth as if the benediction of his lips might heal the shattered bones. The second shepherd turned in time to see their companion's throat rent by the wolf.

She was magnificent. I stood as I might in a theatre, watching the players enact a drama of such intensity that I dared not shift lest I disturb their concentration. The other two stood together, defensive now, not believing what they knew to be true. She circled them once, slowly, and then rushed in, felling them with an axe-like blow of her head. The three rolled on the ground and wrestled but there could be only one outcome. Eventually she shook herself free of the corpses and spun her coat like a hound who has come in from the rain. I watched, knowing somehow that there was more to see.

The wolf had hurt her hind left paw and she limped to the base of my tree. My breath was caged in my chest and I strained to keep it there. She sat against the roots and shook her coat again. The moon passed for a moment behind a cloud, or so it seemed, and suddenly I was looking at a woman, or perhaps a girl. A naked girl at the base of the tree, her shoulders slick with blood, her left foot stretched up to her face where she licked a cut on the soft skin beneath. I had stayed silent thus far but on this transformation I let the night air escape from my lungs in a rush and gasped for some to replace it. The girl's head snapped up and our eyes met, as they had met before. I understood her gaze then, as I had not before. A killer looked at a killer. Like knew like.

In an instant she rolled and before I could say anything, least of all that I intended no violence to one so magnificent, she was gone. She sped across the field, once again lupine, once again perfect. I crept back to the manor slowly, avoiding the blackest shadows, shaking my head as if to dislodge the images of the night from my memory. When I awoke late the next morning, however, they remained as clear as the day which greeted me.

AFTER THAT MY elegant plan had to be postponed and the count's security was doubled. They found the bodies of the three shepherds and the prints in the ground were clear enough that even fat Hugo could read them.

'Werewolf,' he said, grimacing as if he had put his toe into a bath too cold to sit in.

What angered me as I stood there, not far from the tree in which I had perched the night before, was the man's demeanour. An assumption of superiority over something he could never hope to understand. From that moment I decided I was on her side: wild, frightened, perfect killer over fat, tame gamekeeper. After we held a solemn meeting about the best way in which to trap the ferocious beast – my contributions were fatuous and deliberately impractical – I went to seek her.

The farmers and workers on the count's estate lived in a village outside of the walled manor, a collection of huts and thatched cottages huddled around the mill as if they wanted to take up as small an amount of the count's fertile fields as was possible. I felt eyes regard me from dark windows as I walked up, stopping periodically to beat the sticking mud from my boots with a switch of hedgerow. She was not hard to find. I asked a few questions, not to be denied, this man from the manor. The answers I got were not co-operative but the villagers said more than they meant.

I found her drawing water from the well. She saw me and dropped her bucket, ducking behind the barn. I followed as quickly as I could and this time managed to say that I meant her no harm. She knew what I knew from the way I looked at her; it is always in the eyes. She went inside the barn and I stepped in after her, waiting for my eyes to adjust to the darkness, divided by slices of light between the planks. I smelt hay and her.

The wolf's attack took me by surprise and I was lucky to have straw to fall on. She was on me and I remembered clearly enough the fate of an exposed neck to those jaws. But I am not a gormless shepherd boy. I brought my knee up into the creature's chest and gained my feet in time to meet another leaping assault. This time I pivoted on one foot and lashed out with the other. The manoeuvre cost me my balance and I once again tasted the hay but my boot connected with the wolf's ear and sent it sprawling. I leapt up, spitting dust and faced her again. She shook her muzzle, trying to dislodge the straw and a burr which had stuck there and I laughed.

'It seems we both have reason to regret this battle already.' I sounded more confident than I felt but such deceptions are my meat and drink. While we studied each other I was unclasping my cloak and searching the room for a weapon. 'Must we fight until one of us, most likely my good self, is cold meat?' There was a pitchfork holding up the thatch, wedged between two beams above my head. My pleading was having little effect and she lowered her head and crept forward into optimal pouncing range.

I watched her eyes; it is always in the eyes. Hers were yellow and savage, pools of amber malice, but there was a softness as well. I looked harder and almost fell into her trap. There was no softness, a sham designed to distract her sentimental opponent, accurately assessed by her predator's gaze. I recovered as she sprang. She was nearly quick enough, nearly, but I have been a killer longer than her.

I leapt upward, throwing my cloak in front of me and reaching for the pitchfork above my head. She flew head-first into the billowing wool and hit the ground awkwardly. As she skidded across the straw, I yanked down on the pitchfork and it came free. I crashed to the floor in a hail of straw and roof beams. The bundle of cloak and wolf thrashed about and I dealt it a heavy stabbing blow with the butt of the pitchfork. I stepped to the side as a section of the roof sagged dangerously and reversed the pitchfork, pointing the four tines accusingly at my cloak. The bundle therein was now a lot smaller and I released a breath which I did not know I had been holding in when I saw the girl's head emerge from one of the arm-holes. I made sure she remained covered in the cloak. My taste is usually restricted to women of more years and greater curves but I could not deny a certain attraction in this case. Nevertheless, I am nothing if not a gentleman killer. We crouched together in a shaft of sunlight in the corner of the barn, she rubbing a bruise on her shoulder and me working the straw from between my teeth.

Our conversation was short but enough to satisfy me that she was more afraid of her condition than any number of shepherds or farmers. I suggested she might wander farther afield on her night-inspired rampages, or perhaps wreak havoc among the deer of the forest. It seemed she had little control and I vowed to help her. We decided to make it possible for her to leave the village behind, and live somewhere a little more remote. Why? I left the village asking myself this question, suddenly unhappy, uneasy even, with the glib phrases I had made to myself about a killer knowing a killer. Certainly there was that. Perhaps I saw a little of my younger self in her savagery and I wished to help her over the hurdle from random savage into refined artist of death. Perhaps I loved her, though I doubt that. I am not so deeply sentimental.

Whatever the reason, I had determined to help her and would have proceeded along the simple course we had devised, returning then to my employer's task. Except that things did not happen that way, holy father. Another character enters on the scene of this little tale of mine, revered Kaslain, and writes a chapter whose authorship I will rue until my death.

That character and that author is *you*.

KASLAIN STOOD QUICKLY, his heavy robe dropping from his knees to brush the flagstones. The killer on the divan looked at him.

'I have watched you as I told the tale and you knew from the beginning that it was your story, yet you listened. I had counted on your vanity, as sure a thing as any.' He smiled, mouth like a wolf's.

The arch-lector began a brisk walk towards the chamber door, the walk of a man who craves haste but dares not reveal his need. He stopped in response to a noise from behind him and whipped his head around. The man was no longer on the couch. In fact, the priest could not see him at all. A large stain of blood marked that he had lain there and a soft red pillow of flesh, a kidney!

Kaslain stared at it trying to understand. His mind groped in an unfriendly darkness. The kidney was too small to be a man's – a goat's? How many times had he sacrificed a young goat to Sigmar on this holy day or that? He remembered the squeal of the squirming animal and the blood, always so much blood…

The understanding of the ruse came upon Kaslain slowly but powerfully, not to be denied. His face twisted in alarm and he spun around. The assassin stood between him and the velvet bell-pull which would summon his guards. He had divested himself of his bloody cloak and stood, whole and hearty, his face sporting a victor's smile. Kaslain lunged for the door and the killer dropped low, lashing out with the toe of his boot and catching the priest in the knee. The aged lector met the flagstones heavily and rolled beneath the gilt velvet curtains.

The Thousand Faces of Magritta stepped forward and gave the curtains an authoritative yank. They fell, collecting in a heap above the struggling priest. The assassin rolled the priest with his boot, several times, until he was cocooned in velvet. He gave the region containing Kaslain's head a solid kick and the muffled cries ceased altogether. He then straddled the velvet grub and sat heavily. For a second, bizarrely, he adopted the posture of a knight on horseback, hands on imaginary reigns and rocked his hips to the imaginary rhythms of an absent charger. This seemed to amuse him for a short moment but then his face turned serious. He reached into his boot, removing a short stiletto. The Tilean Wasp leant forward with this sting and began to cut a small window in the velvet wrapping. Eventually he exposed the arch-lector's distressed face and made a warning gesture with the blade, telling the priest that he would end his life at the slightest cry for help.

'Your impatience is disappointing, Kaslain, and now you will not hear the end of my story. A story which you wrote parts of yourself, although I am writing this chapter, the last chapter in which you appear. I told you that I must confess how I had killed a priest. You are that priest, though I no longer have time to tell you why you must die.'

MAGNUS CHANGED EYES at the keyhole but otherwise stayed firmly in place, his back bent, his damp palms flat against the wooden doors. He watched the man sit on the arch-lector and angle his knife. He watched as the man slid it into the priest's neck, muffling the victim's scream with a handful of curtain. He watched the man turn and stretch his neck while he looked about for his escape route.

Magnus had seen and heard it all and had not been able to interfere. He hadn't been able to move, until now. But when he began to move he found himself moving the wrong way, his hands on the handle of the inner chamber rather than his feet fleeing down the marble hall. He watched, as if he were still an observer, his hand as it turned the handle. He drew breath when he saw the chamber within as if he had expected that the keyhole might have been showing a different reality to the one which now greeted him.

The assassin sprang to his feet. He moved towards Magnus, measuring his steps, all the time looking at the boy as if he were judging the distance between them so he might spring. After confirming Magnus was alone he gently closed the door and rested his back against it.

Magnus stared at the double line of blood on the curtain where the killer had cleaned his blade, until his concentration was absorbed by need to force air in and out of his lungs.

'The boy with the bucket?'

'Yes. Yes, but…'

'But you are more than that? Yes I am sure. We are each more than we seem.'

A pause. 'You are not injured.'

'So it seems.'

A breath. 'What will you do now?'

'I will finish my story. Isn't that why you came in here?'

EVENTS DID NOT follow my script. The players had their own motives and each proved to be his own author. Even my own script might have been written by another. How often had I been distracted from my work in such a way?

Hugo had a cousin who was a priest of Sigmar. He came, a young wisp of a man with straw for hair and a child's chin. He announced that he would watch the animals by night and he would catch this killer. He had all the eagerness of a soldier before his first battle but he had something else also, the bearing of an officer, though he had no troops. We were his troops and he strode among us imagining that we bowed and saluted.

The shepherds laughed at him, having had little to laugh at in the past weeks. Hugo made an announcement to the effect that his own authority was extended to his young cousin for as long as the priest chose to stay with us at the estate. The priest smiled a tight smile and gave a stiff nod.

He stationed himself in the field on the third night of his stay. He had brought a tome which he consulted before he took up his vigil, then he donned his white robe and strode into the night.

During this time I had not been idle. I had held two further conversations with the girl and each time she had agreed she would leave that night. Each morning I had discovered her, working in the field as if we had never spoken. I do not know for sure why she stayed, killing lambs all the while, but perhaps it was because she had found in me some kinship, some kindness which she would not willingly abandon.

We are complicated creatures and although I do not like interruptions to my plans I cannot say that I was not gratified to have her stay. I was unconcerned about the priest and here it was that I made my mistake – not that he was any danger to anybody, but it was his death which ultimately defeated my strategy.

They brought his body back, damp with dew and bent out of shape. No one had seen the boy die, the shepherds now being far too scared to share the night with the sheep, but the jaw marks left little doubt as to his killer. After that, events moved with an undeniable momentum. The count used his influence to contact Arch-Lector Kaslain in Nuln and appeal to the same sense of pomp and occasion which I was later to employ myself.

Kaslain came south with soldiers and witch hunters and they found her, as I knew they would. The soldiers went among the villagers with clubs and burning irons. Kaslain did not frighten me, though his performance had the desired effect on the peasants and staff at the manor. They bowed and scraped to his face and made furtive warding gestures to his back.

Though their methods were crude, they were effective enough and before Kaslain had spent two nights in the manor he had her. I would have killed him then, but I was more concerned in trying to save her. Helplessness is not a condition I am accustomed to or one which I accept lightly.

Our last conversation had been held in the same barn as our first. I was angry, fearful for her safety and frustrated by her stubbornness. She reacted badly to my anger and the meeting did not go well. I wish now it had been otherwise. I have never been skilled at recognising the actions of fate nor at accepting its whims. I tried to convince her in any way I could think of to leave but I knew it was for me that she stayed.

They came and found her and stuck her with their spears. She took three soldiers with her as I watched from among the crowd of villagers, head bowed and hooded. Her mother was there too, a woman with thin skin which showed the pattern of the blood as it flowed about her face. I never got to know her name. They lashed her to a stake and burned her at sunset. My helpless fingers dug into my wrist and I made a quiet vow.

The tattered body took some hours to burn and produced an oily smoke, which caused the onlookers to cough and shield their eyes. Kaslain spoke a prayer to Sigmar, an obscene stave full of polite hatred and self-satisfied gall, standing with one foot on the ashen skull. I killed a soldier that night, I don't know his name; it is not a deed of which I am proud. I took him as he slept and mixed my tears with his blood.

In the morning I gathered her ashes in a sack from the ruined barn and commended them to the forest.

MAGNUS REALISED THAT the assassin had finished speaking and he lifted his head. The killer was wiping his cheek with a corner of the velvet curtain, cleaning away what might perhaps have been a tear. He stood and looked directly into Magnus's eyes. The stare was not comfortable.

'So that is my tale,' said the Tilean Wasp. 'Here lies perhaps my greatest kill and I feel little satisfaction. You are almost a priest: can you tell me why?'

Magnus chose his words carefully, grinding his sweating fingers against each other. 'I do not wish, sir, to be one of your kills, even one of the least. I have seen what happens to those who hear your confessions.' Dawn clawed at the crack beneath the door. 'Perhaps, however, I may venture, you have seen a little of what others see in death, or perhaps you know that you cannot but kill, even if you would rather love?'

A moment of contemplation, the time it might take for a tear to fall from an eye to the flagstones if there was such a tear, no more.

'Nonsense,' the assassin said plainly. 'I go now to pursue my lucrative trade, leaving you as the only one to have seen me as I am and live.'

'Why?'

'Because I may. You ask a lot of questions, boy.'

'I… I have another. What of the count? He still lives.'

'I go to visit him now. What shall my ruse be this time?'

'Sir, how am I to counsel you in these matters, one who can even disguise himself as himself?'

HUGO BEAT UPON the Count of Pfeildorf's door with fat knuckles. Two men were standing there in the late morning, the stone chamber which attended the count's inner door consumed by their combined bulk. Hugo's girth was natural but the other figure wore the hooded robes of a priest of Sigmar, and judging by their ornate finery an important one at that.

'Awaken, sir!' the wheedling voice pleaded, Hugo a man trapped between two superiors whose wishes were in conflict. 'I would not disturb you, sir, so early in the day, but I'm sure you would wish to receive so esteemed a visitor.'

The answer from within a bark of an inquiry.

'Who is it, sir? Why Kaslain, the Arch-Lector.'

THE BLESSED ONES
Rani Kellock

SIGMAR, STOP YOUR hammering! Jurgen Kuhnslieb thought, as the throbbing pain in his head intensified. He winced and shielded his face as the inn door creaked open, admitting a bright lance of sunlight which seemed to pierce his very eyeballs. Grimacing, Jurgen gestured to the barkeep, who turned and studied him with a dour expression.

'My usual,' Jurgen said; it was more of a groan than a sentence. The barkeep looked unimpressed. The customer slumped before him – with his shabby slept-in clothes, his cropped black hair and dark, blood-shot eyes set into a keen, blowsy face – already owed money and did not look to be paying up any time soon.

'You've not paid your tab from last night,' the barkeep rumbled.

'Come on,' Jurgen moaned, struggling vainly through his hangover to muster some charm, 'just one. For your favourite customer.' The barkeep looked away. 'Look, I'll have the money in a few days. There's this man coming in from Altdorf…'

Jurgen trailed off as the barkeep turned away in disinterest.

Sigmar! Jurgen thought; another place in Nuln he couldn't get served. If this kept up, he'd soon end up barred from every establishment in the city. If only that last job hadn't gone so terribly wrong – Heinrick and Eberhardt betrayed and slaughtered, and Rolf good only for begging since he was caught by Pharsos's men – they would all have been rich, at least for a little while. And Jurgen wouldn't be slinking around in dives like this trying to avoid Hultz the Red-Eyed, the small time crime-baron who seemed to think the whole mess had somehow been his fault; probably for no better reason that he was the only one who had survived the bungled job with all his appendages intact. Then there was the other matter: a few gambling debts which had, well, got out of hand.

No wonder Jurgen was rapidly becoming very unpopular in this city.

Jurgen became aware that a particular kind of silence had descended on the inn, of a sort usually reserved for the presence of the city watch, or strangers who were obviously out of place. Jurgen resisted the impulse to turn around, not wishing to attract attention.

A young man, the apparent cause of the hush, sauntered up to the bar next to Jurgen and gestured imperiously to the barkeep. He was dressed in fine clothes, and clearly in the wrong part of town.

'Tell me, do you know a man name of Jurgen?' the newcomer addressed the barkeep. His manner was languid, but his dark eyes held an intensity that to Jurgen did not bode well. The barkeep risked a glance at Jurgen, who shook his head almost imperceptibly, but the young man caught the exchange and he span like a cat to face Jurgen.

'No need for alarm, sir,' the man smirked, his eyes coming to rest on Jurgen's left hand as it inched towards the knife concealed beneath his jacket. Jurgen paused, waiting for the stranger's next move. 'I've sought you out in order to offer you employment.'

'What are you talking about?' Jurgen said, taking the opportunity to size up the stranger. His dark eyes were set into a handsome, though somewhat pallid face; one which – by both appearance and demeanour – indicated a kinship to one of Nuln's noble families. His head was crowned by neat fair hair which fell loose over his shoulders, which Jurgen noted were somewhat stooped.

'I have come here on behalf of my master, who wishes you to… acquire a certain item for him.' The man studied Jurgen, his voice low. 'A very special item.'

Jurgen leaned forward and hissed: 'Not here, you idiot!' The thief flicked his eyes toward the barkeep, who was standing too close, steadily ignoring the impatient cries of thirsty patrons and cleaning an already spotless glass. The noble's smile tightened, but he nodded to the private booths at the rear of the inn and strode towards them purposefully. Jurgen followed cautiously, quickly checking that the knives secreted throughout his person were accessible.

Both men seated themselves in the enclosed booth and once again appraised each other. There was a moment of charged silence, broken first by Jurgen: 'So who are you? Who's your "master"?'

'My master wishes to remain anonymous, and who I am is not important.' The habitual smirk returned to the face of the young man. 'You may call me Randolph.'

Jurgen suddenly realised where he had seen the stoop-shouldered look that this Randolph possessed: it was common among the students of Nuln's famous university. Being wealthy and unused to manual work, they quickly became hunched when forced to lug about huge tomes of lore. Perhaps this Randolph was also a student at the university; this would explain his pale complexion – the more diligent students barely saw the light of day, spending their time endlessly studying books in the huge university library.

'Alright, "Randolph". What's the job?'

'My master has long wished to acquire a certain object, which recently came to his attention as being in the possession of a local merchant specialising in exotic artefacts,' Randolph paused, and fished a small pipe from his pocket. 'However, the dealer was not willing to part with the piece, much to my master's sorrow. Now we must resort to more discreet methods of obtaining the painting.'

'A painting?' Jurgen asked, incredulous. 'You want me to steal a painting?'

'It's not an overly large piece; you should be able to carry it alone. Once you have the painting out of the place it's stored in, you'll only need to move it a short distance to where we can take it off your hands,' Randolph filled the pipe with a pinch of herbs, and pulled a flint from his pocket.

'What are you offering,' Jurgen grimaced as the lit pipe began to emit sickly sweet fumes, 'assuming I accept this job?'

'Oh, you'll accept. One hundred gold crowns now, and nine hundred more once we have the painting.' Randolph paused for a languid draw from the pipe. 'The amount is non-negotiable.'

Jurgen felt his jaw go slack. This fee was totally out of his league; the old gang would have been happy to pull two hundred crowns for a job. Sigmar! Jurgen thought. Just who does he think I am? Jurgen recovered himself and found Randolph studying him, a quizzical expression on his face.

'S-sounds fair… Hmm.' Jurgen did his utmost to appear casual.

'You accept the commission?' Randolph arched his eyebrows.

'Uh… Of course,' Jurgen smiled weakly.

'Very well. Here's your advance,' Randolph said, rising from his seat and nonchalantly tossing a bag bulging with coins onto the table. 'The merchant is Otto Grubach, of Tin Street, in the Merchant's Quarter. The painting lies within a safe inside his office.'

'What's the painting?'

'The piece is titled *The Blessed Ones*, by the artist Hals,' Randolph said. He carefully extinguished his pipe and replaced it in a pouch by his side. 'I shall meet you in two days, here, to discuss delivery. That'll give you time to examine the premises.'

'Fine.' Jurgen grasped the bag and weighed it in his hands. 'Uh, look: what made you choose me for this?'

'You came highly recommended by a previous employer – a man known as Hultz.' Randolph flashed a knowing grin and strode purposefully from the booth.

Oh Sigmar, Jurgen thought, as his insides lurched with dread.

GETTING INSIDE NULN University was no problem for Jurgen, who had a carefully nurtured friendship with the regular gate guard. It had been some time since he'd last had cause to visit the academy, but the feeling of discomfort he experienced with each visit returned on cue. It was more than just the intellectual and social snobbery of the university's inhabitants which set Jurgen on edge: there were the stories, whispered in the dark corners of taverns throughout Nuln, concerning terrible and secretive goings-on within the academy walls. Of course, Jurgen was too much of a sceptic to believe even part of most of the tales he heard, but he was also cautious enough not to dismiss them out of hand. As the old saying went, Where there's smoke there may well be dragons...

Jurgen was here this time, within the musty dormitory complex, visiting an old friend, Klaus von Rikkenburg II. Klaus was the third-in-line to the Rikkenburg family fortune, built over centuries from the local wine trade. Klaus rejected the traditional third son profession of priest and elected instead to study at Nuln's famous university, a decision his family welcomed.

They were less impressed when he proceeded to almost completely ignore his official studies in order to pursue regular extensive studies into the quality of his family' vineyard produce, and its market competitors, alongside much research into the anatomy of local womenfolk. His family concluded Klaus had 'fallen in with bad sorts', which – as Klaus proudly pointed out – his association with Jurgen was testimony to. Jurgen considered Klaus a good friend, one that had not hesitated in the past to use his influence and intelligence to help him out of not a few tight spots.

'It's good to see you again, old man.' Klaus, having fixed his guest a drink, swept the clutter from an ancient-looking chair and seated himself. 'Where in Ulric's name have you been these last few months?'

'Uh, you know, saving the Empire and all that.' Jurgen glanced around the small dormitory room and shifted awkwardly; he'd made a seat of a low, over-stuffed cushion and was beginning to regret it. 'Well, I suppose I've been in a bit of trouble actually.'

'Really? Jurgen, I am shocked,' Klaus grinned, raising a mocking eyebrow.

'That's not important. I wanted to ask you about someone.'

'Yes?'

'I got approached by this young aristocratic-looking man who wanted me to do this job, right? Only he wouldn't tell me his real name, or who he was working for.' Jurgen paused for a quick sip of the spicy-sweet wine Klaus poured for him. 'Thing is, I reckon he looked a bit like he could be a student of the university, so I thought you might know him.'

'There are a lot of students at this university, Jurgen,' Klaus paused to gulp down a half-glass of wine. 'Well I suppose it's worth a try. What's he look like?'

'About my height, pale, dark eyes, blond hair down to his shoulders–'

'You just described half of the student population,' Klaus smirked.

'Smoked some horrible sickly-sweet weed, smirked a lot, bit of a fool. Come to think of it, he reminded me of you.'

'This tobacco, it smelt a bit like rancid perfume? I don't believe it!' Klaus seemed genuinely surprised. 'That sounds… Tell me, did he walk around like this?' Klaus stood and did an impeccable burlesque of Randolph's haughty demeanour.

Jurgen laughed loudly, almost spilling wine all over himself. 'Yeah, that's the one. Then again, all you aristocrats look that way to us common folk.'

Klaus grinned. 'It sounds like Eretz Habemauer; he was in my art history class. He's been smoking that disgusting Araby weed ever since he took up with Count Romanov last year.'

'Who's he?' Jurgen leaned forward, carefully setting his wine on the floor.

'Lives on the Hill. There are some odd stories about him. There used to be a lot of big parties in his manor, but they stopped because many of the noble families didn't approve of the things happening at them.'

'What do you mean? What was going on?'

'Well, I don't know for sure. But some say that they were taking riffraff – if you'll pardon the expression – off the street and, well, using them for entertainment.' Klaus paused while he carefully refilled his glass. 'Eventually all the bodies began turning up and people started asking questions, so his little soirees stopped. Or perhaps the count has been more discreet since.'

'By the gods…' Jurgen leaned back, exhaling slowly. 'So what's Habemauer to Count Romanov?'

'Romanov seems to have taken him as his protege, and now it seems Eretz shares the count's mania for exotic intoxicants and obscure relics. He really is a clown.' Klaus snorted with derision. 'Did he really ask you to do a job?'

'Yeah. He offered a heap of money, on behalf of his "master", for me to steal a painting. By someone, Halls or something–'

'Hals?' Klaus demanded sharply.

'Um, I think—'

'Not *The Blessed Ones*?' Klaus stared at Jurgen intently.

'Yes. What do you know about this?'

'I studied the finer arts once, mainly to annoy my parents, and gave a dissertation on mythological art: ancient pieces which are legendary, despite the fact that nobody can be sure they even exist. *The Blessed Ones*, by Hals, was one such piece: rumours of its whereabouts keep turning up but the painting's never been found,' Klaus pondered his wine glass for a moment, swirling the contents gently. 'The thing is, well, this old painting was supposed to grant the possessor, erm, eternal life. So, well, naturally, many people are interested in finding it.'

'Then this could be big...' Jurgen was standing abruptly to leave. 'Klaus, I'd better go. Do you think you could find out any more about this painting, or Romanov?'

'I can try.' Klaus sat forward but did not rise. 'So this painting is in Nuln?'

Jurgen offered a guarded shrug of his shoulders by way of a reply. 'Thanks for all your help, Klaus,' he said, before briskly turning to leave.

'Not at all, friend,' Klaus called as Jurgen hurried out of the door, slamming it shut behind him. The impact stirred up motes of dust coating the ancient door frame. 'Not at all.'

JURGEN DODGED HIS way across the city, hurrying through dingy lanes and twisting back alleys. Few knew Nuln as Jurgen did, which was the only reason he had managed to evade Pharsos's men when the last operation had blown up in their faces. Jurgen would be sad to leave this place, but he suspected his departure from this corner of the Old World was long overdue.

As he raced through Nuln's filth-strewn streets, already choked with the first leaves of autumn, Jurgen's mind sped. He knew Hultz was out for his blood, so being hired at his advice could only mean this job was, in one way or another, a death sentence. His every instinct told him to stay away from this strange employer and his obscure artwork. And yet... if this priceless painting really lay within the merchant Grubach's shop, then a solution to Jurgen's cash-flow problems could be at hand.

Jurgen slowed as he reached the end of an unkempt alley, stepping over an unconscious drunkard, to find himself facing the small merchant's house lying at the end of Tin Street. Ducking back into the alley, he squatted down against a broken crate. Fishing a small hand-mirror of beaten brass and a tiny wooden box from the pockets of his jacket, Jurgen proceeded to apply the contents of the box – a pair of dark eyebrows and a styled goatee – to his face. He carefully moulded these new features until he was satisfied they appeared authentic.

Jurgen contemplated his rather shabby clothing for a moment, reflecting that it was a pity he could not afford the time to purchase a more appropriate outfit. Or the money, of course.

Taking a deep breath, Jurgen assumed the bearing of a servant on an important errand and strode purposefully from the alley. He stopped smartly before the narrow, two-storey building, adorned with worn, leering gargoyles. The building was flush with its neighbour on one side, with an alley on the other. Approaching the double front doors, he heard faint sounds from within. He rapped briskly on a solid door.

The noises inside ceased for a moment, then cautious heavy footsteps approached. The clunk of a beam lifting was heard from within, and the door opened slightly to reveal a thick-set man. His face – a jigsaw of scars – held an expression of extreme annoyance, which only deepened at the sight of Jurgen.

'We're closed,' the man growled. Jurgen quickly shoved his foot into the small space. He had to suppress a howl of pain as the man slammed the door on to his leather boot.

'Take your foot out of the door, now, or you'll be carrying it home in a sack.' The scarred man's voice dripped with malice.

'My master would be most disappointed if I returned without having spoken to the merchant Grubach,' Jurgen contorted his voice into the whining-yet-superior speech common to the servants of nobility.

'You ain't hearing too good,' the man snarled, and pushed his face closer to Jurgen's. 'We're closed. Begone, you worm!'

Jurgen struggled to maintain his composure as he felt the man's hot breath on his face, and was about to back off when he heard the faint shuffle of a second figure behind scar-face. Jurgen stretched to peer around the thug's head at the interior of the store, and was rewarded with a glimpse of a rather pudgy figure peering at him from round the corner of an ornate dresser. The figure immediately ducked back behind the antique.

Jurgen raised his voice: 'A pity! Lord DeNunzio will be most upset. I had come to lay a considerable bid for–'

'Lord DeNunzio sent you?' The pudgy figure said, emerging cautiously into the light. Jurgen resisted the impulse to smile; the invocation of the name of one of the wealthiest and most powerful families in the city rarely failed to gain the attention of those of a mercantile persuasion.

'Yes, Herr Grubach. His Lordship was most interested in a piece you have acquired.' Jurgen did his best to speak confidently; not easily done with the thug snarling into his face.

'Well, of course!' The merchant's manner changed, a congenial tone entering his voice, although he still appeared extremely nervous. 'Come in, do! Please allow the poor man in, Hans.'

Hans scowled, but stood back from the door and gestured impatiently for Jurgen to enter. Jurgen stepped smartly into the store, then proceeded to make a show of smoothing down his clothes and examining his boot for scuff marks. Hans's scowl deepened. Jurgen took this opportunity to quickly scan the cluttered store.

'DeNunzio's page boys are lookin' pretty shabby these days,' Hans rumbled sarcastically.

Jurgen ignored him imperiously, as did Grubach. 'Which piece was your master interested in?' The merchant wrung his hands, and glanced about distractedly. Jurgen got the feeling that Grubach wished to get rid of him as quickly, though as politely, as possible.

'A certain vase. Milord provided me with a detailed description... Ah! I believe that is the very piece there.' Jurgen indicated a large vase, which stood at the head of some stairs to the rear of the shop.

'Ah... I'm terribly afraid that piece has been, hmm, sold.' The refusal came haltingly from Grubach, and Jurgen could see he was cursing himself for selling for what must have been a far inferior price to that which would be offered by one of the wealthiest men in Nuln. 'Still, I should think Lord DeNunzio would have nothing to do with such... such an inferior piece. Perhaps he would be more interested in something like this?'

Jurgen was led through the cluttered store to examine various vases, urns and other assorted containers. Grubach became increasingly agitated, casting nervous glances about each time he ushered Jurgen to the next piece. Hans, by contrast, was like a rock, unflinchingly inspecting Jurgen's every move.

A section of the second storey had been cleared of artefacts, and a large tub half-full of water had been placed beneath a leaking section of ceiling. 'Must be quite a hazard in this business,' Jurgen commented pleasantly. Grubach assented, grumbling that the roof repairer was due but had not yet shown.

It took less than twenty minutes for Grubach to show Jurgen every piece of glassware and pottery in the place. Only one section of the shop remained unseen: a door to the rear of the building, which judging by the layout of the building led to a fairly small room.

'Any more pieces through here?' Jurgen asked casually, knowing he was pushing things.

'No! Em, no, just my office.' A look of panic crossed Grubach's eyes for a moment, before he brought himself back under control.

Hans placed a heavy hand on Jurgen's shoulder, gripping it tightly: 'You've seen all the pieces that are for sale,' he said, talking slowly and deliberately, 'and I think it's time you left to consult with your master. Don't you?'

It was Grubach, strangely, who answered the somewhat rhetorical question. 'Er, yes,' the merchant appeared rather distressed, caught between the need for politeness to the servant of a powerful man, and his need to be rid of the same, 'I do have some pressing tasks to attend to, so if that's all…'

'More than sufficient, thank you,' Jurgen began moving towards the front doors, though in truth he had little choice since he was being bodily propelled towards them by Hans's vice-like grip on his shoulder, 'Lord DeNunzio will be most grateful for your time.'

Jurgen was shoved onto the street, tripping and falling into the dust at the final push from Hans. The door slammed shut, and the heavy bolt slid loudly back into place. Jurgen rose and dusted himself off, thinking hard. He was sure from the way Grubach had behaved that the painting was present, and the theft actually seemed relatively simple. There were obviously complicating factors: he would be working alone, for one thing. Grubach's nervous manner did not bode well either. Romanov had probably alarmed him with suspiciously large bids on the painting. Jurgen suspected that if the burglary was not performed immediately – which meant tonight – the piece would most likely be transported to a safer location. That did not leave long to arrange matters…

Jurgen strode off briskly down the street, remembering to retain his servant's poise until he was some streets away.

From the alley opposite the house, a dark figure emerged, looking decidedly sober now. The figure paused to make sure it was not seen, then skulked off after Jurgen.

WOODEN SHINGLES SHIFTED under Jurgen's feet as he stepped cautiously across the rooftop. He checked his movement for a moment, and then crept on more carefully, testing gingerly for loose tiles in the darkness with the point of his boot. His planning would all be for naught if he lost his footing now and plunged to become a bloody mess on the cobbled street below. The faint light emitted by a thin blade of moon, poised overhead like an assassin's knife, picked out the edge of the building in front of Jurgen. He crouched down, crawling slowly to the lip of the two-story precipice. Jurgen looked down into the street briefly and then wished he hadn't: he had never been much good with heights, which was a considerable liability in his chosen profession.

Jurgen steadied himself, slowly unhooking a small device from his belt. It was essentially a compact, three-pronged grappling hook, to which was tied a length of slim and sturdy cord. It had taken almost an hour of cajoling, wheedling, and finally a sizeable deposit of gold before Konrad, a nervous, small-time fencer, had agreed to lend it.

Taking a deep breath, Jurgen regained his feet and concentrated on the stone gargoyle on the roof of Grubach's house opposite. He swung the hook around his head, letting it gather momentum before releasing it to glide across the intervening space. The grapple-iron looped about the statue and caught, one of the prongs finding purchase in the nostril of the hideous effigy. After testing the line, Jurgen secured his end of the rope to a disused flagpole.

Jurgen tried to quell his quickening breaths as he pushed himself gingerly off the roof, dropping a few feet as the line adjusted to his weight. Sigmar save me, he thought, fighting to remain calm as he dangled two stories above the cobbled ground of the alley below. After a few deep breaths, Jurgen settled into a desperate rhythm of hand-over-hand for what seemed like hours, then suddenly found himself dangling against the opposite roof. Jurgen carefully lowered himself to the relative comfort of the tiles below him.

He rested briefly before ascending the slate roof cautiously, to the point at which the roof-leak inside the house had been. Sure enough, some of the tiles had slipped, leaving a small cavity leading into the darkness of the building's attic. Working carefully, Jurgen eased the surrounding tiles out of place, carefully piling them next to him until he had made a sizeable hole.

Jurgen lowered himself though the hole into the cluttered darkness of the attic. After some careful blundering, he managed to find his way to the trapdoor leading down into the building proper. Easing the trapdoor up gently, he surveyed the room below. Lamplight emanated upwards from the ground floor, but Jurgen heard no sign of any occupants. He slithered through, pulled a knife from his jacket, and began a stealthy descent of the staircase, checking cautiously over the banisters for possible assailants; Hans, in particular, he was not keen to face. The room appeared empty, however, the only sign of any occupancy a single lamp burning on a table.

Jurgen crept to the door Grubach had told him led to his office, listening carefully for sounds of occupancy. Once again, there was nothing. What in Sigmar's name is going on here? Jurgen thought, as the unlocked door opened readily to his touch.

Beyond lay a small office, containing a small desk holding neat piles of documents, and a large wooden cabinet. The cabinet had evidently been moved from its regular place, where it had concealed a sizeable wall safe which now stood open and empty but for a few papers. Jurgen was almost ready to weep with frustration – when he noticed a painting, about the size of a large child, which lay propped against a low table in a shadowy corner of the room.

Jurgen carefully approached the painting. A strip of moonlight through a window provided no more than a glimpse of the subject contained within the gilt-edged frame: the green of forest trees, the pale pink of bare flesh, and then an angular face of raw crimson, staring insane and demented from the canvas. Jurgen shuddered and turned away, feeling nauseous. Steeling himself, he turned back to check the small signature in the bottom-right corner of the canvas, and made out the name 'Sena Hals' penned in strange script.

A sheet of black cloth on a table nearby made an adequate cloak for the grotesque painting. Jurgen shouldered his prize and proceeded towards the back door that led from the office to the street.

As Jurgen moved to open the robust oak door, he noticed that it was already ajar, and swinging slightly in the autumn night breeze.

JURGEN EMERGED FROM the building into a narrow lane, its cobblestones slick and gleaming in the moonlight. A light rain had started, and Jurgen had trouble keeping his balance on the slippery surface as he wrestled with his bulky load. As Jurgen stumbled along, he became suddenly aware, by the innate and indefinable sixth sense which had allowed him to survive thus far in his profession, that he was being followed. He took a quick glance over his shoulder, making out a vague blacker-on-black silhouette of a figure as it crept towards him.

Jurgen slowed and peered ahead in the gloom of the lane's end, although he already knew there would be at least one more in front; footpads rarely worked alone. The few Jurgen had ever associated with had been callous, spiteful, stupid cowards. Men who lived by preying on the weak, who all feared – despite their desperate bravado – ending up like their victims: trapped, friendless, alone, bleeding to death anonymously in some dark alley.

There, a second, inching his way through the darkness. Jurgen stopped. He knew he couldn't possibly escape carrying the painting. Yet he could not leave it. The painting was his new-found hope, a way to repay the borrowed time he had been living on. Jurgen backed up against the wall, awaiting a move from the strangers.

The stalkers knew they were spotted and emerged from the shadows. There were only two, which at least Jurgen could be thankful for, and they appeared to be typical street thugs, though well-equipped. Their swords, drawn as they approached, were of a fine make, not the usual rough-hewn barracks-quality usually wielded by street ruffians.

'Good job, Herr Jurgen,' the shorter man said, a menacing undertone belying the compliment. 'We'll handle it from here.'

Jurgen had no doubt the man's tone would not have altered one bit, were he to be uttering the phrase Give us what we want and you won't get hurt.

'What about my payment?' Jurgen spoke casually, desperately trying to formulate some kind of plan. 'I'm not delivering the goods until I get what… what Romanov promised me.'

'Very well. If you come with us to the count's estate, you'll get your payment there. You don't expect us to carry that kind of money around, do you?' The short man smiled, or attempted to; a strange grimace strained his face. The taller thug, who seemed a little slow, guffawed at his companion's wit.

So Romanov is behind this after all, thought Jurgen; at any other time he would have felt pleased with his cleverness. But in the small thug's facial contortions and hard, dark eyes, Jurgen knew that the only payment that would be made at Romanov's manor would be with his own life. He had to get out of there fast. He did the only thing he could think of.

'Here you go!' Jurgen hurled the painting towards the small man, and immediately sprang towards the tall hoodlum, smashing the surprised thug in the face with a quick jab. There was a crunch of cartilage. The man screamed as he reeled backwards, one hand flying to his shattered nose. Jurgen pressed home his advantage, drawing his knife and slashing in one quick motion. The man screamed again and collapsed to the ground, clutching desperately at his side.

Out of the corner of his eye, Jurgen saw the smaller hoodlum, who had dropped his weapon to catch the precious canvas, scrambling forward on his knees to retrieve his sword. Jurgen span and stamped down on the base of the blade, just as the man grasped the hilt. The thug looked up, fear and defiance in his eyes. Jurgen gritted his teeth and brought the pommel of his dagger down on the man's head.

JURGEN SHOOK UNCONTROLLABLY as he raced through the streets with his heavy burden, all caution gone. The immediacy of death never failed to make an impression on him. The two bloodied men he had left back there would most likely survive; Jurgen was not in the habit of killing unnecessarily, and he did not intend to start now. He had two new enemies in Nuln, however, for men like that did not easily forget such moments of vulnerability.

If he had been calmer, the thief would have been rather embarrassed to admit that he had not planned as far as where to go once he actually had the painting. So he stopped, gasping for breath in a shadowy doorway, and considered his options. He could not go to the inn he had been lodging at, nor any others, since the bulky package would start rumours flying immediately. All his regular underworld bolt-holes were off-limits, since there was no one he could trust not to hand him straight to Hultz, or even Romanov.

Jurgen was stumped for a moment, the panic welling up inside like dark spring-water, and then he had it: the one place he could go, where no one would think twice about a man carrying a strange artefact. Jurgen grinned in the darkness.

THE UNIVERSITY GATEKEEPER greeted Jurgen with a nod and detained him a moment with his latest joke, something vile about dwarf and halfling procreation. Jurgen hardly listened, just chuckled politely and strode into the academy, the man still chortling behind him.

He made his way to the dormitory houses without difficulty, though several times he was amicably jostled by inebriated students returning from a long evening at the local tavern. Arriving at Klaus's small dormitory house, Jurgen set down the painting and knocked heartily on the door.

Movement sounded from within, but there was no further reaction. Sigmar, thought Jurgen, he's probably completely smashed.

'Come on, Klaus, it's me! Open up!' Jurgen hammered again.

It had been a long night; he was exhausted, frozen and scared. All of which might help to explain why not until the last, even after the door was flung open, after he was seized by rough hands and dragged into that nightmare room of blood and torment, did he suspect that anything was in the least amiss. By then, of course, it was too late.

Two huge thugs gripped Jurgen's arms, and he hung between them like a sack of grain. The small room was a shambles, although the violence done to the furnishings was minimal. There was some glass on the floor from a broken decanter, and some papers had also been trodden into the rug. It was the blood, which seemed to saturate every surface and piece of furniture in the room, which coated the floor and rug in a sticky mess, that created an impression of such brutal vandalism. The gore was from one source: Klaus von Rikkenburg II, who sat slumped in a bloodied mess, tied into a previously opulent chair by lengths of thin cord. Behind him stood Eretz Habemauer, the one Jurgen had known as 'Randolph', a gore-spattered pair of pliers in his hand and a pouting smile on his lips.

'How fortunate! Who would have thought you would have friends in such circles, Jurgen? And you have brought a little present also, hmm?' Eretz gestured to a third thug, who lifted the cover on the painting for the noble to inspect. 'Ah, how beautiful. Best put it away. Wouldn't want to contaminate the precious thing now, would we?'

The thing in the chair convulsed suddenly, then began moaning piteously. Jurgen's heart turned over; poor Klaus was still alive! Eretz appeared to derive amusement from the display, for his pout became a wry smirk.

'Your friend does have surprising endurance. Had you arrived earlier you could have enjoyed the show; I fear Herr Rikkenburg will not be with us much longer.' Eretz paused with mock regret. Jurgen's tensed with rage. 'Well, we had best be off. I think it's time for you to meet the count.'

'Can I...' Jurgen choked on his words, though with anger or sorrow he could not tell, 'can I have...'

'Hmm? Oh yes, of course. It must be very sad for you,' Eretz said, with the indifference of handing a coin to a beggar.

Jurgen approached the mangled form of Klaus, who was suddenly beset with violent coughing. Jurgen bent to speak to his friend, though the right words escaped him.

'Klaus… I'm… Sigmar!' Jurgen mumbled, his stomach turning. 'I'm so sorry, Klaus.'

The figure jerked his head up at the sound of Jurgen's voice, its ruined face staring straight through him. 'Jurg–' An explosion of coughing. '…Is that you?'

'Yes, friend. I'm–'

'Jurgen… the pain… it's evil. Watch… blood, don't let your blo…' Klaus's body was wracked with an especially violent fit of coughing. When the attack ceased, the figure was still.

The two thugs stepped forward and seized Jurgen, and he was led away. Away from the ruined room, and from his dead, ruined friend.

JURGEN SAW LITTLE of the Romanov estate, crammed inside a darkened carriage. The manor, however, he had ample time to survey as he was pulled forcibly from the coach and shoved up the wide entrance stairs. The exterior gave an impression of ageing splendour: a once-great edifice falling into disrepair, the combination of neglect and the passage of time taking their toll.

The interior, in contrast, contained opulence the like of which Jurgen had never before set eyes on. Its crumbling passages were graced with a plush red pile carpet, and vivid tapestries and silks hung from the walls. The huge, antiquated rooms were decorated with chairs and couches with velvet upholstery, and strange sculptures and statuettes of exotic origin.

Jurgen was led into a large study, with shelves of books lining all four walls and a fire crackling in a sizeable hearth. Reclining on an opulent chair with a large tome on his lap was a middle-aged man, tall, with dark hair greying at the temples. He turned towards the new arrivals with irritation.

'Eretz, what is this?' the count – for Jurgen had no doubt this was he – spoke with annoyance, 'What are you doing here?'

'This is Jurgen Kuhnslieb, your lordship, the thief I hired.' Eretz spoke proudly, like a cat triumphantly depositing the corpse of a bird onto his master's bedroom carpet. 'He obtained the painting, and was attempting to keep it from us, as I predicted, when we intercepted him.'

'You have the painting?' Romanov sat up, his eyes burning with sudden intensity.

'I viewed it myself. We were… interrogating someone, a student, to find out what Jurgen was planning. I knew–'

'Where is it, man?' The count stood impatiently.

'Fyodor and Willem are preparing it as we speak.'

Romanov nodded briskly and stalked past Eretz, who hurried after his master. Jurgen was shoved after them by his large minder.

'So,' Eretz was gabbling, racing to keep up with Romanov's long strides, 'my spies followed the thief to a student's house. I knew this scholar, one of the Rikkenburgs, from my studies. He had even given a dissertation on *The Blessed Ones*. I knew that as soon as this petty burglar found out about the true powers of the painting, he would try to take it for himself. I had to find out what he was planning.'

The group reached a long set of stairs, and began the descent into the bowels of the manor. Eretz continued his report. 'We were fortunate that the thief, having somehow evaded the men I set to tailing him, came straight to the student's room with the painting just as we were finishing up! Of course, I had considered the possibility that he might return...'

The count stopped and turned, directing a piercing look at his excited protégé. 'You took a considerable risk, against my explicit wishes, doing this. You were extremely lucky that things have worked out as they did.' Romanov spoke briskly, with controlled malice. Jurgen seemed forgotten. 'There are more important things to consider now. Be silent!'

The party descended the remainder of the staircase in a hush, only the sound of their footsteps on the ancient stone filling the charged silence. At the base of the stairs, lit by guttering torches, stood a large wine-cellar, containing rows of dusty bottles on racks. Romanov gestured to Eretz, who walked sullenly to the opposite wall and lifted a small flagstone to reveal a short, steel lever. Eretz struggled briefly, then with a grating of stone on stone, a section of the cellar wall swung ponderously outwards.

Beyond lay an unusual sight, a chamber of beauty and horror. One half of the room was adorned with the sweeping silks, extravagant furniture, and fine candelabras common to the rest of the manor.

The other half, set on a cold stone floor, was filled with aesthetically-placed instruments of torture. Jurgen could discern a few of the usual suspects: the rack, vices designed to fit various appendages, and an iron maiden, its exterior decorated with a naked woman carved in alarming detail. Many of the remaining devices were far more bizarre and exotic, and Jurgen could only guess at their uses – though he suspected that guesses would soon be unnecessary.

At the opposite end of the chamber, two men were carefully arranging the covered painting on a large easel, which stood before an altar of stone draped with a silk cloth.

A small jade statuette of a beautiful androgynous figure, a cruel smile upon its lips, stood on the altar, its feet immersed in a low stone dish containing a dark liquid. Jurgen felt the hairs on the back of his neck rise as a feeling of deepest dread filled him.

Jurgen was manhandled over and deftly tied to a large crossbeam planted into the bare stone. At a gesture from Romanov, Jurgen's minder exited the chamber, the stone door rumbling shut behind him. The count turned to Jurgen.

'Listen carefully, vermin. You are about to witness something so wondrous I doubt your petty little mind can even comprehend it. Enjoy the privilege, for your death will soon follow, even as my everlasting life is assured.'

Romanov turned away, and walked purposefully to the painting, the two servants respectfully standing aside. Meanwhile, Eretz had taken a short flaxen whip from a rack of tools on the wall, and was walking slowly towards Jurgen, a coy smile playing across his face.

The first blow caught Jurgen unprepared. A casual flick of Eretz's wrist sent the point of the whip stinging across the thief's right cheek. Jurgen gasped and stifled a cry. A second flick lashed above his left eye, sending blood trickling down his face. This time Jurgen did cry out, equally from despair as from pain. Romanov, who had been stooped in an examination of the painting, turned in annoyance.

'Stop that, Eretz! You can entertain yourself with your trivial games, or you can observe history in the making.'

The count stepped back from the painting, studying it with the eye of an aesthete while Eretz looked on respectfully. Jurgen, blinking away blood, was also drawn to the picture within the frame, his eyes widening in horror at what he saw there. The image was of a forest glade with a shallow pool, in which figures bathed and lounged around in various states of undress. All of the figures were attended by oddly-proportioned red-skinned daemons, who appeared to cater to all the whims and desires of their human masters. The image was disturbing enough to Jurgen, but what induced such terror in him was a figure he recognised within the painting. Even from this distance, Jurgen could clearly make out the merchant, Grubach, lounging by the pool. His face was plastered with a strained grin, but his eyes stared wildly from the canvas in horror and desperation.

Neither Eretz nor Romanov seemed to notice anything amiss. Romanov produced a ceremonial knife from the folds of his robe, and held forth his left arm. He carefully made a light cut, catching the flow of blood on his finger. He studied the crimson drops for a moment before stepping towards the painting. Unnoticed, Jurgen struggled with his bonds, testing for a weakness.

'Immortality is mine!' Romanov cried theatrically, and smeared his blood onto the canvas.

For a moment nothing happened, and Romanov glanced about uncertainly. A light mist then began to seep from the painting, and the frame seemed to glow slightly in the candlelight. The bloody smear began to sizzle, seeping slowly into the canvas. The count stepped back in wonder and a low hum filled the air. The canvas appeared to pulse, the image distending, and abruptly two figures flowed out of the painting, forming before the awed count. They resembled the daemons in the picture: tall, spindly red-skinned creatures, with wide grins painted onto their distorted faces. Jurgen redoubled his efforts, and was rewarded with a loosening of his left wrist's bonds.

The two creatures spoke as one, their horrible sensual voices echoing through the room: 'Lord Slaanesh is grateful for your sacrifice – the eternal service of your immortal soul!'

Romanov stood in stunned horror as the two creatures seized him by the shoulders. One of the guards, prompted into desperate action by the plight of his master, leapt at a daemon with a desperate sword swing. The creature reached out, easily seized the guard's arm with one long clawed hand and twisted it into an unnatural angle. A languid swipe of razor-sharp claws separated the man's head from his body, and he collapsed to the ground.

Eretz and the remaining servant looked on in shocked disbelief as their master was dragged, screaming, pleading, into the accursed painting, flesh flowing like vapour, until all three figures were gone. The room was filled with a palpable silence, though a lingering aftershock remained, like the ringing in the ears after a blow to the head.

Jurgen took his chance. Twisting his freed left arm, he plunged his hand into his clothing, snatching his last remaining knife, hidden on his inner right thigh. Jurgen quickly cut himself free from his constraints, as Eretz and the guard stood staring at the painting in disbelief.

Jurgen lunged forwards and despatched the guard expertly. Eretz span to face the thief, white fury suffusing his face, and lifted his whip. Jurgen raised his arm to defend against the coming strike, only to find his extremity suddenly entrapped in the whip's coil. Eretz yanked the whip, sending Jurgen sprawling on the cold stone floor.

'It's all over now, Eretz,' Jurgen implored from his place on the floor, 'It was Romanov's mistake. There's no need for us to kill each other.'

'You cannot possibly understand!' Eretz screamed with rage. 'You are nothing! Nothing!'

Jurgen received a painful kick to the ribs. He gasped, then jerked the whip from Eretz's hand, rolling quickly away across the floor. He scrambled to his feet as Eretz charged. Jurgen's desperate stab pierced Eretz's shoulder, but did little to stop the maddened acolyte, who seized him by the shoulders and slammed him backwards into the stone wall. Jurgen's head bounced off the chiselled rock, and he slumped to the ground, stunned. A savage kick to his jaw flattened him, blood and pain exploding in his mouth.

Jurgen pushed himself upright, shaking his blurred vision clear, to see that Eretz had picked up a heavy, shoulder-high candelabra, and was advancing intently. Jurgen blinked, attempting to clear the blood from his eyes. He raised his hand up protectively in front of him, the bloodied dagger still clasped in it.

Eretz laughed maniacally at his feeble resistance. 'Good night,' he said, hefting the candelabra.

Jurgen looked up, sighing painfully. His blurred eyes strayed as he awaited the final blow, and came to rest on the malevolent painting sitting just a few feet away. Jurgen continued to stare, as a curious thought struck him. Eretz, puzzled by Jurgen's behaviour, followed his gaze, then quickly turned back, eyes wide as he reached the same thought a moment too late.

Jurgen tensed his arm and flung the bloodied dagger – a wild, inaccurate throw, but it found its mark. The knife clattered against the painting, blood spattering across the canvas, before falling to the floor. Figures began to move within the painting.

Eretz emitted a scream of rage and despair. Jurgen closed him eyes tightly, though he could not stop his ears to the terrible sounds that filled the room.

WHEN HE OPENED his eyes some time later, Jurgen found the room silent, except for the low crackling of a small fire on the plush carpet, started by the fallen candelabra. Jurgen got to his feet slowly, steadying himself against the wall. He stumbled forward towards the painting, then stopped himself. He carefully cleaned his bloodied hands on his clothes, and then gingerly picked the painting up, setting it down on the growing flames.

The search for a mechanism to open the door sent him into a brief panic, but at last the lever was found. Just as he was stepping through the open door, a terrible wail sounded behind him, and he turned back briefly.

From the burning canvas then emanated all manner of horrific screams, some monstrously alien, some undeniably human. He ran, blundering though the wine cellar and scrambling up the stone steps. As he fled, he was certain he heard the anguished cries of Eretz howling in agony once more.

And then, at last, Jurgen stumbled through the still manor house and out into the chill night. The first wisps of flame were already rising into the dark sky behind him.

DEAD MAN'S HAND

Nick Kyme

THE GUARD WAS dead. He fell to the ground at Krieger's feet, his broken neck a pulpy, twisted mass.

Krieger clenched a fist, felt the knuckles crack. It was good to kill again. He regarded the corpse impassively from above, rubbing the angry red rings around his wrists left by the manacles.

A sound beyond the dungeon gate alerted him. He ducked down and slowly dragged the guard's body away from the viewing slit, then waited, listening intently in the gloom. He heard only his own breath and the mind-numbing retort of dripping water from the sewer beneath.

Rising slowly, Krieger felt anew the bruises from the beatings they had given him. He'd sobbed as they'd done it. They'd become complacent and negligent, removing his manacles and leg irons to make beating him easier. The mistake had cost one guard his life, but Krieger's retribution was just beginning.

Krieger heaved the guard's corpse along a stone floor, thick with grime, shushing him mockingly, touching his finger to his lips. He was alone in an interrogation cell. There were no windows and it smelled of vomit and blood. At the back of the chamber was a cot. The rest of the room, dank and filth-smeared, was empty save for a single wooden chair, bolted to the floor. Short chains were fixed to it. Spatters of Krieger's blood showed up, dark and thick, around it.

The witch hunter would be here soon, the guard had boasted of it. Working quickly, Krieger concealed the guard's body beneath a stinking, lice-ridden blanket. The man had the sloping forehead and common features of a low-born; the blanket seemed oddly fitting as a mortuary veil. Donning the guard's helmet, he quickly carved a symbol into the dead man's flesh with his dagger.

After he was finished, Krieger fixed his attention back on the vision slit.

THREE SHARP RAPS came from the other side of the door. Volper sprang to his feet. He fumbled with the iron keys, slipping one into the lock. Bolts scraping, he opened the vision slit.

'I 'ope you spat in that gruel,' he said, peering through it as he eased the door open a crack. A shadowy figure wearing a helmet looked back at him. As it drew close Volper saw bloodshot eyes, filled with murderous intent.

Instinctively, stupidly, the guard reached for his sword with shaking fingers. Looking back through the vision slit, he saw a flash of steel.

KRIEGER RAMMED THE dagger through the vision slit, driving it into the guard's eye. Wedging his foot into the door, he reached around and pushed him thrashing onto the blade. Krieger held him there a moment, waiting patiently for the spasms to subside. Then, opening the door inwards, he allowed Volper's body to fall inside.

Krieger stepped over the guard's body and into the sickly light of the corridor. There was a sewer grate a few feet away. Krieger padded up to it and saw it was embedded with rust and slime. Age and wear had weakened it though. With effort, cold gnawing at him as he perspired, he carved away the filth at the edges of the sewer grate with the guard's dagger, stopping occasionally to listen for signs of intrusion.

Using the fallen guard's sword he levered the grate open, sliding and scraping it to one side. A foul stench assailed him. Krieger ignored it, pushing the grate wide open. He went back to the dead guard, took the man's boots and put them on before pushing the body into the sewer. There was a dull splash as the guard hit the turgid water below. Krieger followed, standing on a slim ledge inside the sewer tunnel and pulling the grate back. With a final glance up into the dungeon, he plunged into the mire beneath.

Effluent came up to his waist and he held his breath against the horrible stink, wading through it quickly. A half-devoured animal carcass bobbed in the filthy water like a macabre buoy. The guard's body was gone; weighed down by his armour the sea of waste had swallowed him.

After several long minutes, the sewage began to ebb and Krieger saw a circle of faint and dingy light ahead. He waded towards it – the hope of his freedom his incentive – and emerged from the edge of the tunnel into the day.

Blinking back the harsh light, Krieger looked down into a rocky gorge. Beyond that, the surrounding land was thick with pine. But from his vantage point he could see a stream. It ran all the way out of the forest and to a settlement, about a mile from the edge of the treeline. Krieger saw chimney smoke spiralling into the turbulent sky. He knew this place.

Climbing carefully but urgently, Krieger made his way down the rocky embankment, negotiating a mass of boulders and slipping occasionally on scattered scree. Gratefully, he descended into the thick forest and kept running until he came upon a clearing. Krieger took a moment to appreciate his freedom, filling his lungs with the smell of it and gazing into the heavens. Clouds crept across the sky, filled with the threat of rain, as the wind steadily picked up.

Without time to linger, Krieger moved on and found the stream he had seen from the edge of the tunnel. He ran into it and eagerly washed away the sewer stench. Following the stream, he soon reached the fringe of the forest. The town was ahead. It was waiting for him. Dark clouds gathered above it, echoing Krieger's mood.

Clenching his fists, he said, 'There will be a reckoning.'

THE TOWN SQUARE of Galstadt was alive with people. Thronging crowds clapped and danced and laughed as jugglers, fire-eaters and all manner of street entertainers dazzled them with their skill and pantomime. Huge garlands hung from windows and archways; acrobats leapt and whirled amongst the crowds and flower petals filled the air with dazzling colour. Even the darkening sky overhead could not dampen the carnival mood.

A massive cheer erupted from the townsfolk and assembled soldiery as a vast and ornate casket was brought into view. Held aloft by six proud men-at-arms, it shimmered with an unearthly lustre. Behind it rode a retinue of knights mounted on snorting steeds, austere and powerful in full armour. The crowds gathered in their hundreds to welcome the return of their count and his brave knights.

As he rode through the town, Count Gunther Halstein regarded the crowds impassively. His steed stumbled on a loose cobblestone and moved its flank awkwardly. A sudden sharp pain seared Count Gunther's chest, just below his heart, and he grimaced.

'My lord?' Bastion, Gunther's knight captain, was at his side immediately. 'Is it your wound?'

Irritably, the count waved away Bastion's concern. 'These people,' he whispered, resuming his smiling façade, 'they know nothing of the sacrifice, Bastion, the danger beyond these walls.'

'No, they do not,' Bastion replied. His voice held a tinge of knightly arrogance. 'But we survived the Lands of the Dead, with the prize,' he added. 'Let them bask.'

Bastion flashed a confident smile, but the count's gaze travelled upward, to the banner of their order fluttering in the growing breeze; a heart wreathed in flames. Framed against a steel sky, it reminded him of an animal struggling for breath.

For Count Gunther, the endless desert was never far from his thoughts. Despite the cold, he still felt the sun on his back, the sand in his throat and the maddening silence of windless days.

Thunder rumbled overhead, rousing the count from his dark reverie. Ahead of the returning crusaders, the great wooden gates of his keep opened. Rain was falling as the knights filed in, filling the great courtyard beyond. Count Gunther was the last of them. He lingered in the gateway and failed to notice the dispersing crowds as he watched the darkening horizon.

'A storm is coming,' he muttered.

The doors closed, throwing their shadow upon him, shutting the outside world from his sight.

LENCHARD THE WITCH hunter stalked from the cell, his hard footfalls resonant against the dungeon floor. He was followed by two templars, wearing the black steel armour of Morr.

The three of them walked quickly down the long corridor from the cell and approached a shallow set of stone steps that led up to the barracks of Thorne Keep. A nigh-on impregnable bastion, the keep rested on a broad spike of rock, surrounded by pine forest. It was a garrison for the Elector Count of Stirland's soldiery, with thick and high walls, so it was also used as a place to hold and interrogate prisoners. Never had one of the detainees escaped – until now.

A guard, a thin, fraught-looking man, wearing a studded leather hauberk and kettle helmet, was waiting for Lenchard and the two templars. The witch hunter emerged menacingly from the gloom. 'The prisoner is gone,' he muttered darkly.

Dieter Lenchard was thick-set, even beneath his leather armour, his facial features bony and well-defined. He wore a severe expression, framed by a tight-fitting skull cap stretched over his head, and the guardsman balked at his formidable presence.

'Where is your sergeant?' Lenchard asked.

The guard tried to muster his voice but could only point towards the steps.

'Captain Reiner,' the witch hunter said, without looking back as he addressed one of the templars, the older of the two, a stern looking man with short black hair and cold eyes. Lenchard marched up the steps, black cloak lashing in his wake, 'with me.'

Reiner turned to the other templar beside him, a bald giant that looked as if he were made of stone, 'Halbranc, wait here until Sigson has finished his work.'

Halbranc nodded and faced the quailing guard.

Like the Black Knights of Morr, the templars' breastplates and greaves were etched with symbols of death and mortality. For many they were a bad omen of impending doom and misfortune.

Confronted with Halbranc, the guard swallowed hard and made the sign of Sigmar.

The massive templar folded his arms and leaned forward. Close up, the guard could see a patchwork of old scars as the shadows pooled into the chiselled depths of the templar's face. Halbranc snarled at him.

The guard shrank away, finding the solid, unyielding wall at his back.

'That's enough,' said Reiner in a cold voice that came from above.

'Yes, Captain Reiner,' Halbranc said dutifully. He looked into the guard's fearful eyes and smiled.

'Just you and me now, my friend,' he whispered.

MIKAEL, A YOUNG TEMPLAR of Morr, waited in the courtyard of Thorne Keep, just outside the stables. His comrades, the twins Valen and Vaust, were with him, standing silently. The three of them had been left with the knights' horses, while Reiner, Halbranc and their warrior priest, Sigson, conducted their investigations. It was to be a short stay it seemed – the portcullis was raised and the drawbridge lowered for their departure.

Reiner emerged from the entrance to the barracks, as impassive and unemotional as ever.

'Make our steeds ready;' he said to them as he approached, 'we are leaving soon.'

The twins moved quickly to the stables and began immediately untying the horses' reins, testing stirrups and checking saddles.

'What happened?' Mikael asked.

Reiner fixed the young templar with an icy glare.

'The prisoner has escaped.'

'How is that possible?'

Reiner kept his gaze on Mikael for a moment. The penetrating silence held an unspoken question. It was one Mikael was familiar with, the threat Reiner saw in all inquiring minds.

'By killing at least one of the guards,' he explained coldly.

A pistol shot echoed around the stone courtyard from the barracks.

All in the courtyard started at the sound. The horses whinnied in fear, Valen and Vaust gripping their reins tightly, patting the beasts' flanks to soothe them. Only Reiner betrayed no emotion, as hollow and deadly as the shot reverberating around the keep. It had come from the direction of the cells.

After a moment, Lenchard appeared, tucking a smoking pistol into his belt. Valen held the reins to the witch hunter's steed, which he'd walked from the stables. Without a word, Lenchard took them, securing his pistols and sabre before mounting up. The young templar bowed his head respectfully.

'Inform your priest,' the witch hunter said to Reiner, 'the guard sergeant is in need of Morr's blessing.'

Reiner gathered the reins of his own horse, utterly unmoved. 'How long do we have?' he asked the witch hunter curtly.

Lenchard steadied his steed. His eyes were dark rings of shadow, his face a pepper-wash of stubble.

'The heretic may have an hour, possibly two hours' head start.'

Reiner turned to Valen and Vaust and said, 'Ride on ahead, find his trail.'

The twins nodded as one. Sometimes their seemingly empathic synchronicity was unnerving, Mikael thought, as he watched them mount up and ride swiftly through the gates.

'Once Sigson is done speaking to the dead guard we will join them,' Reiner said, noting the look of veiled disgust on the witch hunter's face. He ignored it and switched his attention to Mikael.

Ever since that night at Hochsleben, when Kalten had died at the hands of the crazed mortician Merrick, the captain of Morr had watched Mikael closely. The young templar had foreseen his comrades' death in a vision, but spoke nothing of it to Reiner. But he suspected something, Mikael was certain of it. Only Sigson knew for sure.

'He yielded nothing.' The warrior priest Sigson came out of the darkness, face drawn and laboured. Communication with the dead was a gift from their god Morr, protector of the deceased, but it was taxing and often left the priest weak. 'He had a violent death, but that is all I could tell.'

Halbranc followed Sigson. The terrified guard came after, scurrying quickly past the giant templar and into the courtyard.

Reiner was about to mount up when Sigson's voice stopped him. 'However, his face bore some interesting wounds.'

The captain's expression was questioning.

'A mark; carved after death, I believe.'

'A ritual mark?' Mikael asked, abruptly aware of Reiner's gaze upon him, his silence penetrating, searching.

'Perhaps. There was little time for examination. I suspect the other guard was dumped in the sewer. I have performed the binding rites on the body we do have though,' said Sigson, 'and our dead watch sergeant,' he added for Lenchard's benefit.

Reiner addressed the guard who had followed Halbranc out.

'Have your men go down there and find him, it might provide some clue to the fugitive's whereabouts.'

'No,' Lenchard stated curtly, 'I know where Krieger is going. There is but one thing occupying his mind.'

This time it was the witch hunter who received Reiner's questioning gaze.

'The thing that dominates the mind of any killer regarding his captors,' Lenchard said, pausing to steer his horse toward the gate, 'revenge.'

KRIEGER WATCHED THE road from his shelter in the trees. The chilling rain ran off the leafy canopy above and down his face and neck. He crouched, betraying no sign of discomfort. A figure loomed through the downpour, coming towards him. It was a farmer, driving his cart hard, cloak wrapped tight around his body, his hood drawn against the lashing rain. The cart drew nearer, and all other sounds faded. Krieger heard only his own breath. He drew the stolen dagger from his belt and waited until the cart came so close he could see into the man's eyes. The rain smothered Krieger's approach. Lightning cracked. The flash from the blade was the last thing the driver ever saw.

COUNT GUNTHER WAS alone in the dark, empty hall. He sat upon an ornate throne set in the centre of the room. A large window threw grey light into the darkness, illuminating a huge tapestry which dominated the wall before him. The man depicted in it looked just like the count.

Gunther raised a silver goblet to the portrait as he regarded his likeness. A twisted, haggard man bedecked in finery and the coldness of wealth, stared back at him. At the edge of the tapestry were the names of all his forefathers. Soon his would be added to them.

'To you, father.' His voice was edged with bitterness. 'You would be proud.'

Gunther slumped in the seat, exhausted. As the room grew darker he closed his eyes, remembering the desert.

Krieger knelt before him in the stillness of the tent, head bent low. The night was chill and Count Gunther repressed a shudder as he regarded the traitor. Krieger was stripped to the waist; arms and armour removed. Bastion and Rogan waited either side, watching the prisoner. Despite the cold, he did not shiver, nor make any sound or motion.

'You are accused of heresy,' Gunther told him. 'You stole these dark manuscripts from the tomb, why?' He brandished the scrolls before him in a gauntleted hand.

Krieger said nothing.

'Answer me!' Gunther struck his captive hard across the face. Krieger fell to the ground hard but, with effort, dragged himself up.

'What was your purpose here?' Gunther hissed, seizing Krieger's chin to face him.

The traitor's eyes were cold and penetrating. 'To kill you.'

Krieger head butted the count hard in the face. Springing forward he ripped a dagger from Gunther's belt, ramming it into the count's chest.

Bastion and Rogan dove upon Krieger. Rogan punched the traitor in the neck, bringing him down as Bastion disarmed him.

With a grimace, Gunther withdrew the dagger. Blood seeped from the wound onto his tunic. Cries for the surgeon filled his senses as madness and panic took hold.

Thunder resonated around the chamber. Count Gunther awoke, startled. White heat burned in his chest, as fresh pain sprang from the wound. He looked up, suddenly aware of someone else in the room.

Captain Bastion waited in the shadows. He had taken off his armour and now wore a simple grey tunic and leather breeches, though he still carried a sword at his belt.

'Bastion.' The statement held an unspoken question.

'A matter has arisen that requires your attention, my liege,' Bastion said, bowing respectfully. 'This incessant rain threatens the banks of the Averlecht; there is a danger they may burst.'

The count saw the rain thrashing hard against the window. It was the first time he'd noticed it.

'I have workers buoying up the bank with earth and sandbags,' Bastion told his master. 'There is little else to be done.'

'Good. Keep me informed and I will visit the site in the morning.'

'As you wish, sire.' Bastion bowed, and walked away. He was almost at the door when Gunther spoke. 'What of the other matter?' he asked.

'It has been secured as instructed,' Bastion said, without looking back, and left the room.

Gunther nodded, looking far away into the gloom. 'Good. That is good.'

ABOUT AN HOUR after the templars left Thorne Keep, Valen and Vaust found the body of a farmer. He lay in a growing quagmire of earth, face-down and sprawled in the middle of a back road. A cart, presumably once owned by the dead man, lay half embedded in a nearby ditch. The horse was gone; its traces had been slashed.

Mikael crouched next to the farmer in the pouring rain. He'd removed his gauntlet, and rested a hand on the man's neck.

'Still warm,' he said, looking up at Reiner.

The captain had dismounted and was standing with Sigson. Valen and Vaust held the reins of their horses between them, also on foot. The four knights formed a circle around Mikael as they regarded the body. Halbranc was mounted, waiting further up the road, maintaining a silent watch as night crept over the horizon. Lenchard stayed near the other knights, but remained on his steed, preferring not to soil his leather boots with the mud of the road to ascertain facts he already knew.

'This is how you found him?' Reiner asked the brothers.

'Yes, captain,' they answered together.

The farmer's body sank further into the mire. Sigson crouched down next to Mikael and carefully tilted the dead man's head to one side, brushing away the earth clinging to his face.

'We can learn nothing more here,' Reiner said and was about to signal for them to get back on their horses when Sigson spoke.

'There is another mark. Like the one upon the guard.'

Mikael leaned in for a closer look, pulling on his gauntlet.

'Is it a scarab beetle?' Lenchard asked the warrior priest.

'Yes,' Sigson said suspiciously, looking up at the witch hunter. 'How did you know that?'

'It matters not,' Lenchard replied, dismissively, facing the road ahead. 'Krieger has a horse now. We must press on and hope we are not too late.'

'Too late for what?' Sigson asked but Lenchard was already riding away into the darkness.

'To your steeds!' Reiner bellowed, stirring his templars into action.

Sigson seized Reiner's arm, before he could mount his horse. 'What is this? This witch hunter knows more than he's telling us.'

'That is possible.' Reiner's voice was cold and hollow. 'But we are in Herr Lenchard's charge by the order of our temple. It is our duty to deliver him to the heretic.' Reiner looked down at his arm. 'Unhand me.'

Sigson took his hand away and stood back.

Mikael had stood up during the exchange, taking the reins of his and Sigson's horse from Valen, and watched as the two men parted. The tension between the captain and priest was written upon Sigson's face as he turned away from Reiner.

'Do you trust him, Mikael?' Sigson asked quietly as he took the reins of his horse from the young templar.

'I don't know,' Mikael told him, 'but he is certainly hiding something.'

'I agree,' said the warrior priest, then asked, 'Any more dreams since Hochsleben?'

Mikael shook his head.

The old priest held Mikael's gaze a moment, as if determining whether the young knight had told him the truth or not. The rain trickled down his face, tiny rivulets forming in the age lines, coursing to his chin and dripping off the grey spike of beard that jutted out. In his eyes there was a warning. 'Don't ever speak of them to Reiner.'

'I still feel his death on my conscience, Sigson,' Mikael said, watching the others as they mounted their horses.

'As do we all, my son,' said the priest, grunting as he swung himself into his saddle.

Mikael mounted up, trying to crush the memories and push away the dark omens gnawing at his mind.

OVERHEAD, THE STORM wracked the sky with forks of lightning and tremulous thunder, as the silhouette of a man hurried to the outer wall of Galstadt. Unseen by the workers, toiling hard in the downpour, he moved along the wall quickly like a creeping shadow, before plunging into the deepening tributary that fed the town's wells and sewers.

LIMBS ACHING, HIS muscles fuelled by vengeful desire, Krieger swam through the shallow drain in the town's wall, diving deep to crawl through the murky water, beneath the rusting bars that went only halfway to the ground. He emerged into a wide tunnel which was illuminated by a narrow shaft in the wall to his left. Krieger crept into it and climbed up a shallow incline, the water gushing below him. Reaching the top of the shaft, he heaved opened an iron grate blocking his ascent and levered himself out.

He had emerged in a long chamber, probably the lowest level of the keep. Barrels and sacks were strewn about the room. Krieger waited for a moment in the silence, getting his bearings. He was in the east wing storeroom. Across a corridor and up a flight of stairs he would be in the great hall. Padding quietly down the low room, the rain thrumming distantly beyond the walls, Krieger saw a knight ahead with his back to him.

Drawing his dagger, he crept silently towards his prey.

COUNT GUNTHER AND Captain Bastion stood upon a grassy ridge at the outskirts of Galstadt. They wore heavy cloaks, with hoods drawn, to ward off the unrelenting rain.

'If that river is breached, Bastion, it will flood the town, the lower levels of the keep and we'll lose many lives,' the count told him.

'We are doing all in our power to prevent that,' Bastion replied, looking at the workers below as they strived frantically to reinforce the bank.

Men toiled with great heaps of earth as others brought fresh mounds on wooden barrows. Some drove carts through the worsening mire with rocks gathered from the edge of the mountains, some three miles away, and sand-filled sacking. They fought in the constant rain, stripped down to the waist, digging trenches to lessen the river's strength.

Bastion looked back to the horizon, hoping for a sign that the storm might abate. Instead, he saw a rider coming towards them from the town.

'Knight Garrant,' Count Gunther addressed the rider as he approached. He reined in his steed, dismounted and trod steadily up to the ridge. Garrant was a broad man, half armoured with breastplate and vambraces, and wearing a heavy, cowled cloak. When he got to the top of the ridge, he pulled back his hood revealing a noble face, framed by thick reddish hair.

'My liege,' the knight's voice was severe. 'I have bad news.'

The count grew suddenly pale, his eyes questioning.

'It is Rogan, my lord. He's dead.'

GUNTHER REGARDED ROGAN's corpse, slumped against the interior wall of the keep's east tower. He was joined by Bastion and Garrant, the red-haired knight carrying a lantern. Inside, the tower was dark and fairly bare; just a bench and an empty rack for stowing weapons. It was commonly used as a watch station. A stout trapdoor was in the centre of the circular chamber, which led down to the lower levels. Two wooden doors, opposite each other, allowed egress to the walls of the keep – this was where the count and his knights had entered. Wind whipped through a thin window that looked out over Galdstadt, making the lantern flame flicker. It cast ghoulish shadows over Rogan's body.

'In the name of Sigmar, how could this happen?' Count Gunther asked sombrely.

Garrant crouched down next to the body, setting the lantern down and examining the dead man's head. It hung limply at an unnatural angle.

'His neck is broken,' he uttered flatly.

'He was with us in the Lands of the Dead,' Captain Bastion hissed anxiously into his lord's ear.

'I know that,' snapped the count.

Bastion stalked away, clearly disturbed. He went to the window for some air: Rogan was already beginning to stink. He looked through the thin opening and saw something to take his mind off his dead comrade. 'We have visitors,' he said.

Count Gunther and Garrant looked over to him.

Bastion's expression was severe as he peered outwards. 'They are knights of Morr.' It was a bad omen.

'Remove the body and gather the knights,' ordered the count, a grim feeling clutching at him. 'We'll meet them in the town square.'

THE TEMPLARS OF Morr rode wearily towards the gates of Galstadt; they had travelled through the night in horrendous conditions and were at the end of their endurance. They passed numerous workers as they went. Mikael noticed the looks of fear, mistrust and even hatred as the men paused in their labours to regard the Black Knights.

'It is man's nature to fear mortality,' Sigson, who was riding alongside the young templar, told him. 'They fear us and so they hate and distrust us.'

'It is our greatest weapon,' Reiner's voice was like chilling sleet, from the head of the group. 'Never forget that.'

Mikael eyed him carefully and was silent. There was little that escaped the captain's attention. It frightened the young knight.

'A warning, templars,' intoned Lenchard who led the party, his voice powerful even through the downpour. 'The people of Galstadt are devout Sigmarites, their knights are of the Order of the Fiery Heart; they are their protectors and are not well known for their tolerance of other faiths, particularly Morr worshippers.'

'We come to them as allies, though,' said Valen, nonplussed. He tightened his grip on the company standard, partly from the slickness caused by the rain and partly to reassert the grip on his faith, of which the banner was a symbol.

'They will not see it that way. Tread carefully, that is all.'

The templars reached the outer gates of Galstadt, a small party of guards watching them intently, through the driving rain, from atop a high wall.

'Who are you and what is your business?' one of the guards asked, shouting to be heard. He wore a simple grey tunic, leather armour and pot-helmet, and carried a hooked halberd.

'I am Dieter Lenchard, an emissary of Sigmar's holy church,' the witch hunter said, brandishing a talisman etched with the twin-tailed comet. 'Open the gate,' he demanded.

The guard called below and the gate swung open slowly.

THE BLACK KNIGHTS filed through into a small walled courtyard, which was little more than a staging area. There were stables on either side, each protected by a short wooden roof. A second gate at the far end of the courtyard, a stout-looking gatehouse appended to it, led into the town proper. As they entered, the guards waiting for them retreated fearfully and made the sign of Sigmar.

Reiner could barely hide his contempt as the templars of Morr and the witch hunter dismounted, allowing their horses to be led to the stables by grooms.

'Follow me,' Lenchard told the knights, bidding a guard to open the second gate and walking out of the courtyard and into the town itself.

Mere feet into Galstadt, the streets thronging with dour looking people, a beggar stumbled into Reiner, dropping a gnarled stick. The captain reached out and grabbed the wretch's arm.

'My apologies noble lord,' the beggar said, from beneath a thick black hood. The poor creature was obviously blind and pawed at the knight to get his bearings.

Reiner released his grip, disgust on his face, and watched coldly as the beggar slumped to his knees and clawed around in the dirt, searching for his walking stick. Mercifully, he found it quickly and shuffled off into the rain-soaked crowds.

Mikael bit back his anger. Reiner despised the weak and the poor. To him they were little better than the foul creatures they hunted. 'A weak body leads to a weak mind,' was Reiner's creed. 'That way there is only darkness.'

The remembered words of the doctrine in his thoughts, Mikael followed the rest of the knights as they made their way further into Galstadt. When they reached the town square, they stopped. Before them were six mounted knights. They wore half-armour, with the symbol of a heart wreathed in flames over their breast and left shoulder. Their swords were drawn.

'What have you embroiled us in witch hunter?' Sigson hissed accusingly.

Lenchard ignored him, instead addressing the mounted knights. 'I seek an audience with Count Gunther Halstein,' he began, 'on a matter of some import.'

'I am he,' one of the knights, his armour slightly more ornate and arrayed with decorative gold filigree, said from the middle of the group. It was the count. The man had a regal bearing and wore a closely cropped beard that showed signs of premature grey. His eyes were haunted by dark shadows and betrayed the austere façade, as he regarded the strangers suspiciously.

'What is this matter of which you speak?' Count Gunther asked.

Lenchard held the count's gaze. 'A man called Karl Krieger,' he said.

Count Halstein's face darkened briefly, then a mask of indifference slipped over it. 'He was executed this very morning for crimes of heresy, after interrogation by witch hunters. Why should I be concerned about a dead man?'

'Because he has escaped and I was to be his interrogator.'

The count was unable to keep the shock and fear from his face, this time. He instantly thought of Rogan, dead in the tower.

'Holy Sigmar,' he breathed, realising what had happened at once. 'He's already here.'

ROGAN'S BODY LAY on a stout wooden table in one of the keep's halls. It was a sparse chamber with a lofty ceiling, crossed with thick wooden beams. Faded portraits and tarnished militaria clung to the walls. A dust clogged arras hung down one side of the room, on sharp hooks. The dead knight had been stripped of his apparel. A blanket covered the lower half of his body.

Count Gunther and Captain Bastion presided over the body on one side of the table, while on the other Sigson examined the dead knight, the witch hunter having convinced the count that the priest of Morr might be able to learn something useful. Gunther had refused communication with the corpse though.

Reiner, Mikael and the other knights of Morr waited patiently behind Sigson. The warrior priest conducted his work in silence. Mikael caught the dark glances of the Sigmarites – Garrant and two others waiting in the shadows at the edge of the hall – and saw they were still armed. The tension was almost palpable. He didn't need the prescience of Morr to tell him there was danger here. And there was a stench about the place too. Perhaps this was a sign from his god, for it reeked of death.

'Strangulation,' Sigson asserted, pointing out the lividity around the neck. He too had stripped out of his breastplate and arm greaves. He moved the head to one side, inspecting the cheek. 'No mark,' he muttered.

'What do you mean?' Count Gunther asked.

'Krieger has killed two already, that we know of,' Sigson told him, 'and each had a mark carved into the cheek.'

'Perhaps he was interrupted,' Bastion suggested.

'Whatever the cause, Bastion, I want Krieger found and brought before me,' Gunther ordered, before returning his attention to the priest. 'My men and I are tired and their forbearance is stretched to the limit. This is over,' he said, pulling the blanket back over Rogan's body, much to Sigson's chagrin.

'Garrant, conduct a full search of the keep. I want double watches come nightfall.'

Garrant uttered his compliance and left the room.

'And what would you have us do, count?' Reiner said. It was the first time he'd spoken since entering the keep.

'I will make a barrack house available, other than that keep out of our way.'

Reiner nodded, but his cold eyes never left Count Gunther's face.

'I have some questions,' Lenchard said from the shadows then added, addressing Reiner, 'Your men look weary. I suggest you get them to the barracks.'

'Halbranc,' the captain of Morr said, without averting his icy gaze from the witch hunter, 'you heard Herr Lenchard.'

Halbranc nodded and looked over to Sigson.

'I'll follow shortly,' said the priest, washing his hands in a clay bowl. Reiner showed no signs of movement. Clearly, he wanted to hear what the witch hunter had to say.

With that, Halbranc and the other knights left the chamber.

THE BARRACK HOUSE was at the end of a long corridor, past the keep's training ground. Mikael watched as knights paired off and sparred with each other using wooden swords. He felt a sudden pain in his skull – it had happened before, in Hochsleben, just before he'd been attacked by Merrick. Wincing, Mikael saw four Sigmarite knights approaching.

Halbranc tensed beside him, but they continued towards the barrack house.

As they passed, the Sigmarites regarded Mikael and his comrades darkly, and one leant out, jarring Vaust's shoulder deliberately.

'Little better than necromancers,' the Sigmarite muttered.

'What did you say?' Vaust demanded, whirling on his heel to confront him.

Mikael went to lightly restrain him, but Vaust shook the young templar off. 'No, speak up!'

The Sigmarite, a thin-faced, white-haired youth flashed a contemptible smile. 'Those who consort with the dead are not to be trusted,' he spat.

Vaust drew his sword, Valen likewise behind him. Mikael tried to stand between them, but the Sigmarites had drawn their blades too.

'Knights of Morr, sheath your swords,' Halbranc warned, placing his massive form between them. Even the belligerent Sigmarites backed down before the giant templar. But the white-haired Sigmarite felt the presence of his fellows behind him and found his courage. Eyes filled with violent intent, he was about to act when a command stopped him.

'Put down your sword!' Garrant bellowed, stalking towards them. 'What is going on here?' he demanded angrily.

'Nothing, just a misunderstanding,' Halbranc said. 'We'll be on our way,' he added, holding Vaust hard by the back of his neck and turning him around. Mikael followed suite, and as the knights were walking away he heard Garrant mutter. 'The sooner, the better.'

Halbranc stopped. An uneasy silence filled the corridor. Mikael heard the leather of the giant's gauntlets crack into a fist. He could feel the gaze of Garrant and his fellows boring into him. Halbranc released his grip. They walked away. Mikael breathed again.

IT WAS NIGHT. The scrape of Halbranc's whetstone against his sword blade penetrated the frustrated silence. He sat on the end of a small cot and worked hard at the weapon – a mighty zwei-hander and one of several blades he carried – until its edge was razor-keen. He seemed lost in the routine of it as if scraping out past sins that tarnished his blade. Mikael knew little about the giant templar, save that he was a mercenary once and had fought in many armies, across many continents. Halbranc never spoke of it. Perhaps he didn't care to.

The two brothers, Valen and Vaust, were sitting on stools at a low wooden table in the middle of the room. They had found a deck of cards and were playing out a game of skulls. Like Halbranc, they were restless, preferring action instead of prolonged bouts of inactivity.

Reiner and Sigson were still absent, doubtless conversing with the witch hunter, Lenchard. None of them had slept.

Mikael sat on the opposite cot to Halbranc, his attention on the window next to him. Outside, in the flickering light of several lanterns, the shadows of workers still toiled. As he stared up into the blackened sky, Mikael felt his eyelids grow heavy as a dream engulfed him...

A great sun burned down upon the barren desert.

Mikael was alone in a mighty desert that seemed like it was on fire. Yet he felt no heat or wind.

Cresting a mighty rise he looked across a deep valley. An old man dressed in black robes was standing upon a high dune. With a gnarled finger he beckoned Mikael across the valley towards him.

Mikael took a tentative step forward. His foot plunged into a mire of sand and suddenly the entire side of the dune was shifting, collapsing beneath him!

He fell, tumbling down the side of the valley. Spitting sand from his mouth, he looked up into the sunlight. The man had gone.

A sudden trembling began beneath him. Mikael scrambled back, clawing handfuls of sand as he did so. A great spike pierced the valley floor before him, reaching ever higher into the burning sky. A tower of obsidian followed, surging upwards, pushing out great waves of sand. Slowly, a huge black skull emerged like some terrible, mythic beast. Rivulets of sand flowed from the gargantuan eye and nose sockets and as the mouth broke through the churning dunes created by its emergence, a huge black door was revealed. It opened and there stood a towering figure.

Its mummified flesh bore the taint of ages and it wore the armour of a knight of Sigmar. It reached out towards Mikael with a filthy talon-like hand. The creature's mouth opened and uttered, 'Setti-Ra...'

Mikael woke with a sudden start. There was a commotion outside. Halbranc was on his feet, a short sword in his hand, going for the door. Valen had fallen asleep at the card table but sprang up, alert at the sound. Vaust was nowhere to be seen.

Grabbing his own blade, Mikael went to join Halbranc. He pulled the door open and saw three Sigmarite knights running away down the corridor. Another knight was running towards the barracks. It was Vaust.

When Vaust reached the door, he was panting heavily for breath. 'They've found another body,' he gasped.

TWENTY KNIGHTS HAD gathered in the hall of the east wing when Mikael and the others arrived, Count Gunther and his retinue amongst them. They encircled the body of a slain knight and the Morr worshippers had to force their way through.

'Back away,' ordered the count, fighting to get past the throng of knights. 'Holy Sigmar,' he breathed. The knight lay slumped within an alcove, his face covered in shadows.

Reiner and Sigson appeared amidst the crowd. The warrior priest went instantly to the dead knight, crouching down to examine it.

The knights fell abruptly into silence. Mikael heard mutterings of discontent. Valen and Vaust closed in around him, Halbranc at their back. Reiner kept his cold gaze on Sigson but held his sword hilt ready.

'He has been strangled,' Sigson told the count. 'With some force – his neck is broken.' Sigson carefully tilted the dead knight's head, searching for another mark. Light spilled onto the corpse, illuminating the face.

'By the hand of Morr,' Vaust gasped. It was the knight he had confronted in the corridor.

'You argued with this man,' said Garrant, accusingly. 'Where were you tonight?'

'I was restless,' Vaust admitted, 'So I toured the east wing.' He cast a sideways glance at Reiner. There would be repercussions from this. The captain took disobedience very seriously.

'And you met up with this knight,' Garrant continued, 'to settle your differences.'

There were angry murmurings from the Sigmarites. Mikael felt the same tension he had back in the corridor with Halbranc.

'No. I saw no one,' Vaust protested through gritted teeth.

'You drew swords first,' Garrant said. 'I saw it with my own eyes.'

Some of the Sigmarites nodded in agreement. Mikael noticed that the count had moved to the back of the group, Bastion alongside him.

'Is the chamber intact?' he heard Count Gunther mutter above the increasingly belligerent Sigmarites.

The captain nodded.

'You killed him,' one of the knights from the crowd spat suddenly, stepping towards Vaust. Valen put him down with one punch.

The hall exploded into chaos. Three Sigmarite knights waded forward to take on Valen, but Halbranc and Reiner intervened. Halbranc smashed the first two into the crowd, while Reiner brought the other to his knees with a powerful uppercut. Several of the knights of Sigmar bellowed battle oaths and charged in, weapons drawn.

Mikael drew his sword. Valen and Vaust followed his lead.

A pistol shot rang out, reverberating around the mighty hall. Lenchard stood upon a table, smoke rising from the barrel of the weapon.

'Cease!' he commanded. 'Listen.'

From outside there was a sound like thunder.

'The river,' Count Gunther realised suddenly. He turned to Garrant. 'Gather up all the men,' he said. 'If the bank breaks the flood waters will take this keep and us with it.'

Garrant nodded, gave a last dark glance at the knights of Morr, and started bellowing orders.

Reiner approached the count. 'This is what Krieger has been waiting for,' he said. 'To slip away and kill again in the confusion.'

Gunther looked him in the eye. 'I need every man on that river bank.'

'Then let us help.'

The count hesitated at first then nodded. 'Very well.'

Reiner turned to his knights and gestured for them to follow.

As they were leaving Mikael saw Gunther conversing with Bastion once more. 'Take two men,' he said, 'and guard the vault – lock it.'

Mikael had no time to linger and left the hall to join his comrades. Again the strange stench of death assailed him.

'This place reeks of the dead,' Mikael whispered to Halbranc.

'Careful lad,' said the giant, 'they'll be blaming us for that too,' he added, smiling.

THUNDER RAGED IN the heavens and lightning split the blackness.

Mikael carried two heavy sacks of sand towards the breach in the bank. At the river there was chaos.

A cart lay on its side, sinking into the earth. Men heaved at it, trying to free the thrashing horse trapped beneath. Others held ropes onto workers wading into the river itself with sacks and rocks. Workers and knights battled together, heaving great clods of earth into the raging river flow. A great train of them moved from the keep to the riverbank, bringing earth in barrows, pails and tools in an effort to save the keep and the town. The rain battered men down as they struggled to lift the sodden earth, digging the crude trenches ever deeper to divert the water.

Mikael slung down a second sack. Straightening his back and wiping the moisture from his brow, he looked up at the keep. A flash of lightning cast it in stark silhouette. It was a dark and forbidding image. Another bolt lit up the night and through the lashing rain, Mikael thought he saw a figure, away from the river, creeping up a shallow embankment towards the keep. Blinking back the rain and buffeting wind he looked back again, but the figure was gone. He trod back up the shallow rise to the keep.

Halbranc was in the courtyard.

'Works up a sweat eh, lad?'

Mikael nodded. His muscles burned, they'd been fighting the flood waters for over an hour.

They headed towards the cellars, through a trapdoor in the courtyard and down shallow steps, where supplies of sand bags and barrows were kept.

Mikael stopped part way down the stairs. 'Something is wrong,' he said.

'What is it, Mikael?' Halbranc drew his short sword, searching in the half darkness.

Mikael advanced slowly. The torches set in the cellar walls spluttered and cast flickering shadows. The floor shimmered and moved.

'It's flooded,' Mikael said, taking the last of the steps and plunging, waist deep, into the water.

'Can you smell that,' he whispered. The storm outside was dulled down here, resonant and foreboding. Suddenly the rest of the knights seemed very far away.

'Smells like death.' Halbranc watched the darkness ahead.

An ill-feeling grew in the pit of Mikael's stomach as they waded through the flooded cellar.

'Wait,' he hissed. Something was floating down towards them on a light current. Mikael drew his sword.

The thing drifted into the corona of light cast by one of the torches. It was a man's body, partially decomposed.

'Another knight?' Halbranc asked, covering his mouth at the stench.

'I don't know,' Mikael said, leaning in close. 'His neck is broken,' he added, looking back towards Halbranc, 'and I've smelled this stench since we arrived. This man has been long dead.'

A shadow passed over the entrance to the cellar above.

'Down here!' Halbranc bellowed.

Four men entered the trapdoor into the cellar; Lenchard followed by Count Gunther and two of his knights.

'We may have another victim,' Halbranc told them, picking a torch off the wall to illuminate the man's rotting features.

Gunther's eyes grew wide and fearful. 'That's Karl Krieger,' he rasped.

'Then we are looking for the wrong man,' Mikael told them.

Realisation dawned upon the count's face. He plunged into the water, pushing past the templars of Morr and the floating corpse. 'The vault,' he muttered, wading down the flooded corridor, fuelled by anxious desperation.

Mikael sheathed his sword and followed. After a few minutes they reached a corner, around it a shallow slope led up to a massive iron door. Count Gunther stopped. The rain outside throbbed against the walls as the door swung open on creaking hinges.

At Mikael's urging, they moved towards the door. Halbranc gripped it and heaved it open.

Inside was a simple stone room. At the centre rested an ornate throne, encrusted with jewels and worn gold filigree. At the foot of the throne lay three dead knights. Mikael recognised one of them as Bastion. They had all been strangled.

'Just what did you bring back with you from the desert?' Mikael asked Count Gunther, drawing his sword.

The count turned on him, initially shocked the templar even knew of it then said, 'My father... Falken Halstein...'

In the thick shadows at the back of the room, something stirred. Stepping out of the gloom was a creature that resembled Gunther. Its tarnished armour bore the emblem of the fiery heart. Its flesh was desiccated, worn to shrivelled leather by the hostile conditions of the desert. As it lumbered towards them, its eyes flared with remembered hate.

It came at Gunther. The Sigmarite knights rushed forward to protect him. Swinging its mighty arm, the creature smashed one of the knights into the wall with a sickening crunch of bone. From a rotting scabbard it drew a rusted sword and ran the second through, lifting him screaming into the air. As the beast withdrew its sword, the knight slipping off like discarded meat, Halbranc charged at it, hacking down two-handed upon its arm but his blade rebounded.

'Its skin is like iron,' he cried, fending off a blow that almost knocked him down. Mikael went to his side.

The creature held up a withered hand. Mikael couldn't move, halted by the malevolent will of the undead knight. It spoke with a voice that held the weight of ages. 'I am Setti-Ra. A reign of terror shall sweep your lands and beyond at my rebirth. Slumbering legions will rise once more and bathe the deserts in blood. Kneel now before me.'

Mikael felt a terrible weight pressing down upon him. His legs were buckling against it. He tried to mutter a prayer to Morr, but was unable. Halbranc was on his knees; sweat coursing down his reddened face.

'Only fire and the will of Sigmar can purge the creature from this body.'

The voice of Lenchard was like crystal water as it broke the power of Setti-Ra. With the burden lifted, Mikael arose. Halbranc struggled to his feet beside him.

The Black Knights backed away.

Around the chamber, the torches spluttered and died as the water lapped languidly at their feet.

'We must get to higher ground,' Mikael said, 'draw the creature out.'

'No.' It was Count Gunther. Sword drawn, he blocked the doorway. Mikael noticed the creature's gaze was fixed upon the count.

Lenchard saw it too. 'He is under the creature's thrall,' he growled.

Mikael pushed the witch hunter aside, parrying a blow from Gunther's sword. Behind him, Setti-Ra advanced.

'Keep it back!' Mikael cried, hearing the clash of steel as Halbranc and Lenchard fought the creature.

Count Gunther's eyes were covered by a milky white sheen. When he spoke, it was as if he were the creature's mouthpiece.

'The will of Setti-Ra be done, the living shall perish before his–'

The count collapsed to the ground before he could finish. Reiner stood behind him. The other knights of Morr were with him. They had heard the commotion below and gone down to investigate. The captain's eyes grew suddenly wide and a strange keening sensation resonated in Mikael's skull. The young templar dove to the side as, dragging Count Gunther clear, Reiner bellowed, 'Down!'

Lenchard was smashed through the doorway and tumbled down the slope.

'Out. Now!' Reiner cried.

Halbranc backed out of the room, heaving Mikael with him as the beast lumbered after them.

'Seal the doors,' Reiner ordered.

Valen and Vaust pushed the doors shut as Sigson slid down a heavy, metal brace. From within, the distant thudding retort of the creature's blows could be heard almost instantly.

Outside the vault, Mikael nodded his thanks to his captain who responded coldly.

'That door will not hold it long, make ready.'

'Our swords won't kill it,' Mikael said, 'we must get to higher ground and burn it.'

A sudden powerful blow echoed against the iron door as part of it bent outwards.

'The barrel ramp...' Count Gunther muttered, sluggishly. He was slowly coming round and rubbed his head where Reiner had struck him to break the creature's hold. 'It leads to the hall above...' He pointed down the slope where a corridor branched off.

Reiner looked over at it, then back at the count.

'It wants me dead,' Count Gunther said. 'My father killed this creature long ago; in me it sees him and desires vengeance. I can lure it.'

Sigson went over to the count, and helped him to his feet. 'Can you stand?'

The count nodded.

Another blow from within the vault caused a hefty split in the iron.

'We must leave, now,' Reiner told them. 'Vaust, lead them,' he ordered.

The young templar ran to the head of the group and back down the slope towards the corridor Gunther had shown them, his brother following closely behind.

Halbranc hefted Lenchard onto his shoulder as Mikael and Reiner went last with the count. They were backing down the slope, a few feet from the vault, when the iron door finally fell with a screech of twisting metal. Bolts came free from the wall with a shower of dust and debris, and Setti-Ra stepped out onto the slope, driven by primal instincts.

The knights of Morr goaded the creature on. They retreated up the barrel ramp, making sure the creature saw where they were going. Ahead, Vaust smashed through a trapdoor that led to the hall.

CROUCHED IN THE room above, the two brothers heaved an unconscious Lenchard out of the cellars from Halbranc's shoulder. The giant followed, then Sigson, then Reiner, Mikael and the count.

'The creature is close,' the weakened count gasped. 'There,' he said, pointing to another archway.

Heaving the ailing count between them, Reiner and Mikael were right behind the others who stood in the great hall. The tapestry of Falken Halstein loomed large, about to witness his horrifying undead self.

Putting the witch hunter down, Halbranc hefted a massive torch from an iron sconce. Mikael and Reiner did the same.

'Protect the count,' Reiner said to Valen and Vaust. The brothers took Gunther between them to an alcove at the back of the room.

With a bellow of rage, Setti-Ra emerged from the trapdoor opening.

Halbranc lunged forward, thrusting the burning torch into the creature's body. It hurled the templar aside. The torch clattered to the ground, and was smothered. Flames licked over the aging corpse but died quickly.

Sigson stepped forward, the holy book of Morr in his hand.

'In the name of Morr, I compel you,' he uttered, his voice loud and powerful.

The creature stopped as if suddenly held by an invisible bond.

'I compel you,' Sigson repeated, stepping towards it, arm outstretched, his open palm facing towards it. Mikael and Reiner thrust their torches at the beast. Sigson screamed and fell to the ground as Setti-Ra broke his hold.

Though the undead thing burned, the flames were dying out quickly.

'Force it into the tapestry,' Mikael cried, launching himself at the creature. At the same time, Halbranc rammed into it with his shoulder and Reiner tackled the beast's legs. It toppled, slowly like a felled tree, tearing at the huge portrait that caught alight with the remaining flames licking its body. The tapestry pulled free and smothered the foul creature, fire spreading eagerly now over the corpse, as it thrashed and flailed for terrible unlife.

Flames mirrored in his eyes, Gunther looked at the burning form of his father, at the tapestry destroyed and his family history with it.

With the knights of Morr encircling it, the creature gradually stopped struggling and slumped down amidst a pall of foul smoke as it was burned to ash, the spirit of Setti-Ra banished along with it.

'Please,' Gunther rasped, tears in his eyes, 'put him out.'

IT WAS DARK IN the infirmary. Mikael stared from one of the windows onto the town below. The rain had abated at last and the waters were dispersing. Workers shored up the earthen banks, to make certain they would hold. Across the darkened sky, there was a light to the south as the sun began to rise. Looking back into the room, he saw Lenchard was awake. Reiner and the others waited silently in the shadows. Sigson was by the witch hunter's side.

'You owe us some answers,' he said.

Lenchard's head bore a thick bandage and his face was covered in small cuts and bruises. He winced as he smiled back at the warrior priest.

'There is a cult called the Scarabs,' he relented. 'Fanatical men, they worship the Tomb King Setti-Ra, believing the heart of he who defeated their king would bring about his resurrection.'

'Gunther's father,' Sigson asserted.

'Yes, but they need the living heart and since Falken Halstein was dead, they came for his son,' Lenchard said, getting up out of bed.

'Krieger could not have known that Setti-Ra had inhabited the body of Falken Halstein; such a body could not sustain an undead lord. I was wrong; Krieger came here with a mission, not for revenge but to kill Count Gunther and take his heart. He stumbled upon the creature and it killed him, and so we are still no closer to finding the cult,' he continued, strapping on his weapons.

'We,' said Reiner coldly.

From a pouch by his bedside Lenchard produced a scroll of parchment, which he gave to the captain.

'This is a missive from your temple,' he explained as Reiner read it, 'stating that you and your knights are seconded into my service until the cult is found or it is deemed fit to release you.'

Sigson laughed mirthlessly and walked out of the room.

Reiner sealed the scroll up and handed it back to Lenchard. 'So be it,' he said without emotion and left after Sigson. Slowly the rest of the knights followed. Mikael was the last. As he was about to leave, Lenchard said, 'It's Mikael, isn't it?'

Mikael nodded.

'Tell me, Mikael,' the witch hunter said, his expression curious, 'how did you know about the desert? I heard you speak of it to the count.'

A pang of anxiety rose suddenly in Mikael's chest. He thought only the count had heard him.

'I overheard it,' he countered, backing away.

'Of course,' Lenchard said, watching the young templar as he followed after his comrades. 'Of course you did.'

IN THE HALL, the knights of Morr were making ready to leave, checking weapons and armour before heading out the keep and Galstadt for good. The Black Knights had clearly worn out their welcome, and as they fixed blades and tightened belts, a small group of Knights of the Fiery Heart had gathered. The Morr worshippers were standing opposite them, clustered close together, Halbranc putting himself deliberately between Vaust and the glowering Sigmarites. Mikael stood next to the giant, alongside him was Valen. Sigson was sat down, reading his prayer book, while Reiner and Lenchard, who conversed quietly in a nearby corner of the room, waited for Count Gunther so they could observe the proper etiquette for their departure.

As far as Mikael was concerned, it couldn't happen soon enough, his eyes on Garrant, as he and the other knights exchanged dark glances.

'Doubtless, they are making sure we leave,' Halbranc chuckled.

Mikael was about to answer when a door, thudding insistently at the far end of the hall from a strong draught running through the keep, distracted him. Something about it was odd, slightly incongruous.

'Something doesn't feel right,' he said. 'This is taking too long.' Mikael walked quickly over to Garrant, trying to ignore the glare of Reiner, who had been listening to the witch hunter. Sigson saw the young templar too, and put down his prayer book.

'Your lord,' Mikael asked the Sigmarite. 'Where is he?'

Garrant was slightly perturbed by what he perceived as insolence, but something about the young templar's tone got his attention.

'He's in the chapel,' Garrant said, pointing to the door at the end of the room. 'A priest offered to bless his father's ashes.'

'What priest?' Sigson asked, suddenly appearing next to Mikael.

'From the town,' the Sigmarite explained. 'An old blind man.'

The templar and warrior priest looked at each other, with grave faces.

'Show us this chapel,' Mikael said urgently.

THE CHAPEL WAS A small room, little more than an antechamber from the great hall. Inside, there was a stone altar on top of which was an urn containing Falken Halstein's ashes. Count Gunther lay next to the altar. He was dead, his heart removed from his chest. A scarab beetle had been carved into the flesh of his left cheek.

'The blind man,' Mikael said to Sigson, abruptly aware that Reiner and the others had followed them.

'What?'

'The one that stumbled into Reiner at the gates,' he said, pointing at his captain. 'He addressed him as "noble lord". How could he have known he was a knight if he were blind? I saw him on the ridge during the flood, but thought it was my imagination.'

'You're right.' Lenchard spoke with a hint of resignation, standing in the doorway. 'We have been fools; a second Scarab cultist.'

Sigson bent over near the body.

'The blood is still warm,' he said, looking up at Reiner.

A look of disgusted anger passed briefly over the captain's face. 'Get to the gates,' he ordered.

BY THE TIME they reached the gatehouse, it was too late. The guard was already dead, his body propped up on a wooden stool. Protruding from his neck was a curved bladed dagger that bore a gold scarab hilt.

Lenchard examined it.

'They are taunting us,' he said bitterly to the knights of Morr standing around him. 'Get the horses,' he told them, rushing out of the gatehouse, heading for the stable yard. 'They have the heart and the means with which to resurrect Setti-Ra. We must find the cultist's trail. We ride, now!'

The knights followed after him, mounting up quickly and racing through the gates. Driving his steed hard, Mikael looked to the lightening horizon and felt time suddenly ebbing away as if an hourglass were turned and they were all slipping through it.

TALES OF
DEATH & CORRUPTION

SHYI-ZAR

Dan Abnett

As High Zar Surtha Lenk gathers his Kurgan horde for their advance into south, the zars of his warbands compete with one another to gain the honoured and most prestigious rank of Shyi-Zar.

IT WAS DAWN in late winter. The sky was a blur of mauve darkness, broken in the east by a rind of approaching daylight, and the twin moons, like discs of fire-lit bone, were sinking to their setting places. A dawn like any other, thought Karthos, a cold and unforgiving sunrise, but his sorcerer said otherwise. This was an auspicious daybreak. A special time. A time that heralded the future.

Dutifully then, Karthos had woken the men early, kicking away their furs and growling their names. Sullen, they rose, and saw to the fire, which had sunk down to glowing embers in the last part of the night. Karthos took a swig of spirits to warm his belly. The warrior rings around his broad arms were as cold as ice upon his skin.

'What is he doing?' asked Odek. The sorcerer was now on the headland overlooking the camp, walking in slow circles around the goat he had brought with them from Kherdheg, murmuring words they couldn't hear. The goat, its headrope staked to the ground, was bleating.

'He's walking around that goat,' Karthos said. 'And talking to it.'

Odek grinned. 'With these eyes of mine, I see that much,' he said. He had ridden with the zar for nine seasons, and it was as much

553

Karthos's phlegmatic humour and unfailing dryness that kept him loyal as it was the zar's potency in battle. He knew many Kurgan who followed their zars out of fear and duty, but he followed his out of respect and kinship. It was a bond that got as close to friendship as it was possible to get in the blighted North.

'I wondered... why?'

'I know you did,' nodded Karthos.

'So... why?'

Zar Karthos turned to his second-in-command. 'The sorcerer tells me this is a special time. Moonset.'

'The moons set every day.'

'Indeed. But this is a day amongst days. One moon sets, then the sun itself rises before the second moon can fall to its rest behind the plate of the world.'

'This he says?'

'This he says, and I doubt him not. It makes this time sacred. The light of the sun, he tells me, lets him see between the moons on this rare day. There are answers to be read there.'

'Including the answer that we want?'

'That,' replied the zar, 'is what I hope.'

The roused men had gathered by then, all ten of them. Koros Kyr, the standard bearer; Bereng, the horn-blower; T'nash He-Wolf; Odagidor; Lokas Long-ham; Aulkor; his brother Aulkmar; Gwul Gehar; Zbetz Red-fletch and Ffornesh the Dreamer. Furs and cloaks about their wide shoulders, they stood by the warmth of the spitting fire and watched the sorcerer at his rite.

One moon had set, its disc turning pale ivory then smoked silver as it slid down into the haze until it was out of sight. Then a band of flame lit the horizon, and the sun rose, heavy and copper, as if its furnaces had not yet been stoked up.

All of the warband knew the significance. This was Tchar's time. A time of change.

From the headland, the remaining moon behind his head like a halo, the sorcerer called to Karthos, and the zar hurried up the slope.

The sorcerer was called Ygdran Ygra. He was the oldest man Karthos had ever known, thin-limbed and spidery, his skin lined with age. He had been sorcerer to Karthos's father when Karthos's father had been zar.

'Take the blade,' Ygdran Ygra told Karthos. The proffered knife was a sharpened curve of moonstone instead of the sorcerer's usual silver dagger.

'Where must I strike?' asked Karthos. The goat bleated again, more shrill now.

Ygdran Ygra pinched at his own slack dewlap, and for a moment the zar thought he was being asked to butcher his sorcerer.

'The throat, zar, the throat,' the sorcerer instructed.

Karthos did as he was told. The goat ceased its noise. Ygdran Ygra had powdered the grass with chalk, and when the hot blood came out, steaming in the cold air, it ran and blotted amongst the white stalks.

'Good, good,' the sorcerer said, taking the slick blade back. He bent to read.

'Well?'

The sorcerer looked up at the zar. There was a curious fire in his milky blue eyes. 'You must pledge,' he said.

A smile ignited on Karthos's face. Down the slope, his men saw it, and started cheering and whooping even before he could relate the news.

WELL-FED ON GOAT meat, they broke camp and rode into the rising day. There was now an eagerness to the band that Karthos could feel. Sometimes a band dragged and lingered, unwilling, unfocused. But now they were fierce, and fired with a purpose. They were to pledge. Tchar had seen between the moons and licensed them. Lokas Longham and Ffornesh the Dreamer began to sing a war-song, full-voiced into the winter day.

This was how any zar wanted his warrior-pack. Vital, willing, indifferent to danger. Karthos was forced to gallop his steed hard to keep at the head of the charging group. He laughed into the cold wind.

They would follow him. Nothing would stand in his way. They would follow him to eternity.

At the next valley top, they reined in. Below, across a league of gorse heathland, lay the gathering place, staining the white sky with its smudges of smoke.

Zar Karthos raised his left hand, fingers splayed, the sign that meant. 'Let us ride'.

And down they went.

AROUND THE ANCIENT lightning tree that marked the gathering place, the horse clans had assembled in great numbers. Karthos had led his band to gatherings before, but the scale of this meeting took his breath away. He had not known so many men lived upon the plate of the world.

Perimeter fires had been set around the site, around the edges of the old circular ditch that had stood since before men had memories. Within, vast camps had sprung up. He saw the pitched standards of a score of warbands. Some he knew. That was Zar Herfil's, that was Zar Tzagz's, that Zar Uldin's. Kettle drums beat. Near to the lightning tree, the war tents of the High Zar's pavilion had been raised.

It was war then. That much was clear. Not just the seasonal rising of the clans, the annual gathering for raids down into the bloodless South.

The rumours and auguries had been true. Archaon had come, the deliverer, the striker-down of thrones and worlds. He had sent out his word, to transfix the hearts of the warrior bands, to make their very hairs stand up on end, to fire them for slaughter.

When had a High Zar last come forth for a gathering? When had a High Zar commended his clans unto himself for a spring driving? Not in Karthos's lifetime, nor in his worthy father's age either.

Zar Karthos felt his heartbeat rise, in time with the incessant drums. At long last, the promised age of conquest had come. The tempest of fire. The ending-of-times. The Storm of Chaos.

All along the borderlands now, as winter slackened its bite upon the world, high zars were marshalling their clans around them like this. Enra Deathsword, Valmir Aesling, Sven Bloody Hand, Okkodai Tarsus, Zaros Bladeback, all answering the bidding of the strange and marvellous daemon-that-is-also-a-man Archaon.

The greatest of all Archaon's high zars, Karthos believed, was Surtha Lenk, about whom this gathering now swelled. If any warlord might break open the boundaries of the feeble 'Empire' and strike down the tawdry crown of its so-called Emperor... what was given as his name now? Karl-Franz? If any might strike down his crown and dash out his brains, it would be the great and malevolent Lenk.

Karthos's warband rode in through the gathering place. Koros Kyr held the skull standard high. Warriors turned to watch them pass by. Kul, Kurgan, Dolgan, Hastling... all manner of men, all manner of standards. Alien faces in strange wargears watched them go past.

'Be warned,' Odek muttered suddenly. Karthos had already seen the trouble. The banner of the bloody sword-blade on a red field. Zar Blayda's standard.

It was not true to say that no blood was lost between the zars. Far too much had been lost in their lingering clan-war.

Blayda, gaunt and tall in his pitched-black plate armour, etched with the details of his many victories, strode out onto the trackway into Karthos's path. Blayda's sorcerer, a capering, naked fool named Ons Olker, scampered around his master's heels.

Karthos dismounted and tossed his reins to Bereng. He marched through the trail's slush to face the black-armoured chieftain. Blayda drew his pallasz, the long tongue of the sword flashing in the rising sun.

Karthos did not reciprocate, though he heard Odek slide out his sword behind him.

'You know the law here,' Karthos said, staring at the visor slits of Blayda's ink-black helm.

'Do you need me to remind you?' Karthos added. 'In the gathering space of the High Zar, no clan shall fight with clan.'

Blayda lowered his sword. 'You are dung-eating scum, Karthos.'

He was being deliberately provocative. Karthos merely shrugged.

'I will wet my blade with your gut-blood and make you a notch upon my helm,' Blayda added, pointing at a part of his barbute that was not yet marked with an incised gash.

'Maybe. But not here,' Karthos replied.

Blayda raised his visor far enough to spit on Karthos's toes, then strode away, his leaping and cursing sorcerer in tow.

Karthos looked back at his clan. He raised his left hand, fingers splayed.

KOROS KYR PLANTED the spike of their standard into a patch of free ground and the warband settled. They were encamped not far from the pavilions of the High Zar. Water and burning wood was brought to them by the gathering's stewards, along with meat for cooking, wine, and grain for simmering. Karthos had Odek, who was charged with the band's purse, pay them in decent gold.

T'nash came to the zar, suggesting they might also buy a decent fighter from the slavelord Skarkeetah so that they might undo Zar Blayda in formal combat.

Karthos shook his head. There were more important things afoot now.

The men of the warband were drinking wine as their food roasted and night fell. Attended by two of his band, Zar Skolt came to their camp site. He embraced Karthos like a brother, and they drank wine for a while, having many old victories to remember.

'Will you not fight Blayda?' asked Skolt. 'He yearns for it.'

Karthos shook his head. 'No, he may wait.'

'Besides,' said Odek. 'We are to be pledged.'

Zar Skolt sat up as if he had been stung. 'Is that true? Are you pledging?'

'The signs were good. My sorcerer has said it so. Not you?'

Skolt shook his head. 'My sorcerer saw no such good omens. Great Tchar, I envy you. Such an honour no warband could deny.'

'Who else may pledge?' Karthos asked.

Skolt shrugged. 'Uldin, I know. Herfil, Kreyya and Logar. And also Blayda.'

'Blayda?' mused Karthos. 'Indeed.'

ALL THROUGH THE first part of the night, despite a drizzling sleet that came in from the west, slaves worked in processions to build up the bonfires around the lightning tree at the heart of the gathering place.

Great flames leapt up, so fierce that the sleet could not douse them. The hissing of steam filled the sacred place, like unseen snakes. The glow from the fires lit the tree from below, casting a moving amber light up its bald trunk and skeletal limbs. It illuminated the iron cages and gibbets hanging from the branches: offerings, sacrifices and the cadavers of enemies.

Gongs were struck to announce midnight and the time of pledging. Karthos went down to the ring of fire around the altar tree, where a great number of other zars and chieftains were assembling. None brought weapons to that hallowed earth. Herbs and seeds flung onto the fires filled the air with incense and heady smoke. Karthos felt his flesh sweat from the extreme heat. He saw Uldin, also Logar, and others he did not know. Blayda's grim black form was a shadow on the far side of the fire ring.

A hush fell. The High Zar had emerged from his pavilion, escorted by twenty white-robed warriors with horsehair crests. They carried bright lamps on long poles that bobbed like marsh fire as the procession approached.

Surtha Lenk was a monstrous giant of a man, clad in crimson armour. Karthos shuddered at the sight of him. Two goat-headed dwarfs scurried along at his heels. Karthos could not tell if they were children wearing goat-masks, or beastfolk enslaved to the High Zar's power. One carried a casket of jade and gold, the other carried Lenk's war sword. It was so large and heavy, the goat-thing was all but dragging it.

The zars parted, so that their master could reach the fire ring. Surtha Lenk stopped. The brass visor of his horned helm appeared to regard them all, yet to Karthos there seemed to be no eyeslits cut into it.

Lenk raised his massive arms, his huge hands outspread, cased in mail and thorny steel.

'You are to make the pledge,' he said. It was the first time Karthos had heard the High Zar's voice, and his guts turned to ice. It was slight and tiny, like a child's, yet it seemed to come from all around and drown out the crackle of the fire more easily than a bellowing roar.

'Tchar looks to you, warriors. This is holy change you undertake, beautiful to the Eye of Tzeen. Do you understand this pledge?'

'Lord seh!' the zars called out obediently.

One of the goat-things opened the casket and took something from it. Surtha Lenk received it and held it up for them all to see. It was a great claw of frightening dimensions, polished bone-white.

'Look upon it,' the High Zar whispered. 'The zar who brings its like back to me will be called shyi-zar, and he and his warrior band will be accorded the full honours of that title.'

The claw was put away again in its reliquary box. Surtha Lenk took his sword then, and held it upright before himself in one hand.

'Pledge!' he said.

One by one, the zars came to him, and slid their bared right hands down the edge of his warblade without any show of pain. Then each one turned and let the blood drip from their sliced palms into the fire.

Karthos did so in turn, not daring to show any pride by looking up at his master's hooked metal visage. He watched his own blood well up, black in the firelight, and heard the drops of it sizzle in the flames.

DAWN CAME, GREY and sunless, with sheeting rain and a savage wind that shook the hide tents and made the great lightning tree creak and moan. Karthos stretched out his left hand, fingers splayed. The warband left the gathering place.

They were not the first to depart. Some pledged bands, anxious to begin the task, had quit the camp before first light. Odek told his zar of the standards that were missing, Blayda's amongst them.

They crossed the heathlands to the west, into the driving rain, and then turned north, advancing into the haunted hills and miasmal valleys beyond. Here, the crests were granite, and the land suddenly shelved away into steep pine brakes of mist and darkness where the sun never touched, even in summer. They sighted another warband on a trail over to the west, but they were too far off to hail or identify.

Karthos had described the claw to his men, and much debate had followed as to its nature or origin. T'nash insisted it was in fact the tusk of a doombull, but the others shouted him down. It was the talon of a predator beast, a dragon's horn, a sliver fallen off the late moon and all other manner of things.

The sorcerer offered the soundest council. 'Let us not waste effort in fruitless searching, zar seh,' he ventured. 'Let us get truth, and use it.'

So they rode for Tehun Dhudek.

TEHUN DHUDEK WAS a fastness in the lonely hills that many men shunned for they feared it was cursed. But Ygdran Ygra, who knew more of the world's secrets than most men, had been there himself, and scoffed at the common rumours. 'A clan of sorcerers dwells there,' he informed the warband, 'and they have in them great powers of divination. If we please them with our offerings, they will tell us the true nature of the claw, and where we may find it.'

'But the curse...?' Aulkor said.

'Just stories spread by men who have been there to question the oracle and not liked the truth they have learned. To some men, the truth is a curse.'

Karthos hoped that would not be so for them.

* * *

THAT PART OF the hills was indeed lonely. The track wound up through the dismal cliffs of splintered granite, and along deep-cut ravines and narrow gorges. Their only company was a few bird flocks in the pale sky.

'Someone's been this way,' Odek said. There was horse dung on the scree of the trail, and it was not more than a day old.

'A lone rider?'

'No, zar seh. Look there, the soil of more than one animal. A warband, perhaps?'

'One with the same notion as us?'

They rode on a little way further, to the mouth of the sloping gorge that the sorcerer said led right to the fastness itself.

Odek looked round at Karthos sharply, but the zar had heard it too. Hooves, the shouts of men, carried down the gorge by the chill wind. And there, amongst it, the clash of blades.

Karthos drew his pallasz. Gripping it made pain flare in his hand, for though Ygdran Ygra had dressed his pledge-wound, his palm still throbbed.

His men needed no orders. Their weapons came out. Pallasz mostly: long, straight-bladed cleaver-swords. Lokas Long-ham had a horse-spear, and Gwul Gehar the waraxe he favoured. Zbetz Redfletch and Aulkmar took out their recurve horse-bows and slipped on the bone rings of their thumb-guards.

Karthos raised his left hand, fingers splayed.

AT A FIRM gallop, Karthos led the way up the track and into Tehun Dhudek. The mouth of the ravine formed a gateway in a high ringwall of dry stone construction that surrounded a flagged courtyard built upon a shelf in the cliff. The three longhouses of the fastness, along with an ancient and ragged tower, overlooked the courtyard from a promontory shelf, with stone steps running down to the floor of the yard itself.

Murder was underway here. Karthos counted at least nine Dolgan riders assaulting the place, hacking down the defenders with their hooked swords and adzes. The defenders were not warriors. They were shaman, acolytes and slaves, armed with poles and staves. The bodies of many, leaking blood, lay scattered around the gate-mouth and across the courtyard. A number of riderless horses milled around the yard.

'Bereng!' Karthos thundered, and the hornblower at his left side unloosed a mighty blast upon his carnyx that howled around the walled yard like a boom of echoing thunder.

The Dolgan warriors turned, amazed, enraged. Karthos saw their chieftain, a bearded and maned brute with arms wholly covered in warrior rings. Karthos did not know his name, or the name of his warband, for Kurgan and Dolgan were often strangers if not bitter foes except at times of gathering, but he knew the man's face. He had been at the fire-ring at midnight, pledging to the High Zar.

The Dolgans swept around to meet the Kurgan charge, kicking and slashing the fastness's defenders out of their way.

'Into them!' Karthos yelled.

The packs of riders met. Karthos's band had the advantage of surprise and momentum. Reins clamped between their teeth, Zbetz and Aulkmar loosed their first arrows. The shafts went buzzing across the walled yard. Aulkmar's struck a Dolgan through the chest and slammed him off his saddle. Zbetz sent another raider to his doom, a red-feathered arrow through his side.

Lokas Long-ham's spear shattered a Dolgan shield and transfixed the warrior holding it so that he was torn up out of his seat and off his horse. The spear went with him, wedged through his body, and Lokas let it go, reaching over to sweep his saddle-sword out of its long, leather scabbard as the next Dolgan flew at him.

Odek crossed blades with a particularly large Dolgan warrior, and they ripped their swords at one another, their terrified horses circling and stamping. T'nash He-Wolf felled one man cleanly, his pallasz windmilling, and then turned his steed's head hard to engage another.

Karthos, with Gwul Gehar at his right hand, went for the chieftain, but he had two heavy warriors in ringmail and over-plate as body guards. Their wild eyes flashed under the slits of their tusked helmets. They had swords and short, stabbing spears.

Karthos clashed with one, driving his pallasz at the Dolgan's badly timed sword swing, but the man's left hand came around to jab the stabbing spear at the Kurgan zar. Its iron tip glanced painfully off the banding of warrior rings around Karthos's right arm. Karthos, struggling to restrain his frantic horse with the power of his left arm, hacked backwards, and succeeded in breaking the spear haft and severing the thumb from the hand grasping it.

The Dolgan squealed, his maimed hand coming up in dismay, blood squirting from the wound. Better balanced in the saddle now, Karthos struck again, and the man barely got his sword up to block the blade.

From the corner of his eye, Karthos saw that the chieftain was coming for him too now, sword out, moving in from the left flank. Gwul was engaged with the other bodyguard, fighting the awkward, laboured rally that accompanied a duel of sword against axe.

Karthos snarled. He could not break from the bodyguard because the man, due to the pain and outrage of his hand wound, was hacking with a berserk frenzy. The zar could not disengage his blade in time to fend off the chieftain's attack.

The only option left was to avoid it. Karthos threw himself out of his saddle, crashing head-on into the injured bodyguard and tipping him and his horse right over. Men and horse sprawled on the cold flagstones of the yard, winded and stunned. Karthos heard Odagidor cry out his name, fearing his zar had fallen to a blade wound.

Wrestling, Karthos managed to pull free of the frantic bodyguard and regain his feet. The bodyguard had lost his sword, and clawed at Karthos's legs, painting him with crimson blood from his ruined hand. Karthos kicked him away and turned just in time to meet the downstroke of the bellowing Dolgan chief.

The Dolgan's hooked broadsword resounded off Karthos's pallasz with jarring force. The chieftain's bulky horse backed off a pace or two in alarm, and then came in again, and Karthos was forced to leap back to avoid the whistling blade. He was almost slammed off his feet by the tackling charge of the wounded bodyguard, who attacking him, screaming, with a bear-hug. Karthos's left hand was free, so he smacked it round and caught the bodyguard across the face with the iron rings of his warrior bands, breaking the enemy's nose in a spatter of blood. The Dolgan let go. Karthos grabbed him as he staggered, blinded by blood, and pulled him close as a shield, left arm locked around his throat.

The chieftain hacked again and disembowelled his own man. Karthos let the ruptured body topple away and ran across the flagstones to retrieve his horse.

Bereng's horn blew again. A few paces short of his twitchy steed, Karthos looked round. Nearly a dozen more Dolgan warriors were pouring down the steps on foot from the longhouses. That explained the riderless horses.

Karthos ran to meet them. Ffornash and Aulkor leapt from their horses to join with him. Odagidor remained in his saddle and came in close to the steps, scattering the foot soldiers with his hooves. There was a hissing sound, and one of the Dolgans coming down the steps sprawled backwards with a red-feathered arrow in his brow.

Karthos reached the lower steps, and swung his pallasz at the nearest Dolgan. This warrior had a long-hafted adze, and drove it down at the zar like a woodsman with a timber axe. Karthos side-stepped, and the man overbalanced from his desperate strike. Karthos's pallasz opened him from the hip to the armpit and scattered broken links of ringmail across the flagstones. The man fell onto the courtyard floor with bone-cracking force.

Ffornash the Dreamer had famed skill with the long-blade. He was a tall, lithe man who shunned armour because it slowed his limbs.

Both fists around his sword grip, he danced up the steps, ducking an axe and sidestepping a stabbing spear, and sliced his silver sword back and forth, ripping through a neck and opening a Dolgan belly.

Aulkor broke a Dolgan sword against his heavy pallasz, and cut the man through to the breastbone with a side swing. But his blade was wedged. He tried to wrench it free as another Dolgan came down at him with an adze. Karthos flew forward with a howl, and ran the adze-wielder through before his blow could land. The Dolgan thumped away down the steps, his adze spinning free into the air as the dead hands released it.

'My thanks, zar seh,' Aulkor gasped, extracting his bloody sword at last.

Karthos did not reply. The fight was far from done. Now Odek, Odagidor and Gwul Gehar had joined them on foot, battling up the steps into the thick of the Dolgan pack. Another enemy fell and rolled heavily down the stone risers, hit by one of Aulkmar's arrows this time. The steps themselves had become slippery with blood. Dying men clawed at their ankles and shins. Karthos broke a shield away and then cut through the haft of an adze, then a forearm, then a throat. He was changing lives into death. Tchar would approve.

Fighting clear, he reached the top of the staircase. The only Dolgans there were corpses, transfixed by red and grey feathered arrows. He turned and looked back, in time to see the act that finished the fight.

Koros Kyr, still holding the warband's standard high, rode in hard and killed a Dolgan horseman with a wide blow of his pallasz. Then he reined hard around and removed the head of the Dolgan chief. It was a superb cut, all the power of the standard bearer's arm behind it. The brute's helmed head flew off in a mist of blood, and bounced and rolled like a cannonball on the flags. His horse took off, and carried the headless corpse out through the gate and away down the ravine.

Broken, the remaining Dolgans tried to flee, but there were Kurgan swords all around them. Gwul Gehar's waraxe finished two more. The few that made it to the gateway, wailing and screaming, were dropped hard by Zbetz and Aulkmar, who sat astride their tight-circling horses, loosing arrow after arrow.

Zar Karthos, spattered head to toe in gore, lowered his dripping pallasz and smiled. They had destroyed the Dolgan warband, and with no loss to themselves.

Tchar was evidently with them.

THE SORCERER CLAN of Tehun Dhudek had numbered sixteen, an extended family of sons and fathers and uncles. A further twenty acolytes had dwelt within the high stone walls, along with some thirty slaves and womenfolk. Now only thirty lives remained all told, most of them the women, who had been hidden in the fastness caves when the raid began. The Dolgans had sought to learn the truths of the talon from the oracle by force of arms.

Ygdran Ygra had been right. The truth was sometimes a curse, for the Dolgans had found only death at Tehun Dhudek.

The survivors of the fastness clan regarded Karthos's warband with some wariness, fearing that they had exchanged one murdering pack for another. With his sorcerer, Karthos went to meet with the most senior of the surviving hetmen.

'We came to make fair offering in return for answers,' he told the old man squarely. 'We would not have resorted to violence. You need not fear us now.'

The old hetman sat on a clammy stone chair in the draughty hall of one of the longhouses. He had insisted on wearing a golden mask so that the Kurgan would not see his grief.

'What would you have given us, zar, as an offering?' one of his younger acolytes asked. This young man had a bandaged stump where his right hand had been struck off by the Dolgans. He clutched it against his chest like a newborn babe.

'Gold, fine stones from my war chest, salt-meat and wine. Whatever else pleased you that I could provide,' Karthos said.

'But now we have given you more than that,' said Ygdran Ygra. 'By force of arms and the sweat of toil, we have given you salvation from the Dolgans. What is that worth?'

ANSWERS, IT SEEMED. For two nights, Karthos's sorcerer was shut away in the furthest longhouse, probing the secrets of the clan's oracle. A great storm came up during that time, and hammered upon the doors and shutters. The warband sheltered in the first longhouse, their food and drink provided by the grateful clansfolk. The storm's rain put out the pyre of Dolgan bodies heaped in the yard before they were even half burned.

THE STORM CLEARED. A pale yellow light filled the sky above the fastness peaks. The mountain air was alive with the gurgle of water draining and running down the cliffs into the valleys far below.

Ygdran Ygra came out of seclusion, tired and hungry. He refused to speak until he had eaten a platter of pigs' feet and drunk some watered ale besides. Karthos had never seen him so exhausted. For the first time, he looked his years, haggard and worn out.

'It will be quite a thing to do,' he said at last, his voice soft. He dabbed shiny spots of pig grease off his chin with a kerchief.

'How so?' Karthos asked, unplugging a wine flask and pouring himself a beakerful.

'I know where it is and what it is,' Ygdran Ygra replied. 'But now finding it is not the burden. Killing it is.' He shook his old head and tut-tutted. 'Even your father, Kelim Karthos, he who was zar before you, even he would have shrunk from this task.'

'Just tell me of it,' Karthos said.

'A heralder,' said the old sorcerer. 'Tchar wants us to take a heralder.'

KARTHOS FEARED THAT if he told the men, they would revolt and ride away. But they begged to know, and he could not keep it from them. So he sighed, sat down amongst them in the draughty longhouse, and blurted it out.

For a long moment, there was no sound except the moaning of the wind and no movement except the drift of the sunlight on the floor as clouds passed across the sky.

Then Ffornash the Dreamer let slip a low, sad chuckle, and Gwul Gehar spat in the hearth, and the brothers Aulkor and Aulkmar looked at one another and shuddered.

'So, not a doombull then?' asked T'nash He-Wolf.

Koros Kyr slapped him for his question, and the warband broke into laughter.

'You will ride with me?' Karthos asked.

'We are pledged, zar seh,' said Odek simply. 'Riding with you is what we do.'

IT TOOK FOUR days to reach the Wastes. Four days' hard ride, and all of them fatigued and aching from the battle that, they were sure, only Tchar's will had seen them win so thoroughly. Odagidor suspected that Tchar had wanted them to crush the Dolgans because they were the ones who were destined to meet the pledge and take the shyi honour.

But Bereng muttered that they had been spared and granted victory only to give the heralder more blood to spill.

None of them had ever seen a heralder, except for Zbetz Red-fletch, who had been a child when one savaged his home village. He remembered little of it, except its ravening beak that had rent his father in two. He had been a young child. It had haunted his dreams ever since.

Lokas Long-ham said he thought he might once have seen one, circling in the heavens, high up, above Zamak Spayenya, many years before, when he had been riding with the warband of Zar Shevras. An eagle, the others said.

'With the body of a lion?' he replied.

'How could you tell if it was so far away?' asked Odagidor.

'Maybe it was an eagle,' Lokas said resignedly.

* * *

THE WASTES WERE cold and empty. Nothing living seemed to grow or thrive there. At all sides, the dry plains rolled away to the limits of the world, broken only by ridges of crusted rock and scattered boulders. The soil was as dry as dust, as white as a sorcerer's sacrificial chalk. The sky was dark, washed purple by the poisoned light. Thunder rumbled throughout the day, and around the hem of the horizon, slashes of lightning grazed the air and bit into the earth like bright and slender fangs.

The air smelled of decay. Wailing sounds echoed over the desolation, from no obvious source. Amongst the white dust, every few miles, gnawed bones protruded. Horse, man, man-beast.

ON THE FIFTH day out from Tehun Dhudek, Ygdran Ygra rose in his saddle and pointed.

'There! As the insight was given to me. An outfall of rock, spiked in three places, like the front part of a crown. Before it, a steep slope of rocks and stones. In the sky of the west, a crescent of clouds. This is the place.'

Karthos felt fear then, the turning of a long-standing worry into true fear. He sensed it settle upon his men too.

He drew a deep breath and raised his left hand out, fingers splayed.

They rode up into the flinty slope of stones. All of them carried long lances now, fashioned from the cold forests they had passed through to reach the open wastes. Swords would not be enough to do this deed.

According to Ygdran Ygra – and the lore of the Northlands – a heralder was a most feral beast, twisted from nature and combined by the mutable touch of Tchar into a chimera. It was in part a lion, but more massive than even the greatest hunting cats of the Taiga, but its head was that of an eagle or vicious prey bird, hugely beaked. It possessed wings. In the oldest of times, such animals had been plentiful and common, plaguing the realms of man, but they had faded away into the remote corners of the world. Some said the wizards and lords of the Empire had such creatures tamed as war-steeds.

They were called heralders, because their appearance was said to herald great events and moments of history. Ygdran Ygra feared the gods were playing with them. He had read the signs that they should pledge at a special dawn, a heralding moment. It was as if their path had been set from the start. Their doom too, perhaps.

In the language of the tribes, these rare beasts were called ghurphaon, the essence of all beasts.

The warband moved up through the litter of rock, their horses' hooves causing stones to slip and patter away down the jumbled slope. Thunder rolled, distantly. There was an increased stench of death in the air, as if meat rotted close by. Karthos saw the rocks were splashed with great deposits of white dung, like birdlime, but far more prodigious.

'Caves,' said Odek.

His second-in-command was pointing to dark holes in the cliff face above them. Roosts indeed. This place felt like a lair.

Karthos lowered his lance and was about to call back to the band when a shrill cry cut the world apart. It was piercing, as loud as if an eagle had been perched upon his shoulder.

The ghur-phaon showed itself.

It had scented them, located them with its beady eyes perhaps. It came out of one of the deep caves and spread its fearful wings. They were mottled black and white, the lead feathers as long as a horse's back. It took to the air.

Zbetz Red-fletch screamed despite himself, his childhood horrors made flesh. All the horses reared, terrified, smelling the predator coming down upon them. Gwul Gehar was thrown down onto the stones, Lokas too, so hard his neck snapped like a twig. Aulkor's horse broke and ran, despite his best efforts to control it, and carried him away down the long scree slope.

'In Tchar's name...' Karthos heard Odek stammer.

The beast was huge. Its body massed the weight of six horses at least. It leapt into the air on lithe feline back limbs, its hide a mangy grey. A tail the length of the slave master's finest gang-lash whipped out behind it.

Karthos couldn't decide what was most terrifying: the width of the massive, beating wings or the horror of the ghur-phaon's foreparts. Its head, massive and distended, disproportionate to the limber body behind it, was the head of a vulture: a massive ivory beak like an ogre's waraxe, at the crest of which tiny, wild eyes gleamed. The beak clacked like swords striking together, and he saw a glimpse of a thin white tongue.

Around the head and back along the throat, the monster was fletched in black and white down, which became quite shaggy around its breast. Its forelimbs were not the nimble things of a cat. They were scaled bird's feet, huge and armoured in silver. Each of the three scale-encrusted toes on the forelimbs sported a long claw.

Just like the talon Karthos had seen the High Zar lift out of his box.

It came down upon them, keening into the dark sky, beak opened to rake them apart.

Zbetz Red-fletch fired off two arrows before it came upon them, but his darts seemed like tiny red flecks amongst its feathered breast. Aulkmar loosed one arrow of his own before his horse threw him. He broke his left forearm on the stones as he landed.

Odek, Ffornash and Bereng hurled their lances at it. All bounced off.

The creature landed amongst them, crashing out a blizzard of loose stones and chips in all directions. Koros Kyr and his horse were spilled over, and T'nash too, his horse ripped open by the ghur-phaon's talons. It lunged at Gwul Gehar's horse and bit it in two with a savage slash of its monstrous beak. The slope reeked of hot blood.

Odagidor charged into the side of it, the tip of his lance digging deep. It recoiled and lashed out. Odagidor's horse lost its head from the muzzle to the eyes and toppled. Odagidor had his spear shattered and his left arm removed at the elbow. Gwul tried to drag him clear, both of them sprayed with the blood pumping from Odagidor's stump.

Odek tried to recover his spear, but the vast, flapping wings smashed him over. Zbetz fired an arrow that struck the ghur-phaon in the throat. Enraged, it surged forward across the loose stones and seized Zbetz by the right hand and forearm, lifting him off his horse and shaking him in its beak. Screaming in pain, Zbetz flew through the air, his arm shredded.

Karthos raised his lance and spurred his horse on, keeping the tip of his weapon low. The monster's claws had just ripped Aulkor in half at the waist.

Karthos plunged the lance into the beast's upper body from the side, pushing it in with all the force he could muster. The ghur-phaon started to bleat and wail, its body thrashing. It almost tore the lance out of Karthos's hands.

Odek ran to him, and T'nash and Koros Kyr, and they all put their muscles into it, grabbing the shaft and pushing it home.

The ghur-phaon screamed.

'Hold it here!' Karthos yelled, and let go of the lance. He drew his pallasz and ran towards the snapping head of the monster. Double-handed, above his head, he swung the sword down and cut wide its neck, casting scads of down into the air. Blood engulfed him like a mountain torrent.

He sank to his knees.

'Zar seh... it's dead,' Odek said.

Karthos nodded, and went to one of the outstretched forepaws. With a cry, he struck at it, and then raised the bloody claw in his hand.

AULKOR, ODAGIDOR, ZBETZ and Lokas were dead. Their mangled and twisted bodies were bound up and thrown across the backs of riderless horses. Almost every warrior was bruised and hurt. Aulkmar's arm was shattered, but he complained only for his dead brother.

* * *

THE MOONS WERE setting. They rode back along the trackway towards the gathering place. Flies buzzed around the dead strung from their spare horses.

Twenty-strong, Zar Blayda's warband rode out into their path. Their swords were drawn.

Karthos simply raised the talon in his hand. Dried blood clotted its thickness.

'Want to try for it?' he hissed.

Blayda turned his band back and rode away.

THE RING FIRE around the tree was lit. The bands had gathered.

Karthos led his warband up to the pavilion to claim his honour. Drums beat all around them.

'Have you fulfilled the deed?' Surtha Lenk said as he emerged from his tent.

Karthos showed the High Zar the talon.

'You know what this means?'

'It means that my warband and I have done what is necessary. We have made your pledge. We must be granted with the honour of shyi-zar.'

'Shyi-zar. Death zar. You understand what it is I want from you?'

'Yes, lord seh. You ride to war. Should you fall there, you need the best warriors to ride ahead of you into the afterworld, to prepare your place and guard you when you arrive. This is the duty of the shyi-zar. This honour amongst honours I claim for my warband.'

Surtha Lenk nodded.

'Thank you. Ride on to battle, Shyi-zar Karthos,' he said.

And with the ghur-phaon talon, he cut Karthos's throat, and Odek's, and those of all the others, every single soul of them willing.

SLAVES AND SORCERERS banked the ring fires up until the lightning tree was awash with firelight. Slaughtered, gutted and stuffed, the warsteeds were set upon poles, facing east, and the riders of the warband placed upon them, similarly supported.

They had achieved the highest honour, the duty of preparing the way for their High Zar in the afterworld.

Karthos, Odek, Koros Kyr with his standard, Bereng with his carnyx, T'nash, Odagidor and the rest of them.

They would ride into eternity and make it ready.

Karthos's left arm was splinted up on a pole. Raised, outstretched. Fingers splayed.

TYBALT'S QUEST

Gav Thorpe

THE STENCH OF death hung heavily in the cloying fog. The broken shadows of twisted trunks and branches swayed fitfully in the lacklustre breeze. Tybalt dismounted from his great black stallion, his armour dripping with moisture from the swirling mist. Casting his gaze around to find something to fix his horse's reins to, the Bretonnian knight spied what looked to be an old hitching post by the cemetery's gate. As he led his steed towards it, the heavy footfalls of his armoured boots and the horse's iron-shod hooves muffled by the dense fog, Tybalt's eyes and ears strained to sense any other sound. All was still and silent. Even the hoots of owls and the baying of dogs from the village had fallen quiet.

Quickly tying the reins to the rotted post, Tybalt unsheathed his longsword and took one last look around. Above him, the light of the new moon could barely be seen through the misty blanket surrounding the hilltop. The twinkling lights of Moreux had been left far behind as he had made his way to the ancient graveyard overlooking the whole of the valley. Up here, in one of the narrower passes of the Grey Mountains, the air was thin, and even the fit and youthful Tybalt was finding himself short of breath. With a deep inhalation, the knight laid a gauntleted hand on the cemetery gate, the curled ironwork of which stretched several feet above his head, and pushed it open.

The shrieking of rusted hinges rent the air, causing Tybalt to freeze involuntarily . His heart was hammering in his chest, and it was a few moments before he realised that he had been holding his breath. Letting it out slowly, he eased the gate open further, an action accompanied by erratic squeaks and grinding noises. When he'd opened a gap just wide enough for him to pass, he turned sideways and slid himself through the opening, looking up at the gargoyles on the flanking gateposts. Both had probably been identical when sculpted, but now the one to the left had only one of its three twisting horns left, while the lolling tongue of the other had been broken off just outside its fanged mouth.

Treading carefully to avoid the deepest puddles in the uneven path, Tybalt made his way further up the hill, heading towards the blocky, dark shadows of the largest and oldest crypts at the summit. Something scuttling through the darkness banged into his foot, causing Tybalt to stumble in fright. As he fell to one knee, he came face to face with the evil, yellow eyes of a black rat. The verminous scavenger hissed at him and then scampered out of view.

Heaving himself to his feet once more, Tybalt wiped the mud from his left hand on his scarlet and azure quartered surcoat. For a moment, Tybalt wondered if he should go back to his horse to fetch his shield, but decided that a free hand would be more valuable in these treacherous environs. Pausing to collect his thoughts, Tybalt peered through the mist at the looming shapes of the old mausoleums at the cemetery's highest point, wondering which belonged to Duke Laroche, the resting place of the ghost who had appeared to him in a dream five months earlier.

The long-dead duke had warned Tybalt that a great evil was disturbing his rest, and that he should undertake a quest to halt this darkness spreading through the realm. It had taken four months of searching the length of Bretonnia, examining the oldest heraldic records, to identify the arms of the ghost who had appeared to him: a black eagle on a plain yellow field. Duke Laroche was one of the founders of Mousillon, a man whose family dated back to the settling of Bretonnia in the time of Gilles le Breton, the first king. For the last month, Tybalt had searched far and wide for the old duke's resting place, until finally he had come across the answer in the chapel records in the small mountain village of Moreux.

When they had learned that Tybalt was heading up to the old graveyard, the commoners back in Moreux had warned him against going to the ancient cemetery. Local superstition was rife with tales of ghouls and spectres haunting the heights of the mountains. Hearing these accounts had done little to ease the knight's nerves.

* * *

TYBALT'S THOUGHTS WERE interrupted by rustling behind him and he spun around, sword at the ready. Taking a few steps back down the path, his grey eyes tried to pierce the gloom. Shadows drifted in and out of focus with the rolling fog, and Tybalt heard more rustling. Taking another cautious step forward, the knight brought his sword back over his shoulder, ready to strike at a moment's notice. More scuffling swung his attention to his left, and he stepped off the muddy path into the wet grass, which reached up to his thighs. Tybalt could hear an inhuman snuffling noise, accompanied by deep breathing and intermittent grunting. Something was approaching slowly towards him; he could see its vague shadow only a few paces away now.

'Reveal yourself, rascal!' challenged Tybalt, trying to speak with a confidence his shaking hand betrayed he did not have. There was an unearthly squeal and the shadow leapt at him from the darkness.

'Die, spawn of blackness!' Tybalt cried, stepping sideways and bringing his heavy sword flashing down. The blade bit deep into flesh, and blood fountained through the mist, splashing across Tybalt's surcoat and armour. Ensuring the beast was no longer moving, Tybalt took a closer look. At first he thought it some hideous mutant, but as he bent down to look into the thick weeds, he saw that the long tusks did not belong to some creature of the netherworlds and were in fact those of a wild boar. Tybalt straightened up slowly and the tension suddenly released from his body.

'Lady, protect me from fears and nightmares of my own creation,' he laughed quietly to himself, turning quickly and striding back to the path. The sudden action and its mundane end had eliminated all of the knight's trepidation now, and as he looked about, he saw nothing more unnatural than the heavy mist of the mountains, hanging over a place where the dead quietly rested in eternal sleep. With more of a spring in his step, he walked up the twisting path towards the summit.

TYBALT FOUND DUKE Laroche's tomb towards the centre of the hilltop, identifying it by the deep inscription and the coat of arms whose yellow and black paint had been all but obliterated by the ceaseless march of the centuries. Hacking away at the twining ivy and stubby bushes surrounding the crypt, Tybalt made his way around to the back of the tomb, away from the cemetery gates, where ancient tradition dictated the entrance stone would be.

On turning the corner, Tybalt was momentarily taken aback. The portal was already half open! The young knight's ears could hear nothing from inside the tomb, and so he ventured forward once more. Peering into the darkness of the mausoleum's interior, he could not discern anything untoward, and he quickly set to with his tinder and flint to make a torch from one of the many broken branches scattered across the ground. The brand sputtered and smoked badly. The wood was dead but wet from the recent rains and the vapours swirling around the graveyard.

As he was about to step over the threshold of the tomb, Tybalt glanced down and stopped. Muddy footprints could be seen quite clearly leading into the darkness. Kneeling for a closer look, he saw that there were several sets, all overlapping but made by the same pair of boots. Judging from the length of the strides, Tybalt guessed that the man was fairly short. He then noticed scuffing on the imprints of the right boot which could mean that he either had a limp or perhaps was carrying a heavy burden. Tybalt was glad that he had spent much of his childhood with his father's personal huntsman, learning some of the man's tracking secrets. Deciding there was no more to be deduced, Tybalt stood up and took a few steps forward, into the tomb itself.

Looking around in the ruddy, flickering glow of his torch, he could see the walls were hung with ancient tapestries, each depicting some event from Duke Laroche's life. Here was the duke repelling the green-skinned orcs from his castle walls near to what would become the city of Mousillon. Another showed the duke winning the Tourney of Couronne, claiming the silver helm from the Fay Enchantress herself. Another showed Laroche at court with the king of that age, his armour almost white with the brilliance of its polish. There were also scenes from his daily life, such as the duke out hawking in the mountains, his wedding to the Lady Isabon and the knighting of his son. The largest tapestry, almost a dozen paces in length, depicted various tableaux from his Grail Quest. It showed the duke driving forth foul beastmen of Chaos from the hallowed woods of Lapelle, his founding of the Grail Temple at Mousillon and his solitary two-month vigil in the Grey Mountains during which the Lady of the Lake had guided him to one of the Grail's resting places.

Spurred on by the visitation of the duke's ghost, who had given him such dire warnings of evil to come that Tybalt had woken with a shudder and covered in sweat despite the autumn night chill, the knight had vowed to his father that he would seek out this evil, wherever it would be found. It was his father who first directed him to the massive heraldic library at Couronne. During his research, Tybalt had learnt much of the duke and had come to see him as a shining example of the true Bretonnian knight. Records told of a man who was pure and holy, pious in every way, noble to his servants and his peers. His humility had been near-legendary in his time and his ultimate sacrifice, saving the Queen's life from a traitor's blade, had been a glorious end to a glorious life. And now the duke had appeared to Tybalt, asking him for help. Tybalt was honoured that such a hero of his lands had faith in him.

Tybalt noticed that the tapestry at the far end of the chamber was hanging askance, obviously moved by someone. Combined with the footprints by the entrance, this convinced Tybalt that someone had been down here. Or perhaps they were still down here, Tybalt realised with a start. Easing his sword from its scabbard, Tybalt stepped cautiously towards the skewed tapestry, pushing it to one side with the tip of his sword. There was an archway beyond, and in the fitful light he could see that the burial chamber on the other side was empty of life. Glancing up, Tybalt noticed an inscription in the stonework above the arch. Raising the torch above his head, Tybalt read the epigraph: *'In Life I protected thee; In Death I shall Watch over thee.'*

It is true, thought Tybalt. Even from beyond death, the duke has returned to warn us of a growing peril to the realm of Bretonnia.

The inner tomb was unadorned, and in the middle sat the duke's sarcophagus. His shield and sword were laid upon it, along with the silver helm given to him by the Fay Enchantress so many centuries ago. None of his arms showed any sign of the many years that had passed. Looking around, Tybalt could see nothing amiss, but that only served to worry him further. If it had been crude graverobbers who had disturbed the duke's eternal resting place, they would have surely have taken the treasures atop the coffin.

The young knight then noticed something on the floor near to the coffin. It was faint and scuffed, but he could see a tracing of lines and sigils. As he followed them, he realised that they formed some kind of pentagram with the tomb at its centre. They had a reddish-brown tinge to them and Tybalt knew instinctively that they had been drawn in blood. Perhaps human blood, he suddenly found himself thinking, his skin prickling with goosebumps. To his eyes, the enchanted matrix appeared to have faded, the blood at least several days old.

Tybalt was at a loss for a moment. He had finally reached the duke's place of eternal rest, but now what was he to do? Would the duke appear to him again, or was there some ritual he must perform first? Laying his sword to one side and placing the impromptu torch in one of the several brackets hanging from the walls, Tybalt knelt on both knees, bowing his head to the stone coffin.

'By the Lady of the Lake, our eternal guardian, I have sought out this place. I am here to fight whatever dangers await my land. My sword and my life are yours to command, ancient duke. What will you have me do?' he asked, his voice barely above a whisper.

For a moment, nothing happened, but then something stirred in the red-tinged gloom. A faint whispering noise echoed off the walls; a gentle wind sighed around the room. Looking up, Tybalt gasped in surprise. There, no more than two paces from him, stood the shade of Duke Laroche. He looked exactly as he had in the dream, dressed in flowing, yellow robes, the black eagle embroidered onto the left breast, over his heart. A small circlet of gold was placed over his shoulder-length hair, and his dark-brown eyes stared peacefully at Tybalt. The duke's face radiated a knightly air, his hooked nose and strong jaw echoed in most of the aristocratic families of the present day. His face was stern but kindly.

The image was only half-present though. Tybalt could clearly see the coffin and the far wall through the shimmering apparition. A nimbus of white light played around the edges of the ghost, twinkling like distant starlight.

'My lord, I am your humble servant,' Tybalt managed to say. The duke remained silent, beckoning with his right hand for Tybalt to stand. Finally the duke spoke, the words echoing and distant, as if he were speaking from a long way away and some large chamber was magnifying his words.

'I knew thou wouldst come, young Tybalt,' the duke said with a warm smile. 'I knew one of thy great-great-great-great-great-great-great-great-great grandsires! He was a good man, and I knew his blood runneth thick in thy veins. Thou wilst be a fine duke when thy father finally passeth into the care of Our Lady.'

'Thank you, milord,' Tybalt replied, blushing at such praise.

'I expect thou wonderest why I have brought thou here, knight,' the apparition said.

'There is some great evil stirring in this place,' Tybalt answered. 'That is what you have warned me of.'

'Yea,' the ghost agreed, 'a great evil indeed. It hast been long forgotten now, but the ground thou treadst upon is one of the most holy places in all of the sacred kingdom.'

Tybalt stared down at the stone floor of the tomb in astonishment.

'This hilltop is that very spot where Gilles himself rested the night before he descended to claim the lands south of the mountains for his people,' explained Laroche. 'Here is the place that our First King did witness the first visitation of the Lady of the Lake, and from here did all his knowledge and power spring. Even before the coming of the King, this land was a holy one, for our ancestors beyond the founding of the realm of Bretonnia did labour hard here to build the cairns for their dead lords. The very hill itself is but a gigantic tomb of the resting dead, from the time when the elves and dwarfs ruled the lands and our people were but scattered hunting tribes.'

Tybalt gulped heavily in amazement.

'How could such a place be forgotten, milord?' he asked, shaking his head in disbelief.

"'Tis the way of things, young knight,' the old duke replied simply, stroking an incorporeal hand through his dark hair. 'Ages pass, the world changes, the old ways are replaced by new ways; the ancient secrets and beliefs give way to the wonders of the modern age. It is the duty of the Grail Knights to keep that true wisdom alive, but there are fewer of us with every passing generation. A darkness threatens all of our lands, and the realms of others to the north, south, east and west. A time of great change is coming, young knight, a time of war and disorder. We shall need men such as thyself. Verily, there shall be such need of heroes, the like of which time has never seen before!'

Tybalt was about to ask what darkness was coming, but the duke held up a hand to silence him. The knight saw that the duke's gloves were made from the blackest velvet, and on every finger was a golden ring bearing the crests of the eight great families of the founding of Mousillon.

'But that is the future, not thy current quest, valiant Tybalt,' the apparition finally said. 'For now, you must fight against the hideous attentions of a dabbler in the black arts of necromancy.'

'Necromancy, milord?' Tybalt asked, unsure of the word's meaning.

"'Tis the power to summon the forces of Death and Undeath, and bind them to thy bidding,' the duke answered, his ghostly form stepping back to lean against the coffin. "'Tis the power to raise corpses from thy graves to dance in unholy rites and march to war against the living. 'Tis the power to steal life with a touch of the finger. 'Tis the power to gaze past the gates of Death itself and peer at that which lies beyond. 'Tis the power to forever forestall the coming of the eternal sleep, so that thou might never know Death.'

The duke stood up once more, his fists clenched by his sides in anger.

'One who has these powers hath come here,' he spat. 'To this site, that which is the most holy of places. He hath disturbed mine own slumber and that of others of your great ancestors. He yet will raise the bodies of the dead to sweep all before him, his vile blackness spreading like spilt ink across a clean parchment. Thou must stop him, Tybalt; that is why I brought thee here.'

'I should have brought my father's army!' exclaimed Tybalt, raising his hand to his mouth in horror. 'This foul creature would have no chance against a hundred sturdy men and knights.'

'Thou canst not defeat such an evil with battle alone, young Tybalt,' Laroche answered. 'They feed on fear, thrive on thy terror. From the fallen ranks, he wouldst summon more from their graves to do his bidding. Nay, an army is not needed, for is not a knight of Bretonnia strong enough to overcome all obstacles? Is not the Lady the most powerful of allies? 'Tis faith that will break this darkness, and faith does not come from an army, but from one knight who will stand alone against the perils of the world.'

'I do not understand, milord,' Tybalt protested. 'What can I do against a man who can raise an army from the very ground at my feet?'

'You can fight him,' the duke replied shortly, his eyebrows raised in humour. The duke then paused a moment, his head turning as if to look through the wall of the tomb.

'The beast cometh now!' he hissed. 'Gird your arms, and do battle, brave knight. Take mine silver helm, for it wilst protect thee from the worst of the devil's magicks. The Lady is with you, brave Tybalt, so look to your faith for strength, and you will endure and overcome.' With a reassuring smile, the ghost of Duke Laroche began to waver and then was gone.

STANDING ON THE crest of the hill, Tybalt could just make out a faint lightness in the mist, moving slowly towards him. As it grew closer, he saw that it was the glow of a flame, and it was not long before he could make out the figure of a man walking lopsidedly along the path. He had wisely extinguished his own torch, fearing he would reveal his presence too soon, and as the stranger came closer, the knight stepped behind one of the nearby tombs. Another dozen heartbeats passed before he could hear the scuffing of the newcomer's twisted leg as well as the intruder's laboured wheezing and a constant whispering in a tongue the knight did not understand. Pushing himself even further into the shadows, Tybalt waited for his adversary to come closer. The shuffling footfalls stopped at the summit, no more than a dozen strides from his hiding place. Tybalt eased his sword into a position ready to strike, and he waited for his foe to limp within easy reach of his blade. He heard the man give a hacking cough, and then a voice called out in accented Bretonnian.

'Show yourself, knight! I know you are here waiting!'

Tybalt felt his stomach tighten with fear, and he fought down the sick feeling. Blinking quickly to clear the moisture in his eyes, he took a deep breath and then stepped out of the shadows to confront the stranger.

The man was indeed short, no more than five feet tall. His right leg was crooked below the knee, splaying his foot outwards. He was dressed in a heavy, grey robe fastened with a frayed length of rope. In one hand, he held a knobbled wooden staff, the tip of which was glowing with an unnatural flame. Under the other arm, the man carried a heavy book bound in leather and brass. The man was looking the other way, and all Tybalt could see of his face was a bulbous nose surrounded by a wild shock of greasy, grey hair. The stranger then turned to face him, his face old and lined with many deep wrinkles like a carelessly discarded blanket. A scraggly growth of beard sprouted from his chin and cheeks, but the eyes that stared at him from under thick bushy brows were bright and lively.

'There you are!' the figure said, taking several steps closer. 'I came as quick as I could. Did not want you to get cold waiting for me.'

'Approach no closer, creature of evil,' Tybalt warned, brandishing his sword towards the necromancer, who took a step back.

'Creature of evil?' the necromancer replied. 'Who told you such things?'

'The duke has warned me of the vile deeds you are committing,' Tybalt said proudly, lowering his blade slightly.

'The duke?' the magic user replied excitedly, his sharp gaze meeting Tybalt's own defiant stare. 'Then it is true, a spirit can come back across the void! Oh, wondrous!'

'Leave, and never trouble these lands again,' Tybalt told the man facing him in his most commanding voice.

'Leave?' the necromancer replied incredulously, his head tilted to one side in astonishment. 'When I am so near to finishing my work here? I do not think so! Get out of my way, and I will spare you.'

'You shall not pass me while I draw breath!' Tybalt threatened, bringing his sword up once more.

'So be it,' the necromancer sneered, pointing his staff towards the knight. The foreigner spoke two words in a harsh, clipped voice – and a white-hot flame roared out of the staff to engulf Tybalt.

The knight felt Laroche's silver helm growing colder and the flames licked around him without touching, keeping him safe from harm. The flames continued, but the necromancer took a step back in dismay when the uninjured Tybalt strode from the magical fires, his eyes filled with murderous intent, his sword still stained with the boar's blood, raised for a lethal strike. With surprising speed, the evil wizard lashed out with the staff, cracking it against the side of Tybalt's helm.

Dizzied, the knight lurched to one side, his outstretched hand finding the wall of a tomb to brace himself against. When he looked around, the necromancer had disappeared into the mists, the glow of the staff nowhere to be seen. Tybalt could feel a small trickle of blood running down his left cheek from where his helm had broken the skin, and his jaw felt numb. Blinking back tears of shock, he pushed himself upright and began searching for the fleeing sorcerer.

TYBALT HAD WANDERED aimlessly for some time, trying to find the necromancer's hiding place. He had walked back along the length of the path and was sure his prey had not left the cemetery. It was at the gate that he had another revelation. The necromancer had only known he was in the cemetery because of the black stallion he'd tied up by the gate! There had been nothing mystical about his knowledge at all. The man's magic was hardly as all-powerful as the knight had at first believed. Checking on his horse, the knight found it unharmed, and Tybalt suspected that the vile wizard had decided to steal the fine steed once his owner had been killed.

'This is fruitless!' Tybalt hissed to himself in frustration. The grave-yard was large, and in the dense mist it was impossible to see anything at all beyond two dozen yards. What was it the duke had said? Faith would see him victorious? Shrugging, Tybalt stuck his sword in the ground, knelt on one knee and bowed his head to its pommel.

'Oh glorious Lady of the Lake, who watches over our king and lands, guide me to this evil man so that I may slay him in your name,' he prayed, eyes still flickering from side to side, alert from danger.

He knelt for almost thirty heartbeats, but nothing happened. With a sigh, he closed his eyes for a second, and suddenly his mind was filled with a vision. Blinking, Tybalt closed his eyes once more and concen-trated. In his mind's eye, he could see the necromancer in a narrow depression which the knight somehow knew was on the other side of the hill. The wizard had his spellbook open on the top of a low tomb in front of him and was chanting verses of magic from its pages. The air around him was shifting and changing, ruffled and rippled by the movement of unquiet spirits. Focusing his mind even more, Tybalt caught the noise of the wizard's words and, as he opened his eyes once more, he found he could still faintly hear them. Following his ears, Tybalt began to move around the base of the hill, staying close to the high, dry stone wall that served as the cemetery's boundary.

TYBALT WAS CREEPING up the hillside, closing in on the necromancer's ritual. Stealthily he wove his way through the mass of gravestones, glad that his armour was well oiled and did not make too much noise. As he made his way between the graves, Tybalt's foot caught in something, pitching him forward onto his hands and knees. Thinking it a bramble or similar, he tugged hard, but to no avail. Glancing back he gave a high pitched yelp. A bony hand protruded from the ground and was grasping his ankle!

As the knight tried to wrench his leg free, another arm broke through the surface, and then the skeleton's skull pushed free, its fleshless grin leering at the knight from the dead creature's grave. Tybalt smashed the skull in two with his sword, and the dead thing's grip relaxed.

Pushing himself up, Tybalt realised other shapes were pressing through the mist towards him. Preferring not to be trapped in the tightening ring of dead creatures, he jumped towards the nearest, lashing out with his blade. The sword crashed through the skeleton's ribs and spine, toppling it to the ground in two parts. Turning to face the others, he counted four more adversaries. Dodging to one side, he realised that three of the four were armoured and armed with ancient-looking axes and maces. One still carried a shield on its left arm, while all four wore scattered fragments of mail armour.

'Lady, give me strength!' Tybalt hissed as the nearest undead creature lashed out with its rusty-bladed axe, the blow falling wide as Tybalt swayed to his left. Tybalt brought his sword around in a long, backhand sweep, smashing the skeleton several feet backwards. Tybalt stepped forward, thrusting out with the point of his blade, embedding it deep into the creature's chest. The magic binding it to the world of the living severed, and the thing collapsed into a pile of mouldering bones. Fleshless hands grabbed at Tybalt's neck and he spun on the spot, ramming his elbow into the face of the skeleton which had attacked him, its jaw flying into the fog. Too close to use his sword, Tybalt brought his knee up sharply and was rewarded by the sound of splintering ribs.

Tybalt was staggered sideways as a mace crashed into his shoulder, and as he stumbled he brought the pommel of his sword down onto the skull of the unarmed skeleton, crunching through the time-worn bone and smashing it asunder. His next blow crashed against the other's shield and Tybalt was forced to sway backwards as the mace rushed inches in front of his face. With a grunt, Tybalt grabbed the skeleton's shield, pulling the thing's face forward onto the brow of his helm with bone-shattering force. As it flailed backwards under the impact, Tybalt gripped his sword in both hands and cleaved it from right shoulder to pelvis with an arcing, overhead chop.

Tybalt felt something ragged dig deep into his right thigh and he fell to his left knee, the axe in his leg wrenched from the dead grip of the skeleton. Its fingers clawed at his closed helmet, trying to twist his head off. Tybalt grabbed its neck in one hand, battering the thing's temples with the quillions of his sword. The skeleton would not let go though, and with a cry of pain, Tybalt forced himself to his feet, his hand still tightly gripping the creature's neck, blood pouring down his leg from where the axe still hung.

'You died once, you can die again!' Tybalt spat, dropping his sword and thrusting the fingers of his free hand into the skeleton's eye sockets. As its clawed fingers scraped deafeningly against his helm, Tybalt stretched his right arm forward with all his strength, pushing the unnatural monster's head further and further back. He felt the thing's bony fingers scratching at his exposed throat and a flicker of fear struck him when they slid across the veins and arteries which were standing out from his neck with the effort of pushing the skeleton away.

Suddenly shifting his weight to one side, Tybalt pulled the skeleton towards him, throwing it over one hip so that it landed back-first on the ground. Its grip had been broken and Tybalt stamped down on its chest, his heavily armoured boot crushing the unlife from the creature.

Panting with exhaustion and pain, Tybalt grabbed the handle of the axe stuck in his leg and pulled it free, a cry of agony torn from his lips. Tossing the ancient weapon aside, he retrieved his sword from the long grass. Using the blade of his sword, the knight cut a rough bandage from his surcoat and wrapped it around the injured thigh, pulling it painfully tight over the wound to stem the bleeding. Glancing around to ensure that no more unholy denizens were nearby, he started to limp up the slope towards the necromancer.

THE WIZARD'S FACE was a picture of almost comical shock when Tybalt staggered through the mist towards him. He had one hand outstretched, the other pointing towards his grimoire, where he had obviously been following the lines of writing. Around him stood a dozen more animated corpses, all of them ancient and yellowing skeletons. The summoner of the dead quickly masked his surprise.

'Still walking, yes?' he said, a cruel smile playing briefly across his thin, cracked lips.

'I am,' Tybalt replied simply, taking another step towards the necromancer, his sword held across his chest.

'It does not matter, I have more minions to deal with you,' the wizard said glibly, gesturing left and right to the skeletons stood around him.

'And I will destroy them in turn, before I destroy you,' Tybalt answered with utmost sincerity, momentarily surprised at his own confidence.

The sorcerer hesitated for a second, and once again Tybalt noticed doubt creeping into the old man's eyes. The knight took another step forward.

'You think you can stop me? On your own?' sneered the necromancer, but Tybalt caught more than just a hint of false bravado about the wizard's defiance.

'One Bretonnian knight is enough for any evil creature, be it griffon, elf-thing, orc or man,' Tybalt assured the necromancer. A shadow of fear passed briefly across the evil wizard's face. Behind the magic user, two of the skeletons began to sway back and forth and then collapsed into a pile of bones. Tybalt thought he saw a flicker of soul-light and heard a distant cry of joy of a spirit set free once more.

The necromancer turned and looked over his shoulder before his horrified gaze settled on Tybalt once more.

'Your power is fading, old man,' Tybalt said menacingly, pleased with the metallic ring given to his voice by the closed visor of his helmet. He saw the necromancer swallow hard, eyes darting left and right, searching for an escape route. Another three skeletons crumbled into grave dust to the knight's left.

'No, no, no, no...' the foul wizard whispered harshly and then began to babble something in a strange tongue. But this was no otherworldly language of magic, for Tybalt recognised it as the Reikspiel of the Empire, even though he did not understand the words.

'It seems your creations are sparing me the exertion of slaying them again,' Tybalt joked, marching slowly through the long grass. He levelled the point of his sword at the necromancer.

'Your death will be brief,' the knight assured him with all earnestness. With a clatter of bones the magic animating the remaining skeletons was broken, and the necromancer was left standing alone in the thinning fog. Tybalt saw that his foe was visibly shaking with fear now, as the knight stalked across the shallow dell. Once more, the necromancer looked for somewhere to run, but there was no way out. Even wounded, the knight would catch the crippled wizard with ease.

'What powers of magic have you that you can destroy my creations so easily?' asked the wizard, eyes pleading beneath his grey brows.

'I have no magic other than the blessing of the Lady,' Tybalt answered him. 'It is your own weaknesses that have destroyed them, your own lack of will to keep them animated. Your magic is powerful, but you are weak. Without your magic, you are nothing!'

'Have mercy, knight,' the necromancer begged, eyes filling with tears. 'Please do not kill me!'

'Mercy?' Tybalt sneered, stabbing his sword towards the wizard to emphasise his scorn. 'Mercy for the creature who has despoiled and profaned one of the most sacred places of all Bretonnia? Mercy for the beast who would wake the heroes of our past from their eternal sleep to be slaves to his vile purposes? Mercy for a creature that would sweep away the living with his own tide of death? There can be no mercy for such crimes!'

'Please kill me not!' begged the other, falling to his knees in the long, wet grass. 'I cannot bear the thought of death!'

Tybalt paused in his rage-driven advance.

'Scared of death?' the knight asked scornfully. 'Is that all you have in your defence? You have plagued the living and the dead because of your own fear of death? Your fear is the root of your weakness. The very thing that drove you to seek such dark powers has unmanned you.'

'I cannot bear the thought of the final ending of my life,' the necro-mancer admitted, his squinting eyes streaming with tears of fear and loathing. 'I had to find some way to escape. I did not mean harm. That I will one day not be anymore fills me with terror that I cannot face.'

'But death is not an ending,' Tybalt growled, stepping towards the wizard, through the thick weeds once more. 'As the duke has shown me, death is merely a gateway to another place. If we live well, we shall be rewarded: the Lady will take care of us, and we shall be beside her for the rest of time.'

'How do you know of such things?' the sorcerer demanded, his face filled with anguish.

'I do not know such things. I believe in them,' Tybalt answered, standing over the cowering necromancer. 'I have faith that what I have been taught is true. I need no evidence of the land beyond death, for it is faith in its existence that will take me there.'

'And what of those who have no faith?' the necromancer asked fear-fully.

'I do not know,' the knight replied, drawing his sword back. 'Per-haps we all get what we believe in. Perhaps you will just simply cease, or perhaps your soul will be trapped in a limbo between realms. Or maybe there is a hell, and devils will rend your soul for all eternity.' Tybalt stepped to one side of the necromancer and braced his legs in the soft ground.

'You will know, sooner than I!' he cried, his sword arm bringing his blade swiftly across the necromancer's neck, sending the head tum-bling into the overgrown grass.

As TYBALT RODE back along the single road of Moreux, a crowd of peasants began to gather around him. He must have been a fearsome sight, his armour scratched and bloody, his face a grim mask. Reach-ing the open space that served as town square, he halted his steed.

'Foul things have come to this land because we have allowed them to trespass,' he called to the assembled throng. 'We have forgotten that which should be remembered. Hear this, and heed it well. As a knight of Bretonnia, I command you all to send men to the graveyard along the pass, to clear away the ruin of centuries. It shall be your duty to see that it is maintained with dignity and pride. I lay this honour upon you. Do not fail in this task, for I shall return, and I shall demand to know who is responsible if my commands fall on deaf ears!'

As the peasants began to drift away, Tybalt turned to look back at the hill at the top of the pass. The sun was just now reaching over its crest, its golden light spilling down the slope and lending it a beauty it had not had in the dark mists of the night before. He wondered for a moment if the duke was still there looking down on him.

'Farewell, milord,' the knight said to himself. 'You have earned your rest.'

A CHOICE OF HATREDS

C L Werner

ON THE OUTSKIRTS of the small town of Kleinsdorf, a group of raucous men gathered in a fallow field. Before them stood an inverted anvil upon which a burly man garbed in a heavy blacksmith's apron set a second anvil. The man's bearded face split into a booming laugh as one of his comrades lit a hemp fuse that slithered between the anvils to reach a small charge of gunpowder. A hushed silence fell upon the men as the smouldering flame slowly burned its way to the explosive. Suddenly a tremendous boom echoed across the barren fields and the uppermost anvil was thrown into the sky to crash into the ground several yards away. A great cheer erupted from the group and the blacksmith set off at a lumbering jog to retrieve the heavy iron projectile, even as one of his friends prepared another charge.

'It looks like we have chanced into a bit of a celebration, eh, Mathias?' commented a stout, bearded rider on the road overlooking the anvil-firing party.

The man wore a battered and ill-mended pair of leather breeches; an equally battered jerkin of studded leather struggled to contain the man's slight paunch. Greasy, swine-like eyes peered from either side of a splayed nose while an unkempt beard clothed his forward-jutting jaw. From a scabbard at his side a broadsword swayed with each step of his horse.

587

'We come here seeking rest, friend Streng, not to indulge your penchant for debauchery', replied the second rider. A tall, grim figure, the second man was his companion's senior by at least a decade. Where Streng's attire was shabby and worn, this man's was opulent. Immaculate shiny leather boots rose to the man's knees and his back was enveloped by a heavy black cape lined with the finest ermine. Fine calfskin gauntlets garbed slender-fingered hands while a tunic of red satin embroidered with gold clothed his arms and chest. The wide rounded brim of his leather hat cast a shadow upon the rider's features. Hanging from a dragonskin belt with an enormous silver buckle were a pair of holstered pistols and a slender-bladed longsword.

'You are the one who has taken so many fine vows to Sigmar', Streng said with a voice that was not quite a sneer. 'I recall taking no such vows.'

Mathias turned to look at his companion and his face emerged from the shadow cast by the brim of his hat. The older man's visage was gaunt, dominated by a narrow, dagger-like nose and the thin moustache that rested between it and the man's slender lips. A grey arrow of beard stabbed out from the man's chin. His eyes were of similar flinty hue but burnt with a strange intensity, a determination and zeal that were at odds with the glacial hue.

'You make no vows to Sigmar, yet you take the Temple's gold easily enough', Mathias locked eyes with his comrade. Some of the glib disrespect in Streng's manner dissipated as he met that gaze.

'I've not seen many monks with so fine a habit as yours', Streng said, turning his eyes from his companion.

'It is sometimes wise to remind people that Sigmar rewards service in this life as well as the hereafter.' Mathias looked away from his henchman and stared at the town before them.

A small settlement of some thousand persons, the simple wooden structures were close together, the streets narrow and crooked. Everywhere there was laughter and singing, music from mandolin and fife. A celebratory throng choked the streets, dancing with recklessness born more of joy than drink, at least in this early hour of the festival. Yet, none were so reckless as not to make way for Mathias as he manoeuvred his steed into the narrow streets, nor to make the sign of Sigmar's Hammer with the witch hunter's passing.

'I shall take room at the inn. You find a stable for the horses', Mathias said as he and Streng rode through the crowd.

'And then?' asked Streng, a lustful gleam in his eyes and a lecherous grin splitting his face.

'I care not what manner of sin you find fit to soil your soul with', snarled the witch hunter. 'Just see that you are in condition to ride at cock's crow.'

As they talked, the pair did not observe the stealthy figure who watched their exchange from behind a hay-laden wagon. They did not see the same figure emerge from its hiding place with their passing, nor the venomous glare it sent after them.

GUSTAV SIPPED AT the small glass of Tilean wine, listening to the sounds of merriment beyond the walls of his inn. A greedy glint came to the innkeeper's eyes as he thought of the vacant rooms above his head and the drunken men who would fill them before the night was through. The Festival of Wilhelmstag brought many travellers to Kleinsdorf, travellers who would find themselves too drunk or too fatigued to quit the town once the festivities reached their end. Few would be lucid enough to haggle over the 'competitive' fee Gustav charged his annual Wilhelmstag guests.

Gustav again sipped at his wine, silently toasting Wilhelm Hoess and the minotaur lord which had been kind enough to let itself and its horde of Chaos spawn be slaughtered in the streets of Kleinsdorf two centuries past. Even now, the innkeeper could see the gilded skull of the monster atop a pole in the centre of the square outside, torchlight from the celebratory throng below it dancing across the golden surface. Gustav hoped that the minotaur was enjoying the view, for tomorrow the skull would return to a chest in the town hall, there to reside until next Wilhelmstag.

The opening of the inn's front door roused the innkeeper from his thoughts. Gustav smiled.

The first sheep comes to be fleeced, he thought as he scuttled away from the window. But the smile died when Gustav's eyes observed the countenance of his new guest. The high black hat, flowing cape and expensive weapons combined with the stern visage of the man's face told Gustav what this man was even before he saw the burning gleam in those cold grey eyes.

'I am sorry, my lord, but I am afraid that I have no rooms that are free.' Gustav winced as the witch hunter's eyes stared into his own. 'The... the festival. It brings many guests. If you had only come on another night...' the innkeeper stammered.

'Your common room is also filled?' the witch hunter interrupted.

'Why, no,' Gustav said, a nervous tic causing his left eye to twitch uncontrollably.

'Then you may move one of your guests to the common room,' the witch hunter declared. Gustav nodded his agreement even as he inwardly cursed the man. The common room was a long hall at the side of the inn lined with pallets of straw. Even drunkards would be unwilling to pay much for such lodgings.

'You may show me my room,' the witch hunter said, his firm hand grasping Gustav's shoulder and pushing the innkeeper ahead of himself. 'I trust that you have something appropriate for a devoted servant of Sigmar?'

'Yes, my lord,' Gustav said, altering his course away from the closet-like chamber he had thought to give the witch hunter. He led the way up a flight of stairs to one of the larger rooms. The witch hunter peered into the chamber while the innkeeper held the door open.

'No, I think not,' the witch hunter declared. The bearded face moved closer toward Gustav's own and one of the gloved fingers touched the twitching muscle beside the innkeeper's eye.

'Interesting,' Mathias said, not quite under his breath. The innkeeper's eyes grew wide with fright, seeming to see the word 'mutation' forming in the witch hunter's mind.

'A nervous twitch, nothing more,' Gustav muttered, knowing that even so slight a physical defect had put men to the stake in many backwater towns. 'I have a much nicer room, if you would follow me.' Gustav turned, leading the witch hunter to a second flight of stairs.

'Yes, this will do,' Mathias stated when Gustav led him into a large and well-furnished room at the very top of the inn. Gustav smiled and nodded his head nervously.

'It is my honour to serve a noble Templar of Sigmar,' the innkeeper said as he walked to the large oak wardrobe that dominated one corner of the room. Gustav opened the wardrobe and removed his own nightshirt and cap from it.

'I will dine here,' Mathias declared, settling into a large chair and removing his weapon-laden belt. 'A goose and some wine, I think.' The witch hunter stroked his moustache with his thumb and forefinger.

'I will see to it,' the innkeeper said, knowing better than to challenge his most-unwanted guest. Gustav paused a few steps away from the witch hunter. Mathias reached into a pocket in the lining of his tunic and tossed a few coins into the man's hands. Gustav stared stupidly at them for several seconds.

'I did not come for the festival,' explained Mathias, 'so I should not have to pay festival prices.' The witch hunter suddenly cocked his head and stared intently at Gustav's twitching eye.

'I shall see about your supper,' Gustav whimpered as he hurried from the room.

THE STREETS OF Kleinsdorf were alive with rejoicing. Everywhere there was dancing and singing. But all the laughter and joy in the world could not touch the figure that writhed its way through the crowd. The dark, shabby cloak of the man, meant to keep him inconspicuous, was at odds with the bright fabrics and flowers of the revellers and made him stand out all the more. Dozens of times Reinhardt von

Lichtberg had been forced to ward away garishly clad townspeople who thought to exorcise this wraith of melancholy in their midst with dance and drink. Reinhardt spat into the dust. A black-hearted murderer had descended upon this place and all these idiots could do was dance and laugh. Well, if things turned out as Reinhardt planned, he too would have cause to dance and laugh. Before they stretched his neck from a gallows.

Hands clasped Reinhardt's shoulders and spun the young man around. So lost in thoughts of revenge was he that he did not even begin to react before warm, moist lips closed about his own. The woman detached herself and stared up into the young man's face.

'I don't believe that I know you,' Reinhardt said as his eyes considered the golden-haired, well-built woman smiling impishly at him and the taste of ale that covered his lips.

'You could,' the woman smiled. 'The Festival of Wilhelmstag is a time for finding new people.'

Reinhardt shook his head. 'I am looking for no one new.' Reinhardt found himself thinking again of Mina and how she had died. And how her murderer would die.

'You have not seen a witch hunter, by any chance?' Reinhardt asked. The woman's smile turned into a full-lipped pout.

'I've met his surrogate,' the girl swore. 'Over at the beer hall, drinking like an orc and carrying on like a Tilean sailor. Mind you, no decent woman had better get near him.' The impish smile returned and the woman pulled scandalously at the torn fringe of her bodice. 'See what the brute did to me.'

Reinhardt grabbed the woman's arms in a vice-like grip.

'Did he say where Mathias Thulmann, the witch hunter, is?' Reinhardt snarled. The coyness left the woman's face as the drunken haze was replaced by something approaching fear.

'The inn, he was taking a room at the inn.' The girl retreated into the safety of the crowd as Reinhardt released her. The nobleman did not even notice her go, his mind already processing the information she had given him. His right hand slid beneath the shabby cloak and closed around the hilt of his sword.

'Soon, Mina,' Reinhardt whispered, 'soon your murderer will discover what suffering is.'

GERHARDT KNAUF HAD never known terror such as he now felt. The wonderful thrill of fear that he enjoyed when engaging in his secret activities was gone. The presence of the witch hunter had driven home the seriousness of discovery in a way that Knauf had never fully comprehended before. The shock and looks of disbelief he had visualised on his neighbours' faces when they realised that the merchant was more than he seemed had become the frenzied visages of a bloodthirsty mob. In his imagination, Knauf could even smell the kindling as it caught flame.

The calf-eyed merchant with his beetle-like brow downed the contents of the tankard resting on the bar before him in a single bolt. Knauf pressed a hand against his mouth, struggling to keep the beer from leaving his body as quickly as it had entered it. The merchant managed to force the bile back into his stomach and let his head sway towards the man sitting beside him.

'Mueller,' croaked Knauf, his thin voice struggling to maintain a semblance of dignity, even as he struggled against fear and inebriation. The heavy set mercenary at his side looked away from the gob of wax he had been whittling into a lewd shape and regarded the merchant.

'You have done jobs for me before,' Knauf continued.

'Aye,' the mercenary cautiously replied, fingering his knife.

'And I have always paid you fairly and promptly,' the merchant added, his head swaying from side to side like some bloated reptile.

'That is true enough,' Mueller said, a smirk on his face. The truth of it was that Knauf was too timid to be miserly when it came to paying the men who protected his wagons. A cross look from Rall, or Gunther, or even from the scarecrow-like Hossbach, and the mercenaries would see an increase in their wages.

'Would you say that we are friends?' Knauf said, reaching for another ceramic tankard of beer. He swallowed only half the tankard's contents this time, spilling most of the remainder when he clumsily set the vessel back upon the table.

'Were you to pay me enough, I would even say that we were brothers,' Mueller replied, struggling to contain the laughter building within his gut. But the condescending sarcasm in the mercenary's voice was lost on the half-drunken Knauf. The merchant caught hold of Mueller's arm and stared into his face with pleading eyes.

'Would you murder for me?' the merchant hissed. This time Mueller did laugh.

'By Ulric's fangs, Gerhardt!' the mercenary swore. 'Who could you possibly hate enough to need killed?' Mueller laughed again and downed his own tankard of beer.

'The witch hunter,' whispered Knauf, his head swaying from side to side to ensure that no one had overheard.

'Have you been reading things you shouldn't?' Mueller asked, only half-seriously. The look of fear in Knauf's eyes killed the joke forming on the mercenary's lips. Mueller rose from his chair and stared down at the merchant.

'Forty gold crowns,' the mercenary declared, waving away the look of joy and hope crawling across Knauf's features. 'And as far as the boys are concerned, you are paying us ten.' Mueller turned away from the table and started to walk into the main room of the beer hall.

'Where are you going?' Knauf called after Mueller in a voice that sounded unusually shrill even for the merchant.

'To get Hossbach and the others,' Mueller said. 'Maybe I'll see if I can't learn something about our friend as well.' The mercenary turned away. He only got a few steps before Knauf's drunken hands were scrabbling at the man's coat.

'How are you going to do that?' Knauf hissed up at him with alarm.

Mueller extracted himself from the merchant's grip. He pointed a finger to the far end of the beer hall where a bawdy song and shrieks of mock indignation marked the crowd gathered in morbid fascination around the man who had rode into Kleinsdorf with the witch hunter.

'How else? I'll speak with his lackey,' Mueller shook his head as Knauf started to protest. 'Leave this to me. Why don't you go home and get my gold ready?' The mercenary did not wait to see if Knauf would follow his suggestion, but continued across the beer hall, liberating a metal stein from a buxom barmaid along the way.

'Sometimes they confess straight away,' Streng was saying as Mueller inconspicuously joined his audience. 'That's the worst of it. There's nothing left to do but string them up, or burn them if they've been particularly bad.' Streng paused to smile at the woman sitting on his knee.

'So how do you go about finding a witch?' Mueller interrupted Streng's carousing. The lout turned to Mueller and regarded him with an irritated sneer.

'I don't. That's the Templar's job. Mathias finds them and then I make them confess. That way everything is above board and the Temple can burn the filthy things without anybody being upset.' Streng turned away from Mueller and returned his attention to his companion.

'So your master has come to Kleinsdorf looking for witches?' Mueller interrupted again.

Streng shook his head and glared at this man who insisted on intruding on his good time.

'Firstly, Mathias Thulmann is not my master. We're partners, him and me, that's what it is. Secondly, we are on our way to Stirland. Lots of witches down in Stirland.' Streng snorted derisively. 'Do you honestly think we'd cross half the Empire to come here?' Streng laughed. 'I wouldn't cross a meadow to come to this rat nest,' he said, before adding, 'present company excepted, of course,' to the locals gathered around him.

As Streng returned his attention to the giggling creature seated on his knee, Mueller extracted himself from the hangers-on and made his way toward the beer hall's exit. The mercenary spied a familiar face in the crowd and waved the man over to him. A young, wiry man with a broken nose and a livid scar across his forearm walked over to Mueller. The mercenary took the flower-festooned hat from the man's head and sent it sailing across the crowded room with a flick of his wrist.

'Go get Gunther and Hossbach,' Mueller snarled. 'I found us some night work.' The angry look on the young man's face disappeared at the mention of work. Rall set off at a brisk jog to find his fellow sellswords. Mueller looked at the crowd around Streng one last time before leaving the beer hall.

The mercenary had found out all that he needed to know. The witch hunter was only passing through Kleinsdorf; he would not be expecting any trouble. Like all the other jobs he had done for Gerhardt Knauf, this one would hardly be difficult enough to be called 'work'.

A CHEER WENT up from the crowd below as a small boy shimmied up the massive pole standing in the centre of the square and thrust a crown of flowers on the gilded skull at its top.

At the moment, Reinhardt von Lichtberg envied the boy his agility. The nobleman was gripping the outer wall of the inn, thirty feet above the square. To an observer, he might have looked like a great brown bat clinging to the wall of a cave. But there were no eyes trained upon Reinhardt, at least not at present. The few revellers who had lifted their heads skyward were watching the boy descend the pole with a good deal less bravado than he had ascended with. Still, the threat of discovery was far too real and Reinhardt was not yet ready to see the inside of a cell.

Slowly, carefully, Reinhardt worked his fingers from one precarious handhold to another. Only a few feet away he could see the window that was his goal. It had been easy to determine which room the murderer occupied; his was the only window from which light shone. Somehow it did not surprise Reinhardt that the witch hunter had taken a room on the inn's top floor. One last trial, one final obstacle before vengeance could be served.

At last he reached the window and Reinhardt stared through the glass, seeing for the first time in six months the man who had destroyed his life. The murderer sat in a wooden chair, a small table set before him. He cut morsels from a large roasted goose, a wicker-shrouded bottle of wine sitting beside it.

Reinhardt watched for a moment as the monster ate, burning the hated image of the man into his memory. He hoped that the meal was a good one, for it would be the witch hunter's last.

* * *

WITH AN ANIMAL cry, Reinhardt crashed through the window, broken glass and splintered wood flying across the room. Landing on his feet, the sword at his side was in his hand in less than a heartbeat. To his credit, the witch hunter reacted swiftly, kicking the small table at Reinhardt an instant after he landed in the room while diving in the opposite direction to gain the pistols and longsword that lay upon the bed. But Reinhardt had the speed of youth and the martial training of one who might have been a captain in the Reiksguard on his side. More, he had purpose.

The witch hunter's claw-like hand closed around the grip of his pistol just as cold steel touched his throat. There was a brief pause as Thulmann regarded the blade poised at his neck before releasing his weapon and holding his hands up in surrender. Both arms raised above his head, Mathias Thulmann faced the man with a sword at his throat.

'I fear that you will not find much gold,' Mathias said, his voice low and unafraid.

'You do not remember me, do you?' Reinhardt snarled. 'Or are you going to pretend that your name is not Mathias Thulmann, Templar of Sigmar, witch hunter?'

'That is indeed my name, and my trade,' replied Mathias, his voice unchanged.

'My name is Reinhardt von Lichtberg,' spat the other, pressing the tip of his blade into Mathias's throat until a bead of crimson slid down the steel. 'I am the man who is going to kill you.'

'To avenge your lost love?' the witch hunter mused, a touch of pity seeming to enter his voice. 'You should thank me for restoring her soul to the light of Sigmar.'

'*Thank you?*' Reinhardt bellowed incredulously. The youth fought to keep himself from driving his sword through the witch hunter's flesh. 'Thank you for imprisoning us, torturing us? Thank you for burning Mina at the stake? Thank you for destroying the only thing that made my life worth living?' Reinhardt clenched his fist against the wave of rage that pounded through his body. He shook his head from side to side.

'We were to be married,' the nobleman stated. 'I was to serve the Emperor in his Reiksguard and win glory and fame. Then I would return and she would be waiting for me to make her my wife.' Reinhardt pulled a fat skinning knife from a sheath on his belt. 'You took that from me. You took it all away.' Reinhardt let the light play across the knife in his left hand as he rolled his wrist back and forth. The witch hunter continued to watch him, his eyes hooded, his face betraying no fear or even concern. Reinhardt noted the man's seeming indifference to his fate.

'You will scream,' he swore. 'Before I let you die, Sigmar himself will hear your screams.'

The hand with the knife moved toward the witch hunter's body... And for the second time that evening, Mathias Thulmann had unexpected visitors.

THE DOOR BURST inwards, bludgeoned from its hinges by the ogre-like man who followed the smashed portal into the room. Three other men were close behind the ape-like bruiser. All four of them wore a motley array of piecemeal armour, strips of chainmail fastened to leather tunics, bands of steel woven to a padded hauberk. The only aspect that seemed to link the four men was the look of confusion on their faces.

'The witch hunter was supposed to be alone,' stated Rall, puzzled by the strange scene they had stumbled upon. Reinhardt turned his body toward the mercenaries, keeping his sword at Mathias's throat.

'Which one is he?' asked Rall, clearly not intending the question for either of the men already in the room.

'Why don't we just kill them both?' the scarecrow-thin figure of Hossbach said, stepping toward Reinhardt.

Like a lightning bolt, the skinning knife went flying across the room. Hossbach snarled as he dodged the projectile. The mercenary did not see the sword that flashed away from Thulmann's throat to slice across his armour and split his stomach across its centre. Hossbach toppled against the man who had dealt him the fatal wound. His sword forgotten on the floor, the mercenary clutched at Reinhardt, grabbing for the man's sword arm. Reinhardt kicked the dying man away from him, sending him crashing into the foot of the bed, but Hossbach had delayed him long enough. The brutish fist of Gunther crashed into Reinhardt's face while his dagger sought to bury itself in the pit of Reinhardt's left arm. The nobleman managed to grab his attacker's wrist, slowing the deadly blade's strike. The blade pierced his skin but did not sink into his heart. His huge opponent let a feral smile form on his face as he put more strength into the struggle. Slowly, by the slightest of measures, the dagger continued its lethal passage.

Suddenly the sound of thunder assailed Reinhardt's ears; a stench like rotten eggs filled his nose. One moment he had been staring into the triumphant face of his attacker. In the next instant the mercenary's head was a red ruin. The hand on the dagger slid away and the mercenary fell to the floor like a felled tree. Reinhardt saw one of the attackers run through the shattered doorway. The other lay with a gory wound on the side of his head at the feet of the only other man still standing in the room.'

A plume of grey smoke rose from the barrel of the pistol Mathias Thulmann held in his right hand. The other pistol, its butt bloody from its impact against the mercenary's skull, was cocked and pointed at Reinhardt von Lichtberg's own head.

'It seems the last of these yapping curs has not seen fit to remain with us,' Thulmann said. Although he now held the upper hand, the witch hunter still possessed the same air of cold indifference.

'Go ahead and kill me, butcher,' Reinhardt swore, his heart afire with the injustice of it all. To come so close... 'You will be doing me a service,' he added.

'There are some things you should know before I decide if you should live or die,' the witch hunter sat down on the bed, motioning Reinhardt to a position from which the pistol could cover him more easily.

'Have you not wondered what brought me to your father's estate?' Mathias asked. He saw the slight look of interest surface amidst Reinhardt's mask of hate. 'I was summoned by Father Haeften.' Reinhardt started at the mention of the wizened old priest of Sigmar who led his father's household in their devotions. It was impossible for him to believe that the kindly soft-spoken old man could have been responsible for bringing about Mina's death. The witch hunter continued to speak.

'The father reported that one of his parish was touched by Chaos,' Thulmann paused, letting the distasteful word linger in the air. 'A young woman who was with child, whose own mother bespoke the irregularities that were manifesting beneath her skin.'

Stunned shock claimed Reinhardt. With child. His child.

'Upon my arrival, I examined the woman and discovered that her mother's fears had proven themselves,' Thulmann shook his head sadly. 'Her background was not of a suspicious nature, but the Darkness infects even the most virtuous. It was necessary to question her, to learn the source of her affliction. After several hours, she said your name.'

'Hours of torture!' Reinhardt spat, face twisted into an animal snarl. 'And then you took me so that your creature might "question" me!'

'Yes!' affirmed Thulmann, fire in his voice. 'As the father, the source of her corruption might lie within you, yourself! It was necessary to discover if there were others! Chaos is a contagion, where one is infected others soon fall ill!'

'Yet you released me,' challenged Reinhardt, the shame he felt at his own survival further fuelling the impotent rage roaring through his veins.

'There was no corruption in you,' the witch hunter said, almost softly. 'Nor in the girl, not in her soul at least. It was days later that

she confessed the crime that had been the cause of her corruption.'
The witch hunter stared into Reinhardt's blazing eyes.

'Do you know a Doktor Weichs?' he asked.

'Freiherr Weichs?' Reinhardt answered. 'My father's physician?'

'Also physician to his household. Your Mina confided a most private problem with Weichs. She was worried that her condition would
prevent you from leaving the von Lichtberg estate, from joining the
Reiksguard and seeking the honour and glory that were your due.
Weichs gave her a potion of his own creation which he assured her
would dissolve the life within her womb as harmlessly as it had
formed.'

Mathias Thulmann shook his head again. 'That devil's brew Weichs
created was what destroyed your Mina, for it contained warpstone.'
The witch hunter paused again, studying Reinhardt. 'I see that you are
unfamiliar with the substance. It is the pure essence of Chaos, the
black effluent of all the world's evil. In the days before Magnus the
Pious, it was thought to possess healing properties, but only a fool or
a madman would have anything to do with the stuff in this more
enlightened age. Instead of destroying the life in the girl's belly, the
warpstone changed it, corrupted woman and child. When I discovered this, I knew you were innocent and had you released.'

'And burned her!' Reinhardt swore.

The witch hunter did not answer the youth but instead kicked the
figure lying at his feet.

'There is life in you yet,' Thulmann snarled, looking back at Reinhardt to remind his prisoner that his pistol was yet trained on him.
'Account for yourself, pig! Who sends you to harm a dully-ordained
servant of Sigmar?'

Mueller groaned as he rolled onto his side, staring at the witch
hunter through a swollen eye. Carefully he put a hand to his split lip
and wiped the trickle of blood from his mouth.

'Gerhardt... Knauf,' Mueller said between groans. 'It was Gerhardt
Knauf, the merchant. He was afraid you had come to Kleinsdorf seeking him.'

Mathias Thulmann let a grim smile part his lips. 'I am looking for
him now,' he stated. The witch hunter smashed the heel of his boot
into the grovelling mercenary's neck, crushing the man's windpipe.
Mueller uttered a half-gargle, half-gasp and writhed on the floor as he
desperately tried to breathe. Thulmann turned away from the dying
wretch.

'This Knauf has reasons to see me dead,' Thulmann told Reinhardt,
as though the noble had not heard the exchange between witch
hunter and mercenary. 'Reasons which lie in the corruption of his
mind and soul. If you would avenge your beloved, do so upon one

deserving of your wrath, the same sort of filth that destroyed the girl long before I set foot in your father's house.'

Reinhardt glared at the witch hunter. 'I will kill you,' he said in a voice as cold as the grave. Mathias Thulmann sighed and removed a set of manacles from the belt lying on the bed.

'I cannot let you interfere with my holy duty,' the witch hunter said, pressing the barrel of the pistol against Reinhardt's temple. Thulmann closed one of the steel bracelets around the youth's wrist, locking it shut with a deft twist of an iron key. The other half of the manacles he closed around one of the bed posts, trapping the bracelet between the mattress and the wooden globe that topped the post.

'This should ensure that you do not interfere,' Mathias explained as he retrieved the rest of his weapons and stepped over the writhing Mueller.

'I will kill you, Mathias Thulmann,' Reinhardt repeated as the witch hunter left the room. As soon as the cloaked shape was gone, Reinhardt dropped to his knees and stretched his hand toward the ruined body of the mercenary who had almost killed him – and the small hatchet attached to the man's belt.

GERHARDT KNAUF PACED nervously across his bedchamber. It had been nearly an hour and still he had had no word from Mueller.

Not for the first time, the merchant cast his eyes toward the small door at the top of the stairs. The tiny room within was the domain of Knauf's secret vice, the storehouse of all the forbidden and arcane knowledge Knauf had obtained over the years: the grimoire of a centuries-dead Bretonnian witch; the abhorred *Ninth Canticle of Tzeentch*, its mad author's name lost to the ages; a book of incantations designed to bring prosperity, or alternately ruin, by the infamous sorcerer Verlag Duhring. All the black secrets that had given Knauf his power made him better than the ignorant masses that surrounded him, who sneered at his eccentric ways. Before the black arts at his command, brutish men like Mueller were nothing; witch hunters were nothing.

Knauf took another drink from the bottle of wine he had removed from his cellar. The sound of someone pounding on the door of his villa caused the merchant to set his drink down. 'Finally,' he thought.

But the figure that greeted Knauf when he gazed down from his window was not that of Mueller. Instead he saw the scarlet and black garbed form of the mercenary's victim. With a horrified gasp, Knauf withdrew from the window.

'He has come for me,' the merchant shuddered. Mueller and his men had failed and now there was no one to stand between Knauf and the determined witch hunter. Knauf shrieked as he heard a loud explosion from below and the splintering of wood as the door was kicked open. He had only moments in which to save himself from the witch hunter's justice, to avoid the flames that were the price of the knowledge he had sought.

A smile appeared on Knauf's face. The merchant raced for the garret room. If there was no one who would save him from the witch hunter, there was *something* that might.

MATHIAS THULMANN PAUSED on the threshold of the merchant's villa and holstered the smoking pistol in his hand. One shot from the flintlock weapon had been enough to smash the lock on the door, one kick enough to force open the heavy oak portal. The witch hunter drew his second pistol, the one he had reloaded after the melee at the inn and scanned the darkened foyer. No sign of life greeted Thulmann's gaze and he stepped cautiously into the room, watching for the slightest movement in the darkness.

Suddenly the witch hunter's head snapped around, his eyes fixating upon the stairway leading from the foyer to the chambers above. He could sense the dark energies that were gathering somewhere in the rooms above him. Somewhere in this house, someone was calling upon the Ruinous Powers. Thulmann shifted the pistol to his other hand and drew the silvered blade of his sword, blessed by the Grand Theogonist himself and grimly ascended the stairs.

GERHARDT KNAUF COULD feel the eldritch energies gathering in the air around him as he read from the *Ninth Canticle of Tzeentch*. The power was almost a tangible quantity as it surged from the warlock and gathered at the centre of a ring of lighted candles. A nervous laugh interrupted the arcane litany streaming from Knauf's lips as he saw the first faint glimmer of light appear. Swiftly, the glow grew in size, keeping pace with the increasing speed of the words flying from Knauf's tongue. The crackling nimbus took on a pinkish hue and the first faint suggestion of a shape within the light was visible to him.

No, the warlock realised, there was not a shape within the light; rather, the light was assuming a shape. As the blasphemous litany continued, a broad torso coalesced from which two long, simian arms dangled, each ending in an enormous clawed hand. Two short, thick legs slowly grew away from the torso until they touched the wooden floor. Finally, a head sprouted from between the two arms, growing away from the body so that the head was between its shoulders rather than above them. A gargoyle face appeared, its fanged mouth stretching across the head in a hideous grin. Two swirling pools of orange light stared at the warlock.

The daemon uttered a loathsome sound like the wailing of an infant, a sound hideous in its suggestion of malevolent mirth. Knauf shuddered and turned his eyes from the frightful thing he had summoned. In so doing, his gaze fell upon his feet and the colour drained away from his face as the horror of what he had done became known to him.

The first thing Knauf had learned, the most important rule he had found repeated again and again in the arcane books he had so long hoarded, was that a sorcerer must always protect himself from that which he would have do his bidding. In his haste to save himself from the witch hunter, to summon this creature of Tzeentch, Knauf had forgotten to draw about himself a protective circle, a barrier that no daemon may cross.

Knauf's mind desperately groped amongst its store of arcane knowledge seeking some enchantment, some spell that would save the warlock from his hideous mistake. Before him, the daemon uttered its loathsome laugh again. Knauf screamed as the pink abomination moved towards him with a curious scuttling motion.

Thoughts of sorcery forgotten, Knauf clenched his eyes and stretched his arm in front of his body, as though to ward away the monstrous horror even as the fiend advanced upon him. The daemon's grotesque hands closed about the warlock's extended arm, bringing new screams from Knauf as the icy touch seared through his veins. Slowly, the daemon raked a single claw down the length of the would-be wizard's arm, a deep wound that sank down to the very bone. Knauf's cries of agony rose still higher as the daemon's fingers probed the wound. Like a child with a piece of fruit, the horror began to peel the flesh from Knauf's arm, the warlock's howl of torment drowned out by the monster's increasing glee.

Mathias Thulmann reached the garret in time to witness the warlock's demise. No longer amused by the high-pitched wails escaping from Knauf's throat, the pink hands released the skeletal limb they clutched and seized the warlock's shoulders, pulling Knauf's body to the daemon's own. The daemon's giant maw gaped wide and with a formless undulating motion surged up and over Knauf's head and shoulders. The pseudo-corporeal substance of the daemon allowed a horrified Thulmann to see the warlock's features behind the ichorous pink jaws that engulfed it. He could see those still-screaming features twist and mutate as the flesh was quickly dissolved, patches of muscle appearing beneath skin before being stripped away to reveal the bone itself. The hardened witch hunter turned away from the appalling sight.

The daemon's insane gibbering brought Thulmann back to his senses. The witch hunter returned his gaze to the loathsome creature and the fool who had called it from the Realm of Chaos. Atop Ger-hardt Knauf's body, a skull dripped the last of the warlock's blood and rivulets of meaty grease; the body beneath had been stripped to the breastbone. The whisper of a scream seemed to echo through the gar-ret as the last shards of the warlock's soul fled into the night. The pink daemon rose from its gory repast and turned its fiery eyes upon the witch hunter.

Thulmann found himself powerless to act as the daemon slowly made its way across the garret room. The preternatural fiend moved in a capering, dance-like manner, its glowing body brilliant in the darkness, sounds of lunatic amusement emanating from its clenched, grinning jaws. The daemon stopped just out of reach of the witch hunter's sword, settling down on its haunches. It trained its fiery eyes on the scarlet-clad Templar, regarding him with an unholy mixture of hatred, humour, and hunger.

Thulmann forced himself to meet that inhuman gaze, to stare into the swirling fires that burned from the pink face, forced himself to match his own faith and determination against the daemon's ageless malevolence. Thulmann could feel the orange light seeping into his mind, clouding his thoughts and numbing his will.

With an oath, the witch hunter tore his eyes from those of the dae-mon. The horror snarled, no longer amused by the novelty of the witch hunter's defiance.

The daemon launched itself at Thulmann, its mouth still wet with the warlock's blood. Thulmann dodged to his left, the quick action sparing him the brunt of the daemon's assault, but still resulting in the unearthly creature's claws scraping the witch hunter's ribs. Clenching his teeth against the painful wound and the daemon's icy touch, Thulmann lashed out at the beast as it recovered from its charge.

A grip of frozen iron closed around the wrist of Thulmann's sword arm even as the heavy butt of the witch hunter's pistol crashed against the leering head of the horror. The daemon glared into Mathias's face and uttered a sinister laugh. Again, the witch hunter dealt the mon-ster a blow that would have smashed the skull of any mortal creature. As Thulmann brought his arm back to strike again at the grinning daemon, his nightmarish foe swatted the weapon from his hand, sending the pistol hurtling down the stairway.

The daemon's gibbering laughter grew; it leaned forward, its grin-ning jaws inches from Thulmann's hawk-like nose. The witch hunter pushed against the daemon's frigid shape with his free hand, desper-ately trying to keep the ethereal jaws at bay, at the same time frenziedly trying to free his sword arm. Thulmann's efforts attracted the daemon's attention and, as if noticing the weapon for the first time, it reached across Thulmann's body to remove the sword from his grasp. Luminous pink claws closed around the steel blade.

The smell of burnt metal assaulted Thulmann's nostrils as the keening wail of the daemon ripped at his ears. As the horror's hand had closed about the witch hunter's blade, the daemon's glowing flesh had started to burn, luminous sparks crackling and dancing from the seared paw. The daemon released its grip on Thulmann and scuttled away from the witch hunter, a new look in its fiery eyes. A look Thulmann recognised even in so inhuman a being: *fear*.

The daemon's left hand still gave off streams of purplish smoke, its very shape throbbing uncontrollably. The daemon looked at its injured paw then returned its attention to its adversary. The daemon could see the growing sense of hope, the first fledgling seed of triumph appearing in the very aura of the witch hunter. The sight incensed the daemon.

Thulmann slowly advanced upon the beast. The witch hunter had gained an advantage, he did not intend to lose it. But he did not reckon upon the creature's supernatural speed, or its feral rage. Before Thulmann had taken more than a few steps towards it, the daemon sprang from the floor as though it had been shot from a cannon. The monster crashed into Thulmann sending both man and fiend plummeting down the stairs.

Mathias Thulmann groggily tried to gain his feet, ears ringing from his violent descent. By some miracle he had managed to retain his sword. It was a fact that further infuriated his monstrous foe. The daemon scuttled toward the witch hunter. Thulmann struck at it, but the attack was a clumsy one, easily dodged by the luminous being. The horror responded by striking him in the chest with a powerful upswing of both its arms. The witch hunter was lifted off his feet, hurled backward by the tremendous force of the daemon's attack. Thulmann landed on the final flight of stairs, tumbling down them to lie broken and battered in the foyer.

At the foot of the stairs, the witch hunter struggled to rise, groping feebly for the sword that had landed beside him. He watched as the giggling pink daemon capered down the stairs, dancing in hideous parody of the revellers of Kleinsdorf. Mathias summoned his last reserves of strength as the daemon descended toward him. With a prayer to Sigmar, the witch hunter struck as the daemon leaped.

A shriek like the tearing of metal rang out as Thulmann's sword sank into the daemon. The blade impaled the horror, its body writhing in agony before bursting apart like a bubble rising from a fetid marsh. A squeal of venomous rage rose from the daemon, shattering the glass in the foyer's solitary window. Tiny sparks of bluish light flew from the point of the daemon's dissolution. Thulmann sank to his knees, thanking Sigmar for his deliverance.

Daemonic laughter broke into Thulmann's prayers. The taste of victory left the witch hunter as he saw the two daemons dance towards him from the darkness of the foyer. They were blue, goblin-sized parodies of the larger daemon Thulmann had vanquished, and they were glaring at him with looks of utter malevolence.

The foremost of the daemons opened its gigantic mouth, revealing the shark-like rows of serrated fangs. The blue horror laughed as it hopped and bounded across the foyer with frightening speed. Holding the sword before him, Thulmann prepared to meet the monster's attack.

Thulmann cried out as a torrent of pain wracked his body. Swift as the first daemon's movements had been, the other had been swifter still, circling the witch hunter as he prepared to meet its companion's attack. Unseen, the blue horror struck at the witch hunter's leg, sinking its fangs through the hard leather boot to worry the calf within. The intense pain made Thulmann drop his weapon, his only thought to seize the creature ravaging his leg.

The blue thing gave a hiccup of mock fright as Thulmann's hands closed around its scintillating form. The witch hunter tore the creature away from his boot and lifted the daemon over his head by its heals, thinking to dash its brains against the floor. In that instant he realised the trickery the beasts had employed. Scuttling across the floor, its over-sized hands dragging the sword by the hilt, was the other daemon. The monsters had taken away his only weapon.

The horror in Thulmann's hands twisted out of his grasp with a disgustingly boneless motion, raking its claws across his left hand as it fell to the floor. Giggling madly, the blue daemon danced away from the witch hunter's wrath, capering just beyond his reach until its companion returned from secreting his sword.

The two monsters circled Thulmann, striking at him from both sides at once, slashing his flesh with their claws before dancing away again. It was a slow, lingering death, like a pack of dogs tormenting a tethered horse because they do not know how to make a clean kill. Thulmann bled from dozens of wounds. Most were only superficial, but the pain caused by their infliction was intense. Every nerve in his body now writhed at the slightest touch from one of the daemons.

Thulmann's eyes fell upon an object lying upon the floor, its metal barrel reflecting the unearthly bodies of his tormentors. The pistol their unholy parent had taken away from him. If it had not discharged or otherwise been fouled by its violent descent, perhaps the witch hunter could find escape from his agony. Trembling with pain, Thulmann reached for the gun.

One of the daemons slashed the man's cheek as he stooped to retrieve the weapon. Dancing away, the creature laughed and brayed. It licked its fanged mouth and turned to rejoin its comrade in their amusement. It did not see the figure emerge from the darkness, nor the brilliant steel blade that reflected the light of its own glowing body.

The second monster sank its teeth into Thulmann's wrist. How dare the human think to spoil its fun? The blue fiend kicked the pistol away, turning to rake its claws through the shredded cloak that covered Thulmann's mangled back. The daemon leapt away in mid-stroke, turning to the source of the sight and sound that had alarmed it. In the darkness, the sparks and spirals of luminous smoke rising from the death of the other blue horror were almost blinding. The beast scrambled toward the being it sensed lurking in the shadows, eager to rend the flesh of this new adversary who had vanquished its other half. A rusted wooden hatchet sailed out of the darkness, smashing into the snarling daemon.

'The sword,' gasped Thulmann, again reaching for his pistol. 'Use the sword.'

The remaining fiend rose swiftly, its fiery eyes blazing. The daemon lunged in the direction from which the attack had come. It was a fatal mistake. The small creature's hands closed upon the naked blade, sparking and sizzling just as its its parent's had. As the blue horror recoiled from its unpleasant surprise, its attacker struck at its head with a sweep of the blade, finishing the daemon in an explosion of sparks and shrieks. Unlike the pink monster, no new horrors were born from the deaths of its lesser offspring.

'You are mine to kill, Thulmann,' a cold voice from the shadows said. 'I'll not lose my vengeance to anyone else, be they man or daemon!' The witch hunter laughed weakly.

'You shall find your task much simpler now, avenger. My wounds prevent me from mounting any manner of capable defence.' A venomous note entered the witch hunter's voice. 'But you would prefer butchery to a fair duel. That is your idea of honour?'

Reinhardt glared at him, tossing the witch hunter's sword to Thulmann. Thulmann shook his head as he gingerly sheathed the weapon with his injured hand.

'I could not hold that blade with these,' Thulmann showed the enraged noble his bleeding palms and wrist, 'much less combat an able swordsman.'

Reinhardt glared at the witch hunter contemptuously. His gaze studied Thulmann before settling upon the holstered pistols on the witch hunter's belt.

'Are you fit enough to use one of those?' the youth snarled.

'Are you skilled enough to use one?' Mathias countered, slowly drawing one of the weapons and sliding it across the floor. Reinhardt stooped and retrieved the firearm.

'When you see hell, you will know,' the youth responded. He waited as the witch hunter lifted himself from the floor and slowly drew the remaining gun. As soon as he felt the witch hunter was ready, the youth's hand pointed at Thulmann and his finger depressed the pistol's trigger. There was a sharp click as the hammer fell upon an already expired cap.

'Never accept a weapon from an enemy,' Thulmann said his voice icy and emotionless. There was a loud explosion of noise as he fired the weapon he had retrieved from the base of the stairs and holstered while Reinhardt still fought the last daemon. Reinhardt was thrown to the floor as the bullet impacted against his shoulder. Thulmann limped toward the fallen noble. The witch hunter trained his eyes upon the man's wound.

'With a decent physician that will heal in a fortnight,' the witch hunter said, turning away from his victim. 'If we meet again, I may not be so restrained,' Thulmann added as he made his way from the house.

Reinhardt von Lichtberg's shout followed the witch hunter into the street.

'I will find you, Mathias Thulmann! If I have to track you to the nethermost pits of the Wastes, you will not escape me! I will find you again, and I will kill you!'

And the people of Kleinsdorf continued to dance and laugh and sing as they celebrated the triumph of light over Chaos.

WHO MOURNS
A NECROMANCER
Brian Craig

THE FUNERAL CART made its slow and steady way up the hill towards the Colaincourt Cemetery. The day was grey and overcast, and a cold wind blew from the east. The man who drove the cart and the companion who sat beside him both bore sullen scowls upon their faces, and the two dappled black mares which pulled it held their heads very low, as if they too had lost all enthusiasm for the work which was their lot. Behind the cart walked a solitary mourner, incongruous in his isolation.

The lone mourner was Alpheus Kalispera, High Priest of Verena and Magister of the University of Gisoreux. When he went about his normal business he commanded respect and was treated with due deference, but in his present role he drew hostile glances from all those who watched the cart go by. There were not many; although Lanfranc Chazal had been an important and well-respected man in his prime, that prime was now long past, and Chazal's reputation had been badly tarnished in his later years.

Kalispera walked rather painfully. He was old and his joints were very stiff. He kept his hands carefully within the folds of his cloak, for the cold made his gnarled fingers ache terribly.

When the cemetery gates finally came into sight a company of small boys ran from one of the side-streets, hurling mud and stones at the coffin which rested on the cart, crying: 'Necromancer! Necromancer!'

607

Kalispera rounded on them, and would have spoken angrily, but they hared away as fast as their thin legs would carry them. To abuse an alleged necromancer was to them an act of great daring, even if the man be dead in his coffin, unable to answer the charge in any way at all.

A sallow-faced priest of Morr waited by a freshly-dug grave, quite alone. Even the sexton had taken care to absent himself from the ceremony of interment. Kalispera frowned – there should have been two priests, at least. He had been here many times before to see officers of the University laid to rest, and had been witness to occasions when scholars of far less status had been laid to rest by three officiating priests, attended by half a hundred mourners.

The magister took up a position opposite the priest, who stared at him while the two carriers manhandled the coffin down from the death-cart on to the ropes, then lowered it with indecent haste into the pit which had been made ready for it. It was all too obvious from the man's manner that the priest was here under protest, bound by the vows he had taken – which would not let him refuse to conduct a funeral service if he were so instructed. Kalispera felt the man's stare upon him, full of hostility, but he would not bow his head yet. Instead, he met the gaze as steadily as he could.

The priest took objection to this refusal to be ashamed. 'Who mourns a necromancer?' he asked bitterly. 'It would be best if I were left to do this sorry task alone.'

'I was his friend,' Kalispera said evenly. 'I had known him since childhood.'

'Such a man forsakes all claims of friendship and amity when he delves into forbidden lore,' the priest answered him. 'This man has sought to deal unnaturally with the dead, and should be shunned by the living – especially those who deem themselves priests of Verena.'

'He himself has joined the ranks of the dead now,' Kalispera observed, refusing to be stung by the insult. 'He is but a memory to the living and, of all the memories which I have of him, by far the greater number are happy ones. I have come to say farewell to a man I have known all my life, and I will not permit the fact that he has lately been abused by foolish and malicious men to prevent me from doing so.'

'But you have come alone,' the priest replied sourly, gesturing about him. 'It seems that all the others who knew him when they were young have a keener sense of duty to the cause of righteousness.'

Kalispera could not help but look around, though he did not expect to see any others hurrying to the place. He sighed, but very quietly, for he did not want the priest of Morr to know how disappointed he was. All but a few of the magisters of the university had known Lanfranc

Chazal for many years, and had liked him well enough before the evil rumours had taken wing like a flock of Morr's dark ravens. He had thought that a few might be prepared to set aside the vilifications and accusations, for the sake of remembrance of better times. But the university was, as ever, a fever-pit of jealousies and intrigues, in which reputations were considered very precious things, not to be risked on such a chance as this.

Kalispera felt a moment of paradoxical gratitude for the fact that he was old and far beyond the calls of ambition. It was all too probable that the next Magister of Gisoreux to ride up the hill on the creaking death-cart would be himself.

'Please proceed,' he said to the priest. 'You will be glad to get it over, I know.'

The priest frowned again, but consented to let the magister have the last word. Sonorously, he began to intone the funeral rite, consigning the body of unlucky Lanfranc Chazal to the care of his stern master.

But Morr's officer was barely half way through the ceremony when there was a sudden clatter of hooves in the gateway of the cemetery, and though propriety demanded that neither of them should look up, both priest and magister glanced sideways with astonishment.

A huge bay, liberally flecked with sweat, was reined in not thirty feet from the grave. A man leapt down, patting the trembling horse upon the neck to offer thanks for its unusual effort – it was obvious that it had ridden far and fast. The newcomer was a man in his late twenties, plainly dressed, without livery or ornament – but he strode to the graveside with the pride and grace of an aristocrat. He favoured the priest with a single glance of haughty disapproval, but looked at Kalispera longer and far more respectfully. In fact, he nodded to the magister as if he knew him and expected to be recognised in turn, but Kalispera could not immediately put a name to the face.

Who mourns a necromancer? Kalispera thought, echoing the priest's words with a hint of ironic triumph. *Two men at least, it seems, are not so cowardly that they dare not show their faces here. I thank you, young sir, with all my heart.*

Before he bowed his head again, he favoured the younger man with a discreet smile. The priest of Morr saw, and disapproved, but there was nothing he could do save resume the ceremony with all due expedition.

As soon as it was all finished, though, the priest graced the newcomer with a scowl more hateful than any he had previously contrived. Then he hurried off, leaving the grave gaping like a fresh wound in the green hillside.

* * *

THE SEXTON, WHO must have been almost as old as Alpheus Kalispera, and every bit as feeble in wind and limb, shuffled from his hiding place to begin the work of filling in the grave.

The need for a respectfully bowed head now gone, Kalispera looked long and hard at the second mourner – and suddenly found the name which had momentarily eluded him. 'Cesar Barbier! As I live and breathe!' he said.

Barbier smiled, but thinly, as though he had not the heart for a proper greeting. 'Aye, Magister Kalispera,' he said. 'You did well to remember me at all, for it's a fair while since I was a student here – and I have not been in Gisoreux for some years, though I have not been far away.'

'In Oisillon, perhaps?' Kalispera said. 'I remember that we thought you destined to be a luminary of His Majesty's court.'

Now the magister had the name, the rest was not too hard to remember. The Barbiers were one of the great families of the region, more celebrated for breeding soldiers than scholars. But Cesar had been a clever student, more attentive than many to what his teachers had to tell him. Young men of his class came to the university primarily to sow their wild oats at a safe distance from home, and in truth Barbier had certainly done his share of that, but his interests had eventually extended at least a little beyond wine, women and the dance.

Barbier shook his head. 'I have been in Rondeau,' he said, naming a small town some miles to the south of the great city. Kalispera frowned, trying to remember whether Rondeau was part of the Barbier estate – and, for that matter, whether Cesar had yet succeeded to his father's title. A good Bretonnian was supposed to know such things, even if he were a high priest of Verena and a magister of a university, devoted by vocation to more permanent kinds of wisdom. Cesar Barbier certainly did not look like a Tilean nobleman, for he wore no powder and no wig, and his clothes were honest leather – but if he had come to Gisoreux on horseback he might easily have consigned his finery to a saddlebag.

'I am glad to see you here, my lord,' Kalispera said guardedly. He dared not ask whether Barbier had really come to Gisoreux simply to attend the funeral – or, if so, why.

Barbier gave another slight smile when he heard the magister call him 'my lord' – an appellation to which custom had not entitled him while he was a student. 'And I am glad to see you, sir,' he replied in turn, 'though I must confess to a little disappointment that I find you alone. I came as soon as I heard that Magister Chazal had died, but I fear that the news had made slow progress in arriving at Rondeau. Still, it seems that I came in time.'

As he spoke he looked at the ancient sexton, who was shovelling earth as fast as he possibly could, clearly no more anxious than any other to be too long in the company of a corpse of such evil repute.

'Aye,' Kalispera said, 'you came in time. But I doubt that you would have come at all, had rumour of Lanfranc's last years reached Rondeau before the news of his death. I am alone because no other would come. It has been rumoured of late that my friend was… was a necromancer, and I dare say that you know as well as any other what damage such rumours can do. I am glad to see you, as I said – but perhaps I should rather be sorry that you have taken the trouble, if you came in ignorance.'

'I did not come in ignorance, I assure you,' Barbier said solemnly. 'I came because I knew, far better than any other, what kind of man he really was.'

Kalispera felt tears rising to his eyes, and he bowed his head.

'Thank you for that,' he said.

'Oh no,' replied the other, reaching out to take the older and frailer man by the arm. 'It is for me to thank you on his behalf – for you stood by him when no one else would.'

They stood together, silently, for two or three minutes more. When the sexton was finished, Barbier gave him a suitable coin, which the old man accepted without any word or gesture of thanks.

'Is there somewhere we can go?' the young nobleman asked gently. 'I think we both stand in need of the warmth of a fire and a cup of good wine.'

'Of course,' Kalispera said quietly. 'I would be most honoured if you would be my guest, and would share with me in the remembrance of my friend.'

'I will do it gladly,' Barbier assured him. The two went down the hill together, quite oblivious to any inquisitive eyes which may have stared after them.

ALPHEUS KALISPERA TOOK Cesar Barbier to the room where he worked and taught. The sun had set by the time they arrived there, but the autumn twilight always lingered in the room, because its latticed window faced the south-west. Kalispera had always found it to be a good room for reading – and an excellent place for deeper contemplation.

At Barbier's request, Kalispera told him about the shadow which had been cast over Lanfranc Chazal during the last years of his tenure at the university.

'No charge was brought against him in any court, sacred or secular,' he was at pains to explain. 'He was condemned exclusively by scurrilous gossip and clandestine vilification. I have even heard it said that his death was a manifestation of the wrath of Verena, delayed for so long only because Verena was a calm and patient deity who loved her followers of wisdom just a little too well. That was terrible, truly terrible.

'Alas for poor Lanfranc, he had the misfortune to age less gracefully than he might, and he came to suffer from a certain disfiguration of the features which his enemies took to be evident proof of his dabbling with forbidden knowledge. One expects to hear such folderol from common peasants, of course, but I had thought better of Gisoreux and the university. If the men who call themselves the wisest in the world can so easily fall prey to such silly suspicions, what hope is there for the future of reason?

'Long before he was consigned to the grave where we saw him laid today, Lanfranc had begun to take on the appearance of a dead man, with whited skin and sunken eyes. I tried in vain to persuade our colleagues that it was merely an illness of old age, with no dire implication, but my ideas on the subject had always been considered unorthodox, and no one would listen to me. Even his friends were content to accept his disfigurement as evidence of a secret interest in the practice of necromancy. "All illness comes from the gods," they said, "and is sent to educate us." Lanfranc Chazal never believed any such thing, and neither do I, for we had seen too many sick men and women in our time. Alas, we were the only two remaining who remembered the great plague of forty years ago, and how dreadfully it used the magisters of the day. Now there is only me.'

Kalispera realized that his tone had become very bitter, and stopped in embarrassment. The twilight had faded while he spoke and the room was now as gloomy as his mood, so he covered his embarrassment by looking about for the tinderbox in order that he might light a candle. He had mislaid it, and was forced to get up in order to conduct a scrupulous search.

Cesar Barbier did not say anything to him while he searched for the box, found it and struck a light. But when the candle finally flared up, he saw that the younger man was watching him very quizzically from his place by the fireside.

Kalispera resumed his own seat, then smoothed his white beard with his right hand as if to settle himself completely. 'You are probably astonished to hear all this,' he said.

'On the contrary,' Barbier replied with a guarded look. 'There is nothing in it which is news to me, but I am glad to hear your account of it. He would have been very pleased and proud to know that his truest friend did not desert him, even at the end.'

'You knew!' Kalispera exclaimed. 'But you said that you have not been in Gisoreux for some time. How could you know about Lanfranc's illness, the changes in his appearance?'

'He visited me in Rondeau,' the young nobleman said. 'We have seen one another frequently over the years. I always regarded him as my mentor – he was ever the man to whom I turned for advice and help, and he never failed me. He told me more than once how grateful he was for your amity, and I know that it weighed upon his conscience that his claim upon your good opinion was not as honest as he would have wished.'

Alpheus Kalispera started in his seat and his eyes grew suddenly wide. 'What are you saying?' he cried, angrily. 'Do you mean to insult my grief?'

Barbier sat upright as well, but then leaned forward to reach out a soothing hand. 'No, magister!' he said. 'Anything but! Lanfranc Chazal was the best and noblest man I ever knew. I came here to share my grief, not to insult yours.'

Kalispera stared at him angrily for a moment, but then relaxed with a sigh. 'I do not know what you mean,' he said. 'Lanfranc said nothing to me about visiting you in Rondeau – nothing at all. And I cannot believe that he deceived me, even in a matter as small as that.'

'Alas, sir,' Barbier said, 'he did deceive you, even in matters much weightier. I can assure you, though, that it was not because he doubted you that he kept his darkest secrets from you, but only because he doubted himself.'

There was a long moment's silence before Kalispera said in a horrified whisper, 'Do you mean to tell me that Lanfranc Chazal *was* a necromancer, after all – and that you were party to his experiments?'

'That is what I mean to tell you,' the other confirmed, in a low voice. 'But I beg you not to condemn me – and certainly not to condemn Magister Chazal – until you have heard me out.'

Alpheus Kalispera felt that the features of his face were firmly set in a mask of pain, and that his heart was unnaturally heavy in his breast. Nevertheless, he made every effort to speak boldly. 'Explain yourself, my lord,' he said. Despite the title, it was the patronising command of the instructor, not the humble request of the commoner.

'I intend to explain, magister,' said the young man, quietly, 'and I beg you to forgive my clumsiness in going about it. You will remember, I am sure, that I was not the best of students. I was, after all, one of those sent by a pretentious father to acquire the merest veneer of culture and learning, not one intended to learn the skills of a scrivener or the training of a priest. I was something of a noble fool in my early days, and although Magister Chazal taught me in the end to be less of a fool than I was, still my wisdom is of a very narrow kind. Let me tell you my story in my own way, so that we may mourn together the passing of a great and generous man.'

Kalispera had to admit that this was a pretty speech, and he believed that he could hear within its phrases the influence of his friend Lanfranc Chazal. But there was another thought echoing its derision inside his head: *Who mourns a necromancer?*

Could it be, he wondered, that the world had been right after all, and he the lone fool?

'I am sorry, my lord,' he said, however, with honest but troubled humility. 'Please say what you have come to say. I will listen patiently.'

'Thank you, sir,' Cesar Barbier said, relaxing again in his turn. He paused for a moment, collecting his thoughts, and then he proceeded to tell his story.

'You KNOW MY name,' Barbier began, 'and I assume that you know whose son I am. Perhaps you remember my father from his own student days, when I am sure he impressed you with his command of those aristocratic virtues befitting a man whose service to our king has been of the military kind. He is now as he undoubtedly was then: bold in word and deed, with a will and stomach of iron. Neither wine nor passion has the power to disturb his firmness of mind, and I dare say that you found his head quite impregnable to wisdom or sophistication.

'When I first became a student here I set out to do my best to be like my father, and I think that for a while I succeeded well enough to convince almost everyone that I was a perfect example of that kind, save only for Magister Chazal. He saw through my facade of reckless intolerance to the, well, the gentler soul within. He knew what a creature of dishonesty I was, and helped me to use my years here to become a better man.

'In public he never gave evidence by word or gesture that he knew what a poseur I was, but in private he talked to me in a different way. He taught me to trust him, and be honest in what I said to him. With him and him alone I was my true self: full of doubt, full of passion and tender of sentiment – all traits which my father despised, and despises still. Magister Chazal never advised me to break down my public pretence, but was content to give me an opportunity to lay it aside. I cannot tell you how much it meant to me to have that relief.

'When the time came for me to leave Gisoreux and take up the business of accepting the responsibilities of my position, I quickly began to use the gift of lettering – which was one of the valuable things which I had learned within these walls – in the writing of letters to Magister Chazal. I was his guest here in Gisoreux on numerous occasions. He was the one and only person to whom I confided my true feelings, and by degrees I won his confidence too, so that he began to say to me those things which he dared not say to people of his own kind.

'It was from Magister Chazal that I learned about your beliefs, Magister Kalispera. He told me that you had drawn conclusions about the nature of disease which were, if not openly heretical, at least unorthodox. He told me about your sceptical attitude to the medicines and treatments established by custom. He told me too about your insistence that disease and suffering make no discrimination between the guilty and the innocent, and are far less often the result of magic or divine intervention than we are prone to believe. He respected you for holding those beliefs, and for setting what you believed to be the truth over the advantages to be gained by conformity. He thought that you might respect his own opinions, but hesitated to burden you with any more unorthodoxy than you had already accepted.'

Alpheus Kalispera had begun to see where this account was leading, but he kept silent while Barbier paused, and looked at him very gravely.

'It is the common belief,' the younger man continued, 'that any magic but the pettiest is inherently good or evil. Any magic which involves trafficking with the dead or the undead is held to be supremely wicked. Magister Chazal was prepared to doubt that. His view was that although any knowledge might be used for evil ends by evil men, knowledge as such is always good. Ignorance, he used to say, is the greatest evil of all.'

Kalispera nodded his head then, for he had certainly heard Chazal say that on many an occasion.

'For that reason,' Barbier went on, 'Magister Chazal had studied the arcane language of necromancy and had read books written in that language. His intention in so doing was not to become a master of necromantic magic, but to learn more about the mysteries of death – to enhance his understanding. He was not a man to play with the conjuration of ghosts or the reanimation of corpses; for him, the written word was enough. He valued enlightenment far more than power.

'The story of these researches he confided to me by degrees, over a period of more than a year. In return, I talked to him about my own very different problems, which arose from friction between myself and my father as to the managements of our estates and our lives.

'I found myself in disagreement with my father on many matters of principle – on the matter of the unhappiness which he caused my mother and my sisters, for instance, and on the matter of the relentless tyranny which he exerted over his tenants and his bondsmen. But I could not successfully oppose him because I was still forced by convention and circumstance to pretend to be like him. I had begun to hate my father, and in so doing had begun to hate myself too, for being so obviously his son.

'Then, quite out of the blue, disaster struck me. I fell in love.

'Love was not a factor in my father's calculations of advantage, and he had already contracted marriages for my two sisters on the basis of his commercial interests. It would have been bad enough had I fallen in love with a woman of my own class, had it not been the one which he considered most useful to the family interest, but in fact I fell in love with a commoner, who was very beautiful but of no account whatsoever in my father's scheme of things.

'To my father, the very idea of love is bizarre. He has not an atom of affection in his being. I, by virtue of some silly jest of the gods who determine such things, am very differently made, and my honest passion for the girl – whose name was Siri – was quite boundless. I could not envision life without her, and life itself came to depend in my estimation upon my possession of her. By possession I do not mean mere physical possession – my father would have raised no word of objection had I been able simply to rape and then discard the girl – but authentic union. That, of course, my father would never tolerate, and yet it was what I had to have.

'When I said all this to Magister Chazal, he did not presume to tell me what to do, but he gave me every assistance in dissolving my confusion and seeing clearly what kind of choice I had to make. He helped me to understand that the time had come when I must either break completely with my father or utterly destroy the secret self which I had so carefully preserved for many years. I could not cut out and burn my own heart. And so I eloped and married Siri in secret, resolving never to see my father again.

'I anticipated that my father would disown me and forbid my name ever to be mentioned again in his house or his estates. That was what I expected, and was prepared to accept. But I had underestimated him. Perhaps it would have been different had he had another heir to put in my place, but I had no brother and nor had he. He could not face the thought of allowing his lands and his titles to become subservient to another name in being diverted to one of my sisters.

'He sent his servants to search me out, and then to bring me home by force, my... my young wife with me.'

Cesar Barbier paused again in his account – but not, this time, to measure the attitude of his listener. Until now he had been quite calm and very scrupulous in his speech, as befitted a nobleman of Bretonnia, but now his breathing was clotted by emotion, and there were tears in his eyes: tears of anguish, and of rage.

When it seemed that the young noble could not go on, Alpheus Kalispera said, very quietly: 'He had her killed?'

'Had her killed?' answered Barbier, as though the words had been forced out of him with a hot iron. 'Oh no, he did not have her killed! You do not know what manner of man my father is! He killed her with his own hands, while his servants forced me to watch.

'He destroyed her, and the unborn child she carried within her, without any trace of feeling – not because he hated her, but simply because she stood in the way of his calculations. He felt no guilt, nor any fear of retribution. Had she killed him it would have been a fearful crime, for which she would have been burned alive as a petty traitor, but for him to kill her was merely a matter of business, for her father was his bondsman, and she an item of inconvenient property. I saw her die, Magister Kalispera – I saw her *die!*'

Kalispera did not know what to say. He could not imagine that Lanfranc Chazal had known what to say, when the poor man had run to him with the same dreadful tale, four or five years earlier.

'I wanted to kill him,' Cesar Barbier said, when he was capable of continuing his tale. 'And the folly of it all is that if I had been what he wanted me to be, I would have killed him. With a sword or a cudgel or a poisoned cup I would have snuffed out his vile existence, and sent our title to oblivion by surrendering myself to the law and going gladly to the gallows. If his way had been the right way, I would have taken my revenge, and happily so.

'Perhaps I would have done it, had it not been for Magister Chazal – for he it was who persuaded me that I must not waste my own being in destroying my father's, on the two accounts that it would be both futile and false to my own true nature. He implored me to find a better way – and in my turn, I implored him to show me one.'

Kalispera drew in his breath, deeply and painfully. It was all too obvious to him what the result of this mutual imploring must have been. Barbier saw that he had guessed.

'Will you tell me that it was unlawful?' said the young man angrily. 'Will you tell me that it was lawful and just for my father to murder my wife and unborn child because they did not suit him, and a horrid crime to undo the act, as far as it could be undone? Will you tell me that Magister Chazal was evil, and my father's soul quite stainless? Tell me then, Magister Kalispera. Tell me, in so many words, where the right of it lies.'

Kalispera shook his head. The darkness in the corners of the room seemed to close in around them. 'Tell me,' he countered in a steely voice, 'what it was that Lanfranc did, and what its consequence has been.'

'I had not dared to bring the body of my wife into the precincts of the university,' Barbier said, 'nor even through the gates of Gisoreux. I had taken her instead to the house in Rondeau which I had bought, intending that we should live there when we returned from the Empire – for we did not expect to spend our whole lives in exile from our homeland. Magister Chazal accompanied me there and begun his work.

'He had told me that he could not bring my Siri back to life, for if such a thing could be done at all it was beyond his skill. He could not restore her flesh to me, but her spirit was a different matter; he believed that he had knowledge enough to bring back her ghost from the realm of the dead, and protect it from the dissolution which ordinarily overtakes such beings.

'Spectres, he told me, are often bound to our world in consequence of curses, doomed to haunt the spot where they died. What he intended to do was to summon Siri as a ghost, and ask her whether she would be bound of her own free will, not to the place where she had died but to the place where she had hoped to live. If she consented, he said, then he would try to bind her to the house in Rondeau.

'He was not sure that he had knowledge enough to accomplish more, but he promised that he would try firstly to give her a voice that she might speak to me, and secondly to allow her to take on at intervals a certain frail substance which would allow us to touch. For this latter purpose he required to combine together something of her substance and something of mine, and I allowed him to remove from my left hand that finger upon which I had placed my wedding ring.'

Barbier held up his left hand, and Kalispera saw for the first time that the finger next to the smallest had been neatly cut away.

'He bound that finger to hers before we laid her in a tomb beneath the house,' continued Barbier, his voice hushed. 'And he used my blood to write the symbols which he used in his conjuration. When I first saw her ghost I was overtaken by such a terror that I nearly cried out to him to stop, to send her back where she belonged, but I bit my tongue. And when he asked her whether she would rather go to her appointed place, or be bound to this world with me, I felt a tremendous surge of joy which overwhelmed my terror on the instant – for her answer was yes.

'Her answer was *yes*.

'I could not tell what powers Magister Chazal drew upon in order to complete what he had begun. I know that he sacrificed more than I, for I only lost a finger and a little blood, while he seemed to draw upon his own inner life and strength in such a way as to leave them forever depleted.

'What words he spoke, or what dark daemons may have moved to do his bidding, I cannot begin to understand. But his work was successful, and the ghost of my wife now lives in my house, carrying within her the ghost of my unborn child. And whenever Morrslieb is at its brightest in the night sky, she takes on substance sufficient to allow her to caress me, and receive caresses in return.'

* * *

ALPHEUS KALISPERA BOWED his head slightly, and said: 'I had thought the change in him was the effect of an affliction which he had in no way invited. I was sure of it.'

'And are you sure now that it was not?' Barbier demanded, with sudden passion. 'Are you so certain, now that you know what you had not guessed before, that he was marked by the evil of his deeds? I tell you that he worked no evil, but exercised his knowledge only to help his friend. If it was judgment on his necromancy which engraved the death-mask on his features, then it was a cruel and stupid judgment, for he did not deserve it. If there was a debt to be paid, then I should have paid it, and would have done so willingly!

'Have you no faith in your own beliefs, that you would lose them now because of what I have told you? If that is so, I cry shame on you, Magister Kalispera! The man you saw buried today was a man as good as any in the world, and whatever disfigured him was no fault of his, but an undeserved misfortune.'

Kalispera laid his head back and stared off into infinity, before he finally said: 'I do not know what to believe.'

Barbier rose to his feet and looked down at the older man. 'You had best make up your mind,' he said harshly. 'If you will not understand, you must at least keep silent about what I have told you.'

The magister met his visitor's gaze then, and felt a slight shock of fear – but then he remembered that this had once been his pupil, and Lanfranc's friend, and that there was no need to be afraid of him.

'Sit down, my lord,' he said tiredly. 'This is no one's business but our own. I would not denounce you for what you have done, nor would I ever have denounced my friend for helping you. But I cannot say that it was a good thing to do, for it is the most unnatural thing of which I have ever heard.'

Barbier took his seat again, but did not relax. 'Oh yes!' he said. 'Unnatural, to be sure. When a father is utterly without love or compassion – that is natural! When a father murders his son's innocent bride – that is natural! But when a son opposes his father's will and undoes his father's evil – why, that is surely repulsive in its defiance of the laws which the gods have made!

'Tell me, my white-haired philosopher, is it natural for the fops and philanderers of our good King's court to parade themselves in silk and velvet? Is it natural that they should live in gaudy luxury while the peasants who work the soil to produce their wealth go hungry? Are their measured dances natural, or the games which they play with quoits and skittles? Are their manners and hypocrisies natural – or are these noblemen natural only when they ache and bleed like common folk?

'Instruct me, magister, I implore you. Tell me, I pray, why men like you and I should respect and revere what is natural, when everything we are and do is artifice? Your own belief is that disease and illness are but natural shocks to which our fragile flesh is heir, not supernatural punishments sent by the gods or inflicted by the ill-wishing of witches. Lanfranc Chazal's belief was that knowledge of life and death is only knowledge of nature, and that magic is merely control of nature, like other arts and crafts. You could not see a difference between yourself and your lifelong friend this morning – can you really see one now?'

For fully half a minute, Kalispera did not reply. And when he did, it was not with an answer but with a question. 'What will happen,' he asked, 'when you die in your turn, and go to the realm of the dead?'

Barbier laughed, very briefly. 'I cannot tell,' he said. 'If I have the power to curse myself to be a spectre, then I will exert that power with my dying breath, and will be all the closer to my love for sharing her insubstantiality whenever Morrslieb is pale in the sky. And if I have not… then I must wait for her release, as she would have waited for mine, had I not found a necromancer to cast off the chains of nature!'

'And what if you fall in love again?' said the magister, in a low whisper. 'What if you should one day hope for a better child than the ghost of one unborn?'

Barbier shook his head as though to rule the questions impertinent, but Kalispera could see that the man was not untroubled by them. He was a man, after all, and he knew that love is not always eternal, nor the call of duty entirely impotent.

'What will happen when your father dies?' Kalispera said, speaking now as the High Priest of Verena which he also was. 'Will you inherit his title and his estate? And if you do, will you be content to stay in Rondeau, or will you want to show the world how a demesne's affairs could be managed by a better man than your father was? Ten years have passed since you came here as a student, I think, fully seven of them since you left these cloisters – but what did you truly learn, in the three years or the seven, which makes you sure that you are finished and complete, as changeless as your love-deluded wife? What right did you really have to demand of Lanfranc Chazal that which he did for you?'

Barbier was confused now, and taken aback. Whatever he had expected of the old magister, it was not this. 'He was my friend,' he said. 'And a far better father to me than my own parent ever was.'

'Aye,' Kalispera said sadly, 'no doubt that was what he wanted to be. He was my friend, too, but I did not need him as a father. When you combined your catalogue of challenges, you might have asked whether it is natural for priests and magisters to be celibate, so that the only sons they have are those of other men.'

The younger man said nothing.

'Do you love your ghostly wife?' Kalispera asked abruptly.

'I do,' said Barbier boldly. 'With all my heart.'

'And do you think that you can love her forever?'

'I do.'

Alpheus Kalispera shrugged his shoulders, and said: 'Let us hope that your boldness will not let you down, and that your heart is as constant as your father's, after its own very different fashion.'

Barbier bowed his head, and said: 'Thank you for that, magister.' Then he looked up again, and said: 'I hope that you will not think any worse of your friend, because of what I have told you. I did not mean to injure him in your estimation.'

'You have not done that,' Kalispera assured him. 'And I am grateful to know that I am not the only man who will mourn him. If the only epitaph he will have is that which is graven in the memories of other men, I am glad that there are two of us to share the burden of the truth.'

'So am I,' Cesar Barbier said. 'So am I.'

Kalispera got up from his seat and went to the window. He unlatched the glazed lattice, and pushed it back to let in the cool night air. It was not so very dark, for Mannslieb was full and Morrslieb, though by no means at its brightest, was shining from another sector of the vault of heaven. The stars, as always, were too many to be counted. The streets of the city were lit by tiny flames which were similarly numberless, for in a city as munificent as Gisoreux even the poor could afford candles to keep the dark at bay.

'Where is his spirit, do you think?' he asked of the younger man.

'Close at hand,' said Barbier softly, 'or far away. Does it matter which?'

'It is said that the spirit of a necromancer is bound to its rotting hull,' the magister said. 'It is said that such a spirit cannot escape from the hell of that decay, but can sometimes animate the body as a liche with glowing eyes, which spreads terror wherever it goes, and leaves suffering in its train.'

'Do you think that he feared such an end?' Barbier asked, with such faint anxiety that it seemed a mere politeness.

'No man truly knows what he has to fear when he dies,' Kalispera replied. 'Even a man like you, who has brought another back from the life beyond life. No man truly knows.'

Alpheus Kalispera looked at his hands, then. They were gnarled and stiff, and the pain in their swollen joints gave him little rest nowadays. Might it reduce his pain, he wondered, to cut off those fingers which he did not really need? Or was the pain a divine punishment after all, and not – as he had always believed – a mere accident of happenstance?

He had, after all, given succour and sustenance to a secret necro-mancer!

'He was a good man,' Kalispera murmured, not for the first time. 'He was a good friend.'

'In truth he was,' Cesar Barbier said.

And though neither man could know the other's thoughts, both shared at that particular moment in time an identical hope. Each of them was praying, silently and fervently, that whatever god or dae-mon now had charge of the spirit of Lanfranc Chazal would hear their words, and echo their merciful disposition.

THE HANGING TREE

Jonathan Green

THE STURDY OAK door of the inn opened with a crash and for just a moment a gust of what the weather outside had to offer – nothing but foul wind and rain – entered the Slaughtered Calf. It seemed hard to believe that it was early spring. It was more like autumn or winter had a hold of these hills.

Grolst, the thickset, greasy-skinned innkeeper, looked up from wiping a grimy, damp cloth around the inside of an a dirty glass. He cast an unwelcoming grimace from beneath beetling brows at the figure standing in the shadows of the doorway, the evening sky darkening behind him. The man ducked beneath the lintel and closed the door behind him. The foul night's wailing wind and lashing rain became a muffled memory outside the thick stone walls once more. Leaning on a tall, gnarled staff, the figure stepped into the pool of light cast by the cartwheel candelabra.

Grolst surveyed the new arrival suspiciously. The frown on his ruddy face remained. Although swathed in heavy wine-dark robes, the innkeeper could see that beneath them the man was tall and lean, like a hunting dog. His appearance was scruffy and unkempt. He appeared to be into his fifth decade, both his bedraggled black hair, what there was of it on his balding pate, and his long straggly beard greying to white. The skin on his face appeared taught, making his hawkish features even more severe and pronounced.

623

On closer examination, Grolst could see that in places the grey-bearded man's robes were scorched black. There was also the glint of metal from objects hung around his neck and from his robes. Grolst thought he even saw a gleaming bird's skull, a brass key, hanging from his belt – or maybe it was gold – and the hilt of a sword protruding from beneath a fold in his cloak. The stranger's staff tapped against the floor as he approached the bar.

The red-robed stranger peered at the various dusty bottles and earthenware containers displayed haphazardly on the crooked shelves behind the innkeeper.

'A glass of that… luska,' the man said grumpily, placing a pair of copper coins on the bar top. 'I hate the rain,' he added, addressing no one in particular as he shook water from his cloak.

Grolst uncorked a grime-coated bottle and poured a measure of the clear Ostland spirit into a small tumbler. He blinked as the potent alcoholic vapour reached his nostrils. Luska was a fiery Ostlander distillation, not unlike the vodka spirit so favoured by the Kislevites, and as it coursed down the drinker's throat it burnt hotter than a salamander's tongue. It took a certain taste and a fiery temperament in the drinker to even palate the spirit, let alone actually enjoy it.

Perhaps the stranger had some connection to Kislev. From the few words that he had spoken, his accent sounded as though it might come from the sheep-rearing southern provinces of the Empire, but the man wore his moustaches long and drooping, favoured here in the northern realms that bordered the harsh oblast of Kislev, the kingdom of the Tzars. The stranger was well travelled, certainly.

He picked up his drink and took a seat at a table close to the fire blazing in the hearth of the inn's huge chimney breast. From the man's dress Grolst thought that he was most likely a scholar of some field of academic study or other. From the way he travelled alone, without the need for a bodyguard, the innkeeper decided that he probably had some other means of defence that he could call upon in an emergency. Grolst looked at the staff again.

Viehdorf didn't receive much in the way of passing travellers, making their way down from the main road into the wooded hollow where the village nestled. The Slaughtered Calf lay half way between the two amidst the crowding trees and looming hills. Merchants, mercenaries, peddlers and pilgrims mostly preferred to bed down in the larger Scharfen, half a league back in the direction of Middenheim, or press on along the forest road until they reached the stone-walled security of Felsmauern another half a league further along the road towards Hergig.

The sign over the door hardly seemed appropriate for an establishment called the Slaughtered Calf, although it betrayed the reason for the lack of passing trade. The image of a beastman's head depicted on the swaying inn-sign attested to the fact that here, on the Middenland-Hochland border, the forested hill-country was beastman territory. The deep forests hid their camps and herdstone lairs. To stray from the roads in these parts was to invite a swift demise.

Viehdorf was one of those pockets of civilisation clinging onto survival amidst the chaos and barbarity of a land where, whatever the Emperor comfortable in his palace in distant Altdorf might claim, savage nature was mistress – and a cruel mistress she was indeed, red in tooth and claw. The village was a faint, flickering candle-flame in the all-encompassing darkness of wild lands, where the populace were prey to the uncaring seasons and the harshness of survival.

On occasion the animals belonging to the people of Viehdorf gave birth to unnaturally twisted offspring. When this happened, mother and child were culled, their carcasses destroyed, and the matter not spoken of again, for to do so was to attract the attentions of the witch hunters. Such men were not known for their tolerance, understanding or restraint.

If any did stray this way the people of Viehdorf knew what had to be done.

As Grolst considered this new stranger, he gazed across the barroom and took in the other people sheltering from the unseasonable night within the inn. There were the usual regulars; local foresters and other villagers, including the blacksmith, all eyeing the stranger warily, making him feel about as welcome as the plague. There was also another stranger in their midst that night, an armoured roadwarden.

The atmosphere in the tavern was sullen and hostile, talk was restrained to a conspiratorial murmur; there were two strangers in the bar and they were definitely not welcome here. Strangers meant trouble. The people of Viehdorf liked to keep themselves to themselves. That was what proved best and had kept them unmolested by the world beyond the forested boundaries of their village, them and their forefathers before them.

The blacksmith was watching the red-robed stranger but he was also giving the roadwarden on the other side of the bar furtive glances. It was on this man that Grolst's gaze came to rest. The roadwarden was dressed in a tough leather jerkin and hard-wearing trews, and wore an armoured hauberk as well. A lobster-tailed helmet sat on the table in front of him.

He had arrived earlier that same evening and Grolst was just as wary of him as he was of the straggly-haired stranger. The roadwarden had paid for one flagon of ale and had made it last for all the time since. He was enjoying a respite from the harsh, unrelenting conditions outside, no doubt. The leather of his jerkin and his trews dried out in the smoky warmth of the inn's interior, the air bitter with the smell of hops, pipe-weed and wood smoke. No one dared actually challenge the man but the daggers in the stares the patrons were giving him made their true desires perfectly plain.

The Slaughtered Calf hardly ever had any visitors, so to have two turn up on one night unsettled Grolst deeply, making the sullen innkeeper feel even less charitable than usual. The inn had rooms for rent, certainly, but Grolst was hard pressed to remember when they had last been used by a passing traveller rather than by the unfaithful, carrying on their lustful affairs away from the eyes of their jealous spouses. It was too close to the sacrifice for his liking, just when the people of Viehdorf didn't want the prying eyes of the Emperor Karl Franz's authorities, witch hunters or any other stranger looking into their business.

There was one last drinker, sitting alone, who was known to Grolst. The man hardly seemed aware of anything about his surroundings; he just stared mournfully into the bottom of his tankard, shoulders slumped, his face a sagging scowl of sadness. Of course, he had good reason to look so unhappy. The responsibility for the sacrifice had come to rest at his door this time.

The roadwarden raised his tankard and drained the last of the hopsy, locally-brewed ale and, taking up his hammer once again, strode purposefully back to the bar. The soldier fixed the innkeeper with his piercing, steely gaze, making Grolst feel even more uncomfortable. The innkeeper felt his flesh crawl under the unrelenting stare and, in order to break the tension, felt obliged to speak: 'You moving on then?'

'I may be,' the roadwarden said, his voice betraying a cultured accent but also a hint of suspicion in its tone.

Grolst immediately regretted his question but also found himself wondering what had made a man of a highborn upbringing become a wandering warrior, patrolling the Emperor's highways and protecting those who would travel on them with lawful intentions, especially at such a time of turmoil.

The roadwarden's manner made Grolst feel uncomfortable enough to provoke a response. 'Is there good hunting to be had on the Emperor's roads?'

'Good enough,' the roadwarden replied. 'Your village seems to have got away remarkably unscathed, considering there are tribes of man-beasts amassing within the forests and that there is a war coming to the Empire, the likes of which have not been seen since the time of Magnus the Pious.'

'A war, you say? I wouldn't know about that. War doesn't trouble us here. So what brings you to our peaceful village?'

'I'm sorry, I should have introduced myself,' the rugged soldier said offering a smile, though his gaze remained as steely and unforgiving as before. 'I am Ludwig Hoffenbach. Dark times are upon the Empire and all men are called to play their part, to hold back the storm of Chaos that is threatening to break across the land. You have heard, I take it, that the once-great sentinel city of Wolfenburg fell to a Northman horde last year?

'I myself have been called to act as part of an Imperial commission, and I was supposed to meet with my compatriot here. Has a templar of the Sigmarite church visited Viehdorf?'

'A witch hunter, you mean?' the innkeeper said, feeling his scalp tighten.

'By the name of Schweitz.'

Grolst swallowed hard. The blood in his veins felt as if it had turned to ice water. He cast an anxious glance over the roadwarden's armoured shoulder and saw further furtive glances pass around the bar. It was only then that Grolst really realised that the low murmur of conversation inside the Slaughtered Calf had ceased, the foresters, villagers and blacksmith all straining their ears to eavesdrop on what was passing between the innkeeper and the roadwarden. The only one who seemed to be paying no attention at all was the mournful man still staring into the bottom of his pint.

'A witch hunter?' the innkeeper said, trying to keep his tone jovial and the unease out.

Out of the corner of his eye Grolst saw that the crimson-clad stranger was watching the exchange at the bar as intently as the inn's regulars – if anything more so – and fidgeting uncomfortably, apparently at the mention of the witch hunter. Grolst knew how he felt.

'No, there hasn't been anyone like that here.'

The roadwarden lent forward slightly and Grolst couldn't help but notice that his gauntleted hand was resting on the haft of the warhammer slung from his belt.

'Are you sure?' There was the same hard smile on Hoffenbach's lips, the same steel in his eyes.

'Definitely,' Grolst said, managing to force a laugh at the same time. 'I would remember a templar of the Church of Sigmar visiting my poor hovel of an inn. No, no one like that's been in here.'

'Very well,' Hoffenbach said, adjusting his hauberk and making sure that the innkeeper saw not only the insignia of his Imperial commission but also the haft of his warhammer once again. 'Thank you for your... help.' He turned towards the inn door. 'It is time I was gone.'

With that, the roadwarden spun on his iron-shod heel and made to leave the snug of the bar for the wilds of the night outside the walls of the enduring coaching inn. Before he did so, Hoffenbach returned the shifty look the red-robed stranger was giving him.

Then he was gone into the cold, the wind, the dark and the rain.

Grolst went back to occupying himself smearing a tankard with his damp rag, trying to ignore the bewilderment of anxieties and possibilities muddling his mind. They would have to act soon. Grolst would have like to have believed that Viehdorf had seen the last of the roadwarden but he sincerely doubted it.

The grating of a chair on the floor roused Grolst from his thoughts. The innkeeper looked up reluctantly and saw the red-robe taking his turn to approach the bar. Now what? the innkeeper thought resentfully.

'Do you have any rooms?' the wild-haired stranger said. The darker water stains around the hem of his robes were fading as the thick material began to dry out.

As soon as the man had uttered the words, a seed of an idea took root within the innkeeper's mind. He had not thought the red-robe would stay. He had imagined the stranger would have been on his way, like the roadwarden, once he had finished his drink, even if it was after nightfall.

Grolst felt a smile forming on his ugly lips. As soon as he was aware of it, he re-composed the annoyed grimace that made him look like he was irritated by the fact that anyone would dare to waste his time by actually wanting to be served in his inn.

'If you can pay for it, I have,' he said snidely.

'I have money.' The stranger's hand disappeared inside his robe and emerged again holding a bulging leather purse.

Grolst's eyes lit up involuntarily at the sight of it. 'That should just about do it,' he muttered grudgingly, although the twinkling in the black pits of his pupils betrayed how he truly felt. Not that the stranger appeared to notice: he was too busy glancing, fretfully almost, at the stony faces around the bar.

'I want to retire now,' the stranger said, once the innkeeper had taken payment.

'Would you care for another drink before I show you to your room?' Grolst proffered, displaying uncharacteristic generosity.

The stranger's eyes shot Grolst a suspicious glance, his mouth tight-lipped. Briefly, the innkeeper met the man's gaze. For a moment, he fancied he could see fires burning deep within them and the ferocity of the flames made him blink and look away.

'All right then, why not?'

Grolst uncorked the luska bottle again, one whiff of the fiery spirit making his eyes start to water. As he poured a measure of the alcohol into the stranger's glass, he was aware that all eyes in the bar were on him and the unwelcome visitor. Even the mournful man was looking up at him, his red-rimmed eyes no longer gazing at the bottom of his drink. Through one grimy, lead-paned window Grolst could see the white-yellow bloated orb of a gibbous moon, rising between the grey-cast clouds behind the trees at the top of the hill, and he found his mind wandering to consider what would come to pass later that night.

The sacrifice had to be made soon, and it would be. The people of Viehdorf might not like strangers intruding into the isolation of their village, but they did have their uses; Viehdorf had its own method of protection against the predations of beastmen and their ilk.

'Here,' he said as he poured the stranger a double measure into a fresh glass. 'You look like you need warming up on a night like this. This one's on the house.'

GERHART BRENNEND LOOKED around the Slaughtered Calf's guest room. He was unimpressed. It was much as he had expected. It was cramped and sparsely decorated. There was one bed, made of rough-hewn timbers, and a chair with a broken leg. The walls were barely plastered and, in places, the bare boards of the internal walls were visible. There was one crack-paned window, which rattled loosely in the wind and rain battering the isolated inn, that looked down onto the stable yard. The tiles of the stable roof were slick with greasy rainwater that ran into leaf-clogged gutters and poured over into the yard in a relentless cascade onto the rain-darkened cobbles.

As Gerhart sat down on the thin straw mattress of the bed a wave of tiredness swept over him. He felt restless despite the weariness that was threatening to overcome him. For a wizard of the noblest Bright Order to have come to this, he thought to himself miserably. Once he had been the holder of the keys of Azimuth, an honoured position in his order, and now he was brought low like this. In fact, he had never been more destitute. His once magnificent robe was scorched and worn shabby, but at least it wasn't wet anymore. There was nothing a fire mage hated more than rain, other than drowning, perhaps.

Even though he suddenly felt bone-numbingly weary, Gerhart still felt ill at ease. It had been the roadwarden's enquiries that had done it, and the talk of witch hunters. He had met enough of their bigoted, paranoid kind before.

Trying to dismiss such concerns from his mind, he lay back on the bed, his eyelids suddenly heavy. It was as if all his exertions of the last year had finally caught up with him. But, as he closed his eyes, the scowling faces of those whom he had met before, who hunted the practitioners of the dark arts and servants of the fell powers, came unbidden into his mind. First, there was the Castigator of Schreibe, his red face contorted by zealous rage. Next came the cruelly calm features of the tonsure-headed priest of Stilwold, Brother Bernhardt – Gerhart involuntarily recalled the marks of the cleric's self-induced mortification that he had suffered in the name of Holy Sigmar. Religious extremism and intolerance could never really be considered positive character traits.

Gerhart was feeling very drowsy now. Then, of course, there was Gottfried Verdammen, the flesh of his face bubbled, red-raw and blistered from the avenging fires...

A sudden noise in the yard below his window roused Gerhart from the drowsy threshold of sleep. A stable door was banging in the persistent wind that whipped through the courtyard behind the inn. Shaking the slumber from him, he rose from the bed and peered out of the corner of the cracked window into the dark and the rain.

Through half-closed eyes he saw a cloaked figure duck into a stable, the door banging shut on its latch behind him. The wizard blinked his eyes clear, but the figure was gone. Had he really seen anyone?

Another wave of fatigue washed over him and he had to sit down on the bed again, as his legs practically gave way beneath him. What had he just seen? Of course, it could be nothing more than an ostler tending the animals stabled there. Gerhart's heightened sense of mistrust would not let him believe something so innocent or simple. What clandestine activity was taking place out in that stable on a night like this?

He could fight the tiredness no longer. Putting his overwhelming exhaustion down to his long journey and the leeching effect of the continual rain on his powers, he gave in at last, falling asleep as soon as his head hit the musty-smelling pillow.

'YOU'RE SURE THIS is going to work?'

'Don't worry. I've taken care of things.'

'But the sacrifice has to be made tonight.'

'I told you, it's taken care of.'

'So my Gertrude is safe? Truly?'

'She is now. Remember, we owe everything to our protector, just as our forefathers did in years past. We must make the sacrifice. We all have our part to play. It is better that one die than the village die. The good of the many is what matters. The good of the many.'

Grolst took in the furtive group gathered within the dark of the stable, the smell of mouldering straw and stale horse dung strong in his nostrils. There were four of them, their hunched forms outlined by the rain-washed moonlight. As well as the thickset innkeeper, there was the blacksmith and the mournful looking man from the bar, as well as a bearded, burly forester. Grolst looked around the darkened stable.

Everyone in the village, of adult age at least, knew the truth about Viehdorf, but there was something about their dark secret that still made them feel uncomfortable speaking of it openly.

'What do you mean, you've taken care of things?' the broad-shouldered blacksmith asked, an edge of anger in his voice.

'Have a little faith, won't you?' the innkeeper said, his slack smile invisible in the gloom.

'Enough of this goading, Grolst,' the forester rumbled. 'Now is not the time for tomfoolery. I've seen the rise in beastman activity in the forests on the borders of our lands. In fact, I've never seen so much in all my born days. We're all troubled by it. We need to ensure that our village remains protected. We cannot miss the sacrifice.'

'And we won't,' Grolst reassured them with all the guile of a serpent. 'He won't give us any trouble. I put poppy seed juice in his glass. He won't have tasted it under the luska. He'll sleep now until doomsday. Won't nothing wake him before we're done with him.'

'Then we do this now,' the blacksmith said gruffly.

'We do it now,' the others agreed.

Strangers did have their uses after all, the innkeeper mused as the party crept out of the stable into the night.

FROM HIS HIDING place behind the sag-roofed barn, Roadwarden Hoffenbach looked down on the Slaughtered Calf from up amongst the scraggy trees through the sheeting rain. There appeared to be four of them shuffling self-consciously between the half-closed gates of the inn's stabling yard. Waiting on the dirt road outside was a heavy-built saddled shire horse, huffing and snorting irritably in the rain. The men were carrying what, at first, appeared to be an awkwardly packed sack. The only light illuminating their venture came from the moon. An arm flopped loosely from amidst the folds of rough cloth, as one of the men shifted his hold on the bundle, and Hoffenbach realised that what they were in fact carrying was a body. Unless he was very much mistaken, it was the bearded, staff-bearing stranger who had been in the bar earlier that same evening.

Hoffenbach watched and waited, the rain pattering on the brim of his lobster-tail helm.

One of the party, whom the roadwarden was almost certain was the village blacksmith, took hold of the shire horse's reins and put a calming hand on the beast's muzzle, as the other conspirators man-handled their captive onto his back. Was the man dead or merely unconscious? Hoffenbach had no way of knowing. What did intrigue him was that the conspirators were securing the stranger's gnarled staff to the horse's saddle along with a scabbarded sword, which the roadwarden supposed must also belong to the comatose man.

If he acted now he could stop them, he considered, but if he did so he knew that he wouldn't get to the bottom of what was going on here, and might also pass up an opportunity to discover what had happened to the witch hunter Scheitz. Hoffenbach knew the slovenly innkeeper had been lying when he said that he hadn't seen the witch hunter, but just how much did he know? From his involvement in tonight's proceedings, the roadwarden guessed it was a great deal.

No, Hoffenbach decided, feeling the reassuring weight of his warhammer as he hefted it in his hands, he would hold back and see where the Viehdorfers were taking the red-robed stranger. He had seen his type before too, working as part of an Imperial commission, as he was. Practitioners of the Arts Magicae. Spell-casters. Wizards.

As THE MEN led the horse and its burden away from the Slaughtered Calf and off the road along the winding paths of the forest, the roadwarden followed, keeping his distance, unseen. Once the party entered the forest, with the eerily glowing disc of the moon broken by the rain-lashed canopy above them, moved away from the ambient light of the inn, they opened the shutters of the lantern they were carrying and the way through the woods was illuminated by a circle of yellow light.

The ground rose as they travelled south, putting several miles between themselves and the inn. The going was slow as the blacksmith carefully guided his horse over jutting stones and swollen root boles that infringed on the narrow path that they were following. The men were taking care not to slip in the quagmire that the gradually easing rain had made of the ground.

The further they travelled into the tangled forest the quieter the dark woods became, the tree trunks more twisted, the undergrowth more thorny and wild, the path less well defined. Hoffenbach felt uneasy. To him, this was the kind of place that the foul-brood beastmen would call home.

Then, at the top of a craggy hill, they broke through into a clearing. Hoffenbach ducked down behind the stump of a lightning-felled beech, and from his hiding place saw before him something that made the rest of the forest seem like a pleasant arboreal idyll.

The tree was huge, surely larger than any other tree he had seen in the forest; its thick trunk twisting upward and splitting into a mass of warped and misshapen, leafless branches. The top of the tree seemed to point an accusing finger at the cloud-shrouded night's sky, as if in defiance of the gods themselves. Hoffenbach was not able to discern what species the tree must once have been. Its sheer size suggested an oak to him, but the nature of its rough bark, grey and granite-like in the light of the moon that was cast down into the glade between the towering trees, seemed more like that of an ash. Its warped nature was unlike any creation of nature Hoffenbach knew. Perhaps this tree was no creation of nature.

It was not just the writhing form of the tree that lent this place such an all-pervading horror. It was also the bodies, in various states of decay, hanging from its branches. Some were barely more than lichen-flecked skeletons, loosely held together by fibrous ligaments; others mere bones, dangling from moss eaten lengths of hempen rope. Others amongst the tree's grisly trophies were fresher corpses, still clad in the clothes or armour they had worn in life, their flesh grey and greening, heads lolling, eyes plucked clean from their sockets, mouths fixed in rictus grins of death.

There were the bodies of all manner of people hanging here, the cadavers swaying in the wind that wound down through the glade to caress the hanging tree. There were still more rotten strands of rope left trailing forlornly from the higher branches, their bodies having fallen, now lying amongst the mouldering leaf litter that covered the putrid soil of this place. Hoffenbach could see a ribcage here, a shattered skull there.

It was then that he saw, half-buried in the mud and mulch, the red-patina links of the great chains. Each one was secured to the macabre trunk at one end – looped around its great girth or hooked over iron pegs that had been hammered deep into the wood – and at the other to one of a number of boulders that were half-sunken in the earth around the perimeter of the glade. Hoffenbach couldn't begin to imagine why.

A gust of wind carried the vile scents of decomposition to him. He could taste it now on his tongue and he felt the hairs on the back of his neck rise as his unease increased. The rain that had become a gentle patter on the leaves above his head finally ceased. The hanging tree didn't so much seem to grow as to thrust its way out of the putrid earth. The air of the clearing was heavy with the smell of leaf-mould, wet clay and putrefaction – the smell of corruption.

It was only then that he realised that one of the hanging corpses was that of his erstwhile partner, Schweitz.

The witch hunter's body swung slowly like a macabre pendulum, his head tilted to one side at an unnatural angle, his cape torn into tatters, his eye sockets black, bloody holes. Hoffenbach could see that the tips of several branches were buried inside the witch hunter's dead body, as if they had been forced into the corpse for some reason. It almost looked, in fact, as if they had grown that way. What ghoulish practices were taking place here? Perhaps the villagers didn't just hang their victims.

The only half-sane conclusion Hoffenbach could draw, from what he saw here, was that the villagers offered the tree sacrifice in the perversely misguided belief that it somehow protected Viehdorf with its malign influence – the rotting flesh of the corpses feeding the tree's hungry roots. Indeed, on his travels throughout the Emperor's realm, he had heard half-told tales of such barbaric practices before.

Still hidden behind the broken stump, Hoffenbach continued to watch, but still he did not rush to act. If there was anything that his career as a roadwarden on the highways of His Imperial Majesty had taught him, it was patience. He would watch and wait for his moment.

The bushy bearded forester, his axe tucked into his belt at his side, took a noosed rope from a saddlebag and threw half of its coiled length over one of the lower branches of the ghoulish tree.

Hoffenbach continued to watch as the noose was pushed roughly over the unconscious prisoner's head.

Abruptly the man began to stir, shaking his head to clear it of sleep and clutching clumsily at the blacksmith who was trying to pull the noose tight around his neck. Then, when he began to understand the mortal danger he was in, the man started to struggle more violently, arching his back; punching and kicking at his captors to free himself from their grasp.

Now was Hoffenbach's moment. Raising his hammer above his head, he charged into the clearing, leaf mould squelching and brittle bones cracking beneath his pounding footfalls.

GERHART'S EYES BULGED open as he felt a rope tighten around his neck. Reacting on instinct, he kicked out as he tried to free himself from the rough hands he could feel holding him down. He heard a man grunt in pain, felt the hands let go and then had the wind half-knocked out of him as he fell onto the wet ground, landing with a jarring smack on his right shoulder. As consciousness returned to him he became half-aware of men shouting, one as if charging into battle, others in an angry and confused clamour. The wizard managed to get both hands on the knot around his neck and strained at it to loosen the noose and free himself.

Coughing and gasping for breath, he rose onto his knees and pulled the noose free. Well, that was a first. People had tried to drown him, fry him to a crisp and shoot him, but no one had ever tried to hang him before.

A combination of wan moonlight and the orange, flickering glow of a lantern on the ground nearby showed him that he was in a forest clearing. The shadow of a huge, twisting tree loomed over him, even darker shapes hanging from its branches. He heard an angry whinny and realised that, as well as men, there was a horse here. He could smell its animal-sweat stink. There was a man lying on his back in the mud and leaves not three feet away. That must have been the man he had kicked.

How dare they? His temper blazed that these impudent peasants would try to do away with him, a battle wizard of the noble Bright Order of the Colleges of Magic!

The fire wizard scrambled to his feet. Leaves and thorny twigs clung to the hem of his muddied robes. The other man was also back-up on his feet and Gerhart saw that it was the man from the inn whom he had taken to be the village blacksmith. The blacksmith was slipping on the wet ground lunging for something the large shire horse was carrying. With a ringing of steel the blacksmith drew what Gerhart realised was his own sword from the scabbard that had been tied to the horse's saddlebag, along with his staff.

With an angry shout, the blacksmith threw himself at the wizard. Gerhart barely managed to twist out of the way of the enraged man's charge. The tip of his sword landed with a wet thunk where, only a moment before, Gerhart's leg had been, slicing into the knotty tissue of an exposed root. Out of the corner of his eye, Gerhart thought that he saw the root retracted at the blow, as a wounded animal might withdraw its paw from a closing trap.

The blacksmith might be skilled with his hammer and anvil but he was no swordsman. Evading another uncoor-dinated swing, Gerhart stumbled over to the horse and tugged his staff free of the saddlebag. The blacksmith's next lunge was parried by the gnarled wood.

The wizard saw that the roadwarden was already trading blows with the forester, warhammer against axe, whilst the fat, nervous innkeeper was holding back from the fight.

Then there was the last of the men in the lynch mob – the gaunt, sorrowful individual Gerhart had seen drinking by himself – running at him, nock-bladed dagger drawn, wailing like a rabid animal, as if all human reason had left him.

The fire mage swung at the desperate man with his staff but his movements were still clumsy and uncoordinated, even though adrenalin was now rushing though his veins, purging drugged sleep from his body. He clipped the man's arm with the charcoaled end of his staff, but not hard enough to disarm him. The return blow with the other end, however, cracked the sad-eyed man across the chin and he dropped to his knees, blood pouring from his mouth.

Gerhart reeled, his head spinning, as the blacksmith came at him again, his teeth bared in an expression of angry defiance. Gerhart staggered backwards and collided with the snorting shire horse, which whinnied again and broke away, cantering towards the edge of the clearing.

The wizard's sword, still in the blacksmith's hands, connected with his staff, the blow sending jarring pain up Gerhart's arms through his wrists. If the staff had not been toughened by years of fire-tempering and absorption of raw magical energy, the blow would probably have splintered it.

Gerhart knew it was unlikely he would be able to hold off the brute strength of the blacksmith, even if he was an unskilled swordsman. He would need to draw on the other resources he had at his disposal to bring about an end to this battle.

He quickly tried to put some distance between himself and the blacksmith as possible and then closed his eyes on the chaos surrounding him. A spark flared in the darkness of his mind. Gerhart opened his eyes again but looked now with his eldritch mage-sight.

The winds of magic whirled and twisted through the clearing, visible to Gerhart as tormented currents and spinning eddies, bright coruscating ribbons of power. Black shadow-trails were drawn to the tree. Emerald tongues of flame slithered across the forest floor. Slanting, aquamarine bars of sorcerous radiance danced in the sky above the forest, like the fabled Northland aurora. Then he saw what he had been seeking. Hovering in the air over a forgotten lantern, left on the ground by one of the lynch mob, a nimbus of red and orange light, flickering like a candle-flame.

He drew the burnished glow to him, inhaling deeply as he did so, letting the esoteric energies into every fibre of his being, feeling them warming him to the core, as if they were healing his injuries, replenishing his strength. Years of experience fighting upon battlefields across the length and breadth of the Empire helped him focus now. Inside his mind a flame burned, bright and intense, growing in strength as Gerhart's anger fed its ferocity, and a spell took shape there.

At the edge of his field of vision, Gerhart saw the axe wielding forester fall as the roadwarden parried the slicing arc described by the axe blade and brought his own weapon around to connect with the side of his opponent's head with skull-cracking force.

Then the spell was ready and the wizard could contain its power no longer.

In an instant the lurching blacksmith was alight, his whole body, clothes and hair ablaze as if the source of the fire came from inside him. The man faltered in his run, but then stumbled onward, the fire consuming him, dropping Gerhart's sword. A piercing scream rose from the flailing human torch.

Gerhart was aware of other cries of panic.

Seeing what the wizard had done to the boldest of their companions, through the crackling flames curling from the burning blacksmith, Gerhart saw the innkeeper now mounted on the shire horse, having somehow managed to haul his bulk onto its back, kicking his heels into its ribs as the mournful man, struggled to climb on behind him. He could hear a pathetic whimpering accompanying their flight. With a whinny, the horse galloped off into the forest, its hoofs beating a tattoo – like distant thunder on the ground that was swallowed up by the trees.

The blacksmith took two more clumsy steps and then collapsed, his cries silenced. The only sound now was the wailing whine, fizz and pop of the intense fire consuming his body.

Gerhart felt drained. Exhausted, the fire mage slumped to his knees on the leaf-churned ground. He slowly became aware of the road-warden's cautious approach and looked up through weary eyes at the man standing over him, hammer still in hand. The black silhouette of the hanging tree rose up behind Hoffenbach, a sinister, warped per-version of nature, its branches – almost more like rough-skinned tentacles than tree limbs – clawed at the stratus-crossed sky. Blood ran from underneath the iron brim of the roadwarden's helmet.

If it hadn't been for the roadwarden's intervention it was quite likely that Gerhart's body would have joined those other crow-picked carcasses hanging like vile death-trophies from the possessive clutches of the tree. Now the warden was looking at the wizard in shocked surprise – perhaps even horror having witnessed the sponta-neous combustion of the blacksmith. He had risked his own life to save Gerhart from being sacrificed to the tree. Hoffenbach's expres-sion mirrored how his feelings were vying with each other, as he tried to reconcile saving the sorcerer's life with the devastating powers he had seen unleashed. Was it wise to let such a dangerous wizard live?

Gerhart Brennend had seen that expression before. The roadwarden was just as suspicious of wizards as the next superstitious peasant.

Black tentacle-shadows writhed with unnatural life in the darkness. Hoffenbach opened his mouth to speak but the only sound that came from his throat was a gargling death rattle. There was a wet ripping sound and Gerhart felt a warm, cloying wetness splash his face. His nostrils were suddenly heavy with the hot smell of iron. Blood. It was only then that the wizard saw the broken end of a tree-limb protrud-ing from the man's neck above the top of his hauberk.

Gerhart watched in horror, transfixed, as other branches seized the road-warden's arms, body and legs, wrapping themselves fluidly, dis-gustingly around the man with a creaking like a yew bow being pulled taut. Cold realisation leeched the resolve from him to replace it with a numbing chill as he barely dared to believe what he was witnessing. Denied its sacrifice, the hanging tree itself had come to chaotic life. The tree effortlessly lifted the choking roadwarden into the air and then, in one violent eruption tore the wretched man limb from limb. Pieces of Hoffenbach dropped to the ground, offal left dangling from the writhing branches. Then the tree reached for the wizard.

Gerhart recovered himself immediately, the dire urgency of his predicament filling him with renewed resolve. His sword lay close to the still smouldering body of his foolish attacker. Reacting almost instinctively, Gerhart rolled away from the clutching grasp of the branches, stretched out his right arm and snatched up his soot-smeared blade. The pommel was still warm to the touch.

The tree lashed out at Gerhart again, only this time he was able to fend off its attack, blocking strikes from its lower branches with his sword. Where his blade struck the tree, thick dark sap oozed from its wounds like blood.

The branches recoiled from the wizard's wounding blows, giving Gerhart the opportunity to get to his feet once more. He backed away out of its reach. It seemed to the mage that the creaking and groaning of the wood, as it contorted itself into all manner of writhing shapes, was the tree growling at him.

The hanging tree was not done with him yet. With a clanking of protesting rusted metal links, the tree uprooted itself, pulled great splayed roots, dripping earth, from the grave-soil ground of the clearing and began to drag its massive bulk towards him. The boulders secured to the taut chains also came free of the orange flecked mud as the tree heaved the great rocks attached to it across the clearing, gouging great ruts in the putrid loam.

Gerhart had faced all manner of horrors before – slithering Chaos-created spawn-things, a living daemon-cannon, creatures born of nightmares that by rights should never have existed in the waking world – but nothing so primal, so ancient and so terrifying as this hanging tree before. He could feel the malign influence of the Chaos energies fuelling the tree's unnatural vigour all around him. He could feel it thickening the air, feel it raising the hackles on the back of his neck, chilling his spine, freezing the marrow in his bones, taste its bitter gall in his mouth. He even felt its cold, corrupting touch in the dark depths of his very soul.

It was more than that; there was a malign sentience there too, gnawing at the edges of his own consciousness. Gerhart's pre-ternatural senses revealed flashes of visions that were something like memories to him…

He saw blood-daubed, tattooed tribes-men offering the tree sacrifice in the form of enemies bested in battle… He sensed the powers of dark magic being drawn to the tree over the centuries as a result of the blood rites practised before it, and the sacrifices continuing, even as the tribe's settlement become the village of Viehdorf… He shared in the memory when the tree, so imbued was it with warping power, gained some kind of self-awareness… Its influence spreading through the soil beneath the forest, just like its roots, to encompass the village, corrupting the minds of the people who dwelt there so that they continued to feed it human souls, helping to strengthen the tree all the time. In turn its malignancy kept all other threats to its dominance at bay, in an unbroken cycle of corruption, sacrifice and soul-feasting...

Gerhart had overheard the exchange that took place between the greasy innkeeper and the roadwarden back at the inn. Now he understood why the rising storm of Chaos had left this place untouched. Chaos was already here.

His mind awash with disturbing images, in the dark Gerhart did not see the root push itself up out of the ground and snag itself around his ankle. Then he has falling, unable to stop himself. Gerhart plunged down the slope that dropped away at the edge of the clearing, tumbling head over heels through thorny thickets; roots and stones bruised his body, brambles snagging his beard.

He slid to a halt in a bed of nettles, cracking his head against a weatherworn stone. The jolt stunned him for a moment but also helped him shake himself free of the tree's malevolent influence. The hanging tree was crashing towards him, splintering saplings under its weight. Bodies swung wildly from its upper branches, or were torn from it as they snagged in the crooks of elm and silver birch.

It was almost on top of him now. A slimy jawbone fell from the skeletal canopy of the tree into Gerhart's lap as the chaos tree's violent lurching shook it loose from a cadaver swinging high above.

There was no way that he could prevail here armed only with his sword, Gerhart realised. There was only one thing that could save him now. Gerhart looked with his mage-sight again and a glimmer of hope entered his heart. The hollow where he lay was saturated with swirling magical energy. There were places in the world that attracted the winds of magic more strongly than others, like iron filings were attracted to a lodestone.

The fire wizard looked down at the stone he had hit with his head. The tracery of ancient carvings could still just be made out beneath the lichen crawling over its surface, possibly made by the tribesmen who had first offered the tree fealty in times long past. The concentration of magical power was greatest here; drawn to this spot by the ancient stone. Had the primitives who put the stone here realised what effect its positioning would have, Gerhart wondered? It was a potential stockpile of power just waiting to be tapped.

The tree reached for Gerhart for the last time, for now there was no escape for the wizard. As it did so, he breathed out slowly and, ignoring the pain in the back of his skull, focused his mind once more.

So saturated in eldritch force was this spot that the very essence of the winds of magic simply poured into the attuned wizard, the tongue of flame burning inside his mind exploding into a devastating firestorm. Gerhart flung his arms out towards the tree, his hands seeming to burst into flame as he did so. Sorcerous power roared from his fingertips, becoming a roiling ball of liquid fire as it raced towards the hanging tree. Yellow fires blazed within his eyes as Gerhart cast his spell, immolating the tree with his fiery magic. He had not felt power like this since Wolfenburg.

Flames washed over the tree, taking hold immediately all over its grotesquely bulging trunk, fat with the countless souls it had consumed. The tree let out a cacophonous scream, like the splintering of wood, as if myriad voices were screaming in unison with the angry roaring of the flames. The tree writhed in tortured agony as it burned, the rotting corpses hanging from its contorted bow catching light as well. Skeletal forms crashed to the forest floor in a flurry of sparks as their ropes burnt through, the raging inferno lighting up the top of the hill and the forest around it.

His spell cast, his power spent, Gerhart staggered clear of the dying tree. Out of range of its flailing, fiery death-throes, the wizard watched with grim satisfaction as the tree burned. As it burned, he fancied that he could see faces contorted in agony distorting the bark-skin of the tree, adding their howling voices to the tree's death-screams.

Satisfied that his work here was done, his staff and sword recovered, Gerhart left the clearing on the same path the horse had taken with its two riders. The wizard followed its hoof prints back towards the Slaughtered Calf and the corrupted village.

The tree itself had shown the wizard that the people of Viehdorf were party to its evil. The land would not be free of the contagion that was the Chaos growth's malignant influence until the corruption that had been allowed to fester there, thanks to this root of evil, had been exorcised and the wound cauterised.

Before dawn Viehdorf would burn.

TALES OF
MADNESS & RUIN

THE DOOM THAT CAME TO WULFHAFEN

C L Werner

'IT IS TIME,' Gastoen said, his voice deep and commanding, brooking no question. Karel rose from his bed, his head turning towards the open doorway of his room. Gastoen had already withdrawn, however, satisfied that his son would rise from his slumber and hurry to join his father outside.

Or, perhaps, thought Karel, his father knew that he had not been asleep. His body cried out from fatigue, the weariness of long hours spent before dawn hauling lobster pots and fishing nets from the chill waters of the Sea of Claws, a labour which had only ended late in the afternoon, as the small fleet of tiny fishing boats returned to Wulfhaefen, their occupants grumbling about the meagre catch. It was not yet late enough in the year for the lobsters to be numerous, and many of the pots went without an inmate, or yielded such miserable specimens that the clawed creatures were summarily tossed back into the sea. Still, the grumbling was not so very serious as it might have been amongst the fishermen of the many other coastal villages scattered across the Empire, for even if the lobster season was still months away, a far more profitable season was about to begin for the men of Wulfhafen.

Karel quickly dressed himself, emerging from his tiny room into the much larger common room of his family's home. He could see his mother standing calmly in the centre of the room, a clay mug gripped firmly in her tired, wrinkled hands. She smiled at her son, a warm, loving expression, yet with the thread of worry mixed in to tarnish the reassurance the old woman hoped to bestow. When Karel stepped towards her, she gave him the clay mug, its contents steaming; he gratefully accepted the cup and sipped away at its contents. He was not surprised to find that she had mixed some rum into the tea. The alcohol would keep him warm far longer than the tea. His mother was always so very practical.

'Your father is waiting,' the old woman gently prodded as Karel lingered over his tea. The youth nodded and slugged down the remainder in a single gulp, wiping the excess from his chin with the sleeve of his jerkin. Karel handed the mug back to the care of his mother's wrinkled hands and stooped downward to kiss her cheek. He was surprised when his mother tried to slip an object into his hands as he hugged her.

'What is this?' Karel asked, staring at the tarnished steel kitchen knife. His mother pushed his hands and the knife they gripped against his chest.

'You can never be too careful,' she explained. 'Slip it beneath your clothes. Better to have it and not need it, than to be without.' With those last words of warning, Karel's mother manoeuvred him to the door and into the cold night air.

KAREL FOUND HIS father leaning against the side of their hut, staring down the narrow lane that made up the village of Wulfhafen. It was nothing much, as villages went. A scattered mass of simple huts, perhaps two score in total: a large wooden meeting hall, where the village men would spend long summer nights drinking and carousing; a mass of ramshackle boat houses closer to shore; a small warehouse where food would be stored, kept in a community trust; and a small coach house, the domain of Wulfhafen's only wagon and four horses. Gastoen looked up as his boy joined him, smiling and gripping Karel firmly by the shoulder.

'Tonight you officially become a man,' Gastoen said, smiling into his son's face, his tobbaco-stained teeth broken and pitted. Gastoen stared at Karel, reading the youth's features. He thumped his son on the back and began to walk slowly down the lane.

'Everyone is nervous their first time,' Gastoen explained. 'You will do just fine. Why, when I was your age, I was probably even more anxious than you are now.' Gastoen punctuated his remark with a short, cough-like laugh.

Karel looked hard at his father, considering his words. He seemed older now than he had been only this morning, helping his son pull empty lobster pots back into their boat. Karel idly wondered if his father had also been unable to sleep, if he was having problems adjusting to the new nocturnal habit demanded by the long autumn nights. He would have thought that after these many years, his father would have adjusted to the yearly pattern. Perhaps it was something besides the alteration in routine that had upset his father.

'Are you certain that what we are doing is right?' Karel muttered, almost under his breath, as he pursued this last train of thought. Gastoen stopped, turning to face his son, both men, old and young, shrouded in the shadows of the huts to either side of the lane. Gastoen opened his mouth to speak but waited until a figure that had been advancing upon them from further down the lane passed them by, the last chords of the sea shanty the man had been whistling drifting away into the night. Only when the tune could no longer be heard did Gastoen speak.

'I myself asked that question of my father when I was your age,' Gastoen confessed. 'We stood, perhaps, in this very spot. He explained to me the way this wretched world of ours works. He said that in the sea, for the shark to grow big and strong, it must devour thousands of smaller fish. For the kraken, it must consume numberless whales to survive. As it is in the sea, so it is on land. For a man to prosper, he must have prey. It is the way of things, Karel. To have joy, yourself, another must suffer.' Gastoen sighed and put a gnarled hand on his son's head. 'Believe me, we have things much better here than in other places. If what we do brings us such prosperity, can what we do be wrong?'

The question seemed genuine to Karel, as if his father was not certain of the answer himself. The youth would have challenged his father's reasoning further when, suddenly, the shadows in the narrow lane danced away from them, retreating away from the beach. A bright light glared from the shore, dazzling in its brilliance, far more wondrous than the pale, feeble light of the tiny sliver of Mannslieb hanging in the night sky. Karel shut his eyes and flinched away from the sudden brightness, but Gastoen had already gripped the youth by the shoulder and pulled him into sharing the accelerated trot the old man had adopted.

'The beacon fire has been lit!' Gastoen exclaimed as the two made their way toward the shore. 'Our place is on the beach.' Gastoen paused as they passed the last of the thatch-roofed huts. He removed a heavy boat hook from his belt and pressed it into Karel's hands.

'Keep this ready,' Gastoen ordered, his voice heavy with concern. 'Stay close to me. Perhaps nothing will happen tonight, but as your grandfather always used to warn "expect every storm to be a hurricane".'

* * *

THE MEN OF Wulfhafen were gathered around a roaring, blazing fire. The mound of wood rose several feet above the rocks, promising to spend hours before burning out. Karel could make out the figure of Veytman, Wulfhafen's chief citizen, ordering men to stack the empty kegs of oil they had used to douse the wood with into an orderly file some distance from the advancing surf. Veytman spotted Gastoen and Karel as they advanced onto the sand and broke away from the bonfire crew to meet them.

'You are late, Gastoen,' Veytman reprimanded the older man. Thin and powerful where Gastoen was paunchy and frail, Veytman cut an imposing figure. The man's dark hair and rakish looks marked him out as the direct descendent of Wulfhafen's founder, the pirate Wulfaert. The narrow, elegant blade sheathed at Veytman's side was the finest steel in all the village and had been the pirate's when he had plied the coasts of Bretonnia in his sloop The Cockerel. 'We should have been glad for your help in setting the bonfire.'

'I am sorry,' Gastoen began, trying not to meet Veytman's gaze.

'I see you brought your son along,' Veytman observed, focusing his cold blue eyes on Karel for the first time. Veytman studied the boy for a moment and they looked back at Gastoen. 'Are you certain that he is ready for this?'

This time Gastoen did not avoid Veytman's gaze. 'He will do what is expected of a man of Wulfhafen,' the old man snapped, fire in his voice. Veytman nodded and clucked his tongue.

'We shall have to see about that,' the rogue said, running a smooth finger through the slight brush of moustache upon his lip. 'Just be certain that he knows the rules. No hiding anything. Everything that washes ashore must be valued and appraised before it can be distributed equally amongst the village.' Veytman let his face soften, and winked at Karel. 'Then, there is always the Captain's share to consider,' the man laughed.

'Do you think we will catch anything tonight?' Gastoen asked Veytman. Veytman turned, casting his eyes out to the darkness of the nighttime sea. There was motion there, the ceaseless undulation of the waters. But of what might be lurking above or below that undulating mass, there was no clue.

'No,' Veytman shook his head, 'it is early in the season yet. The fog is just now starting to become thick, the wind only now beginning to sound with Ulric's howl. I don't think that we will catch anything tonight. But it is useful to keep everybody in practice. We must let the indolence of summer be forgotten.' Veytman turned away from Gastoen and his son and walked over to the roaring fire, warming his hands before the flames.

'Come along, boy,' Gastoen said, gripping Karel by the shoulder. 'He has the right idea. It will be a long night, and we may as well be warm.'

'LIGHTS ON THE water,' the keen-eyed villager said. Karel was immediately roused from his napping by the sudden activity all around him. He looked away towards the roaring bonfire for a moment, then turned his gaze to Veytman. The rakish hetman of Wulfhafen removed the long, slender tube of his looking glass from within the breast of his coat. Like his sword, it was an heirloom from the pirate Wulfaert, a rare and valuable device looted from an elven ship, if the legends of Wulfaert held any truth in them. Veytman placed the tube to his eye and gazed out at the black expanse of the sea.

'Fortune smiles upon us on our first night!' Veytman laughed, replacing the looking glass within his coat. 'She looks to be a merchantman, a fine prize for so early in the season!' Veytman looked over at a burly villager standing nearby.

'Emil, encourage our friends to come ashore,' Veytman said. Emil took the long, curved horn from his belt and put it to his lips. Soon, the man's bellows-like lungs sent a loud, mournful note echoing into the night. Gastoen and the other men of Wulfhafen stared at the distant lights from the ship expectantly, even Karel becoming caught up in the excitement. The men watched and waited. When the lonely bellow of an answering horn sounded from the ship, the men of Wulfhafen turned to one another, their wide, cruel smiles bespeaking their silent glee.

Karel watched as the lights of the ship came closer towards the shore. The youth understood what was happening, and his excitement abated as his mind made the leap from the scene he was witnessing and that which must surely follow. Emil blasted the horn once again as the ship drew still closer, drawn through the night and the fog towards the promising light of the beacon. Like a moth to the flame.

A captain wise in the ways of the north would never have fallen for the trick. The best charts of the northern coast of the Empire, that neglected, shunned region beyond the Wasteland and the Drakwald, described a craggy stretch of shore as Wrecker's Point. It is a place riddled with sharp fangs of rock, submerged shoals and razor-sharp coral reefs. The refuge promised by dozens of tiny harbours is like the call of the siren, luring ships to their doom and no practised captain would accept their lethal charms. An experienced mariner would take his chances with the sea's doubtful mercy in even the most vicious storm than accept the certain destruction of a landing on the treacherous coastline of Wrecker's Point.

But the evils of geography are not the only dangers to menace the ships sailing the route between Erengrad and Marienburg. A wicked place will often find wicked men all too willing to put to use such a blighted site. Several villages exist amongst the craggy rocks and fangs of the shoreline, tending their small fleets of fishing boats until Ulric's Howl, that terrible, chill wind which heralds the coming winter, brings a more profitable catch to their shores. But the best charts are expensive, and experienced captains in short supply. Far more numerous are the maps produced by cloistered scribes in the cartography shops of Altdorf and Nuln, drawn by men who have never seen the sea or heard the warnings of Wrecker's Point.

The ship continued, Emil and his counterpart on the vessel sounding their horns above the soft roar of the tide. It drew so close that Karel fancied that he could see the bonfire reflecting off the white canvas of the ship's sails. His young eyes tried to pierce the veil of night to ferret out the shape of the ship from the darkness that enshrouded it. A part of him wanted to look away, but he could not. It was not the fear that his elders would think him not ready to become a man that prevented him. It was because the drama was too compelling, too awful for Karel to turn from.

The sound of the ship striking the jagged fangs of rock that lurked just below the waters of the inlet tore the night asunder. It was like the bellow of some bestial god betrayed, a cry of pain and wrath. The cracking snap of the wooden hull as it split upon the rocks was the most horrible sound Karel had ever heard in his life, more terrible even than the cries and screams of the men onboard the ship that followed the death cry of their vessel. Karel focused upon the lights of the ship, trying again to pierce the veil, trying to see the conclusion of this terrible drama he was a part of. He could hear the screams; the cries of terror as the black waters flooded the ruptured hull, as the sea reached up with its amorphous claws to pull the dying ship down to its watery grave.

Long minutes passed and the cries and screams faded away. The men upon the shore watched as the last of the ship's lingering lights was extinguished by the devouring waters and all sign of their victim was lost to their view. Veytman was the first to turn from the beach, striding toward the bonfire and putting flame to the torch in his hand.

'The first will be making shore any time,' Veytman said as the other men of Wulfhafen marched toward the beacon light and ignited their own torches. 'Break into pairs.' The descendant of Wulfaert let a cunning look enter his eyes. 'You all know what must be done.'

Gastoen handed Karel a lit torch, pressing the boy's fingers tightly about the firebrand's grip. 'You come along with me and Enghel.'

Gastoen did not wait to see if his son would obey, but nodded to the grizzled, weather-beaten Enghel and the two men made their way away from the bonfire, holding their torches high to illuminate the incoming tide and the sandy beach.

KAREL WALKED SEVERAL paces behind the two older men, his face pale and bloodless. He had heard the terrible shouts of discovery echoing from other searchers, only their blazing torches visible to his sight. He had heard the terrible screams that followed upon their findings, sometimes preceded by desperate, babbled pleas for mercy. Karel did his best to shut out the sounds of the drama's murderous epilogue, but try as he might, he could not block out the terrible sounds.

Ahead of him, Karel could see a dark object floating upon the white foam. Only when it was deposited upon the sand and rolled onto its back did he recognise the object as being a man. The youth ran towards the body that had come ashore. The ragged figure was tangled in a mass of weeds. Indeed, had he not seen the body wash ashore, Karel might never have noticed the object for what it was. The boy hurried over to the brown mass of vegetation and found himself staring down at a dishevelled shape that had lately been a man.

Who he was, Karel had no way of knowing. Certainly he was no simple sailor, given the extravagance and finery of his clothes. There was a foreign look about him, a darkness of skin that instantly sent Karel's mind wandering to Tilea and Estalia, places that were nothing more than exotic fables to the simple people of Wulfhafen. Karel noticed the man's slender, patrician fingers, locked in a death grasp about a soggy, leather-bound book. Karel bent down towards the body and forced the cold fingers apart, relieving the body of the slender folio.

Karel opened the book, holding it upside down to allow some of the excess water to drool away. The ink had smeared and run in many places, but there was still enough that was intact for the boy to be astounded. The slender tome had been a sketchbook, it appeared, its pages crammed with fantastic drawings of strange creatures and impossible plants. Karel gasped as he saw a drawing of an ugly brutish creature with a warty hide and great horns protruding from its face. He saw weird things that were like bats with the heads and tails of serpents. Karel found that the last pages of the book were missing altogether, lost in the violence of the wreck, denying him the pleasure of whatever sights were depicted upon them. The boy found himself gazing again and again at the drawings. Where had this ship been to see such things? Had they truly been to the terrible Chaos Wastes he sometimes heard his father mention in hushed tones? Or had some other, even more distant shore been the focus of their journey? A wave of guilt swept over Karel. These men had gone so far, and survived so much, only to find their doom on the wasted shore of Wulfhafen, victims of a hideous deception.

The sigh that rose from the mound of weeds caused Karel to nearly leap from his skin. The youth cried out in fright before he saw what had so alarmed him. The man he had thought dead was staring at him, his eyes pleading for help, his slender hand reaching out towards him. Karel bent down towards the man, his hand reaching downward to meet that grasping for him.

'Stand back, Karel,' Gastoen said, his voice strange and heavy. Both his father and Enghel were now looming over the survivor from the ship. Karel did as his father ordered and stepped away from the wounded man.

The youth watched in open-mouthed horror as Enghel crushed the survivor's arm with a savage downward swipe of his axe. The man's arm snapped, hanging limply at a twisted, unnatural angle. All the same, he struggled to raise it to ward off the second blow. He did not see Gastoen come upon him from the other side, a wooden belaying pin in his hands. Gastoen struck the passenger's head a brutal blow with the wooden cudgel, sending a rush of blood seeping from the man's scalp. Gastoen did not pause to see what effect his first attack had accomplished, but struck his victim's head again and again. After what seemed an eternity, Gastoen and Enghel withdrew from the pathetic, butchered thing that had once been a man.

Karel was frozen to the spot as his father walked over to him. His father reached out and took the boat hook from his son. The contact snapped Karel from his horrified stupor and the boy looked away from his father.

'You are tired,' Gastoen said, laying a hand slick with blood upon his son's shoulder. 'Hold the torches. Enghel and myself will attend to the body. ' The old fisherman turned to the body of the murdered man, sinking the boat hook beneath the corpse's ribcage. Enghel followed Gastoen's lead, sinking a second hook into the body's ribcage. Wheezing from the effort, they began to drag the body back towards the bonfire. Karel followed after the grim procession, both men's torches held in his hands.

The boy's mind was in turmoil, reeling from the horror and barbarity of what he had witnessed. Every time he closed his eyes, he saw the horrible scene upon the beach: the murdered man's eyes staring with terror at his father as Gastoen sent the belaying pin crashing against his skull. Karel could not believe that his father was capable of such actions. The same man who had raised him, the same man who had so tirelessly instructed him in the skills of a fisherman, the same man who only the day before had jovially joked with him as they retrieved their lobster pots. How could such a man be capable of doing what he had seen him do? For most of his life, Karel had known what Wulhafen's trade was, but he had not understood what that trade really was until a few minutes ago. Now, more than ever, he thought about the virtue of such a trade, and was unable to reconcile himself to it. How had his father ever been able to embrace so cruel a vocation?

Ås THEY MADE their way down towards the bonfire, Karel could make out the figures of men from the village drifting through the feeble light. He could see them linger before dark objects lying upon the beach, debris from the ship left stranded when the waters retreated back into the sea. Nearer, he could see Veytman and several others standing before a pile of barrels, clothing, and sacks. The men were laughing as Gastoen and Enghel hauled the body towards their position.

'What have we here?' the firm, authoritarian voice of Veytman made Karel stand straight, a look of guilt coming upon his face, as though he had been caught in some mischief. Veytman met the gaze of the men dragging the body. 'Ah, loot,' the hetman of Wulfhafen declared. The hetman walked over as Gastoen and Enghel withdrew their boathooks from the carcass. Veytman stared at the corpse, then reached down towards him. The wrecker's fingers closed around a silver object dangling from the man's throat. With a savage yank, Veytman snapped the pendant's chain and tore it from the man's neck.

'My son found him,' Gastoen stated, looking over at his boy, favouring his son with one of the strange, curious gazes that he sometimes directed upon Karel.

'Congratulations, boy,' Veytman said. 'You have found the best plunder yet.' Veytman turned the pendant about in his hand, allowing the little light penetrating the fog to play across its surface. In shape, it was like a crescent moon, a thin, wisp-like tendril rising from the upward tip of the crescent. Centred upon the crescent was a sphere or circle, as though Mannslieb had been impaled upon the waning Morrslieb. Veytman did not know what the symbol might be, whether it was a talisman of good fortune, a badge of rank or office, or the charm of some foreign god. It did not matter him; it was made of silver, and that was enough for the descendent of a pirate.

THE NIGHT PASSED slowly, and the morning fog was thick upon the beach. In the aftermath of the night, most of the men were gathered around the reduced flame of the bonfire, though a few still prowled the sands, looking for any plunder that might have escaped their notice the first time. Others were gathering broken planks and shards of deck or hull that had been cast ashore, intending to use the wood to bolster the frames of their homes and boathouses. Like the captain of a pirate vessel, Veytman made no move to aid the beachcombers. He stood with some of his closest cronies and examined what had already been collected, principally the salted meats contained within a waterlogged sack and the golden-hued rum within a slightly battered cask.

'We had best keep this away from Una,' Veytman joked as he tasted the rum. 'I don't fancy another night listening to Enghel's wife screaming at invisible goblins.' The comment brought laughs from all, and Veytman turned his attention to the salted meats, lifting a weird creature from the bag. Gastoen reached towards Veytman and took the strange salted carcass from the hetman's hands.

'Hopefully they were carrying something more useful than this,' Gastoen said, allowing the weariness to strain his voice. He turned the strange salted carcass in his hands, holding it by its tail. In size, it was akin to a squirrel, but in shape it was like a salamander. Altogether, Gastoen doubted if he would trust the thing's meat to a dog.

'The rum is good, anyway,' Veytman defended himself. 'And they had some very fine clothing, as well. In fact, Emil found himself a fine set of boots.'

'A wondrous haul,' Gastoen groused.

'There might be more to recover,' Veytman replied, already turning away from the old man and returning to his conversation with the other men.

THE SMALL FIRE continued to burn, fed by dry wood brought down from the village. Much of the kindling was wood salvaged from last season's victims. It was a cruel jest that the same timber should be employed to consume the first victims of the new season. The men of Wulfhafen watched as the blaze devoured all traces of their prey, removing the last vestiges of their crime. It was rare, but not unknown, for a road warden or witch hunter to pass through the village and Veytman was taking no chances that the true nature of their livelihood might be discovered.

'Has everyone come back?' Veytman asked Emil, eager to get to the business of splitting up the loot.

'All except Claeis and Bernard,' replied the grim faced Emil, obviously disgusted by the smell of cooking flesh. There were things even a cutthroat could not get used to.

Veytman rolled his eyes and began to mutter a curse against the laziness of the men in question when, as if on cue, a horrified scream rang out from the beach. As one, the men withdrew from the pyre and ran towards the sound. The fog had still not entirely dispersed from the shore, yet it had thinned enough that Bernard could be seen, kneeling in the sand, staring at the sea and sobbing hysterically. Veytman was the first to reach the terrified man.

'Get a hold of yourself,' Veytman snarled, grasping the front of Bernard's shirt and shaking him roughly.

'What happened?' Gastoen asked, his voice more calm and even than Veytman's savage tone. Bernard turned his face towards the sound of Gastoen's voice.

'Claeis… Claeis,' was all the man could stutter.

'What about Claeis?' snapped Veytman, pulling Bernard to his feet. 'Where is that idiot brother of yours?' Veytman slapped Bernard with his open hand, trying to beat sense back into the frightened man.

'Gone!' Bernard shrieked. 'A daemon rose from the sea and grabbed Claeis in its claws! It dragged him screaming into the sea!'

The men of Wulfhafen cast apprehensive looks about them and fear began to crawl across their faces as they heard Bernard's frightened tale. Only Veytman was unperturbed. Far from fear, the hetman broke out into laughter.

'You expect me to believe that?' Veytman buried his fist in Bernard's belly, knocking the man to his knees. 'A daemon, eh?' A savage kick to Bernard's face sent the man sprawling. 'You and your brother must have found something very choice to concoct that ridiculous tale!' Veytman sent another booted kick into Bernard's ribs.

'I tell you, we were searching the beach and a huge daemon rose from the fog and grabbed my brother!' Bernard shrieked. Another brutal kick silenced the man. The men of Wulfhafen watched as their leader turned away from the unconscious Bernard, uncertain what to make of the situation.

'Two of you drag this thief to the meeting hall,' Veytman ordered. 'And keep him there,' he snarled as an afterthought. 'The rest of you try to find his idiot brother. I won't stand for any man trying to cheat this village of what it has earned!' The gathered men began to break away into small groups to search for the missing Claeis.

It was with great reluctance that Karel joined his father and Enghel in the search. Despite Veytman's contempt for the story Bernard had told, despite the hetman's claim that this was nothing but a plan to cheat the people of Wulfhafen, the boy was not so very sure that something had not in fact risen from the sea and taken Claeis. More than ever before, Karel understood that Wulfhafen was an evil place and that perhaps the Darkness had at last reached out to claim its own.

* * *

THE SEARCH WAS called off after only a few hours. There was no sign of Bernard's missing brother, but neither was there any trace of the sea daemon that had supposedly made off with the man. A furious Veytman had returned to the meeting hall, a murderous look in his eyes. He was quite vocal in his determination to beat the whereabouts of Claeis and the hidden plunder from Bernard and it was not too long after Veytman had entered the structure that the first screams of agony sang out across Wulfhafen.

The other men returned to their homes for the most part, although a few chose to watch the proceedings in the meeting hall. Some, no doubt, did so out of sheer sadistic urges, but Gastoen privately wondered how many did so because they harboured doubts about the honesty of their hetman and desired to be present to hear for themselves what Bernard had to say.

Gastoen and Karel returned to their home, Karel's mother already preparing a stew from one of the lobsters they had captured the day before. Karel, for his part, fell asleep awaiting the preparation of the food, slumping down in his chair. Gastoen smiled, knowing how little sleep the youth had had over the last few days, excited about his trial of manhood. Gastoen rose from his chair, prepared to rouse his boy and usher him to the greater comfort of his bed when he noticed the soggy, leather-bound book tumble to the floor from its resting place within Karel's shirt. Curious, Gastoen picked up the book and returned to his chair.

It was nearing dusk when Gastoen finished his examination of the book. He had scanned every page, trying in vain to decipher the smeared script, a task his own feeble reading skills were not equal to. The drawings were in better shape, and Gastoen gazed at them with a thrill of wonder he had not felt since he himself was a young boy. He stared at the strange pictures, likening them to a curious creature he had once seen in a Marienburg shop: a beast the shop owner had called a lizard, claiming it came from far off Araby. Gastoen could discern no scale for the animals depicted in the drawings, but he could not shake the feeling that the subjects of these pictures were massive, resembling the lizard he had seen in the same way an ogre resembled a man. It was not until he saw the strange plants that a frightful thought occurred to Gastoen. The fisherman and ship wrecker shook his son back into awareness.

'Come along, Karel,' Gastoen said, rising from his chair once again and grabbing his hat from its peg beside the door. 'We are going over to the meeting hall.'

BERNARD'S SCREAMS HAD long since stopped. As Gastoen and Karel entered the large building, its floor composed of looted deck planks, they could see their former neighbour lying hunched in one corner of the main room. The man was unconscious, his chest barely rising. One of his eyes was a darkened hole, the flesh about the burned socket blackened and charred.

'He didn't say anything,' Veytman said when he noticed Gastoen enter. Emil and a half dozen other men stood near the hetman, drinking some of the gold coloured rum. 'He stuck to that idiotic daemon tale of his.' Veytman paused and took a deep swallow from his own leather mug. 'We'll try again when he comes around.'

'I want you to see something,' Gastoen said, walking towards Veytman, the book in his hands. Gastoen opened the volume to a page he had marked and showed it to the hetman.

'Do you see this?' Gastoen asked, pointing to one of the drawings. Veytman glanced at the picture of a strange looking plant and shrugged his shoulders. A few of the other men gathered around to see what was being discussed, staring at the book from over Gastoen's shoulders.

'What am I supposed to see in that?' Veytman sighed, taking another pull from his mug.

'We found a plant just like that washed ashore,' Gastoen answered, one of the other villagers nodding his head in affirmation.

'So? Is it valuable?' Veytman remained confused. Gastoen turned the pages to where the drawings of the animals were.

'Don't you see? If they had some of the plants in this book on the ship, perhaps they also had some of the animals,' Gastoen's voice was on edge, frustrated that he was not getting through to Veytman. Before he could press the point and try to remove the look of confusion in Veytman's eyes, the door of the meeting hall again opened.

'The daemon!' wailed the grizzled, toothless face of Una, the wife of Enghel. The woman closed upon Veytman, beating on the hetman's chest and wailing hysterically. 'A sea daemon, as big as a house! It rose out of the fog and killed my husband!'

Every man in the room except Gastoen, Karel and the unconscious Bernard broke into laughter. One of the men grabbed Una and pulled her off of Veytman.

'Enghel should not have told you about that,' laughed Emil. 'You see enough monsters in your cups without him providing you with more.'

'I shall have to see if all of the rum is accounted for,' joked Veytman, draining his mug.

'I tell you, a sea daemon killed my husband!' the woman shrieked again in protest. A fresh round of laughter broke out.

'As big as a house?' mocked Emil. 'I remember the time you said there was a wolf living in your boathouse and all we found was a

marmot! This daemon of yours is probably just a big ship's rat and
Enghel is sitting in his home right now with a bitten finger!'

Una began a fresh tirade of shrieks and curses causing Veytman to
look across the room at Emil.

'Better go and have a look at it, just to shut her up,' the hetman
declared. Emil stomped across the room and gathered up a wicker
lobster trap. He marched toward the door but paused on the threshold to stab a finger at the sobbing woman.

'When I catch this damn thing, whatever it turns out to be, I am
going to make you eat it, you wailing harpy,' the man warned. With
that, he was lost to the growing shadows in the lane outside.

IT WAS ABOUT fifteen minutes later when the door of the meeting hall
opened again. The pale, drained figure that entered bore little resemblance to the jovial, half-drunk Emil they had last seen. The ship
wrecker dragged the lobster trap across the room, dropping it mid-
way. A stunned silence gripped everyone in the room, even Una, as
the apparition crossed to the elaborate weapons rack that rested
against one wall. Looted from the countless ships that had smashed
upon the reef and rocks, the armoury of Wulfhafen was a haphazard,
but impressive affair. As Emil strode to the weapons, the others in the
room could see the huge, gaping wound in the man's back, as though
the flesh had been peeled away, leaving the wet muscles to glisten
nakedly.

'We're going to need bigger traps,' he stammered before staggering
for a moment, then falling to the floor.

That life had remained in Emil for so long that he had been able to
walk as far as the meetinghouse had been a testament to the hardened
shipwrecker's brutal vitality.

'Sound the alarm!' ordered Veytman, the hetman being the first to
shake himself from his shock. The command brought a fresh wail of
terror from Una, but one of the men hurried to set the alarm bell ringing. Veytman scrambled over to the weapons rack so recently visited
by Emil and began handing some of the carefully hoarded armaments to those men in the room. Even the choice armaments, like the
heavy Bretonnian broadsword and the finely crafted battle axe that
one visitor to Wulfhafen had sworn was dwarf-made were doled out.
Now seemed to be no time to hoard the more elegant weapons.

'What good are these against a daemon?' protested a wide-eyed
fisherman as he was handed a spiked mace.

'It is no daemon!' declared Gastoen, pushing his way to the front of
the group. Already men were rushing into the meeting hall, summoned by the alarm bell. Gastoen raised his voice for the benefit of
the men who had just arrived. 'It is some strange beast from whatever

foreign shore that ship visited!' Gastoen repeated, trying to calm the superstitious dread slinking into the mob.

'Alright,' Veytman snarled. 'Everyone arm themselves, every third man get a torch, and let us see what manner of beast has chosen to die in Wulfhafen!'

THE MOB WAS strangely silent, for all of its numbers, as every able bodied man in Wulfhafen crept through the darkened lane, creeping like a band of thieves toward the all too near row of boathouses and fishing shacks. The fog hung thick about the village, clogging the streets with a misty grey shroud that the torches could pierce only partially. The men kept close to one another and even Veytman could not bring himself to enforce his earlier command that the men break up into teams of five. The sound of the surf striking the beach grew louder as the men pressed on, ignoring the fearful visages that peered at them from behind the windows of the huts they passed.

At last they reached the site where the long row of boathouses and shacks had once stood. The ramshackle structures were in a shambles, looking for all the world like victims of a hurricane. But no gale had blown upon Wulfhafen, for the fog lay thick and unmoving all about them. A strange sense of dread fell upon the armed mob. Veytman and a few of the braver villagers crept towards the nearest of the shacks, staring with horror at the gaping wounds torn into the wood, bespeaking tremendous strength and lengthy claws. In hushed tones, the men discussed the ruin, concluding that whatever had dealt such damage was no such creature as they had ever heard of. Once again, Gastoen said that it was some weird creature captured by the crew of the lost ship.

As the talk continued, more and more men stalked forward, deciding that if Veytman and the others could linger for so long amidst the devastation, then it must be relatively safe. The men spread out, slightly, examining the destroyed boathouse next to the shack. One of the men at once came running back, his hand smeared red with blood.

'It must be from Enghel or Emil,' Gastoen gasped. He rallied several men to his side and ran towards the boathouse. Veytman was quick to follow the older man's lead, bringing the bulk of the mob with him.

A ghastly sight greeted Gastoen's group as they rounded the corner of the partially collapsed boathouse. Looming out of the fog, only a few feet away, was an immense shape of scaly grey and black flesh. The man to Gastoen's right let out a cry of horror as he saw the massive scaly back and tail revealed in the flickering torchlight. The creature turned around slowly, facing the crowd just as Veytman and his followers rounded the corner.

It was huge, easily twice the size of a man. Because it had been hunched the beast's head not been visible over the boathouse, Now it rose to its full height, towering over the structure. Indeed, Una had not exaggerated when she said the monster was as big as a house. In shape it was roughly like a man, though only roughly. Its entire body was covered in grey scales, which faded to white as they came to its belly. Stripes of black, thicker scales criss-crossed its back and shoulders. The head was also scaled, a brutish snout protruding from a thick skull. Dangling from the monster's powerful jaws was the body of Enghel, his head completely within the creature's mouth. Yellow, snake-like eyes gazed indifferently at the mob while thick, muscular arms swayed indolently from the monster's broad shoulders. The reptilian horror worked its lower jaw and the skull of Enghel cracked like a walnut, the loud snap echoing into the night.

THE SIGHT OF the fiend so casually feeding on one of their own snapped some of the men out of their horrified daze. One bold fisherman lunged at the monster with a boat hook, the makeshift polearm sinking into the thick flesh of the monster's shoulder. Another lashed at the creature with a broadsword taken from the armoury, cringing back in fright as the weapon impacted harmlessly against the thick scaly flesh of the brute's leg.

The monster was slow to react. At first it just stared stupidly into the night. Then its lower jaw opened, letting Enghel's body drop to the ground. A thin, purple tongue whipped out of the scaly mouth, flickering in the air for a moment before withdrawing. Then, the seemingly lethargic beast became a blur of carnage.

A huge clawed hand dropped down upon the man who had so ineffectually struck at the creature's leg, the blow crushing the man's collar bone and battering him into a heap of broken bones, a twisted pile of meat recognisable as human only by the screams it still cried. The brute spun about, his powerful tail slamming into the villager with the boathook, knocking him some fifty feet away. The man landed in a crumpled pile on the beach, his head lying at an unnatural angle on its snapped neck. The beast paused, focusing its beady eyes upon the main body of Wulfhafen's defenders. It opened its jaws and from deep within its massive form came a grunt-like bellow that had several men dropping their weapons to shield their ears from the sound.

Before the mob could react, the monster was in their midst, lashing out with its powerful claws and snapping jaws. Swords and axes struck again and again at the brutish reptilian abomination, more often than not failing to sink into the tough leathery hide. The few wounds that did draw blood from the beast seemed to go unnoticed, as the monster continued to deal death and mutilation to his would-be killers. In that same amount of time, the monster had killed or maimed over a dozen men, their dead or broken bodies lying strewn across the beach.

Veytman swiped at the huge beast with his elegant blade. The finest sword in the entire village impacted against the scaly flesh, sinking deep into the reptile's thigh. The brute turned, swiping at Veytman. The hetman dodged the crude attack, but the combination of his manoeuvre and the monster's assault snapped the steel blade. Veytman stared in horror at the broken sword, and the three inches of steel sticking out from the beast's leg, the creature seemingly oblivious to the injury.

It did not take long for the struggle to become a rout. Nor did it seem that the monster was content to allow its attackers to escape. Bellowing its awful roar once again, the huge scaly giant lumbered after the fleeing men, pursuing them into the village. Despite its bulk, the beast was unbelievably fast. Only the fact that it caught some of the slowest early on and stopped to reduce them to mangled piles of meat gave any of the villagers a chance to reach the supposed safety of Wulfhafen's buildings. The feeble structures did nothing to stop the reptile's rampage, however. As the grotesque creature entered the narrow lane, it turned to face the first of the mud and wood huts. The beast's tongue flickered from its mouth, tasting the air, sensing the people cowering inside. The beast bellowed again, battering the wall of the hut with its immense bulk. Two hits were enough to collapse the wall and bring the thatch roof crashing down upon the inmates of the building. The monster paused for a moment, staring stupidly at the destruction it had caused. Then its eyes detected the squirming forms struggling to emerge from the ruins. The beast descended upon the rubble and screams again filled the night.

Gastoen and Karel remained with Veytman throughout the terrified retreat, following their hetman into the more solidly constructed common house. The woman Una gave a cry of alarm as the enraged men entered the meeting hall. A withering glare from Veytman silenced the half-soused biddy.

'It is a daemon!' sobbed Gastoen. 'It has come to punish us for our evil ways!' Veytman ignored the incoherent ramblings and made his way to the stack of tiny kegs piled beside the now empty weapons rack. The hetman lifted one of the kegs removing its stopper. Normally employed to light the evil beacon fires, Veytman now had a very different purpose in mind for Wulfhafen's supply of lantern oil.

'Beast or daemon, I am going to send that thing back to hell!' Veytman growled.

'You cannot kill it! It has been sent by Manann to punish this town for preying upon the sea! No one can defy the judgement of the gods!' Gastoen broke into a trill of mad cackling, his mind crumbling under the years of guilt that now fuelled his terror.

'Karel,' Veytman snapped, ignoring the boy's mad father. 'Help me with this! Grab that torch and follow me! Tonight we will see what kind of man you are!'

Karel withdrew his arms from his father's shoulders and raced to remove the torch the hetman had indicated from its wall sconce. The two men hurried toward the door, determined to put an end to the sounds of death and destruction rising from the street outside, vowing to find the monster preying upon their village and destroy it.

They did not need to find the beast, however. The beast found them.

The front door of the meeting house burst inwards, as if a fully laden wagon had crashed into it. Splintered wood flew in all directions, the shrapnel opening a gash in Karel's cheek. The great grey and black hulk lowered its head and slithered through the gaping hole in the wall. Once inside, the hissing beast rose to its full height, seemingly oblivious to the dozens of wounds bleeding all over its body. The head of the dwarf axe was buried deep in the creature's back, and still it showed no sign of injury. The monstrous brute let its head oscillate from side to side, surveying the room with its reptilian eyes, tasting the air with its slender purple tongue. Then the mighty beast roared, the tremendous sound deafening within the close confines of the room.

The effect was immediate. Una shrieked again, scrambling for the rear door of the meeting hall, disappearing through the portal with a speed and agility that should have been impossible for a woman of her age and health. Roused from his pain-filled slumber, Bernard focused his remaining eye upon the hideous reptile. At once, the man was crawling across the floor, hurrying after the departed Una. The creature made to pursue the fleeing wretch, but a much closer victim gave the enraged brute pause.

Karel could not hear what his father was saying, his ears still ringing with the monster's mighty roar. Gastoen had run forward as the beast broke into the meeting hall and had fallen to his knees before the hulking brute. To Karel, it appeared that the man was actually praying to the huge reptile, a look of insane rapture on Gastoen's wizened face. The creature looked down at the figure bowed down before its knees. The great brute brought one of its enormous clawed fists crashing down into Gastoen's head, the force of the blow making the man's skull and neck sink between his shoulders. Barely ten feet away, Karel watched as his father expired, as his world was rent asunder. The man he had loved, respected and admired was no more. The man he had looked up to all his life had been taken from him in one instant of madness and carnage.

Karel gave voice to an almost inhuman cry of rage and loss and charged the huge beast, the knife his mother had pressed upon him gripped firmly in his hand. The knife impacted harmlessly against the reptile's leg. With an almost dismissive gesture, the hulking brute swatted Karel with the back of its hand, sending the boy flying across the hall. He landed against the far wall, the wind knocked from his lungs. The boy dropped to the floor, groaning the mixture of anguish and agony that wracked his form.

Veytman yelled in fury and ran at the huge monster. The hetman hurled the keg of oil at the beast with his left hand. The object flew lethargically across the room, missing its intended target and breaking apart against the wall behind the creature. The failure of the missile to strike its target did nothing to stop Veytman's attack. The man lashed out at the huge beast with the torch he held, thrusting the flame upward into the monster's face.

The creature hissed angrily, flinching away from the flame. Veytman cackled triumphantly, pressing his attack. But he grew too bold, too certain of the beast's fear. The reptile bellowed again and lashed out with a massive clawed hand. The claws tore through Veytman's stomach, ripping his intestines from his body. A river of blood fountained out of Veytman's butchered flesh, sickly yellow stomach matter staining the crimson cataract. Veytman fell to his knees, blood filling his mouth. The last sight his dying eyes focused upon was that of his own innards dangling from the creature's claws.

As Veytman died, the torch fell from his nerveless fingers, rolling across the floor to meet the spilt oil. Even as the lizardman stomped toward Karel, the flammable liquid caught fire, turning the entire wall into a fiery blaze. The monster turned away from the youth, staring with fear at the blaze behind it, croaking its own terror.

Karel had only moments to act, seconds to overcome the fear gripping his frame, the pain wracking his body. It was a moment to transform a boy into a man. Karel turned towards the rest of the supply of Wulfhafen's oil, smashing the stoppers from the kegs with the end of the knife still clutched in his hand, pitching the ruptured contents to the ground. The incendiary liquid splashed across the floor, rushing to meet the flames on the other side of the room. The creature turned, perhaps sensing what the boy had done, or perhaps merely looking for another way to leave the building. Whatever its purpose, Karel did not wait to find out. Hurling the torch at the pool of oil gathered about the reptile's feet, the young man leapt through the rear door of the common house.

The oil ignited at once, transforming the meeting hall into an inferno. The monster tried to flee from the flames all around it, its primitive brain taking long minutes to realise that its own flesh was on fire. The lizardman's bellows of agony rose from the blaze as the fire seared its scaly flesh.

Outside, the survivors of Wulfhafen emerged from the shelter of their homes; gathering about their burning common house, watching the consuming flames lick into the night sky. The huge beast trapped inside was a long time in dying, its anguished cries ringing into the night for nearly a quarter of an hour. The crowd remained through it all, silent and stunned. There was no sense of triumph in the people of Wulfhafen as the flames consumed the horror that had descended upon their tiny village. Survivors they may be; victors they were not.

KAREL GATHERED THE last of his possessions together and kissed his mother one final time. The morning sun had barely peaked above the horizon; the first birds were only just emerging from their nocturnal sanctuaries. Karel shouldered his pack and made to leave the only home he had ever known. He could almost see Gastoen again, sitting at the table, his weathered, cracked hands resting in a cool bowl of fresh water, trying to soothe the pain from his tortuous labours on the sea. He could almost see his father making ready to join the ship wreckers, with all the guilt and shame that had shrouded the evil things he had done to support those he loved. Karel could now understand the strange and frightened looks his father had sometimes favoured him with. It had been the closest Gastoen had ever come to voicing his truest fear, the fear that his son would become himself one day, that the dark practice of Wulfhafen would live on through his own blood.

'Where will you go?' his mother demanded, trying to fight back her tears. Karel paused and caressed her tired, worn hand.

'I am going to go down to Marienburg,' Karel declared, looking away from his mother for fear that tears would well up in his own eyes. 'I shall go to the temple of the sea god, see if the priesthood of Manann will have me for one of their own. See if they will allow me to atone for the crimes of my fathers, and my home.'

Karel kissed her again, and stepped out into the narrow lane that wended its way through what was left of Wulfhafen.

Perhaps the village would fade away now. Perhaps it would somehow rebuild and endure. Perhaps it would even return to its evil ways. For Karel, it did not matter. He had found the answer to the questions he had asked his father. The beast had not been a daemon, but could it truly be said that it had not been sent by the gods? Had the terrible doom that visited the village not been brought about by their own avarice and greed? Karel could not lead any of his family or neighbours to atone for their misdeeds, for each man was steward of his own soul.

So, the last son of Wulfhafen strode away into the morning light, taking the first steps on the long road of his penance.

HATRED

Ben Chessell

*I am hatred. I am revulsion. If you know me
and do not hate me, you are evil. I have enough hate for myself.*

THE GIBBET IN Kurtbad was unoccupied. Swinging in the gentle breeze, the empty loop of rope regarded the village like a macabre eye. The people of Kurtbad slept, though they had gone to bed afraid. The two guards posted outside the barn which served as meeting hall slumped against the wooden door, blankets wrapped around them like shrouds. Their pitchforks lay discarded on the black Averland soil. If the humble wind which shook the noose had been so bold as to sniff the breath of these men, it would have smelt wine, much wine.

The midnight watch in the midst of an Averland witch hunt was not a duty to face unfortified. The small stocks of wine, kept in Kurtbad for Taal's Day of Spring-return, had been cracked open and distributed to all the villagers. When that day came, and it would be soon, everyone but the children would understand.

Now all that mattered was that a man had been killed.

GUNTER PULLED HIS woollen cloak tighter about his shoulders and made enough noise to wake the form in the bed he had recently left – but got no response. The thin moonlight didn't help Gunter see whether she really was asleep. He buckled on his sword, his since his father had died on a frosty night early in the winter, and drew back the bolt on the door of the house which had come to him the same way. Ice on the stone step cracked under his militiaman's boots and the breeze blew away the last cobwebs of sleep. Gunter found much solace in his duty, the sole permanent militiaman in the village of Kurtbad, responsible for more than a hundred men, women and children. He straightened his back and headed for the barn to see how his new recruits were doing.

Anja waited for the door to close behind him before sitting up and lighting the candle from the last coals which winked like dying stars in the ashen sky of the hearth. She returned to bed via the door, where she drew the bolt again. Gunter's side of the bed was warm but cooling quickly. She crawled back to the corner where she had curled like a cat on the night when Gunter fetched her from her family, telling her mother that she would be safer with him. It was probably even true. How could her mother, older now than most women in the village, tell the militiaman, tall as a bear, he could not take her only daughter. It was for Anja's protection, after all.

Anja and Gunter were not married, and had he not been arguably the most important man in Kurtbad, action would have been taken. As it was, many people in the village muttered after she passed by and looked at her as if to see some sign of her sin worn openly on her garments.

Anja curled up and thought about these things, looking at the candle flame and how the beeswax melted and ran down the stem like tears. The candle cried itself to death.

OUTSIDE THE VILLAGE, on the road to Nuln, the night was shredded by a startled cry and a flash of blades. A man leapt from the back of a horse and stumbled in the mud at the side of the road. Another man rolled on the ground, the winter leaves sticking to his face, his wrist in his mouth. The struggle was as bloody and quick as a dogfight. When it was over, the inadequate moon lit only naked skin and cooling blood.

The victor of the battle rode through the forest toward Kurtbad, searching for something.

OTTO THE BUTCHER slept well that night, despite a nagging feeling of guilt. He was used to that.

KURTBAD NESTLED ON the edge of the Reiksbanks Forest in central Averland, four days' ride from Nuln. It sat beside an old trading route which led from that great city of commerce and industry to a dwarf outpost at Hammergrim Pass in the Black Mountains. There, for centuries, the dwarfs had sucked lead and iron from the guts of the fat mountains. The ore was loaded onto oxen carts and passed through Kurtbad on its way to the markets at Nuln, and thence by river to whatever Empire foundry was prepared to pay the best price: gold for steel. Kurtbad had seen some business in those days.

The greed of the dwarfs eventually exceeded their skill and the bounty of the Black Mountains and the ore dried up like a staunched wound. Hammergrim Pass was abandoned and the dwarfs returned to fight the Goblin Wars or whatever dwarfs do. Kurtbad became a ghost town overnight. The inn was closed and its keeper, who was a business-man, left for Nuln with a girl from Kurtbad he had married. She later returned to the village with a young child, no money and a brand on her arm. The inn was knocked down. Perhaps it was anger or perhaps the people of Kurtbad needed the wood for their sheep pens, living in wolf country as they did.

Nevertheless, in the space of a generation, the village had purged itself of the influence of the dwarfs and merchants, and grass had grown on the road to Hammergrim Pass.

Into this small village, a single black stitch on the great embroidered map which hangs in the commerce hall of the Merchant's Guild in the city of Nuln, came a black horse with hooves of silver. On its back was a tall man clad in dark cloth. He wore a hat the colour of coal, with a plume which must have been dyed because no one knew of any bird with feathers like that. He wore a sword and a knife, in the manner of a gentleman, and his boots were of soft leather, also stained the colour of moonless night. His arms were scarred and scratched, from old battles and new, and he grasped the reins with his left hand as if the right was unequal to the task.

He sat on his horse for some time, surveying the village and its people as they stirred in the dawn grey. He sat there long enough for Wilhelm, chastened for being asleep on duty at the barn, to ring the huge bronze bell. This bell was the last remnant of the dwarf mining days, except for the occasional brightly painted rail which kept the sheep in. It had originally been used to warn the wagons as they left the mountain trail that the road was too muddy for reliable passage and they should wait for a drier day. Now the bell, which bore the crossed hammer and axe stamp of the miners, was struck with a mallet to summon the villagers to the common, the steam mechanism long since decayed.

I am a snake. I am a worm. There is poison in my blood.
I can never die a peaceful death. I am burning now as I will burn then.

* * *

GUNTER HEARD THE bell as he stared for the fifth time at the place where Gregor's body had been found. There were signs to read here, he knew that, answers written in the ground as clear as any illuminated manuscript.

Just as he couldn't read the scratchings in ink which adorned the pages of his father's books, so he couldn't comprehend the signs in the mud which had hardened and cracked since Gregor's violent death two days ago. He had found the pieces of clay from the shattered bottle, but they only served to confuse things further. The only marks he could read reliably were his own deep boot prints, four sets.

He turned away and straightened himself as he made his way to face whatever disaster had befallen Kurtbad now.

ANJA LOOKED OUT between the curtains of Gunter's cottage. The man sat silently on his horse like a sculpture cast in black leather. She thought he didn't look well. He had the balance of a drunkard, and as she watched he shut his eyes and swayed like a young tree in a breeze. Anja pulled on the shoes which Gunter had bought for her on one of his trips to Nuln and unbolted the door.

She was the first of the villagers to approach the man and she straightened her hair as she walked carefully towards him. He made no sign of having seen her, so she moved around to the front of his horse. The big brown eyes of the stallion regarded her critically but the man's head remained slumped. There was a stain of dried blood, Anja knew it by its colour, on the man's right wrist, above his black leather glove. Anja could see he was alive; his chest rose and fell slowly.

She summoned up the courage to address him without considering that she didn't know how one should properly address a witch hunter.

GUNTER DREW BREATH and held the air in until all the goodness had been taken from it. A witch hunter. Just what we don't need.

He sized the man up. Anja had helped the man from his horse, which was now grazing contentedly on the lush grass of the Kurtbad common, before Gunter had banished her inside. Foolish girl. These witch hunters had no purpose but the discovery and destruction of Chaos, he knew that, and although there was a dangerous killer on the loose, perhaps even a monster of some kind, the man in black might be just as dangerous. Didn't she know that? Of course she did.

Even now she watched proceedings from the window and heated water on the stove for the man. Anything to make contact with the world outside Kurtbad, that was what Anja wanted. Why can she not be content with me? Gunter knew that it was likely only his training and foreign postings with the Empire army had brought Anja to his home in the first place, and that was a fragile bargain he was determined to protect.

He turned his attention to the witch hunter. The man sat slumped against the wall of his house like a wilted flower, except that he knew no blooms that were the colour of Death. Gunter addressed him formally, welcoming him to Kurtbad and asking his business.

When the man spoke it was in a voice which sounded like it was squeezed through a throat too small to let the words pass, and he shut his eyes in pain. His name was Dagmar, he was indeed a witch hunter, and he knew about the troubles in Kurtbad. Gunter had no choice but to offer him the hospitality of his cottage.

DAGMAR LAY IN the strange bed and contemplated the rafters. They were oaken and old. Like strong ribs which held the thatched skin of the roof from collapsing, they met at a huge beam, a great rounded trunk which still bore bark in some places. A crossbow hung from one end of it, he noticed, well oiled and maintained. The other held cooking pots and bundles of roots and spices.

Dagmar shifted in the bed and turned his head to watch the girl who stirred the pot. A whip-crack of pain shot through his ribs when he turned his body to the side, so he contented himself with the briefest of glances and returned to looking at the thatching. Grey sunlight filtered between the straw; it lay across him like gashes.

He had allowed the girl to remove his boots but otherwise he was clad as he had been when he arrived, in ill-fitting witch hunter's clothes. The fight in the forest last night had almost been his last and only the overconfidence of his opponent had saved him. Dagmar waited patiently for the girl to return with the stew she was making and wondered if his luck might be changing.

Anja had to feed the man as he couldn't easily sit up. Gunter had not told her his name, saying that he thought it was better if she didn't know such things. He had gone now, to attend to the horse or get wood or something.

She fed the man patiently, noting that he was most polite. He told her his name in an attempt to learn hers. She learnt that he was called Dagmar and freely named herself. What was the danger in that? From what she knew of witch hunters, they were good folk who hunted monsters throughout the Empire. She had never seen one but Gunter had occasionally mentioned them in one of his many travel stories. If he had come here to catch Gregor's murderer then wasn't that a good thing?

She looked at the man's mud-spattered and blood-stained clothes. Normally she would have undressed him and washed his clothes for him. He was clearly wounded beneath the expensive garb. Gunter had not protested when the man had climbed into his bed fully clothed but Anja had seen his face. She did not want to anger him further. Not now.

*I am evil and it is consuming me. There is no place in me but hate.
There is no place in me but disease. Do not touch me.*

GUNTER CUT WOOD as if each log was the head of an enemy. He saw many faces beneath the wedge as he drove it deeply into the chopping block – goblins, Bretonnians, men who he had slain or almost slain. Most of all, he saw what he imagined was the face of the monster who must have killed Gregor: scaled, with tusks and fangs. The creature's head split with a satisfying snap but there was nothing inside. He lifted his axe for the coup de grace but the face he saw became that of his guest and he held the stroke.

Angry with himself for unworthy and inhospitable thoughts, Gunter reasoned, as he gathered the wood, that the witch hunter had done nothing to earn his enmity. Perhaps he could bring resources to bear on the problem that would enable them to catch the killer. He determined to consult with this Dagmar, after they had all eaten, and returned to the house in a better mood.

What he saw as he came through the low door destroyed his good nature as surely as if a daemon-wizard had banished it to another realm.

ANJA MOPPED DAGMAR'S brow with one of Gunter's kerchiefs and sat by him as he dozed. When Gunter returned with the wood she was cleaning the cut on the man's right arm. The wound was not very deep but had bled a great deal and had ragged edges like a newly ploughed track. She tried to take off his leather glove but he clenched his fist; the pain was obviously too great.

She bathed his arm and wrist but did not ask to take off the glove again. There was clearly something wrong with the arm, which had a bulge in it where hers did not. He had talked of a fight in the forest. Perhaps he had broken a bone then. When Gunter suggested she should return to her mother while the stranger stayed in his house, she shrugged him off. Gunter might be a great soldier but he had no idea how to look after a sick man. When he tried to order her, she responded by reminding him that they had taken no vows and that she only need take orders from her mother until such a time as they did.

Things became more heated and Anja was forced to stop stitching her sling and stand up to face him.

Dagmar got out of bed at this point and made excuses about needing to perform his ablutions.

Anja's pointed comment about the stranger's good manners did nothing to pacify Gunter.

WHEN HE RETURNED, she had gone and Gunter sat by the soup pot. Dagmar could not be sure whether the man or the fire glowed more hotly.

The two men found they could talk easily enough and Dagmar imagined that he might have more in common with this lonely man than he thought.

For his own part, Gunter was surprised to find himself trusting the engaging witch hunter, and rethinking what he knew about their kind. This man, Dagmar, although very knowledgeable about mutant creatures of Chaos, was unlike any witch hunter he had ever heard of.

Dagmar talked with Gunter for several hours, making various suggestions for the defence of the village. He suggested, and this is just one example of his useful ideas, that some mutants have thick, strong necks, and might survive a hanging. Dagmar proposed the building of a pyre, with a stake set into it, so that the criminal, when captured, could be burned.

He also said that the mutant was quite possibly living in the village and promised to hunt the man down. Dagmar asked many keen questions about the habits of the villagers of Kurtbad, and Gunter told him who was reliable and who perhaps was not. Then Gunter took a deep breath and told Dagmar his suspicions.

I am unclean. How can you not smell it on my breath? The rot of my body, the decay of my heart. We are so much the same, and so different.

OTTO FLEISCHER WAS a very fat man. He was not a nice man. If the villagers knew everything there was to know about Otto, instead of just suspecting it, they would never have let him be their butcher, let alone their undertaker. When Otto had buried Gregor he had made no secret that he would not grieve for the man.

ANJA THOUGHT THAT the cottage looked like Gunter had been carousing all night with one of his mercenary friends who occasionally came to Kurtbad, most likely to hide from the law, and not like the place where a sick man had been quartered. There were two empty clay bottles next to the fire and Gunter was snoring loudly. He had obviously slept on the hearthstone and his face was covered with a thin layer of ash which lifted in tiny clouds with each snore. The veins on his cheeks were red like a fox and his moustache curled upward on one side.

Anja looked at this man, her lover, as a farmer might appraise a new-born lamb, and turned as if to compare his visage with Dagmar's. The bed was empty.

Anja put the steaming breakfast she had brought onto the scarred table and walked outside.

DAGMAR EASED THE glove off his right hand and washed both in the stream. The small stream ran down from the Black Mountains beside the road from Hammergrim Pass and beneath the stone bridge at the north of the village. The small graveyard for the people of Kurtbad lay on the top of the opposite bank. The water was like knives of ice but the hand was mostly numb anyway. He stared at it in disgust.

He unbuckled his belt and took off his boots. The touch of the water on his feet was agony but he forced himself to stand, unsteady on the slippery rocks beneath the shallow flow. He watched the dirt and blood billow and mingle with the water, quickly lost in the enthusiastic stream. He imagined a purifying experience.

He heard the girl approaching just in time to get the glove back onto his hand.

OTTO SCUTTLED FROM behind Gregor's gravestone and picked up his sack. He knew what he had seen. He took the long way back to the village.

GUNTER PINCHED THE skin above his eyes, his hand clasping together at the bridge of his sharp nose. He shook the ash from his clothes and, wiping his eyes again, looked around the cottage. Breakfast. No Anja. No Dagmar. He took a knife from the roof beam and began to eat the spiced tomatoes. He tried to remember the conversation of the previous evening. Had he gone so far as to mention Otto's name? That was unworthy.

Gunter had long disliked the butcher and declined to eat his meat, preferring to kill and smoke his own, but he had no evidence that the man was a murderer. What had possessed him to tell a witch hunter? Dagmar had been talking about mutations caused by exposure to Chaos he had had experience with and had mentioned that such a man might become extremely fat but otherwise remain normal. That did fit Otto's description.

Gunter had to admit that the Tilean wine was mostly to blame for the liberties he had taken. It was not fair to his guest, who seemed to be a decent man, to burden him with wild suspicions.

Gunter lurched to his feet like a becalmed ship which suddenly finds the wind, and went off in search of Dagmar.

* * *

ANJA SAT ON a dry rock in the stream and listened intently to Dagmar's story. The man was charming, there was no doubt of that, and appeared to be well recovered, almost impossibly so, from his illness of the previous day. There was colour in his cheeks and his beard seemed to have grown overnight.

Dagmar was standing solemnly on the bank of the stream in mock concentration as he related an apocryphal tale about an acolyte of the Temple of Verena in Nuln. The story was convoluted but Dagmar told it faithfully and well, keeping his face serious until the punch-line, which made them both laugh.

Dagmar bent double, exaggerating his laughter and slipped on the muddy bank. He fell heavily on his right arm and his face screwed up in pain. Anja pounced across onto the bank and helped him to sit. Her face was a flag of concern. A great deal of blood stained the sling she had made and she could see bone sticking through the skin below the elbow. He held her away with his good arm, which was surprisingly strong, like a man shielding himself from the sun.

Eventually she calmed him down and they both sat together on the bank. When she went to put her head on his good shoulder, he let her.

GUNTER STOOD ON the bridge and gouged the moss of the low stone rail with his knuckles. He felt the water flow beneath his feet and felt the blood flow through his body. He made himself breathe the air as he watched them. Gunter remembered how he felt when he saw Anja dance with other men on Taal's Day. He stood there for some time.

When he finally managed to uproot himself from the bridge and make his way down through the trees to the stream he walked noisily, so they might hear him and untwine by the time he reached them. Gunter completely forgot his purpose in seeking Dagmar.

Anja met him as he emerged from the trees, smoothing her dress and pulling leaves from her hair. She matched his gaze and her eyes danced.

Dagmar stared into the stream and cradled his right arm like a babe. Gunter could have sworn he was talking to it.

When Anja had gone, the two men looked at each other for a moment, the kind of moment which might be the prelude to anything. As it was, Gunter suggested that they go together to examine the tracks at the place where Gregor was killed.

OTTO KNOCKED ON the door again. He was sure someone was in there. This was the one time he had ever been desperate enough to call on the help of the militiaman. He was dismayed when the door was opened not by Gunter, but by his harlot.

* * *

DAGMAR STOOD BEHIND Gunter as he crouched over the tracks, pointing at various features which he had indicated with muddy sticks in the turf. They stood like a blighted forest, marking the last steps taken by the man called Gregor.

Gunter was trying to understand how Gregor could have been ambushed by the mutant in such an open area as, apparently, he was always a careful man.

Gunter did not suggest that Gregor might have been very drunk on that night. Perhaps the bottle he had found did not fit the fiction of the man's death which Gunter was trying to write in muddy characters on the killing ground.

Dagmar suggested that perhaps Gregor had been the attacker and the mutant had merely tried to defend himself. Gunter was vehemently opposed to the suggestion.

Dagmar explained to Gunter his own version of the tracks. He moved some of Gunter's markers with his good arm, showing exactly where the mutant had been surprised, where Gregor had picked up a stick, and where the broken halves of the stick now lay, stained with the mutant's blood. He finished by showing where the mutant had finally fought back and where the body had fallen.

Gunter concluded that Gregor must have been drunk to be so foolhardy.

I am trying to tell you. I am amongst you. I am Chaos. Destroy me.

ANJA SAT ON Gunter's bed and stared into the fire. She had heard what the butcher had had to say, heard his testimony about the scaled hand of the witch hunter. She had asked him what business he had had in the graveyard but Otto had pressed his case. The man, apparently, had red-green scales on his right hand below the wrist – a sure mark of Chaos. The fat butcher had pointed out how badly the man's clothes fitted him, how he was clearly not a natural rider of that perfect stallion.

Anja had listened to all of this and she saw that it might be true. She promised Otto she would fetch Gunter, and told him to retire to his cottage and wait for them. Then she sat in the dark and tried to recall the taste of the man's breath, as it had been on the bank of the stream.

She tried to remember the taste of decay, of corruption, but she could remember nothing but the sound of the stream and the look in his eyes.

GUNTER CAME SLOWLY back to the house as the burning galleon of the sun sank behind the Grey Mountains. He thought about what Dagmar had said, how he had shown him a different way of looking at the signs in the mud. How he had forced him to see the truth which had all the time been set before his eyes.

More than ever, Gunter felt he was in a great library, like the one he had seen in Middenheim, where all the knowledge of the world was kept and yet he could not read a word of it. He walked past the waiting pyre and smelt the oil. A small group of Kurtbad residents stood about it, like birds of prey who anticipate a kill. Gunter felt it too and began to trot back to his cottage.

Anja was waiting at the open door for him, a sight which grasped his heart. She brought him inside and after looking to see that he was alone, she closed the door. She told him: *I have found the killer.*

DAGMAR STOOD ON the slope above the village in the struggling light. He looked at the cottages and their hearth-fires which sent up vines of smoke from holes in the thatch. He imagined the meals being prepared. There would perhaps be children, certainly animals, underfoot. There would be both happiness and unhappiness in those cottages. He hated them, every one.

I am hatred.

Except her. He thought of her by the stream. Reflected sunlight splashing her face, cooling her eyes. He thought of the way their faces had touched.

How can you not smell it on my breath?

He shattered the picture with the mallet of his hatred.

How dare she?

Do not touch me.

Doesn't she know what she's done to me?

He pulled off his right glove and shook his arm free of the sling. As he flexed it he felt blood course through it and the cuts at his wrist opened again and bled freely.

There is poison in my blood.

How dare she? I am a killer.

I am Chaos.

I will show her.

He drew the witch hunter's sword from the witch hunter's belt and strode down the hill.

I have changed my mind. I will not die. I will live as I am and I am as I will.

GUNTER SURVEYED THE assembled crowd. Fifteen or so men and boys had gathered in the gloom. Each carried a weapon of some kind, many carried torches which they lit from the coals of Gunter's fire.

Anja sat on the bed and said nothing.

Gunter gave his last instructions and the group moved out. Gunter led them. He was the only man with military training and although they felt they knew their quarry, who could tell what strength the curse of Chaos could lend to a man? They were not scared – there were too many of them for that – but there was a thrill which ran through them as they moved closer. They spoke of revenge and justice, though not one was thinking of Gregor.

Gunter gripped his sword and strained his eyes in the dark. He thanked Sigmar that Anja was safe, having come so close to danger. Images of the library returned to him but Gunter no longer needed to read.

ANJA HEARD HIM coming. He was walking loudly and didn't seem to know anything about the mob. She stood behind the door and cancelled her breath while he tried the handle.

Dagmar staggered into the room and she saw that his left hand held a sword. His right hand hung at his side, the fingers moving, almost as if he was not aware of it. It looked as if the first two and second two fingers were in the process of fusing and they did not move independently. Perhaps that was why he no longer wore the glove.

'Dagmar?'

He turned on her like a cornered boar and she saw his face contorted by pain and rage. She brought the iron firestick down on his left hand and the sword bounced off the flagstones.

He moaned, *No*, growled in pain and sank to the floor. He looked at her. Tears of black blood streamed from his eyes.

GUNTER GAVE THE signal and the mob moved forward. They had trapped the murderer in the house and all that remained was to apprehend him. As far as they knew, he was alone. Hardly surprising. By all accounts, Chaos carried a stench that was enough to make a soldier cry.

Gunter steadied himself and kicked the door with his mercenary's boot. It gave way easily and he almost fell into the room. The sole inhabitant of the cottage leapt up in shock, banging his head on one of the butcher's tools which hung from the central beam. The mob piled in behind Gunter, pressing him forward.

Otto cowered away from them, but some spark of unworthy courage flared and he grabbed a cleaver. He wore no shirt and Gunter stared in disgust at the rolls of fat which hung over his linen breeches. The skin was pasty and white and the whole cottage smelt of dead flesh. Gunter disarmed the man with a chopping stroke to his right wrist. The mob grabbed him and silenced his protests.

ANJA MET THEM at the pyre. She held fresh torches in her hands. She watched without flinching as the unconscious Otto was lashed to the stake. It had been easy enough to convince Gunter. He had seen Otto many times with the blood of pigs on his hands. Such a man could kill. There was little distance between the butcher of Kurtbad and the Butcher of Kurtbad.

Otto was a hateful man and Anja told herself that the village would be better off without him.

Gunter was calling for the matter to be settled and judgement to be passed. The eyes of the crowd, hungry and violent, turned to where she stood, supporting Dagmar with her shoulder. His right arm was back in its sling and the hand was tightly bound with linen bandage.

She nudged him forward. Dagmar stepped into the torchlight. He smelled the oil. He looked at the circle of people, death in their faces. He turned to look at the fat butcher tied to the stake like a grub about to be roasted. He thought of the dead, drunk man, buried by the butcher in the graveyard. He thought of the witch hunter, stiffening beneath a pile of forest leaves. He thought of the militiaman, who surely knew and wondered why he stood there amongst the ignorant, blood-driven rabble.

He thought mostly of Anja, of what she had said to him, of how she had looked at him, of what she must have seen when she did, and of how she had again brought him back to himself. He tried to imagine what might happen after this night was over. Someone was forcing a torch into his left hand.

He spread his damaged fingers apart and held the wood as if in a claw, between thumb and forefinger. He hesitated. He asked the crowd: *Why should this man die?*

The crowd told him: *He is Chaos. Destroy him.*

Dagmar's right arm twitched and stretched against the fabric of the sling. Anja touched him gently with her fingers, a reassuring squeeze. The sling tore and scales backhanded her away.

Dagmar leapt onto the pile of oil-slicked logs. He looked at the men and women with their torches and their murderous fear.

We are so much the same, and so different.

The butcher tried to lift his head. Dagmar thrust the torch into the logs and a forest of flames sprang up. Otto screamed and Dagmar howled. He embraced the fat man and locked his claw hands around the back of the stake.

The people of Kurtbad drew back from the thick, fetid smoke and the stench of decay. All except Anja, who stood in the glow of the flames and wept gently, her tears mingling with blood from a cut on her cheek.

Gunter dragged her away, put himself between her and the flames.

Dagmar's body melted like a candle as if the blaze inside him was hotter than the fire of oil and sticks. It took longer for the butcher to die.

I am burning now as I will burn then.

* * *

THOUGH KURTBAD REMAINED a single stitch on the merchant's map it was never the same town. Some believed that they could always smell the stench of the mutant on the common. Chaos had touched them, they said, and that was the reason the crops were poor. The lonely gibbet was demolished and the wood used to make a new sheep pen.

Gunter tried to resign his post but he was forced to stay by the people who said that now they truly understood the gravity of the threat. He tried to learn to read. Anja left the town on the black stallion with the silver hooves, which she was said to have sold for a fair price in the market at Nuln. She never returned to Kurtbad, either with a child or a brand on her arm.

SON AND HEIR

Ian Winterton

'BY THE GRACE of the Lady!' The Grail Knight's voice echoed throughout the forest clearing. The heads of the four beastmen at the entrance to the shrine turned to look at him, claws reaching for weapons. Drawing his own blade, Sir Gilles Ettringer, Knight of the Grail and champion of Baron Gregory de Chambourt, spurred his steed towards the hated abominations.

How dare they tread upon this holy place?

Though righteous anger burned in his heart, he did not let it consume nor cloud his mind, for he was a loyal servant of the Lady of the Lake. Nourished by the water of the holy chalice, his soul was as strong and sure as the steel in his mailed hand. These defilers would pay dearly for their trespass.

The first was dispatched before it even had chance to bring its sword to bear. The second's head, that of a half-starved dog, flew from its shoulders, crashing into the undergrowth.

A goat-headed enemy came at him from the side, baring foam-flecked teeth, scrawny arm preparing to throw a crude spear. Sir Gilles tugged sharply at the reins, sinking his spurs deep into his mount, and manoeuvred it round. The warhorse, rocking forward onto sturdy forelegs, kicked sharply backwards, its iron-clad hooves snapping the beastman's neck.

A spiked mace was swung vainly. Sir Gilles brought his shield up, absorbing the blow, then flicked his blade deftly out, its point sinking for a fatal second into the breast of his final foe.

Hardly out of breath, Sir Gilles surveyed the carnage he had wrought. The only sound was the pounding of his horse's hooves as it pawed the blood-soaked ground.

Darkness came prematurely to this part of the forest, the sun blocked out by the plateau that was Sir Gilles's home. Though the base of the Chambourt was only an hour's ride distant, to be alone in the forest at this time was far from desirable, even for a warrior of his stature.

Before he could resume his journey, there was something he had to be sure of.

Armour clanking, Sir Gilles dismounted. He raised the visor on his helm, revealing the face of a middle-aged man, lined and white-whiskered. He walked towards the entrance of the shrine and knew immediately that his task was not yet over.

From inside he could hear the buzzing of flies.

LYING AT THE heart of Bretonnia, the Chambourt was a vast shelf nestling in the foothills of the Orcal Massif, thrusting high above the crag-filled oaks of the Forest of Charons.

From the window of his chamber, the baron gazed out at his realm with a contented heart. Set against the monotonous, cloud-wisped expanse of the forest, the Chambourt glowed beneath the last rays of the setting sun. Squares of corn caught the fading sunlight, inter-sected with pasture, dotted with healthy cattle. Irrigated orchards flanked the river that flowed down from the snow-capped peaks of the Massif, cutting a life-giving path through the land.

There was a light knock at the door.

'Enter,' the baron said, turning from the window.

Pagnol, his ageing manservant, shuffled into the room, gaze respectfully averted. The baron shuttered the window.

'The banquet hall is prepared, my liege,' said the old man. 'We wait only for your presence.'

'Any word from Sir Gilles?'

'No, my lord. He has not yet returned.'

Taking a robe from his bed, the baron fastened it at his shoulder and stepped towards the doorway, held open by the faithful Pagnol. 'No matter. It is not to be helped.'

At twenty-five the baron was entering the fifth year of his rule. A robust warrior, he was much loved by the people, like his father before him. The year had also seen a record harvest, the best the old farmers said, since they were but boys. The barrels were full of new wine, and along the river the mills ground a ceaseless supply of wheat into flour. Baskets seemingly overflowing with fruit could be seen stacked on every doorstep or rattling to market on the back of wagons.

The baron was overjoyed with his realm. Everything seemed vital and alive, imbued with an astonishing fertility. This, it transpired, included his young wife, the Lady Isobella. A pleasingly attractive princess of the Estalian nobility, she was about to give birth to their first child.

Her labour pains had started that morning. Ensconcing her in a specially constructed birthing chamber, the midwifes attended to her while the priests prayed to the Lady of the Lake for the baby to be born healthy, untainted and, most importantly, male. The baron, as was the tradition, was to spend the time in the banqueting hall. It was a shame that his old friend, Sir Gilles, would not be present. Still, with a wench on each arm and a never-ending supply of wine, the baron felt sure the birth would be over in no time.

ELSEWHERE, THE SEEDS of the baron's undoing were not only sown, but had taken root.

The baron had a sister, ten years his junior. Named Juliette, she was of the same healthy stock as he, though born of a different mother. It was universally agreed by approving men and envious women that she was possessed of great beauty. Always immaculately attired in gowns of flowing silk, she was elegant, demure and slim of waist. Her pale face was delicately featured, painted at the lips and eyes like the finest of masques. With her modest and chaste nature, she was the model of obedient womanhood, sought after by every unmarried nobleman in Bretonnia and beyond.

The baron forbade her to attend banquets, for fear that the sight of such debauchery and routine debasement would corrupt her valuable innocence. Some would say later that this was not a little ironic. Counting Juliette amongst his many blessings, the baron looked forward to the day of her marriage and the excellent alliance it would surely cement.

He could not have known then that his sister was already wed.

ABOVE THE DRONE of the flies there was a chanting: clipped, harsh syllables, of no language Sir Gilles understood, but they possessed a rhythm he recognised, a dread cadence that pierced him to his heart with its evil intent.

The entrance gave way to a wide corridor that led in turn to the main chapel. Within, the knight could see insubstantial shadows, cast by candlelight, slowly writhing. A stench assailed his nostrils, the scent of damp and decay and abandonment. For how long had these fiends been desecrating this holy place? So close to the Chambourt itself, it was not often used by travellers and pilgrims. He himself, amongst the most pious, had not ventured this way in over a year. However long it had been, it would end today.

Shield up, sword at the ready, Sir Gilles stepped into the chapel.

Dead animals. Rats, goats, dogs, sheep, all in varying stages of decomposition, piled high around the room. Dead priests, male and female, lay among them, some not long dead, others grey and rotting. The abominable centre-piece of the sculpture was the lone priestess of the chapel. A thin, middle-aged woman, her body hung by the neck from a rope fastened to one of the roof-beams. Stripped of her robes, the skin had been flayed from her bones, stopping only at the ligature that bit tightly into the skin beneath her chin. A gaping expression of pure terror was stamped on her ashen face. From the glistening blood on her muscle tissue, Sir Gilles guessed that she had been the last to die.

Standing beside her, stroking the priestess's cheek in a mockery of affection, was a man.

A solid block of muscle, he was naked, blasphemous symbols daubed in blood on his body. Long, jet-black hair flowed over his taut shoulders. Eyes lightly closed, he continued to murmur foul homage to his Dark Gods. A blood-soaked, cruelly curved dagger lay at his feet.

With a cry, Sir Gilles launched himself at the fiend.

Eyes snapping open, the man moved with unnatural speed.

Sir Gilles found his blade biting into the marble floor. Recovering his balance, he turned to face his foe.

The man, if man he truly was, was standing a little way off, close to the rotting carcasses, rocking from side to side on the balls of his feet like a wrestler preparing to fight. He made no attempt to reach for the dagger. His dark eyes flashed with venom. An amused smile played on his lips.

Cautiously, Sir Gilles squared up to the man. He was naked, unarmed and yet seemed more sure of himself than any opponent he had ever faced. Was it madness that produced such self-belief, or something else?

Sir Gilles brought his sword back, then struck, this time anticipating the man's agile dodge. The blade hit the man on the side just above his top rib, cutting him open.

Clutching his wound, blood bubbling up between his fingers, the man staggered, knocked against the priestess, setting her gently swinging, and fell on his side. As blood pumped out of him, he started laughing gently, as though the blow had but tickled him.

Kicking the dagger safely out of reach, Sir Gilles moved in to settle the matter. Something leapt at him from behind. From the shrill screams, he could tell that his assailant was a woman. She was unarmed, also, and wearing only a thin cotton robe. She clung with one hand to Sir Gilles's back, while trying to claw at his face with the other. He shifted his weight and effortlessly threw her over him. She smacked against the hard floor, a bone in her leg snapping.

She lay groaning, twisting in anguish on the floor. Nearby, her companion was still shaking with mirth. His wound, Sir Gilles noted with concern, no longer bled and was healing up. This man was well protected by his foul gods. The fire would be the only sure way of ending his evil.

Working quickly, afraid that his quarry would soon recover, Sir Gilles set about tying him up, so as to deliver him to the baron. Considering her of little threat, he did not pay the woman much attention. She continued to squirm in pain, moaning softly.

'Make it stop, make it stop…'

The voice. The voice seemed familiar. Pulling the last of the knots tight, Sir Gilles stood up and crossed the chamber. He knelt by the woman, brushed the hair from her face and lifted her head up.

The old knight caught his breath and whispered a prayer on the holy chalice.

Staring at him with hatred and a snarl on her fair lips, was the Lady Juliette.

Leaving his two prisoners with the castle's militia, Sir Gilles strode into the banqueting hall. A grave expression on his face, his tabard flecked with the blood of beastmen, revellers heads turned to stare at him as he walked the length of the table. By the time he had reached the baron all merry-making and conversation had ceased.

'If I may speak with you, my lord…'

Full of wine, the baron refused to believe the knight at first. 'My sister sleeps in her room,' he guffawed. 'As she has done every night.'

Sir Gilles laid a hand on his master's shoulder.

'Not every night, I fear,' he said.

The baron understood the situation soon enough when he was shown to the cell holding his sister. She was huddled in the corner of the room, broken leg lying at an unnatural angle, hateful eyes shining from the gloom. When the baron approached, she hissed and spat like a cat.

'Show me the fiend responsible for this outrage,' the baron said, his voice shaking with anger. 'And I will have his head.'

* * *

THE DARK-HAIRED man was altogether calmer than his bride. Clothed now in sack-cloth, he sat against the wall of his cell, a serene smile on his lips. Flanked by crossbow-wielding guards, the baron confronted him.

'What manner of daemon are you?'

'None, sir.' The man spoke in a deep, steady voice. 'I am a man like yourself.'

'That I doubt. From where do you hail, witch?'

The man gave a vague wave of his hand.

A headache banging behind his eyeballs from the wine, the baron massaged his temples with one hand. 'Do you, then, have a name?'

The man gave no answer.

The baron was not one to pander to such games. 'No matter,' he said, coldly. 'My torturers will have it from you before long. And after that, you will burn.'

THE WITCH FINDERS set about their task with consummate zeal and efficiency. When the stranger was next brought before the baron, his body was broken, if not his spirit. His long hair had been shaved down to the scalp with a blunt knife. Dried blood congealed over his face and ears. He was missing his top row of teeth. His back flapped open, raw from flogging. But, like the wound in his side, of which no sign remained, the man's body appeared to be healing rapidly. Of small consolation to the baron were the two fingers that the shears had taken. Although hours had passed, they remained stubborn stumps. So he could be hurt. He would be hurt.

The baron, gazing levelly from his throne at the wretched sight before him, ordered the two guards holding the man by his arms to relinquish their grip. The witch did not topple forward as expected, but stood, swaying, his eyes regarding his tormentor defiantly. He spoke mockingly in a clear voice.

'Sir, I feel I must thank you. The pain your lackeys have inflicted upon me is but a small price to pay for the months of nocturnal pleasure your sister has bestowed upon me.'

The baron leapt from his seat, half jumped down the steps and struck the witch across his face, hard with his gauntleted hand. The man staggered back, laughing, fresh blood pouring from a cut over his eye.

'I would kill you here with my bare hands,' bellowed the baron, 'if the law did not demand that you, like all your diseased kind, should be put to the fire.'

'Oh, sir, sir...' the witch cooed. 'Rest assured I will not burn. My master's game will not allow it. I am to be the bane of your life. You do not even begin to comprehend the horror of which I am capable.'

The baron found himself unable to look for long upon the man's face, lest he catch sight of himself in eyes as jet-black and soulless as a viper's.

The witch cupped his hand to his ear as though listening for something. A childish grin spread across his face. 'Oh, sir. I believe congratulations are in order. You are a father at last. And it is a boy.'

In the wake of the terrible events, the baron had forgotten about his wife's confinement. Before he could react, a lad, son to one of the midwives, came scampering into the throne-room. He gave a hurried, unpractised bow and said, excitedly, 'My lord, my mother bids me come tell you the glad tidings: that my lady has been delivered of a son.'

Ordering the guards to clamp themselves back onto the prisoner, the baron strode towards the door. Struggling against his captors, the witch started to laugh once again.

'Baron! Hear me!' he screamed. 'By the Dark Gods I lay a curse upon your house! I will take everything from you, in time. First, though: your wife!'

The baron started to run.

'Go!' the witch shouted after him. 'But you are too late. My master's work is already done.'

THE MIDWIVES AND servant-girls crowded round the newborn, cooing in adoration. None of them thought to check on the baroness.

The baron burst into the chamber.

Responding to his presence by casting their eyes to the floor, the women curtsied and murmured respectfully.

Rushing to his wife's side, the baron took her hand in his. Her head turned slowly to face him. Though drawn and tired from her ordeal, she wore a contented smile.

It was then that he noticed the blood at the corner of her mouth. It trickled out, a small amount at first, but grew steadily. The baroness appeared not to notice, but continued to stare beatifically at her husband.

'Help her,' he said, unable to raise his voice above a hiss. The servant-girls looked up. 'Help her.'

Her head fell onto one side, a dead weight. Blood seeped slowly out, soaking into the pillow and onto the sheet. Her body went limp. But for the soft whimpering from the servant-girls, there was no noise.

The baron freed his hand from his wife's lifeless fingers. Numb and shaking, he crossed the room and picked up the child. He held it to his breast. A boy, thanks be to the Lady. A son. An *heir*.

* * *

THE BARON WENT immediately from the chamber, channelling his grief into thunderous anger. In the cell, he rained blow after blow against the witch's body. Throughout it all, the fiend made no sound.

At last, breathing hard, exhausted, his knuckles scuffed and bleeding, the baron stopped.

The witch sat up, as though refreshed, one eye completely closed with bruising.

'You have a healthy son, my lord,' he said. 'Such a shame that his life will be so short.'

Powered by grief and fear, the baron launched himself again at the witch, pinning him to the wall by the throat.

'You will speak no more!'

From his belt he took a dagger and, forcing the witch's jaws apart, worked his way inside the mouth, cut and carved for a second, then stepped back.

The witch slumped against the wall, blood cascading from his mouth. His face was slack but his eyes still shone with mirth and malice.

WHILE THESE EVENTS had been unfolding, a crowd of the kingdom's finest scholars had been gathered about the Lady Juliette. By now almost mad with grief, the baron received their report in a state of great agitation.

'How fares my sister?'

All reluctant to speak, Blampel the beak-nosed physician was nudged forward. One hand adjusting his skull-cap, he muttered a curse intended for his craven colleagues.

'I fear the news is not good, my lord,' he said at last.

The baron nodded at him to elaborate.

'The lady has lost her mind. Human speech and reasoning are beyond her. Never before have I seen madness consume a person so swiftly.'

Stroking his neatly-trimmed beard with a hand still spattered with the witch's dried blood, the baron said, 'And what of her dabbling in witchcraft? Is she an innocent party or am I to put my own flesh and blood to the flame?' He looked across. 'Tertullion?'

The portly mage, who had been hiding at the back of the group, guzzling from a wineskin left over from the banquet, shuffled drunkenly forward. He dabbed at his food-encrusted whiskers and steadied himself against a pillar. 'My lord. As my friend, the learned man of medicine, has already rightly diagnosed, the Lady Juliette is quite insane. I am of the opinion that because of this, her innocence or otherwise in this matter is now an irrelevance. Any of the Dark Ways that may have been imparted to her by her foul consort are now surely lost, along with the rest of her humanity.'

This was typical of Tertullion. Long-winded, wordy. And wrong.

FOR COME THE dawn, the guards found within the cell, not the witch but the Lady Juliette, her state of mind greatly improved. Somehow fully clothed, she stood holding the trail of her silken dress up, so as to avoid the filth of the floor. Giggling like a young girl, she uttered a single dark word.

Two of the guards fell, screaming, to their knees, eyeballs liquefying, bubbling from the sockets. The third guard, swinging blindly with terror, lopped her head neatly from her body. Escaping from her neck with a hiss like steam, blood sprayed the dirty walls and showered the straw-strewn floor.

Blinking blood out of his eyes, the petrified guard stared at the crumpled body before him as it twitched its last. Juliette's head lay at an angle, partly obscured by the straw, her fine, dark hair framing an expression of surprise.

The witch, her master, was not to be seen for many years.

THOUGH HE WAS born into a house of sorrow, the baron's son, also named Gregory as had been the custom for the first-born son for ten generations, grew into a healthy and well-adjusted boy. His father put at his disposal the finest academics. He soon became the first male member of the line who could read and write, and in several languages, too. But it soon became apparent that the warrior-blood burned brightly within. As adolescence approached, it was to jousts and sword-play that he turned. Even the books he read were tomes dealing with tactics and warfare.

Eager to encourage this aspect of his son's life, the baron put him under the tutelage of Sir Gilles. Though already into his fourth decade at the boy's birth, his sword skills knew no equal and, in the trials, he could still keep several far younger opponents at bay. But it was his tales that made Gregory love him.

Gilles's questing had taken him all over the Old World and beyond. He had fought alongside dwarfs against orcs and goblins in the World's Edge Mountains, done battle with Sartosan pirates, slaughtered beastmen and mutants within the forests, even driven a skaven horde back into the heart of its foul subterranean nest. Every time Gilles spoke of these adventures, Gregory's face lit up in rapt attention.

Shortly before his twelfth birthday, he asked Gilles why he was not allowed to leave the castle.

'That is your father's decision,' Gilles said in his soothing, deep voice. 'And you would do better not to question it.'

But something in the Grail Knight's pale, blue eyes, told the young heir to do exactly the opposite.

'You HAVE BEEN filling his head with your tales!' the baron roared. Gilles, kneeling before the throne on the flagstones, lifted his bowed head.

'I meant no harm by it, my liege.'

The baron, about to shout again, felt suddenly foolish. He put one hand against the side of his head, where the hair had already grown prematurely grey.

'Get up, old friend,' the baron said, sadly. 'I am sorry.'

Gilles got to his feet and looked his master steadily in the eyes. 'No apologies are necessary,' he said. 'But I must ask you why you are so opposed to your son's request?'

'Because I will not allow him to leave this castle,' said the baron. 'And this hunting party he craves? Into the forest? No.' He sighed wearily, adding, 'It is for his own protection.'

'That is as maybe,' Gilles said. 'But do you not think it more dangerous to cosset the boy, to leave him ill-prepared for the dangers he may face?'

'I have made my decision,' the baron rumbled.

THE HUNTING PARTY took place a week later, on the occasion of Gregory's birthday. Though he had relented, the baron was leaving nothing to chance. A retinue of men-at-arms and bowmen, as well as Gilles and his company of knights and squires, all accompanied the noblemen down into the forest. Also, for his magical abilities only, the old bore Tertullion was carried on a litter with the party, his white, oval face flushed with the wine he drank.

They rode away from the shadow of the Chambourt, to an area where direct sunlight broke through the canopy of leaves. Riding between Gilles and his father, Gregory jabbered with excitement.

'Will we hunt boar, father?'

'Yes,' the baron said. 'With the lance.'

The boy turned to Gilles. 'And deer? I would like to test my archery skills on a moving target. Will we hunt deer?'

'Undoubtedly,' Sir Gilles said with a laugh. He flashed a smile across at the baron, and was pleased to see that he shared his good humour.

Tertullion, his goblet refreshed by a servant-girl, bobbed alongside on his cushion.

'I must say, my lord,' he slurred, 'that the effect of this hunting party upon the young prince, already a fine figure of burgeoning manhood, can only be beneficial.' He raised his drink. 'A capital idea.'

It was to be the last wrong thing he said. The arrow entered through his eyeball, cracked his skull apart, and left through the back of his head.

He was but the first.

'Beastmen!' cried one of the soldiers from the front. Horses whinnied as a volley of arrows came from the trees. Screams. The thud of arrowheads on shields.

Pulling the reins of his steed in tight, Sir Gilles quickly assessed the situation. Arrows were coming from all around. They were surrounded. He spurred his house through the confusion of panicked noblemen, to the men-at-arms.

'Form up! Form up!' he yelled. 'Shields high!'

At his word the bowmen scurried forward, taking up places behind the pikes. They fired a volley into the trees. Bestial cries of their victims rang out. Pulling his visor down, Gilles peered into the murk. The shadows moved; suggestions of horns and hooves, tentacles and twisted, Chaos-tainted limbs. This was no opportunist beastman raid, he realised. They were well organised. And there were hundreds of them.

Screaming in their foul, ululating tongue, the enemy burst forth from the trees. Wave after wave fell to the bow and the pike, but each time a gap was left. Under Gilles's command, the soldiers shored up, but the protective circle was getting ever smaller. And the arrows kept coming from all around.

Gilles looked across at Gregory. To the boy's credit he showed no fear. His face, as he kept close to his father, was fixed with a look of stoic determination. He was calm. He had his wits. He would make a fine warrior.

A clamour of clashing armour from one side of the circle announced another attack. The beastmen were concentrating on one area. They hacked at it, burst through, splintering shields and cleaving skulls, cutting down bowmen. They were in.

His horse rising onto its hind-legs, Gilles raised his sword skywards, gave a rallying cry and went to join the fray. An arrow found a gap in his mount's armour-plating, piercing its side. It fell sideways. Unable to free his foot from his stirrups in time, Gilles went with it.

He heard the crunch as his leg dislocated. His sword snapped in two as it connected with a rock. Fighting against the pain, Gilles was unaware of the beastman, a stocky hunchback with the head of bull, standing over him with a club. Raining blow after blow against his armour, it beat him into the blackness.

GILLES AWOKE TO find himself bound. He had been stripped of his armour and was lying on a slab of stone, his arms and legs pinioned by ropes. He was covered in bruises. Blood had dried over his head. His broken leg was numb and would not move. From a torch set on the wall, he could see that he was in some sort of cave. The vicious points of stalactites jutted out of the darkness above him.

'Sir Gilles?' a voice called. It was hoarse as though from sobbing.

'Gregory?'

Gilles craned his head, wincing against the pain. The lad, tied to another slab of rock, appeared unharmed. He was trembling, his face once again that of a frightened boy.

A man entered the room. Towering, his head almost touching the jagged roof, Sir Gilles recognised him of old. He had grown his long hair back. The witch.

He lowered his disfigured face, his hair brushing against Sir Gilles's face. He hissed, opening his tongueless mouth, a string of saliva winding its way down onto the knight's forehead. Sir Gilles gazed defiantly upon the witch, unflinching.

The witch stood up, a rattling, gurgling laugh coming from his throat. He clicked his fingers. Two beastmen lumbered in, hooves clattering on the rock, and took Gregory up from his slab. He started to cry, kicking uselessly against them as they took him from the cave.

'Where are you taking him?' Gilles cried out. 'I warn you now, witch! Do not harm that boy!'

The witch stood in the centre of the room, facing Sir Gilles. He pulled out a knife. Wide-bladed and so sharp its edges shone, it was inscribed with the eldritch signs of the witch's evil master. He held it above his head in both hands, stumps knotting with the fingers that remained, blade facing the floor. He brought it down, plunging it into an imaginary victim. His body shook with deranged, guttural laughter.

The witch strode from the room, dagger at the ready.

Desperately, Sir Gilles began to struggle against his bonds.

In the forest, the cries of the wounded and dying filled the twilight. Soldiers busied themselves digging graves for the dead men. A pyre was stacked high with slaughtered horses, the stench of burning meat all pervading. Subdued and utterly defeated, the men performed their grim duties like automatons. None of them spoke of the likely fates of those men whose bodies could not be found.

Amidst this pitiful scene, surrounded by a circle of troops, the baron sat on a rock, staring into space, his grief by now impenetrable.

'The head-count has been completed, my lord,' the sergeant-at-arms said quietly.

Barely registering the man's presence, the baron waved a cursory hand at him to continue.

'Upon the field are the bodies of thirty men, five of them of name. Ten more are severely wounded and are not expected to live long.'

The baron shuddered, closing his eyes slowly. It was all his fault.

'There is one more disturbing detail,' the sergeant went on. 'As well as your son and Sir Gilles, we could not find the bodies of a further ten retainers. From the testimony of the men, confused by the chaos of battle though it is, they appear to have been taken away alive.'

'But why?' the baron demanded, as much of the darkening forest as the sergeant.

A horse came galloping from the forest, carrying on its back one of the baron's scouts. The man pulled his mount to a halt and dismounted. He stood, panting, trying to find his voice, sweat dripping from his head.

'My lord,' he said, breathlessly. 'My lord, I think I have found them!'

SITTING UP ON the slab, Sir Gilles untied the last of the bonds around his feet. He swung round and planted his good foot on the cave floor. Wincing, he limped up the rough slope in the direction the witch had taken. Supporting himself on the limestone wall, he looked down into another chamber, beyond which could be seen a moonlit clearing in the forest. A bonfire was burning and the unholy mutterings of the beastmen could be heard. Somewhere, drums were being pounded.

Sir Gilles crept out of the cave, hoping that the night and the flickering shadows of the fire would provide enough cover to prevent his detection. It was then he heard the first scream.

Squinting in the darkness, Sir Gilles could make out a terrible sight.

With several flat-topped stones arranged around him in a circle, each with one of the baron's soldiers lying upon it, the witch stood in his robes, his knife in one hand, a severed head in the other. Blood trickled down his arm, glistening in the flames. He moved on to his next victim.

Issuing a silent prayer to the Lady, Sir Gilles called upon his last reserves of strength and courage and took action. He deftly broke the neck of the nearest beastman, took its weapon – a rusted broadsword – and went to work.

Swinging rhythmically, lopping off heads, opening throats, he hobbled forward, screaming out the ancient battle-cries of his order. The beastmen, drunk and distracted by the blood-letting ceremony, were slow to react. And Sir Gilles had his righteous anger on his side. Wounded though he was, he was unstoppable.

More screams rang out as the witch continued to add new heads to the pile at his feet.

Sir Gilles was by now on the other side of the bonfire and could see the witch and his unholy ritual clearly now. The prince was tied to a tree, slumped unconscious, arms above his head and feet crossed over like a martyr of old. The witch was working on the last of the men. The knife, blunted on the other victims, hacked laboriously through windpipe and bone, sending blood rising through the darkness. Occupied with fending off beastmen, Gilles could only listen help-lessly to the strangulated cries of the man's prolonged agony.

Standing back, the last of the heads in his hands, the witch held both arms aloft, the power of his sacrifices flowing through him. He moved towards Gregory.

A beastman came out of the darkness at Sir Gilles, its large hooves kicking up cinders and dead twigs. One arm was a lashing tentacle, the other a thick, almost-human arm, wielding a large club. Its head was that of a horse. Deep-set eyes glowed with rage. Its mouth was crowded with needle-sharp teeth. Expertly side-stepping Sir Gilles's first lunge, it retaliated with an unexpectedly swift upswing that caught the knight in the stomach. Winded, he staggered backwards. The beastman leapt at him.

Beyond the horse-creature, Sir Gilles could see that the witch had not yet harmed Gregory. He stood instead by the tree, freeing Gregory from his bonds, no doubt in preparation for moving him to one of the plinths.

Blocking club with sword, Sir Gilles pulled his arm back ready to punch, but found it held fast by the tentacle. The beast dropped the club and gripped the knight's sword arm instead. Its strength was too great. Sir Gilles felt the blood fleeing his fingers. He dropped his weapon.

A cracking noise. The beastman let its lower jaw dislocate like a snake's, the bone hanging loose in stretching skin. The teeth, coated in spittle, glistened in the flames.

Sir Gilles tried to struggle but the beast held him fast. He prayed to the Lady. *Not this way. Not like this.*

With a roar the horse-head sank its teeth into his neck and bit down hard. Then stopped.

The tentacle uncoiled itself, and the fingers around his sword arm went slack. The beastman pitched forward, a dead weight.

Scrabbling back out from under the monstrosity, one hand to his neck to stem the flow of blood, Sir Gilles saw that an arrow protruded from the back of the creature's neck, lost in the mane.

Not having time to question his good fortune, and losing blood fast, Sir Gilles drew on the last reserves of strength and pounded across to the witch.

Lowering Gregory to the ground, the fiend did not see him.

Gilles knocked him to the side, rolled over with him, pinned him to the ground. One punch destroyed his nose.

Choking on blood that flowed down his throat, the witch stared up at the Grail Knight. His eyes were wild with shock and, though Sir Gilles dare not think it, what looked like fear.

Starting to lose consciousness, Sir Gilles brought his fist down once again. The witch went limp.

More arrows flew out of the darkness, bringing beastmen down as they closed in on Sir Gilles. The others stopped to sniff the air.

Clambering off the witch, Sir Gilles went to Gregory. Felt for a pulse. The boy still lived.

The beastmen started baying in alarm. A crashing of undergrowth. Horses' hooves. The clank of armour. The glint of weapons in the flames. The baron had arrived.

The slaughter was great. Not a beastman was permitted to live. Though the fire burnt still in the centre of the clearing, the baron ordered that their bodies should be left to rot, their heads put upon spikes as a warning to others of their kind. To prevent desecration, the bodies of the ten sacrificed soldiers were taken back to the Chambourt, together with the witch. For him, the flames awaited.

IT WAS A stark, cold morning. The entire town was assembled outside the castle grounds. For a week now, the pyre that would claim the life of the witch had been under construction. Every household had contributed wood. Many trees had been felled. It towered above the crowd, in competition with the castle itself, a man-made cousin to the peaks beyond. A scaffold had been built around it, enabling the chaos-worshipping fiend to be marched up to the stake at the summit.

Having been put to the torture for the entire time his execution was being prepared, he was at last a broken figure. Pale and hunched, head scabbed over where his hair had been burnt off in a bucket of hot coals, he stumbled upwards, each step an agony. From a platform at the base of the pyre, the baron noted with grim satisfaction that the witch's eyes, where defiance had burned so long, now seemed confused and bovine.

'HELP ME TO the window, Gregory,' Sir Gilles said in a faint voice. 'I wish to watch the monster's final moments.'

Pale, drawn and confined to his bed, the Grail Knight's health had deteriorated since his ordeal. His leg had not set well and the bite mark, through which he had lost a lot of blood, was not healing satisfactorily. That morning, Blampel, the old fool, had muttered something indistinct about a possible infection.

In contrast, Gregory, his cheeks ruddy with the flush of youth, was as sturdy as ever before.

He lifted the old retainer from his bed and supported him while he hobbled on his broken leg to the window. Sir Gilles rested himself against the sill, his breathing shallow, his thoughts scattered and vague. If this was a taste of old age, he said to himself, then he prayed that his end would not be long in coming.

Tapestries lifted in the wind as Gregory opened the windows. A low rumble of conversation drifted upwards from the crowd. The occasional cry of a hawker advertising his wares.

The window was level with the top of the pyre, towards which the crippled figure was being marched. The gaoler tied the witch to the stake and made his way back down the steps.

Sir Gilles stared, unblinking, at his hated enemy.

The monster strained forward from the stake, feebly struggling, the filth on his face streaked with tears. A distressed shrieking came from his empty mouth. He seemed more like a child than a man.

THE GAOLER HANDED the baron a flaming brand. All chatter in the crowd died. The witch was screaming down at the baron, neck fully outstretched, eyes bulging, demented. Though his words could not be understood, it was clear he was pleading for mercy. At last, thought the baron. At last.

Making sure he maintained eye contact with his enemy, the baron slowly put the torch at the base of the pyre.

With a crackle of dry tinder, the hungry flames leapt up.

At the sight of the orange glow far beneath him, the witch hysterically started to repeat the same word over and over.

THE SAME WORD, over and over... Sir Gilles felt the hairs on the back of his neck and arms bristle. A prickling sensation came to his face.

The word. The word sounded like–

He turned to look at Gregory. He stood, arms folded, impassively surveying the grim scene. His mouth was curled into a sneering smile.

Sir Gilles started to shake.

The wind brought the scent of burning flesh into the room.

Arms still folded, Gregory waved a dismissive hand at the knight. 'Die,' he commanded.

THE FLAMES LICKED up. The baron forced himself to keep his eyes on the witch. The fire seared his flesh now, billowing through his clothes. Still he screamed out the same word, rasping and harsh.

SIR GILLES STAGGERED back from the window. He dropped to his knees. Felt the air fleeing his lungs. A sharp pain in his head. Tears in his eyes. Blood in his mouth.

Deadly malice flashing in his eyes, Gregory paced around him in a circle.

'Old fool. You did not think to question the nature, the purpose of the ceremony.'

The Grail Knight started to shake.

'The ceremony, the deaths of those ten men, wasn't merely to satisfy my blood-lust. It had a purpose.'

'No...' Sir Gilles croaked. 'No...'

'That night, by the unholy power of my dark master I took the body of the baron's son.' The man that called himself Gregory came close to Sir Gilles's ear. 'And bequeathed him mine.'

Outside, the screaming had stopped. Framed by the small window, Sir Gilles could see all that remained of the witch's body, a column of black smoke.

The darkness of death crowding in on his mind, Sir Gilles locked his hands together in desperate prayer.

He knew now what the word had been.

IT WAS OVER. The people were still silent, awe-struck by the terrible sight they had witnessed. The flames roared on, hungrily consuming the last of the wood.

Suddenly exhausted, the baron let his head drop. The acrid smoke stung his eyes. He moved towards the edge of the platform, his guards stepping aside to allow him onto the steps.

The crowd cheered him as he walked, but he barely heard it. An inexplicable sorrow hung heavily on his heart. He cared nothing for his land, nor his faithful subjects. Only one thing mattered to him now. His son, his heir: Gregory.

WATCHING THE DEAD knight, his aged face contorted with the anguish of his final moments, the witch's eyes flashed with triumph.

The sound of the baron's approaching footsteps on the cold stone echoed along the corridor.

Transforming Gregory's features into a suitable mask of sorrow, the witch opened the door and fell into his father's arms.

Seeing the knight's fallen form beyond the doorway, the baron gave a cry of grief and pulled his son tightly to him.

Face pressed into the baron's tunic, Gregory's muffled voice repeated the same word over and over. Though the sadness was almost too much to bear, the baron took comfort at the word. It was all he had left.

He pulled his son closer, rocking him gently, one hand cradling the back of his head.

The same word, over and over.

'Father.'

ILL MET IN MORDHEIM

Robert Waters

'Amidst the perpetually dank and grotesque scenery of the City of the Damned, they struggled for honour, coin and sport. But some, the nobler and more righteous, struggled for greater causes...'

– Songs from the Eternal Struggle: A History of Mordheim,
by Isabel Rojas

CAPTAIN HEINRICH GOGOL watched the fallen ratmen writhe in pain. They were all around him, their furry forms beaten, twisted and blood-ied. He was pleased with that, despite having been knocked aside as well by the shock of the priest's soul spell. The warhammer strike in the middle of the battle had sent ripples of righteous heat roiling across the charred ground, ending the fight, but leaving a nasty ache in the cap-tain's bones. He rubbed his face harshly, ran his fingers through his thinning black hair and climbed to his feet. He kicked aside a ratman that had taken the brunt of the spell. 'Many thanks,' Heinrich said to the dying beast, then drove a boot heel into its burning throat.

Heinrich focused on a little shrew of a man a few yards away smil-ing with confidence. The old priest hefted the warhammer in his skeletal hands as the mighty weapon popped white with fire that singed the frayed edges of his brown robe.

697

Heinrich sheathed his sword, adjusted his russet-leather surcoat, and joined the priest. 'That was a mighty prayer, Father,' he said, tempering his words. 'We thank you. But perhaps next time you can give us warning first?'

'My apologies, captain,' the priest said with a smile on his pale lips. 'But I had to move quickly. You were in trouble.'

'Nonsense,' said Heinrich sharply. 'I had them right where I wanted–'

An agonising scream pierced the gloom. Somewhere out there amidst the shattered ruins, Heinrich knew, flesh was being torn from bone. Muskets firing, wolves howling, bats screeching, fires smouldering, smoke billowing. An endless cacophony of rage and violence in the city that never slept, the city of damned souls, the city of lost dreams, the city of night fire.

The city of Mordheim.

A chill fog blew in from the east and tugged at Heinrich's thoughts. He looked into the gaunt sky. The sun was setting below the grey spires of the ruins on the western side of the city. Darkness called, and death gave no quarter in the Mordheim night.

'Gunderic!'

A young man appeared before Heinrich, his white tunic and blue breeches smeared with ratman gore. 'Yes, captain?'

Heinrich handed him a blade. 'Cut their throats.'

Gunderic nodded and set to work. Heinrich picked up the warhammer and handed it to the priest who was slowly regaining his strength. 'Let's move quickly, Father,' he said. 'Broderick needs our help.'

They turned their attention to a guildhouse, whose walls were scorched black and pockmarked by the comet blast that had destroyed the city years ago. Its long, rectangular windows were covered in pine slats and thick hessian sheets. Its entrance was a massive double-door archway, heavily reinforced with crates and barrels and rotting meal sacks. High above the doors stood four stone pinnacles whose sharp tips tore through the low passing clouds like claws through flesh. The sight of those pinnacles gave Heinrich pause; they seemed to waver dangerously in the gusting wind. Heinrich breathed deeply, found his courage, and stepped forward.

The ratmen that they had just killed were nothing more than a small detachment defending the building's southern approach. What lay within was what gave Heinrich concern, and the white scar on his left cheek itched. He had no great desire to go inside, but do so he must.

'Let's find the way in,' Heinrich said to Father. Young Gunderic joined them and handed over the blade. 'They've breathed their last, captain.'

Heinrich nodded. 'You're doing Sigmar's work, lad. I'm glad you're with us.'

The young man's face glowed with appreciation, but Heinrich could not share the joy. He hated bringing raw recruits into missions like this, very little training, minimal preparation. Who knew when the fight was on, if newcomers would live up to promise, or tuck tail and run? But live bodies were oftentimes more important than skill. His last mission had cut their strength somewhat, and the idea of facing such a plentiful foe with only five or six swords was madness. *Well*, Heinrich said to himself, *he'll learn as he goes, or die trying*.

Heinrich worked around the massive pile of rotting wood. As he searched for an entrance, he reviewed the plan.

The rest of the men were with Broderick. Their objective was to tackle the northern entrance of the guildhouse, while Heinrich, Father and Gunderic approached from the south. The hope was that the ratmen would assume that the threat lay with Broderick alone and that they would overlook a second danger. With enough confusion, the beasts would panic and make mistakes. The trick, however, was to time the assaults carefully. If they moved into position too early, the ratmen would smell out the trap; arrive too late, and Broderick and company would be dead. But that would never happen. He and Broderick knew each other's moves instinctively, having fought together for years. 'I am the hammer,' Broderick would often say, 'and you are the anvil, my friend. Between us the iron bends.'

They'd been following this group of ratmen – or skaven – for days. Skirmish after unending skirmish through the streets, up and down shifting mounds of rubble, in and out of row after row of dilapidated storerooms, bars, bakeries, and temples. And each engagement had ended the same: minor casualties on both sides, with no conclusion. Heinrich wanted it to end, to pull out of this cursed place, to reform, refit, take stock, catch a warm bath and a good meal. But not until they had won; not until every last vermin they hunted was driven through and planted in the cold ground.

But now their mission had taken on an even greater purpose. If what Broderick claimed were true, if the skaven were in possession of Sigmar's Heart, then the only outcome of this rolling battle *must* be victory… victory for the group, victory for the Empire, and victory for Sigmar.

'Look here, captain,' Father said, pointing to a loose crate in the side of the pile. Heinrich knelt down, pulled away the crate and revealed a small, yet passable, entrance. 'So this is how they get inside.' Heinrich drew his crossbow. 'Arm yourselves and follow me closely… and *quietly*.'

They crawled slowly through the gap in the rubbish. The light in the main hall of the guildhouse was faint and it took a while for

Heinrich's eyes to adjust. With a free hand, he pulled himself through the damaged door. The sickening smell of fermented grain, wet fur and mouldy scat clung to the air and Heinrich wrinkled his nose in defiance. There were also innumerable banterings back and forth between unseen mouths. The ratmen were there just beyond the shadows: mingling, scraping, spitting, snarling; one massive chaotic voice of twisted humanity paying homage to their blasphemous god.

Heinrich pulled himself onto his knees. Father and Gunderic followed suit. Before them, there stood a mountain of old barrels teetering on a lip of steps that descended into the wide belly of the guildhouse. Through the gaps in the barrels, Heinrich could see the angular motions of the ratmen as they mingled about their tasks. He tried to count them, but could not get a proper number. Perhaps two dozen, maybe more. The ceiling had collapsed, and pieces of the roof lay in large chunks on the dirty floor. It was rare indeed for trees and bushes to grow in the poisonous fold of Mordheim, but trees and bushes and thick patches of ivy lay around the edges of the open floor, finding root in the choice cracks and crevices near the walls. And Broderick was right in his reconnaissance: piles of crates and barrels, broken furniture, old clothing, chamber pots, armour and paintings and all the forgotten treasures of the city had been hoarded here by the skaven over their years of scouring the ruins.

If time were convenient, Heinrich thought, it might be useful to look through it all, take stock of the wonders therein, study it and learn about life in the city before its great destruction. Like little windows into the past, each item a discarded memory of someone who once walked the streets. Wisdom lay on that floor, he knew, if one cared to look.

He put these thoughts from his mind and focused on the deadly space below. Despite the ample floor space, there was little open surface. He smiled. A small battle space was best for close in fighting. He rubbed the trigger of his crossbow anxiously and looked beyond the ratmen to the narrow entranceway from which Broderick would attack.

Yet Broderick had not made his entrance. Come on, Heinrich said to himself, make your move. Surprise was slipping away. Any further delay and their position would be sniffed out. Another nervous minute passed, and then he heard the long, powerful howls of his warhounds, Bloodtooth and Witchkiller.

The floor erupted in violence. Squeals, howls, shrieks, shouts, swirling steel and pelting rocks, as Broderick pressed the skaven at the northern entrance. From his vantage point, Heinrich could see his men working their way into the guildhouse. The warhounds took the lead, bounding into the mass of ratmen and taking several down. Roland and Cuthbert followed closely, the spiked balls of their morning stars swirling madly through the air. Both men modelled themselves after flagellants, even going so far as to whip themselves for loss of faith. But they were contrite enough in their devotion to Sigmar to keep it quiet in public. It was exciting to see them in battle. They never disappointed.

Broderick and young Sebastian followed last, fighting off ratmen who were dropping down from atop the huge walls of crates that lined the entrance. Heinrich watched as Broderick swung his sword in answer to every leaping vermin, slicing through bellies and chests in mid-flight. The skill and speed at which he worked his sword was amazing even now, years after leaving the pit fights, and Heinrich felt a great pride. *Push them, Broderick. Push them hard. Show them how Reiklanders fight.*

Father glared at his captain. 'Let's go, let's go!' he hissed. Again, the priest's warhammer, hanging from a white sash at his waist, glowed with magical zeal.

Heinrich smiled and counted off three fingers. 'Now!'

They stood and moved closer to the barrels, each taking positions adequate for firing. Heinrich looked down onto the floor. A mass of fur, claws, clubs, blades and spears swayed back and forth, as men and beast fought to hold their ground. Though the moment wasn't dire, Heinrich knew that Broderick could not hold forever.

He clipped his crossbow to his belt and unholstered his pistol. He leaned out from behind the barrels, aimed carefully into the melee and pulled the trigger. A flash of powder and a mighty *crack*! rang through the space, as two skaven fell dead. For a moment, the enemy was confused as they reconciled to the danger behind them. This gave Broderick and crew time to regroup.

Gunderic and Father sent their missiles into the fray. Volleys of rocks peppered the barrels before them, as ratmen slingers turned away from the main attack to focus on the new threat. Heinrich dropped behind the wall of barrels again, holstered his smoking pistol and drew his sword.

He crouched in cover and noticed that Father and Gunderic had repositioned themselves about ten yards to his right, back to back. They were surrounded by a horde of rats clawing over themselves to sink their fangs. Heinrich had not seen any rats of the four-legged variety on the guildhouse floor; they must have come from holes and tunnels around the walls when they had heard the terrified shrieks of their masters. He cursed himself for not anticipating this problem. He knew better. Ratmen never moved without a horde of rats. And why hadn't Broderick mentioned them in his scouting report?

Swamped, Father wielded his hammer like a man possessed, swinging at every snout that came too close. As each hammer strike found meat, a comet of blood, bone, and fur flew through the air. And yet they kept coming. Gunderic tried desperately to hold his position, but his short sword was no match for the swarm, and some of the creatures had reached his legs. Heinrich winced as he saw blood marks streak the young man's legs. He wanted to help, but he had more pressing concerns. If he stood up now, those slingers would most certainly pound him to death. He needed to create a diversion to throw them back.

He found one. With a mighty lunge, Heinrich slammed into the barrels. They teetered then tumbled down the steps, cracking and tearing apart like an avalanche of ice. He followed closely behind, using the barrels as a shield against the shower of stones. The slingers fell back as the barrels struck the guildhouse floor and bounced like dice. Heinrich locked his eyes on the closest ratman and swung his sword into the rib cage and lifted the beast off the floor. The impetus of the blow, however, put him on uneven feet, and before he could leverage his stance, three skaven pounced.

Heinrich could feel claws on his back, ripping through his surcoat and tunic like razors. Another beast stabbed at him with a dagger gripped in its tail; the blade swiped across the Reiklander's face, inches from his eyes. A third was hitting him on the legs with a club. Heinrich didn't want to lose his sword, but he had no choice.

Dropping the sword, he quickly grabbed the blade-wielding tail, brought it to his mouth, and bit hard. Noxious blood filled his mouth as the ratman let out an agonising screech, dropped its blade, and fell back. That problem solved, Heinrich took his knife and slashed out against the ratman at his legs. But the one on his back grabbed his arm and held it firm.

Heinrich howled and twisted, trying to loosen the beast's grip. He could feel the steam of the creature's vile breath on his neck and its snout pushing into his nape to set its teeth. But as the first fang made its mark, the ratman was rudely yanked away. Heinrich looked down and saw Bloodtooth tearing into its throat.

Turning his attention to the third assailant, Heinrich raised his dagger and stabbed down, aiming for its back, but before steel found its mark, a crossbow bolt pierced its side. But Heinrich could not stop the impetus of the blade, and it hit the ground and snapped at the hilt. He scowled and looked into the direction of the bolt. Broderick stood close, grinning and holding a spent crossbow.

'You owe me a knife!' Heinrich shouted.

Broderick nodded. 'A small price to pay.'

Heinrich retrieved his sword and he and Broderick stood back to back, circling slowly. 'Where did all the rats come from, *friend*?' Heinrich yelled. 'Did you not see them on your reconnaissance?'

'What are you talking about?' Broderick asked, catching a ratman with a swift jab of his sword blade.

'The rats that have taken two of our men out of the battle,' he said, driving the pommel of his sword into a nearby throat. 'Father and Gunderic are fighting for their lives.'

'Aren't we all,' Broderick snapped back. 'What do you want me to do about it?'

'Get us out of this mess.'

'Just shut up,' Broderick said, twisting his body to the left to block a ratman from jumping on Heinrich's back, 'and fight!'

That ended the argument. Through the constant slash of blades and teeth, Heinrich fought to keep his balance. Fighting they were, and valiantly too, but the advantage gained from their initial assault was slipping away. Cuthbert was down, fending off attacks with bare arms, and Witchkiller, though still in the fight, was slowing, her chest a swirl of deep red cuts. Unless a miracle happened, they would never get out of the building alive.

And then as if Sigmar were listening, a flight of arrows flew into the melee and felled several ratmen. The missiles came through gaps in the boarded windows on the sides of the building. Then came powerful shouts as five strange men, attired in richly coloured doublets and tunics, rushed through the northern entrance and gave battle to the enemy. Heinrich stood confused as he tried to make sense of the intruders. What was going on? Who were these men? He turned and looked at Broderick, whose eyes were also seeking answers.

'What is this?' Heinrich asked.

But before he could answer, Broderick's chest exploded in a cloud of green powder and blood. A thunderous roar consumed the space and Heinrich was knocked aside. The crack of the shot rang soundly in his ears as he struggled to stand. He could feel the sting of powder in his eyes and taste it on his tongue. He wiped away the pain and looked at his feet. Broderick lay face down, a black hole in his mangled back, a green mist rising out of the wound as blood pooled around him on the floor. Heinrich knew immediately what had caused the mortal blow.

Warplock pistol!

And just as quickly as it had begun, the battle was over, as the ratmen scrambled for exits. Despite having gained the advantage, the arrival of additional mercenaries were an unwelcome surprise and in seconds, the enemy was gone; all except one lone vermin, standing at the top of the steps leading to the doorway from which Heinrich had entered. Dazed, Heinrich leaned on his sword and stared madly into the beast's foaming maw. It was the white one he had asked Broderick about right before the attack, the one supposedly in possession of the Heart of Sigmar. Its white fur was caked with muddy gore, its chest, shins, and snout wrapped in light leather armour, arms exposed. Warped by Chaos, the creature possessed two tails that tightly clutched two sacks glowing green with wyrdstone, and it waved the sacks in the air. In its left hand was the warplock pistol, smouldering from the shot.

Rage shook Heinrich's body. His heart pounded, his chest heaved as he girded his strength. *You twisted offal,* he screamed silently into the face of the white monster. *You killed my friend.*

As if it understood, the ratman chittered wildly and waved its free hand at the captain. Foaming spit flew from its black lips as it bared its fangs in defiance. Heinrich rushed forward, raising his sword to strike. But it was too late. As he reached the first step, the pale-furred skaven leaped backwards and vanished in the shadows.

An arm blocked Heinrich from going further. 'Easy, sir,' said an unfamiliar voice. 'It's over.'

Heinrich pulled away from the arm, swung around, and drove the hilt of his sword into the sternum of the man. The man fell down, gasping and clutching his stomach. Heinrich stood over the body of one of the strangers that had interrupted the fight. 'Step back!' Heinrich said. But as he stepped away, the man drove his leg into the back of Heinrich's knees, bringing him down. The man followed up with a swift chop to the neck.

'I'd show a little more respect for one that has just saved your life,' the man said, regaining his feet and drawing two poniards from under his cloak.

Heinrich winced against the pain of the blow, rolled over, raised his crossbow and aimed it at the forehead of the man. The man was very tall, sporting a dark complexion, shaved head, goatee and a gold earring in his right earlobe. He wore chestnut-coloured pantaloons and a gold tunic. A tiger fur cloak was draped over his shoulders and clipped at his neck. Black boots with silver points. He wasn't from the Empire.

The man was anxious but steady, like a wild fox, holding his ground but ready to strike at a moment's notice.

'Respect for you?' Heinrich said, holding the crossbow steady. 'And what gave you the right to intrude on my mission?'

'Your mission?' said the man. 'We've been tracking these ratmen for days. The trail led us here. And it looked like you needed help.'

'We were doing fine on our own, stranger,' said Heinrich. 'We do not need your charity.'

The man grunted. 'I beg to differ. If we had not arrived when we did–'

'Broderick would still be alive!' Heinrich shouted.

The man grew silent and looked past Heinrich towards the still body drowning in the pool of deep crimson. His face calmed. 'Yes, perhaps so. That is unfortunate. But let's be rational. Without our intrusion, you might have *all* died.'

By this time, the men from both groups had gathered themselves and were standing around their respective leaders, weapons drawn, eyes glaring at one another over a thin, deadly space. The anger and distrust in the air was palpable; one false move or word could start a brawl. But feeling secure with his men at hand, Heinrich lowered his crossbow and stood. 'Who are you?' he asked calmly.

The man lowered his knives and tucked them back beneath his cloak. 'I am Captain Bernardo Rojas.'

'Where are you from?'

'Estalia.'

Heinrich winced in disgust. Estalia? That hot, mysterious land topped in mountains, shrouded in mystery, and lying far to the west of the Empire. What wicked wind had blown *this* infidel into town? 'Ha!' he grunted and shook his head. 'An Estalian in Mordheim. Is that so? By the looks of your men, however, I'd say you were from further south. I *am* having a bad day.'

'Scoff all you wish,' Bernardo said with eyes glaring, 'but I will gladly pit my men of Marienburg against your Reiklander dogs any time.'

Heinrich ignored the challenge and turned away. He went to Broderick, knelt down, and held his hand above the deep wound. Hot. He leaned over and whispered gently in Broderick's ear, 'I'm sorry, my friend. May Sigmar bless your soul.'

He rose and stretched his back carefully. Night was falling fast and he could barely see his men through the shifting light and shadow. How many are left, he wondered. 'Father? How many have we lost?'

Father appeared at his side, shaken and exhausted. 'Three dead, captain. Young Gunderic and Sebastian, and Broderick. May Sigmar find them peaceful. Cuthbert is alive but his arms are badly mauled. Witchkiller is wounded severely. She may not last the night. I am well, as are Roland and Bloodtooth.'

'You don't look well,' Heinrich said, pointing at scores of tiny bites covering the priest's arms and neck. The old man was stooped over, fighting for air, his bald pate wet with cold sweat. The spells had taken their toll. 'You're lucky to be alive.'

Father rubbed at the wounds. 'Yes, captain. Lucky and cursed I would say.'

Father always said things that did not make sense, but Heinrich did not press him further. He turned away and shook his head. Three dead. What a terrible price to pay without even securing the prize for which they were fighting. He barely had enough men to field. How would they get out of the city alive at night while carrying their dead and wounded to safety?

As if reading his thoughts, the Estalian stepped forward. 'May we be of assistance?' he asked.

Heinrich turned and faced the stranger, uncertain of what to do or what to think. 'Haven't you done enough already?'

'We lost a man too,' Bernardo said, ignoring the jab. 'Young Gabriel fell shortly after we engaged. We should work together to get out of this cursed place, despite any misgivings we may have for one another. Night is falling. Let us help each other.'

'No. No, I will not allow you to touch—'

'Heinrich,' Father interrupted, laying a hand on his captain's shoulder. 'Please, let them help. We can't do this alone, and we can't leave anyone behind.'

'Fine!' Heinrich snapped. He wanted to lash out and smack the old man across the floor, but his words made sense.

'Captain?' Roland came forward, holding Bloodtooth by his massive chain. The dog's muzzle was soaked in ratman blood. 'Should we not look for the Heart before we leave?'

Heinrich shook his head. 'No. It isn't here.'

'But they may have dropped it in the battle. If we could just look through—'

'I said no!' Heinrich snapped. 'The ratmen are vile creatures, but they are not stupid. They know what we're after. They would not be so casual with it.'

'What is this *Heart* you speak of?' the Estalian asked. 'I do not understand.'

'Good. Let's keep it that way.' Heinrich did not try to hide his growing irritation with this pointless discussion. Exhausted, he used his sword to steady himself and wiped sweat from his brow. 'Very well, Estalian. I accept your offer, but that's as far as it goes. When we reach the western gate, we part company. We'll bury our men alone. Understood?'

Bernardo nodded, a quizzical smile on his face.

'And one more thing.' Heinrich leaned in close, his nose nearly touching Bernardo's sharp beak. 'Keep your hands off Broderick. He's my responsibility.'

With that, they began preparing the dead and wounded as the Mordheim night squeezed in.

THE SUN WAS rising in the east and driving away the fog. The air was still and thick. It would be a humid day, Heinrich knew, and he felt comforted by the cool of the stone pavilion in which he stood.

They were in the centre of a Garden of Morr. The garden lay within the moss and ivy-choked ruins of a small keep that stood vigil on a modest hill on the western side of Mordheim. The dead were laid naked on stone benches inside the pavilion. Roland covered each body in turn with a white sheet, while Father, holding a bowl of slow burning incense, whispered arcane prayers and moved among the bodies. He stopped at each, dipped a small brush into the grey ash of the incense fire, and then rubbed the pasty bristles across each warrior's clean-shaven, perfumed cheeks. He knelt down and kissed each lightly on the brow, then covered their eyes with silk cloths.

Heinrich stood in sombre humility and watched the priest work. Few Reikland mercenaries could claim their very own Sigmarite priest, but Heinrich considered it a gift and did not tempt fate by thinking about it too often. The old man's full name was Elgin von Klaushammer, but the men fondly called him 'Father' as befitting his spiritual connections; and at times like this, he was an invaluable servant to the team.

He looked into a dark corner of the pavilion where Cuthbert and Witchkiller lay resting quietly, taking comfort in each other's company. Their evening's wounds had not fully healed, but they had not got any worse. They would live, praise Sigmar, but they would be laid up for a while. Heinrich pulled himself straight, defying exhaustion. He was a leader after all and in times like this he needed to show strength.

It was a tragic thing to lose men on campaign. How many burials had he attended since his arrival in Mordheim? He could not remember. How many more would he attend? It was a fool who did not expect to lose men in such an evil place, but he had lost so *many* good men over the past few months. And now Broderick, his best friend and confidant, was gone. Broderick had always been there to help the group through their grief and to keep them focused. Where Father conducted the ritual of burial, it was Broderick who placed purpose in each death, extolling honour and dignity through his kind and simple words of faith. Faith in Sigmar Heldenhammer, founder and patron saint of the Empire; faith in the Grand Theogonist; faith in their mission. Heinrich looked down upon the rigid form of his friend and whispered, 'Goodbye Broderick. You were a good man and a great warrior.'

Heinrich turned and let Father's prayers drift from his mind. He looked towards the freshly dug graves waiting nearby. He felt sorry for the families of the men he would bury today. They would never know the fate of their kin, and what a terrible burden to bear. Some would consider it blasphemous to bury them within sight and sound of the Eternal Struggle, but it was better than leaving them to rot amidst the ruins. At least they were receiving some dignity and respect with a simple ceremony.

Heinrich placed his hand on the hilt of his sword. He looked beyond the garden to an observation tower. The aged, crumbling stone structure had stood for centuries as one corner of the keep but was now, in its twilight, used to view the city. He and Broderick had climbed the steps of the tower many times. They had looked down upon the desolation and tried to imagine what it might have been like on that fateful day in 1999, five years ago when the twin-tailed comet of Sigmar slammed into the city and eradicated the evil that had gathered.

In his weaker moments, Heinrich would wonder why the Warrior God had allowed Mordheim to survive at all, why he had allowed it to rise from its own grave. Why fill it with that cursed wyrdstone, a currency so valued, so prized that it called thousands into its seedy streets who would kill to possess it? At the top of the tower, Broderick would always answer, 'It is a warning and a test. I believe Sigmar allowed Mordheim to endure so as to remind us of the fine line between order and Chaos. Mordheim is a monument to that thin space between good and evil, and all the other cities of the Empire shoud look upon its devastation with fear and remember that they too could suffer the same fate if they so choose to fall into darkness.'

'And what of wyrdstone, then?' Heinrich would ask, pressing the issue. 'Why would Sigmar fill its streets with that awful temptation?'

'Again, it's a test. Men imbued with both good and bad intentions come here to seek it. What they do with it after they've found it is the test.'

'Have we passed the test, my friend?'

Broderick would smile and say, 'Well, I don't know about you, but *my* heart is pure.'

They would laugh at that and go on discussing issues throughout the night. What is the true nature of Chaos? Of order? Will the provinces of the Empire ever unite under Siegfried, the Grand Prince of Reikland? In the end, Heinrich would allow Broderick to have the last word, for his faith was that of a child's. Heinrich always looked to his friend for spiritual guidance, clarity of thought and consistency of purpose. With Broderick now gone, who would he rely now on to provide that clarity?

'Am I disturbing you?'

It was the voice of the Estalian. Heinrich swung around to face the strange man, his heart leaped into his throat as he considered drawing his sword, but he held steady. 'What are you doing here, Estalian? Don't you have a fallen sword to care for?'

'I have already buried young Gabriel,' Bernardo said, 'but I must speak with you now, before it is too late.'

'You are from a strange, undisciplined land,' Heinrich whispered. 'You are obviously unaware of the dishonour you've brought to me and mine by interrupting this service.'

Bernardo pulled up close, his eyes sparkling with agitation. 'I'm well aware of the sanctity of your burial service, sir, but what I have to discuss with you gives *respect* to those we bury today. Speak with me in private.'

Gritting his teeth, Heinrich grabbed the fringe of the Estalian's tiger cloak and pulled him away. 'Very well. Follow me.'

They walked through the garden and up to the observation tower. Heinrich climbed the wooden steps, carefully placing his boots into the worn places on the planks. 'I suggest you place your feet as I do, Estalian, lest you snap a plank and fall to your death.' Bernardo followed as directed.

At the top, they stood side-by-side and stared down at the mangled sprawl. Several minutes passed in silence. Heinrich spoke first. 'How long have you been in Mordheim, Estalian?'

'Not very long,' Bernardo said. 'Going on seven days now perhaps.'

Heinrich grunted. 'Then you are still clean and unfettered, I see. I've been here all of six months, and I'm already losing myself in its cesspool. I hate it and I love it. Does that make sense to you?'

Before Bernardo could respond, Heinrich continued. 'Broderick and I came up through the pits together, bare-chested fighters for gold and drama. A young man en route to Ostermark, I was captured by brigands and sold off like chattel. I thought I would die in those pits. Broderick saved me. He spoke about Sigmar and gave me purpose to fight on. We bought our freedom and set off for Altdorf to find our lives and to worship the Warrior God. And when we were ready, we set off for Mordheim to do good deeds for the Empire. But it wasn't supposed to end like this. Broderick wasn't supposed to die.'

Heinrich paused for a long moment, then said, 'Right before he fell, I argued with Broderick for not spotting the rat horde that appeared in the guildhouse and cut our band in two. I blamed it all on him, but it was my fault. I should have known better, anticipated it. It's my fault Broderick's dead. All my fault...'

'Why speak these things?' Bernardo said. He tried to lay a hand on Heinrich's shoulder, but the Reiklander pulled away. 'You are not responsible for the fate of every man under your charge.'

Heinrich nodded. 'Perhaps not.' He stared deeply into Bernardo's eyes, trying to measure the man's soul, but everything about him was different. His face was dark and sharp, dirt-smeared but flamboyant. His bald scalp a shiny palette of oily brown flesh. His mouth a thin sliver of pink forming a generous smile that masked... what? Heinrich searched for something more in the kind stare of the mysterious man, but nothing surfaced. The man also had a perfumery about him, a scent of cinnamon and lavender, of rosemary and ginger. It mixed with the stagnant, mouldy smell of the nearby graves and made Heinrich's nostrils flare.

'What brings you to the City of the Damned, Estalian?' Heinrich asked. 'You and your men are very far from the comforts of Marienburg, and, dare I say, from the *fanciful* proclamations of your Lady Magritta.'

If the insult caused the foreigner any agitation, he did not show it. He simply smiled and said, 'I'm not a political man. It matters not to me who sits on the Imperial throne, whether it is *my* Lady Magritta, or a puppet prince anointed by your Grand Theogonist. But I would suggest that you refrain from such observations around my men, as they may take offence. As for me, my kin were merchants. We had establishments in Marienburg, Talabheim, Middenheim, among other places. We were so often on the road that I feel as much a part of the Empire as I do my birth city of Bilbali. When I was old enough to make my own decisions, I returned home and tried to build a life. But it just didn't feel right any more. So I returned to Marienburg, gathered up some swords, then struck out to find my fortune.'

'But why Mordheim? It's such a drastic change from the comfortable life of a merchant's son.'

Bernardo shrugged. 'Mordheim is the place to be if you crave adventure, is it not? And don't take such a simpleton's view of a city and its people, Reiklander. There are two sides to every coin, and the measure of a man goes deeper than a mere prick of his skin.'

I may take you up on that measurement, Heinrich thought to himself, but kept his mouth shut. How dare this fop, this popinjay give him lessons in courtesy? He let the matter drop, however. It would be disrespectful to cause a stir within sight of Broderick's funeral.

A long silent minute hung between them, then Bernardo said, 'So tell me about this *Heart* you seek. I'm not familiar with it.'

Should I tell him, Heinrich asked himself? If such a powerful artefact fell into the hands of a foreigner and worse, Marienburgers, what price would the Empire pay?

Despite his reluctance, Heinrich answered. 'It's called the *Herz des Kriegergottes*, the Heart of the Warrior God, also known as Sigmar's Heart. It's thought to be the last remaining piece of the core of the comet. Many say it does not exist, but they are wrong. It's no larger than the palm of your hand, and flat as a dish. Its face shines brightly even in pure darkness, they say, its aspect shifting green to red and back again, and it's said that if you look upon it long enough, you can see the twin-tailed comet hurling through the sky and hitting the city. The legend goes that a ratman sorcerer first discovered it, and then it fell into the hands of dwarf treasure seekers who took a forge hammer to it and beat it into the shape that it is today, as if it were a mere trinket to be worn around the neck.

'The dwarfs traded it to a brewer for his entire stock of beer, and then it disappeared from sight for a couple of years until the Black

Guard, those templars who seek out and destroy the undead, learned that it had fallen into the hands of a vampire. They saved it from that unholy coupling, but they too lost it en route to Altdorf when a band of greenskins attacked them. The greenskins brought it back to Mordheim during their sweep south, where they too lost it...'

'And you think that the skaven have it again?' Bernardo interrupted.

Heinrich nodded. 'Yes. Broderick confirmed it. He saw it around the white one's neck a few days ago on a scouting mission.'

'But the white skaven last night was not wearing any medallion as I recall.'

'That is true.'

'Then perhaps they've lost it again.'

Heinrich shook his head. 'No. They have it. I'm certain of it.'

'How can you be so sure?'

'Because I am,' Heinrich blurted, growing weary of the conversation. They must have it, he thought to himself. They must, or Broderick died in vain.

'Well,' Bernardo said, 'whatever the truth, it certainly is a well-travelled little trinket. What does it do? What is its power?'

Heinrich shook his head, fighting down painful memories of his friend. 'Immortality. Unimaginable physical strength. Spiritual powers beyond any priest, wizard, or witch hunter of the Empire. There are many speculations. Father says that its true power can only be known by a pure-of-heart, the truest follower of Sigmar. And when *that* person touches it, whomever he may be, the second coming of the Warrior God will be upon us, the Empire will reunite under one banner again and a golden age of peace and prosperity will follow.'

'Really?' The Estalian seemed on the verge of laughing, his thin lips quivering to control an outburst. 'And you believe all this?'

'I trust my *friend*, Estalian,' Heinrich said angrily. 'Broderick said he saw it and that's good enough for me. I've pledged to myself and to the others to find, rescue, and deliver the Heart to Altdorf and to the Grand Theogonist. And that is what I intend to do.'

Heinrich turned away and closed his eyes. He took a deep breath and let his anger drift away with the cool breeze blowing from the east. 'I do love mornings here,' he said finally. 'Just as the sun rises and casts its shadows on the ruins. This is the time to gain the best perspective on the place.' He pointed out to the moist, green mist rising everywhere. 'See how the whole of it has a green glow, as if some daemon relieved itself in the wind? See how the black water of the river Stir sloshes its way through the heart of the city, its depths bulging with the myriad dead of last night's wickedness. The river cuts a fine swathe, a channel dividing east and west perfectly. Sometimes, when I'm down there, I forget which side I'm on.

Sometimes I get lost, drifting around and around the same block until a whiff of meat from a bandit's spit leads me to a gatehouse and to safety. Each ruined shed, each tavern and rookery, each stockyard or tumbled chapel has its own spirit, its own voice, a chorus of the souls that have died – the most *hideous* deaths – within its walls. When you're down there, it's hard to know where the flesh ends and stone and mortar begins.'

'But from here, you can see the whole of the desolation. You can see the deep crater where the comet hit and the destruction that erupted from its impact. Like one great heart of Chaos, pumping to the beat of a madness unstoppable, its veins the criss-cross of cobblestone streets where lost children roam: greenskins and Reiklanders, Marienburgers, Ostlanders and shadowy elves, dwarfs, ratmen, and too many to name. All of them fighting an endless skirmish for the very soul of the world.'

'Do you know what I see?' Bernardo asked.

Heinrich warily turned toward the Estalian. 'I'm afraid to ask.'

'I see a loud, smelly, musty old city that needs a good whipping, and we shouldn't be wasting our time debating about what it is and what it isn't. It is what it is.'

For the first time since they had met, Heinrich laughed. 'Now who's taking the simpleton's view? I see that you have much to learn about Mordheim. You don't show it the proper respect. But you better find humility soon, or you'll pay the price. If you play lightly with the City of the Damned, Estalian, she'll swallow you whole.'

'You said you wanted to talk,' Heinrich continued, not allowing the Estalian a chance to respond. 'What is it you have to say?'

Bernardo's face grew stern and serious. 'We must join our bands and go at the skaven again today.'

Heinrich shook his head. 'I made my position clear last night, Estalian. We can take care of the vermin on our own. We do not need your help. If you will excuse me.' He moved toward the steps. Bernardo held out an arm. 'Please, listen to me.'

Heinrich pulled back, drew his pistol, and held it to Bernardo's forehead. He cocked the hammer. 'That's the second time you've blocked my path. It will be your last.'

Bernardo held still, the barrel of the pistol pressed tightly against his head. 'You fool! I can smack that pistol away faster than you can pull the trigger.'

Heinrich held the weapon steady. 'I'm willing to take that risk.'

By this time, Heinrich's men had gathered below the tower. He looked down and saw Roland struggling to maintain his grip on Bloodtooth's leash, the hound's fatty jowls slathered with foamy spit, its teeth bared and biting the empty air. The rest were looking up, all worn and tattered, but with weapons at the ready. Father's warhammer glowed with power.

'You see, Estalian,' Heinrich said, a rush of confidence flushing his face, 'even if I misfire, you will not get off this tower alive.'

'I will not embarrass you in front of your men,' Bernardo said coolly. 'You have yet to witness and appreciate my quickness. So I kindly ask you to lower your pistol before our emotions get the better of us. I will not block your path again.'

Heinrich lowered the pistol cautiously. 'I pray that you do not. And let me repeat, I do not need your help.'

Bernardo shook his head. 'Despite the number of skaven that fell last night, many more scattered to the shadows. Do you know where they are, and how long do you think it will take to find them?'

'And I suppose you know where they fled?'

'Yes.'

Heinrich's shoulders sunk. 'Impossible. How could you know this? You have not been in the city long enough—'

'With respect, captain,' Bernardo said, 'you are not the only swinging sword in Mordheim with resources.'

Heinrich rubbed his face and considered the Estalian's admission. Could this coxcomb truly know where the ratmen fled, he wondered? Or was this some ruse to keep him from finding their real location? Now that the truth of the Heart had been revealed, perhaps this was some diversion to send Heinrich's men one way, while some of Bernardo's men went another. That was a possibility. Who knew the true motivation of an Estalian, especially one associated with Marienburg and its corrupt merchant guilds? His frivolity and disrespect for things holy certainly did not bode well. But perhaps it would not hurt to hear him out, Heinrich considered, if for no other reason but to reveal the absurdity of the information.

'Alright. Where are they?'

Bernardo turned and pointed to the glowing city. 'My scout tells me that their stronghold is within several blocks of the southern gate. It's an old two-storey mausoleum, with the bottom storey buried beneath rocks. The only entrance is on the first floor behind a marble arcade. It's a long corridor ending at a door leading down to the ground floor. Neither of our bands alone could penetrate the defences. But if we assault it together, we could do it. We could wipe them out and find peace for a time.'

Heinrich tried to find the lie hidden between the Estalian's words, but there was no deception, no hesitation. He was telling the truth... as far as he knew it.

'The southern gate?' Heinrich scratched the scar on his cheek. 'I don't know. That's Sister territory.'

Bernardo chuckled. 'My captain, are you afraid of women?'

Heinrich raised his pistol slightly. 'Take caution in your tone. This pistol is still cocked. The Sisters are not women as far as I'm concerned. At least not like any women I've ever met.'

The Sisters of Sigmar were a convent of misfits and discarded daughters from across the Empire. Self-proclaimed witch hunters and caregivers, their abbey was called the Temple of Sigmar's Rock, and it stood on a single fist of black stone jutting from the poisonous flow of the River Stir. The spires of their home dominated the skyline of the southern districts, and their presence was felt immediately by anyone passing through the southern gate. The thought of facing them did not sit well in Heinrich's chest.

'Do you see this scar?' Heinrich pointed to the white claw-shaped wound on his face. 'I got this souvenir on my first day in Mordheim. A Sister did not appreciate my smile and smacked it off my face with her whip.'

It was Bernardo's turn to laugh. 'The men in my country would have considered that a kiss. You should have kissed her back.'

'I'm not here to frolic and make merry, Estalian,' Heinrich blurted. 'I'm here to serve Sigmar. Given the condition we are in, I've no interest in tangling with harlots.'

'Do not concern yourself with the Sisters,' Bernardo said, 'they will not give us pause. Trust me.'

Can you be trusted, Heinrich wondered? Trust was a rare commodity in the streets of Mordheim. A man had to earn trust, had to put in his time and shed his requisite draught of blood. But perhaps there was no other choice. Looking into the eager face of the Estalian, Heinrich remembered an old adage from his days as a pit fighter: 'No sword, then fight with your hands. No hands, then with your teeth'. *My right hand is gone*, Heinrich said to himself as he thought about Broderick. *Dare I give my left*?

'What is your answer?' Bernardo asked.

Heinrich lowered his pistol, uncocked the hammer, and tucked it away. He looked down at his men. They were a mess: dirty, beaten, bruised, and exhausted beyond a doubt. If he asked, they would find their strength, ready their blades, and head back into the stinking mire. They would fight to the last man if he asked it. But going alone was madness. Alone, they would not survive another day.

'Very well, Estalian,' Heinrich said. 'I accept your offer. What is your price?'

'Half the take of any wyrdstone we find.'

'A third,' Heinrich countered, 'and the Heart is mine.'

'Why is the trinket yours?' Bernardo asked. 'We were tracking the skaven the same as you.'

Heinrich shook his head. 'No, sir. You cannot declare for something that you do not believe exists and by right I claim seniority. I've
been here longer than you.'

There was no such claim of seniority in the streets of Mordheim.
Finders-keepers and winner-takes-all were the battle cries. But does
the Estalian know that, Heinrich wondered?

Bernardo paused, for a long time, then said, 'Okay, a third of the
wyrdstone, plus the lion's share of any gems and jewellery we may
find.'

Heinrich did not like the deal, but reluctantly agreed. 'Gather your
men,' he said, taking the steps and descending, 'and bring them here
so that we may praise our dead. Then let us take a small rest, find a
scrap to eat, and then we'll go. You will lead the way, but let's make it
clear. This is *my* mission. Understood?'

'As you wish… *captain*.'

AFTER A BRIEF respite, they gathered the men and set out to track down
the skaven clan. They moved quickly and quietly outside the stone
wall, which ensnared the city in a ring of vacant ramparts and battlements. The route chosen was of greater distance, but safer by far. Once
you entered the cursed city, there were no guarantees of safety. Brigands, thrill-seekers and treasure-mongers were lying in wait for
passers-by and they could not afford petty distractions en route to the
skaven stronghold.

The men had had little chance to get acquainted with one another
before setting out. Bernardo's men were Marienburgers. There were
three of them: Karl Stügart, an ex-swordsman and deserter from the
Marienburg army, Rupert Keller, a quay merchant who had killed a
rival in cold blood and now, as personal penance for the crime, wore
a chain around his neck attached to a rock hidden in a side pocket of
his orange tunic, and Albert Eickmann, a barkeeper and part-time
burglar trying to stay one step ahead of death and the law. What a
miserable gang, Heinrich thought to himself as he greeted each with
a pensive smile.

They had all shared pleasantries and had kept civil tongues during
their morning preparations, but it was clear to Heinrich that the tension between his men and Bernardo's was as palpable as the gritty fog
that clung to the banks of the Stir. It would take time for the men to
trust each other, and time they did not have. At the moment of
impact, they would have to perform instinctively, anticipating each
other's moves and actions. With only eight strong, no margin of error
was afforded. And with no training or practice, the effective fighting
strength was closer to five men. Heinrich made the sign of Sigmar and
prayed for luck.

They entered the city through the southern gate. The heavily travelled archway was called the Daemon Mouth, and what a ghastly orifice it was. The entrance lay between two stone towers. Tall, sleek and defiant, their arrow slits squinted darkly upon the approach. The massive iron-plated doors had been ripped off and lay adrift in a sea of weeds and brambles beside the road. What remained were the rusty fangs of a portcullis, suspended by equally rusty chains that teetered above the underpass and threatened to drop at the slightest breeze. Heinrich held his breath, stepped quickly beneath the iron teeth, and came out the other side.

Before them lay a narrow cobblestone road that wound through a maze of ruins. Many called it the Street of Madness, for it was believed that no man, not even the most devoted follower of Sigmar, could reach its end at the northern river gate without going insane. One day, Heinrich thought to himself with a confident nod, I will take that challenge.

They set off down the road, eyeing cautiously the desolate architecture pressing down on both sides. They spread out in a loose circle, Bernardo taking the lead, Heinrich holding the centre and the rest pointing bows and swords in all directions. Despite the fog, the sun was hot and the air heavy. Heinrich shielded his eyes from the shifting beams of light that punctured the fog and tossed angular spikes of white heat across his path. He looked to his left and saw an ensemble of bleached skeletons sitting on discarded chairs, huddled tightly in a circle and holding flutes, violins, tambourines, lutes, and harps. In the swirling haze, the bones moved rhythmically, and Heinrich could almost hear notes rising above their unholy recital. He closed his eyes, rubbed them vigorously, and shook his head. He looked again and the band was gone, their music swept away by a chorus of bloody screams from some unseen battle raging in the distance.

An illusion.

Father appeared beside him. 'Captain, are you well?'

'Yes, I'm fine, thank you. I thought I saw... No, it was nothing.' Heinrich rubbed his eyes. 'I'm just feeling a little tepid. The air is thick today, and the dead of Mordheim are playing tricks with my mind.'

Father drew a corked vial of clear liquid from his robe. 'I want you to have this.'

Heinrich looked at the vial warily. 'What is it?'

'Tears of Shallya. Water from the holy spring of Couronne. It will protect you from the ratmen's poison.'

Heinrich shook his head. 'Thank you, but I cannot accept it. You should have it. You are far more valuable than I.'

Father grabbed Heinrich's hand and pressed the vial into his palm. 'Take it, please, I beg you. I fear for your life today.'

The priest's eyes burned with intensity, and his warhammer glowed. Heinrich had seen this look before. There was no arguing with the old man when he had made his mind up. Heinrich nodded appreciatively and tucked the vial into a pocket.

They came to an abrupt halt at a fork in the road. To the right, the way bled into an area of the city once known as the Poor Quarter. To the left, the unassailable towers of the Sisters of Sigmar's abbey loomed large in the distance. Father and Roland began mumbling prayers while making the sign of Sigmar with nervous hands. There was great suspicion and anxiety among Sigmarites towards the Sisters' abbey, Heinrich knew. He shared some of that anxiety himself as he scratched the scar on his cheek.

When the comet had hit the city, it had spread its death and desolation equally, save for the abbey. Neither a scratch nor a speck of dirt fell upon its indefatigable battlements, and many believed that the Sisters had called upon dark forces to ensure their salvation from the holocaust of that dreadful night. Heinrich did not know the truth, but the edict from the Grand Theogonist was clear: No counsel or fraternisation between the devout men of Sigmar and the Sisters. It was an order that Heinrich tried to respect each day.

From behind a lone wall of leaning shale, four figures emerged clad in white and purple habits, Heinrich knew immediately who they were. The men around him trained their weapons forward as the Sisters walked into the road brandishing steel whips. Heinrich's scar ached at the sight of those awful weapons. In a fight, those whips could strike at distances and at speeds impossible to deflect. They could not afford a spat with the Sisters; the ever-watching manses of their abbey guaranteed reinforcements within moments, if more were not already lying in wait around them. Heinrich shot nervous glances at the ruins, they seemed alive with eyes.

He walked slowly to the head of the group, but Bernardo was already on the move. The Estalian raised his hands in peace and wandered up to the armed women. He mumbled a few words to the one clad in all white and gold trim, with silver medallions hanging from her thick neck and pointed towards the Poor Quarter. The Sisters looked at each other, nodded, then moved away. Bernardo thanked them with a generous bow and returned. Heinrich stood there, his mouth open in astonishment. 'Well,' he said as Bernardo returned, 'here's a good reason not to trust you. Would you mind explaining that?'

The Estalian smiled furtively and winked. 'It's a bit complicated. I'll explain some other time.' He said nothing else and reassumed his position at the point.

After passing a few more blocks, they turned off the main route and took to alleys and back streets, forming a tight line, with Bernardo in the lead, Heinrich at the rear, and the rest in between. Cuthbert and Witchkiller had been left behind in camp to mend. It would have been nice to include more help, perhaps hire a sword for close-in fighting or a Tilean marksman to bolster their missile strength, but there was no time. They had what they had, and there was a certain nobility in facing one's foes with your honest strength. The measure of a good man was his capacity to overcome adversity. One Sigmarite equalled ten of the Empire's foes, wasn't that the old saying? Heinrich placed his hand into his pocket and rubbed the vial of tears that Father had given him. He hoped it were true.

They clung to the walls, whenever they came across them, and used piles of debris for cover. Occasionally, a straggler from a nearby skirmish crossed their path, some raving Chaos-possessed brethren or a rotting zombie flesh hunter, but these interruptions caused little delay. A swift spin of a morning star or a carefully placed arrow remedied the problem immediately.

That's how it was sometimes, Heinrich realised as he stepped over the severed head of an orc. The dead city always surprised him. Sometimes, the streets were so thick with thugs that it resembled a tavern in Altdorf and other times the streets were as quiet as a tongueless ghoul. Mordheim took rests, it seemed, little naps to refresh before erupting again. Unpredictable, inconsistent, keeping you off-balance, luring you into complacency and then ripping you back with a deafening clamour of battle through its sordid streets.

They paused for a quick breath and for cover to protect themselves from a hailstorm that blew in abruptly. As they waited for the storm to pass, Heinrich placed his hand upon a section of wall caked in grey dirt. Mere blocks away lay the massive crater where the twin-tailed comet had struck, and this part of the city was smothered in debris. Neither rain nor wind nor goose egg hail seemed capable of washing away the stink of evil here. Heinrich rubbed his hand across his sleeve and realised how perfect this area was for a skaven stronghold. The air was choked with sewer water and silt, hot and humid, and difficult to breathe. A tunnel race could thrive in such torturous surroundings.

When the storm had passed, they set off again. They rounded the corner of a collapsed inn and passed beneath a stone walkway. Below it three human skeletons swung on dry hemp, their bleached bones knocking in the wind like ceramic chimes. The dull clangour sent a chill up Heinrich's spine, and he moved over to Bloodtooth and rubbed the mastiff's broad back. The warhound pushed his slimy muzzle into his master's sleeve and whimpered, nibbling affectionately on his dirty fingers. Heinrich smiled. 'I'm glad you're here, old boy.'

They stopped suddenly. At the head of the line Bernardo motioned anxiously. 'What is it?' Heinrich asked as he moved up.

Bernardo pointed around the corner to a large building that towered above the nearby ruins. Heinrich's eyes widened. He wondered why he hadn't seen it until now; such a massive structure, rising out of the ground like some forgotten temple.

'This is it?' Heinrich asked.

'Yes,' the Estalian said. 'What do you think?'

Heinrich didn't know what to think. It was a mausoleum, a resting-place for the dead, a site of reverence and honour. But the entire structure sat within an enclosed courtyard whose walls were heavily damaged and choked in dried ropes of ivy and nightshade. The remnants of a black iron gate hung limp from the main entrance, and traces of an old stone staircase could be seen amidst a mountain of rocks. Like Bernardo had said, the entire courtyard, and thus the entire first floor, was completely covered by stones large and small, piled high and packed in tight. The rocks formed a pyramid up the sides of the first floor and tapered away to a square granite platform.

Marble arches stood on top of the platform, eight per side, supporting a flat marble roof adorned with beastly gargoyles. The columns that supported the archways comprised capitals and pilasters carved in the faces of dragons and griffons, and the arches themselves were reinforced with spandrels shaped in the letters of some ancient language. Heinrich tried reading the letters, but the distance and the ravages of time had eroded them beyond recognition. Beyond the arches loomed darkness.

Heinrich's temples throbbed. 'I see no guards,' he said.

'If you lived in that fortress,' Bernardo said, 'would *you* need them?'

The Estalian's flippant tone was annoying, but Heinrich let it pass. He studied the rocks. Different sizes and shapes, some seemingly sealed with mortar while others were loose and menacing. 'We must scale those rocks?' he asked.

Bernardo nodded. 'My scout says that behind the arcade lies the corridor leading down to the buried level. The ratmen are there.'

'And you *trust* this scout? He's reliable?'

'*She*, captain,' Bernardo said. 'She had better be, she's my half-sister.'

Heinrich nearly fell over. He could not imagine it. Gods be good, but the neighbourhood was going to the chamber pot. 'Your half-sister? You use your own kin – a *woman* – as a scout? You are joking.'

Bernardo shook his head. 'No, captain. She's honest flesh and blood. Perhaps some day you will meet her. Do not worry, she's the best there is. You can trust her. And me.'

'You haven't *earned* my trust yet, Estalian,' Heinrich glared intensely into Bernardo's deep eyes, 'but I suppose I've no other choice.' He studied the area around the mausoleum. 'There's too much open space around the blasted thing and the other buildings are too far apart. We won't be able to set up a good screen of supporting fire to cover our advance. We'll have to go in force, but I'm worried about those rocks and whether they are stable. If they attack while we're climbing up, will they hold?'

Bernardo shrugged his lean shoulders. 'I have no idea, but a wise old man from Cathay once said, "On death ground, fight"'.

Heinrich's breath caught in his throat. That was something Broderick would have said. He tried to hide his surprise, but a smile crept across his dry lips. 'And if we find ourselves on death ground, I suppose you'll show me your amazing quickness?'

Bernardo drew a poniard and waved it in a circle. 'With pleasure.'

They lined up for the assault, four sets of two. Bernardo paired up with Karl, the ex-swordsman, and Heinrich chose Bloodtooth.

They moved towards the mausoleum. Heinrich held Bloodtooth's chain tightly and stared up the slope of rocks and into the thin emptiness behind the arches. Somewhere in those shadows he knew death awaited.

They moved through the broken iron gate quickly. Heinrich chose to go last, guarding the approach with crossbow trained at the mausoleum. When Bernardo and Karl were safely through and in place, Heinrich followed with Bloodtooth straining madly on the chain. It was all he could do to keep the dog under control, and he considered letting the beast loose. But the sudden stillness of the air unnerved him. This wasn't the usual subsidence of the wind or the occasional acoustical shadow that muffled the city's screams. This was a death silence, a hollowness in the air that had no substance, no mass or form, as if the city no longer existed, all of its parts swept away and a hole left in its place. A cold sweat pricked Heinrich's neck as he tested the rocks with his knees. He pulled Bloodtooth close. The dog's sticky tongue slapped against his face. 'Not now, boy. Save it for the ratmen.'

Heinrich gave the signal and they began to climb, each pair measuring their steps carefully. Bernardo and Karl took the lead, slithering up the rock face like snakes. Heinrich shot the Estalian an angry look, but it did little good. They were at the mid-point before deciding to stop and wait for the rest to catch up. Father and Rupert ascended the rocks slowly and deliberately, the old priest halting periodically to raise cupped hands to the sky. Roland and Albert were moving up on Heinrich's left, when the barkeeper suddenly lost his balance and disappeared in an avalanche of rock and dust. Roland was also swept downward. Heinrich reached out and tried to grab a hand, but Roland cascaded to the bottom and landed squarely on top of his partner.

Heinrich cursed and moved to help, but was abruptly slammed to his back. The absolute silence in the air a moment ago was now replaced by ghostly bemoanings and ululations, as grey and white tendrils of smoke rose out of the cracks in the rocks and wrapped around his body. What devilment is this, Heinrich asked himself? And then he realised it wasn't smoke at all, but spirits, rising from their rocky tomb, swirling around his limbs and pinning him down. He looked around and saw that all the men were grappling with them, swinging their arms or weapons through the air as if swatting flies. He tried to pull free, his heart pounding wildly in his chest, but the spectres' clutch was too great.

What can I do, he wondered? Just as he realised that he'd dropped Bloodtooth's chain, a grey face swirled before him, forming hollow eyes and sharp, smoky teeth. Heinrich whispered Sigmarite prayers and stared breathlessly into jaws that opened and mouthed words. He did not hear the words with his ears, but in his mind. Although the words were thin, raspy and cold, he understood them clearly.

Avenge our humiliation, the ghost said. *Kill the skaven for what they did to us. Kill them all… and give us rest.*

Heinrich nodded obediently as the dark face slowly, slowly dissolved away.

He did not know how long he lay there with eyes closed, humming prayers and breathing calmly, but when he opened his eyes the ghosts were gone and he sat up. Bloodtooth twisted on his back nearby, struggling to right himself. The others were fixing themselves as well, checking their weapons, and beginning the climb again. Heinrich reached over and grabbed the hound's chain.

Unhindered this time, they reached the mid-point together and still no skaven slings or weeping blades slick with poison. Like fireflies drawn to the darkness, they inched ever upward, letting loose stones bounce away with echoes that danced through the ruins. Heinrich held Bloodtooth tight and kept his crossbow ready.

They reached the granite platform and stopped, using the columns for cover. Bernardo was the first to hoist himself up, then Karl and then the others followed. They huddled close, waiting for their eyes to adjust to the darkness. Heinrich squinted and tried to make out the depth of the second floor.

'Estalian?' he whispered. 'Where do we go from here?'

Bernardo pointed into the darkness. 'This way, but we'll need torches.'

Albert pulled torches from his backpack, but before he could light them, the granite floor began to vibrate. Then came a rustle of motion. Then screeching and squalling, high-pitched battle cries flooding the space around the mausoleum and shaking the earth. Heinrich unclipped Bloodtooth from his restraint. The hound growled and leaped into the darkness. The men spread out quickly and brandished their weapons, Father hefting his warhammer in defiance of his fragile form. Heinrich stepped back and braced himself against a pilaster and fixed the stock of his crossbow tightly against his shoulder. 'Great Sigmar,' he whispered. 'Give us strength.'

The platform erupted in a mass of black and brown fur, snarling muzzles filled with yellow teeth, and red eyes blazing with hate. Two dozen strong, the ratmen hurled themselves into the men and slingers let fly a hail of pellets that shattered against the arch above Heinrich's head. He snapped off a bolt and watched it pierce the belly of a slinger. Other missiles fired into the skaven assault as each man worked frantically to hold his ground. Heinrich ducked steel fighting claws and drove the butt of his crossbow into a furry throat. The mangy beast fell over gasping for air. Heinrich drew his pistol and finished it off.

He tucked away his gun and crossbow and drew his sword. He pressed deeper into the darkness, not knowing where the rest of the men were. They were around him, for sure, but the battle was too confused and chaotic to pinpoint exact locations. He prayed for luck and swung his blade forward, cutting a swathe through the shadows. At that moment, Father's warhammer glowed white-hot and pushed away the darkness. Heinrich caught a glimpse of his partner.

Bloodtooth raged a few paces before him, his bloody fangs sunk deep into the crotch of a ratman slinger. The ratman squealed in agony and fell shaking. Other skaven tried to save their clansman from certain death, but Heinrich stepped up and took them down.

'Bloodtooth, enough!' Heinrich yelled. Reluctantly, the hound released its grip, tearing away flesh. Heinrich walked up to the dying skaven and drove his boot into its throat.

The battle ended abruptly as the enemy slipped away into the shadows and down the rocky pyramid. Another swift attack, then dispersal, attack and dispersal, this was how the skaven fought – a guerrilla war, a battle of attrition and Heinrich was weary of it. He sheathed his sword. He turned and saw that the fight was still going. The last two attackers were facing the Estalian and finding their position quite tenuous. Heinrich watched in awe.

He'd never seen a blade move so fast. Bernardo wielded a long, slender sword of curved steel that shined despite little sunlight. It wasn't any kind of weapon Heinrich had seen before. Rumours of mysterious blades forged in far eastern lands had been told, swords that could cleave heads from necks with one swipe, but no one had ever seen them. Save for now. As the ratmen tried to flee, Bernardo felled one and then the other with a single swipe across their chests. For good measure, he counter-swung and lacerated their faces.

Bernardo wiped the blade clean and sheathed it. Heinrich approached. 'What kind of sword is that?' he asked.

'It's a Jintachi blade,' Bernardo said, breathing deeply. 'It was my father's. A gift from a traveller who claimed to have got it in the far east. I call it Myrmidia, after the Goddess of War.'

'You wield it well,' Heinrich said.

'Thank you,' said Bernardo, nodding politely. 'Perhaps you'll let me teach you how to use it.'

Heinrich shook his head. 'I don't think so. Something like that works for you, I suppose. But I prefer something heavier, more traditional.' He placed his hand on the hilt of his own sword.

Bernardo chuckled. 'I guess you're right. A weapon like this requires a delicate touch. Stocky fingers like yours would just get in the way.'

Heinrich's eyes glazed in anger. 'Now see here...' he began, moving forward. But Father, standing close, shook his head and silently implored his captain to remain calm. Heinrich halted immediately. 'We will take this up later, Estalian,' he said. 'Right now we need light.'

Six torches were laid on the floor. Albert lit them and handed them out. Fear spread through the men as shadows were thrown back and terror revealed.

The hallway that lay before them was as tall as four men and immeasurably deep. Along the walls were rows upon rows of crypts embossed with the holy symbols of Morr and Sigmar, the words of ancient prayers and the murals of glorious battles. Though grey dust covered it all, the names of the honoured dead defiantly stood forth from the granite: Siebel Gottard, Hera Ruekheiser, Stephan Voelker.... Names meaningless to Heinrich, but somehow possessing great power, as if the mere utterance of them filled the heart with strength. These people had been laid here in glorious praise to their makers. They did not deserve what the skaven had done to them.

'Oh, my holy Sigmar,' Roland said as he shook in fear beside Heinrich. 'What are we going to do about this? How do we stop such madness?'

Heinrich gnashed his teeth. 'Kill them... every last one of them.'

Hundreds of the crypts had been ransacked, seals penetrated and ripped apart. Piles of skeletons lay on the floor of the hallway, and even more hung out of caskets like twisted scaffolding. The hair of dead matriarchs cascaded down like vines, harbouring nests of baby rats.

With torches raised high, they picked their way through the vandalism. Bernardo passed a nest and set it aflame and watched the embers devour the screeching young. The stink of burning hair and rodent flesh filled the hall.

'That's a mistake,' said Heinrich.

'How so?' asked Bernardo.

'You'll see.'

Stepping over bones and splintered coffins, Heinrich noticed that the walls were suddenly alive with a thousand tiny eyes. Rats everywhere, scampering down the garden of old bones, leaping to the ground amidst the maze of death. One dropped on Heinrich's back. He smacked it off and yelled, 'Run!'

They bolted down the hall, dodging and bounding over a deluge of ripping teeth and claws. 'This is what happens when you set fire to nests,' Heinrich snapped at Bernardo as he ripped a plump one from his shoulder.

'Why didn't you say something?' Bernardo screamed.

'You did not ask.'

Through the shadows a massive postern appeared, and within it stood a mahogany door reinforced with iron bars. 'There is the doorway,' said Bernardo.

Someone at the rear screamed. Heinrich looked back and saw Karl covered in rats. The ex-swordsman howled and fought madly, but the weight of the host was too great. He disappeared beneath them. Heinrich wanted to stop and help, but kept running. If he turned now, he too would be taken down.

They reached the door ahead of the advancing rats, which had stopped momentarily to feast on the downed Marienburg. Heinrich slammed his shoulder into the wood. He cursed. 'It's locked from the inside. We'll need to find another way in.'

'There is no other way in,' Bernardo said, keeping one agitated eye on the rear. 'It's here or back to the rats!'

'I can open it, captain.' Father appeared with hammer in hand, its iron head pulsing white with power.

'Your magic alone will not break the seal, priest,' Bernardo said. 'We'll have to do this together.'

'And quickly,' Heinrich said. 'The horde is upon us.'

The men gave Father room. The priest raised his hammer and brought it down. The black wood splintered. Heinrich wedged his sword into the seal between granite and door and pried as Father delivered a second blow, then a third and a forth. Bernardo and Albert were answering the priest's hammer blows with firm shoulders into the ever-cracking wood. A fifth hammer strike and the door gave way.

'Move!' Heinrich yelled, waving the men through the door and into pitch-black. One after another, they leaped through the doorway as Bernardo and Roland conducted a fighting withdrawal against the relentless swarm. When all were through, Heinrich – feeling the tear of claws upon his legs – slammed the door shut.

The door bowed under the weight of rats and then it stopped as a cold silence set in. Through the smoky torchlight, Heinrich could hear the men gasping for breath. He leaned against the door and said, 'Praise Sigmar. That was close.'

'I'm sorry for torching the nest,' Bernardo said, 'but you could have saved us all a lot of trouble *and* Karl's life if you had just spoken up.'

Heinrich started to say something harsh to put the foreigner in his place, but he refrained. There was nothing that could be said, in effect, to correct the error. Why didn't I warn him, he wondered? Am I so blind with grief for Broderick that I'd risk us all just to humiliate this man? Looking into Bernardo's waiting eyes, Heinrich was ashamed. This was not the behaviour of a good leader. 'You are right,' he said. 'I should have warned you. Will you accept my apology?'

Fighting his anger, Bernardo said, 'Well, it can't be fixed. At least the rest of the men are fine, although we've taken wounds. The hound is cut up, his legs are bleeding.' He leaned in close and whispered. 'I'm worried about the priest, though. He's old and this has been a difficult run. I don't know if–'

'Do not fret for me, Bernardo,' Father interrupted. The priest gave the Estalian a rare wink and a smile, and hefted his hammer in steady hands. 'I may be old, but I'll live.'

Father's confidence quickened Heinrich's blood. 'It's settled then,' he said. 'Where do we go?'

'A stairway leads down here, captain,' Roland said, pointing towards rugged steps winding downward.

Heinrich nodded and reached for Bloodtooth and pulled him close. The dog was performing splendidly, albeit taking the brunt of bites and cuts. With so much enemy flesh for the taking, it was hard for the hound to keep its hunger at bay. Heinrich ruffled his friend's ears. Sadness clutched his chest. Eventually, he knew, the taint of Chaos would take the dog down. It was inevitable in the City of the Damned. A price had to be paid. Bloodtooth would eventually pay that price with his life.

Heinrich moved to the top of the stairs and looked down. The air was cold and clammy and heavy with the smell of rotting wood, rat faeces and blood. It would be madness to go down these steps, he realised. Traps and ambushes surely waited, but perhaps not. What did it matter? A Sigmarite lives to die in the service of his god. Today is as good a day to die as any, he thought to himself. No turning back.

'Did your scout give any clues as to what lies at the bottom of these stairs?' Heinrich turned to the Estalian.

Bernardo shook his head. 'She's a good scout, but she's not an idiot. She would not venture any further alone.'

'I see.' Heinrich grabbed the torch out of Albert's hand and held it high. He drew his sword and started down the steps. 'Let's go and find out.'

Bloodtooth kept at his side and the men followed, torches raised high, weapons ready. They stepped carefully, placing their boots on steps lousy with cobwebs, rat carcasses, and human bones. Heinrich kicked as much filth out of the way as he could, but the going was difficult. With each step, the air grew stale with the sickly sweet smell of the grave, that pungent odour of death and decay for which the skaven were known. Some of the men began to cough and Rupert's torch flickered out. This was the air of the diseased, the breath of mutation and of rot.

They reached the bottom. Before them lay three passages and Heinrich raised his torch and studied their options. The centre passage contained the same architecture as the mausoleum: finely wrought granite, smooth and lined with blind arches. The other passages were crude and misshapen, mere holes carved into the rock. These were skaven tunnels, Heinrich knew, and they undoubtedly linked directly to the maze of passages that ran beneath Mordheim.

'Which one should we take?' Bernardo asked.

'I'm not in the mood to get lost in the skaven underworld,' Heinrich said. 'Let's take the centre one.'

And so they did, slowly and quietly. It was enough that they carried torches, the smell of smoke and the light would sound the alarm anyway, but why tempt fate? Even Bloodtooth, his jowls dripping foamy red-white muck, padded gingerly through the panoply of human remains and skaven waste. Heinrich expected to see more coffins ripped open and strewn along the way, but what he found was even more disturbing.

The walls and barrel-vaulted ceiling were blood-marked in runes and symbols that writhed like twisted souls in the flickering torchlight. The hair on Heinrich's neck stiffened as Bloodtooth pulled on the chain in sputtering yelps and growls. *What have we walked into?*

And then he heard squeals and shrieks coming from behind them and echoing down the stairs from which they had come. The men turned and braced themselves, and Heinrich gripped his sword tightly. 'No turning back now,' he said, more to himself, but the men heard. Rupert fingered the links in his ball and chain, and Albert, Father and Roland backed away from the growing clamour. It sounded like a hundred-strong, but that was likely due to the echoes off the walls. Bloodtooth joined their screeching chorus with a low bass growl. He was angry, straining on the chain so hard that Heinrich felt his feet slip at the pull.

'It's not wise to stand here in the middle of the hall,' Bernardo said. 'We should keep moving and find better ground.'

'I doubt we'll find any of that here,' Heinrich said. But he yanked Bloodtooth away and they moved, faster this time, trying to stay ahead of the oncoming mass.

Around a turn and they emerged into a small circular room, with coffins and bones piled against the walls. A granite pedestal lay in the centre and broken chairs cluttered the floor. Heinrich looked for a passage out, but there were none. This was the end of the line.

'So it's here then,' he said and threw his torch on the pedestal. He sheathed his sword and drew his crossbow. 'Missiles at the ready. Aim straight and true. Down as many as you can, then finish them with steel.'

Torches were tossed aside and bows were drawn. Bernardo drew Myrmidia and climbed upon the pedestal.

Skaven burst into the room from the hallway. A buzz of missiles felled the first rank. The second rank stumbled. That was all the time needed. Blades were drawn and the battle engaged. Heinrich swung low and tore through skaven chest. Bodies piled at his feet, but still they came on. There were no slingers in this group, praise Sigmar, only close quarter weapons: fighting claws, short swords, clubs, and weeping blades. Though the light in the room was faint, Heinrich could see the venomous poison dripping from those dreaded blades. He ducked slashing claws and drove the point of his sword into the tender belly of an assailant, ducked another slash and severed a limb.

It was impossible to know the number of ratmen in the room, as furry shapes leaped in and out of shadows at speeds too difficult to gauge. The screams and shrieks and deep guttural cries of battle were deafening, sounds banging off the walls and ricocheting back to drown out Heinrich's shouted orders. It was futile to direct the fight. No one could hear anything beyond his tiny space of war, and Heinrich shut his mouth and swung his sword.

The nocturnal ratmen were finding the light of the torches unbearable and many were fighting to put them out. But Bernardo and Roland held the pedestal, slashing and crushing every claw and snout that stuck in too closely. Heinrich smiled and kept killing.

Out of the corner of his eye, he saw Father fall under a gang of ratmen, their clubs and spears tearing into the priest's robe. The old man howled in pain as a spear jabbed his chest and Heinrich moved to give aid, but something caught his boot and took him down.

He hit the floor hard, cutting his arms. The impact jarred his sword loose and it skidded into the shadows. Heinrich reached for it, but a force unseen held him down. He rolled onto his back and tried to focus on a small silhouette standing before him. For a moment, he was back on the rocky pyramid outside the mausoleum struggling with phantoms. But there were no ghosts here, only the milky ooze of confusion clouding his eyes and blurring his thoughts. As he struggled to see, the air grew thinner and thinner until a face appeared.

A face belonging to a broken creature, wrapped in a black robe and hood, loomed before him. One eye patched over with a dirty bandage, the other a bright red dot set deep within a puffy socket. Its snout, covered in pus, spit and warts, twitched uncontrollably as its sharp, pink tongue slid across rotten teeth. The skaven sorcerer cackled madly and drew a medallion from its robe.

Heinrich's eyes widened as they set upon the medal. *Das Herz des Kriegergottes*. The Heart of the Warrior God. The Heart of Sigmar. There it was before him, swinging like a pendulum, its sheer surface catching the torchlight and warming to a bright green, then red, then green again. Heinrich tried to raise his hand to touch it, but the invisible force held him down. He stared into the shifting colours as if lost, the sounds of battle around him growing faint. The sorcerer moved forward, letting the Heart swing just above Heinrich's face.

'Is this what you seek, man-thing?' It said, flicking a spider from its lips. 'Yes, look into it. Look and see…'

He tried resisting, but the colours were too beautiful, too powerful. They swirled across the surface, one brilliant strand after another forming steeples, then roofs, then walls, then streets, then a raging river of black, gateways, guildhouses, temples, and defensive towers. Heinrich's own heart leaped into his throat as he realised the city being formed…

And then he was there, standing in a street amidst countless throngs of men and women. The mass pressed in closely, and Heinrich watched as they engaged in degenerate acts of evil as told in the annals of that terrible night in Mordheim many years ago. People dousing themselves with lantern oil and lighting candles, long, haggard lines of old thieves and beggars, chained at the neck, being led up stairs and into the sharp axe of the executioner; village idiots holding pistols to their heads and pulling triggers in a Kislevite game of chance; drunkards and barmaids, priests and parishioners, sharing one and all in an orgy of Chaos that thrust Heinrich's mind into madness. Severed heads danced around him. '*Turn back… turn back… turn back*,' they whispered. Heinrich closed his eyes. A tug at the bottom of his coat; '*Have you seen my mama?*' A young girl looking up with tears in her eyes, a deafening blast and Broderick's chest exploding in blood and green powder, Sisters huddled in prayer deep within their abbey. These things invaded his thoughts.

He tried to run. His legs were stiff. He looked down. The street opened and sucked in his feet. Cobblestones leeched up his legs and turned flesh to stone.

A flash of light appeared in the sky. He looked up. The Hammer of Sigmar burned brightly. The twin-tailed comet, barrelling down, a mighty rock of flame. His skin boiled, little bubbles dancing across his hands and arms, while people nearby burst into fire or shattered into ash, leaving dead silhouettes upon walls. Down and down, the comet hurled.

He screamed.

The world around him collapsed, and Heinrich was ripped from the street. He found himself once more on the mausoleum floor, shaking his head to drive away the fog. The fight still raged around him. He looked up. The sorcerer and the Heart were gone, and in their place the terrifying glare of a rat ogre, its foaming jaws mere inches from Heinrich's face. Hot spittle dripped on his chin, rancid breath burned his eyes. Obviously, the sorcerer wanted to give his pet a taste of man-flesh. But not today, Heinrich thought, as he drew his pistol. He didn't even know if it was loaded, but he pushed the barrel into the chest of the mighty beast and pulled the trigger.

The impact of the shot tore the pistol out of his hand. A white flash, a plume of black powder, and bits of flesh and fur smothered Heinrich as the rat ogre roared in pain and fell back. The shot had blown a crater into the monster's chest. Heinrich pulled up on feeble arms and tried to focus on the death throes. The rat ogre thrashed and scraped at his ribs, clawing away the burning shot, but a swift sword out of the shadows halted its efforts.

Bernardo jumped onto the beast's broad back and plunged his blade through its ribs. The rat ogre wavered in place for a moment, then fell hard. The impact shook the floor.

Heinrich tried to close his eyes and catch a breath, but the floor continued to rumble and pop as a web of black cracks worked their way out from under the rat ogre and across the granite. Heinrich's face grew pale as he realised what was happening. He tried to roll away but it was too late.

The floor collapsed.

He didn't remember hitting the ground, but when he came to, he was smothered in grey dust and rubble. Heinrich sat up and wiped away the grime from his eyes and focused on the shapes around him. Human shapes.

'Is everyone with me?' he asked, coughing.

A brief pause, then men began to answer: Father, Roland, everyone.

'Is Bloodtooth with us?'

'Yes,' said Bernardo. 'Shaken by the fall, but well enough.'

The Estalian walked up and handed over the dog. Heinrich smiled and patted his resilient friend on the muzzle. 'It's good to see you safe, good sir,' he said, using Bloodtooth's back for support.

He gained his feet and picked through the piles of rocks to find his sword. He found it half buried in the back of a ratman, pulled it out and wiped away its blood on his tattered breeches. Where are we, he wondered? He found a torch, waved it in the air for a moment to let it catch a better flame, then lifted it high.

It was a cave. Like the hallway above, its crude rock walls were covered in gruesome skaven script. Heinrich now realised what those symbols represented. This was not just an old, forgotten cave, but a temple to the twelve skaven lords and to their abominable hornedgod.

Bolted along the walls were human skulls containing low-burning candles. Interspersed between the skulls were wooden casks wherein smouldering wyrdstone sent green mist swirling into the chilly air. Heinrich caught his breath; he didn't want to breathe. Wyrdstone could fester in the chest and corrupt the flesh... and the spirit. Though many believed the green substance possessed healing powers, Heinrich knew the truth. Small quantities of the alloy used as currency in the thieves' dens and shantytowns around Mordheim was fine, but if they stayed here much longer, ingesting the fumes, they would change and mutate. But where could they go?

There were many exits. Several tunnels led from the room, large enough for human form, but Heinrich had no desire to test them. They would eventually lead to the surface, but at what risk to the men? Besides, the job was not finished. They had come here for the Heart. He had now seen it, experienced its power and he would not leave without it. Retreat was not possible.

'Heinrich?'

He turned and faced the Estalian. 'What is it?'

'We have to retreat. Despite his courage, Father is wounded and so are others. Look at yourself. We've survived this round, but I don't know how much longer we can go on. We have to retreat now before–'

'Retreat to where, Estalian?' Heinrich glared into the foreigner's dark face. 'Through these tunnels? Not for a moment. I will not stop until this is finished. Until the white one–.'

'Listen to me!' Bernardo hissed, grabbing Heinrich's shoulders and holding tightly. 'This is not a fight we can win. More are coming and I–'

'What happened to your death ground stance?' Heinrich said, pushing the Estalian back. 'Where is your spine?'

'I'm no fool, sir. Valiant rhetoric is fine when the muscle is there to support it. But our muscle is gone. The enemy is too abundant, and we are not on death ground. We *can* retreat, and we must. There's enough wood and rock around here. We can pile it to the ceiling and–'

'If you have no stomach for this fight,' said Heinrich, 'then I suggest you start piling. I doubt you'll succeed. I'm staying ... with or without you and your Marienburgers. No more running! No more retreating! They attack, they retreat, and we die. Enough. I yield no more. And I've seen the Heart.'

'What are you talking about?'

'Sigmar's Heart. I've seen it. The sorcerer had it, and I looked into its core. The things I saw... the things I felt. We must get it.'

Bernardo shook his head. 'I'm not going to die for a silly artefact. Forget about it!'

'No!' Heinrich screamed. 'I told you to learn respect for this city, Estalian, and the things within it. And now I'm telling you plainly: I'm not leaving here until the Heart is mine. Until I've killed them all. Until Broderick is avenged. Be a man and fight... or be a coward.'

Bernardo spat on Heinrich's boot. 'I'm finished with you, Reiklander. Stay and die like a fool, but we're pulling out.'

'Captain!'

Heinrich pulled away from the Estalian and joined Roland in the centre of the cave.

'Hold your torch up, captain, and look at this.'

Heinrich raised his torch high. The bright flames threw back the shadows, revealing a monstrosity of bone.

It was the most terrifying thing he had ever seen. A massive idol of bone stood in the centre of the cave. Bits and pieces of old leather, plate and chainmail covered its arms, chest and legs. Its feet were wrapped in strips of human entrails and oiled cloth. Were these the bones of a giant, Heinrich wondered? No, its body was constructed of human remains, stitched together with twine and sinew, its joints fused by dark sorcery. Human ribs and clavicles, hipbones and femurs, teeth and knuckles pieced together like some daemonic puzzle. On its broad shoulders perched a minotaur's skull, but its horns were coated in sediment that had dripped down from stalactites and had sealed the idol to the ceiling. Heinrich's blood boiled. It wasn't enough that the skaven had disrupted the eternal sleep of the occupants of this crypt, they had to desecrate their memories further by shaping their remains into an unholy reflection of the Horned Rat.

'Enough of this!' Heinrich shouted, letting his voice echo down the tunnels. 'We are here, and we are not leaving. Face us now!'

'You will die, man-thing,' a scratchy, feral voice rang out of the darkness. 'Pink-skins will all die, yes. Leave Mordheim, yes. It is ours.'

'I think not,' Heinrich replied. 'My men and I will reclaim it for the Empire.'

A white, twin-tailed skaven appeared at the opening of a tunnel to their right. A confident snarl spread across its sharp fangs and black gums. It waved a warplock pistol. 'Maybe, yes. But not today.'

With those words skaven poured from every tunnel and circled the trapped mercenaries. More vermin than Heinrich had ever seen. They beat spears and clubs together, scraped daggers against daggers, and slowly, slowly, tightened the noose. White One stepped to the front waving the pistol, a dagger, and fighting claws. At his side limped the one-eyed sorcerer, clearly despondent at the death of his pet, but squeezing Sigmar's Heart in the bony vice of his hand. Bloodtooth barked and snapped at anything that drew near, and Heinrich mouthed a prayer and held his sword high. So be it then, he said to himself. If this is the way it will be, if I am to die, then I will die for you, Broderick.

White One drew close and levelled its pistol towards Heinrich's chest. 'Goodbye, man-thing. Your god is a devil…'

Heinrich waited for the shot, but it did not come. Instead, the skeleton above began to quake and lurch. He turned and saw Bernardo grabbing the Horned Rat's legs and pull himself upward. The climb was effortless, as smooth and graceful as a ratman scaling a wall. The Estalian reached the shoulders and straddled the minotaur's skull as if it were a hobbyhorse. He rocked back and forth.

The skaven horde fell back at the sight of this blasphemy. A pink-skin climbing their lord of lords as if it were a ladder must have been as terrifying to them as the very sight of the skeleton to Heinrich. Even White One had dropped his pistol and had moved aside, glaring up in horror as its god teetered on the verge of destruction.

'You don't believe us, White One,' Heinrich said, 'when we tell you that this is our city? Then let us demonstrate our sincerity. Estalian?'

'Yes, captain?'

'Bring it down.'

Bernardo unsheathed Myrmidia and swung her through the minotaur's horns. Sparks flew as steel sliced through the hardened sediment. He cut the left horn then the right. The abomination seemed to hover in the air for a moment, and then it toppled.

A mountain of bone and chunks of ceiling struck the cave floor and erupted in a shower of grey-white splinters. Heinrich shielded himself from the impact, ducked a rib cage, and drew his sword. 'Attack!' he screamed, and leaped into a mass of ratmen trying to flee in the confusion.

Chaos consumed the space, as skaven routed and swords cut them down. Heinrich prayed to Sigmar that his men had not fallen to flying bones and stone. He looked for them. Roland and Father were fighting hard to his right. Bloodtooth was ripping out throats to his left, and the Estalian was fighting in the centre, holding off a pack of vermin who were trying to recover the minotaur skull. Albert and Rupert were working together on the other side of the cave, defending against a pack with spears and shields. It was a good fight. The men were holding fast.

He worked his way to the centre of the cave, drove his sword through a ratman who squealed in death, and then joined the Estalian.

'That was a foolish thing to do,' Heinrich said, parrying a spear thrust.

'You ordered it, and it got their attention, didn't it?' Bernardo replied, slashing through skaven armour and flesh.

'I thought you were done with me.'

'Well, I changed my mind. I couldn't leave you Reiklanders here alone, and well–'

'Admit it. I was right. There was no retreat.' Heinrich found himself laughing despite the situation.

Bernardo caught a skaven in a headlock, broke its neck, and tossed it away. 'You're beginning to annoy me, sir. I don't like someone who's always right.'

I'm not always right, Heinrich said to himself. Here he was fighting defensively when a more important matter needed attention. He looked around the cave, seeking a black robe and hood. The air was filled with granite and bone dust, green mist and smoke. It was hard to see. But he found the sorcerer to the left being escorted through its routing kin. 'Hold as best as you can,' he said to the Estalian. 'I have something important to do.'

Bernardo drove his sword through the mailed shirt of a ratman and said, 'What's more important than saving our skins?'

'The Heart!'

Heinrich ignored Bernardo's curses and pushed his way through to where the sorcerer was retreating. He sidestepped a spear thrust and responded with a sword hilt, driving the ratman to its knees with a cracked skull. He'd lost his torch, but he didn't need it as the Heart, lying upon the sorcerer's chest, shone bright green and lit the way. The sorcerer tried to drown the glow with its claw, but Heinrich broke its wrist. Its escort, fearing a similar fate, leaped away and left its broken master to die.

Heinrich grabbed the throat of the sorcerer. 'You have something of mine,' he said, hitting the beast's mangled face repeatedly. The sorcerer fell to the floor, its snout bloody, its eyes glazed over, unblinking and unmoving. Heinrich curled his fingers around the leather cord that held the Heart to the sorcerer's neck and yanked it free.

Something flew out of the shadows and hit him square in the side. Ribs cracked and his body skidded across the floor and came to a crushing halt beneath a pile of bones and coffins. Dead teeth and sharp clavicles tore his coat and flesh, while powerful claws reached through and pulled him free.

'You die now, man-thing,' the white one roared above him, its claws slashing through his coat and exposing his chest. Heinrich tried to fight back, tried to hold his arms up to block the assault, but he was too weak. Where is my sword, he wondered. Where is the Heart?

None of it mattered any more, as his eyes winked in pain with each slash. A giddy warmth consumed his body as the space around him swirled. I'm sorry, Broderick. I have failed you.

Through his nausea and sleepy haze, Heinrich watched as White One stood up and stepped back. Its tails pulled two blades from the sash at its waist. Blades long and sharp. Blades dripping green with poison. It held the blades above its head as it squatted down on powerful hind legs. It wavered there for a moment, screamed, bared its teeth, then leaped.

A white and brown blur flew across Heinrich's view. When it was gone, White One was no longer before him, but lying to his side. Heinrich pulled himself up and spotted a warhammer, lying still against the wall, pulsing hot in Sigmarite prayers. Beneath a pile of brown wool lay an old priest with two weeping blades sticking out of his back.

Heinrich's mind snapped to attention immediately as energy poured into his throat. 'Father, no!' he screamed.

It seemed as if he were outside his own body, looking down from the painted dome of the cave. Everything had a black and white sheen. There was clarity now in his thoughts, a single mindedness, and somehow he stood up and lurched across the floor and found his hands upon the warhammer. Somehow he raised the weapon above his head and found White One righting itself from its dishevelment. Somehow he found the strength to swing the pulsing hammerhead. The skaven's head exploded under the strike and its body was tossed like a rag doll against the wall. Heinrich followed and struck again, and again and again, until White One no longer moved. But he kept swinging, until the shape on the floor before him was no longer a skaven or a mutant, but something different, something basic, a singular representation of the City of the Damned, and he felt that if he kept swinging, he could, with mighty strokes, drive the evil away and bring the city back to life. Bring Broderick back to life.

But a hand reached into his space and pulled the hammer away. Arms held him firmly and pulled him back. Whispers from the darkness. 'It's over, Heinrich. It's over.'

Colour returned and he was standing again in the cave. He looked to his right and found the Estalian beside him, holding him tightly. He tried to pull away, but his arms were too weak. 'I'm sorry, Heinrich,' Bernardo said, 'but you will have to kill me this time to keep me from stopping you.'

The last of his strength failed him and he collapsed. Heinrich lay on the floor for a long time, how long he did not know. Perhaps he slept. When he opened his eyes, his men were around him, their warm smiles confirming that he was not dead and this was not the afterlife. Hands propped him up.

'How are you, sir?'

The Estalian's voice was calm and surprisingly comforting. Heinrich turned and felt a sharp pain in his ribs. He gripped the broken bones and groaned, 'Even to a bower like you, it should be obvious.'

Bernardo laughed and helped Heinrich to his feet. 'Well, say a prayer, brave servant of Sigmar. It's over. We've won.'

Indeed it was. The skaven were gone. Obviously the destruction of their idol, the death of their leaders and the loss of the Heart was too much for them to bear. Just as well, Heinrich thought as he took a shaky step. 'How is everyone?'

Bernardo gave a small smile and a wink. 'As if the comet itself sits upon our heads, but we'll make it… all except Father.'

Heinrich saw the crumpled brown robe on the floor and Father's bald head resting upon Rupert's knee. Blood and spittle streaked the corners of his mouth. Bernardo helped Heinrich down and he held the old man's hand. The handles of the weeping blades stuck out of Father's chest, their poison eating his flesh.

'It seems as if I'm finished, captain,' Father said, choking through blood. 'Just as well.'

'You foolish old man,' said Heinrich, gripping the priest's hand tightly. 'Why did you do it?'

'I've lived a long life,' Father answered. 'I saw no better way to leave it than in the protection of my captain.' He coughed very hard. 'We have both won a victory here today, you and me. You will live to carry on against the Eternal Struggle, and I will finally, at long last, die. Tell me true, captain. Did we get the Heart?'

Heinrich didn't know what to say. Did we? He wasn't sure. But he nodded. 'Yes, Father. The Heart is ours.'

'Praise Sigmar,' Father said calmly and raised his hand. He motioned his captain forward. Heinrich leaned in and let the priest's fingers stroke his hair. 'Now close your eyes, captain, and pray for me.' Heinrich cupped his hands together. 'And captain? Be sure to give those tears to someone who will use them.'

The Tears of Shallya. Heinrich had quite forgotten them. He reached into a pocket and found the vial. To his surprise, it had survived. He held it tight, closed his eyes and prayed.

Father's hand slacked.

Heinrich made the sign of Sigmar and crossed Father's arms over his chest. *I will miss you, old man.*

Bloodtooth limped out of the shadows. Heinrich smiled as the hound drew near, but his joy quickly soured as he saw the medallion, the Heart, dangling on its leather cord from the dog's teeth.

'Roland!' he yelped. 'Get that away from him and wrap it in a cloth… now!'

Roland yanked the Heart from the hound's bloody jaw, tore a piece of cloth from his shirt, wrapped the artefact and handed it over.

Heinrich tucked it away.

'I don't understand, captain,' Bernardo said. 'Is something wrong with it?'

Heinrich shivered at images of burning bodies and raining fire. 'It's too powerful for us,' he said. 'We are not worthy of it. It needs a stronger soul than mine to understand it, to harness its power.'

'Then what do we do with it?' asked Roland.

'As I've stated, we will take it to his Grand Theogonist in Altdorf. He will know what to do. And now,' Heinrich said, giving Bloodtooth a little scratch behind the ears, 'let's collect our things and get out of here before they decide to come back. I suspect they will take some time to reconcile to the truth that their god is but a pile of shattered bones, but they'll be back. They always come back. I've had enough of them for a while. Did we get any wyrdstone for our troubles?'

'A full bag of it, captain,' Albert said, raising a sack of glowing green, 'and jewels too. Enough to buy the City of the Damned itself.'

Heinrich chuckled through aching ribs. Maybe, he thought to himself, but I'm not buying.

'How are we going to get out of here?' asked Bernardo.

Heinrich shook his head. 'I've no idea,' he said, looking around. Pieces of the heavily damaged ceiling were still falling, and new cracks were forming everywhere. 'We'd better find a way out soon or we'll be buried alive.'

And then he felt a cool breeze brush across his face. Heinrich stepped back and saw a small shape of grey smoke dart across his view and into one of the skaven tunnels. The shape stopped momentarily and a face formed in its centre. It seemed to smile. Then it disappeared down the tunnel, leaving a trail of faint white light in its path.

'Well, Bernardo,' Heinrich said, 'it seems as if we've made some friends today.'

The Estalian's face flushed with surprise. 'Bernardo, eh? I'm no longer "the Estalian"?'

'Well, we should speak informally if we are to be partners.'

'Partners? Who said anything about being partners?'

'I could use some support on the road to Altdorf. If you and your Marienburgers would care to join us?'

'Altdorf is not my home.'

'But it could be,' Heinrich said. 'You said it yourself... you are as much a man of the Empire as I.'

'What about Mordheim?'

'We'll return. There's much work to be done here. Unless, of course, you wish to fight this city alone. In that case, you're welcome to it. Just let me know who to send your remains to the next time you decide to burn baby rats.'

Bernardo's face blushed deep red. 'You're never going to let me live that down, are you?'

Heinrich shook his head. 'Not likely.'

The Estalian paused for a moment, then said, 'Alright, you win. To Altdorf it is. Then let's fight this city. Friends?'

As Heinrich made his way slowly toward the lighted tunnel, he felt guilty. Am I betraying your memory, Broderick, he wondered, by accepting another as my friend? But as he greeted Bernardo's smile with his own, he knew the answer. This was a test, like Broderick had explained many times before. This was a test to see if his faith in Sigmar's cause could sustain such a loss and survive. And the fight was not over. Today, they had made great strides against the Eternal Struggle, but there would be many more battles to come. Can I fight this city with an Estalian at my side? he wondered. Only time would tell.

'Friends?' said Heinrich. 'Well, let's take it one day at a time.'

Bernardo nodded and together they helped secure Father for transport. As more of the ceiling began to fall, they entered the tunnel with the priest's body supported between them, while Bloodtooth limped ahead, his jowls wet with skaven blood. Together, they followed the ghost light as men of the Empire, Reiklanders and Marienburgers, servants to Sigmar, loyalists to the Lady Magritta, and followers of the Goddess of War, determined to stand firm against the city that never slept, the city of damned souls, the city of lost dreams, the city of night fire...

The city of Mordheim.

TOTENTANZ

Brian Craig

THE LORDS OF Death have but one apparent purpose, which is to raise armies of skeletons, zombies, wraiths and ghouls to fight against the living. There are many philosophers among the living who consider the Lords of Death to be essentially stupid, and their purpose essentially futile. They argue this case on the grounds that the living are bound to die soon enough, whether they do so in battle or in bed, while the dead are far too numerous already to be in urgent need of further company. There are also philosophers among the dead, however, who take a natural delight in the solution of such paradoxes. They declare that the duration of life is an irrelevance by comparison with the manner of its progress and that if life is merely one phase in the long career of a soul, as the existence of armies of the dead surely proves, then it might matter a great deal how the living enter the state of death. Equally important, according to the philosophers of the dead, are the ways in which the living are prepared for death, and the kinds of future that might be mapped out for them thereafter.

Living philosophers are sometimes wont to claim that the central question of philosophy is 'how should men live?' Dead philosophers, not unnaturally, think differently. Were their world a mere mirror of its counterpart, the central question would become 'how should men die?' but that is not the case. Since even the unquiet dead are, by definition, already dead – although victims of an understandable

739

confusion sometimes prefer to call them 'undead' – they take up a more pragmatic viewpoint, which is also more sophisticated. They prefer to ask 'how should the dead assist the living to reap the rewards of death?' – and this, of course, is where the Lords of Death and the Emperors of Necromancy enter into the equation.

Although the living tend to think of battles between their own armies and the armies of the dead as matters of unholy enmity between opposites, only the most imbecilic among the dead think in similar terms. The philosophically-inclined dead think of these conflicts as the entirely natural intercourse of the dead-but-active and the active-but-not-yet-dead, by which the former attempt to embrace the latter and initiate them into the mysteries of their own condition. From the point of view of the philosophical dead, therefore, the crusades waged by their lords are not matters of bitter warfare but affairs of enthusiastic reproduction – which might be as joyous as the kinds of reproduction in which the living indulge, were it not for the fact that the living insist on crying 'foul!'. Given that there never was an army of the living whose extra-curricular amusements did not result in profuse cries of alarm from variously threatened womwnfolk, one might expect them to be more understanding, but stupidity is certainly no monopoly of the dead.

The Lords of Death are mostly practical individuals who are more interested in mass murder than in self-justification, but there are a few of them who deem this narrow-mindedness a tragedy, and firmly believe that if only the dead would take the trouble, they could do much more to help the living understand the rewards of death, and thus make them more appreciative of their necessary fate.

THE GREATEST OF all the Emperors of Necromancy is, of course, Nagash, the Supreme Lord of Death and the architect of the Great Awakening. He resides now in Nagashizzar, the Cursed Pit, but he was born in Khemri, the most splendid of the ancient cities of Nekehara, where he raised the Tomb Kings from their long sleep to serve as his disciples in the Great Crusade Against the Living.

The Tomb Kings are more numerous and more various than the living probably imagine, and the fiefdoms they have established within the barren circle whose circumference the Marshes of Madness, the Black Tower and the city of Quatar are just as numerous and just as various. There is no denying that the greater number of them are not at all philosophically inclined, and by no means intellectually blessed, but there are a few Tomb Kings who take a greater interest than their fellows in matters philosophical, and there is one among them who takes such matters seriously enough to ask questions which are deemed slightly heretical by the majority of his peers. He is the Lord of the Necropolis of Zelebzel, and his name is Cimejez.

Cimejez is by no means an unviolent creature, and he has certainly played his part in the Great Crusade. Because Zelebzel is located in the far west of the Land of the Dead, in the desert borderlands which separate that land from Araby, his armies have abundant opportunities to meet their counterparts. It is by no means unknown for the rulers of Araby to raise armies with which to mount crusades of their own, and Zelebzel has borne the brunt of more than one such incursion. Nagash has never had any cause to complain about the zeal with which Cimejez has conducted his own expeditions or repelled those sent against him. This undoubtedly helps to explain why the Supreme Lord of Death has always been tolerant of the occasional eccentricities of his follower – but it must also be the case that Nagash approves, if only slightly, of Cimejez's attempts to build better bridges between the worlds of Life and Death.

One of Cimejez's eccentricities is the taking of prisoners, which armies of the dead are usually disinclined to do. The dead have little need of living slaves, and no interest at all in sexual congress with the living, so there is no obvious reason for Lords of Death to make captives of their adversaries. Cimejez makes an exception because he is a philosopher, and likes to debate philosophy with the living – although it is, admittedly, rare that he can find one among a hundred randomly-accumulated prisoners who is capable, despite his terror, of taking part in a half-way competent argument. Imagine his delight, therefore, when he returned from one of his raids into territory held by Araby with a famous vizier named Amaimon, who had been travelling in a diplomatic camel-train from one emirate to another, charged with a mission of the utmost delicacy.

CIMEJEZ TOOK SOME delight in displaying to his unwilling visitor the treasures of Zelebzel, which had been accumulated by the best-informed tomb-robbers in history. He had decorated sarcophagi by the score, statues and paintings by the hundred, and thousands of gem-encrusted objects moulded in gold, silver and brass. It was another of the Tomb King's eccentricities to accumulate such useless objects, which most of the Lords of Death disdained to possess on the grounds that they had risen far above such worldly concerns.

'Is there a museum to match this in all the world?' Cimejez asked Amaimon, grinning his rictus smile. 'Has any living man a collection to rival its grandeur?'

'I have not seen or heard of one,' Amaimon told him. 'But I think the living take more pleasure in the works of art they possess.'

'Why, certainly,' said Cimejez. 'Pleasure is a prerogative of the living, which is greatly over-rated by them. Do you not think, though, that there is a certain perversity in taking pleasure in such things as gems, statues and painted images? Do you not think that the dead have a purer and more refined notion of their quality and value?'

'Purer and more refined?' Amaimon echoed. 'Well, perhaps – in the sense that skeletons are purer for the lack of flesh, and wraiths more refined for the lack of substance. Gems are inert, and I suppose there is a certain crucial lack of activity in statues and paintings too – but look at that marble statue of a dancing-girl. I will believe, if you demand it of me, that your kind might have a better appreciation of its whiteness and its stillness, but I cannot believe that you can appreciate the significance of its pose, or the impression it gives of graceful movement. Yes, it is a single moment of frozen time, like death itself; but captured in that moment is the exuberant flow of life with which its human model was gifted. As a bleached white thing yourself, Lord Cimejez, you might feel a particular kinship with the statue's marble substance, but only a living man can see the dance that has crystallized within it.'

'Do you think that the dead do not understand dancing?' Cimejez replied, astonished. 'I can assure you that we do. Indeed, I can assure you that my kind are the only ones who understand the true nature and artistry of the dance.'

Had Amaimon been a less well-travelled man he might not have understood the import of this statement, but he had been sent far and wide as an emissary of more than one emir. He had even visited the Empire, and therefore knew of the fashion within the Empire for depicting the Totentanz or Dance of Death, in which death appears in the symbolic form of a skeleton – a skeleton not unlike Lord Cimejez of Zelebzel, in fact – leading a train of dancers, each one holding the hand of the next.

The point of this representation, Amaimon knew, was to stress the common cause of all humanity against the ravages of fate, by including in the train a wide range of social types: men and women; young and old; rich and poor; knights and priests; merchants and soldiers; scholars and serving-maids. It had not previously occurred to Amaimon that there might actually be dancing in the Land of the Dead – who, after all, would be led away in a Totentanz in such a place as Zelebzel? – but he wondered now whether the image might have some representational value above and beyond the merely symbolic?

On the other hand, it was quite possible that Cimejez was talking about something far more like the kind of dancing that the living enjoyed. In either case, Amaimon thought, surely the Lord of Death had to be wrong about the superiority of the dead, whether as dancers or as connoisseurs of the art.

'I refuse to believe that the dead can dance as well as the living,' Amaimon said to the Tomb King. 'They have neither the grace nor the ability to generate the artistic meanings of which a human dancer is capable. I would stake my life on it.'

'Your life has already been staked and lost,' Cimejez pointed out, 'but I do not mind a contest to settle the manner and timing of its delivery.'

'Alas,' said Amaimon, 'I have no champion to carry forward my cause. There was no dancing-girl among the prisoners your soldiers took, although there were a few musicians.'

'Must it be a girl?' asked Cimejez.

'I think so,' the vizier replied.

'Then you must tell me where to find the one you want. I shall send an army to fetch her.'

Amaimon had not expected this, and he certainly did not want to be the cause of yet another army of the dead descending upon a town in Araby, so he thought hard and fast about what to do next. Eventually, he said: 'That will not be necessary. Fortunately, I have a certain skill in magic, which I have always been loth to use because I have seen what the exercise of magic tends to do to the faces and souls of men. Given that my life is already forfeit to you, I see no harm in making an exception. I am prepared to bring this very statue to life for an hour, in order that the artistry that went into its making may be liberated in performance. Have you a champion here to set against her?'

'Oh yes,' said Cimejez. 'There is not another Lord of Death who could say so, but I have a champion of that kind.'

'But how are we to judge the result?' Amaimon said, dubiously. 'Can you provide an impartial jury?'

'That will not be easy,' Cimejez admitted. 'We might achieve neutrality by taking an equal number of living humans from among the prisoners seized with you and dead ones from among the ranks of my soldiers, but what if a deciding vote were needed? We would need at least one juror with a foot in each camp, so to speak – and if we had one such, we could probably dispense with the rest. Since you have been generous enough to use your own magic to give my statue an hour of life, however, I ought to match your offer by using some of mine, so this is what I propose. Will you accept your own champion as the judge, if I make provision to give her the choice between life and death when your hour expires? If I can offer her a choice between a continuation of the life that you have restored to her, or the opportunity to become a dancer of the same kind as the rival against which she has been pitted, will you accept her decision as an indubitable judgment of superiority?'

Amaimon thought about this offer for a moment or two, but it seemed to him that he would have the advantage, so he agreed. 'And what am I to stake, given that my fate is already in your hands?' he asked.

'That is easy enough,' Cimejez said. 'Should you win, I will let the dancer go, so that the life she has reclaimed can be spent among her own kind. Should you lose, you will become my vizier, and serve me – both before and after your death – as cleverly and as loyally as you have served any living emir.'

Amaimon thought about that too, but again it seemed to be a very good bargain, given that he was already lost. He was already among the dead, and would soon be dead himself, so what else could he hope for but a position of honour and privilege among the dead?

'You are very generous, my Lord,' he said. 'I am glad to accept.'

'The dead do not reckon generosity in quite the same terms as the living,' Cimejez told him, 'but it is good that you are satisfied. If you will work your magic while I summon my court, we can begin the contest as soon as you are ready.'

THE DANCING GIRL's name was Celome. She told Amaimon, when his metamorphic magic had reincarnated her in place of the statue whose model she had been, and her initial shock had waned somewhat, that she had danced in the court of King Luvah of Chemosh, in the long-gone days when Nekehara had been an empire of the living, before its fertile fields had turned to arid desert.

Celome had never been taught to dance; hers was a spontaneous art born of inspiration and nurtured by a natural process of growth. She had danced because dancing was the most natural expression of her vitality, and had danced well enough to win the favour of a king who was known throughout ancient Nekehara as a true connoisseur of that art.

Amaimon was delighted to hear all this. He explained to Celome that she must take part in a competition against a dancer representing the world of the dead – which some called the world of the undead – but that Celome herself would have the privilege of judging the winner.

'I have heard that serpentine lamias are fine dancers,' she said, dubiously. 'I heard, too, that one of King Luvah's courtiers was visited in his dreams by a dancing succubus which charmed the vital fluids from his body. But the real risk is that I might be matched against a wraith who was a famous dancer while she was alive and is now even lighter on her feet.'

'That is a possibility,' Amaimon conceded, 'but the whole point of the wager is to pit the dance of life against the dance of death. I do not think that Cimejez will pick a champion on the grounds that he or she pleased a human audience while alive. You might be surprised by the nature of your rival – but you will be the judge. You have only to desire to continue to be yourself, to live in Araby as you once lived in Chemosh.'

'I cannot imagine wishing anything different,' Celome told him. 'I am a dancer through and through; it is what I am.'

'Good,' said Amaimon.

He was not so pleased by the musicians who had been captured along with him, whose skills were very ordinary indeed and made worse by their abject terror at their predicament, but Celome thought they would be adequate to her needs. She picked out a zither-player, a cymbalist and a drummer, and Amaimon tried to impress upon them the importance of their task.

'Let us show these reanimated corpses what it means to be alive,' he said to the four of them, as they made ready to take the floor. 'Let us demonstrate our love of life. If you can dance as I believe you can, Celome, you might remind them what they have lost, and reintroduce these paradoxical beings to the bittersweetness of honest regret. That is my hope, at least.'

'Mine too,' she said, 'if there is life to be won.' She had found a costume in one of the treasure-chests in Cimejez's museum, which seemed to her appropriate to her purpose. The instrumentalists swore that they would do their best to assist her.

Cimejez had assembled a huge audience for the contest, which he distributed around the great hall of his palace. All the living prisoners recently taken by his army were brought from their cells, and all the soldiers which had taken part in the campaign against them were there too, along with the Lord of Death's ministers, household servants and junior sorcerers.

'You are the challenger,' Cimejez said to Amaimon. 'Your champion must take the first turn.'

'Go to it,' said Amaimon to Celome. 'Make the dead ashamed of their condition, and remind them what it was to be alive.'

And that is what Celome did. She threw herself into the arena and performed the legendary Dance of the Seven Veils.

The vulgar, who have only heard rumour of it, mistakenly think of the Dance of the Seven Veils as a mere strip-tease, but it is far more than that, for each of the seven veils has its own symbolism and each ritual removal is part of a progress from misery to ecstasy. Each garment represents a curse; as each one is discarded, the dancer advances towards a uniquely joyous kind of freedom.

The zither-player, the cymbalist and the drummer had all played the music of the Dance of the Seven Veils before, albeit for performances of a slightly less exalted and terrifying nature. They contrived to get the notes in the right order, and Celome communicated some of her own inspiration to them, so that they improved markedly as the performance progressed.

The first curse afflicting human life, according to the Dance of the Seven Veils, is hunger – which, for the purpose of the dance, includes and subsumes thirst. The first phase of Celome's interpretation was, therefore, the embodiment in body-language of that most fundamental of appetites which shapes the successful quest of the new-born infant for a mother's milk and a mother's love.

The second curse afflicting human life, according to the Dance of the Seven Veils, is cold, so the second phase of Celome's version was the embodiment in movement of the need for clothing and shelter and of its eventual achievement.

The third curse afflicting human life, according to the Dance of the Seven Veils, is disease – which, for the purpose of the Dance of the Seven Veils, also embraces injury – so the third phase of Celome's performance comprised a symbolic celebration of the power of the body to heal itself, and the wisdom of physicians.

The fourth curse afflicting human life, according to the Dance of the Seven Veils, is loneliness, so the fourth phase of Celome's mime was a hymn of praise to society and amity, and the productive rewards of co-operative labour.

The fifth curse afflicting human life, according to the Dance of the Seven Veils, is loss, so the fifth phase of Celome's rendition was a demonstration of the agony of grief, which gave way by degrees to the triumph of resolution and the recognition of all the legacies which the dead convey to the living.

The sixth curse afflicting human life, according to the Dance of the Seven Veils, is childlessness, so the sixth phase – the longest so far – of Celome's extravaganza was a celebration of sexual love, marriage and parenthood.

Amaimon watched all these phases with the critical eye of a connoisseur, and found little to criticise. It was easy enough to see that Celome had not been trained in the conventional devices of Arabic dancing, but it was equally obvious that her spontaneity and exuberance made up for the omission. She was authentically gifted, and her appeal to the emotions of her audience was no less powerful because it lacked a certain refinement and sophistication. Whatever imperfection remained in the playing of her accompanists was easily ignored; the dancer was the only centre of attention, the sole contestant. The living members of the audience followed her with their eyes, utterly captivated by her every movement.

On the other hand, Amaimon could see that the dead were quite unimpressed. Many of the skeletons, most of the zombies and all of the ghouls in the crowd had two good eyes, while the wraiths had more glittering stares than their inhabiting souls could ever have manifested in the flesh. They could all see well enough what Celome was doing, and even the notorious stupidity of death could not have prevented them from understanding the greater part of it – but Amaimon could see that they were unresponsive. They must have been reminded of life, but seemingly not in any way that made them regret its loss.

They did not seem to care at all.

Perhaps, Amaimon thought, that was because they could not care – but he was reluctant to believe it. Dead or not, they had been raised to action, subjected to motive force. Given that they had the capacity to respond to motive force, they ought to have the capacity to respond to the art of the dance. The problem was to reach and activate that potential.

There was still one phase of the dance to be completed, and Amaimon knew that whatever hope he had rested on that – but he suspected that the final phase might seem a trifle offensive to the audience gathered in the palace of Zelebzel, because the final curse afflicting human life, according to the Dance of the Seven Veils, was death itself: not the death of others, as per the fifth curse, but the death of the individual. The final act of Celome's drama was supposed to consist of a heroic defence of creative achievement and a defiant statement of the fact that although a body and mind might be annihilated, the legacy of their attainments could not.

Celome did as well as anyone in her situation could have done. The last and longest phase of the dancing-girl's masterpiece was a celebration of dancing itself, its joy and its meaning; its consummation and climax was the removal of the final veil, and the revelation of the human being beneath, utterly triumphant over every single one of the many indignities which cruel fate had heaped upon her kind. Even her accompanists excelled themselves.

When Celome fell still at last the captive prisoners, all of whom were already in tears, burst into a storm of applause and acclamation – but the dead remained silent. They did not seem to be bored, but neither were they in the least appreciative.

But that does not matter, Amaimon told himself. For they are not the judges who will decide this matter. Celome is the judge, and there was not one among the living observers who enjoyed watching her performance one tenth as much as she enjoyed giving it.

When Celome looked up and met Amaimon's eye he saw that she was pleased with what she had done, and was reassured. Cimejez beckoned to her, then indicated that she should take the empty seat beside Amaimon. The vizier briefly took her hand in his, and squeezed it slightly before releasing it again, by way of congratulation.

Then Cimejez's champion took the floor.

CELOME'S RIVAL WAS, as Amaimon had half-expected, exactly the kind of figure depicted in the art of the Empire: the leader of the Totentanz. He was a skeleton, but not any ordinary skeleton. He was an imperious skeleton, with an eyeless face and perfect teeth set in the permanent smile of the long-dead. He wore a jet-black cape with a hood, and he carried a scythe.

The zither-player, the cymbalist and the drummer had already retired to join the other captives. Their place was taken by a single drummer, also a skeleton attired in a monkish robe – but when he began to caress his instrument with his slender fingers the rhythm he sounded was more signal than dance-beat. Amaimon recognised it as a chamade: the summons used by exhausted armies to call for truce and negotiation.

There were no veils in this performance, no curses and no alleviations. It had only one phase, and even that had no hint of a crescendo.

It occurred to Amaimon, as he watched the skeleton move to the rhythm of the chamade, that he had never been able to make out what kind of dance the Totentanz was. Like the statue of Celome, the carved images of the dance that he had seen in Altdorf and Marienburg had been frozen moments decanted from an unfolding process, but while his human eyes had read an implicit flow and surge into the statue he had been unable to do likewise for the leader of the Totentanz. Now, for the first time ever, he was able to see the evolution and revolution of the Dance of Death, and to understand not merely where it led but how and why.

There were no phases in the Dance of Death because death had no phases. There were no curses in the dance of death because death was devoid of afflictions. There were no veils in the Dance of Death because death could neither deceive nor conceal its essence. There were neither triumphs nor celebrations in the Dance of Death, because death was all triumph, and had no need of any celebration. The Dance of Death was slow, and painstakingly measured, and eternal. The Dance of Death was an inexorable and inescapable summons, whose promise was more truce than release. That summons, addressed by the exhausted to the exhausted, gathered in everyone and everything... except the dead.

Life, according to the symbolism of the black-clad figure's awesomely patient and painstakingly measured steps, was a struggle against fate. It had its victories – which were, admittedly, the only victories conceivable. In death, by contrast, there was no struggle; there were no victories, because none was needed. That was the meaning of the chamade, and the meaning of the dance it accompanied.

Amaimon realised, before the skeleton had made a single circuit of the arena, that he could not win his wager. He could not win because his opponent did not need to win; he had to lose because he was the only one who could lose.

Amaimon realised, without needing to feel the slackness of her hand in his, that Celome would come to understand this too. She had not been able to imagine wanting to be anything other than she was, because that was all she had ever been before she was a statue; she was a dancer through and through. But the failure was in her imagination; she had never seen, imagined or understood the Totentanz. She was watching it now, and she understood exactly how its rhythm intruded itself into the human eye, ear and mind, like a possessive daemon banishing all rival thought and sensation.

Amaimon's fellow prisoners had stopped cheering, but they were joining in the dance.

Soon enough, even Celome was dancing again – but not, this time, the Dance of the Seven Veils.

Now the scythe came into play. As the column of figures wound around and around, doubling back on itself again and again, the scythe offered its blade to the dancing mortals. Hand-in-hand as they were, they could offer no resistance to its seeking blade, but they did not flinch or turn away as it sliced through their flesh and drained them dry of blood. The flesh began to melt from their bones soon enough, as if the dull music of the signal-drum were a fire of sorts, and their whited bones a kind of ash.

Celome made no more effort to avoid her fate than the zither-player, the cymbalist or the drummer, who seemed to be a little more appreciative of the rhythm to which they danced than the unmusical majority of their erstwhile companions.

'That is what the dead have to offer the living,' Cimejez whispered in Amaimon's ear. 'That is what might be attained, if only the living would try harder to understand the nature of the Great Crusade.'

Amaimon was the only living person present who was able to resist the summons of the chamade. He stayed where he was, in his seat beside Cimejez the Tomb King – but the only reason for that was that the careful Lord of Death had rested a bony hand upon his own, forbidding him to move. The pressure was gentle, but it was irresistible. Amaimon was the only living man who was ever privileged to see and hear the Totentanz without being required to join it – and for that reason, he became the only living man in the world who understood the strategy and the objectives of the Great Crusade.

The most remarkable thing about the continuing dance was the reaction of the remainder of the crowd to the performance they were watching. They did not applaud, nor did they sway in time to the rhythm. They remained utterly silent – not bored, but not appreciative either. They had been reanimated to serve as warriors in the Great Crusade Against the Living; they had been given armour, and weapons, and a cause – but the motive force that impelled them to take up arms against the living was nothing like the motives that forced the living to act. Their motive force was like the Totentanz itself, to which they made no evident response because they had no need.

The dead had no need to follow the paces of the dance, or even to approve of them, for the dance was merely a reflection of their nature, like a shadow carelessly cast upon the ground.

'You ought to let me go now,' Amaimon said to Cimejez. 'I have seen all I need to see. I admit that I have lost. I will serve as your vizier – but you should let me go, so that I might join my peers in the Totentanz.'

'Oh no,' said Cimejez, amicably. 'That would not do at all – for then you would be merely one of us, instead of a traitor to the living. The dead have a tendency to become stupid, even when they are recalled by a necromancer as expert as myself. You'll pay out your bargain in blood, sweat and tears, but you'll do it as I require and command.'

So Amaimon stayed where he was, and watched the dance. It seemed to go on forever, but when it was over he had lost far less time than it took a human to be born, let alone to die.

IN THE LONG, hard years of servitude that followed, Amaimon discovered that the first curse afflicting human life is indeed hunger – which, for accounting purposes, might be taken to include and subsume thirst. He discovered, too, the scrupulous accuracy of the estimated hierarchy of needs that had ranked cold the second, disease and injury the third, loneliness the fourth, loss the fifth and childlessness the sixth. He suffered all of these afflictions in their fullest measure, but he was not allowed to die. He helped bring death to hundreds of thousands of the living, and he helped bring the greater number of those he had betrayed into the ranks of Cimejez's army, but he was not allowed the kind of release he devoutly desired, nor any other kind.

Amaimon never forgot that the final curse afflicting human life is the inevitability of death itself, at least according to the Dance of the Seven Veils – but he could find little comfort in the recollection, even though the final phase of Celome's performance was etched so deeply in his memory as to be replayed over and over again in his restless dreams.

He still knew that the sum and climax of his existence, like that of any human being, was supposed to consist of a heroic defence of creative achievement, and of the ultimate inability of annihilation to cancel out the produce of a busy lifetime. Alas, that knowledge had become worthless to him as soon as he had seen a single round of the Totentanz – and worthless it remained to Amaimon the Vizier of Zelebzel, if not to those Lords of Death whose one and only purpose is to raise armies of skeletons, zombies, wraiths and ghouls to fight against the living.

THE ULTIMATE RITUAL
Neil Jones and William King

PROFESSOR GERHARDT KLEINHOFFER, Lector in Magical Arts at the University of Nuln, looked down at the pentagram and the triple-ringed circle his younger companion had just drawn in chalk upon the floor.

'Lothar,' he said nervously, 'surely this is blasphemy?'

Across the chamber, Lothar von Diehl ran bony fingers through his dark beard and paused to give the appearance of reflective thought before replying.

'Herr professor, you were the one who taught me that it is those who seek to hold back the advancement of knowledge who are blasphemous. You and I are men of science. It is our *duty* to perform this experiment.'

Kleinhoffer adjusted his pince-nez glasses and glanced at the leather-bound volume which rested on the lectern standing beside the two men.

'De Courcy's book is an important piece of scholarship, no doubt of that. But Lothar, don't you think that it wanders too close to the forbidden lore of Chaos... towards the end?' He shivered. 'His final chapter is almost the ranting of a madman. Drunk on the wine of stars, false heavens, false hells, all of that stuff.'

Von Diehl glanced at his tutor, fighting down his mounting impatience. It had been Kleinhoffer himself who, years ago, had discovered *The Book of Changes*, written in Classical Old Worlder by the long-dead Bretonnian poet and mystic, Giles de Courcy. Kleinhoffer had spent the rest of his life translating it, worrying away at the cryptic symbolism until he was sure he had decoded it correctly. By then, he had become the foremost authority on magic at the ancient University of Nuln – and Lothar von Diehl, the single person in whom Kleinhoffer had confided, was his most gifted student.

'True,' von Diehl said, striving to keep his voice calm and reasonable, 'but that should not deter us. As you yourself have said, all magic is based, ultimately, on Chaos. The only way to tell if de Courcy was right is to perform this ultimate ritual. And if it works, then it will lead us to the most profound understanding of universe.'

'My boy, I am as committed to the project as you are but... but...' Kleinhoffer's voice trailed off.

Von Diehl stared at the old man's pale, sweating face. 'Herr professor, I thought you understood when I suggested this experiment. The ritual is not something that I can attempt without your help.'

The old man nodded shakily. 'Of course, of course. It's just that... Lothar, my boy, are you sure it's *safe?*'

'Absolutely, professor.'

Kleinhoffer swallowed and once more glanced around the secret chamber in the basement of von Diehl's residence. Finally, he came to a decision.

'Very well, Lothar,' he said with reluctance. 'I know how important this is to you.'

Von Diehl allowed himself a brief sigh of satisfaction. 'Thank you, sir. Now, please, if you will take up your position.'

Von Diehl lifted the rune-encrusted wand which he had carved from a beastman's thighbone and advanced towards the lectern. He lit the braziers and threw handfuls of cloying incense to fizz on them. As the echoes died away he began the chant.

'Amak te aresci Tzeentch! Venii loci aresci Tzeentch! Amak te aresci Tzeentch!'

Von Diehl's chant rumbled on, seeming to gain resonance from the echoes and the constant repetition. The fumes from the braziers billowed around him and seemed to expand his perception. It was almost as if he could see the edges of the world starting to ripple at the corners of his vision.

He continued to chant, visualising in his mind the form of the Tzeentchian steed he was attempting to summon, filling in the details, compelling it to take more concrete form. While doing so, he moved the tip of the wand through a complex pattern, pointing it at every angle of the pentacle in turn.

The effects of the narcotic incense, the constant chanting and visualisation distorted his sense of the flow of time. The ritual seemed to be going on for hours. He felt himself to be a vessel for transcendent energies. Finally, somewhere off at the edge of infinity, he sensed a hungry presence. He reached out with the power of his soul and touched it. The being sensed him and began to move closer, painfully slowly, seeking sustenance.

As if far off in the distance, he heard Kleinhoffer moan. The air was filled with the burnt tin smell of ozone. Von Diehl opened his eyes. The room was lit by a strange blue glow from the lines of the pentacle and circle. Sparks flickered in the air and his hair was standing on end.

'*Venii aresci Tzeentch! Venii! Venii!*' he yelled and fell silent.

There was a rush of air, a sense of presence and suddenly it was there before them: the steed of Tzeentch.

It took the form of a flat disc of sleek, silvery-blue flesh. The edges of the disc were rimmed with small, sardonic eyes. It flickered about within the pentagram as if testing the boundaries of its cage. After a while it seemed to realise it was trapped and ceased to struggle, simply hovering in mid-air.

What do you wish from me, mortals? asked a voice within von Diehl's head.

'We seek knowledge,' von Diehl answered certainly. 'We wish to travel across the Sea of Souls and converse with He Who Knows All Secrets.'

Others have requested this in the past. To their regret. The minds of mortals are fragile things.

'Nonetheless, we wish to go. Once we are safely returned here you will be released from this compulsion.'

Very well. Advance, human, and meet your fate!

With no hint of trepidation von Diehl walked down the corridor of chalk which connected the circle to the pentagram. He stepped over the side of the magical sigil and put one foot on the creature of light. Surprisingly it supported his weight. He felt a strange tingling pass through his foot and up his body.

I will take both of you, the voice said in von Diehl's head. *Both of you or neither.*

Von Diehl turned. Kleinhoffer had not moved. His lined face seemed to float amid the darkness, lit from below by the glow from the pentagram.

'Herr professor,' von Diehl called urgently, 'you must join me. Quickly now!'

Kleinhoffer licked his lips. A sheen of sweat had formed on his forehead. 'Lothar, I can't! I just can't!'

Anger pulsed through von Diehl. 'The book is explicit. We must be two – or else the steed can refuse to transport us, can break the binding spell. You knew. You agreed!'

'I know, but – Lothar, forgive me, I'm old. Old and afraid.'

'But Gerhard, you've worked for this all your life. Ultimate knowledge. Transcendence.'

The old scholar shuddered.

'Join me,' von Diehl commanded. 'Join me, join me, join me!'

Kleinhoffer sighed, and then, almost as if hypnotised, he shuffled down the chalk corridor and took his place aboard the steed beside von Diehl.

Two, the daemon said. *Two in search of knowledge. Now we go!*

There was a screaming rush of air, and the sound of a thunderclap.

VON DIEHL LOOKED down and found they were far above the city of Nuln itself. He could see the University quarter with its aged, many-spired buildings. His gaze wandered to the docks and the dark curve of the River Reik as it snaked northwards. Although he was hundreds of feet above the tallest tower of the Temple of Verena he felt no fear. Standing on the back of the Chaos-steed was like standing on solid earth.

The daemon-thing began to accelerate but there was no sense of motion or of the wind tearing at his clothing. He stood at a point of absolute calm. Only when he looked down at the Great Forest rushing past did von Diehl get a sense of their terrific speed.

In a few moments he saw an open glade where beastmen danced around a great bonfire and a two-headed black-armoured figure looked on. He saw strange monsters moving in the depths where no man had ever penetrated. Their steed hurtled like a meteor until the ground was simply a blur. They gained height until they were above the clouds. It was like skimming over a misty white sea whose surface was illuminated by the twin moons.

Excitement flooded through von Diehl's veins as they flashed along. He felt like a god. It seemed to him that no one could ever have travelled so fast before. The energy of the daemon passed up through his legs, filling him with a tremendous sense of well-being. Perhaps it was the steed's power which protected them from the cold air, he thought. Through a break in the clouds he saw that they were passing over a bleak steppeland only occasionally blotched by the lights of cities. Surely they could not have reached Kislev already?

Soon after, he felt no such doubts. They were moving across snow-covered tundra towards a bleak, stony land. The sky to the north was illuminated by a dancing aurora of dark-coloured lights. They had entered the Chaos Wastes.

Below he could see great troupes of warriors fighting. Champions in the blood-red armour of Khorne fought with dancing lascivious daemonettes. Enormous slobbering monsters pursued fleeing beastmen. The land itself writhed as if tortured. Lakes of blood washed across great deserts of ash. Castles carved from mountains erupted from forests of flesh-trees. Islands broke off from the earth and floated into the sky.

It was a horrific and awesome sight. Beside him, he heard Kleinhoffer call out in fear, but he cared not.

They flew straight towards the aurora, picking up speed as they went. They passed over a flight of dragons that seemed frozen in place so slowly did they move compared to the steed of Tzeentch.

Now von Diehl could make out a vast dark hole in the sky. It was as if the firmament were a painting and someone had torn a square from the canvas to reveal another picture beneath. He peered into a realm of flowing colours and pulsing lights, an area where the natural laws which governed the physical universe no longer applied. Von Diehl pointed the bone wand towards the Chaos Gate and the steed surged forward in response. They crossed the threshold into a new and darker universe.

'Lothar,' Kleinhoffer murmured, his voice full of awe. 'I believe that this must be–'

'Yes,' von Diehl replied distantly, 'we have entered the Sea of Souls.'

For a moment their steed paused on the threshold between the two worlds and von Diehl stared into what was the final and strangest realm of Chaos.

Off in the farthest distance, further away than the stars, he saw the things that he decided must be the Powers. They were vast eddies and whirlpools of luminescence, bigger than galaxies. Their twists and flows illuminated the Sea of Souls. Was that mighty red and black agglomeration Khorne, wondered von Diehl? He noted how its spiral arms of bloody light seemed to tangle with long pastel streamers of lilac and green and mauve. Could that be Slaanesh? It was like watching two nests of vipers fighting.

Then he made out a third pulsating mass that was clearly greater than the many lesser ones in this vast realm. It writhed and pulsed obscenely, and something about this one made the hair on the nape of his neck bristle. From his instinctive reaction he knew that this one had to be Nurgle.

Yet another form came into view. It was the most complex and convoluted of the gigantic structures of energy and he knew it to be Tzeentch, his ultimate goal.

These were clearly the Powers, the Four Great Ones and the many lesser. And this was the true realm of Chaos.

Beside him, Kleinhoffer clutched at his sleeve in panic. 'Lothar, what is happening?'

Von Diehl understood the old man's confusion. His own brain was reeling under this sudden influx of sensation. 'Our human minds are adjusting to the Sea of Souls,' he said happily.

He realised that they were not seeing the whole of this twisted realm. Their human minds were not capable of it. Instead, they were simply imposing their own ideas of scale and form and function on a place where these did not apply. It was a staggering thought.

Much closer than the Great Powers were tiny points of light that von Diehl somehow knew were the souls of mortals. They glittered like stars. Cutting a swathe through them, like a shark through a shoal of fish, von Diehl could see a long streamlined creature, all sucker mouths and questing antennae, a soul-shark. It devoured the small panicky shapes as they swam towards their distant, unseen destinations.

Again he felt Kleinhoffer's hand on his sleeve. 'Lothar,' the old man cried in a frightened voice. 'Lothar, look down!'

Beneath their feet, their daemon-steed had changed shape, so it now resembled the soul-shark. It, too, feasted upon the glittering souls as it swept ever on.

Von Diehl was not surprised. The beast was dangerous. He did not doubt that it would devour the essence of both of them if it could. Very softly, he chanted the words of a spell he had prepared. A thin line of radiance streamed from his bone wand, a pink-hued light that was indescribably richer here in the Sea of Souls. As the light touched the steed it opened up a delicate channel between their steed and himself.

As the creature fed it passed the merest trickle of that energy to him through the channel his spell had created. The energy flowed through von Diehl's veins like liquid ecstasy. He breathed deeply and sucked the pure essence of magic into his lungs. It was a totally exhilarating experience.

'It cannot harm us,' he reminded the terrified old man. 'Not as long as it is compelled by the binding spell.'

But Kleinhoffer only stared down with a look of utmost horror on his face, as if the steed were already dining upon his lower limbs.

The daemon-thing surged forward once more. Von Diehl felt that whatever awesome velocity it had achieved in the mortal world was nothing compared to what it was doing here. It seemed as if the creature was capable of traversing the universe.

As they raced along they passed other great rents in the fabric of the sea. Sometimes what von Diehl saw through them beggared his imagination. Worlds laid waste by war, hells presided over by false gods and heavens of endless serenity.

Suddenly he sensed a change of mood in their steed. He looked back and understood why. They were being pursued. Other creatures chased them, creatures not controlled by any binding spell. More soul-sharks. They could devour their flesh and their souls.

Kleinhoffer followed his gaze and cried out in alarm.

The soul-sharks came closer, their great jaws gaping. They were fast, faster than their own steed, not hindered as it was by two human riders.

Von Diehl raised the wand of bone and prodded the daemon with it. 'Save us,' he commanded the thing. 'Save us or you will never be free!'

A wordless cry of mingled rage and despair echoed inside von Diehl's skull. The daemon-steed suddenly veered and plunged through one of the gates.

Reality rippled like the surface of a pond. They hurtled over a desolate plain on which great pyramidal cities sat. As von Diehl watched, great beams of force flickered between the pyramids. Some were absorbed by huge, thrumming black screens of energy, but one city was reduced to slag in an instant. Their mount swept into an evasive pattern to dodge the webs of force-beams. Several came too close for comfort but none hit them. Von Diehl watched one of their pursuers get caught in the cross-fire and wink out of existence. The others came on.

Their supernatural steed raced through another gate above the greatest of pyramids. There was a sense of space stretching. Now they were above a hell of sulphur pits and dancing flames. Toad-like daemons pitch-forked the souls of some strange amphibian race into the volcanic fires. Von Diehl wondered whether this was real or the dream of one of the Old Powers. Perhaps it was a real hell of a real race brought into being by the imaginations of an alien people stirring the Realm of Chaos.

Their steed dived into one volcanic pit. Beside him, Kleinhoffer screamed uncontrollably, surely convinced that the creature had betrayed them and that they were going to die. He covered his eyes with his hands.

Von Diehl felt only exhilaration.

Once more though they hurtled through a gate. Fewer of the pursuing daemons followed.

They were in the blackness of space, hurtling through a void darker than night over a small world that had been re-shaped into a city. They raced by bubble domes from which creatures much like elves stared out. The workmanship of the buildings within the domes was as refined and delicate as spider-webs. They dipped and swooped into a great corridor holding another gate. Once more they vanished.

Von Diehl had no idea how long the chase lasted. They passed through vaults where rebellious daemons plotted against the Powers; frozen hells where immobile souls begged for freedom; leafy Arcadias where golden people made love and dreadful things watched from the bushes.

They swooped across worlds where great war-machines, shaped like men eighty feet high, fought with weapons that could level cities. They blazed along corridors in doomed hulks that had drifted for a thousand years in the spaces between worlds and where sleeping monsters waited in icy coffins for new prey. They zoomed across the surface of suns where creatures of plasma drifted in strange mating dances.

But eventually their twists and turns through the labyrinth of space-time threw off the last of their pursuers, and they returned once more to the Sea of Souls.

THEIR STEED RACED along the threads of the vast disturbance in the sea that was Tzeentch, picking their way along great arteries of energy until they came to the very heart of it all. They swept past great winged creatures which gave von Diehl knowing smiles. He felt as if the daemons were looking into his very soul and probing his inner-most secrets. He did not care. He was exalted. He knew they were nearing the end of the quest and that soon they would both have what they had come for. Kleinhoffer was exhausted, his face blood-less. But the exhilaration of the chase and sharing their daemon-steed's energy had only buoyed von Diehl up.

They approached a mighty sphere of pulsing light. Colours danced and shifted on its surface like oil glistening on the surface of water.

They drifted closer and slid into, then through the wall. Within was a huge being, larger than a castle. In form it was similar to a man although its head was horned. It possessed great beauty but the shift-ing lights of the sphere reflected dazzlingly off its no-coloured skin and the brilliance caused von Diehl to look away.

Welcome, mortals, to the House of the Lord of Change!

The voice spoke within the travellers' heads. It was calm, polite and reasonable, but there was an under-current of malicious amusement.

Von Diehl peered back at the great figure, looking up into glittering gem-like eyes. He thought that those eyes could take in the entire uni-verse at a glance. Before it he felt as insignificant as a flea.

'Thank you, lord,' he said gravely. He nudged Gerhardt Kleinhoffer with his free hand. The old man mumbled a greeting of his own.

Why have you come here? boomed the voice. *Why have you disturbed my servants who have other more important tasks to perform?*

'We have come,' von Diehl said, 'seeking knowledge, lord.' He ges-tured at his companion.

'Yes,' Kleinhoffer stammered after a moment, a dazed expression on his face. 'That's it. That's why we're here. Knowledge.'

Knowledge. For what purpose do you seek it? To change yourself or your world?

Von Diehl turned and waited for his companion to speak. The old man's gaze went back and forth between his student and the gigantic being. His mouth opened and closed several times but no words emerged. Still von Diehl said nothing.

'Neither,' Kleinhoffer blurted at last.

Lothar von Diehl smiled and turned back to face the Power. 'Both,' he said.

Gerhardt Kleinhoffer blinked, and then finally appeared to realise what von Diehl had said. He jerked around to face von Diehl. His face was ashen. 'Lothar, what are you saying? Have you forgotten the ritual?'

So then, mortal, the gigantic being boomed, addressing only Gerhardt Kleinhoffer now. *Why then do you crave know-ledge?*

'I– I–' Kleinhoffer's eyes bulged. He put his hands to his head, clearly wilting under the gaze of this enormous entity. 'Lothar, for pity's sake, help me!'

Von Diehl raised both hands. 'Lord, he seeks knowledge – for its own sake.'

That is unfortunate. The creature smiled malevolently. *Still, what does he wish to know?*

Again Gerhardt Kleinhoffer's mouth opened and shut and again no words emerged.

Smiling, von Diehl said, 'Everything.'

Suitably ambitious. So shall it be.

Lord Tzeentch reached out and touched Kleinhoffer. The old man went rigid.

At the same moment, von Diehl again murmured the words of the spell which had linked him to the steed as it had fed. Leaning forward, he pressed the tip of the bone wand to Kleinhoffer's temple. Knowledge was flowing into his companion, filling him. And Lothar von Diehl intended to witness it – from a safe distance.

A vast ocean of information cascaded into Kleinhoffer's brain. Von Diehl glimpsed the birth of the universe and the Sea of Souls, the creation of stars and planets, the rise of races, the structure of molecules. He saw the universe burst into a great flood of change and understood the nature of the power that drove it relentlessly onwards. He saw that the universe was never still but constantly altering itself. He knew instantly that he could never know everything because there were always new things coming into being.

Kleinhoffer's face contorted as the flow of knowledge continued inexorably. His mind was drowning in a flood of information, far too much knowledge to cope with. It had stretched his mind to the breaking point and beyond. As if from a great distance, von Diehl sensed the man's personality erode then finally collapse as he descended into screaming madness. And still the torrent of knowledge did not stop.

Slowly, still clutching feebly at von Diehl's tunic, the old man sank down to von Diehl's feet.

Enough, thought von Diehl, sensing his own mind begin to strain. Chanting the words of his spell, he drew back the wand, breaking the contact with the old man.

Lothar von Diehl.

He looked out at the vast unknowable being that was, or represented, Tzeentch.

Your companion's wish has been granted.

'Yes, lord,' von Diehl replied, glancing down at the huddled figure at his feet. He smiled. 'And I offer you thanks – on his behalf.'

A rumbling sound issued from the creature before him that perhaps was laughter on a cosmic scale.

And you, Lothar von Diehl. You have also been granted the gift of knowledge – knowledge that you may take back with you into the mundane world you came from.

'Accept my gratitude for that gift also, lord.'

Of course, for that gift, too, there is a price.

'I understand, lord, and one I am quite prepared to pay.'

You will be bound to my service for eternity.

Von Diehl bowed his head. Tzeentch the Great Mutator. Tzeentch the Changer of the Ways.

'Willingly,' he said.

Tzeentch, his chosen Power of Chaos.

You will serve me in your world. You know what it is that I wish, that I thrive upon.

'I know.'

ONCE MORE THERE was a flickering in the air and the smell of ozone. The steed reappeared in the tiny cellar chamber, a glowing disc of light within the pentagram. This time it bore two riders, one standing, the other slumped at his feet.

Lothar von Diehl stepped down from the daemon-steed. The secret chamber was just as he had left it. The Book of Changes still rested on the lectern, open to the page upon which Giles de Courcy had inscribed the secret of the ultimate ritual, the secret von Diehl had felt it wise to share only partially with his tutor.

In his mind, the memory of the ocean of knowledge still glittered. He had glimpsed at least some of what was to be. Change was coming to the Old World. Elves returning from their long exile in the west, eager for trade, disrupting the nations of men. The Empire itself about to totter as, tempted by that elven trade, its wealthiest province sought to secede from its rule. And a hint, a deep darkness growing in the north. The ancient paths. A shroud removed, to be replaced by the bloodied fog of conflict.

A truly moment for magic to take its place upon the battlefield, to become a weapon of war for the first time in recorded human history.

Von Diehl laughed aloud. The battle magic spells were in his mind now, knowledge Lord Tzeentch had granted to him. He would have a considerable part to play in the events that were to come.

Change.

This was what Tzeentch, the Great Mutator desired – what any true servant of Tzeentch craved more than life itself. And outside this chamber was an entire world, crying out for change. Eager to begin his master's work, von Diehl strode for the door.

Behind him, sprawled across the pentagram, Gerhardt Kleinhoffer raised a thin hand. Pure madness gleamed in his eyes.

'Seas of lost souls,' he mumbled as the door closed on his departing pupil. 'False heavens, false hells. All is change and the dreams of Dark Gods.'

ABOUT THE AUTHORS

Dan Abnett

Dan Abnett lives in Kent, England. Well known for his comic work, he has written everything from the *Mr Men* to the *X-Men* in the last decade. His work for the Black Library includes the popular comic strips *Lone Wolves, Titan* and *Inquisitor Ascendant*, the best-selling Gaunt's Ghosts novels, and the acclaimed Inquisitor Eisenhorn trilogy.

Mark Brendan

Mark Brendan was immersed in his Bumper Book of Black Magic from an early age, and nowadays his writings are considered by many to be 'a shame, a caution and an eldritch horror'. He lives in Yorkshire.

Ben Chessell

Ben lives in the near-Arctic climate of South Australia. He writes one-liners for White Wolf Publishing and Chaosium Inc. He is an avid gamer, and enjoys roleplaying and the Games Workshop game of fantasy football, Blood Bowl.

Brian Craig

Brian Craig is the author of the three *Tales of Orfeo* – *Zaragoz, Plague Daemon* and *Storm Warriors* – and *The Wine of Dreams,* as well as the Warhammer 40,000 novel *Pawns of Chaos.* He has contributed short stories to a range of anthologies, including the *Dedalus Book of Femme Fatales,* edited by Brian Stableford.

Robert Earl

Robert Earl graduated from Keele University in 1994, after which he started a career in sales. Three years later though, he'd had more than enough of that and since then he has been working, living and travelling in the Balkans and the Middle East. Robert currently lives in the UK.

Jonathan Green

Jonathan Green has been a freelance writer for nearly fifteen years. His work for the Black Library includes a string of short stories for *Inferno!* magazine and six novels. Jonathan works as a full-time teacher in West London.

Darius Hinks

After a music career so disastrous it landed him in court, Darius Hinks decided a career in publishing might be safer. He secured himself a position working for the Black Library and over the last five years has written several short stories and the Warhammer background book, *The Witch Hunter's Handbook*.

Andy Jones

Andy has had a hand in such products as *Space Fleet*, *Man O' War* and *Warhammer Quest*, designed games for *The Crystal Maze* TV show, set up the Black Library, headed up Games Workshop's The Lord of The Rings team (lots of essential visits to New York!) and now runs the legal and licensing team within Games Workshop.

William King

William King was born in Stranraer, Scotland, in 1959. His short stories have appeared in *The Year's Best SF*, *Zenith*, *White Dwarf* and *Interzone*. He is also the author of seven Gotrek & Felix novels, four volumes chronicling the adventures of the Space Marine warrior, Ragnar Blackmane, as well as the Warhammer 40,000 novel *Farseer*. He currently lives in Scotland.

Nick Kyme

Nick Kyme hails from Grimsby, a small town on the north-east coast of England known for its fish (a food which, ironically, he dislikes profusely). Nick moved to Nottingham in 2003 to work on *White Dwarf* magazine, but has since made the switch to the Black Library, where he works as an editor. He's written several short stories and the Necromunda novel, *Back from the Dead*.

Nathan Long

Nathan Long has worked as a screenwriter for fifteen years, during which time he has had three movies made and a handful of live-action and animated TV episodes produced. He has also written three Warhammer novels featuring the Blackhearts, several award-winning short stories and the Gotrek & Felix novel *Orcslayer*. He lives in Hollywood.

Neil McIntosh

Neil McIntosh was born in Sussex in 1957. He has contributed stories for the Warhammer anthologies, *White Dwarf* and other magazines, and is the author of several novels.

Graham McNeill

Hailing from Scotland, Graham McNeill narrowly escaped a career in surveying to join Games Workshop, where he worked as a games developer for six years. In addition to seven novels of carnage and mayhem, Graham has also written a host of short stories. He lives in Nottingham, England.

Sandy Mitchell

Sandy Mitchell is a pseudonym of Alex Stewart, who has been working as a freelance writer for the last couple of decades. He has written science fiction and fantasy in both personae, as well as television scripts, magazine articles, comics and gaming material. Apart from both miniatures and roleplaying gaming his hobbies include the martial arts of Aikido and Iaido, rifle shooting, and playing the guitar badly.

Chris Pramas

Chris Pramas is an award-winning game designer whose punk-fuelled writing has infected the game industry for over a decade. He is the founder and president of Green Ronin, a leading publisher of roleplaying games. He is also the designer of the new edition of *Warhammer Fantasy Roleplay*.

Gordon Rennie

Gordon Rennie is the writer of *Missionary Man* and *Glimmer Rats* for *2000AD*, Bloodquest and Kal Jerico for *Warhammer Monthly*, and other stories for *Inferno!*

Neil Rutledge

Neil Rutledge is a veteran of the Games Workshop universe (he still has some of his first Citadel Miniatures, purchased at eighteen pence each!). He lives in Carlisle and lectures in science education.

THE BLACK LIBRARY

BRINGING THE WORLDS OF WARHAMMER AND WARHAMMER 40,000 TO LIFE

ORCSLAYER

Check out all the action happening on the Black Library website!

All the latest news, downloads, special offers, articles, chat forums, online shopping and much more.

Miss it and miss out!

WEB STORE

Pre-order new titles, buy available products and exclusive Collector's Editions.

NEWSLETTER

Sign up for all our latest news and special offers!

DOWNLOADS

Free first chapters of all our novels, wallpapers and loads more.

FORUM

Chat with fellow Black Library fans and submit your own fiction.

Visit :: www.blacklibrary.com

Mitchel Scanlon

Greeted with the words 'Good Lord, it can't be human!' at the occasion of his birth, Mitchel Scanlon would in time confound medical experts and religious leaders alike by mastering the intricacies of human speech and upright posture. More recently, he has embarked on a career as a writer of novels, comics and short stories. His previous credits for the Black Library include *Fifteen Hours, The Loathsome Ratmen* and the comics series *Tales of Hellbrandt Grimm*.

Gav Thorpe

Gav Thorpe works for Games Workshop in his capacity as Lead Background Designer, overseeing and contributing to the Warhammer and Warhammer 40,000 worlds. He has a dozen or so short stories to his name and over half a dozen novels.

James Wallis

James Wallis started his first magazine at fourteen. Since then he has been a TV presenter, world-record holder, games designer, political firebrand, auctioneer, convention organiser and internet commentator. His proudest moment is being called 'slick' by the News of the World. He lives in London, has no cats, hears everything and does not sleep.

Robert Waters

Robert has been an avid Games Workshop enthusiast for as long as he can remember, and has worked in the computer gaming industry for over 12 years. He lives in Baltimore, Maryland with his wife and their young son. Robert is an assistant editor for *Weird Tales* and his fiction has appeared in *Weird Tales* and *Nth Degree*.

C L Werner

C L Werner was born in New York in 1973. An avid and voracious reader almost before he could walk, he began trying his hand at writing stories of his own in grade school and never quite kicked the habit. Extremely interested in by-gone eras, he has been involved in both American Civil War re-enactments and Wild West stunt shows.